The
Foreign Legion
Novels
Part B

The Collected Novels of P. C. Wren
Volume 3B

Fiction Titles by P. C. Wren

Dew and Mildew. 1912
Father Gregory. 1913
The Snake and Sword. 1914.
Driftwood Spars. 1916
The Wages of Virtue. 1916
The Young Stagers. 1917
Stepsons of France. 1917
Cupid in Africa. 1920
Beau Geste. 1924
Beau Sabreur. 1926
Beau Ideal. 1928
Good Gestes. 1929
Soldiers of Misfortune. 1929
The Mammon of Righteousness. 1930 (U.S. title:
        Mammon)
Mysterious Waye. 1930
Sowing Glory. 1931
Valiant Dust. 1932
Flawed Blades. 1933
Action and Passion. 1933
Port o' Missing Men. 1934
Beggars' Horses. 1934 (U.S. title: The Dark Woman)
Sinbad the Soldier. 1935
Explosion. 1935
Spanish Maine. 1935 (U.S. title: The Desert Heritage)
Bubble Reputation. 1936 (U.S. title: The Cortenay
        Treasure)
Fort in the Jungle. 1936
The Man of a Ghost. 1937 (U.S. title: The Spur of Pride)
Worth Wile. 1937 (U.S. title: To the Hilt)
Cardboard Castle. 1938
Rough Shooting. 1938
Paper Prison. 1939 (U.S. Title: The Man the Devil
        Didn't Want)
The Disappearance of General Jason. 1940
Two Feet From Heaven. 1940
The Uniform of Glory. 1941
Odd—But Even So. 1941

The
Foreign Legion
Novels

Part B

by

Percival Christopher Wren

PAPER PRISON
THE UNIFORM OF GLORY

Edited

by

John L. Espley

Riner Publishing Company
Culpeper Virginia
2017

i

ISBN
978-0-9990749-1-6

The text of *Paper Prison* will be in the Public Domain as of 1 January 2035 since it was originally published in 1939

The text of *A Uniform of Glory* will be in the Public Domain as of 1 January 2037 since it was originally published in 1941

Contents

PREFACE v

INTRODUCTION vii

PAPER PRISON 1

THE UNIFORM OF GLORY 401

PREFACE

The Foreign Legion Novels Part A and *The Foreign Legion Novels Part B* by Percival Christopher Wren are the third of a multi-volume series, *The Collected Novels of P. C. Wren*. The purpose of publishing this series is to make the novels written by P. C. Wren more available to the reading public. His novel, *Beau Geste*, is usually recognized by most of the book dealers I have met over the years, but his other works are not so easily remembered.

I have been collecting P. C. Wren for over fifty years, and have been working on a comprehensive bibliography for almost as long. The text of the twenty-eight novels were easily obtained from copies in my own collection. For that collection, I certainly need to thank the hundreds of used book dealers I have purchased items from, and I need to thank some by name: Steven Temple, David Mason, Walt Barrie and, especially, the late Denis McDonnell for the advice and help they have provided over the years.

Mr. John Venmore and Mr. Philip Fairweather, both descendants of the late Mr. Richard Alan Graham-Smith, Wren's stepson, and the executor of Wren's estate, have both been very helpful in providing information about Wren.

As it has been over seventy years since the death of P. C. Wren (November 21, 1941), Wren's works have passed into the public domain in the United Kingdom. In the United States fourteen of the twenty-eight novels are still under copyright. Thanks to information provided by Messrs. Venmore and Fairweather, the heirs to Wren's literary estate, Mr. Danny Adekoya Campbell and Mr. Christopher Oladipo Graham-Smith, were located and permission has been granted to reprint Wren's works.

I also need to acknowledge the help and guidance of my family members: my daughter and son-in-law,

Dawn and Andrew; my son and daughter-in-law, Jared and Claudia; and my long-suffering wife, Cathy. Thank you.

In conclusion, I need to thank Percival Christopher Wren for the many years of great enjoyment that his stories have provided. I know that Wren is not a literary or critical success, but, for me, he is one of the great storytellers of the early twentieth century.

John L. Espley
Culpeper, Virginia
June 1, 2017

INTRODUCTION

Percival Christopher Wren is best known as a novelist, publishing twenty-eight novels from 1912 to 1941, the most famous being *Beau Geste* (1924). Wren also published seven short story collections; *Stepsons of France* (1917), *The Young Stagers* (1917), *Good Gestes* (1929), *Flawed Blades* (1933), *Port o' Missing Men* (1934), *Rough Shooting* (1938), and *Odd—But Even So* (1941), containing a total of 116 stories. There were also two omnibus collections, *Stories of the Foreign Legion* (1947) and *Dead Men's Boots* (1949), containing stories taken from *Stepsons of France, Good Gestes, Flawed Blades,* and *Port o' Missing Men.* All 116 short stories can be found in the five volume collection, *The Collected Short Stories of Percival Christopher Wren.*[1]

Wren was a man of mystery in that the more popular biographical statements about him seem to be more fiction than fact. A typical biography places his birth in Devon in 1885, educated at Oxford, and having a career of world traveler, hunter, journalist, tramp, British cavalry trooper, legionary in the French Foreign Legion, assistant director of education in Bombay, and a Justice of the Peace. Most of the above biography, however, has not been verified.

Wren was born Percy Wren on November 1, 1875 in Deptford, a district of South London on the banks of the Thames. He did attend Oxford University, graduating in 1898 with a 3rd class honours in History leading to a Bachelor of Arts degree. He attained his "M.A." in 1901. In those days, a person acquired a "M.A." after a certain number of years (three in Wren's case) and upon payment of a fee.

After leaving Oxford, he married Alice Lucie

---

[1] For further information on *The Collected Short Stories of Percival Christopher Wren* see rinerpublishing.wordpress.com

vii

Shovelier in December 1899 with whom he had a daughter, Estelle Lenore Wren, born in February 1901, and a son, Percival Rupert Christopher Wren, born in February 1904. Percy worked as a teacher at various commercial schools until 1903 when he and his family left England for India.

From 1903 to approximately 1919 Wren was employed as an educator by the Indian Educational Service (I.E.S.). During that time he published a number of educational textbooks, some of which are still in use in Indian schools today. It was during this period that he started using the name Percival C. and Percival Christopher on the textbooks.

From 1905 to 1915, he also served in the Volunteer Corps (Sind and Poona) in India (see the novel *Drift-wood Spars*, which has a description of a Volunteer Corps), and was appointed a Captain in the Indian Army Reserve of Officers, the 101st Grenadiers of the Indian Infantry, in November 1914. He probably saw action in the East African campaign of World War I (see the novel *Cupid in Africa*, which takes place in East Africa), and resigned from the Indian Army Reserve of Officers in November 1915.[2]

Wren's first novel, *Dew and Mildew*, was published by Longmans, Green in 1912. His first novel of the French Foreign Legion, *The Wages of Virtue*, was written in 1913 and published by John Murray in 1916. One of the many questions about Wren is whether he did serve in the French Foreign Legion. Given the chronology of his documented biography it is hard to see where he had time to actually serve in the Legion. Wren himself always maintained that he had served, and his stepson, Richard Alan Graham-Smith, who died in 2006, "strongly maintained that Wren had indeed served in the French Foreign Legion and was

---

[2] Most of the biographical information about Wren has been obtained through certificates, documents, and original research at the British Library, Bodleian Library, and the India Office papers. Detailed documentation and sources will be cited in the biographical essay to be included in the forthcoming publication, *An Annotated Bibliography of Percival Christopher Wren*.

always quick to refute those who said otherwise."[3]

*   *   *   *   *   *   *

The series, *The Collected Novels of P. C. Wren,* is intended to include all twenty-eight novels in seven thematic omnibus volumes. The number of physical volumes will be fourteen, with each thematic volume divided into Part A and Part B. The individual titles will not be in Wren's original publication order, but will instead have a connecting theme such as characters or locale. The seven volumes are[4]:

> v. 1 - The Geste Novels
> > Part A:
> > > Beau Geste
> > > Beau Sabreur
> > Part B:
> > > Beau Ideal
> > > Spanish Maine
> v. 2 - The Sinbad Novels
> > Part A:
> > > Action and Passion
> > > Sinbad the Soldier
> > Part B:
> > > Fort in the Jungle
> > > The Disappearance of General Jason
> v. 3 - The Foreign Legion Novels
> > Part A:
> > > The Wages of Virtue
> > > Sowing Glory
> > Part B:
> > > The Uniform of Glory
> > > Paper Prison
> v. 4 - The Earlier India Novels
> > Part A:
> > > Dew and Mildew
> > > Father Gregory

---

[3] wikipedia.org/wiki/P._C._Wren
[4] The order of volumes four through seven has been modified since the publication of volume two, *The Sinbad Novels.*

Part B:
Snake and Sword
Driftwood Spars
v. 5 - The Later India Novels
Part A:
Beggars' Horses
Explosion
Part B:
Man of a Ghost
Worth Wile
v. 6 - The English Novels
Part A:
Bubble Reputation
Cardboard Castle
Part B:
The Mammon of Righteousness
Two Feet From Heaven
v. 7 - Other Novels
Part A:
Soldiers of Misfortune
Valiant Dust
Part B:
Cupid in Africa
Mysterious Waye

*   *   *   *   *   *   *

Volume Three of *The Collected Novels of P. C. Wren*, *The Foreign Legion Novels*, contains four novels that feature the French Foreign Legion. There are other novels by Wren featuring the Foreign Legion (the three Geste novels, *Spanish Maine*, *Fort in the Jungle*, and *Valiant Dust*), but they are included in different volumes in *The Collected Novels of P. C. Wren*.

*   *   *   *   *   *   *

The Foreign Legion Novels Part B

The Foreign Legion Novels Part B contains the novels *Paper Prison*, published in 1939, and *The*

Uniform of Glory, published in 1941.

Paper Prison is the story of twin fraternal brothers, Mark and Luke Tuyler, and the woman whom they love, Rosanne. The novel is organized into three parts, with each of the three major characters presenting a first person narrative with over-lapping chronology. The first and longest part is by Mark, being almost as long as the other two parts, by Luke and Rosanne respectively, combined.

The story begins with Luke, the romantic and poet of the two brothers, and Mark, the more pragmatic brother, joining the Foreign Legion while in France at the beginning of World War I. The story starts out as a standard romantic version of war, but quickly becomes more realistic in its description of the trench warfare of World War I, and the horrific results of "shell shock", or as the disorder is now known, PTSD (Posttraumatic Stress Disorder). After being wounded, Luke cannot tolerate returning to the Front, and instead pretends to be blind. Aiding him in this deception is the villain of the novel, Yrotavál, a Spaniard similar to Spanish Maine of the novel, *Spanish Maine* (1935).

In Mark's story (Part 1), Mark tells about his experiences in the war, as both a legionnaire and as a British army soldier. While Mark was in France at the front, Luke marries Rosanne. When Mark discovers that Luke is taking advantage of his fake blindness and is blackmailed by Yrotavál, Mark contrives to have Yrotavál also join the Foreign Legion with him. Eventually, Mark kills Yrotavál, thus removing his evil influence from Luke's and Rosanne's life.

In Part 2, Luke relates how throughout his life, he has always been a "storyteller". He is constantly looking out for "number one", and has always had Mark to look after him and to take the blame whenever he gets in trouble.

In Part 3, Rosanne recounts how she joined the family, when Mark and Luke's father married her mother, and how she falls in love with Mark but marries Luke out of sympathy to his blindness. Eventually Rosanne discovers Luke's deception and the results are tragic (at least for Luke!).

Paper Prison is a complex novel, published (and assumed to be written) in the later part of Wren's life. It is more realistic than most of his more famous novels, with its themes of infidelity, divorce, blackmail, and "killing no murder". At the same time, there are similarities to other Wren novels and stories. For example, the theme of brothers (and their love for each other) featured in the Geste novels.

In *Paper Prison*, the description of Luke's character is similar to the description of Wren himself, which is a little disconcerting since Luke is the villain of the novel (or one of them at least). Luke is described as an artist, poet, story writer, and a psychic. All of which, except for the artist, sounds similar to what is known about Wren. One psychic story told in *Paper Prison* by Luke is the same story published by Wren as a "true" account from his life. This is the story of the Viking ship seen in a vision related in "I Saw a Vision" that first appeared in the magazine *Prediction* in December 1938.[5]

Paper Prison has an interesting bibliographic history. It was originally published by John Murray in 1939. An American edition was published in 1940 by Macrae-Smith under the title, *The Man the Devil Didn't Want*.

For many years there has been two unknown titles attributed to Wren: *Blind Man's Buff* and *None Are So Blind*. In 1953, Hamilton published *Paper Prison* as two separate paperbacks. The first paperback, comprising Part 1 bears the title, *Paper Prison*, and the second paperback, comprising Parts 2 and 3 has the title *Blind Man's Buff*.[6] *None Are So Blind* appeared in a list of Wren's books found in *Twentieth Century Authors*.[7] The phrase "none are so blind" certainly fits the theme of

---

[5] *The Collected Short Stories of Percival Christopher Wren*, volume five, pages 83-86.
[6] One of the rarest, if not the rarest, of Wren's books, the only copy examined was found in the Bodleian Library at Oxford University.
[7] Kunitz, Stanley. *Twentieth Century Authors, a Biographical Dictionary of Modern Literature.* New York, H. W. Wilson, 1942.

Paper Prison. All four of the titles appear in the text of *Paper Prison* in either the exact phrase or a close relative.[8]

Paper Prison has, in comparison to other Wren books, a fairly long dedication.

> To Mrs. John Hardy of Santiago de Chile. My dear Dora, Although I visit you and John with the utmost regularity once every fifteen years, and write to you without fail once every three years, I should also like to dedicate a book to you every decade or so. I am therefore dedicating this one to You, to happy memories and to the famous hospitality of the Coast. Yours, P.C.W. Puerto Montt, S. America, Feb. 1938.

The Uniform of Glory was the last novel published in Wren's lifetime (March 1941). A short story collection, *Odd—But Even So* was published in November 1941, the same month as when Wren died (22 November).

The Uniform of Glory is a humorous novel which has the subtitle of "being the true story of a free Frenchman's night out". It is the story of Denis Ducros, a legionnaire who is the servant of the Colonel, Louis Rochefort. On the night of a Legion fête day, Denis dons the uniform of the Colonel and cleverly impersonates him out on the town. The Colonel is ill and in bed, not to be disturbed for any reason. Denis has a number of adventures pretending to be the Colonel, including giving non-commissioned officers a dreadful time, giving ordinary legionnaires an enjoyable time, helping the Colonel's daughter with her romance, and helping a number of "filles de joie"[9] to escape their environment for the evening.

This story of a legionnaire impersonating a Legion

---

[8] "paper prison" five times herein pages 232, 276, 288, 301, and 315; "the man the devil doesn't want" one time herein pages 108-109; "none are so blind" one time herein page 268; "blind-man's-buffing" one time herein page 99.

[9] prostitutes.

officer might be based on a true story (see subtitle mentioned above). A very similar story is related in *The French Foreign Legion* by John Laffin.[10] Whether Laffin is basing his account on Wren's novel or a true legend from the Legion is unknown.

Two minor characters mentioned in *The Uniform of Glory* have appeared in other Wren novels and stories about the Legion. One of them, Captain Le Sage, appears in the novel, *Valiant Dust* (1932), and the short stories "Mastic—and Drastic", "The Dust That Was Barren", "The Betrayal of Odo Klemens", and "Cafard".[11] The other minor character is a brief mention of Sergeant Major Lejaune of *Beau Geste* fame.

The Uniform of Glory was published in 1941 by John Murray in the United Kingdom, Macrae-Smith in the United States, and Longmans, Green in Canada. It was reprinted in hardback in a London Book Club edition in 1943 and by Gryphon in 1949. It was also printed in paperback by the Australasian Publishing Company (for the British Publishers Guild) in 1945, Kemsley Newspapers in 1951, and Merit Books in 1955. The dedication was "To Dr. James S. and Mrs. Torfrida Robinson and Mrs. Hereward E. Wake, in token of gratitude for incredible kindness. Holnicote, January 1941."

*   *   *   *   *   *   *

The original spelling, punctuation, and grammar, except for obvious errors, have been preserved as found in the latest editions/printings of the stories during Wren's lifetime (1875-1941). The footnotes, in the novels, are also as found in the original source material.

---

[10] Laffin, John. *The French Foreign Legion*. London, Dent, 1974. pages 46-47.
[11] *Valiant Dust* is scheduled for publication in volume 7 of *The Collected Novels of P. C. Wren*. "Mastic—and Drastic", "The Dust That Was Barren", "The Betrayal of Odo Klemens", and "Cafard" can be found respectively in volumes 2, 3, 4, and 5 of *The Collected Short Stories of Percival Christopher Wren*.

PAPER PRISON

CONTENTS

PART ONE

MARK CALDON TUYLER

PART TWO

LUKE RIVERS TUYLER

PART THREE

ROSANNE VAN DATEN

I

MARK CALDON TUYLER

I

I am neither superstitious nor a believer in omens and portents, but I have to admit that to-day's series of events has been rather remarkable. I believe that such occurrences are supposed to "go in threes." That has been the number.

And I cannot avoid feeling that things have conspired, and Fate has intended, to bring Luke to the forefront of my mind, and to keep him there—until I do something about it. He always is in my mind, of course, if only at the back of it. And to-day's events have shown me that, if only for Rosanne's sake, the sooner I get him out of it the better. For he is on my mind as well as in it. On my mind, because, whatever I may have done at the time, I have blamed myself ever since. Blamed myself, and not Luke.

He was spoilt, and I spoiled him more than anybody did; spoiled him more than Father and Mother did; possibly more, even, than Athene and Rosanne did.

I suppose it was, in a way, natural that, in the shock of the discovery, in my first overwhelming anger and heartbreaking misery, I should not only blame him but secretly curse him, denounce him.

Thank God it was in secret; and for it I can also thank my old house-master, Charles Rocke, and his eternal slogan *'Blame yourself, if possible,'* a motto according to which he lived, and endeavoured to make us live.

Rosanne, of course, says that I have nothing whatsoever with which to reproach myself in the matter of Luke's tragedy, but that is Rosanne's comforting way.

Confession is good for the soul. The priests say so, and the psycho-analysts agree; so perhaps I shall feel better if I set it down fully, truthfully, and without bias. I couldn't feel worse, anyhow.

And to-day has made it clear that I must do something or other. Queer that it should have been left for

General Hector Mandrell, of all people, to be the deciding cause or factor. Rather heavy, physically and mentally, to play the part of the Last Straw—man of straw though he is.

It began at breakfast-time. I was sitting staring at Luke's picture, brooding, thinking of him, of course, instead of talking to Rosanne, when—he disappeared—and there was a sudden crash that almost made me jump out of my chair.

"*Look! He has* . . ." I began, as Rosanne sprang to her feet and turned round and we both stared at the blank space on the wall above the long old-fashioned sideboard . . . and realized that the portrait had fallen down behind it, smashing the glass. It was a big oil-painting, done in Paris by the famous Roger Lecomte, when he and Luke were *Quartier Latin* students.

I am *not* superstitious; but it affected me queerly, that sudden crashing disappearance of the face that had been there opposite to mine at every meal . . . the eyes that had looked into mine, seeming to hold a message . . . the lips about to speak. . . .

It is absurd to attach significance to an event caused by a rusted wire, a rotted cord, a nail insecure in crumbling mortar, and I refused to let it affect me, but I could see that Rosanne was troubled.

"We won't hang it there again," she said. "Face to face with you. I ought to have moved it."

"It has moved itself, now," said I, and went out of the room.

Luke's face. The eyes watching me. Eyes that haunted me. The lips about to move; to give me a message. What would he say? That I should not be sitting in that chair? That I should never tell Rosanne? A prayer that I would keep his dreadful secret?

Which shows the state to which this brooding on the past, this entertainment of an *idée fixe*, had reduced my nerves.

And having realized this, and picked up a book that lay on the table beside my armchair, that I might compel my thoughts to turn to some other subject, I opened it and read.

And then the second of the events that started me writing this.

I did not read the book for long, for it was written by one of those lying knaves or besotted fools who in their wisdom and utter ignorance of the facts, tell us that War brings out all the best in us; that War is ennobling; that the fires of War burn out our dross and purify us, and so forth. Presumably, then, a returning army consists of white-souled Galahads whose strength is as the strength of ten because their hearts are pure! That must be why every war is followed by an increase of crimes of violence. This particular fool or knave talked of the beauty added to War by the use of the aeroplane, and spoke of young noble souls swooping like angels through the air, the new cavalry of the clouds; of how War was no longer earth-bound, pedestrian and . . . all the rest of it.

And then he spoke of the beauties of bombing, and suddenly I hurled the book from me, sprang to my feet, and almost lost control. I saw red. I saw that other bomb—that fell at Luke's feet, the bomb that almost blasted the soul from his body, the sight from his eyes, the strength and grit from his character.

"The beauty and poetry of War!"

Had the heroic bomb-dropping poet been before me in the flesh, at that moment, I should have committed murder.

With my bare hands I would have torn his . . .

And I realized that I was trembling from head to foot, sweating like a race-horse—which, for the second time that morning, showed me the condition of my nerves.

War ennobling! Read of what War did to my brother Luke and to me.

And the third occurrence, the little drama at the Club, an hour later, with General Hector Mandrell and little Simms-Dexter as protagonists.

I never used to hate anybody, except Yrotavál. Not a

soul in the world—but I am beginning to hate my neighbour as myself; and particularly I hate General Mandrell for a stupid pompous ass, arrogant and overbearing; a man who always does the foolish thing and never says a wise one. His one idea of conversation is to contradict and, presuming on his seniority, to do it with the utmost rudeness.

Did he but realize it, he contradicts himself more than he does anyone else.

I was sitting staring out of the window seeing nothing that was there, and terrible things that were not. Luke's portrait falling; that bomb falling; Luke flung flaming up into the air; buried alive.

Staring, seeing nothing that was there, I became gradually aware of Simms-Dexter, whose hobby is visiting castles and drawing pictures of their interiors, talking to his friend, Major Johnstone.

"Yes, lovely court-yard and banqueting-hall," he was saying. "Dungeons too. I made a sketch of the place where they kept that chap whose hair went white, but not 'in a single night as men's have done from sudden fright,' whom What's-his-name wrote about in . . ."

"*No-one's* hair ever went white in a single night," interrupted General Mandrell loudly. "No, nor grey, either. Lot of damn nonsense."

"Well, General," faltered little Simmy, instead of ignoring the man, "they say that a tremendous shock will . . ."

"Then they are liars," interrupted Mandrell again. "No one's hair ever altered by the slightest shade in a single night. Nor in a single week either. Nor a month. Damn nonsense."

Little Simms-Dexter, afraid of the arrogant old bully, faltered something about it being doubtless one of those popular fallacies which . . . and sat looking foolish, snubbed into silence. Then, before I quite realized what I was doing, I turned and butted in— partly because I like little Simmy, partly because I detest Mandrell, and mainly because my nerves got the better of me again.

"Not a fallacy at all," I said, pointedly addressing Simms-Dexter. "Established fact. A man's hair can turn colour, to some extent, in a single night, even if it doesn't actually go white."

"*Bosh!*" snorted the General, and I carefully forbore to glance at his over-pink fat face, or meet his cold fishy eye.

"Er—one has heard so, of course," stammered Simmy, "b-b-but . . ."

"Heard so!" snorted the General. "D'ye believe all you hear?"

"And I can tell you of someone to whom it actually happened," I added, looking at Simms-Dexter, across Mandrell's arm-chair.

"Really?" said Simmy, perking up. "Someone you actually knew?"

"Know him still, worse luck," I growled.

"Huh! You 'know someone.' Always a third person!" sneered Mandrell again. "We all know someone else who has heard it or seen it, don't we? Always someone else. Someone else—who has seen the ghost. Someone else—who was there when the Prime Minister told the King off."

Still keeping my eyes on Simms-Dexter's face.

"I'll introduce him to you, if you like," I said.

"Yes! And get his sworn statement that it actually happened," jeered Mandrell, who, entirely unaccustomed to contradiction, was getting angry.

"Will you? By Jove, that would be interesting," chirruped Simmy.

"I will."

"Some day," grunted the General.

"To-day," I continued, to Simms-Dexter. "He's a member of this Club. And a living proof of the truth that a man's hair can change colour in a night."

This was too much for General Mandrell, and he intended that I should ignore him no longer.

"And I suppose you were present when it happened, Tuyler," he scoffed, addressing me personally, in his most sarcastic and offensive manner.

"I was present when it happened," I said—to

Simms-Dexter.

There almost seemed to be an extra glow of light and warmth in the vast room as the General's face crimsoned.

"Good Lord!" ejaculated Johnstone, speaking for the first time. "Who's the man?"

"I'm the man," I replied, turning to Johnstone, who glanced at my prematurely grey, almost white hair, which, while I was in my early twenties, was black one day, greying the next, and quite grey a few days later.

"I *say!*" said Simms-Dexter contritely, "I'm awfully sorry if I have said anything that has led to . . . I mean to say . . . I didn't wish to ask any personal questions . . . or say anything that . . ."

"Not at all," I reassured him. "Entirely my own fault if . . ."

Though, in point of fact, it was the General's fault, with his insolent and ignorant assertions and contradictions on a subject concerning which I was only too well informed.

"My own fault if it were painful. But it isn't," I lied, still addressing Simms-Dexter. "I'll tell you."

And then I could have bitten out my tongue as they stared at me expectant, and Colonel Anstruther strolled over and stood listening. Unspeakable damned fool that I was, to have let Mandrell irritate me into talking, interfering, and *exposing* myself like this.

Of course I couldn't tell them. . . . I must be going mad . . . I must get out of it, somehow.

I could see that Simms-Dexter was sorry for me. Sorry that it had happened. Probably I had gone pale and was visibly sweating.

"An illness?" he said, giving me a lead.

"No. Something I saw."

"*Some* ghost! What?" contributed the General.

"Something I saw, as I looked in at a window. My brother was alone in the room, in perfect health and safety . . . but he . . ." I said, my mind standing aside, as it were, and wondering what my body would do next; what I should say next.

"My brother," I repeated, and stopped in time.

Then I had to go before I disgraced myself. Before I broke down. I couldn't say another word. Fortunately, I hurried from the room and out of the Club.

And then, fully and finally, I realized the state in which my nerves must be, the direction in which I was heading; the life that I was leading, and that I was leading poor Rosanne.

Confession is good for the soul. Confession may save me.

I am ashamed, ashamed to the depths of my being, that I should be so weak. But Luke was my twin.

Incidentally I am much less ashamed of the facts that I deserted from my regiment, and that I murdered a man in cold blood.

II

Although Luke and I were twins, I doubt whether two people were ever less alike, in essentials, than he and I. I don't know whether we were phenomenal in that respect, for there seems to be a very widely-spread belief that twins are always as alike as two pins, both physically and mentally. We were alike physically, though easily distinguishable, but there all resemblance ended.

From early childhood, the tremendous differences between us were patent. Luke was clever, I was stupid. Luke was an artist to his finger-tips, whereas I had no artistic gift or inclination whatsoever. To him a sunset was matter for enthusiasm, joy, rapture. To me, a primrose by a river's brim, or anywhere else, was—just that.

Luke was a genuine poet; and in the opinion of more than one eminent critic, his best poems were in the same class with those of Rupert Brooke, of Laurence Binyon, and of that tragic genius who was our comrade-in-arms, Alan Seeger, whose famous, perhaps immortal, poem, *"I have a rendezvous with Death,"* Luke saw scribbled in pencil, on the back of a letter.

Luke was a musician, and not only a first-class pianist and violinist, but a composer. He understood music, loved music, knew all about music, expressed his beautiful soul and spirit in music. I know nothing whatsoever about it, and don't even appreciate it.

And from babyhood, Luke could talk. He could talk an angry man into good temper, and, what is more, he could talk an angry woman into a good humour. He could wheedle a bird from a tree, as they say. He could talk on any subject, at any time, in any place; and he could change and sway the temper of a crowd. I am rather inarticulate.

And whereas Luke's repartee was brilliant, swift, keen and incisive as rapier play, I could always think of the right answer—the next day.

And, particularly and above all, Luke was *charming*. Always and to everyone he was charming; and I never met the person who could long resist him. In what his remarkable charm lay, one could not say. He was very handsome, and of course that helped; his manners were delightful, and his manner perfect, and that, again, was a great asset; but that was not all, or his charm would have been superficial. True, he could and did use it consciously and openly. He deliberately set himself to please people, and inevitably they were pleased; but there was no harm in that. Surely it is better to charm than to offend, to please than to annoy; better to arouse approval, liking and admiration than to leave a cold surface of indifference untouched and unbroken?

No, it was beauty of face and person, easy pleasantness of manner and manners, combined with his remarkable gifts and abilities, that gave him his charm; and, undoubtedly, it was that perfectly indescribable elusive attribute which we call, for want of a better word, personality, that was the essence of his charm.

And it was only people of the envious and curmudgeonly type who said sneeringly, as though it were a grievous fault in him, that Luke deliberately laid himself out to win popularity. Of course he did—and made the world about him a brighter and a better place by the fact of his doing so.

It was something of a blow to Father, and I think to Athene as well, when he made it perfectly clear, once and for all, that, for better or worse, for richer or poorer, he was going to leave Oxford and be a painter; that he was going to Paris to study, and that when he had learned all the French School had to teach him—in other words, when he was tired of Paris—he was going on to Rome.

I have said that he knew all about music, and the same applies to painting. What I mean is, that he knew all about the various theories of painting, and knew the history of the world's great artists and of their pictures. He had spent days in all the great art-galleries of Europe, and had read, both deeply and widely, the literature of Art.

If only he had gone to any place but Paris, if only he had gone at any other time, he would be alive now. But then Rosanne and I . . . No—this speculation on causality is childish.

As always, he had his own way, partly through the exercise of his irresistible charm, which neither Father nor Athene could ever withstand; partly by reason of his equally irresistible, because inflexible, wilfulness and determination to have his own way. He went off to Paris in his own good time, and the time, alas, was before his twentieth birthday, in the June of his first year at Oxford. I regretted his leaving us, and wanted to go with him. Luke wished to go alone, however, and Luke, as usual, did as he wished.

I think Rosanne hated his going more than anyone did, and literally mourned for him. The big house seemed positively empty, silent, deserted; and we missed him at every hour of the day. Rosanne hardly exaggerated when she said that the sun seemed to shine less brightly and less frequently now that Luke was gone; that there was less to do—and that less worth the doing—since Luke had departed; and that she had *so* earnestly looked forward to four whole months of the Long, with us. And she didn't exaggerate at all in saying that life was the poorer, emptier, less colourful, for his going.

It may be imagined, then, that I jumped at the opportunity of visiting Paris that July of my first Oxford long vacation, when I got a letter from him in which, half-woefully, half-humorously, he admitted that he was in what he called a spot of bother, and would be glad of my help, if only to the extent of good advice.

It was a constant source of amusement and pleasure to me that Luke always behaved as though I were very much his senior, alluded to me as a wise old bird, described me as a very present help in time of trouble, and always turned to me in time of need. Perhaps the tremendous difference between Luke and myself was, after all, accounted for by my being his complement; my earth-bound pedestrian qualities and such few solid virtues that I might possess, supplementing his brilliance, his soaring attributes of grace and beauty, as might a pedestal of stone play its humble necessary part in supporting, sustaining and completing a lovely statue of bronze, nay, gold.

Arrived in Paris, I found that I had come none too soon; that if I could be his friend in need, I should be a friend indeed; for he was in a mess. With his usual impetuosity, his headlong carelessness of consequences, and his undiscerning eye for worth—that went so strangely with his unerring eye for beauty—he had become deeply and unfortunately entangled with a most dangerous undesirable woman.

I had gathered from his letters that he was conscientiously and unconscionably leading *la vie de bohême;* and I had imagined, or rather hoped, that no great harm would follow that common phase of youthful folly. Mere unprofitable culture of the wild oat. Before ever he trod the pavement of the *Boul' Miche,* he had been an assiduous student of Murger and Du Maurier; had visualized himself in *béret* and peg-topped corduroys and spacious studio embellished with the correct furnishings, inanimate and other, and therein leading the life of Loudon Dodd and Jim Pinkerton, of the Laird of Cockpen, Trilby, and Little Billee, and a dozen other heroes evoked by his over-vivid imagination from a vanished past.

That he would have a *belle amie* who was his model, his mistress and his housekeeper was inevitable, the right and proper immorality of his rôle. But that he should ever be in grievous danger of the wrong and improper morality of marriage—to a golden-haired, brazen-faced, steel-mouthed woman, older and abler than himself, I had not dreamed. Nor had he, when lightly he embarked upon his adventure with Mrs. Ogden Lemburg, wealthy, elegant, and vicious ornament of a fashionable expatriate clique. She would have been his utter ruin in every way that matters, rich as she was in everything that does not matter.

As soon as he had told me his version of the affair, and I had seen the woman, I could also see what had happened. Carelessly Luke had turned upon her the battery of his charm; immediately she had seen in him something new and delightful, piquantly fresh, clean, and unspoilt; and, so far as such a woman could, she had fallen in love with him. She wanted him and meant to have him and hold him—in the bonds of an unholy matrimony.

But there is no point in wasting time over her. She merely came into our lives as the cause of my going to Paris; for, within a week of my doing so, War broke out, Paris went mad, all bonds were broken, all values changed, and an even more imperious mistress took him from her—*Madame la République*—and made for him his "rendezvous with Death."

In this universal madness none went madder than the circle that revolved round Luke; French, American, Russian, Belgian, Spanish, Danish, Swedish, Italian and English. Inspired and led by the Spirit of Paris, all the artists were instantly more anti-German than the French; more patriotic, more Francophile than the Parisians themselves.

And, while French eyes but looked hopefully upon the Americans, French tongues assailed the English. What would England do? And at the top of his golden voice Luke told them. With all the assurance and persuasion of his natural gift of oratory, he assured and re-assured them. And as his bosom friend, Réné Barbey d'Aurillac cried aloud, with tears of emotion and alcohol streaming down his face, his *cher ami,* the Apostle Luke, would set England the example.

He did. I don't think Luke slept during those days of August, when France was at war with Germany and England was not. One of the many pictures that will never fade from my mind is Luke, on the day that France declared war, standing high above our heads, in the huge dining room of the *Coq d'Or,* the artists' restaurant in the *Boul' Miche,* one foot on his chair, the other on the table, his glass held high, calling on every Englishman, every American, every Italian, Spaniard, Swede, Dane, or Dutchman present, to fight for France, for Freedom, and for Faith; for Honour, Truth, Beauty and all things that were worth fighting for. England would fight for these things. . . .

"With her mouth," shouted a crapulous, unpleasant looking individual sitting apart at a distant table.

Luke broke off in mid-sentence, and, as always, when confronted with rudeness and unmannerly rebuff, looked genuinely hurt.

"England?" shouted the man. "She'll do what she has always done. Welcome and encourage war, then step aside, sell munitions and profit by . . ."

Then Luke flared up, sprang to the ground, rushed at the man and, as he rose to his feet, knocked him backward across his chair, where he lay stunned or shamming.

Returning and leaping up on to his table, he shouted,

"Listen! To-morrow I shall be in a French uniform! And next week there'll be an English army in France! And next month, it will be in Germany! And . . ."

And when the din of cheering had subsided,

"Who's coming with me *now*—straight to the Recruiting Office?" he cried, and a score of voices shouted in English,

"I am! . . . We all are!" and, headed by Luke, a crowd of us surged to the door, shouting, laughing, waving flags, bottles, hats, chairs—and quickly formed a procession that marched straight from the *Boul' Miche* to the Rue St. Dominic and the recruiting Office of the French Foreign Legion.

III

I haven't the slightest intention of adding another to the plethora of stories of the War, nor do I wish to write an account of Life in the French Foreign Legion, save in so far as is necessary to give a clear understanding of what happened to Luke, of what Luke did, and of the events that led to his doing it.

At the Recruiting Office, we were warmly received, generously praised, and coldly requested to sleep on it; and, if we were of the same mind in the morning, to come again, when, provided we passed the medical examination, we should be enrolled as soldiers of France.

Outside the stuffy little *Bureau de Récrutement,* Luke harangued us in English, for the majority of us were Britons and Americans, and again in French, for the benefit of the others who, among them, represented Russia, Italy, Spain, Holland, Belgium, Denmark, Sweden and, if I remember rightly, Greece and Rumania—bidding us be here, to a man, at eight in the morning; urging us to count ourselves, that we should know if any of us were missing; and generally endeavouring to keep our hot enthusiasm at fever-pitch.

We counted ourselves, made a different total every time, and swore that nothing but death should keep us from returning on the morrow.

I think there were very few defections; and no one failed to pass the somewhat perfunctory medical examination, and be declared *bon pour le service.*

It was very simple, that step which changed us from free and independent civilians into bond-slave soldiers of France. I should think there were a dozen Englishmen, and a score of Americans, who enlisted that day, and at least as many of assorted nationalities. They were splendid specimens and, among the Americans particularly, were men who attained distinction before America entered the War, won decorations and commissions, or obtained a transfer to the Flying Corps and wrote their names large on the blood-stained glorious Roll of Honour of those early days of aviation.

Kniffin Yates Rockwell made flying history, became an ace of the ever-glorious Lafayette Squadron, brought down numerous German planes and, when killed fighting, was buried with all the pomp and circumstance of a French public military funeral.

James W. Condon, after a career of distinction and decoration, became a gunner officer; Bert Hall went to the Flying Corps, won the highest distinctions, and survived the War. But very few others did so.

Like Alan Seeger, the poet, they died for France and Freedom, among them, Russell Kelly, Kenneth Weeks, Dennis Dowd, Jules Harris, Homer H. Conklin, and many others whom I did not know so well, and whose names I have forgotten.

They died, but Luke and I survived, alas. . . .

Each of us having given his name, or *nom de guerre;* age, rightly or wrongly, for we were supposed to be over eighteen; nationality; height and weight; we signed a document, received a stamped form, and were told to be at the Gare de Lyons on the morrow, catch the Lyons train, and report at the Infantry Barracks there.

The first fight of our career in the French Foreign Legion took place on the railway-platform, when we literally fought our way into the train in which there was already standing-room only, and a score of men in each compartment intended to hold six. I know that Luke and I stood face to face from Paris to Lyons, almost without moving; and that, by the time we arrived, Luke was so white that I thought he would faint. Had he done so, it would have been impossible for him to fall. However, release from that awful heat and pressure, and a few deep draughts of fresh air, put him right, and by the time we reached the Barracks, he was himself again, brimful of eagerness, and the acknowledged leader of the English party.

It was delightful to see how popular he was, and how his wonderful charm gave him a kind of ascendancy over, and natural leadership of, our group; and I was very interested and pleased to see that most of the Americans obviously approved and liked him.

So numerous were the new impressions and so swiftly they now came, that my mind soon ceased to be receptive. Everything was so unfamiliar, so strange, and the change was so sudden and subversive, that one's senses became dulled, the result being that I have blurred recollections, and no very clear memory, of the details of our first experiences of the French Army. Yesterday, a quiet and ordinary English civilian; to-day, a soldier of France, a member of the famous French Foreign Legion.

But I do remember that Luke and I were filled high with the spirit of sacrifice, and with a burning desire to excel as soldiers, to get to the Front, and to strike our blow for Right against Might, for Freedom against Oppression. Consequently, when directed from the Barracks to a building that, up to yesterday, had been a Girls' School, we were delighted to lie down to sleep, fully dressed, on straw spread over the bare floor; to spring up at five the next morning, and be the first to answer a Staff-Sergeant's bawl for *deux hommes de bonne volonté.* Two men of good will! There existed no men of better will than Luke and I; but I can see his face now as, with a grin, the Sergeant directed us to seize each a mop and a bucket, and set us to work to swab the muddy floor of his office.

Thereafter our *volonté* was no less *bonne,* but we did not obtrude it.

Contrary to what I had, for some reason, expected, I found that we volunteers for the Legion were formed into national groups, so that there were complete English and American sections, a Russian and a Belgian, and that wherever men of countries less well represented wished to serve together, they could do so. From the very first, I had had a great fear that I might be separated from Luke; and had made up my mind that, cost what it might, in money for bribery and corruption, or in punishment for deserting my own *escouade* and joining Luke's, I would prevent this.

Our English group contained men from all walks of life, though a considerable proportion of them were artists and art-students, the others including clerks, waiters, teachers, shop-assistants, jockeys and stable-boys, and domestic servants thrown out of employment by the mobilization, and one or two nondescript down-and-outs.

The Americans seemed much more homogeneous, a very united band, fine physical specimens, excellent fellows, and magnificent material.

Whatever the Legion may have worn later, it wore the famous old uniform in those early days of 1914; the long heavy blue overcoat, buttoned back to give freedom to the legs; the distinctive baggy red trousers; red *képi*; patent-leather puttees, and strong heavy *brodequins* with a half-inch sole which had one hundred and sixty-two hob-nails in it. Over the overcoat, we wore the wide blue Legion sash, some twenty feet in length, kept in place by a broad leather belt with heavy brass buckle. We were armed with the eight-shot magazine Lebel rifle, and a very long grooved bayonet. Later, the brilliant red trousers being such a conspicuous target, blue overalls were issued, to hide them, as well as a blue cover for the scarlet *képi*.

Luke wore this old-fashioned and romantic-looking uniform with an air, and was not happy until, by repeated exchanges, he had one of which each part fitted him excellently. Had there been time, I have no doubt he would have visited the best Lyons tailor, and either had one made of superior cloth, or that which was issued to him altered until it fitted to perfection.

Scarcely were we equipped, accoutred and armed when, without any drill or training, we were told that we should parade at *réveille* next morning, to entrain for Toulouse, where intensive training would turn us from awkward-squad recruits into real *légionnaires*.

I looked forward with great interest to seeing how the French military authorities would set about this, and how Luke would stand the rigours of the special intensive training. This was bound to be something pretty fierce, inasmuch as there was hardly a man among us who had done a day's soldiering, and the need for us at the Front was imperative.

On the other hand, no drill-instructors were ever presented with better material, or with a body of men of finer spirit and greater keenness.

I was thrilled when I learned that the French War Office authorities—who have nothing much to learn on the subject of military theory or practice—were going to mix five hundred of us volunteer recruits with a thousand trained and experienced regulars of the Foreign Legion who were being brought from Africa.

After four endless days and nights in a cattle-truck, all the hardships of which Luke stood very well, we reached Toulouse and marched to the Infantry Barracks. Here, a number of dug-out *sous-officiers* and elderly officers of the Reserve began our training, taught us our squad-drill, how to make our *paquetage,* do our polishing, and handle our weapons. A considerable part of the remainder of each day was devoted to route-marching, the distances being increased systematically and our loads gradually made heavier.

In a fortnight, we were doing our thirty kilometres a day, carrying the hundred-pound equipment of the 19th African Army Corps.

Luke, still enthusiastically keen, still enjoying life, still full of the romance of being a knight-errant soldier, stood the work, the drill and the marching extremely well. He was quite happy; he was immensely popular; and he was impatiently anxious to get to the Front and join in the fighting.

I think that that period was one of the happiest of his life. He was fully occupied from morning till night, and was thoroughly pleased with himself and everything else. In his uniform he looked handsomer than ever; and was fuller even than usual of high spirits, good humour, and *joie de vivre,* partly owing to the marvellous novelty of the life, and partly to the fact that, owing to the marching, physical-training exercises and the hard work, he was in perfect condition.

§2

And one morning, when we had been there long enough to begin to feel our feet and to look something like soldiers, there marched through the gates and on to the barrack-square, a Battalion of the French Foreign Legion—the *anciens,* real fighting-men, perhaps the best-trained and finest soldiers in the world, bronzed, war-hardened, bearded troops who, for years, had been living in a state of constant active service against the Arabs of Algeria, the Sahara, and Morocco.

I glanced at Luke as I stood watching them march in. His eyes were shining, his whole face alight, as he gazed his fill, breathing the Spirit of Romance. Here was something strange, wonderful, anachronistic. And it was indeed a marvellous Battalion, not only interesting as a military unit, but because it was composed of men, every one of whom had a story. I was stirred as I looked at their lean hard faces, and realized how unique a thing it was; what an incredible collection of men, this Legion of Mercenaries, representative of every country in the world, and of every class and creed and social stratum of that country.

Again I feared that I might be separated from Luke when the fifteen hundred were formed into Sections of sixty, and possibly drafted to different parts of the Front. But we Volunteers were allowed to remain in national Companies, these being diluted, however, by twice the number of trained regulars of the Legion. And amazing men these were; true soldiers, in that they were soldiers and nothing else; men moulded, welded, stamped and sealed to the military pattern; men from whom intelligence, thought, reason, nationality, individuality, originality and all other distinctive attributes had been hammered and excised, that Obedience might take their place and be the soldier's sole mental content.

Obedience their first law—and last. Theirs not to reason why, nor to reason at all, but blindly to obey; so that, supplementing their own indomitable personal courage, there should be that infallible guarantee of unit-courage which is called Discipline.

And from the moment that the thousand trained war-hardened *légionnaires* entered the Barracks, we five hundred Volunteers were absorbed into the body of them, incorporated, became *légionnaires* ourselves, and were treated exactly as they were.

IV

As a rule, Luke and I had hitherto agreed in the matter of liking and disliking people. Almost invariably, if I admired a man or a woman, Luke admired him, or her, equally well; and on the rare occasions when I met somebody whom I heartily disliked, Luke was pretty sure to dislike that person, and for the same reason.

But the man whom Luke introduced to me as *el Señor Don Caballero Yrotavál y Rewes,* and whom he always called Yrotavál, was an exception to this excellent rule, and perhaps that made me dislike him the more.

I wonder if it is possible that I was jealous of the fellow? I hardly think so; but then, of course, I don't wish to think so, and we are wonderful self-deceivers. It is quite probable that I disliked the man himself, for I can truthfully say that I did not take to him at first sight, and had Luke not been there, he was the last man in our *escouade* of whom I should have made a friend.

Either Fate or his own design gave this Yrotavál, as we always called him, the bed next to my brother's; and from the first, he fastened upon Luke and established himself as his *copain.* Luke's charm and perennial attractiveness again, of course. But I doubt whether I did Señor Yrotavál grievous wrong in deciding that Luke's money had more than a little to do with it. These old soldiers from Africa were a thousand minds with but a single thought—wine; and Yrotavál was no exception. Wine was his and their obsession, drunkenness their besetting sin; and for wine they would do anything, steal and sell anything, including their kit and even their hard-earned medals and decorations.

Almost all the Volunteers had private means, if only to the extent of a few pounds, and very many of them had incomes which, in the eyes of the *légionnaires,* were large, indeed enormous, by their narrow standards. A recruit and his money are soon parted—especially when the recruit's comrades are *légionnaires*. In the view of these halfpenny heroes, with their *sou* a day, Luke and I were millionaires, and this Yrotavál promptly appointed Luke as his own private and particular Macenas.

Curious that this little Spaniard who marched into the Infantry Barracks at Toulouse on that August day of 1914 should have affected and influenced Luke's life and mine so tremendously; more even, perhaps, than did Athene, our parents, or even Rosanne herself.

I cannot remember the details of my first meeting with him, but I gradually became aware that Luke was making a new friend; an extremely useful one, who gave him invaluable help with his *astiquage* and *paquetage*, cleaned his boots, polished his buttons, did his washing, gave him invaluable tips, showed him the ropes; taught him how to avoid trouble and how to escape punishment; and generally constituted himself his guide and mentor. He was, of course, invaluable, and the money that Luke paid him for services rendered was undoubtedly a magnificent investment.

I gradually became aware, also, that we two were becoming three; and, quite early, I realized the truth of the adage that two are company and three none. However, as Luke said, he was so extraordinarily useful that it would not only have been ungracious, but foolish, to choke him off.

Whenever I returned from a fatigue or guard duty, I was pretty sure to find Luke and this Yrotavál together, as thick as thieves, Luke usually sitting on his bed, roaring with laughter at his new friend's obscenely foul but very amusing conversation, while the latter did the spit-and-polish work for both of them.

And extremely amusing he assuredly was, partly by reason of the fact that he had a very pretty wit, was blessed with a tremendous sense of humour, and possessed an inexhaustible fund of Rabelaisian stories; partly by reason of the fact that though a Spaniard, a Catalan born and bred in Barcelona, he had migrated to America and lived sufficiently long in New York to have acquired a perfect East Side accent and dialect of English. He had also sojourned in Soho and White-chapel, and learnt the Cockney of the East End of London.

To hear him talk in Legion French interlarded with Catalan, and then suddenly break into the language of the Bowery or Limehouse, was really very funny. It was more so, perhaps, when he would emit a flowing torrent of liquid sibilant Spanish, sonorous and fine-sounding, and then translate it into the most abominable English and American slang.

In appearance, he was a typical Catalan Spaniard, swarthy and leather-faced, with more than a suggestion of a far-back Hispano-Moorish ancestry. He wore his black hair *en brosse* and was clean-shaven, save for bull-fighter side-whiskers; his mouth was an almost lipless straight gash; his eyes, under heavy black brows, were beady, bright and hard, and extremely shifty. Though not big, he was lithe, compact, and immensely strong, wonderfully dapper, quick and deft, especially with his hands, which he never restrained from picking and stealing, and had most assiduously and successfully trained in the use of the knife. This was his favourite weapon and he could also throw it with the speed, accuracy and effect of a pistol-bullet.

As to his antecedents, with varying accounts of which he favoured us from time to time, when under the influence of his favourite drink (a mixture of *vin blanc* and absinthe), he had followed the distinctive Barcelona profession of revolutionist, and had also been either a policeman or a police-agent; probably the latter—a spy, informer or *agent provocateur*. I doubt whether I do him an injustice in believing that, while a youth earning his living at the Docks or in a factory, he had become a Communist, Syndicalist, or Anarchist, had joined in some murderous plot and then betrayed it to the police; that thereafter turning King's Evidence, he had worked with and for the Police against his former associates and other criminal users of dynamite and the assassin's bullet and bomb.

Certainly, when drunk and reminiscently maudlin, he would, on one occasion, tell us how, even in the Legion, his life was not safe from vengeful Anarchists; and on another, how, even here and now, he was in danger of extradition at the instance of the Spanish Police.

On his own showing, he had double-crossed both sides; and one gathered that he had endeavoured to placate his former Anarchist comrades by warning them of projected police-raids upon their meeting-places, or of intended arrests of terrorists against whom the Police had obtained evidence.

On one occasion he would tell how, to escape the Police, he had fled to America; on another, of how, to evade the vengeance of the international Anarchist gang whom he had betrayed, he had fled thence to London, and later to France and joined the Foreign Legion for safety. When sober, he was secretive and completely silent as to his past; but I imagine that when he was drunk and garrulous, it was a case of *in vino veritas,* and that he spoke the truth. Personally, I have no doubt that the same applied to his accounts of his doings in New York, where by his own version he had earned a precarious and dangerous livelihood as a member of a notorious underworld gang. In the spacious days of Prohibition, he would doubtless have been a racketeer and gunman; and would probably have risen to wealth, fame and honour, as a beer-baron or boot-leg king. He certainly had the energy, ability, and utter absence of scruple required for success in that brisk walk of life.

I suppose that such a man as Yrotavál, with his inexhaustible fund of tales of unusual experience, his wit and humour, his ever-cheerful villainy and re-source, was bound to interest anyone so romantic and imaginative as Luke, quite apart from the question of practical usefulness.

But I detested him. He was a specimen of the very worst type of *légionnaire,* and though a fine soldier and extremely courageous, there was something low and obscene and vile about him. Utterly devoid of conscience, morality and scruples, he was essentially bad and base, his character and conduct as foul as his filthy language.

§2

I have introduced this Yrotavál at some length, not because he was more interesting than others of our Section, but because he was to play so unduly important and intimate a part in our lives—Luke's, Rosanne's and mine.

Far more worthy of description and record were Greude, Rassedin, Oberg, Drücke, Araña and several others of our *escouade.*

To my mind, Greude was the most interesting *ancien* of them all, if not of the whole French Foreign Legion, inasmuch as he was a Jew, and, according to all accounts, the only Jew who ever joined *la Légion Étrangère.* Whether this is so, I don't know, but it seems quite probable; for the Jew is not a born soldier, though he can fight as well as anybody when put to it, and he naturally has too much ability, resource and financial flair to sell his services at the rate of a *sou* a day. Usually speaking, he is too practical and too sensible to turn to mercenary soldiering for a living. He is not a romantic, he is not a swashbuckler, he is not a criminal, and he is not a *légionnaire.*

Why Greude enlisted in the Legion, I don't know. It was not because he wished to fight the Germans— although he hated them savagely—for he enlisted some years before the War. He was one of the nicest men I ever met, in the Legion or out, the very antithesis of Yrotavál in every way, and I could not understand why Luke did not infinitely prefer him to the Catalan. One would have expected him and Greude to discover so much more in common, for the Jew had not only a very fine and well-stored mind, but was of definitely artistic temperament, and was fond both of music and of poetry. Whether he had any practical gift and ability as a poet or musician I don't know, but he was a very interesting and obviously competent critic. I often wondered what sent him to the Legion, and also what was at the root of his fanatical hatred of the Germans, and came to the conclusion that the same thing was the cause of both phenomena. He must have been badly treated in Germany, probably on racial grounds. It would not have surprised me to learn that he had been an officer in the German army, and had been persecuted by his brother officers, not only because he was a Jew, but because he was a musician, a poet, and an artist.

Added to his detestation of Germans was a natural loathing—a burning hatred, indeed—of oppression. I suppose that again was racial. Anyhow, the one thing he longed to do was to get to the Front, to get to grips with the enemy, who evidently stood to him for the Enemy of Freedom. He told me that the outbreak of war had delighted him; that he was happier now than he had ever been; and that nothing would give him greater pleasure than to die fighting for the defence of Freedom and the rights of small nations. He longed to do this. His wish was granted.

Greude spoke English and French as fluently and correctly as he did his native German. He was one of the few men to whom one could talk on other subjects than wine, women, war and wickedness (particularly the wickedness of *sous-officiers* and the tobacco ration), and, as I say, it surprised me greatly that he and Luke did not become *copains.* But I suppose this was foolish of me, for there is nothing more incomprehensible and unpredictable than the bases of friendship and the grounds of compatibility. Are we not given constant cause to marvel at the extraordinary people whom people marry? And the same with friendships between those of the same sex.

Anyhow, there it was. Greude, who should have been attracted to Luke, preferred me. Yrotavál amused and interested Luke, and Greude did not. Fate. Our hapless and evil fate. It was written on our foreheads.

Another man whom I liked very much was a Belgian who called himself Rassedin. Although a twice re-enlisted soldier of nearly fifteen years' service, who had earned and won the possibly dubious encomium of *bon camarade et bon légionnaire,* with its implications of boon-companionship and artful old-soldierness, he was, by nature, a quiet and gentle creature who, while taking part in every barrack-room rag and every manifestation of drunken hilarity and cheerful villainy, did so with a sort of mechanical conscientiousness. I believe he thoroughly disliked getting drunk, getting into trouble, and being involved in rows, riots and ruffianism, for, whatever his occasional conduct, he had an essentially orderly and disciplined mind.

I feel pretty sure that he had been an officer in the Belgian Army. If so, he must have been a good one and taken part in the life of the Officers' Mess as faithfully as he did now in that of the Legion barrack-room. He was kindly, dependable and helpful. Like Greude, he was a man with whom one could talk, and I liked him both for himself and for his very obvious admiration for Luke.

That Greude did not seem to share this, not only surprised me very much, but was something of a barrier between the Jew and me. I wondered if it were possible that he and Luke were too much alike, too much of a trade, so to speak, and that each of them found Yrotavál more interesting and amusing than the other, by reason of the fact that opposites attract.

Oberg the Swede, was another likeable member of our *escouade,* because of his sunny temperament and his essential cleanness of mind and body, and beauty of soul. It amazed me that this man should be an *ancien* of the Foreign Legion. I could, of course, have understood his joining to fight for the Cause; but that he should have enlisted in time of peace, and deliberately buried himself in a regiment of mercenary soldiers, was difficult to understand. But here I, not for the first nor last time, talk like a fool; for, later, I did the very same thing myself, and Oberg no doubt had as good, or better, reason for enlisting in the French Foreign Legion. He was one of the most unfailingly cheerful men I ever met. However short other forms of nourishment might be, he always and everywhere contrived to find food for laughter, and inasmuch as his laughter was infectious, he was an invaluable member of our little group.

He, too, was greatly attracted by Luke, and became very fond of him. If only Luke could have reciprocated and made a real friend of him instead of Yrotavál whose interested sycophant toadying he mistook for genuine admiration and affection, our lives would have been different.

Another member of our *escouade* of whom we saw a great deal was El Araña,[12] a poor pitiable creature so low in the human scale as to be a parasite of Yrotavál. He was a pocket Hercules, who, in spite of his enormous physical strength and complete absence of brain, had a curious nervous affliction that impelled him to be for ever plucking non-existent cobwebs from his face.

This was painful to watch, and rather got on one's own nerves. When Luke, irritated beyond bearing, snapped,

"What the Hell are you doing? What the Devil is the matter with you?" he would merely reply, "*Spiders!*" and continue with his ceaseless attempt to free himself from the horrible incubus. Only when asleep, eating, at drill, or cleaning his accoutrements, did his hands relax from this perpetual motion of face-cleansing. I suppose the psycho-analyst of to-day could explain it, and possibly cure it. A big Prussian Guardsman did so, eventually, with a bayonet, death being the German's reward and fee.

Besides being Yrotavál's shadow, butt and slave, Araña was the *escouade's* general factotum, since he was only too pleased to receive so much notice as a request, or order, to clean one's boots. For quite a long time I thought he was dumb. It is instructive to note that this brainless sub-human creature was an entirely satisfactory *légionnaire,* and this statement is a cogent and pertinent comment upon noble and ennobling War.

---

[12] *The Spider.*

Poor Araña. I don't think he ever lifted his eyes to the height of Luke's stature, Yrotavál being a sufficiently god-like superior for his worship. He was a complete animal, his sole mental satisfaction a contemptuous kind word and obscene jest from his adored Yrotavál; and the only taste of physical pleasure that his dull palate ever savoured that of *pinard* and *scafarlati des troupes.*

This last, incidentally, was an incredibly foul and poisonous form of tobacco, by far the worst of even French Government military ration-issues, which is saying something. To the unfortunate *ancien* for whom tobacco was far more of a necessity than a luxury, *Madame la République* issued weekly a small packet of stems; stalks; roots; and the stringy tissue of the largest, worst and cheapest leaves, of the tobacco (or some other) plant. It was practically unsmokeable, not only by reason of its villainous quality, but because of the nature of its form, which rendered cigarette-making impossible. Some of those whose mouths and stomachs were strong enough endeavoured to smoke it in a pipe—and this even before the invention of gas-masks. Fortunately, there was more fire than smoke when a match was applied to *scafarlati des troupes,* or there must have been casualties among the unseasoned troops.

Yes, a queer collection, our *escouade.* The handsome liquid-eyed Jew, with his artistic fingers and sensitive face; the quiet soldierly Belgian, resignedly cheerful *gentilhomme manqué;* the perenially joyous laughing Swede, happy-go-lucky and careless, always merry and bright; the obscene and wicked little Catalan, tricky and cunning, infinitely amusing and the best of bad company; the dumb oaf, el Araña, without a thought in his mind or a nerve in his body, yet cursed with the worst nervous affliction imaginable.

There were others, of course: Bergmann, the admirable Swiss; Dolgorousky, the enormous yet childishly temperamental Russian; Barnefeld, the ever-placid stolid Dutchman; Ericsson, the fine athletic melancholy Dane whom Luke called Hamlet; Drücke, the elderly Prussian, who, after seventeen years in the Legion, denied that he had any country at all, and refused to be left behind at the depôt at Sidi-bel-Abbès when other Germans in the Legion were given the option of doing so. Incidentally, one could not feel that Drücke behaved as a traitor and a renegade in fighting against Germany, inasmuch as he was completely sincere in holding the faith expressed and declared in the Song of the Legion:

> *"Soldats de la Légion*
> *De la Légion Étrangère,*
> *N'ayant pas de nation,*
> *La France est votre Mère."*

So long had he served in the Legion, so completely was he imbued with its spirit, that its *caserne* was his hearth and home, France was his mother, and her enemies, German or other, were Drücke's enemies. He was probably fortunate in being killed and not taken prisoner by his original compatriots.

A queer collection indeed, our *escouade,* chiefly English (good average ordinary Englishmen, who became *bons camarades et bons légionnaires,* but remained *"single men in Barracks, uncommonly like you"*), Belgian, Russian, Swiss, Swedish, Dutch, Danish and French. . . .

V

I imagine that had we Volunteers been ordinary peace-time recruits to the Legion, and gone through the ordinary depôt routine at Sidi-bel-Abbès, we should have found things very different in very many ways. Being Volunteers who had enlisted in the Legion, not for our own ends but simply and solely to fight for France, I think that, at any rate while recruits, we were deliberately treated with leniency, and that to us, the non-commissioned officers somewhat tempered the wind of their usual acerbity. Certainly we got on with them very well, and they taught and trained us with conscientious care and great patience. According to the *anciens,* we did not know what real barrack-square rough-stuff was; and I, personally, was later to experience a far harsher discipline than that of the war-time Legion recruit.

Our Sergeant-Instructor struck me as a man who might well have been a Colonel, so admirable was his bearing, so wise and skilful his handling of the *escouades,* and so clear and knowledgeable his lectures on tactics.

Greude told me that Sergeant-Instructor Marchien had been an officer in the French Regular Army until court-martialled and cashiered, by reason of some irregularity in Mess-accounts, and that he had enlisted in the Foreign Legion as a Belgian.

I was very glad to see that he made rather a favourite of Luke. Later I learned that he had borrowed one hundred francs from him, but I think he liked the boy for himself as well as for his money. To the Sergeant-Instructor it was, no doubt, a considerable sum, whereas to Luke, four pounds was a trifle— especially in view of the value of a Sergeant-Major's warm approval.

As a matter of fact, many non-commissioned officers "borrowed" from Volunteers who were supposed to have money. Most of the Corporals did, with the exception of our Room-Corporal Valence, of whom more anon. Money oiled the wheels in a wonderful way. One gave it to *légionnaires* who did one's cleaning and polishing, who undertook one's fatigues, and who offered themselves as substitutes for guard and other duties. To the Corporals one "lent" small sums on demand, and to Sergeants larger sums on suggestion. All very deplorable as a system and admirable as an investment.

It was amusing to see Yrotavál's indignation when he saw Luke parting with good money thus.

"Huh!" he would growl. "*Con dinero no te conoceras, sin dinero no te conoceran.*[13] Dat Coipril Bjelavitch is de woist ol' boid of de gang. You won't see dem dollars no more. You don' wanna flash your dough here, Bo. *Eh bien! Que voulez-vous? C'est La Légion.* Dey'd pinch your *abatis*[14] for boot-laces. Sure. *Amores, dolores y dineros, no puedan estar secretos.*[15] Dose guys, dey'll skin you alive. Dey's *un abadis du raboin* of thugs. Money! Dey'll steal your teeth."

"Oh, well, it's only a loan in a good cause," Luke would reply.

"*M'Carben Diu!* Like Hell, it's a loan. Say when you wanna lend them kinda loans, you lend 'em to me. See? I do us some good with it, and I do some good for it. I earn it. See? I bark for my supper. See? *A quien no sobra, no crie can.*[16] See?"

"Oh, shut up. You'll get all you are worth, Yrotavál," Luke would reply.

"Sure, and dat Bulgar bed-bug, Coipril Bjelavitch, ain't woith nutting at all. *M'Carben Diu!*"

"What does *M'Carben Diu* mean, Yrotavál?"

"Dat's good Catalan—which is a forbidden language in Spain! It means B'Jimminy Jees. Also it means Holy Peter's Velvet Pants. See?"

In fairness to the Sergeant-Instructor, I think he

---

[13] *With money you will not know yourself; without it others will not know you.*
[14] *Giblets.*
[15] *Love, grief and money cannot be concealed.*
[16] *He who has nothing to spare, should not keep a dog.*

only borrowed once. I don't think any of the Sergeants made more than a second touch. If, in the case of the Corporals, the small loans were numerous, they didn't amount to very much.

One non-commissioned officer who never borrowed from either of us was this Corporal Valence. We were about sixty to a room, and in one corner of each room dwelt the Room-Corporal, a deal table segregating him and cutting his bed off from those of the common herd. Upon him, it depended, to a great extent, whether the *chambrée* was a "happy ship." If the man were a bully, a brute and a trouble-maker, the spirit and general atmosphere of the *chambrée* could be thoroughly unpleasant. If he were weak, slack and drunken, discipline would suffer, petty tyrants and bullies among the *anciens* have their opportunity, and recruits get a bad time. If he were a strong man, competent and of good will, things went well. We were very fortunate indeed in Corporal Valence, an ideal non-commissioned officer, pleasant but firm and resolute, a really conscientious soldier who knew his job, and did it thoroughly, with the minimum of friction.

Here was another man the reason for whose presence in the Legion was hard to understand; for he, too, had enlisted in time of peace, and yet was the last man one would have expected to find serving as a mercenary soldier. Well-educated and extremely intelligent, he obviously could have gone far in a civil career. Another tragedy of a wasted life. And, sorry as I was that he should leave us, I was delighted when he was removed elsewhere, on promotion.

It's a good wind that blows nobody any ill, however, and it was a bad one for Luke, and therefore for me, that brought the Bulgarian Corporal Bjelavitch in his place. This fellow was by any standards a beast. He was an enormous, bear-like man, with a heavy, stupid face, cruel and sensual, thick-lipped, broad-nosed, low-browed and pig-eyed; an ignorant peasant, and doubtless a criminal, who had left his country for his country's good. Yrotavál, who knew all about him, warned us to be careful.

"There's no reason why he should turn nasty, is there?" asked Luke. "I've lent him a few francs and can lend him some more."

"Nasty!" sneered Yrotavál. "Dat guy's sure your woist enemy when he's your best friend. See? You watch out. And you keep close to me. See? Anyt'ing that slob say to you, you tell me. See? You wanna be careful an' watch your step, now. You especial, see?"

"What on earth are you driving at?"

"Huh! It'll be Bjelavitch as'll do de drivin' if he picks on you. Drive you over de edge."

"Pick on me? Why should he quarrel with me?" asked Luke.

"*M'Carben Diu!* Who said 'quarrel'? I said 'pick on you.' "

"Well, isn't that quarrelling?"

"Shucks! Pick on you as a *friend,* Big Boy. Dat's what I mean. Dat Bulgar's a bad guy. You don' wanna cross him. And you won't wanna please him. You wanna be careful. *Paso á paso van lejos.*[17] You stay by me."

I, not unnaturally, imagined that, with this sort of talk, Yrotavál was merely trying further to impress us with his usefulness, and to prove that not only was he valuable as a batman, but invaluable as a protector, adviser and guide among the quicksands that beset our path as *bleus* in the Legion. But I freely admit that here I did him an injustice; for all that he said concerning the Bulgarian was true and less than the truth, so far as decent people, like most of the Volunteers, were concerned. The man was a degraded brute, and should have been a convict in a gaol of the worst kind, instead of a soldier with a position of authority in a fine Battalion. I suppose that apart from his foul habits and vices, he was a good enough war-time non-commissioned officer (which is another indictment of War, if one were needed), for he was a determined and violent driver, courageous and forceful, and was competent to the extent that he knew thoroughly well

---

[17] *Fair and softly goes far.*

what little a Corporal needs to know.

But a change in the atmosphere of the *chambrée* was quickly noticeable, and the tone deteriorated. Bjelavitch took violent likes and dislikes, had great favourites and utter *bêtes noires;* was rough and overbearing in manner, and a great bully. Punishments increased in number and severity; and, whereas everything had gone well and smoothly when Valence was Room-Corporal, there was now friction and ill-feeling. Valence led, but Bjelavitch drove.

Nor was it very long before I understood only too clearly what Yrotavál had meant when he said that Bjelavitch would drive over the edge anyone who thwarted him. What was not, at first, so clear was the true inwardness of his hard saying that it might be worse for a young recruit if Bjelavitch picked on him rather as a friend than as an enemy.

And here Luke's handsomeness, attractiveness and charm quickly seemed likely to be his undoing, for Bjelavitch did pick upon him. He singled him out for praise and favours; and, so far as a non-commissioned officer can, he endeavoured to make a *copain* of him, and ordered Luke's bed to be moved next to his own. At first, Luke was amused, jokingly referred to him as his Friend at Court, and promised to extend his patronage to me. This was all very well, so long as being the Corporal's favourite ensured that he got the minimum of fatigues and the maximum of protection from unjust punishment or bullying. But it was not so amusing when Bjelavitch developed the habit of addressing him as "*Chèrie,*" "*Ma petite,*" and "Lulu," and began to manœuvre to get Luke alone; began to be affectionately demonstrative in a wholly un-English way; to put his arm about his neck and to pat his face.

The first time this happened, Luke thought it nearly as funny as it was objectionable, and imagined that the great bear-like creature, a head taller than himself, was merely exhibiting the normal manners and customs of his Bulgarian breed.

But it did not stop at that, and I came into the *chambrée* from guard, one day, to find Luke speechless

41

with fury, and Yrotavál endeavouring to soothe him with sound worldly advice. Bjelavitch, finding Luke alone in the room, had suddenly flung his great arms about him, hugged him to his enormous breast and kissed him upon both cheeks, as though he had been the pretty girl whom Bjelavitch professed to imagine him.

"My God!" raged Luke. "If he does that again, I'll bash his face in. I'll lay him out, and . . ."

"Spend the rest of the War in gaol?" I asked. "Eight years' hard labour—if you are lucky."

"*M'Carben Diu,*" growled Yrotavál, moved to righteous indignation at such injustice, or at the thought of losing his lucrative job as Luke's henchman, "I'll fix the bastard. I'm sure goin' to *abélardiser* the *sacré soudillard.* But you got to watch your step. He allows you got to be his friend—or else he'll be your enemy."

"But surely," said I, "we can go to the Company Sergeant-Major or the *Adjudant,* and . . ."

"Fergit it!" laughed Yrotavál. "*Dios quiera!* Where do you t'ink you are. *Carramba! C'est la Légion.* You cain't go behind an N.C.O. There ain't no such place. And you cain't go over the head of one neither. He'd be the death of you, even if the Sergeant-Major or *Adjudant* would listen to you."

"But Sergeant-Major Muller is a decent chap and . . ."

"*Ca!* Listen, Big Boy. Dis is de Legion. You complain about a Coipril to a Sergeant, and de Sergeant'll give you de maximum punishment he can, just to learn you not to undermine discipline. See? And you complain to de Sergeant-Major and he'll double it. And then to de *Adjudant* and he'll double dat. And then to de Captain and he'll give you all he's got. And if it gets as far as de Colonel, you'll go before a *conseil de guerre*—and then to prison fer a trouble-making menace to discipline. But it wouldn't get to no Colonel. Potted priests! The N.C.O.'s can deal with any *legionnaire* dat wants to make trouble for one of them. Besides, suppose de Sergeant-Major was a friend of yours because you 'lent' him a wad of francs, and he listens to your tale in private, what then? Skippin' Serpents! If he's feelin' good, he'll tell you—in private—to go away while de goin's good, and not to be a bigger damn-fool than God made you. Good advice, too, *muerte de Dios,* because de Coipril'll get you if you squeal. Get you good an' plenty, every time; get you every day; get you cells— and then some—until you'll soon only be out of cells just long enough to get another sentence. See?"

The situation developed quickly, horribly, and— dangerously. I had a long talk with Greude, who knew the Legion and Corporal Bjelavitch as well as Yrotavál did; and he could only advise the utmost circumspection, wariness and restraint.

"If your brother flares up, well, he'll burn himself, or rather Bjelavitch will. If he antagonizes Bjelavitch, his life will be a hell. If he strikes him, it will be a death-blow—his own."

"But is there no *justice* in . . . ?"

"Justice! My dear Tuyler! What is that? We know nothing of it here. Never heard of it. There's *discipline.* And discipline means that the non-commissioned officer can do no wrong, and the *simple soldat* can do nothing right, if the N.C.O. says so."

"But damn it all, man, suppose a non-commissioned officer robbed him, struck him or . . ."

"Well, that wouldn't be discipline, so he mustn't do it. There is no God but Discipline, and the N.C.O. is his Prophet."

"Look, Greude, what would *you* do?" I asked.

"I? To Bjelavitch? Kill him, probably. Kill him. Drive my bayonet through his throat."

"Discipline?" I sneered.

"No. But we'd both go where there *is* Justice. Yes— I'd kill him."

"That's hardly helpful, Greude. I don't want my brother shot for killing his superior. Can't you . . . can't we . . . can't I do . . . ?"

"No. But we shall be off to the Front before long. Your brother must carry on somehow, till then."

"But Bjelavitch will go to the Front with us."

"Yes, my dear chap. But he won't last there, will he? Not if we don't want him to."

"What d'you mean?"

"Mean? What d'you suppose? When a man like Bjelavitch asks for it, he gets it, doesn't he? At the Front, your brother can shoot Bjelavitch in the back, if he persecutes him; or if you get the opportunity first, or if I . . ."

I stared at Greude in amazement. What had the Legion done to such a man as he, that he could talk like this?

"Yrotavál would do it for five *sous*," he laughed.

Rassedin came over to borrow a brush, and Greude told him what I had been saying; and without hesitation, Rassedin gave the same advice.

"Your brother will have to be careful till we get to the Front," he said. "Damn careful. Then we'll put that *salaud* out. There'll be lots of scores settled, when the shooting begins, besides those against the Germans."

Idle talk, I concluded. The sort of vague and foolish threats probably made in all armies against all thoroughly unpopular superiors.

And that very day, Corporal Bjelavitch was in *rapport* for escort duty to take a man to Fort St. Jean at Marseilles. He at once detailed Luke as one of the escort. The others were a burly bearded *ancien,* one Pere Bossuet, a cheerful old villain who almost lived on *pinard;* and the stunted Hercules known as The Spider.

Directly I heard the orders, I went to Bjelavitch and asked him if I could substitute for Bossuet or Araña.

He looked me up and down.

"Why do you want to go?" he growled.

"To have some fun in Marseilles," I replied promptly.

"*Bogu!* I'll arrange for you to have some fun here," he sneered. "*Rompez*[18]!"

Quickly I found Yrotavál, and told him to substitute for Bossuet, if he could square him and Bjelavitch.

---

[18] *Dismiss.*

"For Bossuet? Sure. Dat ol' *borrachon* would do anyt'ing for wine. He'll be easy. It's Bjelavitch who'll bitch it. But I'll try. Sure.

"How much?" he asked, shooting a sly glance at me.

"Anything in reason. Ten francs?"

"Twenty-five for de Coipril. An' twenty-five for me."

"Damn your hide, Yrotavál. You substitute for Bossuet and look after my brother, and leave the price to me. That'll be all right—so long as my brother doesn't get into trouble with Bjelavitch."

"Okay, Boss."

I had an anxious week-end while Luke was away, and a shock when he returned.

The worst had happened.

He had had a terrible row with Bjelavitch, and, though he had not actually stabbed him, he had drawn his bayonet in self-defence; in other words, he had "threatened the life of his superior in time of war," and before witnesses.

I got hold of Yrotavál at the earliest possible moment. It was a bad business, he admitted. He had done his best, but Luke had been foolish and violent, and Bjelavitch was going to "frame" him. Luke was for it, and unless Yrotavál and Araña gave the evidence that was required, they'd be for it, too—and so forth.

I got as many of the Volunteers of our *chambrée* together as I could, and such of the *anciens* as I thought might be helpful—Greude, Rassedin, Oberg, Bergmann and Barnefeld.

The Volunteers were full of wild schemes, varying from approaching the Captain of our Company, a man whom we had scarcely seen, to threatening Bjelavitch. Réné Barbey d'Aurillac, who loved Luke, suggested that the whole *escouade* should invade the Company Office in a body and protest; and then that they should way-lay Bjelavitch and threaten to beat him up if my brother were arrested.

The *anciens* merely laughed, and pointed out that any one—or any dozen—who lifted a finger to interfere, would merely share Luke's fate. And when asked what we could do, told us that we could do precisely nothing, and the quicker the better.

I could only wait for the blow to fall, and that evening was one of the worst of a life not unchequered with bad patches.

I felt most miserably helpless, and could only determine that I would not leave anything undone of the little that I could do in the way of bribery or threats. I had some hope that the offer of a big sum of money might do something with Bjelavitch; and very little that a faithful promise to shoot him, if anything happened to Luke, would have the slightest effect.

I sat on my bed, that night, awaiting Bjelavitch's return to the *chambrée*; and until Luke went out, leaving me to finish his *astiquage,* I was pleased, not to say surprised, at the calmness with which he went about his spit-and-polish preparations for the morrow. This he had to do for himself, as both Yrotavál and Araña were out.

It was rather he who cheered and sustained me, than I him—until with a laugh he said he must "go and see a man about a dog." I waited, expecting the worst to happen.

I waited in vain. Corporal Bjelavitch did not return that night, or ever again.

He was murdered.

A picket, hastily sent for, found him lying in the gutter outside a low *bistro,* in a narrow slum in the sailors' quarter, with a knife in his back and through his heart.

Police enquiry totally failed to discover any kind of clue. Investigation pursued in the *chambrée* disclosed nothing that could have any bearing on the crime; neither circumstantial evidence nor grounds for presumption of motive.

It seemed that the dead man had no enemies, for example.

All who were questioned bore testimony to the admirable character of the deceased, and the high regard in which he was held. His humble friends and devout admirers, *les légionnaires* Yrotavál and Araña, were possibly more emphatic than anyone on the subject of Bjelavitch's popularity and freedom from enemies. They both wept a little when speaking of their murdered Room-Corporal.

§2

Bjelavitch's place was taken by a very decent Frenchman, Corporal Hervé, who was far too anxious to get to the Front, and to do everything he could to increase the efficiency of the volunteers of his *escouade,* to have any time for other diversions.

Work grew harder, hours longer, and volunteer proficiency steadily greater.

And, after no more than one month of constant intensive training, a Battalion of a thousand of us was ordered to be in readiness to proceed to the Front. This fine unit consisted of five hundred regulars, all old trained war-hardened *légionnaires,* and five hundred Volunteers selected from those who had shaped best at drill, been best behaved, or had had previous military experience.

Luke and I were delighted beyond words to find ourselves included in this *Premier Bataillon de Marche.*

Poor Luke!

VI

I have said nothing hitherto of letters from home. But these had been almost as numerous as they were welcome, my Father and Athene writing frequently, and Rosanne daily, to both of us.

Her first letter, in answer to mine from Lyons, telling her of our enlistment in the French Army, as soon as it was a *fait accompli,* was a curious mixture of a squeal of delight and a groan of agony; of joy and of pride in what we had done and of fear and horror as to what might be done to us. She was obviously both proud and broken-hearted, and begged me to take the greatest care of myself and Luke.

"You are so much stronger than he—in every way," she wrote. *"I expect it was you who made him join; but I'm not going to say a word against that . . . I think I shall die if England doesn't come in. But of course she will, and so you'd have gone, just the same. As it is, you will only get to the Front a little earlier, and you've set a splendid example . . . Oh, how I wish I were a man. I have written to everyone I know, and to a good many whom I hardly know, telling them what you have done, and implying that the sooner they do the same, the better! That is in the case of men. To the women to whom I write, I imply that that's what their sons and husbands will want to do, of course, and all that is necessary is to go over to Paris and ask the way to the Recruiting Office!*

"But England will come in, and I pray that America will, too. But oh, Mark, you will be careful, won't you? And make Luke be careful, too. What an idiotic thing to write, but you know what I mean. . . ."

And much more to the same effect.

Her letters grew more cheerful, or perhaps more resigned on and after August 4th, when England declared war with Germany.

I wrote to her as frequently as I could; but

apparently Luke did not, as she was constantly asking why he hadn't written; where he was now; and whether he were ill. When I reminded him that he ought to send an occasional line home, and that Rosanne was bothered about him, he replied,

"What need for both of us to write? You can give her all the news."

And I was rather angry one day when, in a wine-shop where we were rewarding Yrotavál and Araña, signifying our approval (of their services as batmen) in the usual manner, I saw Luke pull a paper from the pocket of his *vareuse,* glance at it, and light it at a gas-jet, and I knew it to be a letter in Rosanne's handwriting.

I was afterwards surprised at myself for being indignant about it, and yet it seemed to me a rotten thing to do, to use Rosanne's letter as a pipe-lighter in a Toulon wine-shop, in the presence of men like Yrotavál and Araña. Very absurd of me, of course.

As soon as I knew that we were in *rapport* for the Front, with the *Bataillon de Marche,* I wrote her a long letter, telling her that it might be the last she'd get for some time, and that she mustn't worry if she heard nothing from either of us, as not only might we have no opportunity of writing when on the march and in the trenches, but that the posting of letters might be prohibited when we were in billets.

I enclosed a specimen of the cards that had been given to us with the instructions that these only were to be used, from the day that the Battalion left Toulon.

Years afterwards I found this identical card, with a little prayer written on it in Rosanne's handwriting.

Cette carte doit être remise au vaguemestre. RIEN ne doit
y être ajouté, excepté la date et la signature de l'expéditeur;
les phrases inutiles peuvent être biffées. *Si quelque chose y
était ajouté, cette carte ne serait pas transmise.*

Je vais bien.

~~Je suis à l'hôpital~~ { ~~blessé~~ } ~~et suis en voie de guérison.~~
{ ~~malade~~ } ~~et j'espère être bientôt rétabli.~~

J'ai reçu votre { lettre.
{ ~~télégramme.~~
{ ·paquet.

~~Je n'ai reçu aucune nouvelle de vous~~ { ~~dernièrement.~~
{ ~~depuis longtemps.~~

Lettre suit à la première occasion.

Date (*sans indication d'origine*) .... *Sept 1914*

Signature (seulement) : *Mark.*

The news from the Front was not too good. In fact,
it was bad, and this probably accounts for the haste
with which our newly formed *Bataillon de Marche* was
despatched to the Front. Within a week of its
formation, it was notified in Orders, one night, that the
Battalion would parade for kit-inspection in the
morning, and entrain in the evening for an unknown
destination.

It was amazingly quick work, that five hundred
civilians should have been turned into fighting
soldiers, and sent into battle after a month's training;
but the "dilution" system was an admirable one, and
fully justified itself. For the *bleus* had quickly absorbed
the spirit of the *anciens* and the training of the
Instructors.

At shooting, I fear we should have been beneath the
contempt of a British Army Battalion. Definitely we did
not shine on the rifle-range at anything from a

thousand yards down to three hundred; but as most of our shooting was done at something more like a thousand to three hundred inches, this was no great matter. The Legion could pour in point-blank magazine-fire at trench ranges as well as any troops, and could use the bayonet better than most.

So, in the highest fettle, singing at the tops of our voices, we marched out of the Infantry Barracks of Toulon, behind our *clique,* the Legion drum-and-bugle band, through loudly cheering crowds, to the station, where the usual train of "40 *hommes ou 8 chevaux—en long"* trucks awaited us.

Packed like sardines, *Standing Room Only,* once more we made our slow and weary way across France from south to north; across rural France—so unlike England—with her interminable and eternal lines of poplars, her intensively cultivated fields, her endless straight roads, her lovely city-crowned hills, her beautiful old villages, her hideously ugly little villages and industrial towns. Ever north and east, slowly and ever slower, with frequent halts when the train disgorged all over the line, the station and the village, hungry *légionnaires* in search of food and water, the *anciens* bent on loot, the volunteers on purchase— purchase at any price, of cigarettes, bread, meat, beer, wine; the honest would-be buyers usually returning empty, sinkingly empty, the wicked *anciens* laden, heavily-laden, and anxiously willing to sell their surplus—of everything but wine. (No *ancien* has ever heard of such a thing as a surplus of wine.)

At last the train reached Camp de Mailly, where we went under canvas and slept on muddy straw.

It was here that Luke, off duty, fell in with Alan Seeger, talked with him a while and sat beside him, leaning against the station wall, and watched him as he scribbled his "Rendezvous with Death":

> "*I have a rendezvous with Death*
> *At some disputed barricade. . . .*
> *At midnight in some flaming town*
> *When Spring trips north again.*

And I to my pledged word am true.
I shall not fail that rendezvous."

Alan kept his rendezvous with Death.

Next day the Legion marched, and the *bleus,* toward evening, heard in earnest the *"Marchez où crevez"* exhortation from the non-commissioned officers, added to their eternal *"Grouillez-vous! Grouillez-vous!* Hurry! Hurry!"

Incidentally, I remember wondering whether that everlasting *"Grouillez!"* gave us our adjective "gruelling." It was certainly a gruelling march. More than twenty-five miles, with a load of over a hundred pounds, and part of it across country, much of which was soft, sucking mud, horrible stuff into which the right foot sank to get purchase for the pulling-up of the left, and into which the left sank yet deeper as the right foot was slowly and painfully withdrawn like a cork from the neck of a bottle.

This march, of which the conditions grew worse as we penetrated farther through the war-shattered country-side, took us, if I remember rightly, through Verzy, Cuiry-les-Chaudards—an island of mud surrounded entirely by mud—to Fismes, and thence to the front-line trenches, where we took over the most dangerous sector, and plunged straight into the War.

As I have said, I have no intention of writing a war book, nor of describing all over again the ghastly horrors, not of bullet and bayonet and shell, but of cold, bitter cramping murderous cold; mud; mud that was thickly smeared on your clothing from head to foot, as butter is smeared on bread; mud that penetrated to your flesh and clogged the pores of your skin; mud that penetrated to your soul and made it— muddy; rain that drenched till you had not a dry shred, and all but drowned you and filled the undrained clay trenches to the height of a man's waist: noise that deafened you, shook you, shattered you, till you longed desperately for the silence of death: lice that sickened and disgusted you, made you itch and scratch all day, and awakened you at night from such sleep as intervals between bombardments allowed you: hunger, miserable griping hunger, that at dawn rendered you a sick, empty, trembling wreck, fitter for a warm hospital-bed than for desperate physical effort. And constant Death that stalked reaping, right and left: Death whom, personally, you would have welcomed, but who stalked your brother too.

I marvelled to see how splendidly Luke stood up to it. I was proud of him, and ashamed of myself. He was a credit to his country, an example to his comrades. One had expected courage from him, naturally, but not the high physical and mental resistance that enabled him to carry on. But, of course, he was of fine physique; he had never been ill in his life; and was, at any rate until we went into the trenches, in the pink of condition.

Our first actual fight was when Sergeant Paggallini suddenly bawled,

"Aux armes! Aux armes! Load! Rapid fire independent!" and springing to our feet, we saw a wave of shadows swarming from the opposite trenches and bearing down upon us through the dawn mist.

"Aim low! Aim low! Ground level!"

And, cool as on the rifle-range, steady as any of the veterans, Luke, beside me, aimed and fired, aimed and fired, without haste or excitement.

This Sergeant Paggallini was one of the many Corsican non-commissioned officers of the Legion. The authorities like them and promote them quickly—not because they are haloed by the Napoleonic legend, but because they are invariably hard, harsh and severe; men of steel, which takes a fine sharp edge and point; ruthless drivers, violent and cruel; magnificent disciplinarians as the Legion understands discipline.

Unlike the late Corporal Bjelavitch, this fellow took a sudden and violent dislike to Luke, by reason of something in his cool and measuring look, his English aloofness and air of superiority, no doubt; and started to make his life a burden to him as only a Legion non-com can. His childish and petty, though violent and dangerous, persecution did not last long, for Sergeant

Paggallini took an almost equally violent dislike to Yrotavál, who had a wonderful gift for veiled insolence and all the old *légionnaires'* knowledge of the tricks of their trade.

In the incredibly horrible conditions under which we were living, with the "hash-guns"—as the Americans called the kitchens-on-wheels—wrecked by gun-fire; our kitchen-orderlies, with their buckets of coffee and *soupe* shot down as they ploughed their way, slithering, through the mud; and our meagre iron rations devoured, the temper of the *légionnaires* grew increasingly nasty: and when, early one ghastly morning of rain and cold and mud and starvation, Sergeant Paggallini drew his revolver on the dilatory Yrotavál and called him a coward, a cur, stinking scum, and the bastard of a Spanish brothel, he signed his own death-warrant, forestalling the Reaper's regular agents.

That very night, Sergeant Paggallini, a brute as brave as the bravest, took out into No Man's Land a reconnoitring-patrol consisting of the six files to my right, Luke, Yrotavál, Araña, Barnefeld, Brancker and Oberg.

In an agony of anxiety, I awaited their return from their immeasurably dangerous visit to the German trench a hundred yards away, doubly dangerous by reason of the probability of their being seen by the light of a Very star and machine-gunned by the vigilant Germans, and of being fired upon by our own sentries, as they crawled back to our line. They would be all right if they survived to come back to their point of departure; but if, as was most probable, they lost direction in the dark, and approached a different trench section, they were almost certain to be fired upon by our own sentries.

During the hour or two that they were gone, hardly a shot was fired, thank God: and, by great skill and coolness, or greater good luck, the patrol returned to the very spot whence it had set forth.

But not the whole of it. Sergeant Paggallini was missing. And the first thing that Yrotavál did on regaining the trench was to clean his rifle. The others had not fired theirs.

"So I am a *'fils de gadoue de bordel Espagnol,'* am I, Señor Paggallini?" I heard him say as he drew his pull-through from the muzzle of his gun. "And a *'sale gallitrac,'* eh? And you'd pull your gun on me, eh? And you've gone an' missed de boat! . . . Well, well, now! Ain't that just too bad," and grinning amiably he winked at Luke.

Although Luke said nothing to me on the subject of Sergeant Paggallini's failure to return, he obviously knew that we should not be troubled by him again.

VII

As was inevitable in the circumstances, dysentery broke out, and Luke got it badly.

Happily, the remnant skeleton of the Battalion was relieved, after a month of the most appalling existence that human beings ever endured and survived, before he collapsed. With the invaluable help of the powerful and untiring Araña, I managed to get Luke back to the scene of our rest-billets—God save the mark—which were merely second-line trenches and dug-outs, where our restful recuperation consisted in digging from morning till night; deepening and draining the communication trenches; constructing new more-or-less bomb-proof dug-outs; felling, cutting and carrying great baulks of timber; and battling with barbed wire, which to the tired soldier is apt to seem a more devilish foe than the human enemy himself.

Soon typhus or typhoid fever appeared among us, as though we had not sudden Death among us in forms sufficiently horrible and numerous. Luke in his weakness took it at once and was soon too weak to move. Araña, Yrotavál, big Ouspenski and I, lifted him from his bed of mud and carried him up into the woods where we were slaving as lumberjacks. There we constructed an almost rain-proof little shack, in which we laid him and gave him such nursing as was possible between our spells of hard labour.

It was heart-warming, touching, to see the generosity with which survivors of our *escouade* gave of their scanty *soupe,* wine, coffee, and—more valuable—of their brief aching leisure, to take turns in nursing him, for he was very ill indeed. I thought he was going to die, and could I have laid hands on His Most Excellent Imperial Majesty the All-highest, he'd have died too, for my heart seethed with murderous hate of those who had caused this war.

So weak was Luke, that when the order came for

56

the reinforced Battalion to return to the trenches, he couldn't get to his feet, and I was faced with the alternative of abandoning him to starve to death there in the sodden dripping woods, or absenting myself from duty and staying with him.

I stayed.

You may wonder why I couldn't have got him carried back to our alleged rest-billets. I could—and have left him to die there in the mud and water of a trench or a dug-out, not only neglected but trampled underfoot by the almost equally ill, weary, and enfeebled wretches of the next Battalion that staggered back to their second-line trenches for their turn to "rest."

Doctors? Casualty clearing-stations? There were none at that time and place; and only the severely wounded, who might yet be patched up again, were painfully and slowly evacuated on stretchers. Few of these ever reached shelter, bed and medical care.

Things were bad enough in those early days for French troops of the Line. For the French Foreign Legion they were infinitely worse, *Madame la République* being then, as ever, extremely prodigal of the lives of the *légionnaires* whom she could get so cheaply and whom she regarded more cheaply still.

So—right or wrong, criminal dereliction of duty or fulfilment of my obvious and natural duty to my dying brother—I stayed, nursed him, and fed him with such food as I could scrounge, and he could swallow. I made a sort of gravy with scraps of bully-beef and paving-stone biscuit. I bought or stole an occasional egg and mug of milk. I travelled long distances, furtively and by night, and contrived, in the words of Thomas Atkins, "to find, win or wangle," at farm, *estaminet,* camp and bivouac, enough of the right sort of food to keep him alive.

From our own rest-billets I kept away until I thought our Battalion would have returned to them; but, on cautiously reconnoitring, I found, to my dismay, that they were occupied by a Line Battalion. This was bad. Were I caught and questioned by the

Military Police, I stood an excellent chance of being arrested as a deserter, tried by drum-head court-martial, and shot at dawn. The French have a very short way with deserters or suspected spies, their motto being, Better shoot the wrong man than no man at all—*pour encourager les autres.* A plea that I was nursing my dying brother would have earned a sarcastic bitter smile and a death-sentence.

Nor, in the event of Luke's dying, could I march up to the front trenches and, with a broad grin and a wag of my tail, say, like a Lancashire comedian, "Ah've coom."

With one exception this fortnight was, I think, the worst period of my life, for I touched the very nadir of wretchedness. It seemed impossible that Luke could recover; I was a deserter from my regiment; my comrades were fighting and dying, while I lurked in ignominious safety; the rain poured night and day incessantly; it was bitterly cold, with the penetrating deadly rawness of a French November; and we were almost starving.

When not scavenging and reconnoitring for food, I sat leaning against a tree-trunk, sunk in the lowest depths of depression and, having covered Luke's shivering body with my overcoat, unable to do anything further for his comfort. It was impossible to keep a fire of wet wood alight in that pouring rain; impossible to keep him dry, much less warm.

From time to time, I must have fallen into a kind of daze or a state of coma; and I remember a sort of waking nightmare in which I thought I was a rotten wooden peg being driven into the sodden clay of that charnel-place by two giants wielding sledge-hammers, one of which bore as in a cartoon, the legend, *"You are a deserter,"* and the other, *"Luke is dying of typhoid fever."*

These were the two thoughts that hammered on my brain when I was awake, and they pursued me in what was but a substitute for sleep.

I suppose I grew light-headed toward the end of this almost sleepless and foodless vigil (for what little food I could get was barely sufficient for Luke), for I occasionally seemed aware of the presence of a third person, a woman. It was Rosanne.

I must, of course, have dozed sometimes, for I also dreamed of her: and, when fully awake, I found myself thinking of her frequently, and then, toward the end, almost continuously. Suddenly I realized that, next to Luke's recovery, what I wanted most was to see Rosanne again. Or, to be strictly accurate, perhaps I should say that what I wanted most in the world was to see Luke restored to health; that what I wanted next was to find myself back in my *escouade* without being court-martialled as the deserter that I was; and that thirdly, more than anything else, I wanted to see Rosanne; to speak to her; to have her sitting beside me in the deep old settee in front of the log fire in the hall at home, my arm about her, her head on my shoulder, while Luke played something on his violin—just as we three had been doing any evening until a few months ago.

I was only beginning to realize, now that I had leisure—or rather, a ghastly hell of nothing-to-do—how much I missed Rosanne. I had only left her for a day or two, as we thought, almost without farewells; and then had come the hectic time in Paris and our enlistment; and from then until now there had been no time to think of anything at all. . . .

What should I do if Luke died? Slink back to the trenches and be shot next morning, blindfolded and tied to a post, as spies and deserters were, by the dozen? Or really desert, and try to make my way back to England—to Rosanne? I think—or let me be perfectly honest and say, I hope—that I decided to rejoin and take my chance of being shot for cowardice.

A fine end to our romantic and glorious adventure into a Holy War for Right against Might—Luke dead in the mud, of a foul disease; I shot at dawn as a cowardly deserter, by a firing-squad of my own comrades.

"I could not look on Death. This being known,
Men led me to him blindfold, and alone."

It was Yrotavál who saved the situation. A more decent-minded man than I would give him full credit for a brave deed and a bright idea. I'm afraid that, rightly or wrongly, I attribute what he did to his besetting avarice and greed. On the Battalion's second retirement to rest-billets, in the ruins of a village a mile or so to the north of where we were, he took the first opportunity of visiting the shack and warning me that Luke and I were posted as deserters, inasmuch as, though missing, we were not known to have been killed by shell-fire while in rest-billets, and could not have been taken prisoners.

On discovering the true state of affairs, and learning that neither of us had the faintest intention of deserting, he at once propounded a clever scheme for our salvation.

As soon as Luke was so far recovered as to be able at least to stand up, Yrotavál was to "discover" us in the wood, almost dead of dysentery and starvation. He was then to "rescue" us by bringing some friends who, partly supporting, partly carrying, us, were to contrive to get us back to the new rest-billets. There we were to lie recuperating, until the Battalion moved again. . . . With any luck, we should get away with it, inasmuch as we were Volunteers and men of excellent conduct and unblemished record.

From that moment, Luke began to recover, and made remarkably rapid progress. Next day, Yrotavál and Araña came, bringing a *bidon* of wine, another of coffee and a *gamelle* of *soupe;* and, the following day, he returned with Ouspenski, Araña and Oberg. The giant Ouspenski and the herculean Araña carried Luke; and, as we neared billets, I put my arms about the shoulders of Yrotavál and Oberg and was impressively supported down what had been the village street to the cellar in which the remains of our *escouade* was billeted. Obviously we had risen almost from our graves and returned to duty as soon as we were able to move with the help of the comrades who had discovered us lying at death's door.

It would nevertheless have gone hardly with us had Sergeant Paggallini been in command of the Section, for he would have denounced us and done his best to get us court-martialled and shot as deserters.

Fortunately Corporal Hervé had been promoted in his place, and he actually welcomed us back from the dead, without a word of question. The numerous poor devils who had died of dysentery in those ghastly rest-billets had not died in vain, so far as we were concerned.

By the time the Battalion returned to the trenches, Luke was able to march, his accoutrements and kit being distributed among his friends.

§2

It did neither of us any good when the *vaguemestre* gave us each a letter from home, written by Rosanne, telling us that our father had died.

He had been ill for a long time, and the blow was not unexpected.

Poor Father. . . . He had not had a very happy life. Luke was always his favourite, but I loved him very much. Luke's going to the war broke his heart, and he never got over it.

There was no time for mourning—and little sensitiveness left in us, for suffering much grief.

§3

By the fortune of war and the mercy of God, we were only in those flooded open sewers, called trenches, for another fortnight, two weeks of indescribable and incredible hell, during which men died hourly and horribly—and were envied by the living. Just when I was beginning to wonder how much longer Luke's nerves would stand up to the incessant bombardment, the bitter cold, hunger and sodden misery, we were relieved and, by way of a rest, marched under driving rain, through squelching sucking mud, toward another sector of the line.

What would it be like? Of one thing we could be certain, grinned the *anciens,* and that was that it would be a change for the worse, to a place too bad to be held by the troops of the Line, otherwise the Legion would not be sent there.

As a matter of fact, it was only worse in point of intensity of bombardment, and was a great deal better from the view of comfort—a curious word to use in such a connection—for it was a quarry, and the dug-outs were almost dry, being excavated from a kind of gravelly chalk soil. Here, our death-rate was higher, but so were our spirits. Luke's health improved, in spite of constant and terrific din, for we slept dry, got our food regularly and in adequate quantity, and enjoyed the warmth of brazier fires. But it was a terribly anxious time when half our *escouade* marched away to the rear at night to draw our rations for the week, leaving the rest of us on duty in our trench. It always seemed to happen that Luke and I were separated, and I never knew, from minute to minute, whether I should see him again. It was bad enough when we were side by side, but as most of our casualties were from shell-fire, there was always the hope that we might be killed together by the same explosion.

The days passed and we both survived.

One day, having been relieved in our quarry by another Battalion of the Legion, we marched to garrison a Château, which had already changed hands about half a dozen times. For some good reason, the authorities were particularly anxious that it should now remain in French possession; and our Commandant guaranteed that, so long as it was entrusted to the care of the Legion, it would do so. He told us this himself, at evening parade, and it was a case of " 'Nuff said." The Legion dies but does not surrender.

And the very next day, I saw a battle-picture that remains as an imperishable memory—hand-to-hand combat, with rifle and bayonet, between French troops in the uniform of 1870, *képi,* blue overcoat and baggy red breeches and all, against burly Germans in field-grey with *picklehaubes,* though these were now concealed beneath cotton covers.

It was at dawn on a foggy morning. Our *escouade* was on duty, guarding a door in the park wall of the Château. Greude was on sentry, standing on a wine-barrel filled with earth, so that he was able to look over the wall beside the door. The rest of the *escouade* were making coffee, washing, cleaning kit, or pursuing the coy reluctant louse to his fastnesses in the seams of their garments, when suddenly Greude shouted, threw up his rifle and fired. Almost simultaneously there was a loud explosion, the door was blown inward, and a swift rush of German soldiers followed it.

It was a soldiers' battle. With a shout of *"Aux armes!"* the *légionnaires* sprang to their feet, seized their rifles and dashed at the doorway.

At the moment that it happened, I was walking toward the rough lean-to shelter built against the wall, in which the men off-duty had slept; and, as I rushed toward it to get my rifle, I saw this picture that will never fade.

Luke, who was seated on the ground drinking coffee from his *quart,* put it down almost carefully, snatched up his rifle, sprang to his feet, fired at, and killed, the leading man, and then leapt like a tiger, long bayonet well advanced, just as though charging at bayonet-exercise. I had no time to be frightened, no time to think or feel. With a quick and clever feint and dodge, he evaded the second German's point and drove his own through the man's breast. Beside him was Araña, who, ducking under a German's darting bayonet, gave him a hay-maker that transfixed his throat.

As these two Germans staggered back against those behind them, Ouspenski, swinging his clubbed rifle, brought it crashing down on the head of another German who had just bayoneted poor Réné Barbey d'Aurillac. Another gigantic guardsman—for men of a Prussian Guard Battalion they were—drove at fat and beaming Père Bossuet who, parrying, made swift return and got his man, while another over the collapsing German's shoulder, drove his bayonet through Père Bossuet's chest.

All this happened in the few seconds during which I was running to the shelter. By the time I had seized my bayoneted rifle and looked again, more Germans had thrust in through the doorway, and our outnumbered *escouade* was being thrust back.

As I reached the *mêlée,* a great tall Grenadier, a handsome man with blue eyes and a golden beard, had thrown his rifle like a spear backward across his right shoulder, butt uppermost, and was putting all his strength and weight into a downward drive at Luke, who, bending over the man he had stabbed, was endeavouring to withdraw his bayonet. It seemed to me that time stood still and that this swift and silent struggle took place in slow motion; for, as the tall Prussian's bayonet-point descended, I took the liberty of blowing his brains out, and seemed to have plenty of time in which to do it. Luke's bayonet came out of the fallen German, and, side by side we stood for a moment, thrusting, parrying, grunting, panting and swearing. With the tail of my eye, I saw Luke's bayonet again go in, his enemy stagger back, saw the man drop his rifle and seize Luke as he did so, pulling him to the ground. Simultaneously, someone behind fired his rifle within an inch of my ear, deafening me and filling me with wrathful indignation, but shooting between the eyes at point-blank range, a man who was in the act of bayoneting me. As he fell back, I thrust with all my strength at the German who was fighting Luke, my bayonet striking his cartridge-pouch and bending almost double. Clubbing my rifle, I brought it down on the man's head, and then whirled it round and round with all my might, shoving forward, and clearing a little space as I did so. If you are tall, fairly strong, and your blood is up, a rifle held by the muzzle and used like a flail is, to my mind, a more effective weapon than a bayonet.

Anyhow, the Germans gave ground. Luke, Yrotavál and Araña beside him, charged forward with me, big Ouspenski, Oberg, Barnefeld and others, and we drove the enemy back, through the doorway, and out of the

Château park.

Evidently it was only a raid for the purpose of getting *képis,* shoulder-straps, regimental badges, notebooks, letters, and other evidence as to the identity of the garrison of the Château.

As I sat on the ground beside Luke, gasping, panting, whooping for breath, as distressed as though I had won the half-mile in a sprint and record time, I felt happy; happy that I was a re-instated self-respecting soldier, instead of a skulking deserter; happy that Luke was again so well, strong and active; and I felt prouder of him than ever I had been before, and that is saying something.

I am not of a literary turn, I am not particularly well-read, but there came to my mind some lines learnt by heart when I was at our Prep. School, of which the Head was a keen Shakespearean scholar:

> *"I do not think a braver Gentleman,*
> *More active-valiant, nor more valiant-young,*
> *More daring, or more bold, is now alive,*
> *To grace this latter age with noble deed."*

With noble deed! Poor Luke. . . .

VIII

Well, as I have said, I have no desire to write a war-book, or to give an account of Life in the French Foreign Legion under war conditions. So I will just say that our Battalion was in the thick of the fighting the whole time, was decimated and reinforced a dozen times, was kept in the Line until it was a skeleton battalion of skeleton men, withdrawn, re-fitted, brought up to strength and sent back again, time after time; and that Luke and I seemed to bear charmed lives.

Bullets tore our clothes; Luke's *bidon* was drilled twice as we dashed across No Man's Land under machine-gun fire; my *képi* was shot from my head as I peered over the parapet at dawn, one morning; and during a night raid, my right ear was torn by a bullet and my left fore-arm deeply scratched by a bayonet.

Greude died, saying something in a language which I did not understand, a bullet through his chest, giving his life as he had wished to do, fighting against Oppression.

Rassedin, decorated and promoted to Sergeant, was killed by a shell which blew his right leg off. He lingered for hours, dying of shock and loss of blood, his last words being,

"Well, well, *mon ami,* life's been very amusing. . . . Death is probably more so. . . ." In the breast pocket of his tunic was a valuable and beautiful miniature, in a gold case or locket, of a very lovely girl. There was a crest and motto on the case.

The last I saw of Oberg was in a German trench. Ten of us, with blackened hands and faces, made a night raid to get regimental badges, in order that the authorities might identify the enemy battalion that had that day taken over the trenches opposite to us.

Three of us returned, Araña, Brancker and I.

Drücke was wounded, patched up, sent back to the

Battalion, and shot through the head the next day.

By the time that Luke succumbed to strain, hardship and illness, and was sent to hospital, only I, Yrotavál, Araña and Hervé remained of the original *escouade.*

In point of fact, I was glad when Luke cracked up. Our luck had lasted too long, and every time he went back from rest-billets to the trenches, I thought of the Pitcher and the Well. It was too much to hope that this charmed-life business could continue indefinitely, with Death waiting for him in a dozen forms and in a hundred places.

We were at a place called La Roche Something-or-other—La Roche Nazaire, I think—when Luke fell ill. Dysentery—unless it was typhoid—again. And it was quite obvious that he was not only far too weak to march, but utterly unfit for duty. By that time, things were much better organized, and medical arrangements were not too bad, even in the Legion.

As we were in real rest-billets, and actually resting —save for a trifle of daily drill, route-marching, bomb-throwing training, bayonet exercise, rehearsal for new kinds of trench-attack and mopping-up work by *nettoyeurs des tranchées,* and the eternal digging and building of dug-outs, cook-houses, officers' quarters, casualty-clearing-posts and so on—the sick could get proper attention, especially if their friends knew how to get it for them. I haven't a word to say against French Army doctors, as a class, but I do say that the War threw up one or two of the type who were more than willing to profit by it.

Anyhow, having been informed by an American comrade that our temporary *Médecin-Major* was amenable to a certain form of argument, I interested him in Luke, whom he promptly declared unfit for duty, as of course he was, and ordered him to be sent at once to hospital. It was with almost undiluted joy that I saw him carried on a stretcher, by a couple of *brancardiers,* along the *boyeau* to where a motor-ambulance awaited its load of sick and wounded.

Had I but known what I was doing for him!

§2

In the peace of the quiet hospital at Pont Mailleul, fifty kilometres from the Line and forty from the war-zone, Luke made slow but steady recovery, as I heard from time to time, when other sick and wounded men rejoined us from that same hospital.

When he was convalescent, he used to sit, with other flotsam and jetsam of the wreckage of war, sunning himself and preparing to take up Life again; to take it up exactly where he had laid it down; to resume the crushing weight of the cross which, voluntarily, he had laid upon his young shoulders. And on the very day before he was to return to that nerve-and-mind-and-soul-shattering Hell from which he had briefly escaped, a German aviator—flying *"high above War's sorrows and seeing only its beauties"* perhaps—saw among them a defenceless hospital, plainly marked with a colossal Red Cross, a hospital full of doctors; and of those, perhaps noblest of all human beings, nurses; and of wounded sick and shattered men.

And on this hospital the young hero released his bombs.

A young hero, soul-mate and blood-brother of him who torpedoed the hospital ships with their cargo of wounded men, doctors, and the ministering angels we call nurses.

One bomb fell almost at Luke's feet. The marvel is that he was not blown to pieces. I had almost written, in my bitterness, the pity is that he was not blown to pieces, as his manhood was, his character, his self-respect, his self-confidence, his very self itself.

When I feel that my Luke, the *real* Luke, was left in that hole from which they dug his blinded body, I want to kill every cursed, bellowing, bullying Dictator and War-monger in the world. I wish that all the Dictators and War-Lords had but one throat—that I might cut it with a blunt knife.

It was, of course, part of the very pattern of our fate

that on the same day that it happened I was sent away, our Battalion was moved to Verdun, and plunged into that unique Hell of man's mad destructive folly, that long-drawn battle of heroic maniacs which was the bloodiest, most brutal and most horrible that the world has ever seen, and that I pray God the world may ever see.

I will not re-tell its story, but merely say that I survived, physically uninjured, and that the poor pitiful remnants of the Battalion were again brought up to strength and transferred to the Somme.

In point of fact, I don't remember very much of this last phase, this campaign which was one long battle, for my mind was as deaf as were the ears of my body, as shaken and as shattered; and I was too stupid for the reception of other impressions than those of hunger and pain and horror.

After the battle of the Somme, what little was left of the Battalion was disbanded. Soon a rumour spread that the whole Legion was going to be returned to Africa, and there built up again from the nothing that it almost was. In point of fact, this proved to be true. Our own Battalion was paraded, addressed by the Colonel in a speech of such eloquence as only a real hard-bitten fighting French Colonel can use when addressing his men; and the tiny handful of surviving Volunteers was given the choice of going to the depôt at Sidi-bel-Abbès, leaving France for ever, and becoming regular *légionnaires;* of being transferred to a French Line Regiment; or, in the case of those whose countries were already fighting the Germans, of joining their own national Army.

Most of the Legion Volunteers chose the second course, and a small draft of Americans, Britons, Belgians, Russians and Italians was transferred, and the young veterans became French Infantry soldiers in the 170th Regiment of the Line.

I personally elected to quit the French Army and join my own, the real inducement being neither that I wanted to get a respite from war nor that I desired to begin again as a recruit in a British Regiment, but that

I felt I must go home or go mad.

I must see Luke.

For I had had a letter from Rosanne telling me that Luke was at home and that Luke was *blind!*

Luke was blind.

I must see Luke and I must see Rosanne. I must see them both—and the seeing of Rosanne might soften the blow and mitigate the agony of seeing Luke, shell-shocked and . . . *blind.*

One curious little memory I have of the terrible time before the frayed and tattered remnants of the Battalion was disbanded, is that as I marched, as I stared out over the parapet, as I worked at the innumerable fatigues, as I lay in the mud of my dug-out, I repeated endlessly to myself—and not only to myself but aloud, for my comrades would turn and stare at me:

> *"And neither the angels in Heaven above,*
> *Nor the demons down under the sea,*
> *Can ever dissever my soul from the soul*
> *Of the beautiful Annabel Lee."*

I don't know much poetry, and I doubt whether Luke would admit that this is poetry; but, whether poetry or prose, whether jingling rubbish or beautiful verse, it expressed my feelings then and it expresses them now. . . . Rosanne.

The actual disbanding of the Battalion was to me a heart-breaking business, rendered a little less poignant by the fact that my oldest and best friends among the *légionnaires* and Volunteers were dead: Greude, Rassedin, Ouspenski, Oberg, Barnefeld, Dolgorousky, Ericsson, Drücke, Hervé, Brancker, Barbey d'Aurillac, Père Bossuet. Of the men with whom I had eaten and drunk and marched; laughed, worked and drilled; fought, lived and had my being at Toulon, and in the early days of the War, the only survivors were Yrotavál (who had been in the bombed hospital at Port Mailleul) and Araña, who took a literally tearful farewell of me. Unashamedly and unrestrainedly, the poor Spider cried like a child, put his great arms about me and kissed me on both cheeks as though I had been his brother, nay more, as though I were his own Yrotavál. It was probably a case of "transference," for since he had lost Yrotavál, he had been lost indeed.

I loathed going but I could not stay, much as I would have preferred to do so, for not only did I feel that Rosanne's letters told me less than the truth about Luke's condition, but I really and honestly felt that I should not much longer be of real use to any unit in which I continued to serve. Although bodily I was in not too bad shape, mentally I was near the end of my tether.

I was in need of healing.

The bomb that struck Luke blind—and, for all I knew, paralytic if not insane—had stricken me. It had done something to me that I could not understand, but which had, I knew, placed me in jeopardy. I realized that I was in need of healing, and I believed that only Rosanne could help me. If Luke were, as I feared, not only blinded but shell-shocked to insanity, not even Rosanne could heal me, but she could help. She could help me—as she was helping Luke, God reward her. And it was possible that I, too, could help him.

Anyhow, go I must, for Luke's sake and for my own sake. I must know the worst about him and the best about her, the best for me, that is to say—that she loved me.

I needed no assurance, of course, that she loved me in one way. She had always done that, from the very first, almost from the time we met in Switzerland, and certainly from the earliest days of her coming to live with us at Courtesy Court.

But I wanted more than that.

§3

I reached England and home safely, to find Luke not so badly shell-shocked as I had feared, broken and wrecked, but resigned; infinitely brave and patient; *blind*; devotedly nursed by Rosanne; and valeted, guarded and waited on, hand and foot, by—*El Señor*

Don Caballero Yrotavál y Rewes.

§4

I don't know that I was myself shell-shocked, but I was so shocked by this blow, this appalling tragedy of Luke's blindness, that I was as stunned, stupid and disorientated as if I too had been blown up and buried alive. I felt numbed.

There is something merciful about such numbness of mind, but nothing about the awakening from it.

Apart from being blind, poor Luke was so strange. I shall never forget how, the afternoon of my arrival, when we were sitting in a circle about the fire, having tea, he suddenly burst into speech, almost as though he were delirious. No, it was more as though he were a prophet or a seer, and I felt inexpressibly uncomfortable and miserable. Besides Luke, Rosanne and I, there was our local medical man, Dr. Watson (whom Luke insisted on addressing as "my dear Watson"); the Harley Street nerve-specialist Abernethy, who was waiting to be driven to the station to get his train back to London; the Vicar and his wife, who were most kind and helpful; our friend and neighbour, Giulia Brent-Grayleigh, and Athene who had, as she said, dashed down to hear Dr. Abernethy's latest report on Luke.

Suddenly Luke, who had been sitting silent staring with his blind eyes at nothing, turned and pointed with levelled finger unerringly at my breast. Of course he knew where I was, from the sound of my voice, but it was uncanny.

"See the Conquering Hero," he said. "Behold his medalled breast. Medalled, not muddled. Would that you all could behold also the scene which I can see. The remnants of the Moroccan Division on parade; with a battery of the Colonial Artillery on the right of the line; a Squadron of Chasseurs d'Afrique next; then Zouaves, Turcos, Tirailleurs and the Legion. A blaze of colour. Light-blue shakos; scarlet fezzes; blue dolmans; red trousers. . . . The bugles blow the *Garde à vous.* Splendid *Chefs de Battalion* bawl their orders, and the beautiful herbaceous border forms itself into a brilliant flower-bed.

"More booming shouts of *Faites les faisceaux* and *Sacs à terre.* The skeleton Division stands at ease, forming three sides of a square. A distant bugle warns the Commandant that the great General Lyautey himself approaches. Again fife and drum sound the order *Garde à vous.* More shouts.

" '*Rompez les faisceaux. Sacs à dos. Á droite, alignement. . . . Fixe.*'

"And the flower-bed of glowing colour, over which the wind had rippled, is now motionless, frozen solid. Another roar:

" '*Baionettes au canon.*'

"As though a flash of lightning had crossed the flower-bed, a thousand bayonets leap from their scabbards and are fixed to the rifles. And again there is perfect immobility and silence.

"And then the great General gallops up, followed by his glittering staff. The *clique* of the Legion shrills and crashes forth '*Le Générale.*'

"Simultaneously on the order '*Présentez armes!*' every man brings up his rifle to the *present,* and stands like a rock. The General, with eyes like those of an eagle, trots round the three sides of the square, inspecting the veteran survivors, takes up his place in the centre of the blank side, and sits at attention, while the massed bands of the battalions play *Au Drapeau* followed by the *Marseillaise.*

"And then, out from the ranks of the Legion battalion marches our Mark, and salutes with the precision of a Guardsman.

"The great General dismounts from his horse, pins the *Médaille Militaire* beside the *Croix de Guerre* on Mark's broad bosom, and kisses him on either cheek. . . . Serve him right for being such a bloody hero.

"Mark, blinking back his tears and swallowing a lump in his throat, salutes like two Guardsmen, and returns to the ranks.

"Then, to roars of '*En avant par quatres. En avant. Marchez,*' and to the strains of the March of the Legion,

Mark (and the other *légionnaires*) go by. To the air of *Sidi Brahim,* the Zouaves, Turcos, and Tirailleurs follow; and our Mark . . . Mark. . . ."

Suddenly Luke bowed his head almost to his knees and, covering his face with his hands, burst into tears.

Dreadful.

I learned then the meaning of the word 'heart-rending.'

§5

"Is there no hope for his eyes?" I asked Dr. Abernethy, as I saw him out to his car.

"I am not an oculist," he growled, for there was nothing of the bland Society Physician about this man. "He ought to see one, later on. The best in England. I suggest Sir Theophilus Grant. Your brother says he is satisfied with the verdict of the Paris specialist, Renier; and I suppose he's about the best in Europe. But he could have another opinion. Keep the idea before him, anyway."

"There's always hope, I suppose," I begged him to admit.

"Hope? Hope's free. And easy. But after what Renier said . . ."

"He's getting better otherwise?" I said.

"Oh, yes . . . Yes. He'll be all right—in time. Absolute rest and . . . It may sound foolish to say it . . . freedom from anxiety, worry. He mustn't brood. So far as it can be prevented, I mean. He's getting the best of nursing, but it is mental nursing he needs most. Wants taking out of himself, cheering up. He must have some sort of occupation and constant cheerful companionship . . . You staying here?"

"For the present," I said.

"Miss Van Daten?"

"Yes. She'll stay at home. On purpose to look after him."

"Splendid . . . Right. I'll see him again in a week's time. Meanwhile Doctor Watson knows what to do."

And with what was almost a twinkle in his cold grey

eye, very nearly a whimsical smile on his tight mouth, he added,

"And Miss Van Daten knows what to do—I think."

IX

It is useless for me to attempt to give the slightest idea of how I felt about Luke—and Rosanne.

For a start, I was in the very queerest mental condition myself, as I imagine all were who survived Verdun, not to mention the Somme.

In the second place, had I been perfectly normal on reaching home, the blow that I received on seeing my poor brother so changed, so quiet, so broken and *blind,* would have knocked me out completely.

And in the third place, I was just dying to take Rosanne in my arms and . . . well . . . give way; loosen the string of the over-taut bow that soon must break; tell her how I loved her, or rather, try to do so; hear her say that she loved me; marry her at once; to have a honeymoon that should be a heaven upon earth even more ineffably glorious than the Legion, the trenches, Verdun, and the Somme, had been an indescribably bitter murderous hell. A War wedding, a brief honeymoon, and then back to my duty; the plain duty, simple and inescapeable, that I must perform until my brother was avenged, Right had conquered Might, and Liberty was assured.

But how could I contemplate such a thing as love and marriage, with blind Luke hanging, not so much between life and death, as between sanity and insanity, salvation and destruction? For, quiet calm and self-controlled as he was, one knew that it was unnatural, his quiet air but a mask, that his apparent normality was but the crust over the seething lava of the white-hot volcano which sooner or later must explode, erupt —with God knew what consequences to his sanity, his health, his life.

How *could* such a temperament as Luke's resign itself to *blindness,* to eternal darkness and blackness? Luke, who so loved beauty, and whose pleasure and joy came to him so largely through his artist's eyes.

It would have been impossible had he been normal; but he had been through all that I had been through, had suffered all that I had suffered—and I was anything but normal.

I knew that what I needed for my salvation was a rest-cure in a place of perfect peace and silence, where I could have the help of the best of those wonderful doctors who really understand the inter-relation of mind and body, and who can save the poor, trembling, shaken, shattered, though unwounded body, by ministration to the mind that governs it. I wanted, and indeed I needed, that; but even more I needed something else, something far more efficacious. I needed Rosanne. Rosanne's mere presence. That alone, without Rosanne's love and care and ministration and sympathy, would have been enough.

But who needed it the more? Luke or I?

Luke. For he was every bit as ill, mentally and physically, as I; and he was blind.

And slowly it dawned on me, with a pain greater than any that I had ever suffered or ever should suffer, that not only did Luke need Rosanne's presence as much as I did, but *wanted* it.

And of course, it was possible that he wanted her quite as much as I did.

There is a vast difference between needing and wanting, for one may need something infinitely distasteful. But suppose Luke did, as I feared, want her as much as he undoubtedly needed her, *could* I, could *I*, try to come between her and my blind brother, for my own joy and delight and benefit? Could I try to take that which was, quite probably, his only chance of salvation? And if I could do it, and if Rosanne could consent to my doing it, where would be the joy? How could I ever have a happy hour, even with Rosanne?

And so I tried to kill this love that had grown to be the most powerful factor in my life; tried to throw the cold water of common sense, common decency, and perfectly common unselfishness upon the raging, fiery furnace of love that consumed my heart.

What made it ten times more difficult than it would otherwise have been, was the fact that Rosanne was so kind, so affectionate, so loving. The kiss that should have been an ineffable and soul-melting joy was a torture; and one of the hardest things that I had ever had to do was to place my hands upon her shoulders and kiss her soft, sweet, lovely mouth, morning and night, as might the most affectionate of brothers—and not take her in my arms, crush her to my breast, bruise her lips with burning kisses and ask her to marry me. How could I bear to sit beside her on the old deep settee before the log fire, with my arm about her shoulders, as we had done a thousand times before the War, and not gather her up to me and pour out my love?

How could I, with Luke there in his chair beside the fire, a black bandage about his eyes, sitting there so remote; aloof; alive, but dead to all that made life lovely; sitting there in that ancient panelled hall in which he had grown up, of which he knew every tiny detail as he knew his own face, and yet, at the same time, sitting there in that prison of eternal night, that dreadful cell of black velvet darkness from which there was no escape? It was, in a way, worse than being in the worst prison cell, inasmuch as there was no end, no escape from it, for it must go with him wheresoever he might go, unto the last day of his life.

Could I make love to Rosanne—no, I hate that expression—could I tell Rosanne I loved her? Could I show her, by any act or word or deed, that I *worshipped* her; while Luke sat there needing her, depending on her, wanting her perhaps as much as I myself did?

Yet that seemed to me to be impossible, for every man thinks, and tells the woman whom he loves, that no one could ever love her as he does; that no man has ever loved any woman as he loves her.

Well then, as I must remember, did not the same apply to Luke? Did he not feel—as he sat there, silent, with that awful, eternal blackness pressing down upon him, the darkness that would have made me shriek like a tortured child—did not he too feel that no one could love Rosanne as he did; that no man in this world had ever loved woman as he loved Rosanne?

Looking back, it was strange to realize that neither he nor she had yet said anything of this to me. But I knew it; and I had the strength to hold my peace.

Yes, Luke was changed. He was utterly different from the Luke that I had known. This was not to be wondered at; but it was terrible, it was heart-breaking, to contemplate this new and different Luke.

How shall I describe it? Best, perhaps, describe him, and it will be seen that I am speaking of a different man.

In the first place, this laughter-loving jester, so inconsequent, so irrepressible and irresponsible, now never laughed. Very, very rarely did he smile; and when he did, it gave one a heart-ache to see it—so patient, so resigned and gentle, on the face of the man who had been so merry, so happy, so full of life and laughter, the man who had been my brother Luke. He spoke but little, and that soberly and seriously. Before, he was an incorrigible jester who made fun of every-thing and, with witty speech, kept his hearers ever on the verge of smiles, chuckles or downright hilarity. Unconsciously, one always looked for the double-meaning, the sly allusion, and the humorous twist. When he appeared serious, it was only that his sober mien might add point to the outrageous nonsense that he was talking.

All this was gone, and that fact alone told anyone who knew him and loved him as we did, how changed he was.

And he was *blind.*

Freely I admit that I would not have believed that Luke, the frivolous, the volatile, the effervescent, could ever have borne so terrible an affliction with such stoicism, such uncomplaining patience, such noble dignity. I knew that I could not have done it. If I had formerly admired as well as envied him, what was now the measure of my admiration for such courage, such wonderful self-control? Luke touched the heights, and the least that I could do was to watch that I did not touch the depths—by trying to win Rosanne from him, trying to make her love me, marry me, go away with me upon that incredible honeymoon that in the trenches I had pictured, before I knew that Luke was blind.

How could I compete with him when he needed her so? I could as soon have struck a child and robbed it of its treasured necklace. I could as soon have stolen the coppers from the tin that hung about the neck of a blind . . .

Oh, my God! . . . *Blind, blind, blind.* Luke was blind . . . and loved Rosanne.

I am sorry for this outburst.

Almost always Luke wore a black silk bandage bound about his eyes and head. Sometimes, especially when he was taken out of the house, he wore big spectacles of black glass instead. Just occasionally, especially when we were alone, he and I and Rosanne, he wore nothing at all over his eyes. For, thank God, except for discoloration and a look of soreness, they were apparently undamaged and he was in no way disfigured.

He managed wonderfully; grew extraordinarily clever at so managing; and unobservant visitors who knew nothing of his tragedy might well have come into the drawing-room, stayed an hour for tea, and gone without knowing that he was blind.

The only abnormality about him, save for the fact that his eyes were often red and bloodshot, was the way he held his head, slightly raised; and the fact that, although he looked straight toward you when you spoke to him, he looked (or rather appeared to look, of course) over your head. It was as curious as it was painful, to notice how he always looked a little too high.

I was immeasurably thankful, in a situation where, God knows, there was little enough for which to be thankful, that his wonderful eyes were not destroyed. It would have been even worse than it was, if he had had unsightly cavities, hidden by permanently closed, red-rimmed, eyelids. He was, of course, fine-drawn and haggard-looking, for that was inevitable after what he had been through; but he was still handsome, handsomer than any man I have ever seen. Did I not dislike the word intensely, as applied to a man, I could say, with truth, that he was beautiful.

How could Rosanne do other than love him?

It was as lovely as it was painful to see her with Luke, to whom she was nurse, mother, sister and sweetheart in one. I say "sweetheart" because the brotherly love he must always have borne her, even though he had not shown it much, was now quite obviously changed, developed and increased. Before he went away, he had but rarely kissed her, even with a perfunctory good-night; had scarcely ever touched her, save to administer a fraternal thump; and he had sought her society but little—not that there had been any need for this, so assiduously had she sought his.

But now he could not see enough of her. (God, how one uses that word—of him who could not see her at all.) He could never have enough of her presence; was never happy when she was away from him. It now gave him most obvious delight to touch her, to sit with her hand in his, to stroke her hair and to kiss her.

In her sweet thoughtfulness and consideration, she would often come and sit beside me too, or perch on the arm of my chair, her arm about my neck; she would stroke my hair, stick a finger against the corner of my mouth and say,

"Turn it up at the corners, darling. It used to smile so nicely," and things of that sort.

Imagine what it cost me to refrain from responding as I yearned to do.

Don't think that Rosanne was one of those girls who "paw" people. Quite the reverse. No one could be kinder, more gentle, more responsive; but she was not what could be called demonstrative. With all her sweetness, there was, indeed, an astringent quality about

Rosanne. She had the wonderful saving grace of faintly
sardonic humour; and was endowed with what I might
perhaps call a very puncturing wit. There never lived a
human being less patient of pretence or falseness; or
who was less of a humbug. And oh, how she despised
and detested humbug of every kind! Beyond anything,
she loathed the false, the unreal, the specious; and if
any of her friends, acquaintances or relations were
marred by those defects, or indulged in anything of
that sort, they obtained from sweet Rosanne a sharply
acid reaction.

I am quite certain that she had more use, as they
say, for an out-and-out cheerful villain than for a
mealy-mouthed person of ostentatiously blameless life;
for a big, bold crook than for a mean swindler of lesser
calibre. And, as she once remarked, she definitely
preferred a bad man of the best sort, to a good one of
the worst kind.

I don't want to idealize and apotheosize Rosanne. I
fully and freely admit that she was no angel—except
when nursing and guarding and solacing Luke, when
she was ministering angel incarnate. She had a
temper, and she was a good hater. She was no believer
in meekness—possibly because she had no desire to
inherit the earth. She was no admirer of the poor in
spirit—perhaps because she had not the faintest desire
to possess the Kingdom of Heaven. But she was a
merciful lover of mercy; a peace-maker before all
things; and pure in heart as purity itself. Nevertheless
she was not religious. In point of fact, a person who
was known to be very "good" and strictly righteous,
started heavily handicapped in her sight, and had to
prove that goodness and religiosity were not incom-
patible with human humour, sportsmanship, good
fellowship, broad tolerance, wide sympathy, and deep
understanding of the frailities of common men and
women.

She had a splendid sense of humour, loved a joke,
wasn't too easily shocked, and never never pretended
to be shocked when she was not—though I should be
sorry to be the humorist who gave her real cause to

take offence.

No, with all her great gift of sympathy, kindness and love, her real fundamental goodness of heart, Rosanne was not perfect, thank God, and there never lived a woman less faultily faultless, icily regular, splendidly null.

Nor would I say that Rosanne was particularly forgiving toward anyone who had once really roused her anger and resentment. And that, doubtless, was part of her tenacity. For remarkably tenacious she was, and it was even more true of her than of most women, that you might convince her against her will and she'd be of the same opinion still.

Why did I love her so? I suppose, in the first place—human nature being what it is—for her very piquant beauty of face and figure, the great attractiveness of her little ways, her personality as well as her person, her vivacity; and partly for her *responsiveness.* She was so enthusiastic about things, so warmly inter-ested, and so appreciative. She entered into things with such zest. She never failed you; and you always said to yourself, at once, "I must tell Rosanne" or "I must show Rosanne," knowing that, whatever it might be, Rosanne would be as interested and appreciative as you were yourself.

Rosanne understood. Rosanne was with you. What-ever you did or saw or enjoyed was of double value if Rosanne were there; and if you did or saw anything alone, you immediately, if unconsciously, thought how much more enjoyable it would have been if Rosanne had been with you.

No wonder Luke loved her.

No wonder he loved her, even before she became his nurse, his mother, his guardian angel, the light of his darkness, the invisible yet shining light that must paradoxically have illuminated that blank black night of horror in which he lived.

And when I had got my breath, so to speak; recovered from the numbing blow of seeing Luke blinded and changed; had to some extent got the better of my selfish agony at realizing that Rosanne was for Luke and not for me; and had begun, in a numbed way, to accept the terribly abnormal as the normal, the new and ordained and inevitable way of life, I had time to consider the phenomenon and portent of the incredible presence at Courtesy Court of the amazing El Señor Don Caballero Yrotavál y Rewes.

<h2 style="text-align:center">§2</h2>

Luke told me that he owed more to Yrotavál than ever he could repay. The Catalan had saved his life, saved his reason, and had got him home. Not only did Luke feel that what Yrotavál had done gave him a claim upon Luke for life; but the fellow had, moreover, made himself indispensable. He was not only the perfect valet, but an admirable male nurse; and did for Luke all those things that Rosanne could not do. From the time he brought him his morning tea, shaved him, turned on his bath, led him to it, helped him bathe and dress, to the time he put him to bed, he was his constant companion, guide and guardian, when Rosanne was not with him.

She gave him every minute that she could spare, and spent the greater part of almost every morning, afternoon and evening with him; but there were times when she had to leave him as she had other duties and calls upon her time, for not only was she nursing Luke, straining every nerve to bring him back to health and normality, but she was running Courtesy Court. Since our father's death, Athene had done this very competently, but, directly war broke out, she had plunged into a whirl of Red Cross, and other, activities, and left the care of the house and estate to her daughter.

I gathered from what Rosanne told me, and Luke hinted, that Athene had rushed down from London the moment she got Rosanne's wire telling of Luke's return and of his condition, but had been unable to stay for long. It appeared that she had been simply and genuinely unable to bear the sight of Luke, whom she had always loved devotedly, blinded and shell-shocked. And in the light of its effect upon myself, I was able to see how terrible it must have been for Athene, who was essentially tender-hearted and loving.

Anyhow, having seen how devotedly and successfully Rosanne was able to nurse him, and how efficiently his Spanish valet looked after him, she had returned to her important duties at Lady Angela Kinloch's hospital.

Although my mother's death had been my first real grief, and was indeed one of the great griefs of my life, I was now positively glad she had not lived to see Luke like this. It would have broken her heart, for she worshipped him. It would have been bad enough for Father who was devoted to Luke, but it would have killed Mother, or broken her for life. She was not strong, and whenever Luke cut his finger or had a sore throat, it was a tragedy that temporarily reduced her to the very lowest depths. This would have been a murderous and fatal blow to her, poor darling.

Yrotavál's attitude to me was interesting and a little puzzling, with its mixture of the old familiarity of the comrade-in-arms and the new deference of a household servant to the *patrón,* the head of the family. In the Legion, as an *ancien* and a man of vast experience, he had treated me with familiarity—tinged with the natural contempt of the old soldier for the recruit, but diluted with the miserable respect of the extremely poor man for the comparatively rich.

Now he addressed me as Señor, and his attitude was one of deference, if not respect. But I was conscious of something else in his manner, something of an elusive quality which was not quite irony. Yrotavál never obviously had his tongue in his cheek, but he had a glint in his eye, though there was nothing whatsoever to which one could take offence.

Sometimes I wished there were.

His manner to Luke was perfect. To me it was imperfect. To Luke he was unreservedly respectful, attentive and solicitous. To me he was reservedly respectful and neither attentive nor solicitous.

I think I can honestly say that I am one of the last people in the world to care twopence about the attitudes of other people toward myself. I don't use ceremony or desire other people to do so; I don't stand on my dignity, for I can imagine no more insecure footing for any sensible and self-respecting person. I take not the slightest pleasure in bows, salutes, and greetings in the market-place; I like to give and receive civility, but I detest servility; and had Yrotavál been an ordinary valet or male nurse engaged by or for Luke, I should not have been in the slightest degree interested in the question of his attitude to me, in his manner, respectful or disrespectful.

But this was different. I knew a very great deal about Yrotavál, and most of it to his disadvantage. He was, on his own showing, a damned abominable scoundrel, and of all people whom I had ever met, the very last one I would have chosen to see installed in the same house with Rosanne, especially a house of which she had the responsibility and care.

On the other hand, he seemed to suit Luke splendidly and to serve him perfectly; and after all, that was what he was there for. Realizing this, I would take myself to task for my prejudice and suspicion, put the matter from my mind, and then have it all brought back again by some word from Yrotavál, some look on his sinister leathern visage. He was tough, and one expected him to be tough; and I was surprised to find him so much the soft-footed, soft-voiced valet and nurse. But what one did not expect was an occasional glimpse of what perhaps I might call the iron hand in the velvet glove, a certain masterfulness just under the deference; positively a hint, at times, of the whip-hand; of a too robust self-confidence and self-regard.

I decided, in the end, that I was fanciful and foolish, and that, had I been in normal mental and physical health, I should not have been so sensitive to atmosphere and attitude, and should never have noticed or fancied anything of the sort, and if I had, should not have given it a second thought. Doubtless I was entirely wrong, and even if Yrotavál sometimes wore an air of one who acted a part, he *was* acting a part, and a very novel one.

Of him, more than anybody I ever met, it was surely true that each man in his time plays many parts. But surely this rôle of deft *valet de chambre* and ministering angel was a new and strange part for a scoundrelly gunman, crook, terrorist, police spy, gaol-bird and toughest of tough *légionnaires*. Surely that would account for anything "different" in Yrotavál's manner, for he could hardly be leading a more different life from that which he had been leading. *Autres jours autres moeurs.*

Nevertheless, when I had said it all, the fact remained that there was something faintly disturbing about Yrotavál's attitude as of one who—what shall I say—bides his time, has something up his sleeve, knows more than he says, could say a lot more than he does—and all that sort of thing.

One day I asked Rosanne how she liked him.

"How do I like him?" she replied. "I cannot tell you how, Mark, because I don't like him at all. In point of fact, I detest him."

"My dear, if he has ever said one word, or . . ." I began, feeling my blood begin to boil and my fists to clench, wretched nerve-symptoms all too ready and frequent in those days.

"Heavens, no! His manner is perfect. And it makes my flesh creep. The way he looks at me . . ."

"But, Rosanne! If ever he gave you so much as an insolent look, I'd . . ."

"Insolence? Not a bit of it. I could deal with that myself. Oh, no, quite the reverse."

"Then what?"

"Nothing. Absolutely nothing. No complaints. I haven't a word against the man, except that I hate the sight of him. He makes my blood run cold. There is something absolutely repellent about him. I feel that he is evil incarnate. And I am very grateful to him for the splendid way in which he manages Luke, and for all he does for him. But oh, how I wish . . ."

"Look here, Rosanne, he's not the only pebble on the beach. First-class valets can still be got, and so can trained male nurses. I'll speak to Luke."

"No. No. Please don't, Mark. It would be an awful thing to get rid of the man, just because I don't particularly like him . . . when Luke likes him so very much. He seems to suit him perfectly."

"And that's something in his favour," I said.

"It's everything," agreed Rosanne. "Absolutely everything. At any rate, while he's still suffering from shell-shock."

"Yes, yes. But there are others. I'll have a talk with him about it," I said.

Rosanne was right and I was wrong, as usual; for when I spoke to Luke on the subject of replacing Yrotavál by a properly trained English male nurse, who could also do what valeting was necessary, he seemed absolutely horrified at the mere idea of parting with him, and literally implored me to put any such idea out of my mind. From being suppliant he became absolutely angry, and spoke as though I wanted to upset him, disturb such peace as he had attained, and generally do him harm. I was amazed at the importance that he attached to Yrotavál's services, presence, and company.

"My dear chap, I simply could not carry on without him," he said. "If Yrotavál were turned away, I should . . . I should . . . well, I should go with him."

I begged him not to talk like that, and assured him that nothing was further from my thoughts than to do anything to which he would not agree; that my sole object was to replace an amateur nurse and valet by a professional; and to find somebody less alien, less exotic, and who would fit better into the scheme of our quiet life at Courtesy Court.

"But I don't want anyone better," objected Luke. "He suits me perfectly. Besides, don't you realize that but for him I shouldn't be here? I owe him my life! . . . What has he done that you want to start hunting and hounding him out of . . ."

"But, my dear boy," I assured him, "nothing in the world is further from my thoughts than to get rid of Yrotavál if he is necessary to you. We'd do anything to keep him, so long as you feel like that about it."

"Well, I do feel like that about it. . . . What is your objection to him? What has he done? Some damned prudish house-maid or scullery-wench think he's cocking a wicked eye at her? So long as he looks after *my* eyes . . . These damned country bumpkins with their *'Here's a foreigner, let's chuck a brick at him'!* It's absolutely sickening and disgusting that . . ."

"Listen, old man," I soothed and assured him, "no one has a word to say against Yrotavál's work or conduct; and he'll be here until you yourself turn him out, or he himself says he wants to go. I only wanted to ask whether you wouldn't sooner have an Englishman."

"Well, I wouldn't. And if he doesn't go till I kick him out, he'll be here for ever. And if he doesn't go until he himself wants to, he'll be here just as long and a bit longer. . . . Where would he go? He couldn't go back to his own country. You know the Spanish police want him, not to mention those damned Anarchist and Communist thugs who pride themselves on always getting their man if he turns informer. And he can't go to France or he'll be arrested as a deserter from . . . I mean to say, he'd . . . Well, he's got to earn his living somewhere, hasn't he? And talking of which, where would he earn as good a living, or earn it as easily, as he does here? No, Yrotavál won't leave me in a hurry, Mark, so don't you think it or try to make him."

" 'Nuff said, old chap," I soothed him. "Yrotavál's here for life, since you want him to stay. What about a turn in the garden?" And putting my hand beneath his arm, I led him from the room, out on to the lawn.

So that was that, and we must regard Yrotavál as a fixture. Nevertheless, there was nothing to prevent my taking what steps I could toward making that fixture adapt itself to its surroundings. If Luke had told Yrotavál that he had got a job for life at Courtesy Court, I could do my best to persuade him that it was, at any rate to some extent, dependent upon his conduct and general attitude. Sort of *quamdiu se bene gesserit,* like a Bishop. But he'd have to please me as well as pleasing Luke. For, after all, in the ultimate resort, I was master of Courtesy Court. It belonged to me, and although God knows I'd be the last person to parade the fact, or even to refer to it in Luke's or Rosanne's hearing, there might be no harm in my letting Señor Yrotavál know who was the master. Not that there was really much in the idea, as I quickly realized, for he was quite cunning enough to know that, though I might be the *de jure* master of Courtesy Court (and, were I so disposed, could make a clean sweep of him and everybody else in it), the *de facto* master was Luke, by reason of his being my brother.

Luke's blindness was the main factor of the situation; Luke, in his stricken weakness, the real master of Courtesy Court—and Yrotavál knew it.

Nevertheless, before I went, a word with Yrotavál I would have, a word of good advice, of warning, and of scarcely veiled threat.

Why threat? I asked myself. And was able quickly to answer—Because I don't trust the man; because I detest him; because I hate leaving him here with so much power in his hands; himself, indeed, the power behind the throne of the poor blind king of this little domain; because I know him for a vile, foul-minded and villainous rogue who, on his own showing, was a cur who had the currish habit of biting the hand that fed him; a double-crosser, badly wanted by those on both the sides that he had served.

And not only was he a treacherous villain, base and evil, but he was undeniably bold and resolute as well as intelligent, a man with the nerve and brains and guts to carry out whatever villainy his mind conceived. How could I leave a creature like that, not only in charge of Luke, but in the same house with Rosanne when I went away?

For go I must. In a morass of uncertainty this was certain. On all grounds and for a dozen reasons, I must go. Cowardice drove me; misery impelled me; and, a faint and feeble will-o'-the-wisp across the morass, shone fitfully a sense of duty. For I was rested and was fit to fight again.

This, Watson, our excellent local doctor, one of those general practitioners who, from the extent and variety of their practice, become specialists of every-thing—quite strongly contradicted, and got the support of the distinguished nerve-specialist who came down from London periodically to see Luke. These good fellows talked about nervous lesions and strains, rest-cures, sea-voyages and what-not; and no doubt from their point of view they were right. From mine, they were wholly wrong. What I needed was action; absorp-tion in constant, and preferably violent, physical occu-pation that, while giving me no time to think, would so tire me that I must sleep at night. Occupation I must have, if I were to gain salvation, retain my balance, carry on, behave reasonably and decently, and keep on an even keel.

I was afraid of what I might say and do, if I re-mained any longer under the same roof with Rosanne. To realize that I must not come between her and Luke, must not take her away from Luke, was one thing; but to see her with him, to see her at all, was quite another. And I was frightened by the violence and strength of the emotions that surged up in me when she kissed me good night and good morning; put her arm through mine, or sat down beside me in our own place on the old settee.

And the unbearable pain that it gave me to watch blind Luke; to see his pitiful brave efforts to be brave; his clever attempts to do things for himself; to find his way about the house; to go to his room unguided; to feed himself at table; to wander about the garden that he had always loved.

God! It made my eyes tingle when I saw him fingering the books he could not read; feeling and stroking the favourite gun that he would never fire again, he who had so loved his shooting; touching the wheel of the car he would never drive again; fumbling for his pipe and tobacco and matches, filling and lighting it, and, a minute or so later, putting it down, with a little sigh for the tastelessness of unseen smoke, he who had been so fond of his pipe.

Little things, but oh, how big are little things, and gifted with what power to wring the heart.

No, I simply could not bear it, and misery joined with cowardice to send me back to the wars.

I could no longer hide from myself the fact that here was I, young, healthy, very strong, and already well-apprenticed and trained to the trade of trench-fighting; the fact that so long as I could pass a doctor or a medical board, I had no right to be here, loafing and scrimshanking, while others were fighting for me.

It was not as though I had been badly wounded or otherwise incapacitated; not as though I were married or forty years of age. Our own doctor and Luke's specialist, doubtless influenced by Rosanne, said I was not yet fit to go back to it. Well, let an impartial and unbiased judge decide, a Recruiting Office doctor.

If I failed to pass him, well and good. Very well, and damned good. I would take another six months for rest and recuperation.

If I passed him, well and good also. I should be very well out of that house, and it would be a damned good thing for me to be occupied again. But I must be careful lest I find myself in some back-water of more or less leisurely training, some relatively easy way of life that would give me time for thought. I simply must not have time to think, to realize, to remember, to suffer with Luke the agony of his blindness. Not at present. Not yet. I should be able to bear it better later on, perhaps. So I wouldn't go to our very old family friend, General Sir Henry Brent-Grayleigh, and ask him to recommend me for a Commission. That would mean at least six months of O.T.C. training work, with a certain amount of evening and week-end leisure. Nor did I feel that I should, after six months, have the knowledge, experience and ability to warrant my taking an officer's responsibilities and having the lives of good men dependent on me. The very best man in every unit must be its officer, and the men must know it. I had seen officers from below, heard how their men spoke of them, seen how they regarded them and judged them; and I knew that, for a man to be a good officer, he must have his men's respect for his superior knowledge, experience, training and ability. His resolution and courage must at least equal theirs, and to do so they must be great. To exceed theirs they must be remarkable. But there must be no question whatever as to the officer being infinitely the men's superior in all the arts of war. They must realize and admit that their leader is in every way fit to lead them, in every way the best man among them.

I knew perfectly well that, in my own Company of the Legion, I should have been entirely unfit to command and lead those magnificent fighting-men, and I had no reason to suppose that I was, at present at any rate, fit to command and lead Englishmen.

I decided, therefore, that I would again enlist as a private soldier.

The next question was the arm and the unit. Obviously Infantry, as I was a trained infantryman, and if I enlisted in the gunners or cavalry, most of my training would be wasted. As to what Infantry unit, it seemed to me that a Guards Battalion was indicated. Why were they admittedly the best infantry regiments in the British Army? Because of their superior discipline, smartness and efficiency. And what did this superiority indicate but more, longer, and harder work; more intensive training? And it was work, constant thought-killing, mind-dulling work that I needed.

The Guards it should be, if they would have me; and, inasmuch as I was not Scots nor Irish nor Welsh, the Grenadier Guards appeared to be indicated.

I would offer myself at their Recruiting Office and let their doctor be the arbiter of my fate.

§3

Having come to this decision, I felt better—less cowardly, less miserable, and no longer the victim of a sense of dereliction of duty.

I would go almost at once; just as soon as the

specialist had again reported on Luke; but I would first have my final interview with Yrotavál. And with Rosanne. That I really dreaded. Whatever self-control was left to me, whatever manhood and self-respect remained, must help me to say good-bye to her without saying anything else. That she loved me dearly and that she had always done so, I knew. I lacked the self-conceit to think that she would respond in kind if I threw off my—what shall I say . . . brotherliness—and told her I loved her, worshipped her; and begged her to marry me. But it was possible that she loved me as much as she did Luke, and Luke as much as she did me, and that the one of us who "made love" to her first would marry her. If it were possible, it was a possibility that I must not risk, for it would be a kind of stealing. It would be horrible; it would be taking advantage of Luke's blindness; winning her behind his back, so to speak.

But of course, if I spoke words of love—love of that sort—she would not listen. If I poured out love before her, at such a time and under such conditions, she would be shocked, even if she had been disposed to love me.

So I dreaded saying good-bye to Rosanne even more than parting with Luke.

The morning after my decision I went into the library, seated myself at the big writing-table, and sent for Yrotavál. I would treat him as a servant, keep him standing while I spoke to him, and try to put into him —if not the fear of God—the fear of me and of losing his job.

He came in, closing the door behind him gently, treading softly, and conducting himself as the discreet servant and trained valet. Among other things he was a good actor. It was wonderful how quickly he had changed, adapting himself to his new rôle. Even his speech had, like his manners, improved enormously. There were only traces of his Cockney and East Side idiom and accent; and visitors to the house, who saw him with Luke, imagined him to be an ordinary

Continental courier-valet and confidential servant.

But the leopard cannot change his spots, nor could Yrotavál his face, his shifty wicked eye and steel-trap mouth.

"You sent for me, Señor Tuyler?" he said, bowing and standing in the deferential attitude of the well-trained servant, everything perfect save for the faintly ironical gleam in the eye and flickering smile on the thin lips.

"Yes. I'm going away, Yrotavál, and . . ."

"Not back to the Legion? *M'Carben Diu!* Don't you be no bloody . . ."

This was a lapse. The real Yrotavál peeped through the veneer. There was nothing of the imperturbable impassive servant about the start and quick question.

"I will do the talking, Yrotavál," I interrupted, and stared him out, until his eyes dropped. "Don't forget you are a servant here, and that a servant you will be until you go. Understand me?"

"Si, Señor."

"I am going away to-morrow or the next day, and may not be back for some while. Miss Van Daten will, of course, be in whole and sole and complete charge of this house, and although you will be Mr. Luke's servant, you will be entirely under her orders."

"But, *Señor*, if . . ."

"No 'if' about it. Miss Van Daten will be absolute mistress here, and in the unlikely event of her orders differing from any that Mr. Luke may give you, it is her orders that you will obey—if you wish to remain here. Understand me?"

The restless reptilian eyes flickered up, darted a look into mine and fell again.

"Sin duda, Señor. Without doubt, I quite understand. Sure thing. Mr. Luke's orders are to be disregarded and . . ."

"Listen, Yrotavál, and watch your step. You will do exactly as Mr. Luke tells you. You will be his servant and nothing else; and you will behave as a servant should. If Miss Van Daten sends for you and says '*I don't think Mr. Luke ought to be allowed to do such-and-*

such a thing,' or '*I want Mr. Luke to do such-and-such a thing,'* you will give her every help in your power, and make it your business to see that her wishes are carried out. Understand?"

"*Si, Señor.*"

"Of course, should Miss Van Daten send for you and say '*Yrotavál, you are in the habit of doing such-and-such a thing. I don't like it,'* you will never do it again. Or if she gives you an order such as '*Go up to London to-morrow and bring me this or that,'* you will go. In other words, you will absolutely obey Miss Van Daten, and do your utmost to please her in every way. If you wish to stay here, that is. Do you?"

"*Sin duda, Señor . . . Por Cierto!* . . . Sure thing. I wanna stay with Mr. Luke . . . always."

"Well, that is the only way you'll do it, then. For I give you my solemn promise, Yrotavál, that if I get one word of complaint from Miss Van Daten, I'll make it my business to come back here, *pronto,* and turf you out—on your ear, and ack over tock. . . . Got it?"

The suddenly raised eyes again shot a look into mine and a leathery-looking tongue darted like a snake's across the thin lips.

"*Si, Señor.* I get you."

"Good. We understand each other, then. Don't forget. You may go."

And with a glance that had nothing in it whatever of humility or acquiescence, no faintest suggestion of the trained and respectful servant, Yrotavál turned and went from the room—leaving me anything but satisfied about him.

§4

I had said nothing definite to Rosanne on the subject of my immediate plans. Time enough to tell her what I was going to do, when I was going to do it.

After we had seen Luke to his room, on what was to be my last night before going to London to enlist, I asked her to come along and have a talk with me before she went to bed.

"I wish he wouldn't lock himself in at night," she said as we sat on our favourite settee in front of the fire in the hall. "He *will* do it."

"He oughtn't to," I agreed. "Suppose he were suddenly taken ill, and we couldn't get in there to him. Supposing there were a fire. Yrotavál sleeps in the next room, but it would take time to break Luke's door down, if there were need. Suppose he fell asleep in bed, with a lighted cigarette in his hand . . . I'll try to talk him out of it," I promised.

"I've done my best," said Rosanne, "but he simply won't hear of it. I suppose it is—what's the word . . . when you feel you must be alone? Not only alone but safe in a place of your own where no one can get at you. It's a phobia. I know—agoraphobia."

"Yes," I agreed, "I've heard the word."

"It's the opposite of claustrophobia," supplied Rosanne. "That's the fear of being enclosed, trapped, isn't it? One can quite understand Luke suffering from agoraphobia, after living perpetually in public, so to speak, always with a crowd, night and day."

"Yes, and as he was hating life in the trenches like hell, and in the so-called rest-billets, which were nearly as bad, one can understand his being 'struck like it,' so to speak, when the bomb got him," I agreed.

"Yes, poor Luke," murmured Rosanne. "Never a moment's privacy, from the day he enlisted till the day he reached here. Barracks, trains, marches, trenches, billets, hospital; no wonder he has an absolute craving for privacy, and insists on locking his door. I suppose it is what psychologists would call symbolic."

We sat silent a while.

"It is dangerous, nevertheless," she mused. "Do you know what I think I'll do? Have a ladder fixed from his window to the ground."

"What, a sort of fire-escape?"

"Yes. A sort of staircase. Iron, with a hand-rail. There could be a little railed platform just outside his window, and in an emergency he could get out and go down the stairs—just as he does alone inside the house."

"Oh, I don't know that all that is necessary," I said. "A fixed ladder, by all means. It would be perfectly easy for him to use it. He'll get accustomed to doing all sorts of things like that, poor chap."

And I could scarcely speak as I visualized the things he'd have to learn to do.

"If we made a real permanent external-staircase of it, he'd probably object as strongly as he does to having his door locked."

"Yes. But I must do something about it or I shan't sleep in peace, with him behind that locked door . . . *blind* . . ."

A silence fell between us.

"I'm off to-morrow, Rosanne," I said, after a while.

"Up to town?"

"Yes."

"For how long?"

"I don't know. I'm going to enlist in the Guards, if they'll have me."

"*Mark! . . . Oh! . . .*"

Rosanne began to cry, a thing I hadn't seen her do thrice in all the years I had known her.

"Oh, Mark, you *mustn't,*" she sobbed. "You're not fit . . . Sorry, snivelling like this. But it is the last straw. Mark, I can't carry on if . . . *Must* you, Mark?"

"Yes."

"Oh, God! Mark, I . . ."

And then, visibly, brave Rosanne pulled herself together.

"You must if you must, Mark. But, oh . . ."

I steeled myself not to gather her into my arms. Luke wanted her. And who knew better than I what it was to want Rosanne? Luke needed her. And who knew better than I what it was to need Rosanne? And though he could not want her more than I did, he needed her a thousand times more.

Inevitably she must love Luke, with his wondrous charm, beauty and wit, more than she loved me. I could not be such a cur as even to *try* to compete with him . . . But if I stayed there another minute with

Rosanne beside me, her arm through mine . . .

"Good night, my dear," I said, and rose to my feet.

"Good night, Mark," she said.

That night I did not kiss her. I couldn't. Not in a brotherly way.

§5

Next morning I went to say a last good-bye to Luke. He was still in bed, and I thought he was looking better, but it wrung my heart again when he put out his hand to take mine and missed it. I could have kicked myself for my clumsiness.

"Where are you going?" he asked.

"For a sojer," said I.

He shot up in bed.

"Not back to the . . . ?"

"No. To support Home Industries. Bold British Grenadier."

"Good Lord! Sir Henry got you a commission?"

"No. Going to trail a pike."

"Good God! I say. What, '*Quo Fas* and *Gloria duck-hunt?*' "

"Yes. Or '*Try a juncter in—you know.*' "

He smiled. "I say, Mark, come back safe and all that. I don't want to inherit. We don't want me blind-man's-buffing at Courtesy Court."

"I'll come back. Under the *alias* of Bad Penny, Esquire," I said. "Good-bye, Luke. Keep a . . . Keep your pecker up. You'll . . ."

I met his blind eyes and hurried from the room.

I tried to avoid saying good-bye to Rosanne in private and alone, but she defeated this. Taking my arm and drawing me into her morning-room, she shut the door and faced me. She had no faintest idea of how hard she was making it for me.

Putting her hands on my shoulders, she raised her face to mine.

"Mark," she said. "*Mark* . . ."

I am not an emotional man, I trust; but I found it

difficult to say anything. Indeed there was nothing to say.

As we held each other thus, without kiss and without embrace, it seemed to me that her eyes tried to speak words that her lips did not say.

Should I tell her that I understood that she and Luke . . .

"*Mark!* . . . *Mark!* . . . Kiss me good-bye, then."

I kissed Rosanne a quick good-bye and went.

X

What I write now is not in criticism of the intensive war-time training-system of our truly magnificent Guards' Battalions, but of foul War and its vile compulsions and necessities.

I have no hesitation in saying that I found depôt life in the Guards harder than in the French Foreign Legion at Toulon. Whether it was because the Volunteers there received preferential treatment and had an easier time than the ordinary *legionnaire* who gets his training at the depôt at Sidi-bel-Abbès, I don't know, but I do know most definitely that I found recruit-training at the depôt more thorough, more strenuous, more violent, than at Toulon. I found the Drill Instructors much more aggressive, harsh and strict. I would say more brutal but for the fact that they probably only seemed more brutal because their curses, objurgations and insults were uttered in English; and an insult in one's own language is infinitely more—insulting—than one uttered in a foreign language. It is a case in point that "*sale cochon*" seemed little more than a term of endearment, but "stinking bloody swine" seemed much more or less.

If a French Sergeant told me in his own tongue that to gaze upon my face must always have given pain to my mother, I was in no wise offended; but I did not like it when a huge ruffian with suffused countenance and bristling moustache stuck his coarse and brutish face close to mine and roared aloud that of all the things my mother ever dropped, I was the filthiest.

One of course told oneself, trained oneself, to take no notice of any noises that came out of Drill Instructors' mouths, save military orders; to ignore insults; to regard oneself as above and beyond verbal hurt from these people. But it was difficult. And, at first, their appalling oaths and foul epithets got one down.

Some of the Drill Instructors were worse than others—which I suppose implies that some were better. But I came to the conclusion that the whole abominable business was part of the system, the definite policy of breaking before making; of crushing the raw material, that it might be pressed into the mould; or, to change the metaphor, of harrowing *(harrowing,* my God!) and clearing the soil that the ground might be prepared for the sowing of the good seed, the dragons' teeth of Cadmus.

Beside the breaking-in-order-to-make aspect of the system, there was also that of breaking now what might otherwise break later; unnatural selection, so to speak; and the survival of the fittest.

Yes, it was a harder life than that of the French Foreign Legion *bleu.*

I did not positively enjoy the eternal shining of ration-tins, the scrubbing of floors, the scouring of tables, the black-leading of grates; nor demand more than I got of latrine fatigue, cook-house fatigue, nor other bristle-broom, scrubbing-brush, mop and swab fatigues; but I hated the parade-ground drill and the eternal cursing, blustering and bullying of louts whose Lance-Corporal stripe gave them power to hurt, injure, humiliate and degrade, as well as to instruct in squad-drill and the use of the rifle.

Oh, that rifle! At Toulon I had been through a pretty small-grinding mill and liked it, but there were times in England when I could almost have wept when, for the hundredth time, we were made to,

"*Slap* it, you b—— b——s! *Hit* it. Break the b—— stock—or bust your b—— hands, but *slap* it! *Hit* it! Hit it as b—— hard as you b—— well can, you herring-gutted tripe-hounds. Hit it till you *bleed.*"

That I had been in the trenches and had fought in many battles (which the Lance-Corporal had not done) was as nothing beside the ability to slap the rifle with sufficient force if not to break it, at least to make my hand bleed. It was not sufficient that one should make one's hand "tell" on the rifle when bringing it to the *present.* One must hit it, literally, with all one's strength. Presumably, the more violently one could slap one's rifle when doing the manual, the more efficient a defender of one's native shores would one become.

Nor was it only foul language that we had to suffer. I was amazed, literally astounded, when I saw a Drill-Sergeant strike a man on parade. Not a push, a shove, or an unpleasantly over-playful prod in the chest, but a violent blow in the face. This was, of course, utterly illegal, and was never done within sight of an officer or the Regimental Sergeant-Major. But there were fifty-five minutes in every hour in which any Instructor was not within sight of an officer or the Regimental Sergeant-Major.

And if the act were utterly illegal, why was not the Law invoked? Because there was no man fool enough to invoke it—and the literally fatal enmity of every Drill-Instructor, Sergeant, Corporal, and Lance-Corporal at the depôt.

One fool, less foolish than to report a foul-mouthed diabolically insulting brute of a Corporal who struck him, struck back; and in the blow was the pent-up hatred and resentment of days and weeks and months. It was a noble blow. The man must have been a trained boxer, for when "with sense of wrong and outrage desperate" he struck at last, he knocked the Corporal senseless and fractured his jaw.

I have often wondered what became of him when he completed his prison sentence.

§2

I am not complaining and I am not accusing.

The proof of the pudding is in the eating, and the proof of the excellence of the system is in the super-excellence of the discipline, smartness and terrific military efficiency of a Guards Battalion. That a system of brutality and terror is the best for turning a mob of men into a magnificent military machine is only one more unnecessary comment upon the villainy and monstrosity of War, that most abominable of all insane human activities; and the person who complains and accuses, should complain of War and accuse the makers of War. It is childish folly to blame Military Authorities because a system of brutality and terror is the best system that can be found for making men brutal and terrific, turning men into trained professional killers.

It will at once be objected by the ignorant that more can be done by gentleness, kindness, and encouragement than by roughness, strictness, and driving carried to the point of brutality and terror. So it would for any other purpose than War—and that is War's condemnation. The highest killing returns are obtained by the best-made killing-machine; and, in the turning of gentle kindly men into killing-machines, gentleness and kindness have no place.

All of which aside, I should be a fool and an ingrate to complain because the Guards gave me what I went for—work to the limit of human capacity; constant endless drill and training, so intensive that the long day was a solid block of tiring work, the short night a solid block of tired sleep.

Some Drill-Instructors, Sergeants and Corporals were less violent, brutal and menacing than others; and I am afraid that the honest truth is that these men were less successful than those whose one idea of recruit-shaping and soldier-making was the use of terror, shock, brutal insult and savage threat. These men seemed to live in a state of overwhelming military wrath, irrepressible bitter contempt, and savage rage at finding themselves asked to make men, much less soldiers, of what they regarded as the pitiable human offal given them as material.

We liked and admired the occasional kindlier Sergeant; and we feared, with a pitiful shrinking as of beaten hounds, the more efficient ones. And alas, for these latter we struck our rifles the harder, "jumped to it" more swiftly, drilled ever more energetically, and worked more desperately. And by this undeniable fact the system is justified and proven for its purpose of making slayers.

War is hell. The most disciplined unit does best in war. Perfect discipline must be absolutely mechanical. Violence, brutality and terror are the best agents for making men mechanical; for turning thinking, reasoning, and decent men into iron machines.

The best material were the men of most strength and least intelligence; outdoor manual workers; unskilled labourers accustomed to long hours of hard and heavy work, such as navvies, dockers, field-workers, porters and men of that type. Not only were such men accustomed to great physical effort, but were devoid of nerves, and better able to stand the monotony, the mechanical pettiness of the life, and the absence of mental exercise and relaxation. Even for these men, the life was very hard; but it was infinitely harder for the educated men of the black-coated professions, who were unaccustomed to the strenuous muscular life, for they suffered both physically and mentally. I was more than sorry for the clerks, musicians, writers, lawyers, artists, students and such people. I was particularly sorry for a splendid youngster named Rawlinson who had come straight from Cambridge and who died under the strain. He was killed on the Barrack Square, but he died for England as much as any man who was killed in a Flanders trench.

Yes, during the War, it was definitely a much harder life of far stricter discipline and more intensive training than that of the French Foreign Legion, but the aims and ideals of those respectively responsible were different. For the Guards, the uttermost ultimate polish and finish of perfect mechanical smartness and precision that inevitably connotes discipline. For the Legion, endurance, endurance and again endurance; gallantry, initiative and *élan,* with repressive iron discipline expressed in harsh punishment for military offence.

In the Guards there were tremendous *esprit de corps* and intense nationalism as well as patriotism, with the "Bill Browns" (Tommy Atkins becomes Bill Brown in the English Guard Battalions), the "Jocks," the "Micks" and the "Taffies," each perfectly certain that the men of his Regiment are superior to those of the others.

But before a Bill Brown, Jock, Mick or Taffy could be turned into the perfect Guardsman, confident, aggressive and swaggering, he had to be bullied and brow-beaten until he was broken and cowed, that he might be re-made on the new model; drilled to breaking-point and drilled again; drilled until the only impulses that his mind could feel, the only calls that it could hear, came from the Drill-Instructor; and he was the complete robot.

And all this suited me finely.

The mere physical hardship of it, bed, board, housing, fatigues and so forth, were luxury compared with what I had been through in the trenches; and the endless drills, exercises, classes and marches gave me no time to think, no time to suffer.

While hating every aspect of the system and deploring its necessity, I was grateful to it. My mind was so dulled, my thoughts so confused, my sensibilities so blunted, that I lived in a curious state of "being about to"; being about to suffer rather than suffering; being about to think of Luke and the horror of his tragic life, rather than actually thinking; being about to realize that I could but rarely see Rosanne again, scarcely ever stay with her, and never again live under the same roof. For, apart from the fact that I was far too desperately in love with her to be able to do this, I had not the courage and endurance to bear the sight of Luke blind . . . fumbling . . . broken. . . .

When thoughts of Luke and Rosanne came to me by day, they were very promptly driven out by the urgency of action, the necessity of straining every nerve to pay the utmost closest attention. For it is not until a thinking man has been killed and an unthinking machine has been made, that the resultant product can work mechanically.

And at night, physical fatigue mercifully dulled mental suffering; and between waking and sleeping there was no twilight borderland.

§3

After a few months of this drastic kill-or-cure, make-or-break intensiveness of training, the awkward-squads of recruits coalesced into a company of trained soldiers, and was transferred to battalion barrack-life in London. And, after further training, there occurred, one day, a small event of great significance. Red strips of cloth, on which the name of the regiment was embroidered in white letters, were issued to those men whose names had appeared in a list headed with the familiar formula:

"The following are warned to be in readiness to proceed overseas."

On this list in due course appeared my name. Forthwith the scarlet tabs were sewn below the shoulder-straps of my tunic and I was marked as sacrifice acceptable to the Red God of War.

My first thought was that this would mean a brief spell of pre-embarkation leave, and an opportunity to go home and say good-bye to Rosanne and Luke, as it was rather more than probable that I should never see them again. Expectation of life at the Front in the Guards was not at that period high—not nearly as high as expectation of death.

Should I go home or not? Could I see Rosanne again without making love to her—to use an expression I detest? Did I dare to see Luke again? Certainly I could not see him and then ask the woman whom he loved to marry me.

But no leave was granted, and to this day I do not know whether I should have gone home if I had been able to do so.

XI

"Back to the trenches again, Sergeant." A raw recruit with more trench-fighting experience than most of the veterans.

Once again I will resist the temptation to let this account of my part in Luke's tragedy develop or degenerate into another war book. Suffice it to say that life in the trenches with the Guards differed mainly from that with the French Foreign Legion in the fact that I was now serving with a purely working-class British Regiment and not with one composed of men from every walk of life and almost every country in the world; and secondly, in the fact that we were treated with more humanity, that is to say, more humanly and humanely, and as though our lives were of some value and account to our officers.

We were far better fed, far better looked after, and, when sick or wounded, received much greater care and attention. But Death noticed little difference between us and the *légionnaires,* feared not to blunt his scythe, and mowed among expensive guardsmen as freely as among mere ha'penny-a-day *légionnaires.*

I was now better off and worse off; better because I did not suffer the constant strain of worrying about Luke, hourly expecting to see him killed or mangled; worse off in that I had this constant ghastly spectre lurking at the back of my mind and ever ready to spring to the front, the knowledge that the worst or almost the worst had already happened. Perhaps in a way, knowledge of the worst is not so bad as its anticipation.

Being absolutely indifferent to whether I were killed or not, if, in point of fact, my taste did not lean perhaps to the side of a quick death, I was spared where so many were taken, survived innumerable hot encounters and became something of a joke or by-word among my comrades as The Man the Devil Doesn't

Want, and among our officers as The Immortal.

It was considered to be a safe bid that if I was sent out on a raid or night-reconnoitring expedition, I should return, if only as the sole survivor, a thing which happened several times.

Partly because trenches were now vastly improved and trench life better organized, partly because we were so much better fed, clothed and cared for, my health remained good, and though I was still aware of a certain mental numbness, a kind of living in a state of suspension or in a vacuum, I was not wholly and always wretched and depressed, nor what might be described as perpetually miserable. I did my best to live the life of my comrades, but found it difficult, inasmuch as we had so little in common—which was my loss. As I have said, it was a purely working-class battalion, every man of education having been promoted and given a commission—an offer which I received and declined. The "Bill Browns" who remained in the ranks were ignorant, uneducated, stupid men of incredibly narrow outlook and interest, and very many of them amazing by-products of our system of free and compulsory education. Let me hasten to add that they were splendid fellows, the salt of the earth, staunch and sound, solid and reliable. They had their code of honour, and, albeit a different one from that of the officers, they observed it as strictly as the officers did theirs.

I admired them and loved them, was unfeignedly proud to be accepted by them—and lived among them utterly alone.

§2

I did not know whether we were winning the War on the Western Front, but the Germans seemed to be making a frantic effort to win it on our Home Front. Gothas were now over London, as well as Zeppelins.

I could sympathize most deeply with the terrific indignation, felt by my comrades, at this bombing of civilian homes, with its accompanying slaughter of women and children. How ridiculous such scruples seem nowadays, when it is the recognized pastime of poetic young heroes. Many of the "Bill Browns" were London men, and although immune to the horrors of their own war, they were aghast at the thought that their little homes, their wives and children, might be blown to bits.

For one unhappy day of bitter east wind and driving rain, I received a letter the contents of which put me utterly and wholly *d'accord* with them and deepened my savage sympathy, for in it Rosanne tersely told me that Athene, bright-plumaged happy bird of (earthly) Paradise, had been killed by a bomb; happily—she died, since stricken she had to be, for her beautiful body was torn and mangled, and she would have been a cripple for life, maimed, ugly and deformed.

I am somewhat ashamed now to think that my reaction was an increase of the burning resentment that I felt against the Germans, an increased desire to kill and kill and kill, preferably with a bayonet, the men who had blinded my brother and killed poor beautiful Athene who had been so kind. It was an utterly irrational hatred, for these Germans were but soldiers like myself, doing their noble duty of slaying their fellow-men, just as I myself was. On the other hand, the German Army was the German people in arms, and the people wanted the war, acclaimed it from the house-tops, cheered it spontaneously, marched to it singing songs of joy and gladness with flowers on their rifles. But, of course, they had been misled by a governed Press and lies about Germany's encirclement and her danger from the dark machinations of evil Belgium, wicked France and menacing Serbia.

At times I am still ashamed: at others I am not, when I think that those same Germans would again to-day consent to death while conquering agony—the death of millions and the agony of millions, including their own—should a house-painter's patience be exhausted! God give me patience when I think of it.

So Athene, about her Red Cross work, was

butchered.

I was glad I was a Battalion marksman and a sniper.

§3

With unexpected rapidity I was growing a shell and living inside it, as does a tortoise or a snail. Perhaps I was also becoming mentally as slow as these recluse individualists. This condition of calloused sensibilities may have stood me in good stead when, after being cut off from our postal delivery for some days, I received two letters, one from Rosanne and one from Luke, announcing that they were about to marry.

I had expected it, of course, but the impact of the blow was not greatly lessened by this. The fact that one expects to be shot does not lessen the shock when the bullet strikes. It was, of course, by far the best thing that could happen to Luke. He would not only have someone to look after him for the rest of his life, but that someone would be the person whom, above all others, he would desire to have as his constant companion. She would be not only his wife, his lover, and his nurse, but his medicine, his cure, the perfect cure for everything but his blindness. Dr. Abernethy had seen it, had hinted at its being the best thing that could possibly happen. What was it he had said? I should remember, for it had so hurt me at the time:

"Miss Van Daten knows what to do—I think."

Of course it was the obvious and perfect solution of Luke's ghastly problem, and would be his salvation and cure of all but—the incurable. I could almost hear poor Luke's infinitely sad and bitter voice murmuring,

"That's all. Only blindness. Cured of all but that trifle." But no, I wronged him, and should be ashamed of myself. His heart would leap for joy, and he would be so happy that he'd feel precisely as I should have done myself in such circumstances. Better blind with Rosanne than have perfect sight without her. What else was worth looking at?

But I prayed that it would be impossible for me to

attend the wedding. Almost certainly it would be impossible, for they would be married soon. What reason was there for waiting? The only thing that could set me free to attend the wedding, in the present condition of affairs at the Front, would be a Blighty wound or the outbreak of Peace. Even so, I did not feel that I could go through with it. Let anyone who cannot understand this, wait till he loves a woman absolutely and for always, with a love so consuming that life without her is something devoid of interest, a matter that is neither here nor there nor anywhere else, and can be spent in a coal-mine, on a desert island, as a soldier, a sailor, a beauty-chorus boy or an all-in wrestler, in wealth, or poverty, or anyhow else. Let him, I say, love a woman like that, and then propose to attend her wedding to his twin-brother, or rather the shattered wreck of that other-self.

Luke's letter wrung my heart. That is a trite and silly *cliché* and perfectly accurate. The pain I had was that of an iron hand grasping, twisting, and crushing my heart; for he had typed the letter himself, with many mistakes. I could repeat it to-day, every word of it from beginning to end, but prefer not to do so. It was a fine brave letter, resigned and stoical, while gallant and humorous—and dreadful.

Nevertheless, it was obvious that, so far as happiness could come to such a man in such a state, he was happy at the thought that Rosanne so loved him that she could marry him in spite of his hideous handicap; in spite of his being, as he described himself, "a sheer hulk; a blind mouth; a tuppenny Samson in Gaza who had been a man in Israel."

I was glad that he realized that Rosanne must love him greatly and truly to be able to assume the part of what he referred to as "a blind man's dog."

There was one thing—terrible beyond imagination as it must be for an artist who lived mainly through his eyes, to be for ever sightless, to be for ever in need of a blind man's dog—there would never be the necessity for the dog to carry a tin money-box for alms. Rosanne would be very rich now, and one thing that Luke would not suffer, who suffered all things else, was poverty.

As things had been up to the time of Athene's death, Luke, like myself, had very little money, and that only pocket-money. Courtesy Court was not self-supporting, and, until my father married Athene, money had been definitely tight. But for his marriage, we should only with difficulty have gone to Oxford, and should have had to earn our livings professionally, in the open market.

Luke would doubtless have done splendidly as an artist, painting being his great gift. But now that he was blind, he would have had nothing on which to live, save what I could have given him. Now, thank God, he would be a wealthy man, would have every comfort, including the greatest of all luxuries, freedom from financial anxiety; and in his blindness he need have no idiotic scruples about being the penniless husband of a rich woman. It was all splendid; perfect, from Luke's point of view.

And Rosanne's? Rosanne tied to a man who could take but little part in so full a life as such a woman as she would naturally lead; who could join with her in none of her sports and pastimes, in none of her work and occupations? Would she be happy?

Of course she would; simply because she loved him; loved his happiness. And as for occupation, what better would she desire than that of looking after Luke? That would constitute her happiness and be her whole-time job. Rosanne loved him, and being Rosanne, would love him the more for his blindness; would never, never let his dreadful handicap be a recognized drag, an admitted and resented brake on the wheels of her life.

Yes, it was for the best from the point of view of both of them, the best possible thing that could happen; and, unless I were a base mean-hearted swine —I must rejoice.

I did not rejoice.

But I can truthfully say in self-defence that I would not have lifted a finger to have prevented it or to have beckoned Rosanne to my side, if I had had the power to do it.

A small mercy, in what was to me a somewhat unmerciful situation, was the fact that Luke and Rosanne were married at a time when all leave was cancelled, when men were scraped together from every quarter and, while none left France, all who could be spared, were being poured into the country.

So Luke and Rosanne were married.

XII

When I was demobilized, there was nothing for it but to pay a visit to Courtesy Court. I longed to go there, almost as much as I feared to do so. I wanted to see my brother, even more than I dreaded the meeting with him. I knew that I must see Rosanne and that I must *not* see Rosanne.

But I owned Courtesy Court; and all that I loved was there. To keep away when there was no ostensible reason for doing so, was to hurt both Luke and Rosanne cruelly. I could offer no excuse for not going home.

I went.

§2

Luke was marvellously improved, and my heart rejoiced. So wonderful had been the effect of his marriage that he was a changed man; almost light-hearted; so brave; so resigned—without any air of resignation.

And so amazingly clever with his blindness. His finger-tips were as ten minor eyes, so much could he see by the sense of touch. At times, it almost seemed that he could read plain surfaces, surfaces on which there was no embossment. To read the surface of a coin, of the back of a book, the raised print on good visiting-cards and note-paper, these things were possible; but at times it almost seemed that he could read such things as letters on which the writing was thick and heavy, the pattern of a crest, the denomination of a stamp, things like that.

It really was amazing.

Certainly he could do marvels in the matter of appreciating form and shape, and could identify faces by means of touch. Of course, he knew people by their voices, but if a stranger were introduced, if a new maid came, Luke would always say that he would like to know what they looked like, and if they wouldn't mind his just touching their face with his finger-tips he would know.

I thought it was perhaps a form of self-protection, or reassurance.

Anyhow, he was continually surprising us with his cleverness. Though, after all, there was no reason for any uncomplimentary degree of surprise that anyone so accomplished, artistic, and sensitive as Luke should have made such an astonishing conquest of blindness.

Another small mercy was the fact that he was obviously endowed with an unusual sense of direction, and could find his way about, whether indoors or out, in a remarkable manner. Give him his stout, white-painted, steel-shod stick, and he did not seem to be blind at all. Tapping his way along with it, using it to give him warning of obstacles, while his acutely attuned ear gave notice of the approach of people or vehicles, it seemed to serve him as yet another eye. My weight of sadness was slightly lightened; my crushing misery somewhat assuaged by the fact that my brother was coping so nobly and successfully with his cruel affliction.

To Rosanne, much of the glory and the praise; Rosanne whose love had saved him.

Hope for his future? None.

At least he had none. And who should know better than he? So far, there was not the faintest lightening of his darkness. To stare at the window on a brilliant summer day was to receive as much sense of light as he had when he sat with his black silk bandage bound tightly about his eyes.

Nor had Rosanne been able to persuade him to visit an oculist or to allow her to bring Sir Theophilus Grant to the house.

He had had enough of it, he said; had accepted the verdict of the world-famous Renier once and for all. And Rosanne had accepted Luke's own verdict, feeling, as she told me, that it was cruel to talk of hope where there was none; to buoy him up with a false and treacherous support that, slowly becoming water-logged, would but tend to sink him more deeply in the ocean of despair.

Faithfully he had promised to tell her if, and when, he received the very faintest hint of a sensation of light; and he would then instantly go to any or every distin-guished oculist in London. Meantime, she must leave him alone and not tantalize him with the hope deferred that maketh the sick heart yet more sick.

Brave Rosanne and braver Luke. They were facing life wonderfully.

But it was more than I could do. Some day, per-haps, but not now. And not at Courtesy Court. For a while I must rest, and then I must go. Whither and to do what, God alone knew.

XIII

Yes, I must go. I must leave this nightmare of delirious happiness and torture. I must have the strength and courage to leave Rosanne's presence, the weakness and cowardice to turn my back on Luke, the sight of whose brave agony I could not much longer bear. How and when and whither were my constant questions and preoccupation, my insoluble problems. How could I go without hurting and offending Rosanne who was so thankful that I had come; who told me I was a tower of strength to her; who declared that she did not know how she had carried on without my help; who was so happy in my company, and who constantly assured me that Luke also was the happier for my being at Courtesy Court.

It was obvious that, like most women, Rosanne hated ultimate responsibility; the feeling that she had no support, and must be self-sufficient. To manage Courtesy Court would have been her delight under normal conditions, with a husband to give her authority, strength and power; a man to whom she could refer every problem, doubt, and difficulty with which she could not cope alone.

As it was, she had as much responsibility as though she were unmarried, and the owner of Courtesy Court; for she was still in sole charge of it, of course, as she had been in my absence.

What she would have liked and considered the ideal solution was that I should remain at Courtesy Court, its owner and master; that she should be its chatelaine and mistress; and that the welfare of Luke, her husband and my brother, should be our joint care. Part of her day she would always devote to him; part of mine I would always spend in his company. With me to be the man-friend and companion; she the woman-friend and nurse; and with Yrotavál to valet him, his life should be as happy as that of a blind man can be.

But it was a dream that I must shatter.

And when she spoke of Yrotavál, I could see that some small part of her joy at my coming concerned him. She made no actual accusation or complaint, but she did, when describing her ideal programme for our joint lives, say,

"And you'll be here to deal with Yrotavál. Oh, how I wish Luke would bring himself to get rid of that man. But he won't hear of it, and I hate to press the point because he is so dependent on him. Time after time I have told him he can get somebody just as efficient, and a great deal more acceptable in the house; but he only says that Yrotavál is efficient enough and to him entirely acceptable. . . . And after all, that is the main point. It would be horribly selfish, as well as a great mistake, to dismiss the man while Luke feels like that about him. Besides, I can't very well dismiss him, since Luke engaged him, and he is Luke's servant. . . . Yrotavál is in a strong position and he knows it."

"What have you against him?"

"Nothing . . . much."

"Well, what does he do that annoys you?"

"Makes my flesh creep."

"How? Why?"

"The way he looks at me. He insults me with his eyes. His false politeness. He obsequiously promises to do exactly as I order and never does it or intends to do it. . . . His beastly personality. Without one word that I can object to, he points out to me that what Luke says *goes,* in this house; and I somehow get it quite clearly that what Luke says is what Yrotavál wants him to say. . . . And Mark, do you know what he has done to me?"

"*Done* to you?" I sprang up.

"Yes. Done to me. What no man or woman has ever done before. He has made me a coward. I am afraid of him. I fear him as much as I hate him. And oh, how I hate him. I *hate* him!"

"Rosanne, I'll fling him out, neck and crop. I'll break his damned . . ."

"Break nothing," interrupted Rosanne. "Fling

nothing. So far, and at present, it seems that he is absolutely essential to Luke. The poor boy gets into quite a state if I so much as suggest that Yrotavál . . ."

"I'll speak to him. I'll speak to both of them."

"Don't upset Luke. He's extraordinarily—well—touchy about it. Do you know—when I wasn't feeling too good, and Yrotavál had so got on my nerves that I thought I couldn't bear him in the house another day, I went and told Luke so. I don't often fly off the handle, as you know, Mark, but I did then. I felt murderous about the skunk. I said more than I meant, of course, and used the idiotic words,

" *'Either Yrotavál leaves this house or else I do.'* And what do you think he said?

" *'If Yrotavál goes, I go with him.'* "

I was shocked; shaken; and a dumb, cold anger arose and grew in me. . . . Yrotavál! By God, I'd . . . I'd . . . what—since Luke was so dependent on him?

"What did you say to that?" I asked.

"I said the best possible thing. Nothing," replied Rosanne. "I can't be too thankful that I had the sense to go out of the room. As I think you know, Mark, I don't often get really mad, and I'm not angry for long. When I cooled down, I was more thankful than I can say, that I hadn't let it come to a quarrel. Fancy me quarrelling with Luke! Fancy a conscientious nurse quarrelling with a patient, a sick man; for Luke is still mentally sick, marvellously as he bears, and copes with, his blindness. Fancy a reasonably decent self-respecting woman quarrelling with a blind man—and him her husband! Oh, Mark, I'm so ashamed and . . ."

I could see that Rosanne was near to tears; Rosanne who never cried.

('And' *what?* What was that last word which she had not uttered? Surely it was not *'unhappy'*. *'I am so ashamed and——'* What? Not *'unhappy,'* surely?)

My dear good Señor Don Caballero Yrotavál y Rewes, I'll have a reckoning with you yet. You may be in a strong position. But wait till you are out of it.

It was an impasse, but to Luke I would talk in one way and to Yrotavál in another. I'd tell Luke that while there was no question or suggestion of Yrotavál leaving him, he must see that Yrotavál behaved himself; that it was Yrotavál's plain duty, as well as to his interest, to make himself as indispensable, as much *persona grata,* to his mistress as to his master.

And to El Señor Don Caballero Yrotavál y Rewes I would speak a language he understood, a language at which my training in the French Foreign Legion and His Majesty's Foot-Guards had rendered me reasonably adept.

But I must not make the mistake of promising what I could not perform, uttering threats which he would know that I was unable to implement.

And what could I do to the fellow, so long as Luke declared him indispensable? Perhaps the other tack would be better. Swallow my wrath and use promises rather than threats, promises that would be easy enough of fulfilment, such as a raised salary, a bonus, so to speak, so long as Rosanne had no complaint to make of him.

And then again, what were the complaints? Of what was I to accuse him to Luke?

"What shall I tell Luke that Yrotavál does to annoy you?" I asked Rosanne.

"My dear Mark, he does nothing to annoy me. A cat may look at a king; and a dog may look at a woman. . . . A wolfish evil dog . . . cur . . . hound. . . . Oh, how I *loathe* him."

"Look here, has he ever said one word that . . ."

"Not one word. But every word he says makes my blood boil."

"Can you tell me anything of which I can accuse him to Luke? Anything he does or ever has done? Something I can lay hold of. . . ."

"Nothing. He has never done a thing. It is only that everything he does makes me . . . Oh, Mark, can't you understand, it is not what he says or does, it is his . . ."

"Manners?"

"No, manner. Atmosphere. I hate the word 'aura,' but that's it. It's the man himself. He's a reptile, poisonous, dangerous . . . *evil*. I can't *bear* him to be near me."

"Yes. Yes. I do understand, Rosanne. I understand perfectly, for he affects me rather in the same way. Always has done. But, of course, I can deal with him in a way a woman can't. I understand, my dear. But what I wanted was something that Luke would understand. Something concrete in the way of an accusation. Since he simply cannot bear the thought of parting with him, it is not much good my going to Luke and saying,

" 'Look here, I'm going to kick Yrotavál out,' and when he says,

" 'Why?' to reply,

" 'Oh, you know, *"I do not like thee, Doctor Fell, the reason why I cannot tell, but have the goodness to get to hell"—out of this.'* It would seem so unreasonable . . . Unkind to Luke."

"Exactly. Didn't I say he was in a strong position; impregnable? It must sound a lot of fuss about nothing."

"But it isn't 'nothing'."

"No, Mark, it isn't. And don't get the idea that I am jealous of the creature! You wouldn't, of course; but some people might think I was jealous of his influence over Luke and, still more, of his indispensability. I don't think it is unreasonable of me to feel a little hurt that Luke should say that if Yrotavál went, he'd go too."

"He didn't mean that, Rosanne. Of course he didn't. You know he didn't. It was only a figure of speech. Just a way of saying how frightfully he'd miss him. One is always using exaggerations of that sort. If I told Yrotavál I was going to wring his neck, or break every bone in his body, I shouldn't actually mean that I was going to kill him, I suppose."

"Luke was serious when he said it."

"And I shall be serious when I say what I am going to say to Yrotavál. Very serious; but I shall probably use a few *façons de parler*. Luke meant that, just as much as he'd have meant it if he said,

" 'Rosanna, I'm about to bite your ear and then give you a good beating.' "

"Comforting Mark! Nice Mark!" smiled Rosanne and took my hand.

I promptly withdrew it, being merely human.

"Look here," I said, as I did so, "you've been doing too much nursing and too much worrying. You've been through a dreadful time, and your nerves are all to pieces. I know how that feels, and what it can do to one. Now listen. I'm going to put Yrotavál where he belongs; tell him where he gets off; and without upsetting Luke. I'll send for him, and, speaking as the owner and master of Courtesy Court, I'll tell him that if he wants to live long and die happy, he had better watch his step."

"Live long *here?* And die happy *here?*" mused Rosanne.

"Live here at all. If he wants to stay here, he's got to please you as well as Luke."

"Yes; and he'll grin behind his face and assure you that to please me is the one thing he lives for," said Rosanne bitterly.

"And I'll tell him he had *better* live for it, if he wants to live here. . . . Have you told him that you dislike him?"

"No, no need. He knows all right and he knows that it doesn't matter. Mark, I don't know what to do."

"I do, though."

"And there's another thing that troubles me about Luke," she went on. "I can't get *at* him, Mark. I have a horrible feeling that there is something between us. I don't mean a row, a quarrel. It's an obstacle, a wall. . . . He still locks himself in that room."

"Sleeps there?"

"Yes—whenever he feels like it. And as you know, he goes there most afternoons and almost every night, between dinner and bedtime for an hour or two, and shuts himself up. It's bad for him and it's dangerous."

"I'll have a talk with him."

"Darling Mark, you are such a . . ." and she slipped

123

her arm through mine.

"Nothing of the sort. . . . I want my pipe," said I, and got up from the settee.

I must walk and think.

And I must go.

But before I went, I must deal faithfully with friend Yrotavál.

I ground my teeth and clenched my fists as I thought of what Rosanne had said. *El Señor Don Caballero Yrotavál y Rewes.* . . . God! I could have stamped upon his face.

§2

After dinner that night, we sat over our coffee and cigarettes in the hall until a visitor, our neighbour Giulia Brent-Grayleigh, went home.

Luke then retired, leaving me with Rosanne. For as long as I dared, I stayed with her, but soon made the excuse that I thought I would like a turn on the terrace before going up to bed.

I tried to bring myself to tell her that I must go; that I was leaving Courtesy Court again; and that I must go soon.

Once again I had procrastinated.

Standing in the door-way, I filled my pipe, lit it and strolled out into the moonlit night.

I am not a great thinker, as may be apparent, but such thinking as I do is best done while I am walking. If I walk long enough, I generally arrive at some sort of solution of whatever is troubling my mind, come to some conclusion, and settle the matter once and for all.

Whether it be habit formed by innumerable periods of sentry-go as *légionnaire* and as Guardsman, I subconsciously walk up and down when I am exercised in mind and pondering a problem. I walk up and down, to and fro, rather than go for a stroll.

Fate, Chance, or God, willed that on this occasion I should pace the terrace like a sentry on duty, save for the fact that I walked with head bent and mind abstracted. I paced the length of the side of the house sunk in a brown study, oblivious of my surroundings. How long I walked I don't know, but my absent mind was suddenly recalled to awareness, and from heavy brooding on the problem of Yrotavál, to the actual sound of his voice, raised and angry, and that of Luke answering sharply; to the noise—it was nothing less—of an altercation.

I halted in amazement. That Luke should raise his voice to Yrotavál and tick him off was very well, very right and proper and no novelty, but that Yrotavál should not only answer him back but actually shout him down, was entirely the opposite, and something very new indeed.

So far as I knew, this was the first time, and, by God, it should be the last.

They were actually *quarrelling!*

I looked up at the lighted uncurtained window, more than twenty feet above my head, the window distinguishable as Luke's by the little platform beside the window-sill from which descended the iron staircase that Rosanne's love, anxiety, and forethought had had permanently fixed.

I would go up. The insolent hound! The snarling dog! How dare he raise his voice to Luke! Perhaps this would give me an excuse to do what I would have given anything for the power to do, to thrash the brute and throw him out—with Luke's consent. If I could step in while Luke was angry, he might agree. He might sack him himself.

Before I was half-way up the ladder, the sound of the raised and angry voices stopped suddenly.

I paused. Too late now. Yrotavál must have gone out of the room and shut the door. Heaven grant that Luke had sent him out—and with orders not to return. Out of the room and out of the house. I hung in doubt for a minute and turned to go down again. Whatever I did I must not butt in, must not give Luke the sensation he loathed above all others, that of being spied upon.

Luke's voice had fallen very suddenly. Was he all

right?

Anyway, he'd never know if I crept up very quietly and just looked in. I need not actually go on to the platform, need make no sound that would reach Luke's ears.

I would take one glance to assure myself that all was well, and then go down again.

My head came above the level of the window-sill.

I saw that Luke was reclining in his deep arm-chair, his feet raised on to the pouf which was a detachable part of it. On the book-rest attached to the side of the chair was a book, and Luke, his eyes uncovered, was reading it.

Of course he was not reading it.

Poor Luke! He would never read again.

The pity of it, the agony of it.

He was sitting there *pretending* that he could read. Fingering a beloved book, as he sat in the black night of his blindness. Just touching and fondling the book that he could not read.

He turned a page of it; and, as I was about to look away before my own eyes were briefly blinded, a fly settled on the page. . . .

And Luke did what I had seen him do a thousand times before, in the trenches, in the school-room, in the nursery. Slowly, gently, he raised his hand, his fingers curling. Suddenly and swiftly his hand swooped across the page of the book, closing as it did so.

Carefully opening his clenched fist, Luke took the captured fly between the finger and thumb of his other hand, looked at it, and dropped it into the ash-tray.

He then turned to his book and read on.

And as I clutched the railing of the ladder for support, he turned the leaves back, read something on a previous page, and again resumed his reading.

Almost before I realized and accepted the horrible truth, he turned the page that he was reading.

I was trembling. I felt too ill, too weak, to move.

He was reading.

He could see.

No! Fool, fool that I was! *Devil*, to insult my brother

with so base and foul a suspicion! . . . He was *pretending* to read. . . . *Playing* at reading.

And the fly?

He had heard it buzz. It was purest chance. In his blindness he must have tried a thousand times to catch a maddening fly that came near him, and once in a thousand times succeeded.

He was blind. . . .

He was blind. . . .

And better *that* than be the vile, lying, swindling, impostor that my filthy mind had dared to think him. I was unfit to live. . . .

And as I turned to go, Luke reached out, took a pencil from the table beside his chair, underlined something, and wrote a note in the margin of the page.

It was in that minute that my hair began to turn grey.

XIV

God knows I am no saint and the Devil knows I have no desire to be one.

For a while I was stunned.

When I had sufficiently recovered from the blow to be able to realize the incredible truth, my first sensation was one of fierce and bitter anger, my first impulse to blow Luke's edifice of lies and deceit sky-high. It was spontaneous and quite natural, I think, and free from any *arrière pensée* of benefit to myself. It was a swift repulsion, an utter revulsion of feeling—and feeling, of course, came before reason, emotion before thought; and, under the influence of emotion, I almost went straight to Rosanne.

I cannot be too thankful that I did not act in the violence of my great anger and disgust; and I owe a debt of gratitude to that discipline that had so irked me. I realize that I had cause to be thankful to those who so recently and for so long had trained me, mechanized me, so that I did not immediately act upon impulse.

Instead, trembling slightly, feeling weak and shaky in the legs, I made my way to my room, locked my door, sat down in my arm-chair, lit my pipe, and tried to think calmly, clearly, and logically; tried to give Reason a fair field, unhindered and unobstructed by Emotion.

It was not easy at first. Wrath, indignation, contempt; a sense of most cruel hurt, disillusion, and sick disappointment, all had to be overcome and eliminated. It was a desperate struggle, but the battle was half won by the time I had reached my room, seated myself, and lighted my pipe. By then, I had got myself under control; and I knew that if I could keep myself in that chair until I had finished my pipe, whatever I then did would be done in cold blood and not in hot anger, done in the steady light of reason and not in the fierce flickering glow of rage.

And by the time I knocked out the ashes of that memorable pipe, symbolic of the ashes of my world, I was sufficiently calm to make a decision and honestly to judge my own motives for the course of action upon which I decided in that terrible hour, by far the most important, as it was the most poignant and painful, of all my life.

And I think that, had I taken a day or a week in which to think over the situation, I should have come ultimately to the same conclusion and decision.

First of all, the feeling of anger that followed the incredulous bewilderment, the refusal to accept the evidence of my own sight.

On what was that anger based? Was it a noble, indignant wrath, the righteous man's pure and unadulterated hatred of any deceit, swindling, trickery and baseness?

Not it.

There was a strong element of selfishness present. I personally had been injured, and much of my anger was plain, personal resentment.

And was I angry on Rosanne's behalf? Not wholly, solely and genuinely. For it could be argued that he had done her no wrong, inasmuch as it gave her great pleasure to look after him, to protect him, and to stand between him and the asperities of a life of blindness. Besides loving Luke, Rosanne loved giving, loved helping; and he had provided her with a permanent object for the exercise of her infinite capacity for giving and helping.

Secondly, what of the feelings of fierce contempt and sick disgust?

They too were mainly selfish. By doing this perfectly incredible thing, Luke had hurt me. He had shocked me. He had disillusioned me. He had destroyed my faith in him. He had all but killed my affection for him. He had struck me the heaviest blow that I had ever received.

Yes, there it was. "*I*" and "*me,*" the whole time.

And suppose that, in my pain and anger, I had denounced and exposed him. What should I have done to Rosanne who loved him so? With my own hand I should have struck her exactly such a blow as I myself had just received. I should have inflicted upon her the kind of miserable agony which I was now enduring, similar in kind but perhaps even worse in measure— which God forbid. For it was possible that she loved him even more than I did, and it was quite certain that she was less fitted than I to withstand such a shock, to bear such an intensity of suffering. It would have been an abominably cruel thing to do, even had I acted from the purest sense of duty. And I hate those people who always find it their duty to tell the truth at any cost; at any cost to anybody. I loathe the type of man and woman who will never allow their friends' ignorance to be bliss; who would never, for example, allow a mother's blissful ignorance of a son's misdeed to remain undisturbed; would always find it their duty to open the eyes of a husband to the truth and fact of some error of his wife's, or *vice versa*.

I had recently, and for long, been in contact with the type of man whose chief joy in life is the catching of his fellow-man in some alleged fault of omission or commission; who goes about looking for trouble—for other people; who thoroughly enjoys the noble sport of catching-out. Personally I hate catching people out. I would far sooner be caught myself. Wrong-doing has to be punished, we know, but I should never, in any cir- cumstances, find any pleasure in the rôle of the discoverer of wrong-doing. . . . No, to expose my brother to his wife would be an utterly beastly thing to do, and mine a loathsome part to play.

By the time my pipe was cold, the fires of my anger were cold, and it was perfectly clear to me that, rather than expose Luke's deceit, I should do everything I could to hide it, because the blow to a woman like Rosanne, so honest and straightforward, so trusting and unsuspecting, might have a terrible personal effect, quite apart from its result upon her married happiness, to which it would, of course, be simply fatal.

If I knew my Rosanne—and who knew her if I did not—she would be so angry, so resentful of the cruel joke that Luke had played on her, so enraged at his abominable trick, that she would never forgive him. Rosanne did not suffer fools gladly, and still less gladly would she suffer one who fooled her. Among Rosanne's virtues, meekness was not the most prominent. She was extremely good-tempered and even-tempered, but a temper she had, and when it was justly aroused, it was a warm and a strong one. Like many people who are splendid friends, she could be a redoubtable enemy; and few things would arouse her enmity like trickery, deceit, humbug, and false pretence.

She would never forgive him. Never. She would, at first, feel positively murderous toward him; and it would be the end of their married life. In other words, the end of her happiness. Her marriage would be wrecked, her life spoilt. For how could she go on living with him when once she knew the truth?

It was the sort of thing which would affect Rosanne's mind and nature; which would, in turn, affect her body and make her ill—if only by killing her trust in all mankind, her faith in human nature. ("Only"!)

That lovely, simple mind, so forthright, honest, trusting, so apt for hero-worship, would henceforth be warped and twisted. There would be a danger of her becoming as cynical as I now felt myself to be.

Imagine Rosanne, of all people in this world, becoming suspicious, sceptical, distrustful of Life, through a mean and selfish act of mine!

And again Luke himself. What would be the effect upon him—sensitive, self-centred perhaps, intolerant of accusation and criticism? I did not see how he could possibly go on living after the exposure; how he could permit himself to survive it.

The blow which I had received on discovering his imposture would be lighter than the one which he would receive on learning of the discovery. Its result would be terrible, and would do him the utmost possible harm. It would be a mortal wound, not only to his pride and self-esteem but to his very self. It would kill him. And if it did not, he would commit suicide. A nice thing for me, his brother, to drive him to his death. I should feel that I had murdered him. I should indeed have murdered him.

And from an angry and resentful

"Serve him right. He needs punishment. The more severe it is, the more good it will do him," I came gradually to an entirely opposite conclusion. Not only because I saw the expediency of refraining from denouncing him, but because, as I grew calmer, affection came back to the hurt mind from which it had been driven. Surely if anybody could understand, it was I, I who knew him better than anybody else; and, moreover, I, who had been through that same hell of suffering that had tortured him into doing this. This shameful trickery and imposture was, after all, only his way of escape from a world and a situation that had become too much for him. It was symbolic. It was like protective colouring. Quite probably it had been begun on the spur of the moment, on impulse, with no other thought or intention than to escape immediately from what was killing him, escape from what he could no longer bear.

And another idea occurred to me. Inasmuch as he had done it after being blown up and buried alive, driven almost to lunacy and to death, it was a direct result, a definite symptom, of the appalling mental illness known as shell-shock—and sometimes derided by those who have never seen or heard a shell.

He would never have done it but for that shattering concussion. He had begun it while suffering from shock; and, realizing that he could not possibly return to those or any other trenches and retain his sanity, he had kept up the deception.

If I exposed him, he would feel that he must flee—and never come back.

Hour after hour I sat and thought, thrashed the matter out in all its dreadful details.

Having sat so long and got so far upon the road to unbiased reason, I would go further yet; sit all night; completely calm down; see the matter with the clear eyes of quiet disinterested reflection, crush every angry impulse, feeling of resentment and bitterness; thrust away from me the thought that he had won Rosanne under false pretences; had made, with his sham blindness, an appeal which she could not refuse. I would try to understand that, if I had suffered, he would suffer far more than I had, if I exposed him; admit that my loss of my hope of Rosanne would be as nothing to compare with his loss of Rosanne herself. For lose her he would, if she knew what he had done.

Exposure would be more terrible, more injurious, for him, even than for her. Where she would receive a blow to her trust and love, a blow from which she would never wholly recover, he would be exposed to so shrivelling a blast of bitter contempt that life would be impossible. Yes, exposure would do literally that, leave the proud man utterly naked to so icy a wind of loathing and condemnation as would be too deadly to be borne.

So, round and round, went my slow mind.

And if he had taken a false step, made a terrible mistake, and done a great wrong, he had not deserved a punishment as heavy as that which discovery would bring upon him—so thin-skinned, so sensitive, so easy to hurt. Ever impatient, resentful and rebellious beneath the rod of criticism and the whip of rebuke, what would he be under the scorpion-scourge of his little world's utter disgust and contempt?

I could not bear to think of him thus facing Rosanne whom he loved, and whose love and admiration were so necessary to him.

Dawn lightened my open window through which I had stared unseeing—and dawn lightened the darkness of my mind. As the sun rose, I made my final conclusion.

If he had done a base thing, I should be doing a baser one if I denounced and exposed him.

Even apart from the ugly fact that I might profit from my act and deed, I could not do it and I must not do it.

But neither could I countenance and support the vile swindle. If I could not denounce Luke, I could not pretend that I did not know. I simply could not play the ghastly hypocritical rôle of the kind sympathizer and helper whose great desire was to strive in every way to ameliorate his dreadful lot. I had neither the skill nor the grace to play such a part, and I would not do it if I could.

For after I had said all that I could in his favour, the fact did remain that it was a vile imposture, and I could not possibly countenance and support it.

I must go. Go without seeing him. For I could not trust myself to speak to him as though I had not found him out. In point of fact, I felt that I could never speak to him again, never see him again.

And that would mean that I must never see Rosanne again either.

§2

But there was one person whom I must see again, and see quickly.

Yrotavál.

Yrotavál must be Luke's accomplice. That completely accounted for his manner, his otherwise inexplicable air of importance, self-confidence and knowledge of his own power and the strength of his position. Yrotavál the indispensable and unassailable.

Of course, without his help, Luke could never have carried on the deception in France and got to England. Without Yrotavál's help, Luke could never have carried on as a totally blind man. Without his constant, ever-watchful care, guidance and connivance Luke could not have kept others at arm's length, as he had done, and managed without a professional nurse, companion and valet. Undoubtedly Yrotavál must know that Luke was not blind. So cunning a rascal, in perpetual contact with Luke, must have discovered his secret—if he had not known it from the first, which I did not doubt.

That entirely accounted for Yrotavál's conduct, attitude and bearing. He had Luke exactly where he wanted him. He was on velvet for life. Of course, he was the unshakeable power behind the throne, and his power was his knowledge. Poor Luke was absolutely in his grasp, and nothing but the death of one of them could end the appalling situation. Yrotavál could blackmail Luke as long as he lived; and if Luke died first, he could blackmail his relatives with the threat of posthumous exposure.

My poor brother was absolutely at the mercy of the only man whom I hated; the man whom I trusted least in all the world.

I heard sounds of life about the house. I must make up my mind what to do, and then act quickly.

Was it possible that I was wrong about Yrotavál, and that Luke had deceived him as completely as he had deceived me, Rosanne, and everyone else?

The more I thought of it, the less likely it seemed. I had an intuition, an instinctive feeling, that Yrotavál knew.

Why otherwise was he there? Why should Luke have brought him to Courtesy Court? Why should he keep him here, in spite of all Rosanne had said? Of course Yrotavál knew.

Of course Luke feared to dismiss him—or the man would have been out of the house within an hour of Rosanne's complaining of him and saying that she strongly objected to him and his presence about the place.

An idea occurred to me.

Did Luke intend his blindness to be only "for the duration"?

Now that the War was over and there was no

question of his having to fight, would he pretend gradually to recover his sight? That might, of course, be his idea—but what was he going to do with Yrotavál then? He couldn't turn round to him and say,

"I've recovered my sight. Get out," and expect Yrotavál to go. Or at any rate to go without a huge bribe—and leaving behind him the perpetual fear and danger of blackmail.

I could imagine no more competent blackmailer than Yrotavál, none better qualified, none less hampered by scruples of decency or mercy.

Of course Yrotaval knew. Of course he was Luke's accomplice, and I must act accordingly.

If I were wrong, and he was absolutely ignorant of the fact that Luke was blind, no harm would be done by my removing him from the house, inasmuch as Luke—who was *not* blind—had not the slightest real need of him, and Rosanne most strongly objected to his presence there.

If I were right, as I knew I was, then it was essential that Yrotavál should go, and it was my business to see that he went, or rather, that he came. Since I must go, Yrotavál must come with me; and come with me to some place whence he could not return and make himself a menace and a danger at Courtesy Court.

Suddenly I rose to my feet, as it dawned on my somewhat slow mind that it was useless for me to shield Luke and keep his secret from Rosanne, if Yrotavál were free to expose him!

Inevitably such a man as Yrotavál would blackmail Luke. His demands would equally inevitably increase; and should they at length reach the point at which Luke either could not or would not meet them, Yrotavál would first torture and then destroy him, would put him through the mental agony of the blackmailed, and, when finally rejected, denied and defied, would have his vengeance. I had lived too close to this sewer-rat of the slums of Barcelona, this deadly and dangerous product of its underworld, to have any illusions as to his real character and nature. He would exhibit all the gratitude, friendship, forbearance and mercy of a hungry wolf, a wounded snake, an injured scorpion. I should soon know, as certainly as if it had been proven, that he was Luke's accomplice his partner— and therefore his master.

Besides, even if I could satisfy myself beyond shadow of doubt that Yrotavál was for once innocent and had no part in this particular piece of villainy, the fact remained that Rosanne wanted him to go; and, since he was not necessary to Luke's welfare, go he should.

Round and round went my slow mind until I came to this conclusion.

That was that, then. I must go at once and Yrotavál must go with me.

And having come to that decision, I took off my evening kit, had a bath, and dressed for my journey.

§3

I suppose that, different as we are, I have in me the same strain of weakness that Luke displayed in his flight from reality. For I also fled, fled from him, from Rosanne, from the situation, from my home—and without a real farewell to Rosanne. I could not face Luke at all, to say good-bye to him, because I feared that I should show him that I knew. I was not equal to acting the part. The hypocrisy would have made me sick.

Breakfast was a movable feast, between eight and nine o'clock, and Luke was invariably the last, which of course was considered natural, right and proper, inasmuch as it takes a blind man so much longer to prepare for the day. As a rule, I avoided Rosanne, breakfasting at eight o'clock punctually.

As I sat down to breakfast that morning, I said to old Johnson, the butler,

"Tell Mr. Luke's valet I want to speak to him, will you?"

"Yes, Sir. Here, Sir? Now, Sir?"

"Here. Now, please," I replied, and a few minutes

later, Yrotavál crept quietly, cat-like, into the room.

"You sent for me . . . Sir?"

"Yes. I want you to go up to Town with me this morning. I shall be catching the ten-fifteen. The car will be at the door at nine-fifty sharp. I don't expect we shall be coming back to-night."

"But Mr. Luke . . ." began Yrotavál.

"You are going to Town with me by the ten-fifteen. Be ready at nine-forty," said I, fixing him with a very cold eye indeed. "Don't keep me waiting."

"Very good, Sir," replied Yrotavál, with a puzzled, questioning look in his shifty eye, and a slight further compression of his tight lips. "Not returning to-night, Sir?"

"Probably not," replied I briefly.

And as he bowed and turned away, I added to myself,

"Nor for ten thousand and one nights. Nor ever again, unless . . ."

When old Johnson re-entered the room with some letters, I gave orders for the car, and none for the packing of a suit-case. I was going to travel light. A pair of pyjamas, a clean collar, shaving-tackle and a tooth-brush would satisfy my brief and simple needs.

As I rose from a light and hurried breakfast, I again considered the question of Luke.

Ought not I to let him know that I had found him out? I could do it without any harsh accusation and reproach. . . .

I recoiled from the thought. Absolutely shrank from the idea. I could not face the scene. I could not hurt him so. I should be so ashamed *for* him.

It was sheer cowardice. I had not the strength of mind to do what I could not help feeling was, in some mysterious way, my duty.

It would hurt him so. It would be a mortal wound, not only to his self-esteem and self-regard, but to his self-respect.

I could not suddenly abandon my rôle of Luke's protector and guardian; the fender and buffer, when possible, between him and the world's roughness and the blows of Fate. It would be like brutally kicking a pet dog, like drowning a kitten; and though I can kill a man, I cannot drown a kitten.

No, I hadn't the courage, the nerve, the high sense of duty, thank God. What I could do, if later on I felt ashamed of myself for my cowardice, was to write to him. . . .

And then the idea again occurred to me, and I grasped it thankfully. Now that the War was over, it was more than likely that he would gradually "recover" his sight. That is what he would do; and he would never have the life-long miserable shame of knowing that I had discovered the truth.

And if he did not pretend to recover his sight? Suppose he preferred to remain in the lime-light of universal sympathy? Suppose he preferred his safe refuge from responsibility and the ordinary cares and duties of life; found he could not relinquish this protective colouring that he had assumed?

I could write to him.

I could give the matter long and careful thought, and let a sort of instinctive decision slowly crystallize in my mind, and then I could act upon it. And if the decision was that I must let him know, then I could still play the coward, spare myself the horrible pain of watching myself strike the blow, and write to him— stab him by post, so to speak. Equally then I could never meet him again.

How could we ever again be to each other what we had been up till last night—equal halves of one whole; twin brothers who had hardly been out of each other's sight, sound and thoughts, for the whole of their lives. Whatever happened, whatever course I chose, our brotherhood was finished.

But face him and denounce him now, I could not and would not.

Rosanne came into the room and my heart leapt— and sank.

"Finished? You are a greedy gobbler, Mark. Have another cup of coffee and talk to me while I eat."

"Can't. Going up to Town. Car will be here in a few minutes. Got to put a tooth-brush together. Staying away to-night."

"Hark at the man of affairs! All sudden and mysterious-like. Got a date?"

"Yes, Rosanne. A date."

"And you'll be coming back to-morrow?"

"Not before to-morrow certainly."

"I say—what about taking Luke with you? Don't you think it might do him good?"

"No. Sorry. Can't. Not this time."

No, not this time, nor any other. Never again would Luke and I set off together.

"Good mind to go with you myself, old son. . . . Ah! That made you jump, didn't it? I'm a bit suspicious of this 'date,' Mark."

I strove to grin feebly.

"Oh, by the way, can you spare Yrotavál to come with me?"

"Yes, I can spare Yrotavál—for a long while. For the rest of my life, in fact. Why?"

"I want to take him with me."

"Shopping for Luke? Take him, darling, and lose him. Take him, and don't bring him back. I'm perfectly certain that I could look after Luke and do anything for him that Yrotavál can do. Until he got another man. You know, Luke could really do without him altogether, only he won't realize it. He can shave himself now. He manages his food splendidly. He uses his typewriter every day. . . . Giulia does all his correspondence, with him. How I wish he'd let me be his valet. . . . Well, take care of yourself, Markie. When shall we see you again? Lunch to-morrow?"

"Don't know exactly. I'll ring you up or send you a wire."

"Well," said Rosanne, rising from her chair. "I must see Cook. Good-bye, Mark."

"Good-bye, Rosanne."

Yes. It was 'Good-bye, Rosanne.'
I nearly failed—her—and Luke—and myself.

XV

"A First Class for you, Sir, and a Third for me?"

No, Master Yrotavál, that's not quite the idea. I'm not going to let you out of my sight till I've got you where I want you, or at any rate, until I have made up my mind about you.

"Two Thirds," said I, "since there are no '40 *hommes ou* 8 *chevaux—en long,'* " and gave him a five-pound note.

Faintly puzzled, Yrotavál took the money with a non-committal grin, and got the tickets.

When the train came in, I made for an empty carriage, motioned Yrotavál in, and sat myself down opposite to him.

Slowly and subtly his manner changed as, unconsciously, our environment affected him. If not a case of *'Back to the Army again, Bo,'* it was definitely a step back to our former democratic level. Before the end of our first hour together he had dropped the 'Sir,' had shed some of his newly acquired refinements of speech, and begun to lapse back in the direction of his normal Cockney-East Side-Franco-Spanish dialect.

Producing cigarettes (Luke's, I noticed) he patted his pockets.

"Forgot me goddam *allumettes*. Gotta match?"

Getting on nicely together. Soon be quite matey. . . .

As we approached London.

"Where's we goin', *Patrón?*" he asked.

"For a binge," I replied. "At least, I am. Got to blow off steam."

"*M'Carben Diu!* You've said it. Gotta blow off steam? I gotta blow off steam too, or blow me block off."

"Oh, you'd like a binge, too, eh? I thought you would."

"You've said it, *Patrón*. I was gettin' near the end of me bit o' rope. If I don't soon wrap myself round a few pinard-and-absinthes, not to mention a *crevette—a* nice blonde one—I shall . . . I shall . . . cry. Go nuts. *J'aurai une chambre à louer.* Take a runnin' jump at a cop and bite him in the stomach. *Il faut faire des bosses. Carajo!* Bo, you sure gonna save my life. . . . Where we goin'?"

"Where would you like to go?"

"Where I can't. Never no more."

"Where is that?"

"Barcelona."

"No. Can't go there. But we can go to the next best place."

"What . . . ?"

"Yes, Paris. Know a 'better 'ole' than that?"

"Sure. One. Marseilles. Jimminy-jees! Luke and I had a helluva time there with old Sunnavabitch and the Spider."

"We'll go there. If we can get you through with Mr. Luke's passport, should you need to show one. I have got both his and mine in my pocket. And anyway, we're going by 'day-excursion' to Boulogne. No passports needed for that. And we'll book from Boulogne straight through to Marseilles."

"Marseilles? . . . Boss! . . ."

And sinking the petty differences of caste that had obtruded between us, Yrotavál seized my hand and wrung it.

"Jees!" he whispered. "I'll show you something, there, Bo."

"And if all goes well, I'll show you something, Yrotavál," I promised, a statement which brought an amused, half-pitying grin to the shark mouth and leathern face.

"You show *me!* Anyway, you've saved my life, Bo, you sure have," he continued. *"Nous allons 'diner en ville'!* Say! Dey knows me there in every *bistro* and every *burdel* down-town! We'll show de gals a time. *Nous en allons avaler le bon Dieu en culotte de velours!* Boy! What a helluva goddam riot it'll be! Will we whoop it up in the Vieux Port! *Attaboy!"*

§2

We did not whoop it up in the Vieux Port.

Proceeding without let, hindrance, or loss of time, we headed straight for our happiness. We lunched early in London, supped in Paris, slept in the train, breakfasted sketchily at a wayside station buffet, and lunched late in Marseilles.

I gave Yrotavál an excellent meal at the *Hôtel de Noailles,* and not only good, but assorted, wine and liqueurs. Thereafter, letting him not out of my sight, I took him on a Cannebière café-crawl, and marvelled at the amount of cognac that he consumed. We were preparing for the evening; getting ourselves into trim; into the right frame of mind and body. We would dine well, drink well, and then sally forth in good time for the opening of the haunts where we were really to see Life, really to enjoy ourselves at last. And *then,* Señor Yrotavál . . .

After fatiguing hours of Yrotavál's company and conversation, we returned to the hotel, ate well and drank better. We then retired to our sitting-room for further attention to whiskey, cognac, pinard and pernod—to kill time, if not ourselves.

It took a wonderful lot and a remarkable mixture to make Yrotavál drunk, but I think that when suddenly I sprang it on him, he might, by ordinary standards be so described.

He gave me a suitable opening.

"Las' time I was *hic*-here, it was Fort St. Jean for mine, not the *Hôtel de Noailles,"* he grinned. "Barracks —not a posh joint all plush and palm-pots.   . . . And it was good ol' Luke—not you."

"Yes. He could see then, couldn't he?"

"Sure. Good ol' . . ." and Yrotavál emptied his glass again.

"How long have you known that he's not blind?" I asked quietly, naturally, although my heart was thumping fast.

"All the time, you mug. . . . Eh? . . . God's Velvet

Trousers! What? *What* did you say? *You* know! *Votre frère a débiné le truc!*[19] How long have you . . ."

The shock sobered him to some extent.

"Oh, yes, I know all right. How long have *you* known?"

Yrotavál slumped back in his arm-chair, liquor-defeated.

He laughed stupidly.

"Longer than you have, *muchacho!"* he grinned.

"Not you!" I jeered.

"No? Did you know before you came home? Before he came home? Before he left the hospital? *Disparate."*

"You knew then? You knew from the first?" I asked.

"Me? Know? Bejezus! It was me first thought it up!" replied Yrotavál—and sealed his own fate.

I too leaned back in my chair; and I heaved a sigh of relief.

I do not know why relief should have been my first sensation. I suppose it was because I now knew where I was; knew that what I intended to do with Yrotavál was, in the first place, justified and, in the second place, necessary. It was, I suppose, the sense of relief that comes to one when suspense ends and the anticipated blow falls: suspense is over and one knows the worst.

Relief was followed by a cold and deadly anger. I could have killed the drunken ruffian then and there, but I had no desire to be publicly guillotined outside a French prison.

"So it was your idea, was it?" said I.

"Sure, Bo! And it woiked. The Luke kid plays blind, and me deaf and dumb! We has one pair of eyes and one pair of ears and one voice between the two of us— till we gets safe to England. I did de lookin' and de boy did de listenin' and talkin'. B' Jimminy Jees, some ramp! We sure put it acrost de Froggies!"

"All your very own idea, eh, Yrotavál?"

"You said it, Boss. . . . Me own little frame-up!"

---

[19] *Given the show away.*

I half-filled his tumbler with neat cognac, and, with the air of one doing the most natural thing in the world, then filled the tumbler up with neat whiskey.

"You're a clever man, Yrotavál."

"Sure, Boss. You said it. . . . Any time you want— *hic.* Thass good hard liquor."

"Splendid. Have some more."

And again I filled his tumbler with equal measures of brandy and whiskey. Quite a cocktail. Easy to do, but equally easy to over-do. I didn't want Yrotavál to pass out. Not yet.

"Well, what about a move?" said I, after his second tumbler of assorted spirits had joined the forerunners.

"Sure. We'll grab us a *fiacre* and start with a class joint that I know. Some dive! Down by the Docks. Best booze in Marseilles—smuggled stuff. Bouillabaisse. Bouillabitches too. Then to Marie's."

By his thickened speech, glassy eye and slight uncertainty of movement, I judged that the psychological moment had arrived; and, with my arm firmly through his, steered him down the stairs, across the *foyer* and out into the Cannebière.

"We'll walk," I said, as with a lurch and an airy, somewhat wild, flourish of his arm he attempted to hail an elegant private car driven by a frozen-faced chauffeur.

Purely from the standpoint of the fact that it assisted me in my purpose, Yrotavál's expansive wave of the arm was most fortunate, for his hand caught a passing stout citizen of Marseilles a remarkably smart smack on the ear.

With a snarl of wrath the man wheeled upon Yrotavál and returned the blow with hearty goodwill and even better aim.

Yrotavál kicked him, and the fight was on. I hoped that Yrotavál was too drunk to do himself justice and the citizen some cruel injustice, for, as well I knew, Yrotavál was an extremely dirty fighter.

So was I on that occasion, I hope the first and last in my life. For rushing into the fray, I smote both protagonists impartially, fell to the ground between them, flung my arms about the Frenchman's legs, brought him down on top of me and—poetic justice— received in my ribs a kick which Yrotavál aimed at him. Seizing his foot, I contrived to upset him also, no difficult matter in the condition in which he was. The three of us rolled, struggled, smote and swore, upon the ground. The swiftly gathering crowd surged about us, uttering loud cries of joy, alarm, protest, encouragement and "Police." I had been waiting for the last cry, for it was the Police that I wanted, and I now joined in with all the strength of my lungs.

It does not take long to summon gendarmes in the Cannebière of Marseilles. Within a couple of minutes of Yrotavál's unintentional blow upon the citizen's plump countenance, I was seized, hauled to my feet and confronted with that affronted Frenchman, who at the top of his voice gave evidence that I was an assassin, a bandit, an apache, a robber, a murderer, a *pompier*[20] and a foreigner. Then removing his outstretched accusing finger from its place beneath my nose, he thrust it beneath that of Yrotavál and shouted to the crowd, the Police and the heavens that Yrotavál was an assassin, a bandit, an apache, a robber, a murderer, a *pompier* and a foreigner; also that he was drunk.

I was sorry that Yrotavál, beneath the stress of circumstance, now went wholly Catalan and spoke only in that language, for I felt that what he was saying was worth hearing and understanding; altogether too good to be missed.

A *brigadier* of police marched up majestically, as the assaulted Frenchman finished his tirade; and, in the manner of Police-Sergeants the world over, enquired as to what was all this.

Having heard the wild plaint of the eminently respectable Marseillaise, he asked me what I had to say in reply. What I had to say was that it was perfectly true, that I was extremely drunk, and most disorderly; that my friend was even more drunk and more disorderly; and that the right and proper place for us both

---

[20] *Drunken ruffian* (slang).

was a police cell.

"I am inclined to agree with Monsieur," observed the *brigadier* politely, and made it so.

Followed by a crowd and accompanied by the apoplectically indignant citizen, we were taken to the nearest *poste de police,* Yrotavál singing loudly if not tunefully.

After a brief interrogation, brusque and menacing, by a *Commissaire de Police* or some such portent, we were informed that we were under arrest, that we would be detained, and that our case would be considered by the Magistrate in the morning.

On hearing this news Yrotavál smiled, thanked the *brigadier* and observed that had the poor *crétin* been born in different circumstances, had a wholly different education and upbringing and been completely unlike what he unfortunately was, he would doubtless have been a gentleman. Having been delivered of this opinion, he suddenly cast his arms about the gendarme who was holding him, smilingly observed "*J'ai un coup d'bleu,*" slumped, fell to the ground and passed out.

Had I been Fate itself I could not have managed and arranged things better.

§3

"Put him in Double Cell Number Three," said the official in charge of the *Commissariat de Police,* a little later, "and perhaps Monsieur"—glancing at me—"will be good enough to accompany him."

"*Avec plaisir, Monsieur,*" quoth I, speaking the truth. And we were personally conducted to Cell Number Three by four uniformed *agents de police,* three of whom frogs'-marched the unconscious Yrotavál.

Having dumped him on the floor of the cell, and each bestowed upon him a more or less gentle application of a stoutly shod foot, the gendarmes turned to go.

"*Messieurs,*" said I, putting my hand into my inner breast pocket, "*un moment, je vous en prie.*"

Coldly, angrily—and hungrily—the policemen

regarded me.

"There is something I forgot to mention. Stupid of me. We are foreigners. We are drunk. We were the cause of a disgraceful fracas in the Cannebière. And why? Because it was our last night of freedom before joining."

"Joining?"

"Yes. The French Foreign Legion."

"*O-h-h-h!* . . . Why didn't Monsieur say so? . . . Ah! But that is different. That arranges itself."

Of course it was different. And of course it arranged itself. For it was fifty francs Government grant for these worthy men, if they could personally sponsor, introduce and produce us as recruits for the French Foreign Legion.

"And possibly you could get us a cup of coffee?" I proceeded, handing each of the worthy fellows a ten-franc note.

A few minutes later, the *agents de police* returned with the *brigadier.* So he had to be in on it too? Well, the more the merrier and the greater the certainty of the success of my scheme. The face of this excellent official had suffered a sea-change, for there was something remotely like a smile of geniality upon it.

"But how foolish of Monsieur!" he said. "Not to admit that he and his friend are recruits for the French Foreign Legion."

"To tell you the truth, *Monsieur le Brigadier,* I and my friend have been celebrating."

"Undoubtedly that one has," agreed the *brigadier,* nodding at Yrotavál, who lay stertorously snoring on the floor, and kindly adding, "Dump the body on the planks," an order tenderly obeyed by the *agents.*

"Monsieur enlisted in Paris?" he continued. "*Mais oui.* Without doubt. Certainly. Of course. And received his railway warrant and sustenance money and instructions to proceed by a certain train to Marseilles. And the train was not met by a non-commissioned officer of the French Foreign Legion at the Marseilles Station?"

"No. To tell you the truth, *Monsieur le Brigadier,* we

didn't come by the train on which we should have come. We—er—celebrated in Paris also."

Still eyeing Yrotavál's carcase, the *brigadier* found nothing improbable in my statement.

"And not being met by a non-commissioned officer of the French Foreign Legion at the Station, you proceeded—er—to celebrate again in Marseilles? I see. . . ."

The *brigadier* eyed me thoughtfully for a moment.

"Have you any papers, Monsieur? Instructions? *Carte d'identité?* Passport?"

"Yes, I have our passports here," said I, producing mine and Luke's.

"Well, you won't want those in the Legion . . . But didn't they give you any papers at the *Bureau de Récrutement* in Paris? Any *feuilletons de route?* Did you give up your railway-warrants at the Station? Have you nothing wherewith to prove that your story is true, and that you did actually enlist in Paris and are genuine recruits for the French Foreign Legion?"

"*Monsieur le Brigadier,*" replied I, "consider! As one man of the world to another. Let me remind you that we—er—celebrated after leaving the *Bureau;* and my memory is not at all clear as to what happened. Moreover, any papers we may have had were stolen from my friend here, along with his wallet. Some wretched pickpocket took his note-case, either in a restaurant or . . ."

"The gutter, perhaps, eh? And so you have no proof whatever?"

"I'm afraid not."

"Well then, it would seem that the best thing for you to do would be to join all over again, here at the depôt in Marseilles. If they raise any difficulty, or want to ask any awkward questions . . . not that they will . . . But it's like this. If you are recruits for the French Foreign Legion, having already joined in Paris and signed your attestation documents there, you are soldiers. Thus you come under Military Law, and your case must be settled in Fort St. Jean, not here, in the *Commissariat de Police.* D'you see?

"Be much better for you," he added.

"Quite so! Quite so!" I smiled gratefully.

"They are lenient with *bleus*—until they are in uniform. It might be an awkward business for you here. Criminal case tried by a magistrate; assault and battery; accusation of robbery, I understand. Very nasty. Heavy prison sentence perhaps. Whereas the Commandant at Fort St. Jean would probably give you nothing more than the rough side of his tongue or at the worst, eight days' *cellules.*"

"A thousand thanks, *Monsieur le Brigadier.* May I leave it to you? That is to say, may I now formally declare that we are recruits for the Legion; that we wish to join at once; and that we came here on purpose to do so? As for our offence, we intended no harm. My friend only jostled our accuser. We very greatly regret any trouble we've given, and only ask to be treated as the recruits we are, and handed over to the Competent Military Authority."

"It can be arranged," smiled the *brigadier.* "In fact, it arranges itself."

"Then are we free to go along to this Fort St. Jean, or rather, can we be taken there?"

"By no means," was the cold reply. "You are not free to go to this Fort St. Jean. Neither can you be taken there."

"But . . ."

"But I should not be surprised if you are sent for tomorrow morning. It is for the Military Authorities to come and take you over from the Civil Authority, thus assuming the responsibility for you and for your trial and punishment for the alleged offence."

"But who will notify the Military Authorities that there are two recruits for the Legion here in your *poste de police?*"

"That will also arrange itself," replied the *brigadier.* "I repeat, I shall be surprised if you are not claimed tomorrow morning."

"How can I thank you, *Monsieur le Brigadier?* My friend and I are indeed anxious to join the French Foreign Legion with the least possible delay."

"I don't doubt it," replied the *brigadier* coldly.

He lingered, though the interview seemed to me to have terminated itself—and most satisfactorily. Would it be a fatal error or a very sound move to offer this Police Sergeant a *pourboire?*

Turning my back and contorting myself as one who struggles to extract money from an inner pocket, I took a fifty-franc note from my case, put it inside my passport and presented that book-like little document, closed, to the worthy fellow.

"Perhaps *Monsieur le Brigadier* would care to study my passport at his leisure?" I suggested.

"Ah!" observed the *brigadier* and departed with the others from the cell.

A little later the heavy door was unlocked, and another *agent de police* entered, bearing two of the mugs called *"quarts"* filled with coffee. These mugs he put down on the flap table attached to the wall, produced my passport from his pocket, handed it to me and retired.

The French police are, like our own, wonderful. Also incorruptible. But the fifty-franc note had gone.

Seating myself on the other plank bed, I looked at Yrotavál. Sadly I gazed on the face of the drunk and bitterly thought of the morrow; and of all the morrows to come.

The one drop of honey in my cup of bitterness was the thought that I had succeeded in the matter of the damnable scoundrel lying there. I had indeed got him exactly where I wanted him, or should have, in a few hours' time, if all went well. That this would come to pass I had little doubt. The French petty official is an economist, a *ramasseur de sous,* and knows exactly how many francs make fifty. Yrotavál and I were worth fifty francs to those who delivered us to the Legion; and I felt certain that we should be safely delivered.

Since my tale of enlistment at Paris was purely mythical, and as we had not enlisted, there would naturally be no documentary evidence concerning us. The gendarmes, *agents de police, gardes mobiles,* or whatever they were, could truthfully claim the honour —and the cash—for recruiting us.

We were, thank Heaven, neatly in a cleft stick; for, should Yrotavál recover his senses in time to protest that he hadn't the faintest intention of joining the French Foreign Legion, it would be pointed out to him that he had already done so; that according to our own account, and on our own admission, we had enlisted in Paris. Also that we had got drunk, missed our train, arrived at Marseilles, and got drunk again on our way to Fort St. Jean, as I myself had borne witness.

But by the look of him, Yrotavál would be a member of the French Foreign Legion a long time before he was a sober man who knew what he was saying and doing.

Suddenly, I realized that I was very very tired, and, lying back and resting my head on a folded horse-blanket, thin and filthy, I fell asleep.

§4

I dreamed a most amazingly realistic dream, of which I have never forgotten the least detail, so deeply did it impress itself upon my mind.

Now Luke had always been a wonderful dreamer, from earliest childhood. Quite frequently he dreamed of events to come, quite unlikely events; and they did come. There was no trickery and no doubt about it; for he would tell me of the dream, and I would say, "Well, that's not very likely," and would be amazed when it proved to be prophetic.

As a rule, they were not important things, but the fact that he had dreamed them was. For example, he said to me one day at school,

"I dreamed about you last night, Mark. Rotten dream. You were drowned. I can see you now lying face downwards. I can see you there on the ground—muddy grass—and somebody waggling your arms about. You seemed to be dead."

And within a week I very foolishly went after a dog that some brute at the mill had thrown into the river with a brick tied round its neck, a brick not heavy enough to keep the poor beast under and drown him properly. If I had stopped to think, I shouldn't have done anything so damned silly, for it was a very cold day and the river was swollen and swift. . . . Anyway, it was a case of artificial respiration on the part of the village policeman who pulled me ashore.

That was one of a score of Luke's prophetic dreams.

Then again he would often dream of something that was actually happening somewhere else, and would "see" a death-bed, a house on fire, a ship sinking, or a fight; that sort of thing.

The third kind of dream that he frequently had was a dream about something that had happened in the past, and he would dream it so vividly that he could describe the historical dress, weapons, acts and words of the people about whom he dreamed. (Incidentally, he once saw a vision, or thought he did. But perhaps he was dreaming then.)

Well, although I am not in the slightest degree gifted in that way, this dream was so curious, realistic and detailed that it soon became almost indistinguishable from actual memories of real events. That is to say, I sometimes found myself subconsciously, as it were, looking back upon this dream, and wishing to God that I had not done what I did—in the dream. I expect I wish this so earnestly because I realize that if I had thought of it in time, I might actually have done it.

I wonder?

My dream carried on the story of my life, so to speak, from the time of my discovery of Luke's deception.

Seething with bitter anger and resentment, I went down to the hall and seated myself in front of the fire.

Luke came in at once and sat down in his favourite arm-chair on the left, almost facing me, and I stared at him while he, with despicable and cunning hypocrisy, gazed in my direction but just above my head, eyes apparently unfocussed, seeing nothing, and occasionally blinking.

And as I looked at him and he refused to look

straight at me, I knew that he had married Rosanne
under false pretences; had won her pity, her sympathy,
and love—won her herself—by a villainous trick; for
she did not love him sufficiently to have married him
had she not believed him to be blind and terribly in
need of her.

And as I sat there wondering that he did not read
my savagely angry and bitter thoughts, Rosanne came
down the broad staircase, crossed the hall and seated
herself beside me on the settee, Luke's gaze wavering
above the heads of us both, as she did so.

And suddenly an evil impulse of revenge, of
punishment for Luke, a means of impaling him firmly
on the sharp horns of a dilemma, entered my mind. If
he could not see us, I'd give him something to—not
see; if he could see us, I'd give him—something to
think about.

Placing my left hand on Rosanne's, I put my right
arm about her, drew her close to me and then pressed
her head down upon my shoulder.

As we sat thus, I felt that she was filled with
wonder, at my extremely unwonted demonstrativeness.

Luke stiffened and stared—just above our heads.

Relinquishing her hand, I put mine beneath her
chin, tipped her head back, bent over and kissed her—
again and again.

Once she returned my kiss. Then her lips stiffened
and she made to draw back.

Strengthening the pressure of my right arm which
was about her, I drew her yet closer, kissed her again,
and then, taking her left wrist, I raised her arm and
put it about my neck.

There she left it. And as her head lay against my
right shoulder, her face upturned, I kissed her
repeatedly, hotly, but softly and without sound. Then
with both my arms about her, I clasped her to me with
all my strength.

And there, in front of Luke, her arms about my
neck, mine about her body, his wife and I sat silent.

For one second Luke had hung on the verge of self-
exposure; his hands had gripped the arms of his chair;

he had drawn in his feet as though to rise, and his face had flushed and then turned pale. His dilated eyes had at last come down to normal level, and he was staring at us, astounded, shocked, aghast. And then, in the act of springing to his feet, he had remembered; *remembered that he could not see.*

And so in silence I tortured him, Rosanne consenting to, or at any rate suffering, my kisses and embrace.

And as I turned to gaze at the swindler whom in my dream I hated fiercely, the door behind him opened and I awoke as a uniformed *agent de police* entered, followed by a Corporal and a file of soldiers in the dress of the French Foreign Legion.

"So these are the birds, are they?" said the Corporal.

"There they are. All present and correct," grinned the *agent.* "In fine plumage, if not in good song."

"Oh, I wouldn't say that," said the Corporal as Yrotavál emitted a stertorous snore. "How are we going to get that one along? If he weren't a *bleu* in *pékin* dress, I'd have him dragged along on his back, but . . ."

"What about a bucket of cold water?" suggested the *agent.*

I thought it was time that I contributed my suggestion to this symposium. It seemed to me that Fort St. Jean would be a much more desirable scene for Yrotavál's restoration and recovery.

"If I might make a suggestion, *Monsieur le Caporal,* what about a taxi?"

"A great thought! Brilliant!" admitted the Corporal. "What about a taxi each? That would only be six. Do you suggest that I or the State should provide them?"

"Well, I think we could do with less than six. Say one or two to start with. And I'll pay for them."

"What with?"

"Money."

"What's that? Haven't seen any lately. Have you?"

"Yes. I've got some here," and I produced my wallet.

At least four pairs of eyes regarded it with interest and favour.

"A *bleu* of the right sort," observed the Corporal.

"Good. We'll have at least one taxi from here to the Fort. And we'll stop *en route* for a cup of coffee, eh, *bleu?*"

"With something in it," I agreed.

And with no more than reasonable violence, Yrotavál was hauled from his plank bed to an uneasy seat in a taxi which was quickly called.

My farewells to the occupants of the *poste de police* were cordial; our journey to Fort St. Jean, broken by a call at a *bistro,* was pleasant; and our reception by the Sergeant of the Guard as recruits for the Legion, prompt, unmistakeable, and—final.

When El Señor Don Caballero Yrotavál y Rewes recovered sufficiently to realize the state of affairs and grasp the situation, he was, to say the least of it, surprised.

He was also furious to the point of violence, revolt, mutiny, madness.

At first, I believe, he positively entertained a suspicion that I had some hand in the matter; and I am sure that he never changed his opinion that, but for my incredible stupidity in getting drunk when he was drunk, this appalling catastrophe would never have overtaken us.

A brief conversation-piece, which interested me, between a hard-faced *adjudant* receiving us into the fold, and Yrotavál, still bewildered:—

"*Señor!* . . . Sir. . . . *Monsieur l'Adjudant!* This is an outrage. I wish to protest. I do not want to join the French Foreign Legion. Advantage was taken of me when I was drunk."

"So? Isn't that just too bad . . . That being the way of it, we'll keep an extra-watchful eye on you, my friend. . . . *Silence, you dog, before I . . .*"

XVI

Once again I must resist any temptation to write a book about Life in the French Foreign Legion, even from this new angle, that of an ordinarily enlisted man at the Sidi-bel-Abbès Depôt.

As I am trying to tell the story of Luke, and of what I, in my wisdom, did regarding him, I will only tell as much of my second Legion venture as concerns my subject.

Rosanne having kept all the letters that I wrote to her, and some that I wrote to Luke, I can correct my memories and make them absolutely accurate.

§2

I had a splendid start in the Legion, inasmuch as I not only knew the worst but knew the ropes; also because I positively wanted all the hard work, fatigues and constant occupation that I could get—and those are matters of which there is no dearth in the Legion; and because I was fortunate in having private means which, though definitely small in my own walk of life in England, amounted to great wealth in that regiment of the poorest of the poor, whose pay is negligible, mere inadequate tobacco-money. It is but slight exaggeration to say that, in the Legion, no man who has money need do anything that he doesn't want to do, and can count on being able to do anything that he does want to do— except buy himself out.

I was again lucky in having had the Guards' training, to which the depôt recruits' course at Sidi-bel-Abbès and Saida is inferior in rigour, stress, strain and intensity; and also in having had four years in the trenches. They had inured me to real hardship, beside which any that I was likely to encounter in Morocco would be quite bearable.

What was new and severe was the combination of

great heat and the terrible monotony of outpost life.

So, all things considered, I realized, and was thankful, that few men ever joined the Legion under more favourable conditions.

From the very first, I determined to win promotion as quickly as I could, in order that I might have control of Yrotavál; and as soon as I had got my uniform and had settled down at Sidi-bel-Abbès, I put in for admission to the *peloton de Sous-Officiers.* I was warned by Yrotavál, who, after all, knew infinitely more than I about the Legion, especially in Africa, that I should be making a great mistake in doing so, because it meant double the work and quadruple the responsibility, not to mention the fact that I should lose many privileges and, worst of all, much of the pleasure of his company and that of my *bons camarades* of our *escouade.*

Did I want to be a *sacré animal avec sardines sur ses jambes,* he asked—in other words, a damned non-commissioned officer with stripes on his arms?

I replied that that was precisely what I did want to be, but forbore to add that my main reason for this was that it would give me what I wanted almost more than anything—power over him, opportunity to keep my eye on him, and, to a very great extent, the ability to regulate his comings and his goings.

As a Corporal, with Yrotavál in my room and my *escouade,* I should have him as much in my charge as is a child in that of its father. As a Sergeant, I should be in a position to do with Yrotavál what I would. And what I wanted and intended to do with him was to have him always with me. Practically never out of my sight. Where I went, there Yrotavál should go, and of what he did I should have complete cognizance.

Meantime, to stick closer to him than a brother sticketh, to be with him night and day, and if any orders threatened to separate us, to use whatever money might be necessary to get those orders modified. To square a Corporal would be extremely easy, a Sergeant easy but more expensive, a Sergeant-

Major neither difficult nor costly, an *Adjudant,* save in very rare cases, not too difficult and not beyond my means. And the *Adjudant,* so far as the *légionnaire* is concerned, is all-powerful.

To the Officers, the men hardly exist as individuals. They are not known to them by name, and the personal contact is of the slightest. It would be a strange and unusual case in which I could not influence the Corporal to influence the Sergeant to influence the Sergeant-Major to influence the *Adjudant* to arrange that I and my *cher copain* Yrotavál were not separated.

§3

It would, of course, be entirely false to say that I was now happy; but I can truthfully state that I was not always and wholly unhappy. One cannot be that when one literally has no time to remember, is too tired to think, and is fully occupied from waking till sleeping. And in the Legion one sleeps, whatever one's troubles.

And I set myself to conquer unhappiness, to get the better of this misery that tried to get the better of me, overwhelm me, defeat me, and turn me into a soured cynic and a wretched hypochondriac.

I meant to make the Legion my career, set myself the high and difficult ambition, rarely achieved (by a foreigner), of winning a Commission from the ranks. With that aim and object to strive for, my constant work to do, and my unending watching of Yrotavál, I should have no time for self-pity.

And I might pause here to remark that if any man in this world gets an all-round training in the duties of the Compleat Soldier as private, as non-commissioned officer, and as officer (should emergency cause him to take the place of one), it is the man who passes through the Legion's *peloton de Sous Officiers.*

It is not a crushing, grinding, gruelling drill-training, such as he gets in the Guards, with the object of turning him into the perfectly disciplined machine. It is a training in all that the private soldier should know and do, followed by a training in all that the non-commissioned officer should know; a training in initiative, resource and leadership; a very sound, thorough and wide training too; and the intelligent man who goes through it, if he have initiative and ability of his own as well as resourcefulness and resolution, should be able, if called upon to do so, to command a Company in action or a *poste* in state of siege.

I had sent post-cards to Rosanne from Paris and Marseilles, as I saw no reason why she should have occasion to worry about me as well as about Luke; and I now wrote to her regularly.

It was difficult. It was painful. It made me feel a hypocrite; but though I could not and dared not say much to her when I was with her, on paper I could let myself go, put it all down, and give rein to my longing for self-expression, open my heart, and relax the repression and suppression from which I had so long suffered. I do not, for one moment, mean that I made love to her, that I wrote a line that Luke was not most welcome to read; but I did write to her as though she were more than my sister, my very dearest friend whom I had always loved.

Not only did I write to her because it was a relief and a joy, but in order that I might get answers to my letters.

I told her (God knows how truthfully) that I had come away because I could no longer bear to see Luke in the condition in which he was; that I had not the fortitude and courage to remain at home with him; that, moreover, I had to do something, and soldiering was the only thing I knew how to do; that I was ineligible for a commission in the British Army, save through the ranks, a long, slow process doubtful of success, and that a not particularly desirable one. I had no wish to be a grey-haired Lieutenant-and-Quartermaster. Nor, even if I were eligible for re-enlistment in a British regiment, did I want to soldier in peace-time in an English garrison town. I had had enough floor-scrubbing, grate-blackleading, ration-tin-polishing, pipe-claying, and barrack-square drill. So I had come to the Legion which was always on active service; where one could have a life of colour, variety, sunshine and romance; where a professional soldier might make himself a career, and get, on the field, that promotion for which he might have to wait twenty years in England, and wait in vain. And so forth. I had to make it convincing and it was partly true—for there really was sunshine (when there wasn't heavy rain, bitter cold wind, and, in the Atlas Mountains, sleet, snow, and conditions of almost Arctic severity).

I also assured Rosanne that she need not have any anxiety about Yrotavál; that he was here with me in the French Foreign Legion; that he would be here for the next five years and, at the end of that time—we would see. There was one thing she would not see, however, and that was Yrotavál back at Courtesy Court.

I also wrote to Luke, and it was a difficult letter to write.

I felt that I must not give him the slightest inkling of the true state of affairs—that I knew all about his imposture—for otherwise I might just as well have denounced him to his face. He would suffer quite as much misery, shame, anxiety and fear of exposure, if I told him by letter (or raised any doubt in his mind) as if I had told him in so many words, face to face. But at the same time I had got to explain Yrotavál's defection, and I hesitated between two courses; one of saying that I had more or less kidnapped him because Rosanne detested him and hated his being at Courtesy Court; and the other of saying that Yrotavál, tired of the humdrum peaceful life of respectability, had not only volunteered and begged to come with me, but had said that he had intended to quit before long, in any case. The former seemed to me somewhat undesirable, as implying that Rosanne put her likes and dislikes before (the supposedly) blind Luke's necessity and comfort. The latter seemed undesirable because Luke could hardly imagine that such a man as Yrotavál would throw up a position in which he was in clover, on velvet, and as he himself would express it, sitting pretty, to come back and rough it again in the French Foreign Legion. It didn't sound convincing.

Finally I decided on a sort of combination of these two and a third, in which I took the blame.

I said that I couldn't help seeing that Yrotavál was something of a disturbing influence at Courtesy Court; that the servants detested him—especially the women-folk—and threatened to leave; that I had noticed that his manner to Rosanne was anything but that of a well-trained valet of her husband's; that, having had a talk with him, I realized that he was, at any rate for the time being, weary of the monotony and restricted life of the country; that he was tired of respectability and virtue; that he was bored to extinction, and really yearning for a return to the flesh-pots, yea, even the cook-house *soupe*-pots of the French Foreign Legion. That, moreover, I had felt for some time that Yrotavál had served his purpose, come to the end of his use-fulness and was really more harmful than beneficial to Luke; that he was to Luke a constant reminder of the trenches, of his terrible tragedy, and of all sorts of other things better forgotten; and, finally, that Luke could get an English valet quite as good as Yrotavál in some respects, and a very great deal better in others.

I then hinted at a piece of selfishness on my own part, a desire to have Yrotavál with me as a batman again in the French Foreign Legion, to which in my own utter boredom and unfitness for any other profession than soldiering, I had returned.

I begged Luke to forgive me for my gross and unwarrantable interference with his affairs, and begged him to believe that, at any rate to some extent, I had acted for the best and in what I thought to be his own interests.

It was the best I could do; and I saw no reason why Luke should suspect the truth and fall into a state of perpetual worry and anxiety as to what might happen.

That I was fit for nothing else but soldiering he

would readily believe; that Yrotavál was sick, sorry, and tired of respectability he would believe; and that I had bribed Yrotavál to come with me he might imagine.

If, at first, Luke's conscience pricked him, and uneasiness and fear beset him, that surely would gradually pass off, as all went well, nothing transpired concerning his secret, and my regular letters to Rosanne reassured him and lulled him into a sense of security. He would conclude that the worst that could happen was that at the end of five years Yrotavál might return and, holding out a beseeching hand of iron, well covered with a velvet glove, beg, menacingly, to be taken back into his comfortable and easy billet as valet to his old friend and master.

Yes—it seemed to be the best I could do; and to the best of my ability I did it.

I awaited Rosanne's first letter with painful eagerness; opened it with mingled excitement, joy, and anxiety; and found it to be much as I expected.

She was shocked, stunned almost, she said, at finding that I had cut myself off from her—from her and Luke—for five years, which would be years of the greatest danger to me; and to her, years of anxious fear for my safety. *Why, oh why, had I not told her what I was going to do, and at least have talked it over with her before taking so irrevocable a step. That I felt as I did about Luke she could quite understand; and that I must have employment she could quite understand; but surely I could have found something to do in England, something other than soldiering, something that would have left me free to come, from time to time, and stay at Courtesy Court which, after all, was not only my home but my own house.*

(Didn't she guess, didn't she for one moment dream, the real reason; understand it all—realize how difficult, how impossible, it was for me to do just that; to come and see her from time to time, and stay under the same roof with her? Apparently not.)

She thanked me for taking Yrotavál away, and assured me that there, at any rate, I had done her a real kindness and a very great service.

Not only was Luke resigned to his loss, but she was perfectly certain he was the better for Yrotavál's departure. He seemed easier in his mind, more light-hearted, happier; and the tiny cloud that had arisen on their horizon and threatened to spread, had been entirely dissipated.

Yrotavál had been not only a bone of contention but a source of irritation and, long as she had borne it, hard as she had striven to hide the fact from Luke, the man really had been something of a danger to their domestic happiness. It had been absurd and ridiculous that such a position should have been allowed to arise, and she couldn't be too thankful to me that I had taken the bull by the horns, or rather Yrotavál by the ear, and removed him. And the splendid thing about it all was that, not only was she rid of the loathsome moron, but that his departure had really not upset Luke at all.

So things were, on the whole, better at Courtesy Court. Luke was coping marvellously with his blindness, the house was happier than it had been since he came back to it, and Luke's blindness aside, her only trouble now was the thought of my long separation from them and the danger in which I should be, on active service in the French Foreign Legion.

Well, that was that; and, on the whole, good; and if I had really served Rosanne, that fact was my reward.

Luke's letter was a curious document.

Reading between the lines, I could see that he was a little puzzled, not to say anxious. While evidently having no idea as to the true state of affairs, he obviously could not quite understand my action with regard to Yrotavál, nor Yrotavál leaving him as he had done—without a struggle or even a word of protest.

Poor Luke had to put up a pretence of missing Yrotavál terribly, *Yrotavál, who had become a second pair of eyes to him*; but his reproaches were half-hearted, and he admitted that *doubtless he would, sooner or later, get accustomed to a new valet, though he hated changes and was by no means sure that he would not try to do without a valet altogether.*

As I could see by his typewriting, said he, *he was making great progress along the blind man's path through the dark Valley of the Shadow—not of Death nor of Life—but of something between the two.*

I was ashamed for him. I suffered for him, and with him, to think that he had to descend to this; had to be such a hypocrite; had to write these packs of lies to bolster up the deception—which he had undertaken, I was sure, in a moment of terrible weakness and over-whelming temptation.

And until he began the gradual recovery of his sight, he must, of course, continue to weave this tissue of lies and deceit.

§4

To shorten what might be quite a long story, both Yrotavál and I, being not only old soldiers but rejoined *légionnaires,* completed our recruits'-training in the minimum time and heard our names read out in *rapport* one evening, as members of the next draft for Morocco, where the Riff campaign was in full swing. We were not sent to Morocco direct, however, but to a place called Saida, where a battalion was undergoing intensive training in the particular methods of warfare being pursued in the Atlas Mountains. After a few weeks here, we returned to Sidi-bel-Abbès and thence entrained, by narrow-gauge railway, for Oujda on the Algerie-Maroc border. Here we underwent more intensive drill, training, and rifle-range work, and then marched to a concentration camp for troops of all arms. From here, we marched again, entered the danger-zone, and after skirmishes and affairs of outposts, took our place in the battle line of a *groupe mobile,* and were soon in the thick of the fighting.

Letters from home became irregular, not because Rosanne grew tired of writing, but because the field postal-organization broke down from time to time, and the delivery of letters to *les légionnaires* not unnaturally was a matter of much less importance than the delivery of rations and ammunition. The lines of communication were long, difficult, constantly threatened, and frequently broken by the extremely active Riffian *harkas* under the command of Abd-el-Krim.

One day there arrived at the *poste* which our company had built and garrisoned, letters which were distributed at *rapport* that evening, and the *vague-mestre* handed me a batch from home. Quite a little packet, and more welcome to me than food, wine, or even tobacco. More welcome indeed than anything on earth could possibly have been. So wonderful, so precious, that instead of tearing them open instantly, and reading them through from beginning to end, I thrust them inside my tunic, almost literally hugging them to my breast, hoarded them up, and waited for an opportunity to read them in peace, to re-read them a dozen times, to savour and enjoy them, and to learn, almost by heart, every word and sentence.

But when I came off duty and had cleaned my rifle, bayonet and accoutrements, finished all work and fatigues and settled down in a corner of the *enceinte* really to enjoy myself for an hour and for the first time in weeks, I suffered disappointment once again.

There was fresh trouble.

Yrotavál was at the bottom of it; and as I read, I again felt that cold and deadly anger and hatred under the influence of which I had removed him from Courtesy Court and decoyed him into the Legion.

Blackmail—as I had feared while he was at Courtesy Court.

But I had not, I admit, visualized the possibility of long-range blackmail, so to speak. Installed in what he considered an impregnable position as Luke's nominal servant and real master, blackmail in one form or another would be easy, and to a man of Yrotavál's type, natural and obvious, indeed almost inevitable. But it simply had not occurred to my stupid mind that—once I had got him not only out of the house but out of the country and buried alive in the French Foreign Legion on active service in Morocco—blackmail was possible. I had imagined that I had not only removed him from the scene of his offence, but had completely eliminated him from Luke's life; liquidated him, so to speak, so far as Luke was concerned.

But I had under-estimated the villainy and re-sourcefulness of El Señor Don Caballero Yrotavál y Rewes.

"I am worried about Luke," wrote Rosanne. *"That sounds rather an under-statement, because I have naturally been worried about him from the day he returned here from France. What I mean is that there is a new anxiety. He is getting letters from Yrotavál and they are bad for him. They upset him, each one more than the last. He won't tell me why, or what's wrong; but now, even if I didn't see them, I should know when he got them.*

As you know, he is terribly susceptible to annoy-ance, is very easily disturbed and troubled, and is prone to make mountains out of mole-hills. That is my hope—that this is really some sort of a wretched little mole-hill. But it's a mighty great mountain to poor Luke, whatever it is. If it goes on, I shall take it upon me to interfere, intercept all letters from Yrotavál, and destroy them, instead of letting Giulia read them to him in the course of her 'secretarial duties.' For two pins, I'd open one and read it.

I'd hate to be such a dishonest meany as to read a blind man's letters. It would seem a terrible thing to do; but surely it would be a case of the end justifying the means—and the meanness—wouldn't it? I have asked Giulia and she says that Luke gets no disturbing letters that she knows of; and that Yrotavál's are just respect-ful letters from an ex-servant to a good master and friend. I can't make it out. Tell me what you think, Mark. Shall I open one, read it, and send it to you, if it is obvious that Yrotavál is deliberately worrying and disturbing Luke? And it's no good my saying 'if,' for Luke is worried and disturbed and troubled.

I can't think how such a man could be in a position to do this to Luke—how he should have the power to upset him. But there it is, in spite of what Giulia says. . . ."

Yes, there it was.
And I must deal with it.

I opened Luke's letter with considerable trepidation, tinged with sympathy and some curiosity. Poor Luke!

Poor devil, how he must be suffering. The fear, the worry, the miserable and crushing anxiety of the blackmailed. And how could Luke account plausibly for the fact that Yrotavál was in a position to worry him?

I read Luke's letter.

Oh, that was the line he took, was it?

"One can quite understand Yrotavál's wanting to come back," he wrote. "The first soft job he had ever had. The first time in his life he had had a good home, good food, good treatment and everything he wanted. And best of all, peace and security. He found Courtesy Court a bit of a change after Barcelona, New York, Chicago, Soho, Limehouse, the Legion and the trenches. And now he finds the Legion and the Riff campaign a bit of a change after Courtesy Court. He's not only dying to come back, but he'll die if he doesn't. Not only wants to come, but intends to come. As soon as he can, too. Says he can't stick five years of it, and he's going 'on pump' at the first opportunity. . . ."

Good Lord! What a fool I was. It had positively never entered my head that Yrotavál might solve his little problem like that; desert—and make his way back to England and Courtesy Court.

"And I don't want him back here now. I've got used to being without him. I manage very well indeed, with

Rosanne's help; and the more I have to do for myself, the more I can. And Rosanne, for some reason or other, is so thankful that he has gone that it would be a shame to let him come back, especially as he is no longer necessary.

So I want you to make it clear to him that, in the first place, if he does desert, it is no good his coming here. Job definitely not kept open. No fat-headed calf here awaiting the return of the prodigal valet. Perhaps he won't want to desert if you can make that quite clear to him. But best of all, old chap, see that he doesn't do it. Butter his feet, as Rosanne did the kitten's. It wouldn't take very many francs' worth, to do it. I've no doubt that if you gave him a salary which naturally ceased if he bolted, he'd think twice—and then not do it. Probably it's the salary that attracts him back here. Suppose you promised him as much as I used to pay him, so long as he stays with you. . . ."

Somehow I didn't think that it would be a salary that I should promise Yrotaval. Something quite different.

Nor was I able to console myself with the thought that such a salary as I could offer him would weigh for a moment against the profits of blackmail and the comforts of Courtesy Court. If I read Yrotaval aright, his idea of velvet would not be the khaki of the French Foreign Legion; his notion of a bed of roses would not be a sack of straw on a plank in a Moroccan *poste;* nor a dole from me his idea of the exploitation of a good thing in blackmail.

I was badly worried.

Had all my efforts been in vain and was the situation worse than ever? Had his contentment with the fair and reasonable bribery, corruption, and illegal gratification at Courtesy Court now turned to anger and stark threat, open blackmail, with terrible danger to Luke's peace and Rosanne's happiness?

Thanks to changes, Yrotaval had hitherto, fortunately for him, escaped recognition as a deserter, the man who had mysteriously disappeared and been posted as missing, after the bombing of the hospital at Pont Mailleul. This was not remarkable, as the personnel had completely altered since August 1914, the Legion having been destroyed and reorganized so many times that there was scarcely a man, an N.C.O. or an Officer left, not only of our Battalion de Marche formed at Toulon, but of the Legion itself.

I admit that while considering my original plan, I had glanced at the idea, once safely in the Legion, of laying information against Yrotavál as a war-time deserter who had escaped to England. This would have earned the fellow, at the very least, an eight years' Penal Battalion sentence, and would have almost certainly disposed of him once and for all, so far as Luke, Rosanne and I were concerned, as well as giving him a fitting punishment for what he had done to my brother.

But I could not do it. I recoiled from what seemed to me the treachery of such a course. It was a foolish scruple, no doubt, but I felt that I had done quite enough in the way of preventive punishment in getting him back to the Legion, which was, after all, the life which he had originally chosen for himself. Denunciation would have served him right, and been no more than his due, but my inhibition was too strong—partly because Luke himself, whether induced by Yrotavál or not, was just as bad as he; and I had, for a time, been a deserter myself. And even if I had not avoided the heavy fighting in those terrible trenches in order to nurse my brother, and even if Luke had been genuinely blind and completely innocent, I still could not have done it. Instead of well-deserved punishment it would have seemed like treachery, betrayal.

To me there is something horrible about the very words "laying information," and the act of being an informer. I suppose it is a relic of one's schoolboy training and prejudice against the tale-bearer and the sneak.

It is a curious phenomenon; for although I quickly and totally rejected the idea of punishing and defeating Yrotavál in this way, I eventually did something far worse. I don't know that it was worse for him than a sentence of eight years' *travaux forcés* in a Penal Battalion, but it was worse for me, from the moral point of view, and should have been far more strongly condemned by my own conscience.

In fact, considered without prejudice and reference to schoolboy conventions, the one would have been an entirely blameless course of action, while the other, the course I actually followed, was utterly indefensible. It was simply criminal.

And yet I should have been ashamed to do the one, while to this day I feel no shame with regard to the other.

Now—should I suddenly confront him with my knowledge of what was going on; warn him and threaten him; tell him that if I heard that he wrote Luke one more letter I would . . .

Would what? What could I do? Tell him that he must transfer his attentions from Luke to me? Blackmail me instead of Luke?

Hardly. I somehow couldn't imagine Yrotavál regarding me as a likely and suitable subject for blackmail. I could scarcely say to him,

"Just let me know how much you thought you would get out of my brother, and I'll pay you the amount for him," apart from the fact that I was fairly sure that the first item in his bill would be a return to the safe haven of Courtesy Court, where he'd be not only hidden from, but beyond the reach of, the Spanish Police, the French Police, his implacable Anarchist and Communist "comrades" whom he had betrayed, and all other enemies whomsoever. Money he would want, of course; all he could get. But of what use would money be to him if his life and liberty were endangered, as they would be almost anywhere outside of England?

Which would be the better? Promise or threat, bribery or punishment? I must find out, for whatever happened, Luke must receive no more threatening letters.

What about a combination of the two? Reward for

good conduct and punishment for bad. The reward would be simple enough. Ten francs a week, so long as I received no further complaint from Luke. And punishment? Yrotavál was not easily daunted, and was not the sort of man to pay the slightest heed to a threat of being beaten up, or of any other act of vengeance. It would rather amuse him (it almost amused me) to think of my endeavouring to brow-beat, threaten and terrify him. No, there was no hope in threats of personal violence, and in point of fact, two could play at that game. My talking "rough stuff" to him would be the amateur competing with the experienced professional, tyro versus past master.

§5

Under the influence of my fear that Yrotavál might escape me, might desert and return to Courtesy Court, I provided the gentleman with a body-guard. Carefully, and one by one, I selected half a dozen men whom I liked and trusted and who, as I believe, liked and trusted me.

In the sight of each of these I rendered Yrotavál precious. For, so long as he was with us, present, if not correct, in our midst, they each received on our Thursday pay-day a little addition to their official emolument, a sum small to me but very considerable to them in terms of wine, tobacco, postage-stamps or canteen feeds.

Having explained to them individually that I simply could not bear it if Yrotavál went away and left me, I pointed out to them collectively that it would be quite simple to arrange that at least one of their number always had an eye on him.

The first man I approached was one Mallen, a magnificent American, taciturn, grim-visaged and reserved, a man who drank all that he could get and never appeared the worse for it; drank, I imagine, because he had something to forget, and in wine found his only anodyne. Like others of his type, he heartily disliked Yrotavál, and when I to some extent explained the position to him, Mallen assured me grimly that should Yrotavál, in spite of his care and attention, succeed in deserting, he would himself desert—for the sole purpose of catching him and bringing him back.

Another man into whose care and keeping I committed Yrotavál was a wild Australian whose name, real or assumed, was Charles O'Malley. He was quite mad, quite fearless, a very desperate fighter, and a man who would do anything for a bottle of wine. As soon as he realized the situation and grasped the idea, he addressed Yrotavál by such terms of endearment as his standing-drink, his walking wine-bottle, informed him that inasmuch as he could "shake him down" for a franc's worth of wine every Thursday, he'd shake the indescribable teeth out of his unmentionable head if he ever caught him so much as thinking of deserting and abandoning us to our fate.

A third man, Sanson-Fayette, was a very queer fish, remarkable even in this school of queer fish, a man who had been a police officer of the rank of Detective-Inspector or Superintendent, whether of the Paris *Sûreté* or of the Belgian Criminal Investigation Department. What had caused his downfall I don't know, but he was a very nice man and undeniably extremely clever. I think that of all Yrotavál's body-guard he was the most valuable from my point of view. Certainly he contributed nothing to Yrotavál's peace of mind or sense of security. In fact, he did to some extent for Yrotavál what that scoundrel was doing for me. He worried him. And I think he frightened him, for he watched and shadowed him in a manner that Yrotavál, as an ex-police spy himself, must have admired, if not appreciated. He also found out something about him, and the fact contributed nothing to Yrotavál's remaining peace of mind.

It just occurs to me—and I rather wonder that I never thought of it at the time—that quite possibly Sanson-Fayette was on duty, so to speak, in the Legion, seconded from the French or Belgian Police for some special purpose.

Anyway, he was one too many for the clever

Yrotavál and kept that criminal guessing.

The fourth was a man whom I chose for very different reasons, a Swiss named Dreiner, who almost certainly had been a pastor of some kind, probably the minister of some obscure village sect. His mind may or may not have been permanently unhinged, but it swung on one remarkably solid and unbreakable support, an utterly incorruptible and unwavering sense of duty. To this and to his undying love of the Legion that had given him a home and a refuge, I shamelessly appealed, after giving him more than a hint that Yrotavál was contemplating desertion, that Yrotavál must be prevented from deserting, and that Dreiner was the very man to see that he did not do it.

The other three members of Yrotavál's body-guard were men who disliked Yrotavál, liked a joke, and rather more than liked a weekly carouse and a sufficiency of tobacco. Whether it was the constant watchfulness of these seven friends that prevented his escape, I don't know; but my fears that he might desert proved groundless, and in time, he and I found ourselves, still together, in country and conditions which made desertion impossible.

XVII

My promotion to the rank of Corporal was very welcome because it gave me an enhanced sense of power over Yrotavál; partly because I could do a great deal to prevent our being separated; and partly because, as a Corporal, I was now a person worth placating.

I don't think that, hitherto, he had had any sort of respect for me, even when I was the master at Courtesy Court and he was a servant. There he felt, no doubt, that through his knowledge of Luke's secret, it was rather I who was in his power than he who was in mine. Now there was no question as to who had the power, and I looked forward to the time when I should be a Sergeant and perhaps Sergeant-Major—when Yrotavál should be my batman and live in my shadow.

What did worry me was the thought that, in one of the frequent attacks on our *poste,* our skirmishes on patrol and reconnaissance duty, or in the next battle, when the *groupe mobile* was re-assembled into a striking-force, I should be killed and Yrotavál would be free to recommence his blackmailing activities. That was an ever-constant anxiety and fear. There was, of course, the other aspect of the fortunes of war. Yrotavál himself might be killed, and I felt that nothing would give me greater pleasure than to attend his funeral.

The thought that Yrotavál might be killed found permanent lodgment in my mind, and from it I drew what comfort I could.

Meanwhile, what I had said to him seemed to have borne fruit, for in none of his subsequent letters did Luke make any complaint whatsoever about him. His letters were by no means regular or very frequent, but from time to time it seemed that he must let off steam, must get himself down on paper, as he expressed it. I suppose it was a natural, and indeed inevitable, urge to self-expression, for he must have found life terribly restricted and circumscribed.

Although Rosanne's letters were anything but complaining and miserable, were indeed cheerful, it was quite evident that she was still very worried and unhappy about Luke. I told myself that, in the circumstances, it could hardly be otherwise and that life could be no more normal for her than it was for him. She was not the sort of woman to live her own life and go her own way, as it had always been her mother's profession and practice to do; not the sort of wife to leave a blind husband to his own devices, while she sought amusement and distraction elsewhere. Loving Luke as she did, and having married him to look after him, nurse him, and help him in every possible way, that would be the life she would wish to live and the way she would want to go; it would be her chief pleasure too—provided Luke responded and the only trouble they had to face was the handicap of his blindness. The *only* trouble! I felt sick when I thought of the grief and pain that he was causing her.

But I was quite sure that there was something more than this; that Rosanne had difficulties, troubles and worries of which she was not telling me. I was very much afraid that instead of doing so, she was taking the view that I had trouble enough of my own without her adding to it, especially as I could do nothing to help her.

One day, however, on return from escort duty with a convoy, I found awaiting me a long-delayed letter of hers, which showed me that I must take drastic and final action, if I were to be Rosanne's friend in deed.

". . . . *So I decided that the end justified the means,"* she wrote, "*and intercepted the next letter addressed to Luke from Morocco.*

"*It was quite evident that Yrotavál had taken no more notice of what you said to him than to write and warn Luke that if ever he complained to you again, it would be the worse for him; that* 'he wouldn't stand for any of that sort of double-crossing, and that if Luke hadn't any gratitude for what his old friend and comrade had done for him, he ought to have. Anyway, it would be just too bad for him if he acted that way again. This had nothing to do with brother Mark, and if Luke was the wise guy, he'd leave brother Mark out of it; and unless a regular salary were paid him there would be trouble. He himself didn't want to make trouble—never had—but if Luke wanted it, there was plenty of it about; not only the Big Thing which, even if it didn't interest the Police, would interest all kind friends and relations—*M'Carben Diu,* it would!—but one or two other things that might interest the Police a lot. The French Police, that is to say. And had Luke ever heard of a dirty little police-trick called extradition? They do it for murder. Had Luke forgotten one night at Toulon when a man named Bjelavitch met with an accident, and did he remember a couple of *copains* called The Spider and The Bull? Because they were still alive, and in possession of all their faculties, especially good memory, and a good thirst too, if Luke would like to do anything for them. Then there was that Corsican bastard, Paggallini. Had Luke forgotten what he did to him? Well, Luke might think that Yrotavál was the only witness of what happened that night, but as a matter of fact, there was another one. . . .'

"*Then there were further references to other mysterious doings, of which one could not make head or tail. But it is quite clear why Luke is worried. The man has got some sort of hold over him, and is actually blackmailing him. Can you imagine anything more abominable, more fiendishly awful than to attempt to blackmail a blind man? No wonder I always hated the creature instinctively. He must be an absolute monster of cruelty and wickedness.*

"*What I cannot understand is why Luke should take any notice. If the man were in England, he could hand him over to the Police, of course. As it is, there is nothing he can do. Without for one moment believing that he* knows anything really discreditable to Luke, I imagine that he has got hold of something that can be twisted that way; some accusation which Luke would find it impossible to disprove. One has heard of such things, of course, and that it is a regular trade with a certain class of criminal—tricking and trapping people into apparently compromising actions or circumstances, and then blackmailing them. Yet why is Luke so terribly worried and anxious—in fact, it wouldn't be too much to say frightened?

"I think I had better intercept all letters from Yrotavál. It couldn't do any harm; and it certainly doesn't do Luke any good to receive them. I think all blackmailers should be treated as murderers are; and those of them who blackmail innocent people who fall into their clutches, and over whom they have got some hold, should be punished more severely still. Hanging is too good for them. Can you conceive of such devilish wickedness as torturing a blind man? For blackmail is mental torture—the worst kind of all."

Yes, blackmailers should be treated as murderers are.

This one should be.

§2

It's an ill wind that blows no one good, and an ill wind for thousands and thousands of Riffians, as well as for hundreds and hundreds of French soldiers, brought in its hot, dusty, and evil train, a measure of good for me.

A prolonged period of desperate fighting in the Riff Campaign brought me further promotion. My being left, through the death of my superiors, in charge, and in sole command, of a small but important *poste* which I managed to defend successfully, won me another stripe. The first thing that I did when promoted to Sergeant—and in the French Army a Sergeant is an extremely important man, saluted as an Officer by private soldiers—was to appoint Yrotavál my batman.

Fortune favouring me again, I was in charge of a convoy of food and ammunition that, suddenly surrounded and desperately attacked by Chleuchs, I contrived to bring safely through to its destination, a *poste* which, but for its arrival, must have fallen.

To the initiative and ability of two Corporals who had been German Officers in the Great War, and to the desperate valour of the escort of *légionnaires,* the credit for the defence of the convoy is due; but it was I who reaped their reward, for I was promoted to Sergeant-Major.

Doubtless my record as a Legion Volunteer in the Great War, my Guards' training, my rejoining the Legion, and my consistent good luck in this campaign, contributed to this quick promotion.

But far greater good than this, the ill wind of War blew me; for it kept me occupied, not only occupied and busy from morning till night, but so over-worked and over-strained that I had no time for worrying. I was constantly so mentally and physically employed, and so weary when the opportunity for sleep came, that I had no time for private grief and misery by day and slept like a log the moment my head touched the pillow, or more often the pack, on which it rested.

It was the hardest part of a hard campaign, and the Legion as usual bore the brunt of it. When my battalion was, for very shame on the part of the authorities, withdrawn to rest and re-fit at the Fez camp, we marched from our place in the *groupe mobile,* a ragged regiment of scarecrows, our clothes in rags, our toes through our boots, gaunt, hungry, diseased, strained to breaking-point, and everything but daunted and defeated.

After a brief space for recuperation, refitting and re-inforcement, we marched out again to the scene of what was now a guerrilla war of infiltration and attrition; and, a few months later, I again found myself in temporary command of an advanced *poste* in mountainous country.

My garrison of two Sergeants, eight Corporals and

fifty men, of course included my faithful batman Yrotavál.

Life in Fort Boulanger quickly settled down to a dreary monotony of hardship, short commons, long days and weeks of dreadful dullness broken only by occasional sudden and swift attacks by the bold and hardy warriors into whose mountain fastnesses the French forces were thus "peacefully penetrating."

In spite of the stagnation of the war, we were sniped by day and our sentries occasionally stabbed by night; we could only go outside our mortarless stone walls with proper military protection as though moving in open warfare through enemy country; and the water-party, which daily went to a neighbouring stream with half a dozen mules and a dozen sixty-litre barrels, must always have its route picketed and be accompanied by a strong escort.

Nevertheless, life was, as I say, dreary and monotonous beyond belief and almost beyond bearing. There were many cases of *cafard,* and I am not certain that I was very far from it myself.

And Yrotavál was busy again.

Yrotavál was hatching something. He was in funds, and each convoy that reached us bringing our precious, nay priceless, wine and tobacco, our cases of monkey-meat as the French *poilu* calls bully-beef, our biscuits, coffee and sugar, our ammunition and our letters, evidently brought him good news and good money. Our Yrotavál was becoming a personage, apart from his importance and prestige as the acting Commandant's batman.

He had money to burn, money for wine, money to hire the services of the penniless.

Luke's money.

And although here I was monarch of all I surveyed and (were I the average and normal *légionnaire)* should have had every reason for satisfaction, contentment and happiness as a successful man whom kindly Fortune had carried to the top of his tree, I was far worse off than when, under authority, I was over-driven, over-worked and harried almost to death. In this relatively peaceful interlude, when life for me was quiet and easy, though responsible, I should have been happy. In point of fact, I was more wretched and uneasy, more anxious and miserable, than I had been during the months of mobile and "open" warfare, when the campaign was at its fiercest, life at its hardest and most dangerous.

I had too much time to think, too much time in which to read, and re-read, and brood over, Luke's letters—and Rosanne's.

All was not well at Courtesy Court and Rosanne was not happy. Very far from it.

§3

And one day, after we had been in Fort Boulanger for months that seemed like years, I got, in a batch of others from her and Luke, a letter from Rosanne which told me that Yrotavál had written to Luke telling him that I had reviled and threatened him for attempted blackmail, and announcing that, whereas he had promised me he would never do it again, it was now up to Luke, if he valued his peace, safety and happiness and anything else, to make special amends—in cash. Unless he wanted to be exposed, to his wife and brother, he had better keep his trap shut on the subject of blackmail, and never try that sort of game again and never admit that he, Luke, was getting any letters whatsoever from him, Yrotavál.

And reading between the lines of Luke's latest, it was perfectly certain that that was the position; that Luke wanted me to know that he was still being blackmailed, but even more wanted me to understand that I must not let Yrotavál know that Luke had again complained to me of what was going on.

Obviously Luke was anxious, frightened, nay terrified; and equally obviously, Rosanne knew it and was just as anxious, frightened and terrified on his behalf.

And there was Yrotavál all about me, pervading and

poisoning the atmosphere I breathed, my batman in closest hourly touch with me.

And I bore it. How, I know not.

XVIII

I am, I admit, a little slow in making up my mind, but once it is made up, my decision stands.

Three events which happened almost simultaneously combined finally to decide the problem of Yrotavál. Rosanne's latest letter, Yrotavál's intention to desert from the *poste,* and Yrotavál's knife.

As usual I had kept this letter until I could read it in some measure of peace and privacy. As convoys had arrived with some regularity and letters had not accumulated, there was only this one. I took it to my quarters, my mortarless stone-walled, earth-floored room in the long one-storey *caserne* in which we all lived, closed the door, sat down on my ammunition-box bed, read it from end to end, and in great perturbation, rose to my feet, subconsciously impelled to do something . . . something . . . anything . . . though there was nothing that I could do.

I was not in the best of health, and, owing partly to fever and dysentery, partly to the reading of the letter, my hands trembled and shook, and the letter fell from my twitching fingers. Quickly I stooped to recover it, and as I did so, something struck the door with a thud.

As I rose from my stooping position, I saw that a long-bladed heavy knife was deeply embedded in the door at about the level of my heart. It must have passed above my bent back, missing me by an inch or so, as I stooped for the letter. It must have been thrown through the glassless window opposite the door. Knowing that it was quite useless to do so, I nevertheless flung the door open, dashed round the corner of the *caserne,* along the short side of the building, and looked to see who might be between the *caserne* and the wall of the fort.

No one, of course. It would have been an idiotic idea, had I entertained it, that I was likely to see Yrotavál running for his life or standing about looking innocent, and chatting with some kindred spirit who would provide him with a few minutes' alibi.

Hurrying along to the door of the *caserne,* I looked into the big *chambrée* which was the Section's dormitory. It was empty, of course.

A hasty tour of the *poste* showed that Yrotavál was not in the cook-house, store-room, N.C.O.s quarters, nor apparently anywhere else. Running to the gate, I asked the sentry if anyone had come in or out during the last five minutes. No one. I then made a quick tour of the walls and questioned the sentries at the four corners. With apparent truthfulness and some surprise, they assured me that no one had dropped down over the wall during the last few minutes, nor at any time since they had been posted. With equal certainty they assured me that neither had anyone climbed up over the wall and into the *poste.*

Evidently Yrotavál had cleverly evaded a sentry and got away while his back was turned; or else was, equally cleverly, hiding within its walls.

Well, it didn't much matter. I knew that it was he who had attempted to murder me, and but for my sudden stoop would have succeeded. He alone had the motive to do so, and the skill to throw a knife with such accuracy and force.

Returning to my cubicle, I pulled the knife out of the wood; and it required considerable effort to do it.

Naturally, it was not Yrotavál's knife. I recognized it as Dreiner's, the one he used as a wood-working tool— a deadly weapon with a long, strong, double-edged blade and sharp point, a very heavy handle and a spring device whereby the blade could be prevented from closing into the handle.

Had I not suddenly bent to pick up that letter, with my face toward the door, that knife would now be planted to the handle below my left shoulder, the blade through my heart.

I remembered how Corporal Bjelavitch had been found in the gutter of a slum in the sailors' quarter of Toulon, with the handle of just such a knife protruding from his broad back.

Well thrown, Yrotavál! . . . Well saved, Rosanne! . . . And I laughed with a sense of happiness compounded of gratitude and relief. Gratitude to God and Rosanne. Relief that, once and for all, for good or for ill, the problem of Yrotavál was settled.

The knife and the letter had combined to put an end to anxiety, worry and indecision.

The letter was as follows:

DARLING MARK,

This really is an S.O.S., but what is the use of my sending it when you are too far away to help me. Oh Mark, why did you go, and why did you cut yourself off so completely and for so long? When, when, when will you come back?

I am at my wits' end, and just about at the end of my tether too. I can't tell you how terrible things are here now; and I don't think I would if I could. And Yrotavál has written to Luke to say that he can expect him to arrive at Courtesy Court quite soon now, as he has completed—with the help of Luke's money—all arrangements for deserting successfully when you return to Fez. He says he has disguises and a fast car. . . . Luke is dreadful nowadays . . . I am ashamed of myself to be writing to you like this, but I have simply got to do it. I must, or I shall go mad. No, I shan't do that, but I shall break down. To whom can I turn but you—although you are so far away? You have always been my tower of strength. You have always been there. One has always felt you were there, either for immediate help or in the last resort.

And, oh Mark, this is the last resort, and even though you cannot help me, I am helping myself by writing to you. I can't tell you everything. I won't! But, oh Mark, if you can come, do. If you can help me, help me. I pray you to. Something has happened to Luke. He has gone utterly and completely to pieces. Mark, it is as though he is going mad. Really mad, I mean. He seems to be terrified literally to a condition of insanity.

Mark, it is terrible. It is heart-rending, and yet at the

same time—oh, I can't write it—but he . . .

And, oh Mark, there is something else.

But that is my trouble, and I will say nothing about it —though I feel I would give years of my life to come to you and tell you. I won't post this wretched letter . . .

There was much more like this. Something had happened. Something terrible. And it had happened to Luke—and through Luke to Rosanne.

Yrotavál?

I felt cold and sick and horror-stricken.

Could I have been mistaken about Luke? Could he through genuine blindness have met with some accident? Run over? . . . Burnt? . . .

Of course not. He *wasn't* blind.

No blind man can read a book, and turn page after page, then turn back to read something and compare statements, then pick up a pencil from a table, underline two or three sentences, and write something in the margin of the book. No man can slowly and carefully and accurately make a swoop with his hand and catch an ordinary house-fly that has silently settled on the top of his book. Utterly impossible and absurd.

Besides—Yrotavál. Had the faintest shadow of doubt remained in my mind, his story would have removed it completely.

And had I never seen what I had seen through Luke's window, and had I had no evidence save Yrotavál's confession of complicity in Luke's deception —was not that amply confirmed by Luke's submission to his blackmail, by Luke's attitude to him, and by Yrotavál's own attitude of security, power, and importance at Courtesy Court?

No, of course Luke was not blind. What had happened was that he had at last broken down under some threat of Yrotavál's, some monstrous increase of blackmailing pressure.

What Luke was doing was fighting, struggling, *acting*—to prove to Rosanne and the rest of his world that he really was blind. Fear is the deadliest microbe that attacks the mind of man, the most poisonous, destructive, fatal. And as the poisoned mind suffers and deteriorates, so does the body. Fear kills; mind, body, and soul. Fear was killing Luke, driving him mad.

Yrotavál was killing Luke.

And, a few minutes ago, Yrotavál had almost killed me.

And Yrotavál had reduced Rosanne to a state of stricken misery, grief and agony of mind.

Yrotavál!

XIX

The indecision ended, my mind at peace, my determination irrevocable, my will adamant, I acted quickly.

Next morning, I marched as in a dream along the mountain path, preceded by Yrotavál whom I had ordered to accompany me on a short expedition from the *poste.* He was unarmed but carried entrenching tools.

In spite of my fierce determination, unalterable purpose, and my grim errand, I marched, as I say, in a dream, myself walking beside myself, wondering at me, at what I was about to do, and the manner in which I intended to do it.

Arrived at a spot which I decided was suitable, deep in the live-oak forest, out of sight of the *poste,* I gave the order.

"Halt! . . . About turn! . . . Ground entrenching tools! Stand properly to attention!"

With the promptitude of the old soldier, Yrotavál, whatever may have been his surprise, obeyed.

"Yrotavál," said I, "you attempted to murder me yesterday. *Silence!* You are doing something worse than murder, to my brother. You have driven him to insanity, perhaps suicide. You actually did murder Corporal Bjelavitch and Sergeant Paggallini, and by your own account you have murdered other men. Any Court of Law before which you were tried would convict you and sentence you to death. I am now going to take the Law into my own hands. I sentence you to death."

"It is murder!" shouted Yrotavál, as I drew my revolver from its holster.

"Silence! Stand back!" And I levelled my revolver at his face. "Murder or not, I'm going to kill you—as you tried to kill me."

"You can't prove . . ." began Yrotavál, his voice high and hoarse.

"No. I can't. Though I know it; and you know it. But I am not killing you for that. I . . ."

"*It is murder! Murder! . . .*" screamed Yrotavál. "You talk about *me* being a murderer and . . ."

"Murder or execution, Yrotavál, I'm going to kill you now. . . . Even if it brings me down to your level. I have warned you. I have tried to stop you. You've been blackmailing my brother again. . . ."

"*It's a lie. It's a lie.* I haven't written a word since . . ."

"That's enough. I know that you have. It was you who persuaded him to sham blindness and you've blackmailed him ever since."

"*It's a lie.* He began it. He asked me to sham deaf and dumb and . . ."

"You yourself admitted that it was your idea. You yourself admitted blackmailing him and . . ."

"*I stopped.* I stopped it when you . . ."

"About turn!" I roared, and, so strong was the habit of years, the force of mechanical instinct, that Yrotavál obeyed.

Should I bid him kneel? Should I bid him pray?

Yrotavál kneel! Yrotavál pray! I thought of Luke. I thought of Rosanne—and pulled the trigger.

With a convulsive jerk and jump he fell forward. Placing the muzzle of my revolver to his ear, I shot him again.

With the entrenching tools I made a shallow grave, thrust his body into it, shovelled the earth and gravel back into the hole, and covered the place with large loose stones.

I was cool, nay cold, collected in mind and calm in spirit.

Having finished my task, I marched back to the *poste,* taking with me the light pick and shovel.

On the way, I visited the sentry-groups posted to guard the passage of the water-fatigue party to the stream.

"Did you hear a shot?" I asked Corporal Mallen, the American tough guy and Bad Man, for whom I had much admiration and a high regard.

"Sure, Sergeant," he said. "Two."

"*Légionnaire* Yrotavál has been shot," I informed him.

Corporal Mallen appeared to bear the bad news bravely.

"Isn't that just too bad!" he said.

As I turned away and he saluted, a smile flickered for an instant across his grim face.

§2

I slept particularly well that night, perhaps because I felt that I had done something that might enable Luke and Rosanne to sleep their nights through also in peace.

Next morning, as I sat at the egg-box table in my dry-stone, earth-floored cell, I looked up to see Corporal Mallen standing in the doorway like a statue at the salute.

"Come in," said I. "What now, Mallen?"

"*Légionnaire* Dreiner has a request to make, *mon Commandant.*"

When we were being formal and official, Corporal Mallen always addressed me thus, though when alone, marching at ease with our minds off duty, so to speak, we talked as man to man rather than as insect to tin god.

"*Cafard?*" I asked, knowing my Dreiner.

"Nothing special," smiled Mallen. "Only wants to erect a tomb-stone to the late, unlamented *Légionnaire* Yrotavál, and to conduct a service over his grave!"

This Dreiner, called The Pastor, of whom I have already made mention, was an interesting man whom I liked as much as I pitied; one of those gentle simple Swiss who are so transparently honest and straightforward that one marvels how any of them survive in the wicked world outside their own villages.

One's chief wonder concerning him was how on earth he ever got to the Legion or found himself in the position that made such a step seem advisable. A love-

190

affair probably.

Never, I imagine, of very strong intelligence, his mind, affected by the War and Legion service, was now definitely feeble. A very good soldier indeed, he was queer, and lived in an almost permanent state of *cafard*. With him as with me, it was a case of occupation being salvation, and he was quite happy when on duty, on the march, or busy with his *asti-quage* and fatigues. At other times he was miserable, morose, and depressed to the point of madness, save when he was doing something with a knife and a piece of wood. He had been a wood-carver as well as a preacher and was invaluable as a handy-man during the construction of a *poste*. He could make doorways, window-frames and simple furniture as well and quickly as a carpenter.

He was not the kind of man to boast of anything, but had he wished to do so, he could have boasted that the grave of every one of his comrades who had been killed, save in battle or on the march, had been marked by a well-made cross on which at least the name and *matricule* number had been neatly and deeply carved.

In the case of friends or comrades whom he had approved, there would frequently be a text or some brief encomium. Such were *"God is Love"*; *"He giveth His beloved sleep"*; *"Requiescat in Pace"*; *"The Bravest of the Brave"*; *"A Noble Comrade"*; or *"Mort sur le Champ d'Honneur."* When possible, he would carve this text or epitaph in the language of the country of the dead man.

"Certainly," said I. "Anything to keep poor Dreiner happy. Bring him along."

A minute or two later the two reappeared at the door of my hut, or hutch, and saluted like guardsmen.

"Le légionnaire Dreiner to speak with *Monsieur le Commandant,"* announced Mallen.

"Well, Dreiner?" said I, studying the curiously Christ-like bearded face of this gentle and kindly Swiss who must have killed hundreds of his fellow-men, thinking as I did so of Luke and myself at

Oberammergau and of Anton Lang, the famous actor who took the Christ part in the Passion Play.

"So you want to make a cross for Yrotavál's grave?"

"*Oui, mon Commandant, je vous en prie.* I have never failed a comrade yet. Not when he died at a *poste* or in camp, so to speak."

"Was Yrotavál a friend of yours?"

"*Mais non, mon Commandant. Au contraire!* But he was of the Legion, and a comrade though not a friend. I should not like to fail him, especially as he was killed by the enemy."

"Excellent," said I. "Yrotavál was, as you say, of the Legion—and he was killed by an enemy. Have you decided on his epitaph?"

"I have decided that there shall be no epitaph, *mon Commandant.* A text would be inappropriate, for he was an enemy of God. Nor can I praise him. But I will not blame him. What was Yrotavál when he was alive? He was Yrotavál. What is Yrotavál now that he is dead? He is still Yrotavál. Then let his name be his epitaph, and, at his graveside, let me say a prayer for his soul. *Mon Commandant,* I often think. . . ."

"Silence!" cut in Mallen quietly. "You haven't come here to think but to ask the Commandant's permission to make a cross for Yrotavál."

Mallen was neither brutal nor harsh, and he was not unkindly; but he knew his Dreiner, and that unless he were cut short, he would, in Mallen's idiom, be delivered of a mouthful and myself enriched by an earful and then some.

"Very good, Dreiner," said I. "You make Yrotavál the best cross you can, and carve his name on it; and we'll give him a military funeral—and you shall conduct a short service."

"Plant the old bastard good and proper, in fact," I heard Mallen observe while marching Dreiner from the Presence.

Considering the difficulty of tools and materials, Dreiner made an admirable job of it; and, partly for something to break the monotony of life at Poste

Boulanger, partly as a reward and encouragement and tonic to poor Dreiner, partly in a cynic spirit of bitterness that would have amused Luke, I gave orders that the placing of the memorial cross should be an official function and parade, although Yrotavál himself was already well and truly interred; in short, that he should have a solemn and official, if belated, military funeral.

Soon after morning Stand-to, I sent out skirmishing and scouting parties, made reasonably sure that there were no Riffians in the neighbourhood, and then, after posting sentries and taking all precautions against surprise, I ordered Corporal Mallen to parade, as a funeral-party, all who were not on duty.

It was one of the weirdest occasions of my life, and looking back, I realized that whatever Dreiner may have been, I was myself more than a little mad, suffering from more than a slight attack of *cafard.*

As the funeral cortège marched from the *poste,* with Dreiner carrying the cross and looking more than ever like the unique actor of Oberammergau, I wondered whether, ever before in the history of the world, such a ceremony had been conducted in such a way, such a cortège marched to a grave, bearing the cross of a murdered man, with his murderer, in the post of honour, bringing up the rear.

And the end of the ceremony was truly worthy of it.

After Dreiner and his two assistants had, with spade and mattock, firmly planted the well-made cross at the head of the grave in which I had buried Yrotavál, I gave Dreiner permission briefly to recite a Burial Service and offer up a prayer.

It was most moving and pathetic. Poor Dreiner! Evidently he had once been an eloquent and impassioned preacher of the revivalist type. He had also conducted many Burial Services. . . . When he began to wave his arms, froth at the mouth, and wax incoherent in prayer and exhortation, Mallen laid a hand upon his wrist and whispered to him to conclude the Service. Like one awakening from a dream, Dreiner, with a simple dignity, ceased to pray and orate, quietly said the *"Au Père, au Fils, au Saint Esprit"* valediction, observed that, after all, it was the undeniable truth that Yrotavál was an old soldier who had fought for France and died in French uniform far from his native land—and then collapsed.

At Mallen's orders, the party fired a volley and then, with arms at the Present, saluted the memory of the dead.

As we left the hallowed spot, I gave the order *March at Ease,* and, when I did so, Corporal Mallen fell back from his position, saluted and joined me.

"Just glance back, Sir, will you?" he said, a wry smile curling his tight mouth, a twinkle of humour lighting his cold grey eye.

I looked round.

In the level morning rays of the African sun, the cross stood out boldly against the dark mountain background of grey stone and tree trunk.

From the cross stood out starkly the one word,

"Read it backward," said Mallen, and hurried off to his place at the head of the funeral cortege.

Luke's humour! . . .

Luke's voice here in the heart of the Atlas Mountains. . . .

So "Yrotavál" had an epitaph after all. Suitably and appropriately provided by Luke.

XX

"How does it feel to be a murderer?" I imagine it depends to a great extent on the murder, the murdered man and the murderer himself. Speaking for myself, with apologies to all moralists, I experienced a feeling of the utmost relief and, believe it or not, a sense of satisfaction, of something accomplished, something done, to earn a life's repose for Luke and Rosanne.

I had committed a murder, the brand of Cain was on my brow, and I was prepared to wear that brand, if not as an honourable scar, at least as a spot and blemish that worried me not at all.

From that day to this, I have never felt one twinge of remorse or of regret. In cold blood I killed Yrotavál. In cold blood I would kill him again, in similar circumstances.

Doubtless my years of war, my training in bayonet-fighting, my sniper's practice, my life in the trenches, my daily experience of death, mutilation and horrors unspeakable, have blunted my sensibilities, have caused a deterioration of my moral fibre and weakened my respect for the sacredness of human life.

At any rate, I have, I hope and believe, remained honest, and I honestly and truthfully admit that I have no horror, no spiritual fears and forebodings in the matter of my killing Yrotavál. And time having enabled me to see the matter in perspective, to regard it calmly and dispassionately, I know now that I did not so much take the Law into my own hands and presume to punish Yrotavál for what he had done, as assume the right and duty of protecting Luke from a danger which to him would be worse than death, and Rosanne from the destruction of her happiness—at the cost of taking human life. To call Yrotavál human.

No, I have no regrets, no remorse and not the slightest sense of a need for repentance.

§2

I could begin here and write a big book about my further experiences and adventures in the Riff Campaign but have no intention of doing so. In fact, having made my confession, I shall not write more. I have done what I set out to do, and it has been painful. Nevertheless, I feel the better for it.

What would be even more painful would be to dwell upon what happened shortly after Yrotavál's death.

The Chleuchs cut the lines of communication between our *poste,* Fort Boulanger, and the base, and besieged us, with the result that not only did we nearly all die of starvation and the strain of constant siege, but, until the *poste* was relieved, we received no letters.

When at last these came, one from Rosanne, almost incoherent in its horror, misery, and grief, brought me the news that had more than a little to do with the fact that I left Fort Boulanger—scene of so much suffering and agony of mind, scene of battle, murder and sudden death, literally of murder, so far as I was concerned—on a stretcher, and that I have no knowledge of how I eventually reached the Base Hospital at Fez.

No, I'll write no more—save to say that in that letter poor Rosanne contrived to tell me what she had to tell concerning Luke.

"*Then I spake unto God in my grief: My wine and my bread*
And my staff Thou hast taken from me—my friend who is dead."

(Shane Leslie).

Mark Caldon Tuyler's manuscript here ends thus abruptly.

II

LUKE RIVERS TUYLER

I

So they have given me a typewriter to play with. A special machine with rubber caps on the keys, each letter nicely embossed, that my finger-tips may learn to distinguish it!

Pity the Blind.

What shall I write?

Apologia pro vita mea?

I don't know that I really have so very much for which to apologize, after all. Or perhaps I will amend this by saying that doubtless I have, like everybody else, a good deal for which to apologize; but that I have had good cause and reason—or, rather terrible cause and reason—for what I have done.

At school, we had a somewhat self-righteous, somewhat pompous old fool of a master, who was full of such counsels of perfection as *"Never explain"*; or again, *"Justify yourself to yourself and to nobody else,"* and, one that was his especial favourite, and which he repeated *ad nauseam,* like a parrot, *"Blame yourself."*

Why should one blame oneself, if the blame lies elsewhere? Why should not one justify oneself, since Justice is desirable? And why should one never explain, when explanation is obviously indicated?

A pretty mess and muddle one would make of one's affairs and of one's life, if one were careful never to explain. I can conceive no better method of creating every sort and kind of misconception, misunderstanding and impasse. So, without any idea of white-washing myself, or of hypocritically assuming blame that is not my due, I am going to explain why I did—what I did.

And I will begin at the beginning of my life, for that is where the chain of causality starts—so far as our own free-will influences our lives that is, and our own rough-hewing of our ends affects their shape.

I will, to the best of my ability, avoid casuistry; and I freely admit that our acts our angels are, our fatal shadows that walk by us still.

I used to know an amusing, cynical chap in the French Foreign Legion, a Belgian named Rassedin who, seeing a devout Dutch youth praying very busily beside his bed one night, remarked to me,

"I never have prayed and I never shall, but if I ever did offer up a prayer, it would begin like that lovely one that the Pharisee prayed in the temple—

"*God, I thank Thee that I am not as other men are, extortioners, unjust, adulterers, or even as this publican.*"

Personally I do not return thanks that I am better than other men, but I *am* definitely glad that, in one or two ways, I differ from the very vast majority. There is no sense in denying obvious facts about oneself, nor indulging in stupid false modesty—such as distinguishes dear old Mark, for example.

So I freely admit that I have been blessed, not only with a great gift, but also with a great advantage; the gift being my marked psychic power, and the advantage my undeniable membership of both of the two classes into which men are divided, the physical and the mental—the low-brow and the high-brow. For I have been endowed with the physique of an athlete and with the intelligence, perception and understanding of an artist, and I am a painter, a poet, a musician, an essayist and a story-writer.

Perhaps I can best indicate this wonderful advantage with which I have been blessed, and for which of course I take no personal credit, by mentioning that, had I worked my hardest when at School, I could undoubtedly have won a scholarship; and that had I played my hardest, I could have been Captain of Cricket and Captain of Football, as well as Captain of the School. Also, had I remained at Oxford and chosen to work my hardest and to play my hardest, I could easily have got a Double First and a Double Blue—and the man who can do this is, I submit, unusual, to say the least of it.

And let me make it clear once again, that besides being an artist to my finger-tips, I am abnormally psychic. For this explains a very great deal—and it is at honest explanation that I here aim.

Of my great *advantage,* my combined physical and mental endowment, I only become gradually aware; but from very early childhood I was cognizant of my *gift,* my psychic power to see and hear what are known as ghosts; and to dream amazingly interesting dreams that were sometimes prophetic, that were sometimes glimpses of what was happening elsewhere at the time of dreaming, and that were sometimes what must have been absolutely accurate pictures of events that had happened in the past, whether recent or far-distant.

And then, from a very early age, I occasionally saw visions as well.

By this I don't imply that I, like so very many other children, merely fell into brown studies, as they are called, and indulged in idle day-dreams. I mean that I had real objective, conscious experiences.

I'll give you an example of this:

I will describe the phenomenon exactly as I saw it, and I shall ask none, and shall expect few, unreservedly to believe my statement.

To such kindly folk as will say soothingly, with a large-minded tolerance and forbearance,

"Yes, yes, my good Luke Tuyler, we are quite sure you think you are speaking the truth as you remember it; but memory is a very tricky thing, and it all happened a very long time ago," I reply most gratefully,

"It is very good of you to make allowances. The fact remains, however. And memory is not a tricky thing when it is renewed and renewed again; when one thinks of the event repeatedly, frequently; and when, time after time, one recapitulates its every detail without change; and can shut one's eyes and see it again as clearly as the actual scene that was plainly before one at the time of happening."

In point of fact, I am not greatly concerned as to whether my account of this vision is believed or not.

But nevertheless, I shall write it down, as I shall write whatever else interests me, for my own satisfaction and justification.

§2

When I was a very small boy, my brother Mark and I were taken by our nurse, nursemaid and governess, as usual, for a long summer holiday by the sea. Young as I was, I enjoyed the most conscious awareness of the utter and unutterable beauty of sea and sky and sands, the last, at low tide, apparently illimitable.

I did not use this kind of language, of course, as a small boy, but looking back, I know that even then I was, as I have said, an artist to my finger-tips, full to the brim of artistic appreciation and delight in beauty.

I have only written two slim volumes of poetry hitherto, or, to be exact (and in this *apologia* I passionately desire to be exact in every detail), I should say I have only published two volumes of my collected poems. But I have written hundreds of poems, short and long, and at this place, especially at dawn of a perfect day, I was undeniably endowed and endued with the authentic poetic fire and the yearning to express in words the feelings that filled my soul, the appreciation of the ineffable beauty of Nature here displayed.

So far behind me now, so far from me to-day, is that high capacity for that fine frenzy, that I have a curious sense of shame in confessing to it, and in writing of it here. But the fact remains.

In the mornings, I did not get out at dawn, or as early thereafter as I could, in order that, equipped with spade and pail and shrimping-net, I might build sand-castles or pursue the minor fauna of the deep. These things I did, and did with zest, later in the day, with Mark and other young barbarians at play; but in the early mornings there, I would arise, dress myself and, noiselessly escaping from our bedroom and the house, go across the road to the beach (praying that I might have it to myself) and simply . . . *gaze.*

I would gaze—myself the very least and lowest of artists—as does a great artist on a great picture.

I had no desire to do anything but look; and I was, doubtless, completely unconscious of that desire and of the fact that I yearned to steep my soul in beauty, in unsullied pure loveliness; fill myself with it, and at the same time, enter into it and be one with it.

Of course, I was conscious of nothing of the sort. All I knew was that I loved to see those illimitable sands and sea and sky at dawn, and especially at time of low tide when there was an added beauty, a fourth element, as it were, besides the sky and sea and sand—a combination of the last two, a rippled, pool-adorned, wave-marked, boundless tract that was neither sand nor sea.

And one day, walking to the edge of this ephemeral lovely realm that was neither land nor water, but born immaculate of both, I beheld my first vision.

A dream dreamt by a sleepy little boy who had risen from his bed at early dawn, and had naturally and unconsciously lain himself down with a yawn to sleep again? On sands so wet that every foot-print filled immediately with water? Lain down, where to stand still was to sink a little? Lain down at the water's edge, where the turning tide would lap about him and in a few minutes cover him?

No, that is all patently absurd.

Do believe me when I say that there is no question, no possibility, of my having slept and dreamed. On the contrary, I was walking along the water's edge, bare-footed, wondering whether I should catch the tide in the very act of turning—a thing I loved to try to do—and enjoying with my whole being, and with a pleasure denied to adults, the simple sweet and lovely delights provided by every sense; sight providing the joy of the marvellous colouring of golden sand, palely blue sky, greenly blue sea, goldenly yellow gorse, and distant green-tipped snow-white cliff: smell providing the joy of that unparagoned scent, compact of ozone, salt and sea-weed: touch giving the delight of the caress of the light breeze on cheek and neck and naked limb, of soft wet sand and cool water on foot and ankle: sound enchanting the ear with merry music of the little ripples, the happy baby waves, the pleasing soothing susurrus of the gentle back-drag of the tiny pebbles of the occasional patches of fine shingle: and the sense of taste providing the sweetness of the faint flavour of the air and the tang of salt upon the lips.

Awake? Conscious? I was as widely awake, as keenly aware, as truly and actively conscious, as ever I have been in all my life.

And, suddenly lifting up mine eyes and looking out to sea, I beheld—the Ship.

It was as real and actual as any ship that ever I saw in all my life. Not a phantom ship, such as the Flying Dutchman, but concrete and solid-seeming. It was about the size of one of those life-boats carried by liners, and optimistically labelled as "For the accommodation of 56 persons." Perhaps it was a little bigger. And it was of a different shape, inasmuch as the high bows were extended to be themselves their own figure-head, crudely dragon-like, and the stern was square and also high. The short, stumpy mast supported a long yard and a heavy sail, torn, stained and dirty, of which some device had been roughly limned in tar and red paint, a bird or beast or dragon. Over each gunwale hung a row of shields, whether of wood, or hide stretched over metal, I could not be sure; for they were dirty, sodden, and salt-encrusted.

Seated on the thwarts of this boat or long-ship, their backs to me, were two rows of oarsmen. Standing up in the stern was the helmsman who grasped a tiller, or perhaps a long and heavy oar resting in a deep niche or rowlock and serving as a rudder. Other men of better sort and superior rank stood in the bows, sat in the stern, or moved, balancing themselves between the thwarts.

Now what interests me most of all perhaps about this vision is the fact that it was evident and present as much to the ear as to the eye. For suddenly I heard a man shout a command, the heavy sail was let down with a noisy run, and, a little later, at another order which was distinctly audible, the rowers backed water.

Every sound was natural, loud, and clear; and they were precisely those that one always hears when a big boat or small yacht is thus handled. There was nothing whatever silent or ghostly about this ship and its crew.

Soon it grounded gently in shallow water, and the attention of its occupants turned to a man whom hitherto I had not noticed. He half lay on the stretchers or bottom-boards, half leant against the mast, until a man, standing beside the helmsman, pointed at him and gave another peremptory order, whereupon three or four of the crew pulled him roughly to his feet and thrust him headlong overboard into the shallow water. There were loud shouts of rude laughter, as the man, apparently revived by the cold douche, rose painfully to his feet, staggered ashore, and collapsed at the water's edge. A seaman in the bows, thereupon picking up a pole or boat-hook, thrust the boat off. The rowers plied their long heavy oars, the helmsman put the tiller over, the sail was again hoisted, and the boat made out to sea.

Now, it is another very interesting fact that it did not vanish like the morning mist, or suddenly disappear as does the figment of a dream when the sleeper awakes. It "proceeded," as they say in the Navy. It simply sailed away like any other boat.

The man left behind was lying in the posture of the Dying Gladiator, and turning to him, I realized that he was either badly wounded or mortally sick.

As I stared—not frightened, bemused or amazed, but accepting the whole impossible affair as the right and proper sort of thing to happen, just after the pearly dawn of a perfect lovely morning by that magic faery sea—the wounded or dying man raised himself on his elbow and looked straight at me.

In my memory it is no vague and nebulous dream-face. I can see it now, and most distinctly; bronzed, weather-beaten, lined and deeply wrinkled beside the eyes; the moustache and beard fair; the hair long and unkempt, and, where it protruded from beneath a rusty iron head-piece like a skull-cap, it was bleached to a still lighter hue than that of the moustache and beard; the face and head, save for the long locks, just such as one might see any day on the quay of a Devon fishing-village.

And here enters a somewhat incongruous element which seems to me to protrude into this realm of Vision from that of Dream. For the man now spoke, using what language I know not, presumably some Norse tongue, and I clearly understood what he said.

It would have been normal and usual enough, had I been dreaming, for a foreigner whose own language would actually be some form of early Scandinavian, to speak modern English; but this queer fact does not fit in with the Vision, and spoils otherwise simple and acceptable theories.

What I saw in the Vision were real things. What I heard were real sounds. But reality ceases when a Viking speaks modern English.

It is possible, of course, that the man did not really speak English at all, but his own Norwegian or Danish, and that I was given the power to understand his meaning, in some occult and inexplicable pentecostal fashion. The simplest solution lies in the theory that there was telepathic communication between his mind and my own; though, on the other hand, I freely admit that I may well be mistaken as to this detail, and after the lapse of so many years, I may have forgotten the relevant facts on this one point. But, as I remember it, the man distinctly uttered the following words, plainly understood by me:

"Battle in strength and strive in guile if you must! But beware the arrow that you shoot at the sky."

I know that that was the message he gave me; and I believe, as surely as I believe in Beauty, in Love, and in Death, that he said these words to me.

As he said them, his eyes seemed to film over. They closed, and his head sank down upon his arms.

Filled with pity, the deepest sympathy and some alarm—not at these supernatural and fantastic happenings—but at the sight of a man dying as I knew this Viking to be, I sprang forward with outstretched hands and . . . he was not there. There was nothing there at all, and I was standing stupidly, my extended arms and empty hands pointing at the equally empty sand at my feet.

Quickly I looked to where the ship should have been tacking toward the horizon; but the ship had now disappeared as well.

This is the simple truth of what happened to me that morning, an exact account of what I saw, of what I heard, and of what I did. I have never forgotten it. And I can still, to this day, see and describe every detail of the ship and of the men: and I can give a faithful eye-witness account of the event—for an eye-witness I was.

The explanation? It is gratuitous folly to try to explain the inexplicable. It is a waste of time, albeit an attractive and interesting way of wasting it, to specu-late concerning the cause of such a phenomenon, to wonder whether the Time Machine slipped a cog, and I then saw something that had actually happened exact-ly there in Space, but a thousand years ago in Time. Doubtless Professor Einstein could shed a little helpful light on the subject.

Did my Unconscious Mind, which, throughout my whole life, has been inclined to be officious and self-assertive, produce from the depths of its immeasurable and inexhaustible store of personal, family, and tribal history, actual knowledge of this real incident and cause the physical retina to behold what was in the mind's eye? Did the time and the place (and the anni-versary, perhaps?) cause the Unconscious Mind to per-form one of its incalculable and apparently miraculous gambols?

Or was it a ghost ship manned by ghosts?

This last suggestion I reject. It was too stout a ship, and the sounds made by its oars and the fall of its yard and sail, too real; the men too loud and hearty and of too too solid flesh; the whole event too simply normal and natural—save for its utter super-normality and super-naturalness.

But for the incident of the man who spoke to me

and died, I should, looking back upon it, endeavour to imagine that I had been hoaxed by a boat-load of fishermen masquerading in strange disguise and in a strange boat.

What, I wonder, would have been the result had I possessed and used a camera when that ship of my Vision dropped sail and grounded gently not fifty yards from where I stood? Presumably the film would have been no less sensitive than the retina of my eye, and would similarly have recorded the image?

Now I have told the true story of this Vision at some length, for two reasons: first, that you may understand how differently constituted is my make-up, physically speaking, from that of the average man; and secondly, that I may tell you of Mark's reaction to my account of it.

He flatly refused to believe a word of my story when I returned to the house and told him all about it!

He did not call me a little liar, as some brothers might have done, but he enjoyed and approved the story *as* a story. When I declared that I was not making up a tale, as I frequently did for his amusement and diversion, but was describing an actual occurrence, he laughed and said,

"Jolly good, old chap!" And whenever, in later years, I again and again described the amazing event, he always adopted the same maddening attitude of,

"Jolly good effort, old chap! Wonderful imagination you've got. You'll be a great writer some day—a novelist."

He would never take the account seriously.

Queer that *my* twin brother should be so utterly devoid of imagination, so matter-of-fact, so stolid and earth-bound.

I'm afraid he is one of those people who believe in what they see, and are really incapable of comprehending anything occult, any such things as telepathy, clairvoyance, second-sight and similar psychic phenomena. I admit that he is extremely intuitive, sympathetic, considerate and all that; but, to be quite frank, he is of commoner clay, dear old Markie; and without being in the least a materialist in the sense of self-indulgence and grossness, he is not only out of touch with the occult, but has always been incapable of believing in its existence.

For example, there was another personal experience of psychic phenomena which showed how closely I was in touch with what is known as the Spirit World, and served to prove that Mark was totally unable to make any contact with it.

This experience was my repeated, indeed regularly recurrent and periodic, hearing of what I must call ghostly sounds; for that is what they were. I never saw anything on these occasions, but I heard something, and always the same thing; and what is also remarkable and interesting—always at the same time, somewhere about five minutes to ten in the evening.

Whenever it happened, I was suddenly aware of what is only to be described as a rushing noise; wind whistling down the corridor outside my bedroom, as though through unglazed or open windows, accompanied by the sound of the pattering feet of dogs, most distinct and audible, and, clearest of all, the thudding of the feet of someone who ran. Not someone shod in modern boots with heavy sole and heel, but in something soft, so that the feet, as I say, thudded or thumped, rather than clattered, making a noise little louder than that of the dogs, but of a heavier and deeper note.

Then, after fleeing along the corridor, the man and dogs rushed through the room in which I slept; and most definitely I felt the coldness of that wind which I could hear.

Thinking back, I realize that I grew up with this phenomenon, so to speak, and accepted it as something which was just as ordinary and natural as the moon-light which shone into my room; something as usual and ordinary as the distant slamming of a door or the sound of voices from the stairs, which voices I recognized as those of my relations or of the servants.

It was only when I was about old enough to go to

Prep School that I began to realize it as something abnormal, and recognized it as a psychic experience. I did not, at that time, use those terms with regard to the matter, of course; but during my first holidays from school, on hearing it all again, I took special notice of the phenomenon and wondered as to its cause.

Of course the Wise Man will at once say,

"Central-heating, my good ass! Wonderful what a performance an accomplished radiator can put up, in the way of funny nocturnal hissings, gurglings, splutterings and rumblings. And some of them do actually clank—just like knights in armour. All very ghostly in the middle of the night."

True. But in that old house of ours, there was no central heating.

"Very well then, my dear chap," replies the Wise Man, "just ordinary water-pipes. They, in their more modest way, can do their bit too, when they give their mind to it. Varying temperatures; or the turning on and off of water-taps far away in some other part of the house."

True again. But there were no water-pipes on that storey, nor on the one below it.

"Well then, what about rats in the wainscoting?" asks the sceptic, and the reply is—Rats! For, intelligent as those rodents undoubtedly are, I never yet heard of a family of rats that staged a wild hurroosh at perfectly regular intervals and always at five minutes to ten at night. Nor have I ever encountered a troupe of rats so gifted that some could whistle like the wind, some give a perfect rendering of the sound made by running hounds, while others could make their footfalls thud as heavily as those of a running man. No.

What about birds in the eaves? Precisely the same objections apply, apart from the fact that there were no eaves adjacent to this room.

I once talked this matter over with a prominent member of the Psychical Research Society, a man with a fine sceptically-inclined mind which could sift evidence; and he having, of course, rejected all the above solutions, suggested gas-pipes. He, personally, had known of a persistent and troublesome ghost that turned out to be water in a gas-pipe which passed under the boards of the haunted room and produced very weird sounds whenever a tap was turned on to light the gas in another room on the same floor.

But this solution also we were unable to accept, by reason of the fact that in this part of the house no gas was laid on; lamps and candles then being our sole means of illumination.

But we did glance at the chimney, metaphorically speaking; starlings, cowls, direction of the wind, and so forth coming under discussion. But suddenly and simultaneously we agreed, with wry smiles, that it would indeed be strange if any of these three agents operated with periodic regularity, and always, and only, at five minutes to ten at night.

No, there was absolutely no getting away from it.

A man and two or more big hounds rushed along the corridor and through my room, accompanied by a cold wind; and the man was dressed in the fashion of a bygone age, with soft-soled shoes upon his feet.

As I grew older, I liked the experience less; or let me say that I began to dislike it a little when I became more and more conscious of it as something super-natural. And it was no use my trying to get to sleep before it happened, because the noise was always sufficient to wake me—if it were the noise that did so, and not what one might call my *awareness*.

What surprises me now is the fact that I never took the trouble to work out the periodicity of the event. It is curious that I did not make a note of dates, and establish to my own satisfaction the incidence, the cycle of recurrence. But I had a pretty good idea of when it was coming; and as I grew older, I rather took to endeavouring to avoid being in the room when it was due to occur. And although it was as real to me, as regular and actual a part of my life as going to church on Sunday or having a half-holiday on Saturday, it never existed at all for Mark.

I only told two other people about it; and I did want him to share this experience with me, for it began to get a little too much for me to cope with alone, if you understand me. I don't know whether I told nobody else because I am naturally secretive; whether it was because I didn't expect to be believed; or whether it was because it was so familiar a phenomenon that, until I was quite a big boy, I simply paid no attention to it.

And when I did tell Mark, he treated it much as he did my account of my experience with the Ship and the dying Viking. Perhaps he did his best to believe that what I said was true. If so, it was obviously without success. For his reaction to my account of my ghostly experience was, at first,

"Quite a good effort, old chap! Throw in a groan or a shout or a bark, next time. . . ."

And when, later, I again and again begged and besought him to believe me, he adopted the attitude of,

"All right, all right! I'll believe you. Honestly, I don't doubt that you think you hear it. But it is pure imagination, you know."

"Right!" said I, one night, in reply to this sort of thing. "Come and hear it for yourself, then."

This he most willingly agreed to do; and for several nights he surreptitiously crept into my room and lay down beside me.

On the third or fourth night of our vigil it happened. The ghostly wind whistled as distinctly as ever did the real wind on a wild rough night; the two or three hounds made as much noise as ever real dogs did when scampering down a corridor; and I could have sworn that a man in soft leather shoes, or only his silken hose, was running with them. Familiar as I was with every sound of it, I once again experienced the physical sensation known as goose-flesh.

"There!" said I to Mark, lying silent beside me, "what do you make of *that?*"

"Of what?" he asked, as the noise died away.

I could have burst into tears of chagrin, disappointment and anger, for he had heard absolutely nothing at all.

I think it was on that night that I first realized that

dear old Mark was not in the same mental category with me. And though I wouldn't have used a disparaging word about him, I did feel that, in comparison with myself, he was, if not something of a clod, at any rate of coarser and commoner clay. It was not his fault, of course. But facts are facts, and there it was. I realized that I had perceptive powers far finer than his, and that I dwelt on a different spiritual and psychic plane. . . . Dear old Markie! . . .

It is amazing how unlike each other, brothers can be, even twin brothers.

Incidentally, one of the other persons whom I told was my father. He was not sceptical or surprised, but was obviously shocked and very grieved in spirit.

"My *poor* Luke!" he cried, and took me in his arms. "But *you're* not the heir. Not *you*, Luke," he kept saying. It was as though a doctor had told him that I was stricken with some incurable and mortal illness.

He would never explain this curious attitude to my psychic experience, and he hated me to speak of it. Very strange . . .

II

Intimations of immorality? Or of a bent? Both, perhaps, for one's bent may be toward immorality. I'm afraid mine was.

Certainly I showed, at a deplorable age, a literary bent which was a tendency toward, and an ability for, the telling of stories. The Young Story-Teller. Already an awful little story-teller at the age of four! An aptitude for the telling of stories . . . an intimation of immorality.

I still consider that my first story, told at the age of four, was a good one, as stories go. Where it failed, as such efforts so often do, was in the author's lack of sufficient knowledge and understanding of his material, particularly his local colour.

My mother had an ermine coat that was her pride and joy. It was a taste in fur undoubtedly shared by moths, as to her infinite regret and annoyance, my mother discovered one day, on going to take out her coat from the cupboard in which it had been hanging.

Hearing the tale of woe which she told to my father, who seemed to bear her suffering bravely; and to maids, relatives, guests, callers and all who had ears to hear and tears to shed, I gathered that The Moth had "been at it," had got into it, had eaten right through it, had made great holes in it. Wondering at the limited and curious tastes of these enterprising yet stoic epicures, I also bore my mother's trouble bravely, and stored this new, interesting and, to me, remarkable, knowledge in the recesses of my receptive and retentive memory, whence later it issued forth to my undoing.

For, as it happened, in that very week, if not on that very day, I fell from grace. Also from a stout if rusty nail on which I had hung for a brief but most unpleasant period, by the seat of my nether garments.

Mark and I had been playing in the grounds when I had tried to climb a fence. Instead of climbing I scrambled, went to drop instead of to climb down, and found progress suddenly arrested by the above-mentioned nail which must have been both long and strong, for it supported my weight and kept me dangling ignominiously, hanging without dignity or grace, in the position nautically known as "bottom upwards."

Stoutly as Mark helped with all his strength and wit, for an age of æons I hung suspended thus in great suspense, the seat of those innominate garments presented to the gaze of the All-Seeing Eye.

Suddenly, and only just in time, I verily believe, to save my life, there was a sound of rending, and no longer was it the seat of the garments that was presented to the Unwinking Eye. I fell and (oh, how symbolically!) I fell on Mark, unhurt—though the wind was knocked from his young carcase. Homeward we made our way, I with keen consciousness of draught, if not of sin.

Fate was unkind, and at the very threshold of the hall, Nemesis overtook me.

"You are to go straight to the drawing-room, Master Luke," said Johnson, our severe, impeccable butler. "Your aunts have come to-day. You too, Master Mark," he added as an after-thought.

This was bad. Very bad.

Putting a bold front upon the matter, since I could do nothing about the back, I entered the drawing-room, marched up to the tea-table and, after behaving as I had been taught, endeavoured to fade unobtrusively away, though only too well I knew that children must be seen more than heard. "Seen" I was, alas, as I retired, and it was impossible for me to leave even these great ladies, dignified and awe-inspiring though they were, in the manner in which one quits the presence of Royalty, by retreating backward down the drawing-room to the far-distant door.

Having backed and backed until I feared that I should run into something and cause catastrophe, perhaps the overthrow of an occasional table laden with fragile bric-à-brac that was precious in my mother's sight, I turned about, and in the very act of doing so, knew that the worst had befallen me. There was a loud and sudden shriek, expressive of incredulity, pain and shock, from Aunt Matilda. For, after all, love me though she might, she was a Victorian spinster lady with a reputation as such to maintain. The other aunt, Elizabeth, cast in a sterner mould, did but call upon her Maker in his manifestation of the Gracious.

"*Good Gracious!*" she cried aloud, "look at the boy's bottom."

"Come here . . . come back!" cried my mother, anguish and horror apparent in her voice. "What on earth . . . ? Why . . . how . . . what have you been doing, Luke?"

Desperate and foolish, I feigned complete ignorance as to the unmentionable.

"Luke! That great rent! Why, the whole *seat* . . ." ejaculated my mother, regaining breath.

And then and there did I enter upon my career as novelist, teller of tales, weaver of imagination's warp and woof.

"Oh, that!" said I. "Oh yes. The Moth, Mother. You know. The moth—er—got at it. A great moth came and ate it, while I was sitting reading."

That first step along the path that, often since, I trod, was innocently taken; and I am certain that, but for Mark, it would have availed me nothing toward escape, and the exercise of what faculty I have in the telling of tales and stories would then and there have been most firmly discouraged. But Mark, as usual, stepped into the—well—the breach. And even as three pairs of hands were raised in horror that one so ingenuous should utter lies so ingenious, my brother, until then silent and not so much ignored as over-looked, lifted up his voice in confirmation of my story.

"*It did!*" he said stoutly. "*I was sitting behind him and I saw it.*"

And the lightning was deflected.

To this day I smile when I think that it was Mark who was the culprit, the little liar, the wicked boy, and upon whom the bolt of punishment descended.

The incident shows how early I displayed my gifts

as a novelist, and how early Mark assumed his rôle of guardian angel and my protector from blame and punishment, where he could possibly assume it all.

In fact, even from this early age, he shielded and spoilt me; and, albeit with kindest intent, began the undermining of my character.

III

It is indeed amazing how unlike each other even twin brothers can be. I should think there never were two who differed more widely than did Mark and I.

For example, he had no literary gift or real appreciation of literature. Poetry gave him no pleasure whatsoever; and he frankly and freely admitted that, with a few exceptions, it bored him to read it. Kipling was about his highest level; and almost the only other poetry of which he knew anything at all were the stock recital-poems and those Shakespearean plays that are treated as lessons and enforced upon reluctant boys as tasks at school.

He found no mental joy and satisfaction in words for their own sake; whereas to me, words are what jewels are to women.

In this respect, I was extremely fortunate in the English Master at our Prep School, a chap we called The Badger. He really loved his subject; and a boy with an appreciative mind, an ear for words and a literary bent was an abiding joy to him. I was his favourite, whereas he rather disliked the stubborn Mark.

With the Headmaster, a very religious man, however, the reverse was the case. He recognized Mark's sterling qualities, and undoubtedly liked him very much indeed—until he fell from grace with a truly hideous thump.

Me he disliked and distrusted from the time I misunderstood a line of his favourite hymn.

Our good Headmaster was very strong on Religion, and took a senior class every Sunday, for what he termed Divinity. A short weekly essay was an unpopular corollary.

On one unfortunate occasion we had to write all we knew about Eli. This did not take us long. Personally I found that my material for a Life of Eli was meagre, so drew upon my imagination and a pretended belief that the line

"His watch the little Levite kept"

disclosed a lapse from grace on the part of Samuel, and the loss of his gold repeater on the part of Eli. The Head was not amused nor I thenceforth approved.

Poor old Mark! He offended the Head too. The cause of *his* fall from grace was not his fault, really. It was partly mine, and partly that of a groom who looked after our two ponies, a very bad little man who, albeit low-browed, squint-eyed, bulbous-nosed, bat-eared, loose-lipped and prognathous-jawed, rejoiced in the incredible name of Valentine Marmaduke Jermyn. Presumably he had been born on St. Valentine's Day; probably his mamma had known and admired a gentleman rejoicing in the name of Marmaduke; and possibly he was a degenerate descendant of some bastard offspring of a Restoration Jermyn.

Anyway, he was a man of limited vocabulary, who referred to a misguided or misbehaving horse—or indeed, to any man, woman or child—as a fool of one unvarying hue. He used this expression (then uncommon, if now a favourite allocution of babes, sucklings and débutantes) impartially, as a condemnation, an approval, an appraisement, a passing reference, or merely as a term of endearment.

When in his company—and I sought his company assiduously, since it was prohibited—I heard the phrase constantly applied, whether to my father's hunter that he loved; my mother's carriage-horses that he admired; the governess-cart hack that he hated; our riding-ponies that he despised; the Vicar of whom he disapproved; the head coachman whom he feared; the village publican whom he revered; Sir Garnet Wolseley under whom he had served but whom he had never met socially; or to his own wife whom he tolerated when sober.

Since I had been strictly prohibited from unnecessary intercourse with Valentine Marmaduke Jermyn, it was really my disobedience, assisted by Mark's treacherous memory and slight mental slowness, that led to his own dreadful downfall; and it was just too bad that it was the Head himself who was the astounded and affronted witness of Mark's unintentional crime.

Now the Head was a fanatical Shakespearean, and did his utmost to give the young barbarians a play for their edification, every term, and more than a glimpse of the literary wonders and glories to which, had they the perception and intelligence, they might be the heirs. It was no fault of his if any boy went on from that admirable Prep School to his Public School under the impression that Shakespeare was a weary task, an unfortunately necessary evil, something to be "done" and happily forgotten thereafter. So, each term, we read a Shakespearean play with The Badger, the English Master, worked it up, were allotted parts, if worthy, and at the end of term, the Head would devote a solemn evening to seeing and hearing us enact it, with such costume and scenery as we could conceive and procure.

Macbeth was the play that particular term, and Mark, being one of the most outstanding and commanding personalities of the top form, had been miscast by The Badger to act the title-rôle.

It was really a combination of Macbeth, Valentine Marmaduke Jermyn, and my own evil suggestion that caused poor Mark's downfall.

I can see it so clearly to this day, and smile at the memory. Three boys, most weirdly garbed and be-wigged, seated about a camouflaged waste-paper basket, had gabbled, or rather very creditably chanted, their incantation as the three witches:

> *"Double, double toil and trouble,*
> *Fire burn and cauldron bubble."*

Another boy, listening in the wings for his cue, tottered on as a wounded soldier from the battle-field, and Mark, with dramatic gesture, raised his hand to shade his eyes, stared, gazing upon him; and instead of declaiming Shakespeare's line,

"*What bloody man is that?*"

Mark cried aloud and ringingly, "*What bloody fool is that?*"

Nor was it until a shuddering gasp went up from the assembled school, and the Headmaster, rising in his wrath, turned upon Mark like a wounded lion, that the poor old chap realized that, in all his lovely honesty and innocence, he had quoted me (who had so often quoted Jermyn) instead of Shakespeare.

I don't think the Head ever forgave him, for he never spoke really kindly to Mark again. And this so worried dear old Markie that I nearly went to the Head and told him that it was partly my fault inasmuch as, when we were privately rehearsing the play, and I was hearing Mark's part, I had always made a point of thus correcting him when he followed the true Shakespearean reading!

But I didn't do it, nor did Mark expect me to. As a matter of fact, he would not have allowed it; wouldn't for one moment have considered my interviewing the Head and explaining that I was partly to blame, for he knew how I hated that sort of thing. And besides, I'm quite sure it gave Mark tremendous pleasure to take the blame whenever he could. And who was I to deny Mark pleasure?

Looking back, I can see that I must have afforded him lots of that kind of satisfaction.

Yes, from very early days, although almost invariably I meant no harm and did no intentional wrong, I got into trouble incessantly; and incessantly Mark either got me out of it or shouldered as much of the blame as he could secure for himself. He enjoyed doing it.

There was the terrible case of the explosion in church.

Who would have imagined that so well-meaning, right-minded and innocent a child as I was, would have caused a tremendous detonation in a church, and during Divine Service?

Yet such was my fate.

Had it occurred elsewhere, the adjective "tremen-dous" would not be quite the *mot juste:* but in church, during Morning Prayer, and at a moment of almost perfect silence, the explosion was tremendous. It was shattering, ear-splitting.

Why should such things happen to a virtuous small boy whose fervent desire was to enjoy life, incur the dislike of no-one and the blame for nothing; to seek peace and ensue it, and go on his way rejoicing?

Now, a favourite toy of the period was a pistol that, while neither attempting nor professing to expel any sort of projectile, fired a percussion cap. These pistols ranged from penny cast-iron affairs, at one end of the scale, that fired a cap consisting of a tiny square of pink paper in the middle of which was a small brown spot of some detonating compound, to, at the other end, a very colourful imitation of the real pistols of the day, and firing a cap identical with that used in the cartridge of the genuine fire-arm. This cap was a thing resembling a tiny copper thimble which fitted over a steel projection or nipple that stuck up from the barrel just beneath the hammer.

To my boundless joy and utter undoing, my adored mother, who spoilt me shamelessly and most delight-fully, gave me one of these magnificent dummy pistols from the very apex of the scale, and a box of percus-sion caps. The thing was in no wise dangerous, for though it looked exactly like a Wild West "gun," the nipple was not bored, and in any case, save for an inch of the muzzle, the iron barrel was solid all through. This naturally made it a fine heavy weapon, as within a week of possessing it, I was to realize only too well.

What a pity it is that adults cannot remember, or rather recapture, the ineffable joy that children feel on receiving some coveted object; a thing so insignificant to the grown-up, so colossal to the child. We should be more concerned to provide that joy more often if we more often tried to re-live our own childhood.

In this instance, I honestly and truly believe that I

would have given a finger, if not a hand, a pint of blood, and almost anything that I possessed in the world, rather than have lost that pistol.

I was literally never parted from it; for it went to bed with me, and lay beneath my pillow, its butt ready to the grasp of my hand. And at the slightest sound, perhaps of someone shutting a door down below, I would stealthily draw the pistol from beneath the pillow, cock it, and peer into the gloom.

What was it? A questing leopard; a great python; a stealthy dacoit; a Red Indian; or a mere burglar, masked and horrific?

Then with infinite care, the hammer would be lowered on to the percussion cap and the pistol replaced, to be withdrawn as I woke at dawn—the hopeless dawn that found me sitting beneath a tree which, with my broken leg, I could not climb, my back against the trunk, watching and waiting while the circle of wolves closed in, and their red mouths and evil glinting eyes drew nearer and nearer . . .

And when those holidays ended and Mark and I had to return to school, my pistol went with me, smuggled, to my great discomfort, inside my exiguous trousers: and for less than a week, it was the admiration of all beholders, among whom masters were not included, as they were given no opportunity of admiring it. High as I had hitherto stood in the estimation of the other fellows, my standing in the school improved yet further. For those few days I was almost as happy at school as I had been at home. When in class and unable to handle, I might say to fondle, my pistol, I thought of it the more.

Of course, it went abroad with me upon our walks, and in a rash and foolish moment, I, impulsive ever, decided that there was no reason why it should not go with me to Church, this being the early days before our School Chapel was built.

It went—in my overcoat pocket, into which it fitted but ill.

The temperature of the church that morning was unexpectedly high, and grew steadily higher, whether by reason of excessive zeal on the part of him who stoked the furnace in the crypt, or because of the coming out of the sun and the waxing of its heat. At any rate, as we settled down before the sermon, a nod and a whisper from the master in charge of us encouraged such as so desired, to remove their overcoats. Many of us preferred to do so, I among them.

Folding my coat once, I put it over the back of my chair, seated myself and, a minute later, did, in common with every other member of that large congregation, suddenly leap high at the sound of a crashing, shattering and rending explosion!

My heavy pistol had fallen from my overcoat pocket, and the first part of it that struck the stone floor must have been the back of the hammer, for never before or afterwards did that pistol go off with anything like so loud a report. It was terrific, ear-splitting, and of course, the sound was infinitely greater inside the closed and echoing church where, through the long-drawn aisle and fretted vault, there pealed that fearful noise.

The whole school was paraded, before lunch, in the Hall. . . .

I really don't think that the Head could, for one moment, have supposed that so outrageous and foul a deed was intentional. But he behaved exactly as though it had been; and as though both he and Mark knew it to have been not only intentional but premeditated. Had a boy risen from his seat, pointed a pistol at him, or at the very preacher in the pulpit, and fired it off, he could hardly have taken a more serious view of the matter. But he kept on what was, of course, absolutely safe ground by defining the crime as "being in possession of a pistol and of taking it, loaded, to Church"—which undoubtedly *Mark* had done.

Or so he promptly said!

Although words would have failed me to tell the Head so, I should as soon have contemplated taking a police-whistle to Church and blowing it with all my might in the middle of a sermon, as taking my pistol to Church, had I for one second envisaged the possibility of so ghastly a contretemps. I explained this fully, afterwards, to Mark—as I was spared an interview with the Head—and all that he could reply was,

"Well . . . Shut up . . . And don't take a pistol to Church again, or a police-whistle either."

I stoutly objected to Mark's interference, and wanted to go to the Head and confess that the pistol was mine; but, as Mark at once pointed out to me, he would cop it most frightfully for having told a thumping lie in saying that the pistol was his.

Poor old Markie! . . .

Had he anything to say before the passing of sentence, asked the Head?

Mark had nothing to say, especially as the offence of which he was accused, and to which he pleaded guilty, was the taking of the pistol to Church. Whether the explosion were an accident or not wasn't the question. But there could be no question as to the truth of the indictment as the Head framed it. A loaded pistol had been taken to Church, and Mark had confessed to having taken it—before I could get to my feet and utter a word.

So the Headmaster, as Jury, found Mark guilty; and the Headmaster, as Judge, sentenced him to the cat, to a term of imprisonment with hard labour, and to the confiscation of his property; and the Headmaster, as Lord High Executioner, carried out the sentence.

The cat had more than nine tails, being a birch—and it was a bad business. I think I can honestly plead that it hurt me more than it did Mark . . . No? . . . Perhaps not! . . . Imprisonment in an empty class-room, while other boys played football, and to work at the hard labour of writing an imposition was worse, and I must in decency visit him in gaol and spend some time with him.

But in point of fact, the worse of all fell on me, as was only just, for the pistol was confiscated. This was, I think, the greatest of the sorrows up to that time suffered by me, a child almost unacquainted with grief.

It was quite a bad week. It must have been, to

remain thus clearly in my memory which has had so many other and so much worse sufferings to drive it out or obliterate it.

But there were compensations. Out of evil cometh good, almost inevitably.

And in this darkness of suffering, childish, but as real in its degree as was the agony of Samson, there shone a light, that light of human kindness that is the true *lux mundi,* and shines farther than does any other light, and gives far greater warmth.

Mark, as so often before and since, was its source, for he suffered with me and for me in my mourning and my loss, and was my comforter. Nay more, for whether aware or not of the excellent proverb which states that Pity without Relief is like mustard without beef, he gave me concrete pledges of his sympathy—his own little pistol and caps, bought by himself with his own money.

Compared with my own, my loved, my lost, this pistol was but a poor thing, albeit double-barrelled. Cast-iron in all its works and parts, it resembled a real pistol only in shape, and that distantly. Beside mine, it was without form and void, and it fired mere, miserable pink paper caps. But poor old Mark loved it, and this giving was the token and the measure of his great goodness of heart. I could not accept it because, in the first place—and I hope that this feeling really took the first place—it was a poor thing but his own, almost as dear to Mark as my wonderful pistol was to me; and in the second place, I could not accept it because really it was so very inferior a substitute.

But for a day or two I kept it. In Mark's presence I used and praised it, and going for a walk with the rest of the school on a Sunday afternoon, I carried it in my overcoat pocket, and used it when we reached the Common, our Sunday destination, in repelling an attack of spear-brandishing savages upon our stockade.

An excellent game this, always popular, and of my very own invention. About a magnificent old tree the inappropriate authorities had erected, for its protection, a particularly futile and ineffectual ring of chestnut-wood stakes, joined by a single strand of wire. Inside this, those who possessed pistols and caps, formed a thin pink line of heroes, few but staunch, and were promptly and grievously and over-whelmingly attacked by lesser breeds without the fire-arms.

If a foeman rushed at you with brandished spear, which might be a raspberry-cane, a light walking-stick or anything else of that nature, and could prod you in the chest ere you fired your pistol, you were, in honour bound to collapse upon the bloodless trodden earth, writhe, groan and die.

If, on the other hand, you fired your pistol as he rushed at you, that histrionic duty was his. Inasmuch as our caps rarely missed fire, the garrison usually won and, ere the fight ended, the enemy dead were thickly piled about the stockade.

I loved this game and so did Mark.

And an interesting point about this pistol incident is the fact that it was I, and not Mark, who was oppressed by a sense of injustice. Why should I lose my pistol, which was the thing that I cherished beyond all else that I possessed? I remember that the text of the sermon in Church on the following Sunday was that deeply intriguing and somewhat sinister question,

"*Were they sinners above all men upon whom fell the tower in Siloam?*"

Was I a sinner above all boys, that this blow should have fallen upon me; that my pistol should have been taken from me?

It struck me, a schoolboy in my earliest teens, even then, as unsatisfactory that towers and blows should fall upon some and not upon others, upon the just and the unjust alike. Were they sinners? And if not, why were they the chosen victims of this catastrophic mischance? Or were they chosen victims? Because, if so, it was not a mischance. And if it were not a mischance it was intentional, and if Christ Himself had to ask the question "*Were they sinners beyond other men*" there would appear to have been doubt in His own mind on the subject.

The question remains in the air, looming portentous and vitally important. Are we victims of accident and chance? Are we playthings of a mocking Fate, or the cherished children of God, rewarded and punished fairly and exactly, according to our deeds and misdeeds?

Were they sinners beyond other men? A hard saying, and, what is worse, a fundamental question asked by God Himself—and left unanswered.

Was I a sinner beyond other boys? Of course I was not.

I think it was while pondering the text of this sermon that, of such Faith, Hope and Charity as I possessed, Hope superseded Faith and took the leading place.

By some, it may scarcely be believed that so young a child would be interested, nay, arrested, by a question of this nature.

The fact remains. I was.

And I accepted the blows of Fate and of my Headmaster as in the nature of things, inevitable, ineluctable, falling upon the good man and upon the wicked.

Before I was much older I decided that this, though a dreadful thing, was to be recognized and dealt with wisely; that since one could not be justified of one's Faith, and could only cling to Hope, one must also help oneself; one must keep one's eye upon all Towers of Siloam, watching lest they totter; and when they did so, stand from under. If the eighteen upon whom the Tower fell were not sinners above all men, they were, at any rate, supine and fatalistic beyond such men as knew enough to avoid insecure Towers, and to go while the going was good. Without putting my thought into words, I did then and there resolve to be a nineteenth, so to speak, where Towers of Siloam were concerned. And inasmuch as the rain, on good authority, falleth upon the just and the unjust, I resolved to preserve at least enough sense to come in out of the rain.

Yes, that explosive Sunday together with the next, and its disturbing sermon (so poignantly appropriate to me, who had just lost my pistol), marked, I believe, a turning-point in my life, and had a great effect upon my character.

Faith? What about faith in Life's Towers of Siloam?

Hope? Hope they won't fall on you.

Charity? In this case, charity was not called upon to function. Toward the Head there was no need to exercise forgiveness as well as the compulsory forbearance, since one realized that he was but an instrument; a noble, if necessary, instrument in the hand of that same capricious Fate that, either behind God's back or with God's knowledge and consent, allowed the Tower to fall upon the just and unjust men of Siloam, and again, this blow to fall upon me—in spite of Mark's altruism.

Yes, I decided, walking home from Church, beside Mark, if Heaven helps anybody it is those who help themselves.

Ever since then I have helped myself to the best of my ability, and gratefully accepted any outside help, whether from God or Mark.

And I did so when we went on from Prep School to Public School, and again when from Public School we went on to Oxford.

Mark and I were inseparable, I with my quicker intelligence usually the leader, Mark with his unfailing loyalty the follower, and, with his solid stolid love and devotion, only too often the scapegoat.

All very nice, but all very bad for me, of course, and a continuation of the spoiling that I got from my mother, and to a slightly greater extent, from my father, and after my mother's death, from Athene if not from Rosanne. As a matter of fact, it had always been more or less the same from everybody, with the exception of the hard-faced hag, my Aunt Elizabeth, the Headmaster of my Prep School, Rosanne perhaps, and one or two other rare people.

Mother always let me have my way, and indeed saw that I had it. I must never be thwarted, and whatever I said or did was right, when it wasn't marvellous. And on those occasions when things were not right, Mark must have been at the bottom of whatever was wrong.

Poor old Mark! For him life was one damned stile after another—and I the lame dog he helped over them all . . .

§2

And speaking of help, I must speak of Rosanne. For her other name was helpfulness. She was a marvel; and I really think she was never so happy as when joining in our plots and plans and multifarious activities; her assistance and support being the more welcome in that she was almost as good as a boy. She was a very attractive kid, and not the less intriguing because she could be an aggravating little bitch when she felt like it.

To be quite fair, I must admit that this was only when she was made to feel like it; and as a rule, it was I who was the cause of her feeling that way. We squabbled a lot, partly because I loved to tease her, and partly because she always took Mark's side when he and I differed. Almost from the time of her coming to Courtesy Court, we regarded her as a sister and, paradoxically, treated her as a brother.

She was like a boy in her code of honour, and was quite unfeminine in her sense of fairness, in her straight, lucid, and logical mind; in many of her interests; in her preference for out-door things; and particularly in her preferring our company to that of girls.

Nevertheless, I liked Giulia, of whom we saw nearly as much, even better than Rosanne, for she was more appreciative, more understanding, more of an artist.

To be frank and self-critical, it is possible that the chief reason for my great affection for Giulia was the fact that she was my perfect audience.

It was to Giulia I turned for approbation; it was to Rosanne I went for help.

From Giulia I was certain of getting what I wanted— neat and in full measure. From Rosanne I was equally certain of getting what I wanted—but not without criticism. If Giulia was honey, what was Rosanne? Carbolic soap? Yes, not a bad simile; helpful, cleansing, purifying, very good for you. Perhaps Giulia was something of a luxury and Rosanne, at times, a good deal of a necessity.

Nevertheless, there were times when I hated Rosanne; and if Giulia were occasionally cloying, she was never detestable.

But always, even when I told her that, in bringing her to Courtesy Court my father had put a critic on my hearth and domesticated my Recording Angel, I admitted that he had done a wonderful thing for us all when, having married Athene, he brought her and Rosanne home.

I realized, even then, that Athene's money made a marvellous difference to Courtesy Court, if it did not actually save it; and though only a boy between Prep School and Public School, I very warmly welcomed the fact and appreciated Rosanne. Within limits. Out of doors she was splendid, delighted to fag for us, to take second place as a member of the inferior sex, to play minor rôles and to do as she was told.

Indoors it wasn't so good, for she held her own— and something that hitherto had been mine.

The extraordinary thing about Rosanne was that she was so sterling, so clean, simple, straight and honest, in view of what her mother was and what her upbringing had been.

It is really very difficult to say anything about Athene. *De mortuis nil nisi bonum* is bunk; but there are things one doesn't want to say about persons who have been kind, even when they have been inordinately so. For the trouble with Athene was that she was a damned sight too kind. To me, at any rate. Especially when I came home, very grown up and all that, at the end of my first year at Oxford. It was partly on that account that I pushed off to Paris. What amazing and unexpected consequences spring from small causes—if one is to call that a small cause.

But for Athene's utterly uncontrolled, indiscriminate, and promiscuous what shall I say—self-expression in love—I should not be sitting here in my self-made paper prison.

In a way, it was a terrible thing that she did; unthinkable; an incident and theme worthy of a Greek tragedy and comparable with the *Œdipus* situation. And yet at the same time—paradox again—Athene was a good woman, to the extent that she was of loving-kindness, good-will and generosity all compact. There never lived a more liberal soul. The trouble was that she was too liberal.

She was a dear kind friend to her friends, though over-kind to her men friends. She was an excellent wife to my father, who only wanted to be left alone in his selfish peace while somebody ran his house, paid his bills, adorned his table, entertained his guests, looked after his sons, and relieved him of what he regarded as the carking cares and crushing burdens of widowerhood in a big house.

She was a good mother, to the extent that she gave Rosanne everything except a good example, and grudged her nothing but her time and the care, guardianship, teaching and training that only a mother can give.

She was an excellent mistress (here the fault lies with the English language and not with me, if my meaning is obscure) for the servants gave her a first-class character, and never contemplated dismissing her from her position as their employer. Even Johnson, who had really loved my mother, was quickly won over, forgave her for being a foreigner and an incomer, and approved her generous management of the house.

She was an admirable hostess, and soon became very popular in the County.

In short, there was nothing whatsoever wrong with Athene except that she was an utterly amoral unprincipled wicked woman.

Amazing that Rosanne should have been not only her daughter but the product of her upbringing!

Well—I will only say that Athene spoilt me and not

that she might have ruined my character altogether had I not escaped her.

She spoilt me, and I loved it and loved her sympathy with my temperament, and her encouragement of my gifts. She understood me better than Mark or Rosanne did, and it is to those who understand us that we feel the highest gratitude. She really loved my poems and stories, would listen to me by the hour— and ask for more. Dear Athene—my evil genius . . .

IV

No, in my rôle of poet and juvenile novelist, or shall I say story-teller, it was not from my twin-brother nor from Rosanne that I got understanding, sympathy and encouragement, any more than in my manifestations as a clairvoyant and psychic. It was from Athene and also from Giulia Brent-Grayleigh, a child who, if she did not exactly grow up with us, grew up very near us. Very near to me, certainly. How far this was by reason of the fact that she was so appreciative an audience, so much in sympathy, and of such similar tastes and disposition, I do not know. No one enjoyed my stories more than she did.

Giulia, as well as believing in my psychic experiences, was always most encouraging to my literary efforts, professing to find, and I think really finding, greater pleasure in the stories that I told and afterwards wrote, than in any that she found in the books and magazines that she read.

Not so Rosanne. She was critical, and instead of accepting the story as a story, the fancies as facts, and the poetic licence of the weaver of tales as permissible, she must put an unerring finger on improbabilities, discrepancies and inconsistencies. Moreover, if Giulia were over-endowed with imaginative power, Rosanne was a little lacking in imagination, and much too literal. Not only was she an unsparing critic, but she made Mark critical, Mark who until her coming had held the admirable creed that whatever Luke did was perfect, whatever Luke said was right, and that whatever Luke produced was above criticism. (In point of fact it usually was above Mark's.)

Right from the days of my Moth story, I had been noted as a weaver of spells and a spinner of tales, a fact that accounted for some of my great popularity among our friends at home, and in our circle at School. I was in great demand in the dormitories, both at Prep and Public Schools.

To Giulia and to Mark, before Rosanne's coming, my stories were joys undiluted, shining examples of perfect entertainment which no breath of criticism must ever dim.

Rosanne changed all that.

Particularly I remember my wonderful story of the Wolves and the Three Children in the sleigh. We all knew the story of the Faithful Russian Servant who saved his master's life by throwing himself to the Wolves, and had read it *ad nauseam:* but I produced a brighter and a better story in which Lukeovitch, accompanied by Markovitch and Rosannski, drove a *troika* sleigh across the boundless Steppes, pursued by a tireless pack of Abominable Wolves. Nearer and nearer they came. Slower and slower went the weary horses. The children's ammunition was exhausted. Everything that could be thrown out for the distraction and hindering of the wolves had been thrown.

Must they all die? Should Lukeovitch sacrifice himself for them, and leap to a dreadful death?

No, he was the only one of the three who could drive and control the maddened horses.

Should he sacrifice one of these? He must. With swift strokes of his hunting-knife the boy severed the traces; and the horse, instead of galloping gaily off, directly it was released from the burden of the sledge, unaccountably fell behind and was pulled down by the wolves, its piercing screams curdling the blood of Lukeovitch, Markovitch and Rosannski who had loved the poor faithful animal.

The delaying device gave but a temporary respite. A second horse was sacrificed. Again the relief was but brief; and now they had but the one horse to take them for the hundred versts that lay between them and home.

Now the wolves had drawn level, were beginning to forge ahead, and soon the leaders of the pack would spring upon the remaining horse.

Suddenly Lukeovitch, to the horror of his companions, again drew his hunting-knife, severed the remaining traces and released the third horse.

"You've killed us!" cried Markovitch.

"Leap out!" cried Lukeovitch as the sleigh slowed down; and, when they did so, putting forth all his tremendous strength, Lukeovitch, with a superhuman effort tipped the sleigh up on one side, so that it stood erect.

"Quick! Under!" he shouted, as he began to lower it to the ground, and the other two, realizing what he was doing, flung themselves down in the snow, as Lukeovitch, crouching beneath the sleigh, lowered it over their three prostrate bodies.

They were saved. . . .

There was breathless silence, as I finished my tale.

"Oh no, they weren't," said Rosanne suddenly. "They were suffocated, and died miserably. Just as well, perhaps, for they'd only have been frozen to death. Or if they had huddled together and kept warm, they'd have starved," she said. "Sad."

Little bitch. How I hated her.

I remember, too, my almost uncontrollable anger when she brought me down from the heights of the creator's joy, after my story of the noble young Trumpeter who saved his Officer's life at the cost of his own, in the massacre of the Khyber Pass.

His name was Lucas and he was the son of the grey-haired coachman who had so long served Sir Markham's family.

The fugitives from Kabul were pouring through the Khyber Pass; the Battery of which Sir Markham Tuyler's son was Captain, suddenly came under heavy fire from the hordes of Afghan sharp-shooters concealed along the rocky sides of the gorge; the horses plunged in wild confusion and fell, dead or wounded, blocking the passage of the guns. Gunners and bombardiers fell from their seats on the limbers; men ran hither and thither, some trying to escape, some trying to get at the enemy, others trying to manhandle the guns.

On to a boulder sprang Captain Sir Markham Tuyler and shouted clear directions. Upon him the

Afghans, who were picking off the officers with fiendish cunning, turned their fire, and he fell wounded. Soon they would swoop down, hacking and stabbing, slaying and slaughtering, but specially reserving the officers for hideous tortures by the women-folk.

Lucas, his Trumpeter, sprang to his side.

What could Trumpeter Lucas do? He gazed into the face of his beloved officer, as he held his water-bottle to his pale lips.

"Leave me, leave me," murmured Captain Sir Markham. "Save yourself."

Instead of obeying him, Lucas sprang to his feet, hastily stripped off his uniform and laid it on the ground. Then, with unexpected gentleness, he unbuttoned the handsome, heavily braided tunic of his wounded officer.

With almost womanly care he undressed him and re-dressed him in his own plain uniform of a private soldier. Having done so, he hastily donned the officer's kit, his gold-braided tunic with its furred dolman and his tall, plumed busby.

Scarcely had he finished, when, with a wild yell, the hordes of tribesmen sprang to their feet and rushed down the gully brandishing their tulwars, and shouting "Kill! Kill!"

"Keep the officers alive!" roared their leader. And desperately as he fought with his master's sword, Lucas was overborne, struck down, seized and carried off. Of his fate let us not even think.

When the relief party from Jellalabad, led by Dr. Brydon, reached the pass, Captain Sir Markham Tuyler was still alive. He recovered—but he never smiled again.

A long silence.

It was broken by Rosanne.

"Onions!" she said. "Never smiled? I should have thought he'd have laughed all day. What did the fool Trumpeter want to put his officer's uniform on at all for? Couldn't he have scrammed—bunked in his little short shirt?"

I could have wrung her neck, a fact which I did not

withhold from her; and a deed to which Giulia would have raised no objection.

§2

As well as enjoying my stories and unreservedly praising them, no one understood, or more fully believed in, my occult experiences than did Giulia.

We shared one together. And to be quite frank and honest, as I desire to be, we shared on that occasion more than a psychic experience; for psychic in inception, it proceeded, young and passionate as we both were, through spiritual, emotional and physical phases to a passionate conclusion.

I cannot remember when I first knew Giulia Brent-Grayleigh. We probably exchanged bubbling salutations from our respective perambulators, but I have known her as long as I have known anybody, and, save for Mark and Rosanne, as well as I have ever known anybody. Better perhaps. It was truer of her and me than it was of Mark and me, that we were, even as kids, two minds with but a single thought, so extraordinarily well did we get on together, so delighted was she to do anything that I was doing, and so content, indeed happy, merely to be in my company. She was the only person except Mark, whom I ever told of my Viking-ship experience. This she fully accepted and understood, as she did that of the man and hounds who rush down the corridor and through my bedroom.

There was something un-English about Giulia, which is not remarkable in view of the fact that her mother was an Italian lady *née* Contessa della Mirandola. Giulia was all that is the opposite of stolid, stupid, slow-witted, conventional; nothing of the English bread-and-butter Miss about her at all.

The shared experience to which I refer happened on the occasion of her birthday celebrations, her eighteenth, I fancy. Being an only daughter, her parents made a tremendous fuss of her, and every year there were great doings at Grayleigh House on this anniversary, the place being filled with young people. On this occasion, there was the usual gay house-party and dance in the evening; and although we lived so near, Mark and I had to join the house-party, for Giulia wouldn't hear of our merely coming over for the Birthday Ball.

Grayleigh House is a pre-Elizabethan building, one wing of which is quite old, the remains of a house rather rich in historical associations. General Sir Henry and Lady Brent-Grayleigh did things very well, and it was reluctantly, though sleepily, that the party broke up, and those who were staying in the house dispersed to their respective rooms. Mark and I were in the old wing of which the upstairs floor consisted of a row of bedrooms so numerous and small as to suggest that they probably had been at one time a monks' dormitory.

This wing had character and atmosphere, both of which appealed to me enormously. I could feel that I had lived and slept here hundreds of years ago, or that if I had not done so, an ancestor of mine had, which in point of fact was quite probable.

Having undressed, I blew out the candles on the ancient stone overmantel, yawned my way to bed, blew out the remaining candle on the little table beside me, and fell asleep almost as my head touched the pillow.

I was awakened by someone gently shaking me.

"Sh-h-h," whispered Giulia, who was standing over me and dropping candle-wax on to my bed.

"What's up, Giu?" I whispered.

"The ghost. . . . I'm frightened."

This woke me up quite effectively. I sat up, rubbed my eyes and pulled myself together. Giulia wasn't a liar (at least, she didn't tell me lies) and I knew all about the Grayleigh House ghost.

"Seen it?" I asked.

"No. Same thing again. This is the third time I have heard it. . . . I had gone to sleep and was awakened by a noise in the room."

"What sort of noise?"

"Somebody crying. A woman, I should think, sobbing as though her heart would break."

In view of my own experiences of hearing inexplicable sounds, I forbore to suggest radiators, water-pipes, gas-pipes, chimneys, birds, cowls and such origins, because they did not apply to this wing of Grayleigh House any more than they did to my room at home.

"What did you do?"

"Although I've heard it before, I was too petrified to do anything, at first. She just went on sobbing. It was absolutely clear and realistic. Then I was certain there was somebody alive and real in the room. One of the girls upset about something."

"Why didn't you strike a match?"

"Just what I did do, because she had a catch in her breath, just like Beatrice Miller has when she cries, and I was reassured. I felt quite angry with her, coming and frightening me like that, and I said, *'Oh, shut up, Beatrice!'* and felt for the matches. And then, *'Is that you, Beechy?'* I said as I struck a match, and—there was nobody there. I managed to light the candle, and the room was quite empty."

"Did the crying stop?" I asked.

"It faded away as though, not liking the light, she had gone out of the room."

"Here, put that candle down. . . . How your hand is shaking. . . . You'll get your death of cold. . . . Come in here." And as Giulia sat down beside me, I raised the warm bed-clothes and put them about her shoulders.

Turning gratefully, she freed one arm and pulled the eiderdown about us both. Putting my arms round her, I hugged her to me until her shivering stopped.

"Oh, Luke," she whispered. "I . . . I'm so frightened," and raised her arms about my neck.

"You were, you mean, silly," I said, and gave her a brotherly hug and kiss.

The hug was returned with interest. The kisses grew less brotherly.

We sat for I know not how long. . . .

"Darling, *darling* Luke," murmured Giulia between kisses. In fact, she only took her lips from mine to whisper endearments, until suddenly,

"My feet are cold," she said, making me feel

thoughtless and inconsiderate, a selfish brute indeed, for mine were warm enough.

I raised the bed-clothes and Giulia crept into bed with me.

Next day, as Giulia and I sat, after lunch, ensconced in a deep arm-chair in a corner of the library, where for a while we should be undisturbed, I told her that I wanted to spend a night in her bedroom, to see whether I too might experience a psychic manifestation. Inasmuch as Mark completely failed to hear my ghostly hounds, I had a theory that, just as beauty is in the eye of the beholder, so ghostly experience is in the capacity of the observer. In other words, one man can see a ghost, while another cannot; just as one ear can hear and appreciate the beauties of a Chopin Prelude or a Bach Fugue where another ear cannot. Giulia was psychic and so was I. Giulia had heard, but not seen, the ghost. Perhaps I could hear it, and possibly I could see it too.

Promptly she flung her arms about my neck and pressed her soft moist lips against mine.

"Darling, darling Luke," she whispered; and it was not until I had repeated the statement, that she grasped that what I wanted to see and hear was a discarnate ghost and not a fleshly Giulia. I, with some difficulty, forbore to point out that Giulia I could see as often as I liked, possibly oftener, whereas occasions for encountering a disembodied lady of bygone years, a wraith from beyond the centuries, a relic of old unhappy far-off things, were all too rare.

Did I really and truly want to see, and perhaps hear, a ghost? asked Giulia, in a little hurt withdrawn voice, as she arose from my lap.

Yes, most definitely I did; and if she had been speaking the truth, and the ghost had manifested in that room last night, there was at least a chance that it might repeat the visitation to-night. There was a still greater chance that it wasn't so much a case of the ghost visiting the room and making its presence known to the occupant, as of a person of receptive and perceptive psychic powers visiting the room and being aware of the ghost that always inhabited it.

Giulia pondered for a moment, gnawing her little finger-nail.

"All right," she said, "we'll go to bed as usual, after the doings to-night, and change rooms when everything is quiet."

Some time after two o'clock that night, Giulia crept into my room in nightdress and wrapper, and I, pulling on my dressing-gown, hurried off—to Giulia's ill-concealed chagrin.

I lay down in her warm bed and remained awake for I know not how long. I probably fell asleep, for I was suddenly aroused, if not awakened, by Giulia acting the goat in the darkness of the room.

I might mention, by the way, that this was not her own bedroom. It may have been due to the upheaval caused by the big influx of guests for the birthday celebrations, that she had turned out of her own. It may, on the other hand, have been by reason of the fact that the room next to the one allotted to me was vacant and available. Anyway, it was a room very rarely used, and carefully not alluded to as the haunted chamber.

I was a little bit annoyed that she should have come and played the fool when I was really engaged in a little private and practical psychical research on my own account, and it was with somewhat bad grace that I observed, as I felt for the matches,

"Oh, *very* funny! Very humorous! Great joke, Giulia. I feel a laugh coming on."

Sulkily striking a match and lighting the candle, I saw that the room was empty. And I heard the sound of a deep sob and a catch in the breath, as some invisible person turned, went toward the door, apparently through it and down the corridor, the sounds of suppressed sobbing dying away as he or she did so.

I found that I was trembling, but my emotion was not fear or horror so much as excitement. I experienced the same phenomenon later when under heavy fire, and nothing was further from my thoughts than fear and terror.

What an extraordinary thing that twice I should have so distinctly heard what were, without the shadow of a doubt, ghostly sounds, and yet on neither occasion did I see the ghost associated with them.

Having slowly returned to earth and to my normal calm, I got out of Giulia's bed and went back to my room. For the sake of added certainty and making absolute assurance doubly sure, I accused her of having played the fool and the ghost, an accusation which she warmly denied. And, as I have said, Giulia never lied to me.

I apologized, and my apology was more than warmly received. It was not till daylight that Giulia could contemplate returning to the haunted room.

§3

I love to get the *mot juste* and the apt simile. I think I have both if I say that Giulia was my nightingale and Rosanne my lovely mocking-bird. Giulia so sweet, so tuneful, so alluring to the poetic soul; Rosanne so piquant, so stimulating, so aggravating.

Giulia was like a lovely songster, and I, for one, but rarely had enough of her sweet music.

Rosanne's music might be charming, delightful, soothing even, for a bird of so many notes must inevitably be attractive; at times with the attraction of sheer delightfulness, at others with that of the unexpected. Rosanne was always *en surprise,* at once sweet and savoury; sweet, sharp and vinegary; sweet, peppery and burning, but never cloying, uninteresting or dull. Natheless, it is not always pleasing to the palate to encounter cayenne where you expected jam; to find an onion in your apple-dumpling, chillies or garlic in your cream-bun. Nor should an apparent glass of sherry prove to be a prairie-oyster or a dose of quinine.

And yet here is the strange thing. It was Rosanne and not Giulia whom I wanted to please. Giulia I pleased inevitably, invariably. Rosanne I did not. For her to be pleased, one had to please her. Giulia was always pleased with *me*, Luke Rivers Tuyler. Rosanne was not by any means always pleased with me. I could charm her, of course, and I did charm her, but I had to do it. Perhaps that was part of her tremendous attraction—and repulsion.

I loved Giulia for loving me. Far more I loved to please Rosanne; and I hated her for not loving me for myself; for making me please her; and for making me want to please her.

As I have said before, I do desire to be honest with myself, and I am going to get this straight in my own mind, for it is as puzzling and as interesting as it is important.

I have said that I had to please her, and that has a double meaning, each of which is true.

When I say that I had to please her, I mean that to please her I had to make an effort. I had to be the Luke that she wanted me to be. I had both to be and to do, to be her ideal Luke and to do the things that her ideal Luke naturally would do.

Again, when I say that I had to please her, I mean that I was under an irresistible compulsion to do so. I simply *had* to please her or be miserable. When I was not pleasing her, I was wretched, piqued and annoyed. I was unhappy, and I hated her for making me unhappy. And when she made me unhappy, as she so often did, I went to Giulia for comfort, and Giulia never failed me.

I don't thereby imply that Rosanne ever failed me in the sense of letting me down. She was incapable of that sort of thing. But she did most undeniably and quite frequently fail to approve, applaud, admire. Perhaps I am a little harsh on myself when I use the word admire, and seem to complain that Rosanne was not filled with uncritical admiration of everything I did. Perhaps "accept" would be a better word.

Giulia accepted whatever I did as admirable; and she always approved and applauded, whereas Rosanne was much more critical.

Or let me say, rather, that Giulia was never critical and Rosanne always was.

I don't mean that she was always disapproving. She could give praise most generously where she thought it was due, but she was far too fond of her own opinion, and she presumed to sit in judgment when not qualified to do so.

Giulia, for example, loved my poetry, and enjoyed nothing more than hearing me read it to her, especially when she and her beauty were its subject.

Rosanne, on the other hand, would, in the same breath, frankly confess that she knew nothing about poetry, and that she considered mine to be tripe; that *vers libre* was not poetry at all, and that any fool could write it. Nevertheless, she was most generously and stoutly appreciative of my effort to please her when I wrote a poem *To Rosanne on the occasion of her Eighteenth Birthday*.

There wasn't a word of criticism of that poem and I knew, with the utmost certainty, that this was not because it was dedicated to Rosanne, but because she realized that I had given thought and effort to pleasing her. So warmly appreciative and grateful was she that I really felt a slight sense of guilt in the knowledge that this poem had been written for Giulia's natal anniversary. But Rosanne is a very much easier word for which to find rhymes. In fact, I had, in this very poem, been despairingly driven to the ghastly depths of making "peculiar" and "truly your" rhyme with Giulia!

Having perpetuated this awful poem and realized that Giulia would simply love it, I was almost ill upon the paper—and turned to rhymes for Rosanne. . . .

But on ordinary occasions, though she gave praise where praise was due, she obviously preferred to criticize where criticism was possible. It was good criticism—and damned impudence, too, very often.

I remember particularly, doing a water-colour of the rose-garden with the house in the background. When it was finished, it proved to be one of my successes, and I was very pleased with it. So much so, that I decided to have it framed in narrow gilt and give it to Rosanne for her sitting-room. She accepted it gratefully, thanked me very warmly, and admired it generously. When I said,

"Well, little Miss Clever, any complaints? Any fault to find, this time?" she said,

"Well, looking a gift horse in the mouth is a lousy trick, but since you ask—I am quite sure that trees silhouetted between you and the sky-line couldn't be as green as that. This would be a lovely green if the sunlight were on them, but with the light behind them, they'd be almost black."

"Thank you, Madam Corot," I said, taking the picture from her and putting my heel on the glass with all my weight.

Had I given the picture to Giulia, she would have "simply loved" it, praised it without stint; and had I pretended to ask for criticism, would very rightly have observed that I knew a thousand times more about painting than she did, and that she would not dream of attempting to find any fault. And the incident would have provided nothing but mutual delight, and would have ended in my being thoroughly pleased with myself and with Giulia.

I don't want to give the impression that Rosanne and I were constantly quarrelling, or that she was difficult to live with. Nothing could be further from the truth. She was delightful to live with, and we bickered quite cheerfully and amicably, for she was an extremely difficult person with whom really to quarrel, or indeed to argue. As she so often remarked during our married life,

"Discussion I enjoy; argument I loathe; and quarrelling I abhor. In fact, I utterly refuse to do it."

No, as a girl she was a delightful person, one of those rare women who have not only beauty, but brains and character, all of the very first class.

But among her gifts of golden silence, of silver speech, of sparkling wit, of perfect sincerity, of generosity, sympathy and kindness, she had a rare gift of mockery and provocation. She could be most annoying and irritating, to me at any rate, the damned darling.

As a boy, I always looked forward to seeing her at the end of term, and at the end of hols I was generally jolly glad to see the last of her, and openly thanked God that boys and girls did not go to the same school.

And yet I missed her, and quite frequently decided that next Sunday I would write to her telling her all about myself and my doings. She'd be glad to get a letter at her school, and would show it to the other girls. I never did, of course, but the fact that I contemplated doing such a thing showed that Rosanne was not the sort of person whom one could easily put from one's mind.

It was lovely to see her again when one got home; sheer delight until I would tell her about some prize that I had won, and she would ask whether the other competitor got the second one, or something of that sort. She would *not* be impressed, and appeared to take more pleasure in digging the confession from Mark that he had succeeded in something or other, than in listening to my Troubadour Song of Triumph.

If Giulia did me good by encouraging me to express myself, in being a wonderful audience, and in giving me more and more self-confidence, I suppose Rosanne was equally good for me in another way, inasmuch as, quite unintentionally, she goaded me, by her very indifference, to further and further effort.

To be perfectly frank, honest and self-revealing once again, my chief ambition was to impress her. I *would* impress her, I *would* make her admire me, I *would* make her admit that I was—I don't say a genius, but— what everybody else admitted me to be. If Mark thought me wonderful; if my father had the greatest admiration as well as love for me; if my mother had thought me perfect; if Athene proclaimed me simply marvellous, and if Giulia thought there was no one on earth to equal me, surely they were not all wrong and Rosanne right?

And did she but know it, Rosanne was the cause of my joining the French Foreign Legion. Admittedly, I was carried away by a generous indignation for the wrongs of Belgium and of France, by a burning wrath against the appalling gospel of the right of Might, by the beautiful folly of youthful romanticism; but the real underlying motive was my determination to impress Rosanne.

It was a yearning, an *idée fixe*; and when, drunk with enthusiasm, words and wine, I sprang on a table and poured forth my soul in a torrent of eloquence, calling on all decent men to follow me and to fight for France, I said to myself as I stepped down,

"What of *that*, Rosanne? What do you think of me now?"

§4

Well! I have shown you the vast and fundamental difference between Mark and myself. I have given you some idea of the higher type of man to which I belong— sensitive, psychic, intellectual, artistic, poetic, highly strung—and I ask you to judge whether I was fit to endure what followed. I ask you whether I could be expected to bear, as Mark could bear, the prolonged physical and nervous strain, the agony of suffering, to which my rash and foolish act condemned me.

Hear my story, and judge for yourself—and for me.

V

Even yet I hate to write about my experiences in the French Foreign Legion. I get enough battle-dreams, nightmares and attacks of the horrors, without raking all that up again. It was all very well, all very thrilling, interesting and romantic, until we got into the trenches, but we had not been long in that unbelievable hell of mud, cold, noise, stink, starvation, lice, illness, mutilation, death and misery unspeakable, when I began almost to hate Rosanne for being the real cause of my being there.

Well, I bore it as long as I could, and no man can bear anything longer. I did my utmost, and no man can do more. Let no one cast a stone save him who experienced, and survived unbroken, the indescribable hell of the first winter of the War in the trenches with the French Foreign Legion—whose lives were squandered without stint.

I worked and marched as cheerfully as anyone. I fought as desperately and bravely as anyone, until nerve and heart and sinew broke. When that happened—well, I was broken too. Finished. Thereafter I could no more stand up to it than a man with fractured legs can stand up.

I don't blame myself and I expect no one to blame me unless he is in a position to judge; unless he has lain for weeks under bitter cold rain, not in a ploughed field but in a deep and stinking sewer, a latrine, in fact, in the mud of which he sinks almost to his knees as he tries to move, and up to his waist when he had to sit down: unless he has lived without being able to change his stiff and stinking clothes for forty days and forty nights on end: unless he has never had more than a couple of hours' sleep at a time, under these conditions: unless he has had inadequate food and none of it hot throughout such a period: unless he has been so swarming and crawling with lice that, when he could find a place of relatively hard clay on which he could lie down without fear of drowning, he could not sleep for the constant itching and burning of the whole of the skin of his body: unless he has stood on rotting corpses, lain down beside them, been sickened to the depths of his soul by the hideous sight and horrible stench of those unburied dead beside and beneath and around him: unless he has lived, for interminable days, with the noise of ten thousand thunderstorms shattering his ear-drums, as great shells burst by the parapet and parados, and in the trench itself: unless, daily and hourly, he has seen the men with whom he had eaten and drunk, worked and marched, slept and sung, killed, mangled and torn; and had their blood and brains and entrails splashed over him; been called upon, when almost too cold, sodden, weary, sick and weak to stand, to climb out of the flooded clay ditch and, with sinking empty stomach and aching head, take part in a "glorious" bayonet charge. . . .

At the end of my tether, I had the choice of going mad, killing myself or—escaping. I escaped, and care nothing for the condemnation of those who have had nothing from which to escape. Death I would have welcomed, but from suicide I shrank, and only escape was left.

I first realized that I could go no further, give no more of myself when, in what were humorously called rest billets, I got a touch of dysentery during a typhoid epidemic. It was the last straw. There is nothing that takes the heart and courage and grit out of a man like illness of that kind. I gave up, and said I had typhoid fever. I had reached the point where I simply did not care what happened, if only I could lie down and keep still. Mark and some of our comrades carried me from the wretched dug-outs in which we sheltered when not tree-felling, road-building and trench-digging, and made me a sort of bed with branches, sand-bag sacks and a ground-sheet under a bush over which Mark hung a lorry-tarpaulin or something of the kind, which he had scrounged. Mark covered me with his overcoat, went on with his digging, and left me to it. When the

Battalion was warned for return to the line, he absented himself without leave, hid as they marched off, and when night fell, came and joined me. There we hid in the woods, deserters, and while I lay and rested, Mark foraged for food—an extremely risky business, for if he had been caught he would have been court-martialled and shot, out of hand, as a deserter.

As a matter of fact, poor old Mark was just about as weary and ill as I was, but he is tougher than I am. He has little imagination, and his brain takes no toll of his nerves.

Because I had ceased to care what happened and would as willingly have been shot as not, we were not discovered and arrested for what we were, deserters from our Battalion that was holding a bad sector of the front line, miles away. But after a time, I came to hate lying-up starving in those dripping woods almost more than being in the trenches. In the end, I think it was healthy hunger more than anything else that reconciled me to the prospect of our return, and I professed to feel better, declared myself to be convalescent and staged a quick recovery of my strength.

Far from being arrested and denounced, we were welcomed as though returned from the dead—of whom there were only too many in that typhoid-stricken death-trap that had been our "rest" billets.

Improved weather, better organization and the Battalion's transfer to a drier and healthier part of the line enabled me to carry on once again. It was noise, more than anything else, that caused my second breakdown. Had we been otherwise living in comfort and luxury, feasting like the friends of Lucullus, and sleeping in feather-beds, with nothing to do but enjoy life, that hellish din would alone have rendered preferable the vilest conditions imaginable, provided only that there had been silence.

The ghastly toll of lives, the hideous wounds, the imminence of mutilation and death, and the other horrors of the shells were less terrible than their noise. It wasn't merely that one was deafened, one was dithered shaken, stupefied, *shattered.* One was unable to think. Not only was one unable to hear, one felt unable to smell, taste, touch, almost unable to see. It sounds a kind of stupid exaggeration to talk of noise being so colossal that it affects the senses of touch, taste, smell and sight, but, after all, the senses are dependent entirely on the nerves, and the noise so shattered my nerves that they ceased to function—otherwise than as instruments of torture.

Again I reached a point where I could bear it no longer, and decided that I must get out of it, once and for all. Not only had I had enough, but I felt that I had done enough. I had played my part, I had taken my share. Now let someone else take my place. Why should I go on to destruction, mental and physical, while there were hundreds of thousands, millions, who had taken no part at all. . . . *Gentlemen in England now abed.* . . .

Well, I would have some sleep—abed too.

I had shrunk from the thought of suicide and still do so, but I knew of another way.

Although at first my mind rejected the idea as contemptible, I dallied more and more with the thought of self-mutilation. Sooner or later, I was certain to be shot. Almost every one of our original *escouade* had been killed. Mark and I were positive veterans, and could not possibly last much longer. Why wait till a German shot me, perhaps killing me, perhaps blinding me, perhaps maiming me for life? I determined to anticipate the German bullet.

I had a horribly narrow escape, and was almost miraculously saved. I shudder still to think of it.

One loathsome dawn, cold, wet and foggy, when my vital forces were at their lowest ebb and I was, both physically and mentally, depressed to the very depths, I was on sentry, staring through the fog at the German lines, not a hundred yards distant. The temptation was overwhelming. I was alone and there was no one in sight. Owing to the fog, I was invisible. But I must be wary. The penalty for self-mutilation was death. If the sound of a shot brought Sergeant Hervé, I must not be found wounded in the shoulder—with a burnt and smouldering coat. . . . I would fold my handkerchief into a pad, fix it against my left shoulder by tucking a corner under my cross-belt, lay my rifle on the parapet with the muzzle close to the handkerchief, lean forward and press the trigger with a finger-tip . . . In spite of the shock, I must then stamp the handkerchief into the mud beneath my feet. If it were ever found, it would merely be a torn and muddy rag. . . . I must then snatch up my rifle and fire it toward the German trenches. Hervé or Corporal Ouspenski, whoever was nearest, would come at once and find me wounded. Before I staged a collapse or fainted from loss of blood, I would say that a reconnoitring German, or one who had lost his way in the fog, had approached the trench, fired at me and vanished into the mist. It might have been a sniper who had lain out all night between the lines. I would do it, and in a few hours I should be . . .

Bang! . . .

Another sentry, a few yards to my right, had fired his rifle, and I jumped as though actually caught in the actual commission of a crime, the guilt of which could only be punished with a death-sentence.

Sergeant Hervé must have been but a short distance away, for he passed me as I took my hand from the pocket in which I was fumbling for my handkerchief.

"*Sacré Dieu!* The *salauds* have got you, eh, Pelotti?" he said.

I heard Pelotti, a slender youngster who should have been at school, swear in Italian.

"*Iddio!* . . . *Cospetto!* . . . Through the arm, Sergeant."

"Through the arm, eh? The bastard must have been very close—by the sound of the shot."

"*Si! Si!* A few yards from the trench. . . . *Dio mio,* it hurts!"

"You were keeping a good look-out, of course?"

"*Si! Si!*"

"Then you saw him coming?"

"*Si! Si!*"

"Why didn't you fire, then?"

"I hadn't time."

"He had time, though, hadn't he? Here, let me look at your coat. Ah, I thought so. Scorched. Burnt. Open the breach of your rifle."

"*Dio non voglia!* . . . I can't! . . . I can't. . . . My arm."

"Pick up that rifle. Open the breach."

I heard a sobbing groan and the sound of a breach-bolt being worked.

"*A-a-a-h!* So you didn't shoot, eh? Hadn't time, eh? How did that *empty* cartridge-case get into your breach, then?"

"Sergeant, I . . . I . . . I must have fired at him without realizing it."

"There was only one shot fired, Pelotti."

"*Si! Si!* Sergeant. . . . It was mine."

"Then how do *you* come to be shot? Yes, it was *yours* all right, Pelotti. . . . Come with me. . . ."

I felt sick. But not one-half as sick and faint as I felt at dawn next morning when I, with five other men of our *escouade,* stood ten yards from a *poiteau d'éxécution* to which Pelotti, with bandaged eyes, was bound.

I had sinned in imagination, and I suffered in ghastly reality. Had the proceedings lasted another minute, I should have collapsed in a dead faint.

The officer's sword fell just in time, and I endeavoured to control my swaying rifle sufficiently to be sure of firing over Pelotti's head. Others of the firing squad were not so merciful—or were more merciful. But shoot him I could not.

There, but for the grace of God, stood Luke Rivers Tuyler.

There, a moment after the fall of the officer's sword, hung his riddled body.

§2

This incident gave me a real shock, and it was some time before I quite recovered from it. Apart from any

question of malingering, my nerves were quite genuinely in a bad way, and I was the victim of a succes-
sion of nightmares in which I was bound to the
execution-post, blindfolded and *awaiting* the volley. No
words can tell how terrible, how mercilessly racking,
was that awful suspense, waiting, waiting, for the
volley of bullets that would shatter my chest. Waiting
blindfolded, seeing and hearing nothing.

I got a kind of blindfold complex, and it had much
to do with what followed.

A repeated variation of this dreadful nightmare was
one in which poor little Pelotti was bound to the stake
and I was his sole executioner. There he stood, weeping, begging and pleading for his life, while I was con-
strained slowly to raise my rifle and point it between
his eyes while he shrieked,

"No! No! You'll *blind* me! You'll *blind* me!"

What with insomnia and a horrible internal
condition of pain and weakness—dysentery, I suppose
—I really was in a bad way.

It was Mark who saved me; Mark and a French
military *médecin.*

It was not so much that he magnified my illness as
that he secured me the treatment that I needed, and
that a hundred others needed more than I did, and
which they did not get.

I was evacuated from rest-billets, where we were
being worked to death, to an advance Base Hospital at
Pont Mailleul.

Here that merry, merry Fate that watches over me
arranged that I should have the next bed to a man
from my own *escouade,* a Spaniard whom I had named
Yrotaval y Rewes, and who had accepted the sonorous,
high-sounding name with delight, and called himself
Yrotaval thenceforth.

This man had fastened on to me at Toulon,
appointing me his patron and employer from the very
first, and sticking to me thereafter like a leech. A leech
he was, too, but an uncommonly useful one, being an
ancien who knew the ropes perfectly; who knew when
and how and whom to bribe; who was a deadly,

dangerous enemy to one's enemies; and who had a faithful following of desperados of his own kidney, among whom were a brainless creature of gigantic strength called Araña and a villainous ex bull-fighter called Toro.

Why I allowed this Spaniard to constitute himself my combined mentor and servant, my cunning guide and humble follower, was because he was at once the most amusing and the most interesting chap I ever met. He was really witty, extraordinarily funny, and even so, was even funnier than he knew, by reason of his amazing Hispano-American-Franco-Cockney speech. And he was interesting by reason of the life he had led—or the nine lives—of which were his double lives as a police agent and a police victim; a Communist plotter and a betrayer of Communist plots; an obscure limb of the Law and a far from obscure limb of Satan; a notorious criminal, in fact.

I should think he was unique, a genuine museum-piece of villainy; utterly conscienceless, shameless, and callous. Paradoxically, he did no wrong, for nothing to him *was* wrong. He was so amoral that he was incapable of dividing human actions up into two main classes of good deeds and bad deeds. The only classification he could make would be into the possible and the impossible. Nor would he ever have used the words legal and illegal, because, as a professing Anarchist born and bred, he recognized no such thing as Law and held that the curse of a people is a Government. Nevertheless, his high principles of Anarchism did not prevent his betraying his brother Anarchists to the Police, nor from earning an honest living as a police agent and spy. When he left his country for his country's good and fled for his life to America, he became a criminal pure and simple, and without any ideological nonsense about it.

Prudence later indicating the wisdom of abandoning America to its fate, he fled to London, thence hastily escaped to Sunny Spain, but found it too sunnily hot to hold him, bolted to Marseilles, his real spiritual home, and, thither still pursued, found refuge in the

French Foreign Legion.

I freely confess that, in addition to finding him most amusing and extremely interesting, I found him very useful indeed, and not only as self-constituted batman, body-servant and body-guard. He steered me past all sorts of trouble, and, more than once, got me out of it, when my headstrong and impulsive folly had, despite his warning, led me into it.

There was the case of Corporal Bjelavitch, a loathsome Bulgarian blackguard with whom I foolishly went to Marseilles against Yrotavál's advice. It seemed to me a wonderful opportunity of seeing the genuine underworld of the wickedest city on earth, inasmuch as Yrotavál was a member there, in good standing, and could play Virgil to my Dante in a tour through that lowest *cercle* of Hell. He did to admiration, and I shall never forget the *cinema bleu*; the night-club of the *Nervis*; the amazing, incredible and appalling brothels; the thieves' kitchens, Marie's House, and other underworld rendezvous that we visited.

That I might stay the course and see all the sights, I kept myself pure and unspotted and reasonably sober, while Corporal Bjelavitch, Yrotavál and his henchman Araña, made whoopee, revelled, wallowed, in fact. Never before had Yrotavál and Araña haunted the stews and purlieus of the Vieux Port in any other rôle than that of members of its underworld, *habitants,* natives, vendors, *solliciteurs, procureurs, souteneurs,* bullies, pimps and panders. Now, thanks to funds supplied by me, they came in the rôle of visitors, purchasers and patrons. But patrons with what a difference! Not pigeons to be plucked, but *cognoscenti,* connoisseurs who knew exactly where to go, what to demand and what to get—and what to pay for it.

And truculent! *M'Carben Diu!* as Yrotavál would say; it was not they who were in danger in that jungle of savage and dangerous human beasts.

Among the many virtues of Yrotavál and Araña was the ability to carry quite a lot of liquor like gentlemen. Up to a point, the more they drank the more tight-lipped, wary, and quietly sinister they became. The swinish Bjelavitch, on the other hand, went completely to pieces, became violent, pugnacious and extremely objectionable; and, but for Yrotavál and Araña, would have been thrown out from, if not done-in at, more than one decorous and respectable haunt of depravity, vice, and villainy. . . .

When at long last we made our way back to Fort St. Jean whence (by grace and purchase) we had late passes, this animal Bjelavitch assaulted me in such a manner that I had no choice nor desire but to smash his face. Luckily for me, the powerful, bear-like brute was sufficiently drunk for this to be possible, and I beat him up in style. But next day he remembered. Doubtless he had a racking headache, a rebellious stomach and a congested liver. Certainly he had a vile temper, a vengeful spirit and a firm determination to compass my downfall, if not destruction. A properly worked charge of attempted desertion and violent assault upon a zealous non-commissioned officer who endeavoured to prevent it, should, he knew, get me anything from eight years' penal battalion to a death sentence. Almost certainly the latter, since the crime had been committed when on escort duty in time of war.

That, at any rate, was the view that Yrotavál took and, as I miserably realized, he should know.

"Sure boy," he growled, "dat buzzard would hang you in your own tripes. He'll frame you—and get you."

And both Araña and Toro, albeit inarticulate, made it clear to me by a wealth of gestures, what would happen when we got back to Toulon, Bjelavitch turned in his Fort St. Jean papers, and then made his report on my conduct. And if by the wildest chance and utter improbability, the Authorities did not support him to the full and punish me to the utmost, the N.C.O.s (a close corporation that would act as one man in the event of a member of the guild being offended) would see to it that if I did not die an early death, it would at any rate be the consummation I would most earnestly desire.

Within an hour of reaching the *chambrée,* Yrotavál drew me aside.

"It's you or dat *batteur,*" he growled. "It's you on the spot or dat b—— up de spout. . . . What's it worth?"

"What do you mean?"

"Talk Turkey, Bo. Dis is serious. What's de rake-off if dat goddam guy gets his, *pronto?* . . . And it has got to be to-night. . . . If Bellybitch is alive when Orderly Room opens to-morrow, it's *tckkk* for you," and with the unpleasant sound he made a yet more unpleasant gesture and grimace, as of one who dies in some discomfort of a hempen or steel affection of the throat.

"There are no witnesses that I hit the swine."

"No witnesses hell! Dere's t'ree."

"You'd give evidence against me? You and Araña and Toro would give evidence in his favour?"

"We gotta live, ain't we? If we didn't get a hard-labour stretch for beggaring-up de Court Martial and defeating de ends of Justice by perjury, the N.C.O.s would get us. Get us for keeps too. We gotta live."

And eyeing me sideways, with a slow smile breaking the straight gash of his lipless mouth and creasing his leathern face, he added,

"But dat sunnavabitch ain't gotta live."

Well, I had realized that the French Foreign Legion was an interesting institution, and that life therein held its little surprises, but I had hardly imagined that a reversion to the days and customs of the hiring of *bravos* was among them. And if it were, I had no inclination for the pastime.

"It's you or him, Sonny," murmured the tempter.

"What's the least I'll get from a Court Martial?"

"Death, anyway. In chains, boulder-carrying on the Colomb-Bechar Road, any time during the next eight years if you are unlucky; or next week, the day after the *Conseil de Guerre* has given you the Thumbs-Down."

An unattractive prospect.

"It's you or him, Son. *P'quoi faire l'andouille?*[21]

---

[21] *Why play the fool?*

What's it worth—for de bastard to meet wit' an accident?"

"Oh, an accident? I don't mind an accident," I said.

"Could you lend me t'ree hundred francs?" smiled Yrotavál. "See, there's t'ree of us—me and Araña and Toro. If it's to be a bad accident . . ."

Twelve pounds. Yes, I could certainly afford twelve pounds. Much cheaper price than eight years, or as much of eight years as I might survive, in the notoriously murderous Penal Battalions (which are not to be confused with the Bat d'Af, wherein life is said to be bearable). If twelve pounds was to make the difference between my destruction and the foul Bjelavitch's meeting with an incapacitating accident, well, twelve pounds be it—or twelve hundred.

"Er—yes, Yrotavál. I could lend you three hundred francs if you'll promise to pay me the . . ."

"Pay! I'll *pay* all right," growled Yrotavál, pocketing the wad.

People who read examples of its manifestations are apt to sneer at the long arm of coincidence. It is, nevertheless, a fact that that very night Corporal Bjelavitch was killed. Inasmuch as he was stabbed in the back, one might safely say he was murdered.

A wonderful piece of good luck for me and another marvellously narrow escape.

After our trip to Marseilles, Yrotavál quite finally adopted me as his *copain.* Literally, and somewhat to Mark's annoyance, I fear, he hardly let me out of his sight. I don't for one moment suggest that Mark was jealous of the good Yrotavál, but he did not seem to think that he was the most desirable of companions for me, nor that his influence was wholly for good!

Poor, dear old Mark, he never appreciated Yrotavál at his real worth, although the little Catalan kept him in fits of laughter with his wit and humour and inexhaustible fund of stories. He was indeed a fellow of infinite jest; of most excellent fancy.

§3

I confess that I missed him horribly when he was wounded and evacuated from the trenches, and that I rejoiced at finding him in hospital; for not only would he keep me amused there, but would fag for me and look after me like a father, or better still, like a damned good servant.

Of course he was what my brother called him, an utter scoundrel and villainous blackguard; but, as I was wont to point out to dear old Mark, whose business was it, save that of his victims?

Granted that he was a murderer, he didn't murder me; agreed that he was a thief, he didn't rob me; admitted that he was as treacherous as hell, he had been a faithful friend to me. So what?

"A bit of a viper in the bosom, I should say," Mark had growled in his best heavy-father style.

"Wrong there, Cocky," I had replied. "The bosom is nice and warm. It would be when you went to chuck the old viper out into the cold that he might snap."

"A damned bad man to cross."

"Right, old chap—don't let's cross him," was my wise conclusion.

He *was* a bad man to cross too, as a certain Sergeant Paggallini discovered—if he lived long enough. He was one of those admirable Corsican N.C.O.s, efficient, competent, trustworthy—and brutes to their fingertips. He had bullied, threatened and insulted Yrotavál in a way in which a very senior *ancien* should not be insulted by a young Sergeant, and he had struck me brutally in the face when we were in the trenches. It had only been Yrotavál's hand on my wrist that had prevented me from hitting him back—and being shot dead, on the spot, for he was an N.C.O. who kept the flap of his pistol-holster open.

"We'll get the bastard," he whispered later. "Wait till we're all out in the front garden together, late one night. I dunno who'll come home wit' de milk in de mornin'—but I know one who won't. . . ."

Within the week Sergeant Paggallini was sent with

six men to make a reconnaissance patrol to the German lines, with orders to report on the condition of the wire, and bring back what evidence he could as to the identity of the battalion opposite to us.

Crouching, creeping, crawling, wriggling, we made our way, unobserved, across No-Man's-Land, lying flat and freezing solid whenever a Very light shed its baleful brilliant glare over our part of the Line. At the end of an hour or so, we were near the German trench and Paggallini slowly wriggled forward. The voice of the man lying close beside me whispered.

"Now we got de bastard—goin' or comin'. *Il va avaler ses batuettes.*"[22]

Some distance away a Very pistol was fired and by its faint light I could see in front of me a silhouette that slowly, gently, moved. French—not German.

A rifle beside me cracked. There was instant activity in the trench; Very lights went up; sentries promptly shot at nothing in particular; ragged rifle-fire broke out; and a machine-gun suddenly started its hideous staccato coughing.

Among the unburied dead we lay, face downward, motionless as the corpses.

The firing died down, and soon the night was again as quiet, or as noisy, as usual. It was hopeless now, of course, to attempt to make a surprise raid on the trench.

"Looks like de Sergeant's got lost, don't it? *Il a son affaire!*"[23] whispered Yrotavál, after a long interval of immobility. "Just too bad. Me for home."

Of the reconnoitring patrol six returned, Sergeant Paggallini not being of their number.

Later, Yrotavál took it upon him to remind me that he had committed two murders in my interest and at my instigation!

Well, such was the man Yrotavál of whom I now made real use, made the instrument of my salvation,

---

[22] *He's going to hand in his checks.*
[23] *He has got his!*

the occasion being the inexcusable, shameless, and shameful bombing of Pont Mailleul Base Hospital.

VI

To be quite honest—and once again, that is my sole object and firm intention—the bombing of Pont Mailleul hospital was, so far as Yrotavál and I were concerned, a mere nothing.

In the trenches we had had more shattering experiences and narrower escapes a hundred times; and although on the occasion of this bombing, scores of splendid doctors, noble nurses and brave, wounded men, met their deaths or received ghastly wounds, all I got was an idea.

Yrotavál and I, convalescent and due for return to the Line on the morrow, were sitting side by side in the sunshine, outside our ward, I listening with one ear to his very funny stories, tall yarns, amusing locutions and intriguing blasphemies, and with the other to the droning of an aeroplane, while I pondered ways and means of prolonging this ineffably lovely and gracious period of respite from the horrors of mud, blood, wounds, hunger, filth, lice and the rest of the hell of war.

Suddenly it dawned on us that the aeroplane was a Boche . . . that a bomb was falling . . . that people were running for their lives.

Yrotavál, swift as a panther, flung himself on the ground and promptly I followed suit. There was the usual shattering concussion and hellish bang, a roar of sound almost too loud to hear, and we were covered with earth, while all about us walls fell, windows were blown in, roofs were blown off, and tiles came clattering down.

For us of the Legion, straight from the hottest of the fighting, it was almost routine. Getting up on all fours and shaking the earth from my head and hair, I took my hands from my face where I had almost instinctively placed them when expecting an explosion, and saw Yrotavál kneeling up, face to face with me.

A string of oaths, each more curious than the last, issued from the corner of his twisted mouth. He spat mud and shook himself like a dog.

"Say, Bo," he suddenly grinned. "We'll sure get something outa dis. Me, I'm suffering from shock. Shell-shock. Month in hospital down Monte Carlo way. Nix on trenches to-morrow. God bless dat blasted Bosche."

And suddenly the Great Idea was born in my mind, sprang, fully developed and complete, strong, unde-featable, armed *cap-à-pie,* as sprang Minerva from the brain of Jove.

But it was from the brain of the Devil that it came, that temptation, sudden, utterly irresistible.

Perhaps, had I slept on it, I could have found the strength to resist; but impulsive ever, I fell instantly, and my fall was irretrievable. I spoke and my words were irrevocable.

"Yrotavál—*I am blind,"* I whispered.

My *âme damné* stared open-mouthed.

"Blind!" he whispered. And then the mouth closed like a steel trap, twisted in a leering grin, and partially opened again to whisper,

"Sure! Sure you're blind! You said it, Buddy. An' I can give you some dope that'll make you a helluva lot blinder too! . . . And me? I'm deaf and dumb. Sure! *Ca fait ma balle!*"[24]

And collapsing again upon the ground, he closed his eyes and emitted piteous animal sounds, while, I kneeling, bent double, covered my eyes with my hands and sobbed aloud with hysterical tears and laughter

When the hideous mess was cleared up, the dead and the dying separated from the wounded, the shell-shocked and comparatively unhurt *légionnaire* Luke Rivers Tuyler L.M. 6752, English, was found to be totally blind, while *légionnaire* Ramon Caballero L.M. 9886, Spanish, was both deaf and dumb. Two pitiable

---

[24] *That suits me fine.*

cases of acute shell-shock.

§2

There was soon no doubt about the efficacy of the stuff that Yrotavál gave me for causing an inflamed and ugly condition of the eyes. There was no mistake about the pain it caused, either. I felt I was doing a foolish thing, but I also felt that I should be doing something a thousand times more foolish if I allowed myself to be sent back to the trenches. That way madness lay. Agony, mutilation, death, were one thing: madness was another. And I felt it was worth the risk.

I was under no illusions as to Yrotavál being a thorough-paced scoundrel, but there was always a reason as well as a method in his villainy, and he could have no possible object in really blinding me. That he was profoundly ignorant, I of course knew; but he swore by God, His Mother, His Son, and all the Saints, that he knew, from long and wide experience, that the stuff was harmless. It was used by all the best beggars who earned their livings by sitting in the sun on Cathedral steps; and although their eyes were hideous to look upon and they were blind all day, they could see well enough when they went off duty; and they died, at a ripe old age, with their sight unimpaired: it was used by all the best criminals (who could get hold of a supply of it) when they wished to go blind in gaol, whether with the view to evading punitive tasks such as the work of the oakum-picking and mail-bag-making variety; or that they might evoke the pity of the visiting Justices and obtain amelioration of circumstances or remission of sentence: and it was used by young men who wished to evade the draft when the time for their conscription arrived, particularly when war threatened or was in actual progress. According to Yrotavál, there was a terrible lot of this blindness at the time of the American-Spanish War and when there was active campaigning in Morocco.

Under the influence of the acute pain caused by its first application, I assured the blackguard that I would shoot him if it really blinded me.

"Sure, Bo," he grinned. "You'll be able to see to do it on a black night in a dark room in which I ain't. *M'Carben Diu!* It will improve your sight . . . But don't use it if you can't take it. It wants just a little guts—like any old Spanish beggar-woman's got."

What the stuff was I don't know to this day, for whether by reason of superstition, idiotic mystery-mongering, or some kind of gleam of honour among thieves, Yrotavál firmly and finally refused to give away the secret of his precious preparation. But among its ingredients were cordite, tobacco-juice, soap and something to which Yrotavál mysteriously alluded as "sumpin from the chimist." (Possibly atropine?)

Certainly it was more efficacious when compounded with the anonymous something-from-the-chemist, but without this ingredient it was, I can testify, sufficiently painful and inflammatory. And certainly no one, I thought, not even an ophthalmic surgeon, could doubt that one's eyes were in a terrible condition, whether caused by injury or disease.

§3

What, under normal conditions, could be a more fatiguing, hopelessly boring, well-nigh heart-breaking way of killing time than hanging about in the waiting-rooms of French provincial railway-stations, the corridors of hospitals, the ante-rooms of medical officers' bureaux, waiting, hungry and tired, for long weary hours, and then being peremptorily dismissed and told to return on the morrow?

What, under the conditions to which Yrotavál and I had grown accustomed in the trenches, could have been more peaceful, restful and delightful than such waiting about—I, with a bandage about my eyes and a luggage-label, on which was scribbled *Aveugle,* tied to a button of my tunic; Yrotavál with dirty cotton-wool in his ears, a look of bravely borne suffering on his face, and a label marked *Sourd et Muet* on his coat. When evacuated from the ruins of the Pont Mailleul Hospital we received every sympathy and kindness. At the "Shell-shock" Hospital we got little sympathy, no kindness, and considerable suspicion. Fortunately, the administrative Medical Officers were worked almost to death; were too harassed and over-driven to find proper time to eat and to sleep.

The *Médecin Major* who examined me there was frankly sceptical. Having heard all I had to say, which was a good deal, he examined my eyes which Yrotavál's 'dope' had made extremely painful as well as repulsively ugly. In the middle of this swift and somewhat cursory examination he said abruptly,

"You are lying."

"I cannot see, *Monsieur le Major,*" I replied quietly but firmly. "I am totally blind."

"None are so blind as those who won't see, are they?" was the sarcastic reply. "Unfortunately I haven't got an ophthalmoscope here, or I would soon make absolutely certain whether you are malingering, as I know you are . . . You say the bomb fell in front of you, there was a blinding flash and a terrific concussion, and you have seen nothing since? . . . Well, I wonder if you can explain why it is that the pupils of your eyes contract as I shine this light into them, eh? If you were blind, they wouldn't change. You may be quite clever at refraining from blinking, but the muscles of the eyelids are voluntary muscles and those of the iris are involuntary. Can't stop *them* from contracting, can you?"

"I can't see, *Monsieur le Médecin Major,*" I repeated.

"To my mind there is no lesion whatsoever, not the slightest sign of one. It's your heart that is wrong, not your eyes. You are *bon pour le service.* And I . . ."

"I cannot see, *Monsieur le Médecin Major,*" I repeated.

"Perhaps you can feel, then," he shouted, springing up and aiming a blow at my face with his open hand.

Had I been blind, I should not have known that he was about to strike me, and my eyes would not have moved. Not being blind, I could see that the blow was about to fall, and contrived to refrain from flinching or blinking. He didn't strike me, of course, but he could not, as he had hoped and expected, triumphantly shout,

"There! You flinched! How did you know my hand was approaching your face?"

For a moment he regarded me thoughtfully. Then suddenly picking up a pen from the table beside him, thrust it straight at my right eye.

I could have told him that Yrotavál and I had practised that game until practice had made me perfect. Not the faintest flicker of an eyelid answered the sudden dart of the pen-point, which stopped a fraction of an inch from my eye-ball.

Again the doctor, who was not an oculist, regarded me thoughtfully. Then he picked up the printed form which had been given me at Pont Mailleul and read it again.

"H'm . . . *Volunteer.* English . . . *Shell-shocked. Blind.* . . . So you volunteered, did you?" he said.

"On the outbreak of war, *Monsieur le Médecin-Major,*" I replied.

"And now you regret it, eh? Well, I'll send you to Orleans. They've got oculists there and all the apparatus. They'll soon settle your hash. And if you are malingering, as I think you are, they'll know what to do with you."

On the whole Yrotavál had an easier time than I did. If a man chooses to go dumb, no doctor on earth can prove he isn't, and it is nearly as difficult to convict any wily individual of shamming deafness.

I wasn't present at Yrotavál's examination by a choleric and over-worked doctor; but, according to his story, they accepted his deafness when no light of joy suffused his eye on being asked whether he'd have a mug of wine, and when he refrained from giving a start of surprise as a pistol was fired just behind his head.

After a few simple tricks and obvious traps, he was given three months' medical leave and instructions to proceed to the same medical-observation convalescent-camp-hospital at Orleans.

§4

But at Orleans, where my hash was to be settled by Army Medical Corps oculists with their malingerer-detecting apparatus, and Yrotavál was to be kept under observation until inadvertently he heard the voice of some charmer and replied in his own, we never arrived.

We lost ourselves.

And, away from the cold official atmosphere of cruel suspicion, a blinded soldier led by his deaf and dumb comrade, two pathetic, shell-shocked orphans of the storm of war, we received nothing but sympathy, and were treated with nothing but kindness by all who encountered us on our *via dolorosa* to—wherever we might be going. Refraining from using our railway warrants, I bought our tickets in the ordinary way, and having set off toward Orleans in the rôle of *réformés* proceeding to convalescent hospital, we changed our route, and eventually took train for Le Havre in the guise of English *légionnaires* going on leave.

It was at Le Havre that Yrotavál, skilled in such quests, discovered a doctor of the type we wanted The war threw up quite a number of them in France men whose temporary army-pay was insufficient for their luxuries, not to mention their necessities, and who drove a thriving trade, in pronouncement of physical unfitness and provision of documents to that effect, on behalf of those who could pay for them.

We had some bad scares, we had some good luck, and we had the immeasurable advantage of the times, so abnormal, so out of joint, that what would have been utterly impossible in peace-time, was relatively easy.

Curious eyes stared at us as we approached the leave-boat, and friendly voices sympathized with us when it was learned that we were two Englishmen discharged by *Conseil de Réforme* from the French Foreign Legion.

At the foot of the gangway we were questioned, for

the last time, by an A.P.M. not accustomed to seeing French soldiers travelling to England in uniform. To him I explained that we were not French soldiers going on leave, but a couple of Britons discharged from the French Foreign Legion.

Yrotavál, as one mechanically performing an over-familiar rite, produced his bogus forms, one of which bore the words:

Nom :	John Brown.
Régiment :	Premier Regiment.
	Premier Bataillon de Marche Legion Étrangère.
Déclaration :	Congé de Réforme
	Retraite 25%

and the other:

John Brown.*

Né—12. Août 1884.			
À Londres.			
Canton de Londres	Etat		Signalement.
Département de Londres.			
Resident à Paris.		*Cheveux*	Noire.
Département de Seine.		*Yeux*	Brun.
Profession de Palefrenier.		*Front*	Normal.
Fils de		*Nez*	Rectiligne.
et de	Civil	*Visage*	Long.
Domicilié à		*Poids*	55 kilos.
Canton de		*Taille*	1 mtr. 70 centimetres.
Département de			

Où Engagé, Volontaire ; durée, guerre ; le 15 S'bre 1914, à Paris, département de Seine.

Numéro de la Liste Matricule 9886.

* A deceased comrade whose body Yrotavál had robbed.

Fumbling in the inner pocket of my tunic, I also produced my forged discharge and my matricule certificate.

A minute later we were *free*.

VII

It was all simply wonderful.

Never before was there such a return of such a hero. I enjoyed every minute of it.

The great thing, of course, was the inevitable bliss of the sense of *escape,* and the unspeakable joy of the return to peace and plenty, to safety and sanity, from what must surely be the worst hell that man ever made for himself on this earth.

And in addition to this was the tremendous fun of it all, the sheer enjoyment of the immensity of the colossal joke; and, I freely admit it, the very real, if deplorable, pleasure of being in the limelight, of being the very centre and cause of the tremendous fuss that everybody made of this wonderful occasion. Even I almost grew tired of the perpetually played air of "See the conquering hero comes"; and almost I had a surfeit of veal by the time the last fatted calf had been sacrificially killed in my honour.

But in time the excitement died away, and I settled down to the completest appreciation and enjoyment of the marvellous life of perfect peace and luxurious glorious ease. Or almost perfect, for naturally I had to be on my guard, and at first, to be very careful indeed. Not that it was as difficult as might be imagined by anyone who has never tried shamming blindness, because I indentured myself to a very thorough apprenticeship by keeping myself actually blind for some time. Whenever I left my own room, I wore a bandage over my eyes, and quickly learned from practical experience exactly how a blind man behaves. When tired of this, I had only to make my way back to my room, lock the door, remove my bandage and settle down for a quiet read, smoke or nap.

For weeks and months I could never have too much rest, and I desired nothing better than to while away the greater part of the day in my own private room, my peculiar and personal place apart, that gloriously safe and happy haven where none could disturb and bother me.

When, with returning health and strength, I grew more restless and desirous of more active life, I got Rosanne to procure for me a pair of the blackest sunglasses that could be got, and sometimes wore these instead of my bandage. I felt safer when wearing them when I removed my bandage, as they were a constant reminder that I must not see. Even so, in the early days, I was more than once on the point of doing something which no blind man would have done, or of realizing the presence of someone or something, of which only by sight I could have been aware.

However, I never aroused the slightest suspicion in the mind of anyone, and in course of time, felt quite safe in venturing out of my room for a little while, without either the bandages or the dark glasses.

My first trouble was with Athene. Her truly kind, sympathetic and generous heart was affected to its shallow depths; and her one idea was to get me the best of advice, the best treatment procurable; and it was her constant demand that I should come to Town with her to see various Harley Street wizards who, by her account, could raise the dead, and to whom the restoring of sight to the blind would be a matter of no difficulty.

I assured her, with perfect truth, that I had seen all the doctors whom I wished to see, that I was entirely satisfied that they were right, and that I had not the slightest intention of seeing any more. . . .

In the end she had to be content with my promise to visit her pet oculist, if my eyes pained me, if I realized that any change in them was taking place, if I found I was becoming sensitive to light, and finally, if and when I felt differently about it and equal to a journey to London for the purpose.

Fortunately, she had to hurry back to resume the Red Cross duties from which she had obtained, or taken, leave on hearing from Rosanne what had happened to me and in what condition I had made my way back to Courtesy Court.

Rosanne. . . .

Rosanne was marvellous. She rose to the occasion as though it were *the* occasion of her life. Perhaps it was. And if, at times, I was really rather ashamed of myself for the genuine grief, pain, and mental suffering that I was causing her, I comforted and reassured myself with the realization of the compensatory pleasure and joy that I was giving her.

No, I will withdraw "pleasure and joy" as not being the *mots justes*. . . . No, again, I won't. . . . For Rosanne did undoubtedly find a high and noble form of pleasure in ministering to me, and a sort of sacred or religious joy of the purest and least earthly kind, in lightening my terrible burden, assuaging my dumb suffering, and doing for me anything and everything that one human being can do for another. (Or almost everything.)

I cheated Rosanne, and, did she know the truth, she would probably feel that I wronged her—but in point of fact, I did her good. Naturally, I am not so egotistical a self-deceiver as to take credit for it, but the fact remains that I provided Rosanne with what most she needed.

I gave her a purpose in life, and a great and noble purpose. I brought out all that was best in her. Nothing could change my mind on that point; no one could possibly convince me that my return to Courtesy Court, apparently blinded, was anything but an unmixed blessing for Rosanne. She quickly, and one might say visibly, turned from a somewhat flippant, slightly hard, faintly superior and self-centred girl, whose day was a trivial round of hospital-visiting, charity-bazaar-running, committee-attending, and other petty war-work-pursuing, into a warm-hearted, devoted nurse, a real ministering angel—a woman with an aim in life, a single aim, on which she concentrated the whole of her energy, thought and love.

She had always loved me, up to a point, although we bickered from morning till night. Now she really loved me, I knew, with all her heart and soul and mind.

From the moment I walked into the hall, guided by Yrotavál, and heard her cry of shocked horror, I knew it; and it gave me no surprise when she dropped everything to devote herself to me, and from that moment stopped her training and abandoned her intention of becoming a V.A.D.

So, though I tricked her rather disgracefully, she deserved well of me for turning her from a young girl into an adult woman, from a girl who had never felt much, into a woman over-brimming with feeling; and from a somewhat useless atom in a world of uses, into an actual force with a living purpose and determination for good—the good of the man she loved.

She, too, of course, kept on at me about doctors and oculists, but, more quickly than Athene—being far wiser and more understanding than her mother—understood my attitude, my reluctance to go through it all again, only to hear at the end of it the same death-knell of a sentence. I had no need to tell her that she might be quite sure that the French Army doctors would not have invalided me out of the Army, as totally blind, unless I were so. And when I assured her that, on my own initiative and at my own expense, I had gone, when passing through Paris, to the great Renier, an eye-surgeon and oculist of European reputation, and that he had confirmed their diagnoses, she appeared to accept the situation and my word, though doubtless she did so with the mental reservation that she would get me to go and see the best oculist in London, later on.

Who, that knew Rosanne before and after my return, could doubt that I had done her anything but good? I repeat; she was a different girl. So different that whereas, before, I loved her as a brother and admired her with reservations, I now had no reservations whatsoever, and could have loved her as a lover.

Could have done—but for Giulia Brent-Grayleigh.

It is an amazing thing, this aberration of the mind, this madness of the soul that is called love.

Can a man love two women at once? I believe some men can, because some men are naturally, instinctively, and fundamentally polygamous. Had there been no Giulia, I believe I should have loved Rosanne wholly and completely; or, at any rate, should have thought I did. Had there been no Rosanne, I am quite certain that I should have loved Giulia completely. And that last is a somewhat foolish observation, because I did love Giulia thus.

So I did Rosanne.

Did I?

I don't know; and it is a pointless and unprofitable pursuit, this cold-blooded analysis of my feelings.

Still, I am out for truth, and I should like to get the matter straight. There's a wonderful satisfaction in getting things down in black and white and having them clear in your mind. At least I find it so, nowadays, driven in upon myself as I am; dwelling as I do in my paper prison.

Yes, I loved them both; but there was more passion in my love for Giulia; more gratitude, regard and respect in my love for Rosanne.

Was it pompous old Tennyson (I've never wallowed very deeply in the sloppy slush of his alleged poetry) who said that we needs must love the highest when we see it?

Of these two women, I was well aware that Rosanne was the higher, but I did not love her the more.

Or, damn it, did I?

Definitely I knew that Rosanne was the finer woman of the two; that she was noble, splendid; and that I owed her a deep debt of gratitude. But it was Giulia who stirred my blood. It was for Giulia that my heart beat faster. It was Giulia to whom I turned for— what shall I say? Let me be honest and say—for approval, unquestioning and unqualified; and for that warm, unstinted, ungrudging *passion,* that human passion of love which human passion demands and needs.

Like Rosanne, Giulia was not only willing, but

anxious, to give up everything else and concentrate on doing all she could for me. She, too, had filled her days, since war had broken out, with the kind of work that most such girls of the leisured class did to the best of their ability. I don't think she would ever have joined any uniformed organization such as the V.A.D.s even if she could have got her mother to agree to her doing so. She had led a sheltered life and was very much of a home bird. She liked her little comforts, lacked initiative, and had no yearnings for the rough realities of Life, nor for self-sacrifice. Nevertheless, she was anxious to help, and most willing to do whatever she could, within limits—the limits of home and the life to which she was accustomed.

All these little hospital-visiting and similar activities she now dropped, and placed herself at Rosanne's disposal for sharing in the work of looking after me. Rosanne must appoint her as confidential secretary, first-assistant, second-in-command, head nurse or what she liked, and count upon her as being ready, willing and able to come at any time, and for any length of time, to entertain me, talk to me, write letters for me, read to me, play to me (for she was an accomplished pianist), take me out for walks, or drive me in her car on shopping and other expeditions.

Rosanne was only too grateful, for, of course, she could not devote the whole of her time to me, being as she was, since my father's death and her mother's departure to London, in sole charge of the running of Courtesy Court.

Giulia was of course in love with me, as Rosanne was; and although her love could not exceed Rosanne's in breadth and depth and strength, in sympathy and loving-kindness, and the desire to serve, to help, to protect, it did exceed hers in passion. I do not say that Rosanne, with the Scottish and Anglo-Saxon strain in her American ancestry, was cold; but I do say that Giulia, half Italian and wholly Italianate, was warm— indeed hot-blooded and passionate—as who should know better than I to whom she had frequently given the ultimate proof that her love was volcanic, a thing of passion and of fire.

So here was I in a situation of which the comfort approached perfection, a position of almost Paradisial luxury and delight; and, moreover, loved by two lovely women whose one desire and great happiness was to wait upon me hand and foot.

Almost. Not quite. There was a fly in the precious ointment of my blessed joy and glorious peace.

Yrotavál, my fellow-conspirator and partner in innocent crime—for I still maintain that my deception was harmless, nay positively beneficial to those to whom I gave occasion and opportunity for self-fulfilment and self-expression in lavishing upon me their devotion—was troublesome.

Who hath a partner hath a master, and, quite soon, Yrotavál became masterful. It was all right at first, and I could jokingly refer to him as some people do to the cook or butler who has been with them for half a century, as having "turned from a good servant into a bad master, or at any rate from a fine and faithful servant into a difficult and exacting master."

At first he was only too thankful to find himself safe; and safe, moreover, in a place where he had every kindness and consideration, and a life of real ease and comfort, such as he had never known.

But one day, after we had had "words" on the subject of his attentions to Rosanne's own personal maid, he came right out into the open with a remark to the effect that should he tire of this dull and humdrum life and decide to live elsewhere, it might be awkward for me, unless we parted on the best of terms—his own terms, to wit.

With a grin and an inimitable leer, he remarked that with all our experience, we had never seen a bomb burst with quite such effect as the bomb-shell of his exposure of me would have, if it burst in this quiet little corner of England.

"*Si, si, Patron!*" he smiled. "*Ça va faire un drole d'effet.*"

And I reflected at leisure, and at length, on the

truth of his statement, his under-statement, that the results of exposure would be uncommonly droll for—me.

Like Jeshurun, the brute began to wax fat and kick; to give trouble in the servants' hall; offend the maids; annoy the cook, by what she considered outrageous and outlandish demands—such as for his favourite mess of bread-crumbs, mutton-fat and garlic; and thoroughly to upset Johnson, the butler.

And in some way, he completely failed to please Rosanne. In point of fact, that is also something of an under-statement; for he did more than fail to please her. He succeeded in making her absolutely loathe him. How, Heaven knows! To my mind it was just a piece of feminine unreasonableness on her part, for she could never bring any definite charge against him.

Nor did it seem greatly to improve matters when I pointed out to her, what was the simple truth, that Giulia, far from taking the same view of Yrotavál, rather liked him; did like him, in fact; found him very interesting and really rather charming.

VIII

What did upset Yrotavál and, to some extent me, was Mark's return from the Front. I was, of course, truly delighted to see him home again, safe and sound, but was shocked at his condition. So far as such a powerful man as Mark could be—and he was very tough indeed, of rock-like strength of mind, body, and soul—he was a bundle of nerves; and I must admit that the sight of me didn't do him any good either. He had evidently had an appalling time, had lived face to face with death, night and day, under about the worst conditions that a human being can endure and survive, was just about at the end of his tether, and scarcely equal to the blow of seeing his beloved Luke—broken and blinded.

He being so ill, shattered and worn out himself, the fuss he made of me was really rather pathetic.

But glad as I was to see him, his coming didn't really improve things for me, beyond making a little change and excitement in an existence that was already becoming rather humdrum.

In the first place, he, of course, started the bother and annoyance that I had already gone through with Athene and Rosanne about seeing oculists and getting not only the best opinion available but several of them; and he conspired, for my own good of course, with our own chap Watson and with Abernethy, the nerve-specialist whom Rosanne brought down periodically to deal with my shell-shock and general mental and physical condition. I was, of course, pretty ill by the time I got home, and no nonsense about it, whether one called my symptoms those of shell-shock or of the neurasthenia that inevitably follows intolerable stress and strain, or just the results of general weakness due to malnutrition and prolonged excessive tension and fatigue.

This Abernethy was a queer, cross-grained chap,

and although he was never actually offensive to me or difficult with Rosanne, he seemed to think that anyone, who wasn't either obviously unhinged in mind or mortally stricken in body, must be something of a *malade imaginaire.* He bluntly told Mark that what he would like to do would be to send me to a nursing-home run by a famous neurologist who was supposed to be affecting wonderful cures by means of psycho-therapy, especially cases of shell-shock, to which, incidentally, he always alluded as "alleged" shell-shock, professing to believe that there was no such thing! Fortunately Rosanne would not hear of my going to a nursing-home, and it did not take me long to persuade Mark that it was just plain cruelty to pester me with oculists in my present condition.

Of course, I wouldn't have dreamed of agreeing to anything of the sort, but in point of fact, it was never even proposed to me, as Rosanne put her foot down heavily and immediately, when Abernethy suggested it. She could and would do all the nursing that was necessary!

There is no doubt that Abernethy was a brilliant alienist—too brilliant from my point of view—and I am not sure that I completely deceived him. Of course I was in a pretty bad way when he first saw me; but perfect rest, good food, and Rosanne's nursing had very quickly and rather marvellously improved my condition—had put me almost right, in fact; and it was none too easy to continue to play the nerve-shattered invalid in front of Watson, much less Abernethy. As to the blindness, I simply insisted on wearing either my bandage or my dark glasses when either doctor was present, and any suspicion that might have been entertained on that subject could only have been based on my refusal to let them examine my eyes.

They did not want to do this from the professional-oculist point of view, but because, by an examination of the retina, they could learn a good deal concerning my nervous condition, and whether there was any symptom of cerebro-spinal sclerosis or anything of that kind.

As I got better and stronger, the less I enjoyed Abernethy's visits and Mark's anxiety to bring him down oftener and to hold long consultations with him and Watson about me. Mark was too solicitous altogether—for my liking and comfort—and I had to make it quite clear that nothing upset me more, nothing set me back more surely, than these medical attacks and invasions—attacks on my slowly built-up self-confidence, invasions of my painfully erected mental defences, and of my precious privacy.

Fortunately for me, Mark's mind, unlike my own, is more notable for strength than for subtlety.

In the second place he started another bother with his attitude to Yrotavál. He had never liked the old scoundrel, and now he seemed positively to hate him. In point of fact, I think he was a bit jealous that I saw so much more of Yrotavál, my valet and constant attendant, than I did of him.

I think, too, that Rosanne turned him against the rascal, for Mark had not been in the house a month before he was talking about my sacking him and getting a male nurse who was also a trained valet. God knows that, by that time, I'd have been glad to see the back of Yrotavál, but the irony of it was that, while I agreed with every word that Mark said, I was compelled stoutly to defend the blackguard, to swear that I simply could not get along without him, and that whatever else they did to me in my blindness, they must not deprive me of the one person who was now the prop and mainstay of my existence.

Mark hated that, even more than I disliked saying it.

"*What!* Yrotavál the mainstay of . . ." he protested. "Surely Rosanne is *that.* So far as I can see, she simply lives for you; thinks of nothing else but you and your comfort and welfare and happiness."

"So do I, old chap," he added. "You know that. And when I say 'happiness,' you understand what I mean, Luke," he faltered. "Happy as we can make you . . . in the circumstances. . . . Surely Rosanne and I . . ."

"But, my dear old boy," I interrupted, "neither

Rosanne nor you can be my valet. You can't come in at seven in the morning and shave me. Neither you nor Rosanne can very well bathe me and dress me every day of my life. Damn it, Mark, I don't want either Rosanne or you . . . er . . . buttoning up my trousers! . . . Rosanne and you are the best friends I've got in the world, the best friends a man can have, but I must have a servant too. I must have someone on whom I can make demands at any hour of the day or night—in return for cash payment. I don't know how I should get on without Rosanne, of course; and I shall hate it when I've got to get on without you; but I simply cannot get on without Yrotavál."

"There's the little matter of gratitude too," I added. "I owe him my life. But for Yrotavál I shouldn't be sitting here at this minute."

Poor old Markie was obviously between the devil and the deep sea—Rosanne's wishes and my needs—and about as comfortable as a herring on a griddle.

"Yes," he agreed, fidgeting like a small boy in the presence of the Headmaster whom he fears won't accept his excuses, "of course you want a valet, old chap. Neither Rosanne nor I would dream of suggesting that you should do without one. But what about letting us find a really first-class man who is a well-trained servant as well as a professional nurse; a man who would fit in with the rest of the staff and wouldn't cause friction? You know what's the worst accusation that a butler or cook can bring against any fellow-servant? They say they 'give trouble'—and as far as I can see, Yrotavál gives trouble to everybody, every day, in every possible way.

"Of course they are a silly, narrow-minded and hide-bound set of half-wits," he hastened to add, "but . . . well . . . there it is. I don't suppose Johnson or Cook or Rosanne's maid would go the length of giving notice—but they give tongue, all right."

" 'Here's a stranger, heave half a brick at him,' eh?" I said, with apparent bitterness.

"Well, you know what servants are. And after all, old Johnson came here as a page-boy in grandfather's time. Cook used to speak of father as Master John, to the day of his death. And Old Janey used to wash his neck for him when he hadn't done it himself. And Rosanne's really fond of Jeanette."

"And Yrotavál professes to be, eh?" I interrupted. "Look here, Mark. I can see what it is. And I simply am not going to be a disturbing element in the house. I'm not going to that loony-bin, for psycho-therapy or psycho-analysis or whatever they call the mumbo-jumbo, but surely you could find some quiet place—some Devonshire farm-house or seaside place—where Yrotavál and I . . ."

"*Shut up!*" growled Mark, coming and standing with his hand on my shoulder, rocking me gently to and fro, and patting me on the back as though I were a child. And although I could not look him straight in the face, but only glance at him as I fixed my gaze just above his head, I saw there was a look of dreadful pain in his eyes.

"Don't talk like that, Luke," he begged after a moment's miserable silence. "There's nothing in the world we wouldn't do. . . . You misunderstood me completely. . . . I . . . My dear chap, we'd sooner. . . ."

I fumbled for his hand and—heard no more about dismissing Yrotavál, damn him.

What bothered me most was the thought of what I was to do about the foul brute when the time came for me to recover my sight. However, that certainly wasn't going to be before the War ended, so there would be plenty of time to cross that bridge when I came to it.

No more war for me! No. Whatever happened, nothing on this earth would induce me to go back to it. When Peace came, I'd decide what to do about recovering my sight and losing my Yrotavál. Cosy as he was at Courtesy Court, I had no doubt that there were other places where he would enjoy life just as well, or even better—and at a reasonable price. Sufficient unto the day . . .

But it was very annoying to have him constantly grumbling about the way Mark treated him—like a dog, like dirt, like a criminal—and threatening that he'd show him where he got off if he weren't more careful how he insulted a Spanish hidalgo. Who did Mark think he was, anyway? Was this the French Foreign Legion and Mister M. Tuyler a Sergeant-Major or what?

Much of this was both artificial and artful of course —an excuse to demand compensation in the form of a rise in salary—but it was all very annoying and disturbing, for although Yrotavál knew on which side his bread was buttered, he was, like all criminals, a fool. A man wouldn't be a practising criminal if he weren't a fool, and Yrotavál was a criminal all right, and I never knew what form his folly might take when some alleged insult injurious to his Spanish pride filled him with brooding anger and smouldering resentment. To think that such a low ruffian should have anything so fine as pride! I suppose it was really conceit and touchiness rather than true pride, though.

Anyway, I grew to hate him more and more, for Mark's treatment of him had turned him from an expensive luxury into a nuisance, nay an incubus, an absolute Old Man of the Sea, and clamped upon my shoulders apparently for life.

So it was with some fortitude that I bore the bad news of Mark's intention to return to the Front. Positively the old lunatic was going back to it all; back to the trenches; and as a private soldier again!

I would sooner have been put up against our own park wall and shot, then and there—and that's the simple truth.

§2

Yes, all of a sudden our Mark, in the good old Markian way, was delivered of what was doubtless the product of long and painful gestation, one merry morn —an announcement to the effect that he was going to enlist in the ranks of His Majesty's Foot-guards, forthwith or sooner!

I could scarcely believe my ears.

It seemed to me to be something really superhuman

that he, having survived the dangers and horrors of that unbelievable and indescribable Legion hell, from which barely one in a hundred returned safe and sound in wind and limb, not to mention mind and soul, should voluntarily return to the trenches, and long before he was fit to do so.

And to go back as a private soldier, when he could have got a commission in any regiment in the British Army! With his fighting record, the *Croix de Guerre and* the *Médaille Militaire*—and General Brent-Grayleigh's recommendation, he could have gone to the Guards as an Ensign or the Life Guards as a Cornet, or whatever they call them.

But to go back to the trenches as a Tommy, when not only were Abernethy and Watson willing to give him a medical certificate of unfitness, but positively anxious to do so . . . well!

I couldn't quite make up my mind as to whether he simply wanted to get killed—though God knows why he should—or whether he had developed a real taste for personal Hun-slaying. Surely he had "done his bit," to use the vulgarism of the day. And if not, why go back as a private soldier? There again, I couldn't quite make up my mind as to whether it was his excessive modesty, combined with a lack of self-confidence; or whether, at the back of his funny old mind, there was some idea about scourging himself and wearing the metaphorical hair-shirt. And again, God knows why he should want to do that.

However, there it was! Back to the wars he'd go, and with a rifle on his shoulder rather than a sword by his side. Perhaps our Markie, being out to kill, felt that he could do more killing with the .303, for he had turned out to be a really first-class shot, as good with a rifle as he had always been with a twelve-bore.

Rosanne took it very hardly and, had I been in love with her, I should have been quite jealous. As it was, I confess to a slight twinge of—not jealousy, of course, but a sort of feeling of not greatly enjoying quite all the *See the Conquering Hero goes* stuff, while his brother sat by the fire in carpet slippers and black glasses.

It was Mark for the lime-light and Luke for the back seat, for once in a while, with a vengeance.

I was astonished at the way in which Rosanne positively moped after he had gone. I really began to wonder if she were actually in love with him, whether the sisterly love that she had doubtless always felt for him, had changed in nature and intensity.

Not that she was in the slightest degree less loving, kind, and attentive to me, of course. I should be giving an absolutely false impression if I so much as hinted that. I don't want to give that idea at all, for although his going certainly caused a change in Rosanne, she did not change toward me. No, on the whole, poor old Mark's departure made things none the worse so far as I was concerned, and I lost nothing by his absence. On the contrary, things rather improved, for Yrotaval ceased to grumble and threaten; Rosanne had less to distract her attention from me; and Giulia and I had more time together. There, Mark had, with all the goodwill in the world, overdone the "mustn't let him mope; must take him out of himself and make him cheerful" attitude and treatment a little. A lot in fact— for it had never dawned on him, of course, that three could be an awkward number; nor that when Giulia was with me, it was a case of two being excellent company. I was only too delighted for him to come and smoke a last pipe with me when she had gone home and Rosanne had said good night; but at other times, when Giulia and I had settled down for a *tête-à-tête* in the library or my room, he was, at that particular time and place, at any rate, just about one too many.

Of course, neither Giulia nor I ever admitted that we were glad when he went off and enlisted, but undeniably we settled down for our afternoons together with a sense of, what shall I say—privacy and security —which was very pleasant. No, we never admitted it, nor did we even once, when we set off for a drive in her car, say, "Isn't it lovely to be alone together again!"

Darling Giulia!

Nevertheless, delightful a companion as Giulia was, warm-hearted, responsive, kind and loving as only she could be, it was not so very long before I began to suffer from a sense of boredom. Definitely I was cribbed, cabined and confined; and though any nerve-trouble with which I may have come home was completely cured, this sort of life was beginning to get on my nerves, and I was really suffering now from sheer *ennui.*

The walls of the paper prison that I had built myself began to look and feel like granite; and at times I wondered whether I could keep my blindness up until the end of the War.

God alone knew how long the war might drag on. What should I do if it went on for years? If that did happen, Conscription was bound to follow, according to General Brent-Grayleigh, and as he was a member of the Army Council or something terribly important at the War Office, he knew what he was talking about.

I was in a quandary; for on the one hand, I couldn't very well recover my sight and hang about in safety and idleness at home, while Mark was at the Front again, fighting in the trenches as a private soldier in a Guards' Battalion; nor could I leave home, go into hiding, and spend my time in dodging the beastly press-gang when Conscription came into force.

And if I partially recovered my sight, so that I could lead a somewhat wider and more spacious life than that of a blind man, I might get hauled before some Medical Board who'd hand me over to their pet fiend whose verdict on draft-dodgers would be final. It would be pretty rotten if Luke Rivers Tuyler of Courtesy Court were pronounced a liar, a fraud and a scrimshanker by some Military Tribunal's eye-specialist.

No, I must stay blind, at any rate for the duration. Better that than exposure and a beastly scandal; and a thousand times better that than the trenches again.

I told myself I was simply getting morbid through not having enough to do. Better go outside and shake myself.

Nevertheless, the Perfect Life was beginning to pall.

I was getting tired of doing nothing; getting tired even of Giulia.

Man cannot live by love alone.

Another thing was beginning to worry me, and that was the question of my future. Courtesy Court would be my home as long as Mark lived; and Mark would say, as the Spaniards do (with the slight difference that he would mean it from the bottom of his heart), that everything in his house was mine. That would be all right, and I should have the run of my teeth and everything that I wanted, including pocket-money. But suppose Mark were killed, as was extremely probable? Courtesy Court would then be mine, and that would be all right too—so long as Athene chose to run it as her home. But suppose she married again, a thing she might do any day? She was a very wealthy woman, still extremely attractive, and definitely given to the practice of matrimony. As she had had enumerable husbands (three) and innumerable lovers (three score at least), there was no earthly reason to imagine that she would long remain in what she would not consider a state of single blessedness.

Suppose she married some damned fortune-hunter who got hold of all her money? Or some fellow who would view her expenditure on the upkeep of Courtesy Court with complete disfavour? Or some chap who had already got a place of his own, and would naturally want her to live there? Or some American officer who would take her back to the States? In short, suppose she made some marriage which put an end to her interest, financial and other, in Courtesy Court? It would be calamity, absolute ruin, especially in view of the fact that there would have been a second lot of death-duties to pay when Mark was killed.

At times—generally about four o'clock in the morning—the future would look anything but rosy, and I would imagine Athene married and gone to America. Rosanne gone with her, or Rosanne married and gone God knew where. Courtesy Court derelict, deserted, uninhabitable. Luke Rivers Tuyler ruined, crushed, penniless, broken.

Crushed and broken? I was that already, mentally and morally speaking. There was no fight left in me at all. I could no more get up and go out and earn my own living now, than I could go back to the trenches. As I think I have made clear, I am a very different man from Mark. If he is a battle-axe, I am a razor; and you can't fell trees with a razor, any more than you can shave chins with a chopper. What Mark will be like if and when he ever comes back, remains to be seen; but I am finished so far as fighting goes—fighting for bread, fighting for my life, apart from any question of fighting Germans.

Thus thought I to myself in the dark small hours when vitality is at its lowest ebb.

Nor, in these black moods, did I see any hope for me in Giulia or Rosanne. Giulia, like myself, had nothing more than pocket-money; and her parents might live another forty years. Rosanne had plenty of money to spend, but it was Athene's money—which she might never inherit. And apart from my having no particular desire that Rosanne and I should be pensioners on Athene's bounty, there was no telling what might happen to us when Athene married again. Sometimes, before merciful sleep put an end to these miserable fears and anxieties, I actually contemplated marrying Athene myself, which merely goes to show the gloomy depths of horror and depression to which I could sink. And, other things apart, it was rather more than doubtful that Athene would wish to marry a man twenty years younger than herself, a crock who was also her stepson!

I'm not sure whether the Bishops in their wisdom have decided that it is not lawful and right for a man to marry his stepmother, but I am quite sure that Society has, and with the strongest ban of all—ridicule.

No, even if I could go to Athene and say, with a becoming blush,

"Darling, isn't it time you made an honest man of me?" I somehow didn't think I could bring myself to ask Rosanne at breakfast one morning to pass me the toast and become my step-daughter-in-law.

No. Money isn't everything.

It's a damned lot, though!

§3

We suffer most from the calamities that never happen to us.

Out of the sky fell the bolt that was to change my life, settle my future, and relieve me of all fears, doubts, and anxieties concerning it. A bolt from the blue indeed, a cowardly woman-and-child-slaughterer's bomb; and poor Athene was less fortunate than I, for the explosion mangled her so that she died within a few hours.

It was a great shock to me, and I genuinely grieved for her, as must anyone have done who knew her fundamental kindliness. I had almost said goodness. Incidentally, why should one not call good anyone whose heart is kind, whose nature is generous, and who is a person of good-will? I cannot pretend that Athene did me any good, but she never wished me any harm. Perhaps nothing in her life became her like the leaving of it, for she died very bravely, thinking of, and for, others; and sending them messages. It is no bad epitaph for any man or woman which says that he or she, dying in great agony, thought of others and gave instructions for their welfare.

Her death was a shock to me. It was a greater shock to Rosanne. Although she had been most filial, she had never really loved her mother, perhaps because Athene had never loved Rosanne—or if she had done so, had given remarkably little evidence of it. One of the things I admired about Rosanne had been her attitude to her mother. Not only did she refrain from criticizing her, but she would never listen to any criticism of her; and now that Athene was dead, Rosanne, while making no pretence of great personal loss, undoubtedly mourned her and grieved for the manner of her death.

Except for pleasant legacies to Mark and myself, Rosanne was her sole heiress.

§4

Another anxiety that, having effected lodgment at the back of my mind, steadily grew and pressed forward, was the question of the real truth as to the condition of my eyes. I was using Yrotavál's concoction less and less frequently, and I intended shortly to do without it altogether. What worried me was that, whenever I removed my bandage, I found that my eyes were definitely more inflamed and painful than when I put it on. They were at their best in the mornings and on such days as I relied entirely on the dark glasses and forbore to use the bandage altogether.

Frequently I decided that I would abolish the use of the latter entirely, but no sooner had I done so, than I would realize that the time was not yet, that I still lived dangerously when I could see, even through glass darkly. No one who hasn't tried it would believe how numerous and easy are the pitfalls that await one; how instinctive it is to do things which it would be impossible to do if one were really blind.

By the use of the bandage, by extreme care with the dark glasses, and by acting hard, consciously, and with the utmost concentration, when my eyes were uncovered, I had avoided suspicion while gaining a reputation for extreme cleverness.

But only while using the bandage did I feel safe.

With my eyes completely covered I could make no mistake. While wearing the dark glasses I was on tenterhooks, though life was of course much pleasanter. While going about with my eyes uncovered, I bore a strain that was almost unendurable, and lived in constant fear. Nevertheless, I had to do it sometimes, for there were occasions when I felt I must, at any cost, see sunshine, colour, the sky, the grass, the trees, my fellow human-beings, Giulia, Rosanne, the house, inside and out.

Here the pain was, of course, helpful, a constant

reminder that while seeing and most thoroughly enjoying what, for some reason, the pious call the lusts of the eye, I was blind. I must do nothing that a totally blind man could not do.

Let me here once again be perfectly honest, frank and truthful, and admit that what I disliked most of all was the disfigurement. At times, my eyes looked simply beastly, and, when this was so, I would bathe them, use an eye-wash, retire to my darkened room and wait till they were less of a disfigurement, were, in fact, quite normal, and no disfigurement at all. This meant complete retirement into my shell for a day or two.

It grew less and less easy to restore them to normality, and my worry and anxiety about them were at length sufficiently strong to make me at last decide on a course which I had long considered, that of visiting an ophthalmic surgeon.

I must not visit Sir Theophilus Grant, for fear Rosanne and Mark should conspire behind my back to bring him to Courtesy Court, and suddenly confront me with him.

I must go incognito to some excellent but less-famous man.

I would go to two, and make assurance doubly sure.

§5

Telling Rosanne that I was going up to Town with Yrotaval to do a little shopping, and that I neither desired nor would tolerate any other company, I contrived to get away without much fuss.

That was one thing about Rosanne. Never did woman argue, nag, thwart, wrangle or reproach less than she did. In point of fact, she sometimes angered me by her complete refusal to quarrel, be it never so mildly, and thus give me an opportunity of justifying myself when I was in the wrong.

She was a dear, and it was a damn shame to bother her.

Mr. Household of Wimpole Street was a most pleasant, kindly, and sympathetic person, and although I do not imagine that Ophthalmic Surgeons do a great deal of bedside work, he had the most perfect bedside manner that I have ever experienced.

He accepted my word for it that I was totally blind, and, when I removed my bandage, he expressed grave concern over the external condition of my eyes, spoke of purulent conjunctivitis and staphylococcic infection.

We had quite a time together, and he gave me a prescription for a nice eye-wash that would cure the conjunctivitis in no time. Gravely he warned me against the use of nitrate of silver, as, although an excellent and soothing disinfectant, it would, in time, stain the eyeball and render yellow and bilious-looking the healthy young clearness of the white of my eye. He was interested to know what had caused my blindness, and was very sympathetic and understanding when I told him of the explosion.

"I thought as much," he said. "There's absolutely nothing to indicate blindness, and had you not told me what you have, I should have said that your sight was perfect. . . . But I've known of lots of such cases. . . . Terribly sudden. . . .

"Concussion. . . . Sudden severe nervous shock. . . . Occasionally *purely psychological*. . . ."

"No retina spots, no indication of a dead end of the optic nerve," he murmured to himself, or words to that effect, as sadly he sighed and shook his head.

"No sign of disease, Doctor?"

"Absolutely none. The eyes are *not* diseased. Pupils give good light reaction. . . . Nothing wrong with hinder part of optic-nerve system. . . . But we know now that men can be struck blind by shock—and by *mental* shock, too, without any physical concussion. . . . No one but yourself could say that you are not blind. And, equally, no one but yourself could say that you are. But you will have to be careful of this infection. And don't, *don't* bind the eyes up again, whatever you do."

We parted on the best of terms and a three-guinea fee.

So far so good, but while I was about it, I would have another opinion.

Certainly, it was extremely interesting and most reassuring to learn that nobody but I could decide whether I was blind or not: but, on the other hand, nobody but I knew the effect that Yrotavál's filthy concoction was having on my sight; nor how infernally painful it was.

Mr. Struthers of Harley Street proved to be an extremely unpleasant person. Having taken my name (Captain Arthur Holbeach of Willoughby House, Linfield, near Warwick) and asked a number of questions about my eyes and those of my ancestors unto the third and fourth generation, he thoughtfully screwed up a sheet of paper into a ball, balanced it on his thumbnail—and suddenly flipped it straight in my face! Mad as a hatter! I was positively alarmed.

Thereafter he examined me much in the way that Mr. Household and the French *Médecin Major* had done, but with a more formidable array of instruments and apparatus.

Throughout this examination he appeared to be possessed of a devil of dumbness, one which, as the expression of his face grew more unpleasant, I would fain have cast out. At length the look on his saturnine visage became definitely sceptical and contemptuous.

When he did speak, he was sarcastic, if not insulting.

"Are you in receipt of any disability pension?" he asked.

"I am not," said I.

"Oh, I thought perhaps you had been invalided out of the Army by reason of the condition of your eyes, and that you were in enjoyment of partial-disability compensation—and hoped to increase it to a total disability."

"What you think must inevitably be very interesting," I replied, "but I didn't come up to London for the pleasure of hearing it."

"No? Not to hear what I think about your eyes?"

"That, certainly. But not what you may or may not think about compensation. If you will kindly tell me exactly what is the matter with my eyes, I shall be obliged."

"I'm afraid I can't. I thought at first glance it was phlyctenular conjunctivitis due to active-service malnutrition, strain, and some sort of infection. . . . Staphylococcic probably. . . . But it isn't; and if you'll excuse me 'thinking' again, I am inclined to think that you know better what is wrong with your eyes than I do. I should say that you are putting something in them, and I would most strongly recommend you to stop doing it."

"I'd be glad if you'd stick to what you actually know," I began.

"Well, I know one thing. You are no more blind than I am. You can see perfectly well. Had you been a pensioner, it would have given me considerable pleasure to have had a chat with my friend, the ophthalmic referee at the Ministry of Pensions. However, as you say you are not . . ."

I rose to go.

"Since, admittedly, you cannot tell me what is wrong with my eyes and appear to be ignorant of the fact that there are eye-diseases of which not every ophthalmic surgeon is aware, I must try elsewhere. I should have gone to Sir Theophilus Grant, perhaps. It may interest him, after he has made his examination, to learn that you are 'perfectly certain' that there is nothing the matter with my eyes, and that I can see as well as you can. It may also interest your eye-specialist colleagues and the general public. It is just possible you may hear more about this."

The man laughed unpleasantly:

"I doubt it," said he. "Good morning. There will be no fee."

"Would it be asking too much of you to beg you to be good enough to conduct me to the door?"

"Far too much. You can see that door-handle as well as I can."

"Perhaps you'd be so kind, then, as to call my man,

who is in your waiting-room. Or must I shout?"

"I will ring for your—er—confederate," replied the fellow.

And as, led by Yrotavál, I walked out of the room, he added,

"Next time you try to trick an oculist, don't go straight to a chair that you can't see; don't flinch when he throws a paper-ball at your face; don't, in your blindness, accurately place your hat on a neighbouring table and put your gloves in it."

What a fool I had been—but what a useful lesson!

A damned unpleasant experience, but it again reassured me as to the condition of my eyes. No signs of other than superficial damage caused by Yrotavál's filthy concoction.

§6

It gave Rosanne great satisfaction to know that I had been to two Ophthalmic Surgeons; but the news that both found me totally blind and that neither held out any hope, brought the unready tears to her eyes.

She thanked me very sweetly for having done what she had so long wanted me to do, and praised my kindness and consideration in going through the painful fruitless ordeal, just to please her and ease her mind of the constant fear that there might have been any stone left unturned.

IX

Whether Rosanne married me out of pity, or because she loved me, or because she loved Courtesy Court and it seemed the obvious thing to do, only Rosanne knew.

Of course she loved me, but I doubt whether she was in love with me in the sense, say, that Giulia was. Perhaps I caught her on the rebound, if I rightly understand the meaning of that remarkable phrase—in other words, asked her to marry me just at the moment when she was feeling particularly lonely, unsettled and depolarized. When I say lonely, I do not mean physically lonely, so to speak. She had my company; Giulia Brent-Grayleigh had almost lived at the house since I returned; and there were plenty of visitors and callers.

It was the position of lonely responsibility without actual and established authority, I think, that troubled her. While her mother was alive, Rosanne was the daughter of the house. Now that her mother was dead, she was merely a rich woman living at Courtesy Court, of which the owner was her absent step-brother, who was more than likely never to return.

I suppose that, after Father's death and Mark's inheritance of the place, Athene had been in a somewhat similar position; but Athene was a very different woman from Rosanne.

Anyhow, after having waited for a reasonable period, and without having shown indecent haste, I now begged her to marry me because I loved her; because I simply could not contemplate life without her, if she married and went away; because, apart from that, I simply could not bear the thought of her marrying anyone else; and finally because Mark would rejoice and would be so much easier in his mind if he knew that I was happily and permanently provided for, and that she would still be mistress of Courtesy Court.

I shall never forget how, when I urged the last

point, Rosanne, resting her hands on my shoulders, looked into my eyes, while tears welled into hers.

"You think *that,* Luke? You really believe that Mark would—what was the word you used—rejoice—if I married you?"

"I'm certain of it," I said. "Of course he would."

"Yes, of course he would," said Rosanne, "but oh, Luke, how I wish you could look into my eyes as I am looking into yours. . . . No, I'm sorry I said that, dear Luke. . . . But oh, how I wish I knew whether Mark really . . ."

And suddenly it dawned on me that she had been extraordinarily quiet about Mark since he went away. I don't think she had ever initiated a conversation about him. Could it be that Mark . . . ? Of course not. Wouldn't he have said so? Would he have gone off again, without a word?

"I didn't want to have to say it—to urge you, Rosanne," said I, putting out my hands to touch her face, "but Mark . . . told me. . . . *This is what he hoped for.*"

And Rosanne, unexpected ever, smiled as she still gazed at me as though she longed to read my thoughts, longed to see into my soul. She smiled—though it was scarcely a smile of ecstatic joy—and said,

"We mustn't disappoint Mark, must we?" and kissed me.

On hearing the news, Yrotavál raised his wages.

§2

When Giulia heard the news, she went very white.

"Oh, Luke! Luke!" she whispered. "I have been afraid you'd . . ."

"You won't let it make any difference?" she added.

"To our friendship, Giulia?" I said. "No."

And Giulia began quietly to weep.

I suppose that being abnormally intuitive and having, like most true artists, a streak of femininity— which is by no means the same as effeminacy—in my character, I understand women as well as most men do, and I was not surprised at Giulia's attitude. We had loved each other for years.

Now that I had returned to Courtesy Court, blind and helpless (not to mention the fact that I was far too poor to give Giulia Brent-Grayleigh the establishment that she must have), I am perfectly certain that nothing would have induced her to marry me. On the other hand, I am quite certain that her love had increased and that it had changed in kind and nature. I know, without the shadow of a doubt, that, although she loved me more, and more truly, by reason of her deep womanly pity, there was also a sadistic quality in her passion and her love, or perhaps in the passion of her love. She loved being loved by a blind lover, my Giulia who was half Italian. It was entirely subconscious, of course, and she was fond of reassuring me that she loved me more than ever now, for the simple reason that she felt that I was her child as well as her lover.

Rubbish!

Although no crude statement of fact was ever made, we both clearly understood that I was marrying Rosanne for her money. If this were balm to Giulia, why deny it to her? If it gave her comfort to lay such flattering unction to her jealous soul, let her take that comfort.

I was thankful that she took the news as well and quietly as she did, for I had been a little anxious. Definitely I did not wish to lose her friendship, her company, her appreciation, her love, and, let me be frank, her admiration. Giulia supplied me with something that I badly needed, something that Rosanne either lacked or withheld. And even more definitely, I did not want trouble, recrimination, possibly the most delicate nuance of something threatening in her attitude. Giulia was a gentlewoman and utterly incapable of anything in the nature of amorist blackmail, but it would have been rather terrible, as well as dangerous to the success of my plans, if she had taken the news badly, flung off in a rage and, inspired by jealousy, had made some unforgivable and unforgettable remark to Rosanne. Happily, her English blood and English training triumphed over her Latin temperament and temper, and she accepted with quite a good grace what she must have foreseen as the inevitable.

And so Rosanne, my fairy-godmother, and I, her Prince Charming, were married, settled down to live happy ever after, and had been doing so for a time that, to me in my paper prison, had begun to seem quite long, when the War ended and—Mark returned to Courtesy Court.

X

At first sight of Mark I almost gave myself away. It was on the tip of my tongue to say,

"My God! You look . . ."

It was, I think, only the shock that kept me from speaking, and making an appalling slip of the tongue that would have exposed me and been the ultimate tragedy. One talks of being struck dumb with horror. Fortunately I was. And before the words came I remembered.

He really looked simply awful; so terribly changed, gaunt, haggard and wasted; and he looked so—for once I am at a loss for a word—I suppose "haunted" meets the case as well as any of them, but I don't like it. He looked tortured and suffering; though I could see that his pain was far more mental and spiritual than physical; for he was neither wounded nor actually ill, beyond being weary, fine-drawn, and fatigue-poisoned, the sort of thing that rest and treatment would soon have put right if that had been all.

§2

It would not be true to say that Mark's coming brought a great deal of sunshine into the house.

For one thing, it upset Rosanne, and in a curious way. Once again I observe that I understand women as well as most men do, but I was at a loss to decide exactly what was troubling Rosanne; what she was thinking and feeling. She annoyed me rather, but I frankly and freely admit that this may have been because, although she in no way neglected me, she gave so much of her time and attention to Mark, and wanted to nurse him as though he were really ill. Apparently this did not please Mark any more than it did me, for he told her quite plainly that there was nothing wrong with him, that he didn't want to be coddled, and that if she fussed over him he'd clear out again.

Methinks he did protest too much, for he seemed to bear it very bravely when Rosanne came and sat beside him on the settee, leaning up against him with her head on his shoulder, just as she had done any evening for the last ten years.

He had always been terribly fond of her, and yet he was quite brusque and short in his manner now.

"He has met another woman," thought I.

And gradually something of the sort seemed to dawn on Rosanne, for she grew much less demonstrative, suffered a little from pique, and undeniably obliged him in the matter of ceasing to fuss.

But of course women are unaccountable as well as changeable, and there were times when you'd have thought he was a combination of her only child and her first lover. At others, she was cold, distant and short. I got infinite amusement from sitting and watching them.

Once Rosanne put her hand on Mark's, or rather into it. Mark kept his perfectly still. Then Rosanne drew it toward her and old Mark snatched it away. I wished that the light had been better, so that I could have seen Rosanne's face, but she obviously stiffened when he rebuffed her little advance.

"Poor old Mark," smiled I to myself. "*Cherchez la femme!*"

What interested me more, and less pleasantly, was his attitude to Yrotavál. That villain had settled down to a peaceful life of perpetual discord, annoyance of Rosanne, and friction with the staff, all of whom loathed him, except the old scoundrel, Valentine Marmaduke Jermyn, who still looked after the couple of horses that Rosanne kept. He and Yrotavál were birds of a feather.

I imagine that Rosanne had said something to Mark about Yrotavál, for he made a dead set at him without seeming to realize that he thereby also made trouble for me. Never was the old boy more clumsy, tactless and blundering, and he contrived to make things difficult all round and to put everybody in an awkward position, and to make mine most uncomfortable of all. For I, of course, could do nothing with Yrotavál except appeal to the sense of decency which he had never had, and to the better nature which he did not possess.

When I tried to talk to him as master to valet he would grin and say,

"Cut it right out, Bo. Can it. If you ain't sure which of us is boss—I can soon put you wise all right, all right. Sure."

When I told him that it was not only part of his job, but the most important part of it, to avoid giving any offence to Rosanne, he'd eye me coldly and out of one corner of his straight, tight mouth enquire,

"And what's biting that dame now? Say, kid, shall I lie down flat on my back each time I meet her so that she can wipe her feet on me or go for a walk on my empty stomach or something? Or shall I fall on my face so that she can't think I looked at her. Gee! I . . ."

"That's enough, Yrotavál."

"You've said it, Bo. More than enough."

And he would remark that—talking of enough—he did not think he was getting enough dough to pay for the insults and annoyance handed to him in this dump.

And one day, Mark actually sent for him and told him off—and Mark could do that sort of thing remarkably well when he gave his mind to it. Yrotavál simply blew up. I was really alarmed, and it cost me more, both in conciliation and cash, than I liked.

I had no option but to go for Mark and to put it to him plainly that if my valet were so objectionable, and he and I gave so much trouble, we must go away. I said I was sorry to put it like that. I could not get on without Yrotavál, but at the same time I realized that it was Mark's house and that he was master here. Rosanne, of course, could . . .

A very few words of that sort were enough! Poor old Mark simply went up in the air, or rather, nearly broke down. There were almost tears in his voice, if not in his eyes, as he told me I must not talk like that. He'd do anything in the world rather than give me cause to say such a thing: of course Yrotavál must stay with me; I must never never dream of doing such a thing as contemplating for one moment the possibility of my leaving Courtesy Court: he couldn't say how sorry he was that he had spoken a word against Yrotavál; that I had misunderstood him; and, finally, that he would a thousand times rather leave Courtesy Court himself than that I should have occasion to talk so.

And metaphorically we embraced—and all was well.

Still, it put me in an awkward position.

Rosanne, too. With Mark to back her up in the matter of Yrotavál, she got more difficult, and thereby made Yrotavál more so, keeping the vicious circle going round and round nicely. So much so, that one day, when the brute had been saying what he would do and what he wouldn't do, if Rosanne didn't "lay off" him a bit, I had to take the same line with her as I had done with Mark, and hint that rather than she should suffer the hideous inconvenience of my having a valet whom she did not much like, I would take him out of her way, find some place where he could look after me without troubling her—and then we should both be happy. All three of us, in fact, not to mention the fourth.

And that put Rosanne in a difficult position.

And naturally Yrotavál did not want to leave Courtesy Court, where he was not only in the most perfect clover but in perfect safety. Naturally he did not want to lose his job as the highest paid valet in the world. And although I was a bit anxious and worried, I didn't quite see him doing it. But I knew that if, in a fit of Spanish wrath, stupid irresponsibility and criminal folly, he did one day suddenly walk out in a rage, he'd leave chaos behind him. He'd see that I regretted it as long as I lived.

So between his annoyance and his cupidity he was in a difficult position too.

And of course Mark put himself in an awkward situation by his interference, because he could do simply nothing at all except regret it. Doubtless he had told Rosanne that he would soon squash Yrotavál, tell him where he got off, and threaten to give him the sack and the order of the boot with his heavy foot inside it. But in point of fact, he could do precisely nothing at all. So long as I stood by Yrotavál, that is, which was just what I had no option but to do.

Poor, dear old Mark! I hate to say a word against him, for he meant so well though he frequently did so ill. He was all that was kind and considerate, affectionate, loving, brotherly and—boring.

Oh, how tired I got, too, of his eternal nagging at me about fresh doctors and more oculists. I was on tenterhooks lest one day he marched into my room leading Sir Theophilus Grant by the ear and setting him on me before I could put my fists up, in other words, get my bandage round my eyes and refuse to move it. The man Struthers had given me a nasty shock—and a fear of artful oculists.

Constantly he pestered me to come up to Town with him and see another eminent eye-specialist, or if I would not do that, to let him bring one down.

I think he and Rosanne must have put their heads together over that too, for between them they again gave me a bad time and I really began to wonder whether my excuses for refusal were quite convincing. However, all I could say was,

"As I've told you a thousand times, I have had four opinions, two in France and two in London—among them the very best opinion in the world, Renier's, and they have proved to be right. Now that I have accepted my blindness and am doing my best to bear it and adapt myself to it, why try to unsettle my mind? It isn't as though I had cataract or anything that an operation could cure or even improve. You cannot give a man a new optic nerve. . . . I'll go to another ophthalmic surgeon fast enough when I find that my eyes are in the faintest degree sensitive to light. Meanwhile, do leave me alone to make the best of it. . . ."

"We only want to do our best for you, darling," Rosanne would reply to this sort of tirade.

"I know, I know, my dear," I would answer. "And that is why I try to be patient when you . . . unsettle me, and make life more difficult for me by . . ."

"Luke, old chap!" Mark would break in, "*don't*. Don't talk like that."

"I don't want to," I would reply. "And I shan't, if you will only leave me alone. . . . But when one has got a certain distance along the path of resignation, it's a bit hard. . . ."

And he'd come over and stand dumb, his hand on my shoulder, gently shaking me.

Poor old Mark. . . .

And one day he suddenly disappeared again! Took it into his head to clear out, and just vanished. One day he was there, perfectly normal and quiet—and the next he was not. Talk about here to-day and gone to-morrow! Moreover, he had gone for good—or for what was practically that, since he had rejoined the Foreign Legion. Five years—and no discharge possible.

XI

But the really marvellous thing was that he had taken Yrotavál with him!

It took me some time to realize that.

Imagine my joy when I did so!

Free for five years—and almost certainly free for ever! If Mark had cleared him out because he was a nuisance to Rosanne, and because he guessed that Yrotavál was something of a fly in our domestic ointment, he'd take damn good care that Yrotavál never came back. It wasn't Mark's way to do things by halves, and if he had made up his mind that life at Courtesy Court would go along better without Yrotavál, the place would never see him again.

But when my first feelings of joy subsided, I began to be a little bit worried. Exactly why had he done it—after speaking so apologetically about upsetting me in the matter of Yrotavál? And how had he induced the fellow to leave his happy haven—not to mention making him join the French Foreign Legion again?

Eventually I decided that Mark *had* come to the conclusion that it would really, in the long run, be a good thing for me to break away from Yrotavál's influence; that it was a bad thing to have the Spaniard about me as a constant reminder of the trenches and the cause of my tragedy; that whatever might be the fancies of my sick mind, a far better valet-nurse than Yrotavál could be obtained, especially now that the War was over: and, of course, the fact that Rosanne couldn't stand Yrotavál and that he was the cause of constant discord in the general household harmony *had* weighed with him.

And then again, I argued, Yrotavál might have grown heartily sick of the humdrum life of Courtesy Court; and it was only natural that a man who had lived as he had always done, should crave for excitement, drink, dissipation and violent forms of self-expression.

Anyhow, he had gone. And a damned good riddance!

Not so good, however, when the brute started writing me blackmailing letters; the implicit threat veiled at first, but growing more and more open as most of the letters remained unanswered, and I sent him but a tithe of what he demanded.

Luckily the threats were veiled, and when Giulia read one of his letters, she could make nothing of it. But I took care that she saw no more—and I lived in a state of constant anxiety.

§2

However, save for a certain growing fear as to what Yrotavál might do, my life flowed along smoothly and pleasantly enough at Courtesy Court.

Rosanne was still the perfect nurse, companion and friend; the perfect mother, I was going to say; and in the goodness of my heart I allowed her to persuade me to do without a valet, and agreed to let her wait on me hand and foot, be my constant guide and guardian, my attendant and my servant. And when she had to leave me, there was Giulia ready, willing, and able to take her place at any time and for any length of time.

They arranged a sort of schedule between them so that, except at night, I should never be alone. They relieved each other like sentries, Giulia coming on duty when Rosanne went off, which was usually in the afternoons, so that, on most days, Giulia (who was supposed to read me all my letters) and I could count on having the time between lunch and tea to ourselves.

To some people this way of life must sound ideal, especially for a war-worn warrior back from a period—which, in memory, loomed illimitable—of incredible hardship combined with boredom insupportable.

It sounds, and it was, an almost Paradisial existence. But in my Eden there was the inevitable serpent—that same boredom, a condition that from childhood has always seemed to me to be one of the most unbearable that can afflict a human being, especially one who is intelligent, active-minded, and artistic-souled.

I had everything on earth that a man could want, except what I wanted most, the opportunity to *express* myself in the way my self insistently demands—in painting. I am an artist to my finger-tips. But those finger-tips must be used; for first and foremost I am an artist of the brush. In my blindness I could still play my piano; I could compose my poems; I could write. But what, for my health's sake, for my very salvation, I needed to do was to *paint*—and a blind man may not paint.

Thank God for this typewriter. It gives me something to do with my hands. Thank God for books, but I could only read them, of course, in the privacy of my room and with my door locked.

What I should have done without Giulia, I don't know. Probably have recovered my sight!

With this idea I dallied often and long, but came to conclusion save that of the desirability of postponement. Some day I must recover my sight, of course. But not yet. I could not put off my protective colouring. I could not emerge, and face life again. I could not sacrifice the sympathy, the constant attention and ever-thoughtful consideration that Rosanne and Giulia lavished upon me. I could not leave my lime-lit stage and walk off into the cold dark wings and ordinary every-day existence; descend from my pedestal; cease to be the centre of attraction and attention.

And I had an uneasy feeling that, with the going of my blindness, something of Rosanne's love toward me might also go. For I realized in my heart of hearts not only the truth that Pity is akin to Love but that Pity is, far more often than we think, a part of Love. We are prone to love what we pity—the crippled child more than the healthy child; the wounded relative or friend more than the unwounded one; the grief-stricken, fate-pursued victim of disaster more than him whose head is neither bloody nor yet bowed.

I am intuitive, and intuition told me that when Rosanne pitied me less, she would love me less.

And interested in myself as I am—as, indeed, all sensible people are interested in themselves—I was intrigued by the fact that, although I did not love Rosanne, or rather was not in love with Rosanne as I was with Giulia, I could not bear the thought of her love for me decreasing or changing.

So indefinitely I postponed the recovery of my sight, and basked in the warmth of the protective loving care of the two women both of whom lavished now upon me *all* that they had to give.

But oh, how bored I often was!

Oh, how satiated, at times, with Rosanne's kindness and care; with Giulia's adoration and passion; with the wearing of that blasted bandage and those accursed glasses; how worn with the strain of the constant watchfulness against betraying myself when I wore neither of them; with the circumscription of my life; and with the narrowness of my orbit.

At times, I was almost mad with the desire to rush out into the open country; to drive my car at eighty miles an hour; to follow the hunt in the front rank of the thrusters; to bring down a brace of rocketing pheasants with a left and right; to cast a fly; to see a good play; and, above all, to paint . . . and to paint . . . and to *paint*. . . .

God! How hard I earned the laziness and luxury that I enjoyed.

And that damned Yrotavál. I could have murdered him. I grew to dread the sight of his letters, and at times felt sick with the fear that Rosanne might open one of them, and read, in plain black and white, the blackmailing threat of exposure.

From the first, I had insisted that all my letters should be brought straight to me, and had given Johnson strictest orders personally to attend to this. Every letter that came to the house, addressed to me, was to be brought immediately to me. The theory, at first, was that Yrotavál read them to me, a thing he was quite competent to do.

Now, after his departure, the same procedure obtained; but instead of Yrotavál, Giulia was my amanuensis and secretary. She read all other letters to me and I dictated to her the answers or, in some cases, typed them myself on the machine in the use of which I was supposed to have become even cleverer than the average blind man. In point of fact, I can type quite well with my bandage on.

Yrotavál's letters I, of course, now put aside and read privately, and completely destroyed.

I never fully complied with his demands. Once or twice I wrote to him, flatly refusing to give him more money or to have anything further to do with him, and conveying veiled but quite intelligible references to the Spanish, French and English police. I also made allusion to the weight of Mark's vengeance should I complain to him, and I concluded one letter by stating that I had made to my wife the completest confession of my little deception. I also told him that if he accused me to Mark, my brother would not only refuse to believe a word of it, but would knock his teeth down his lying throat.

Still, I was nervous and anxious.

On the whole, a mixed-grill of a life—as Life is apt to be.

§3

I was beginning to take him really seriously and to lose sleep over him, when a letter came from Mark saying that he was very angry and upset to learn that Yrotavál had been worrying me, that it was just like the blackguard to presume on my former kindness, to write begging letters, and to make himself a nuisance; that I was to take no notice of them, however, and to put them right out of my mind, for now that he knew about it, he was going to put a little salt on Yrotavál's tail. This was an old expression of Mark's, one that he had always used when he really meant business. He scarcely ever threatened anybody, and when he did, it was nothing more bloodthirsty than a promise to put salt on his tail. But from Mark that meant a lot; and when he did have to apply salt, it was invariably painful and effectively deterrent.

Undeniably Yrotavál was for it, but this again raised the worrying question in my anxious mind as to whether Yrotavál, in his anger and resentment, might tell Mark the truth about me.

Mark would not believe him, of course, but one knows how rapidly a seed of doubt germinates, sprouts, and grows into a tree of sinister certainty; and although the innocence of Mark's mind was of the most limpid simplicity, I did not want the seed to be planted there.

Here I took some comfort from the thought that, once the blackmailer has parted with his secret, it is of no further value to him, and the last thing he really wants to do is to fulfil his threats of exposure.

No, I decided, he wouldn't tell Mark. Had he been going to do so, he would have told him already, and there was not the slightest sign or suggestion in Mark's letters that he imagined Yrotavál to be doing anything worse than writing more or less impudent begging letters.

XII

Does God hate to see us happy? Is it a Law that man must suffer? Can the cranky-minded warped theologists, who pray and rant and groan about original sin and inevitable damnation, be right? Surely not. Surely any sane man, with an intelligence higher than that of a ju-ju-worshipping savage, demands a nobler and a better God than one who says,

"You are born full of original sin. If you sin you shall suffer here and be damned hereafter."

And yet, even though Mark promised that he was going to squash Yrotavál; even though I was a wealthy man, with every want supplied and every anxiety assuaged; even though I had the perfect home wherein not only my needs and desires but the least of my whims were forestalled and satisfied; even though, with Giulia's loving help and comfort, I could fight my boredom and weather the brain-storms caused by the thwarting and circumscription of my instinct, desire, and urge for self-expression—perfect happiness was withheld and denied.

Yrotavál was still the great trouble. Fear (that Mark and Rosanne might come to know of my deception, and I stand naked and exposed to the cold and cutting wind of their contempt) was its ancillary disease. And now that fear was lulled, even if it had not gone for ever, there was a new disturbance of the even tenor of my way, a threat and menace of discomfort.

For Rosanne was changing.

Her attitude toward me was growing different. She was not like the same woman. She was less affectionate, less considerate.

Worst of all, she was less sympathetic.

What could it be? Could she suspect that Giulia and I . . . ? But no, that was absurd.

314

Could Yrotavál have written to her? . . . No—what utter rubbish!

All my foolish morbid fancy. What I needed was exercise!

§2

And so the days and the weeks and the months went by, not perfectly happily, but with nothing worse to disturb my peace of mind and the beautiful peace of my way of life than this boredom, and idle fears about Rosanne's attitude; occasional berserk fits in which I felt I must paint or die; times when I thought I must burst the tenuous walls of the paper prison in which I had so inescapably immured myself, apparently for life; periods of madness in which I felt that, unless I did so, I should change this dungeon of my own construction for the padded cell of a lunatic asylum; and days of dread and doubt when I received letters from Yrotavál promising dire vengeance upon me if ever again I complained to Mark. In these letters he threatened not only the exposure of my swindle, but referred to my complicity in the murders of Bjelavitch and Paggallini.

At times, I cheered up and realized that Yrotavál had not spoken, had been faithful to one of the tenets of his faithless tribe—*'Thou shalt not squeal'*; preserving the one gleam of honour that dully shines among such thieves.

An unmitigated scoundrel; an unredeemed criminal; loathsome villain of the deepest dye; a murderer, swindler, robber, traitor and blackmailer—he had not yet betrayed me.

Torture me by blackmail he might, but betray me he would not, surely? Anyhow, so far he had not.

For obviously Mark did not know. And again— thank God for that. Reassuring myself, I would breathe freely once more, and settle down to cope with my only remaining trouble, boredom, those fits of depression increasingly frequent and of depth immeasurable.

And here, once more, let me thank God for Giulia.

For when these terrible fits attacked me, she could charm me with her fascination, comfort me with her love, and with the passionate words of her golden voice do for me all that David did for Saul.

§3

Well . . . I yawn . . . and I yawn . . . and I yawn. . . .

And there seems nothing more to write in this *apologia pro vita mea,* unless I start to keep a diary. That would be something to do! A form of self-expression and a substitute, however poor and faint and feeble, for my painting. If I keep it fully and faithfully and try to put colour, feeling, depth, atmosphere, chiaroscuro, into my words, I can perhaps delude myself that such word-painting will, to some extent, assuage my burning desire to express myself on canvas with the brush.

I might even make it a book for publication, and thus attain the fame that is denied to me as a painter. *The Tuyler Papers . . . The Diary of Luke Rivers Tuyler* . . . I would call it *De Profundis, By Luke Rivers Tuyler,* if a greater than I had not already taken that title. What about *Lux e Tenebris* with a translation underneath—*Light out of Darkness*—for the information of the ignorant. Something of that sort.

Yes, something to do. As old Mark is so fond of saying, Occupation is Salvation.

I will write a diary that, on publication, shall be hailed as the Book of the Hour, referred to later as the Book of the Year, and in days to come, recognized as a Classic. The brave patient diary of a blind man who was a thinker, a philosopher. . . .

*   *   *   *   *

Oh, God! Oh, God! Oh, God! I am blind! . . . I am blind! . . . *I am blind!* . . .

Oh, Son of God! Help me! Forgive me! Intercede for me!

Oh, Christ, my Saviour! . . . I am blind . . . I am in

eternal darkness. . . . A fearful blackness . . . It suffocates me. . . . Day is Night. *I have gone blind!* I have been *struck* blind!

Oh, God! Help me! Forgive me! Save me! . . . Give me back my sight, oh God.

I am going mad.

Oh, God! Oh, God! I am blind. I am *utterly* blind!

Oh, God! Forgive me and do not punish me thus. It was a harmless deception.

Oh, God! I hurt no one! I injured no one! I was driven to it. How did I know what war would be like?

God, I would not do this to a dog.

Oh, Christ! Pity me! Intercede for me! *I am blind.* I have to feel my way. I can do none of the things that I pretended I could do. *Please* God . . . please. . . . Oh, God! I will devote my life to doing good. I will spend my life in Your praise and honour and glory.

Oh, Christ, I will . . .

*   *   *   *   *

*   *   *   *   *

*   *   *   *   *

Oh, Rosanne, I am blind. *And you will not believe me.* Was ever man so punished, so caught, so cunningly entrapped?

Oh, God! How *can* You do this to me . . . ?

Rosanne, Rosanne, Rosanne, you discovered that I was not blind. You scourged me for what you called my lying, swindling, filthy hypocrisy and theft. You said I stole you, stole you from my brother—by my lying swindle. When I thought that you were changing, you were suspecting me. Your suspicion grew and you laid traps. Rosanne, how *could* you? . . . And you found me out. . . . You learned that I could see. And you were terrible in your anger and contempt. And now that I *cannot* see, *you will not believe me.*

Rosanne, you shall live most bitterly to regret that you struck me down with your contempt, that you spurned me, that you called me a whining crying child, a weakling, a liar, and a rogue—when I was truly,

really, actually *blind. Blind,* I tell you . . . *Blind.* . . .
Oh, God! . . .

*   *   *   *   *

*   *   *   *   *

*   *   *   *   *

That oculist was right. . . . *Shock.* . . .

It *was* shock. *The shock of seeing you, Rosanne, when you came upon us so suddenly.*

Rosanne, how could you *spy* upon me?

I remember him saying that blindness could be caused by mental shock.

And it was you who caused it. You, Rosanne.

I looked up from Giulia's breast and saw you. *And your face was the last thing I ever saw. The last thing I ever shall see.* Your face, a bitter mask of contempt and cruelty and anger.

You, Rosanne! *You* have struck me blind.

Oh, God! I cannot see.

Rosanne! Rosanne! I cannot see. I am *blind. I am blind.* . . .

*   *   *   *   *

*   *   *   *   *

*   *   *   *   *

And you, Giulia! Now that I am really blind you will have no more help, comfort, salvation for me than your stupid empty vapid,

"*But you've been blind for years!* And you've always been so brave and clever about it."

*   *   *   *   *

*   *   *   *   *

*   *   *   *   *

How noisily those hounds rush through my room. Louder and louder grows the thudding of the feet of the man who hunts with them.

It is a sign. It is a sign. When calamity and death

threaten the heir of Courtesy Court he hears them, and as catastrophe approaches, they come more frequently and with greater clamour.

Calamity. . . . Catastrophe. . . . Death. And I am the heir of Courtesy Court.

Oh, God! Forgive me and *help* me.

*   *   *   *   *

*   *   *   *   *

*   *   *   *   *

Oh, God! *Did I aim an arrow at the sky?* At You? At Fate? And has it fallen back and struck me through the eyes? I have battled in strength and striven in guile.

That Vision . . . that warning!

"Battle in strength and strive in guile if you must, but beware the arrow that you shoot at the sky!"

Oh, God! You would not punish me thus. Not thus, oh, God! If I mistook . . . forsook . . . denied . . . your warning.

Forgive me, oh, God!

Forgive me and help me.

Intercede for me, oh, Christ, and save me.

Give me back my sight.

Believe me, Rosanne. You *must* believe me. I *am* blind. I *am* blind. *I am blind.* . . . Mark! . . . MARK! . . . *MARK!* . . .

III

ROSANNE VAN DATEN

I

Can a woman be in love with two men at the same time, or is it absolutely impossible?

I know that she can dearly love two men at the same time. I was in love with Mark Caldon Tuyler and I loved his brother Luke Rivers Tuyler.

I fell in love with Mark almost at first sight; and I loved Luke from the beginning to the end, the very bitter end when he killed my love.

I would have married Mark at any time. I would at any time have given anything for him to have asked me to do so.

Had there been no Mark, I should not only have loved Luke but have been in love with him.

And yet two more different men never existed, in spite of the fact that they were twin brothers; and, immeasurably different as they were, there never lived two more attractive men from the point of view of the ordinary woman; never two more lovable.

But they evoked different kinds of love.

I loved Mark—as a man; for his strength, force and dependability.

I loved Luke—as a child; for his attractiveness, his weakness, his waywardness and need of protection. There was a great element of mother-love in one's devotion to Luke. Luke made you feel that he needed you, and a woman loves to be needed.

Mark made you feel that when *you* were in need, it was to him that you could turn with absolute certainty.

I rather like finding the right adjective for people, the word that sums them up. There are, of course, a dozen descriptive words for everybody, but there is always a master word, if it is only one that describes their indescribability.

The adjective for Luke was "charming." He was, without exception, by far the most charming person I ever met. It is easy to belittle charm and say that it so often goes with insincerity; but it is not so easy to estimate the amount of real good that a charming person does, merely by being charming. It is no small thing to be given a good conceit of yourself by a pleasing and delightful flatterer, no small thing to be soothed and smoothed when you are irritated and ruffled. The person who habitually and constantly drops lubricating-oil into the machinery of Life does as useful a work for the society in which he moves as does the engineer for the engine that he oils. But don't think that there was anything oily about Luke, or that he was a greasy and ingratiating sycophant or creeper. Nothing would be farther from the truth. Such a person could not possibly be charming, and that is what essentially Luke was; a charming and fascinating boy, youth, and man.

And like so very many charming, easy and delightful people, he had the vices of his virtues, for his best friend—and how much I should love to think I had really been his best friend—could not call him reliable.

You couldn't depend on Luke. But to be quite fair, I don't think this was due to any inherent badness in his character. It was just that he was volatile, effervescent and changeable. His grandmother was Irish, a Miss Fitzgerald-Rivers, and a favourite remark of his, intended to be roguish, broguish, humorous and exculpatory, was "Oi'm Oirish and onaccountable," when taxed with the disastrous results of some wild and hare-brained escapade. He had a splendidly Irish sense of humour, high courage, dare-devilry, and alas, irresponsibility. And with it all he was so lovable that one loved him for his very faults. And they were numerous enough to secure him a double portion of love.

He was not only one of the most likeable of human beings, but one of the most forgivable. Personally, I found it very easy to forgive him seven times and seventy times and seventy times seven, and to keep on until he committed the unforgivable offence and did what no woman could possibly forgive or forget.

Poor Luke! So gifted, so clever, so witty and high-spirited, and so insatiably avid of praise and approval. One of the many faults that were, after all, the mere complements of his graces, was his absolute hatred of criticism. Less excusable was his refusal to take blame.

To him it was hurtful, it was unfair criticism, if anything he did should be considered deserving of adverse comment; hurtful punishment that he should even be deemed worthy of punishment. Approval was the breath of life to him, and only by unstinted uncritical approval could you win and keep his love.

It was a real misfortune for poor Luke that so many people loved him so very much; and that all around him were those who praised him so highly and with so little discernment.

By all accounts, including his own, his mother spoilt him terribly. That his father did so, I saw with my own eyes; and, for Luke's sake, I regretted it. As bad as either of them was Mark, who loved him so devotedly that not only would he have given his life for him, but would have given it cheerfully to have saved him from harm or unhappiness. No one could ever use the word "weak" in connection with Mark. He was not weak where Luke was concerned, but he was devoted to an extent that ended only this side of idolatry.

And the same with all his friends, especially girls, chief of whom was Giulia Brent-Grayleigh, who I should think never once, from early childhood, contradicted or criticized him. He could always be sure of sympathy, approval and adulation from his Giulia.

And Athene, when we came to Courtesy Court, carried on the good work, ably aiding and abetting in his spoiling, if she were not the worst of them all, if, indeed, she did not do him more harm than the rest of them put together.

And this, of course, was all as bad for Luke as it could be. Without it, he would have been conceited and wilful; rash and headstrong, though weak; over-eager for approval and praise. With it, the only marvel is that Luke was as lovable and charming as he was. No one should blame him without including his mother, his father, his brother, his step-mother and his Giulia in the indictment, and apportioning the condemnation among them all.

I may be, probably am, what Luke frequently called me, a cocky and conceited little bitch; but I do think that if I could have arrived earlier on the scene, I could have done him some good. I simply hated to see him so mishandled, so wrongly treated, so cruelly spoilt. It was a sin and a shame. It made me sick, and I made up my mind, from the very first, that I would not join the ridiculous chorus of praise and adulation that would have turned a stronger head than Luke's. Why, it would have spoilt Mark himself, and that is saying something.

Although I loved him very dearly, or perhaps because I loved him so well, even in Switzerland, before ever we came to Courtesy Court, I determined as soon as I realized what was going on, that I would have no part or lot in it. On the contrary, I would do what I could to counteract it; do my best to prick the bubble of his conceit whenever I saw it swelling, throw water on the flames of his ardent self-approval; drop a little acid in the sweet draught of praise that he so greedily swallowed.

It was a thankless task, a distasteful and a difficult one, and if I hadn't loved him so much, I couldn't have done it. It would have been so easy to have joined the choir that eternally hymned his cleverness, gifts, abilities, and achievements, but though I was twelve months younger than he, I was twelve years older, and frequently I felt much more like slapping him for a silly child than kissing and lauding him for a wonderful hero, as Giulia did. Compared with Luke, the school-boy, I was Rosanne, the woman of the world. I had seen and heard so much, travelled so far, and knew such a great deal about Life, that when I came to Courtesy Court and into Luke's orbit, I was a fish coming from the great ocean to a minnow in a tiny pond—monarch of all it surveyed in that puddle.

I loved him and hated his weaknesses, his silliness, conceit and impatience of reproof. He loved me and hated my criticism. Nevertheless, if he went to Giulia for approval he came to me for advice; and if she was sweet salve for his abraided self-esteem I was his antiseptic, if stinging, ointment.

And what was Mark's adjective? There are so many, but I think "reliable" is the chief. Whatever else Mark was—ruthless, dominating, compelling, powerful, solid —he was reliable. Charming he was not. I don't think I ever heard anybody use the term in connection with Mark. But he was something better. Valuable and desirable as are the charming people of this world, and great as is the good they do with their lubricating *politesse* and courtesy, the really reliable ones are more useful.

Before all things Mark was dependable, a rock-like, solid, static person. Being solid, he was stolid; and being powerful and compelling and dominating, he was a little—formidable.

I distrust generalities, but I think I am right in saying that greatly as a charming man attracts women, there is something about a formidable, or at any rate potentially formidable, man that attracts them even more, because it intrigues them.

The charming man is not enigmatic and incalculable.

The formidable man generally is, because he may be dangerous; and I should say that, on the whole, the average woman's favourite pursuit and pastime is playing with fire, when she can find any nice fire to play with.

Although no one could call Luke effeminate or in the least degree womanish, there was a good deal of the woman in him. There was nothing of the woman in Mark. He was male and masculine all through. Charming, delightful, lovable, Luke was a mine of faults. The only serious fault one could find in Mark was his weakness where Luke was concerned. No, I must withdraw that. One simply cannot use the word "weakness" in conjunction with Mark. Let me say folly. The way he spoilt Luke was foolish and stupid and wrong. The way in which he tried to take the blame for all Luke's misdeeds was idiotic, and thoroughly bad for Luke, who needed punishment more than anything.

(But how can I talk like this—I who know how terribly Mark paid, how cruelly and bitterly he suffered for his part in spoiling Luke!) And there again, one must try to apportion the blame justly, for he had been brought up to do it, trained and taught and, in a way, compelled to do it. Although Luke's elder brother by only a few minutes, he was always treated, by both his parents, as though he were ten years older than his twin brother; as though he were in charge of him and responsible for him, when Luke was out of their sight. Generally, when a mother has a favourite child, the father favours another, and the balance is kept even; but in this case, Luke was the favourite of both parents, and so much so that, by comparison, Mark was as nothing in their sight, except as a guide, guardian, and protector for the infant prodigy.

And all the while Mark was worth two of Luke, really lovable as Luke was. It was incredible and simply sickening, the way in which everything that Luke did wrong was Mark's fault, and everything that Luke did right was no credit to Mark.

It was wonderful and rather pathetic to see the way in which Mark accepted the situation. I suppose one does accept that to which one is born, and is inevitably reconciled to the conditions in which one grows up from the cradle.

Luke was cleverer than Mark, no doubt. He was mentally and spiritually a Celt of the brightest type, and was undeniably endowed with the artistic temperament. But, much as I loved Luke, I grew a little tired of temperament. I came greatly to prefer Mark's equanimity, calm and evenness of temper. You may call solidity stolidity, and coolness phlegm and stupidity; but having tried both, give me solidity and stolidity before temper and temperament.

Was I jealous of Luke because Mark loved him better than he loved me? Quite probably. I have been saying a lot about the faults of other people and I should not forget my own—whereof one thing can be said; Luke gave me ample occasion to remember them.

But what I want to do is to give a fair account and clear picture of my two lovers; those two men whom I loved so much, and who both in their so different ways loved me.

II

I was born in the Crescent City, to me the loveliest, most intriguing, most attractive town in the world, New Orleans in Louisiana—lovely names, New Orleans, Louisiana—and though I love England, adore Courtesy Court and worship my husband, I am American to the backbone, American to the depths of my soul, and back to New Orleans some day I will go.

I must once again see the Cathedral; Chartres Street and the Napoleon House; the Cabildo; the Calabozo; the old French market; the Ursuline Convent, one of the oldest buildings in America; I must walk again down Pirates Alley from Royal Street to Chartres Street, with little old balconied shops on the right and the garden on the left; Pirates Alley between the Cabildo and the old St. Louis Cathedral. It is so many, many years since I was there that I begin to forget my geography, and mentally, I have lost my bearings. But how it will all come back to me! My heart will almost burst when I return, and show it all to Mark. How I wish I could show it to those Europeans who think that the whole of America is necessarily new, young, stark, crude and materialistic; lacking in history, romance, colour. I would give anything to show all of them an American town with such names as the Spanish Arsenal, the Place d'Armes, Vieux Carré, Pont d'Alba Building, Madame John's Legacy, St. Anthony's Garden, the Duelling Oaks, the Haunted House of Royal Street, St. Roche's Chapel, Toulouse Street, the Gate of the Two Lions, Fencing-Masters' Houses, Perdito Street. . . .

It is fragrant with the very Spirit of History and Romance.

Did not the Marquis de Lafayette himself stay in New Orleans as a guest of the lovely and glamorous Madame Lalaurie, when the city fêted him at the Cabildo?

And oh, how my baser nature longs at times for some New Orleans food and cooking. Mark smiles when I speak of red beans and coffee. But coffee means something in most people's lives, and there is no coffee in the wide world like that you get in New Orleans. It dyes the cup. There's nothing fainting about it. And if you don't know what 'fainting' means in this connection, it means pale and thin and washy, as you get it in Europe.

No one knows what chicken is who has not tasted it as we cook it. Why, even our eating-houses have such names as Patio Reale, Galatoire's, La Louisiana's, Antoine's. Even our food is romantic. Oh, how I pray they haven't spoilt my lovely city in the years that the locust has eaten.

It gave me quite a heart-flutter to read the other day in a paper sent to me by a dear friend,

"Tattered and beloved old pages from long-ago Spain and France linger in the memory as one walks about the streets of the older part of the city. Shadows still cast their dancing feet upon old pavements, touching little courts and patios and creeping over quaint roofs and through balconies, reminding the visitor of the glamorous days of romance and chivalry which gave this city its birth and which to this day clothe it with charm. . . ."

But this won't do. . . .

I can just remember my father, and I love his memory. I can just remember the big roomy home we had, the lovely Old Colonial house in which I was born. And I can remember the sick agony of suffering that prostrated me, even as a little child, when he died.

Well . . . he died. And life changed. Mother changed too. I shall never understand how she could have sold our beautiful home and left our lovely city. For what? To live in hotels.

From the time I was a shy, awkward, spindling child until I came to Courtesy Court, I never knew a friendly room. I hardly knew a friendly face.

I'm not going to criticize mother, or say a word against her. I am not lost in admiration of those who pillory their parent in print, and I'll only say that her ideas and tastes, her aims and ambitions, her opinions and her standards all differed from mine, were indeed generally diametrically opposed to mine. She loved living in a world of noise and movement. I hate it. She loved hotels. I loathe them. She seemed absolutely afraid to allow the tiniest growth of root, whereas the one thing for which I yearned was to dig in, to settle, to take root, and there to remain most firmly *planté là*. Oh, how I thanked God when she married a man who owned a historic home, and went there at last to live and settle down. Though even there, poor darling, she did more living than settling.

I don't say that we stayed in every hotel in America and Europe, but I do say that we lived in practically every famous hotel in every famous town in the States, in Canada, in South America, and in the Capitals of Europe.

What an education I got in those hotels! Education in Life.

I had almost no schooling at all, though I was occasionally parked at a school when Mother was having a honeymoon; and I did occasionally have a governess for a brief period, until Mother began to feel that she had been in one place long enough.

"Not move on again, child?" she would answer my protest. "*Bon Dieu* and Martha Washington! We've been in this god-forsaken hole ever since we came. Jimminy crickets! I'm so covered in moss that I smell like a goddam graveyard . . . Celestine, start packing."

And next day we would be gone. The Wandering Jew had nothing on us. He was a mildewed stick-in-the-mud compared with the Wandering Gentiles who were Mrs. Athene Van Daten and her daughter Rosanne.

The length of our stay in any particular place depended on the men we met. Particular place, but not very particular men. Mother wasn't blessed with the gift of discrimination.

Oh, God, how I came to hate men! The brutes, the beasts, that have pulled me into their fat laps, slobbered my face with their cigar-and-alcohol-stinking mouths, called me Momma's Own Cutie and endeavoured to curry favour with me as an approach to her. How many of them, releasing me, rumpled, resentful and sick, have said,

"Now what about the biggest box of chocolates they've got on the stand? And you'll tell Momma what I said about her, eh?"

And to how many have I replied,

"I don't like chocolates, thank you. And I'll tell Mamma what I think of you."

And therein I spoke the truth. For I was sick of chocolates to the depths of my young stomach, and I did tell Mamma exactly what I thought of the beastly would-be Sugar Daddy.

I hated all men until I met my two boys.

§2

It was at Montreux that it all came to an end, and at the Grand Imperial Hotel of that lovely little town that I had my last adventure with one of the beastly, fat, gross bar-flies and lounge-lizards who were my *bêtes-noires*.

On the first floor of the Grand Imperial is a colossal landing from either end of which interminable-seeming corridors run to either end of the building.

Mooning miserably about in this vast corridor I waiting for Mamma—I estimate that up till then I had spent quite half my life waiting for Mamma in hotel foyers, lounges and corridors—I was suddenly seized as I passed a big deep settee. I had not noticed the man sitting there, or I should have been more wary; a great fat, hulking brute of the type I call bulgers—stomach, neck, cheeks, eyes.

I had seen him before when sitting in the entrance-hall pretending to read a magazine, and had actually heard him making enquiries of the hotel-clerk about Mamma. He was more hateful-looking than most of his type, and as he pulled me on his lap I stiffened from head to foot, shut my eyes, set my mouth and prepared to be kissed as usual, petted and propitiated and then questioned about Mamma.

But this creature was the worst I had ever encountered, which is saying something, and in a very few moments I was varying my defensive technique and screaming at the top of my voice. I don't think I had ever really screamed before in my life. Just as this loathsome brute, alarmed at the row I was making, was in the act of putting me off his knees, trying to rise, and to get his fat hand over my mouth, two very big boys who had just come up the main staircase looked to see what all the row was about, grasped the situation, and with wild whoops, rushed and grasped my persecutor likewise. It really was an amazingly scientific assault. Hurling themselves at him, they pushed him back on the settee; each seized a foot, yanked him on to the floor, and began dragging him along the carpet to the stairs. The noise that I had made compared most unfavourably with that emitted by the creature, and was as the squeak of a mouse compared with the roaring of a lion.

Down the stairs the boys bumped him, dragged him across the tiles of the foyer, and would have had him down the steps and out into the road but for the officiousness of the hall-porter, the lounge-waiter, the booking-clerk and other unsporting characters.

There was a terrible row, and when the Manager went with him to the boys' father and lodged a complaint, demanding apology and the infliction of severest punishment, the boys did not improve matters by declaring that it was all true, and worse. "It was a hold-up. They had made Herr Pilsenbrauer put his hands up for half an hour, had frightened him almost to death, so that he, collapsing, had knelt and wept, imploring them for mercy, and had only let him go after relieving him of his wallet, which contained one hundred thousand francs, and they were going to do it again twice a day so long as Herr Pilsenbrauer remained in the hotel." In short, they were not repentant, much less remorseful and apologetic, and it was quite evident that their father had no control at all over the one who was the ring-leader and spokesman.

I told Mamma all about it. She insisted on my bringing the boys to see her, declared that she had fallen in love with the lively one, and wished to meet their father, to tell him my version of what happened.

Mr. John Tuyler, the father of the two boys, Mark and Luke, was something new to Athene, and I think she really fell in love with him. It is quite possible, for she had an infinite capacity for taking love just as some people have for taking colds.

Anyway, she—no, I won't say—followed him to England. But she did take me to that country very soon after the Tuylers left Switzerland, and she accepted the invitation to visit them at their home.

Meanwhile, I had become a different girl. Actually I had, at last, an interest in life, and life was interesting and worth living; worth living if I could see those two boys again, the boys with whom I had fallen desperately in love during the month that we all spent together at Caux, Jaman and Chateau d'Oex.

One of the really dark days of my life was the day when they left Switzerland. On the platform, seeing them off, I was like a stupid stone image of grief, and when they had gone the image turned into a fountain, for I wept as I had never wept before.

And one of the bright days of my life was the day on which Mother said she was going to England and that she wished to see the Tuylers again.

Whether Mother had fallen in love with Mr. Tuyler I don't know, but most undoubtedly she fell in love with Courtesy Court at first sight. That, too, was something new to her, a house nearly six hundred years old, in which the same family had lived for centuries. Mellow stone without, and ancient black oak within, set in a park of emerald grass and glorious trees, it was a sample of England at its best. The place had originally been called Tuylerston, the name having been changed after Queen Elizabeth had stayed there on one of her royal progresses; for, on mounting her horse (the mounting-block is still beside the wide steps leading up to the front entrance), she had remarked to her host,

"We thank you, Master Tuyler. And since you doubtless consider yourself too big a man to desire the bauble of knighthood, we confer a title upon this your house. Let it be known henceforth as Courtesy Court, for we have found great hospitality and fine manners herein."

I believe there is a house in Kent called Satis House because the same Good Queen Bess, on being, perhaps foolishly, asked by her host whether she had found all things to her liking, replied succinctly,

"Satis" (or "Good enough"), the house being known thereafter, and to this day, as Satis House.

Mr. John Tuyler was like the house, aristocratic, a relic of other days, a beautiful anachronism, and falling to decay. He was a most lovable creature, with perfect manners, lofty character, weak will and feeble purpose. It makes one doubt the theory of heredity. Personally, I began to doubt it very strongly indeed when I knew that Mark and Luke, so virile, active, forceful, so full of life, health, strength, energy and *joie de vivre,* were his sons.

I wish I could have known their mother, who must have been very much younger than their father, and doubtless a woman of much character and beauty.

He died suddenly, soon after the outbreak of the Great War—of anxiety and a broken heart, I believe, because his beloved son, his Luke, his Benjamin, had enlisted in the French Foreign Legion and gone to the Front.

The more I saw of the boys, the more I loved them. Both of them. Mark for his gentle strength and protecting kindness; Luke for his charm, beautiful manners and lively wit.

I have no words to tell how marvellously life changed for me when my mother married their father, and we became one family and settled down to life at Courtesy Court.

It seemed all too good to be true, and I felt that such happiness could not last. It did, however; and, moreover, it promised to improve, as I could look forward to the time when the boys would be at home permanently. This thought sustained me when they went back to school, and Mother, in one of her rare attacks of maternal conscience, decided to send me to school as well, and arrangements were made for me to go with Giulia Brent-Grayleigh, the daughter of very old friends and neighbours of Mr. Tuyler's, a girl of whom I did my damnedest not to be jealous.

I think I succeeded better than she did in the matter of conquering jealousy, for she had known the boys from babyhood—had almost grown up with them, in fact—and was as fond of them as I was. It really was a little hard on her that I should not only appear suddenly on the scene but actually come to live in the house with them. Every time that the visiting Giulia said good-bye and went home, she made me feel that it was I who should be departing rather than she.

She and I never quarrelled. We were excellent friends indeed, but there was always a slight feeling between us, an undefined attitude on Giulia's part of "I was here first," and an unexpressed accusation that I was an interloper.

I liked her father, General Sir Henry Brent-Grayleigh, very much indeed, and her mother not at all. One felt that she was definitely critical of Athene, if not of me, and that she would certainly do nothing to soothe any slight feelings of resentment that Giulia might entertain.

What saved the situation and prevented the slightest manifestation of any discord was the fact that Giulia preferred Luke to Mark, and did not very greatly resent my preferring Mark to Luke.

Thus we were, on the whole, a very happy and harmonious quartette; and I really got on very well with Giulia, who was quite decent to me, especially at school.

III

Why did I marry Luke Tuyler—when I loved Mark so much? Why *did* I marry Luke?

Because I loved him.

And, to be quite honest with myself, partly because I loathed the thought of going away and living somewhere else. I could not bear it. And yet the whole time I knew, though only subconsciously, I suppose, that I loved Mark as much as I loved Luke.

No, that is not the truth. I loved Mark far better, but it was quite obvious that Mark did not love me, or rather, that he was not in love with me. He left me in no doubt on that score.

And I did love Luke. I loved him in spite of the fact that I saw through him; realized that he was the supreme and perfect egoist; knew quite well that all the goods were in the shop window, and that while he dazzled one with his brilliance he did it deliberately; did it as deliberately and intentionally as does a man who switches on the headlights of his car, or as a tradesman who makes elaborate and lavish display to catch the eye of the passer-by—to catch it for his own profit. Luke dazzled me as much as he did the rest of us, but with the difference that I knew that I was being deliberately dazzled, fascinated, and bewitched. He realized that I knew it, and he resented it, for, in a spate of true self-revelation and confession, he once said to me,

"Rosanne, I believe you are the only person whom I totally fail to deceive; and I believe that is the greater part of your charm and attraction for me. Dear little bitch."

Well, if he went on loving me in spite of the fact that he knew that I saw through him, equally I went on loving him while I did so, even though I knew that he was utterly selfish, self-centred, and unreliable.

Poor Luke! Brilliant, charming, lovable, he was also spoilt, luxurious, deceitful, a little malicious, and rather false.

Can a woman love a man whom she despises? She can and she does. Not that I ever despised Luke until the very end when he showed himself despicable beneath contempt.

And can a man love a woman whom he hates? He can and he does, if only in spasms and flashes. Not that Luke hated me for long; but there were times when his temper flared up; and then, while he was in a rage, he would hate me fiercely and make the curious accusations, far more revealing of himself than of me,

"You don't understand me—and you don't try. You intrigue me deliberately. You think you are an enigma, and you are just a little beast. And I'll tell you this, young Rosanne, I never, *never* forgive anybody who makes a fool of me."

For poor Luke, the keenest and cleverest of malicious wits and practical jokers, loathed being fooled by anybody else, simply could not bear a joke against himself.

And he utterly hated to see anything being done better than he could do it himself, and I don't think it was in him to take pleasure in another person's triumph. It was he who must have the great success, he who must excel, and for any of the rest to do so was an exhibition of bad taste.

And yet it was utterly impossible, even for me who steeled myself against his fascination, to be angry, or even annoyed, with him for long. One was ashamed to damp the gaiety of his ardent high spirits, to put up a surly defence against his beautifully worded sweet apologies for any offence. In fact, one felt that one simply must fall into line with the rest and give him preferential treatment as a privileged and superior being; he was so beautiful, his manners were so lovely, he had such endearing ways, and did such charming and delightful things.

And then he would do something that made you ashamed of him and ashamed for him, until he turned the battery of his charm upon you, a long look from his brilliant blue eyes that seemed to glow; a bewitching smile from his really beautiful mouth, a warm and brotherly hug from his strong arm, and a charming little apology from the depths of the (apparent!) sincerity of his limpid and lucid soul.

He was wont to refer to me as a poker-faced little enigma when I provoked him, but—merciful Heavens! —if ever there were an enigmatic bundle of contradictions it was he. And I suppose this was due very largely to his artistic temperament. For at times, he was essentially the "cat that walks alone," dwelling apart in a deep and dark seclusion, while at others, more frequent, he was the ebulliently high-spirited leader in every sort and kind of wild hurroosh of his own invention. For quite long periods, he was the sweetest thing alive, completely irresistible—hard as I personally struggled to resist him—completely lovable and dear.

And at times, he would have fits of depression when we must all spend ourselves in comforting, cheering and diverting him. Yet, with all his wonderful and genuine charm, he had an amazing power to crush and a dreadful gift for wounding. His wit was like a diamond, it was hard, it sparkled, and it cut.

I never knew anybody whose way pursued a less even tenor, with its terrific bursts of energy and its curious little patches of dull lethargy; its deep and serious engrossment in some such pursuit as painting, music or writing, followed by utter and absolute indifference to any pursuit whatsoever, a lapse into sheerest laziness, when he would join in nothing, was interested in none of us, and dwelt brooding apart, devoid of ambition, unresponsive to challenge, sunk in apathy.

It always worried Mark dreadfully when this fit took his adored Luke. He became most pathetic in his anxiety, his spending of himself; and he would squander all his time in trying to coax Luke out of his dark fit. He was positively maternal, and reminded me of our spaniel Diana, licking her pup, her only child. I believe that had Mark thought it would have done Luke any good, he would, like her, have licked him all over.

It was then that I loved Mark so much more than I did Luke, realized his complete unselfishness, and admired his unfailing, undemanding kindness and the real sterling goodness that lay beneath his self-contained, detached and reticent stolidity.

It was just as well for Luke that Mark was somewhat stolid and apparently thick-skinned, for one of Luke's chief joys was in scoring off him, playing practical jokes on him, and trying to make a fool of him. In this last he never succeeded, for Mark had an amazing natural dignity. And as for the sells and "sucks" and practical jokes on Mark, the best of any joke was the way Mark himself enjoyed it.

I suppose I could sum it all up by saying that my attitude to Luke was, that while I recognized his faults, I loved him tremendously; loved him *for* his faults; loved the sinner while I hated the sin. I tried to harden my heart against him and I completely failed.

When he suddenly went off to Paris, I was amazed at the awful blank that his going made in my life. When Mark went too, there was more blank than life. I scarcely had any life at all, and crept about like a dead thing. When Mark wrote that they had both enlisted in the French Foreign Legion, I got an actual physical pain. I wish I could say that this pain was romantically in my heart. In point of fact, it was in my stomach; and it made me feel sick for days and weeks. It made me feel horribly ill; and whatever, and however, the boys suffered, I don't think they suffered more than I did. But that is nonsense, of course, for their physical sufferings must have been incredible, whereas once the physical sickness had passed, mine were only mental.

But it was a dreadful time; and on many a night, after I had had a letter, I was unable to sleep at all; on many a day, quite unable to swallow food. For I had enough imagination to know how terrible it must be for Luke. Luke whose nerves were so very close to the surface; Luke who, both literally and metaphorically, was so terribly thin-skinned; so easily offended, hurt, thrown out of gear; so hopelessly vulnerable. To think of *Luke* up to his neck in mud and blood and horror; Luke—who should be painting his pictures, playing his violin and piano, writing his poems and stories—living like a beast, unwashed, unshaved, filthy, devoured by lice; Luke who felt everything so much more intensely than anyone else, whose senses were so terribly acute. How could he bear it! And how could Luke, so impulsive, hasty, resentful of criticism, bear army discipline, especially the iron discipline of the French Foreign Legion?

It was unimaginable.

§2

And when, one day, he walked into the house . . . *blind* . . . led by another soldier, a single glance at his face showed me what he had been through. Had his eyes not been bandaged, the sight of his face would have been enough.

My heart stopped and then turned over, and before I could utter a word, I knew that there was nothing on earth I would not do for him, that my life would not be long enough for me to do all that I should yearn to do for him.

And in that moment I loved him with, I think, a perfect love; perfect because passionless.

That this should have happened to my poor Luke! To Luke of all people. To Luke who lived through his eyes.

If, that day, he had asked me to marry him, I should have jumped at the chance to do so. I should not have hesitated for one second. Any doubts as to whether I loved him as well as I loved Mark, any doubts as to whether Luke would not prove a difficult husband, would have been swept away in the rush of feeling, the overwhelming pity that almost deprived me of speech, and of sober reason.

Many and many a time had Athene, eyeing me appraisingly, said,

"Well, you are like me in one thing, my girl—your

head will never rule your heart. Still, you are not all heart and no head, like your silly mother, so that's *something* to be thankful for!"

But when Luke came home blind, so stricken and pitiful, I was all heart and no head, and there was no sacrifice I would not have made for him.

Nor was there, of course, any question of sacrifice. Nothing was too much trouble, strain or tie. It was a pleasure and a joy to do anything and everything that would in the least degree lighten his terrible lot. I even did my best to endure the presence of the horrible man whom he had brought home, or, perhaps, who had brought him home. I tried to share Luke's belief that the man had done him incalculable service, had indeed saved his life. This latter I doubted; and, as to the services, I felt perfectly certain that, if any, they had been done with a view to the maximum remuneration. It was only intuition on my part, for Luke was somewhat reticent about what had happened from the time the bomb fell on the hospital, but I was quite certain about it, nevertheless.

I had many adjectives for this Yrotavál, the principal one being *reptilian.*

He had the cold, glittering eyes of a snake, the straight, hard, bony mouth of a snake, the look of repellent, lurking, dangerous cruelty and inhumanity, threatening and horrible. A more ophidian face I never saw on a human being, and I really do not think I should have been surprised if at any time the thin, forked tongue of a snake had come out through those thin hard cruel lips and flickered at me. I hated him on sight, and hated him more and more every time I saw him. Possibly that was why he also hated me, though I have no doubt that the fact that I took charge of Luke and did my utmost to curtail Yrotavál's influence and activities, had as much or more to do with his attitude. I had an instinctive or intuitive feeling that he was bad for Luke; that he had some hold over him, and that I should be doing Luke a service if I could get rid of the man.

I honestly think that I should have felt as I did,

even if he had not been insolent to me, as he always was in manner and sometimes in words. At first, I tried to excuse this to some extent on the grounds that he was a rough soldier who was unaccustomed to dealing with decent women, something of a misogynist, and possessing all the soldierly and Spanish pride that forbade him to accept and obey orders from a woman. But it wouldn't do. Had he been an American soldier in like circumstances, he'd have been polite and helpful, respectful and probably chivalrous. This man was utterly hateful, and there was not a soul in the house, save Luke, who did not hate him, and with good reason.

And a thing that really hurt me was Luke's attitude when I spoke to him about Yrotavál's attitude to me, manners to the butler and cook, and conduct to the maids.

However, I realized that Luke, blind and shell-shocked, must not be thwarted in anything, must not be crossed in any way, and if Yrotavál was essential to his comfort, Yrotavál must stay.

So I keyed myself up to endure him.

Well, one cannot live at concert pitch; and, more-over, we are all so adaptable that in time we grow accustomed to almost anything. I grew accustomed even to Yrotavál. I even grew accustomed to Luke tapping blindly about the house; and though I didn't pity him less, and although my heart ached for him as poignantly, I gradually came to realise that part of my love for him *was* pity; and when Mark returned, I allowed the counsels of my head to mingle with the warm promptings of my heart.

For, in his way, Mark was almost as pitiable as Luke, if only because he was so difficult a man to pity, so impossible a man to mother; and was suffering for, and through, Luke almost as much as Luke himself suffered. My first sight of him shocked me nearly as much as did my first meeting with Luke. He had aged ten years; and ill, wasted, and nerve-shattered as he was, the sight of his blinded twin-brother was perhaps the worst of all the blows that he had received.

And he was so selfless, so unconcerned with his own condition, that I just ached to nurse him and mother him as I had done Luke. But whereas Luke would take all that one could give, and ask for more, Mark seemed to resent pity, to hate being nursed, and, not irritably like Luke, but somewhat coldly, said that he did not want to be fussed and coddled, and was quite all right, thank you. Both our local doctor and the consultant neurologist whom he brought down from London seemed to think that Mark was in a worse way than Luke, and needed complete rest, nursing, nourishment and relaxation, quite as much as Luke did; and indeed Luke had made a pretty good recovery, except of course for his sight, by the time Mark came home discharged from the French Foreign Legion.

Poor Mark! He had never been as articulate as Luke; he had always been quiet, patient and averse from claiming anything, explaining anything, and demanding any sympathy. But now he seemed—not crushed and broken, for nothing could crush or break Mark—but driven in upon himself, irreparably hurt in some way, so that it was almost as though he had grown a protective shell. Try as I might I could not get *at* him; get *close* to him, as I used to be. It wasn't that he was impatient, rude, or even cold. It was more that he was not much interested in me. It was as though a wall of glass separated us.

I had doubly regained Luke in a most terrible way.

I had lost Mark in an almost equally terrible way, and I was surprised at the effect this had on me.

I was glad beyond words that he had come back; glad and thankful and happy. It sounds an amazing statement or confession, but I was happy while Mark was at home, and I did not understand it. Why should I be so happy because he was there, and so hurt because he kept me at arm's length? Perhaps it is an exaggeration to say he kept me at arm's length, but he certainly didn't cast his arms about me to any noticeable extent.

I put it down to his grief and horror at the state in which he had found poor Luke. That was the real internal wound from which he was suffering. What I hoped was that, in time, he would—as I myself had done—become reconciled and accustomed to the blindness of his brother. And although his mind could never become callous and immune, it could grow resigned. And as Luke receded a little, possibly I might find a place in it.

That is the frank unpalatable truth of how I felt. It was a strange, weird, bizarre time and situation—I loving Luke dearly, and jealous of him; I loving Mark dearly, and hurt and almost angry with him. I loved them both so much. What was to be the end of it?

Mark put an end to it. Quite casually, but with inflexible determination, he just rose up and departed; enlisted in the British Guards and went back to the Front!

It was while he was away that Athene was killed in an air-raid over London. I had never loved her as a daughter should love her mother, but it was a great shock to me and something of a blow.

Luke comforted me wonderfully, and out of the depths of his own darkness and suffering, found room for understanding, a beautiful and winning sympathy.

Rather crushed by these three blows—Luke's blindness, Mark's departure and Athene's death—I turned to Luke. Very hurt by Mark's casualness and lack of response to my love and desire to mother him, I turned the more warmly to Luke, and when he begged me to marry him, I agreed at once. I listened to my head and closed my ears to my heart.

For my head told me that this was wisdom; that I should live always at Courtesy Court (and I could not bear the thought of permanently living anywhere else); that Luke really loved me and that I really loved Luke; that I should be Mark's sister-in-law and that he would not go out of my life; that I should have the joy and privilege of spending the money that Athene had left me, on keeping my adored Courtesy Court as it should be kept; and many more things.

My heart told me only one thing—that I was

marrying Luke while I loved Mark.

But I couldn't refuse him. I can hear him now.

"*Oh, Rosanne, do marry me. . . . Do say you will. . . . Oh, Rosanne, you can't refuse. Rosanne, I shall die, if you don't. . . . Rosanne, you couldn't leave me. You couldn't leave Courtesy Court. . . . My dear, how could I live without you. . . . You do love me a little, don't you, Rosanne—poor blind old Luke? . . . It would be cruel, after all you've done for me. That gives me a claim on you, you know. You've done so much for me that you must do more, do all. You must look after me always. . . . You must marry me, Rosanne. Do you think I could bear any other woman near me, ever? I shall go away, Rosanne, if you don't. I shall go away with Yrotavál and live in some wretched lodgings. . . . Answer me, Rosanne. And it would make Mark so happy. He told me he hoped for that more than for anything . . . Say something. Quickly. . . . Rosanne, I shall die. . . . I shall kill myself. . . .*"

"Hush . . . hush . . ." said I, stroking his poor head. "I will marry you, Luke. Of course I will."

IV

In the circumstances I could not and did not expect a honeymoon of perfect rapture and romance. Blessed is she who expecteth little, when she marries a man with whom she is not in love with all her heart and soul and mind and body. I did love Luke, but I had no sooner married him than I knew, beyond a shadow of a doubt, what I had already imagined and suspected—that I loved Mark more and in a wholly different way.

However, I had married Luke—whether out of pitying love or loving pity—and I set myself to make the absolute best of it. I have said that I set myself, and I might almost have said that I set my teeth, to make the best of it, for Luke grew increasingly difficult, and there were two flies in the ointment; two flies which grew and increased till they began to assume the proportions of mammoths.

One was Yrotavál, who, after our wedding, seemed to consider himself even more firmly established as the power behind the throne, to find himself even more deeply embedded in the soil of our very earthly Paradise. The fellow really seemed to be trying to run the house, through Luke, knowing that whatever Luke said "went," as he expressed it; and knowing, with equal certainty, that whatever Yrotavál said "went" with Luke. Had I not been as tactful as it was possible for me to be, and really forbearing and long-suffering, our ship would have been wrecked quite early on our matrimonial voyage.

I am not of a suspicious nature, but I could not help a horribly unpleasant and disloyal feeling that Luke had somehow put himself in Yrotavál's power, and had not the strength, honesty, and courage to struggle free; that he feared Yrotavál more than he loved me; that he was willing to sacrifice my peace and happiness, not to mention my position and dignity, to Yrotavál's wishes and desires—in fact, instructions. It worried me constantly, and a great deal more than Yrotavál's scarcely-covert insolence did.

It was a most difficult and unpleasant position. Maids who had not been with me long, having taken the place of two footmen and a pantry-boy who had enlisted, all gave notice on account of Yrotavál. Old servants, who had been with the Tuylers for ages, begged me to get Master Luke, as they still called him, to dismiss his nasty, dirty-minded valet, and had to be content with my promise that I would do the best I could. I think that, had not Luke been blind, even they, though with deepest reluctance and regret, would have given notice too.

And the more I tried to make Luke understand how impossible it was to carry on, the more difficult and irritable he got, and the more clearly evident it was to me that Luke could not dismiss Yrotavál if he would, although he pretended that he would not if he could.

The other fly in the ointment was Giulia Brent-Grayleigh. Her attitude toward me now changed in some curious and indefinable way. I honestly and firmly believe that I had never paid Giulia the compliment of being jealous of her, though she had always and obviously been jealous of me, which was perhaps quite natural and to be expected. Now she seemed to do her best to give me cause for jealousy and, though I hate to use the expression, to trade on Luke's blindness. At times, it was almost as though she took a leaf from Yrotavál's book, and behaved as though she too were a power behind the throne, the throne of Luke's unassailable position of Him Who Must be Obeyed, of Him Who Must not be Thwarted in the Slightest Degree.

Had I been really and truly and passionately in love with Luke, it would have been almost unbearable, so possessive was she, so much the interpreter to me of Luke's needs, Luke's character, Luke's personality. She was Giulia, the Indispensable; Giulia, the Only One who really understood him.

That was all very well, and if it pleased Giulia and soothed Luke, it did me no harm; but I did not like it, and still less did I like her growing air of importance, her attempted usurpation of the head nurse's and chief companion's position. Had I not made a fight for it, I should have been an absolute cypher in the house run by Yrotavál and Giulia, the cosmopolitan Spaniard and the Anglo-Italian of whom firmly I forbore to think, '*L'inglese italianato é il diavolo incarnato.*'

But quite a good fight I did make, and the training of the life of self-reliance, self-dependence and self-protection, which I had lived with Athene, stood me in good stead. But my hands were tied behind me by Luke's infirmity. And almost everything that I did to thwart Yrotavál's and Giulia's unwarrantable and increasing interference seemed to be an interference on my own part with Luke's wishes, his quietude, peace and happiness. I, Luke's wife, in the house of which I was chatelaine, was the disturbing element, the cause of friction, the troublesome Interferer! Heaven knows I did not mind how long Giulia spent with Luke, nor how much she did for him. On the contrary, I was only too thankful that she could interest and amuse him; that she took him for walks or drove him out in her car, read his letters to him, helped him with his correspondence, or played or read books and poetry to him. It never for one moment entered my head to feel the slightest twinge of jealousy. I should have been utterly ashamed, and felt myself beneath the contempt of both Luke and Giulia, had I for one moment entertained one base thought or unworthy suspicion—unworthy of Luke or Giulia, I mean. But any woman likes to feel she is mistress in her own house, and would surely be either superhuman or sub-human if she allowed it to be run by her husband's valet and his girl-friend.

I don't know how to define Giulia's change of attitude to me personally, but I can give a good idea of it by describing it as one of,

"You may be his wife now, but I am still his best friend. It is I who understand him, and if you want to manage him properly, you do it through me. Don't for one moment imagine that this wedding has made the slightest difference between me and Luke."

That sort of thing. A kind of self-assertion which had not been necessary before, but might be necessary now that Luke had raised me up to be his wife. There was a sort of implication that I was very well on the domestic plane, quite useful in the house and for material matters, but that it was she who was his true companion on the higher mental and spiritual plane, his soul-mate and his One Thing Needful.

All very well; but all very annoying. At times, more than annoying when Luke supported Giulia against me, and moaned something about her being his *Lux e tenebris*. (I suppose it didn't further endear me to Luke when I was moved to murmur, "And my *Nux e vomica*.")

What a wonderful thing it would be if we could always act and speak in the light of the question,

"How will this look and sound to me ten years hence?"

How bitterly I regret that I have not done that.

And added to these wretched little troubles and trials and irritations was my constant anxiety concerning Mark. Daily I opened the paper and scanned the Casualty-lists with a sinking heart. Daily I found my heart seeming to stop dead and then sickeningly turn over in my breast, whenever I caught sight of a telegraph-boy or heard a ring at the bell.

And I knew that, had Luke been Mark, I should have cared nothing for what Giulia did, less than nothing for Yrotavál's intolerable conduct and unbearable insolence. But there would have been no Giulia or Yrotavál had Luke been Mark.

§2

And at last, November 11th, 1918, arrived and the War was over. Mark was still alive, and the household machinery of Courtesy Court was still groaning and creaking and bumping along in difficult and uncertain fashion. But it was functioning, and I have no doubt that to any outsider it appeared to be working with the smoothness of a dynamo.

How well I remember, and with what difficulty I could describe, my feelings; for I longed to see Mark, and I almost hoped he would not come. I prayed that he would come straight home, and I feared his coming. For having married Luke and lived with him as his wife, I knew that, although I loved him—I was in love with Mark.

Mark came, and I shall never forget the shock that the sight of him gave me. He looked ten years older still; and it was only by means of a conscious and difficult act of self-control that I avoided making a fool of myself, throwing my arms round his neck, and giving my secret away to both the brothers.

And then began another amazing phase of my life at Courtesy Court. My heart simply sang with happiness. I cared nothing at all about Giulia Brent-Grayleigh's silliness, and as for Yrotavál, I felt I had only to tell Mark of my little troubles for him to sweep them away.

Oh, Mark, Mark! What a tower of strength and harbour of refuge! But what a weather-worn tower and storm-beaten harbour! What a wreck and a ruin of the boy who went to France in 1914!

But much as my heart ached for him, I'm afraid it ached more for myself, when I found how little he really cared about me. He had always been cool and undemonstrative, quiet, reserved and self-controlled. Now he was positively icy. He wasn't unfriendly. On the contrary, he was too perfectly friendly—just pleasantly and kindly friendly. And that was the trouble. Perfectly friendly without being in the least affectionate, much less loving.

And suddenly, a second time, although the War was over, he simply got up and went; walked out on us, without a word. I was almost as much amazed as I was hurt, grieved and desolate. I think I should have been almost broken-hearted had not a certain feeling of anger come to my assistance. For a time I was really angry that Mark should behave so. Did I mean nothing to him that he should just go, and without a word of farewell, when I was doing my very best to give him everything that he so sorely needed in the way of care, nursing, rest and sympathy?

Then such better feelings as I possessed asserted themselves, and I decided that his going was due to sheer inability to bear any longer the sight of Luke fumbling and tapping his way about in his dreadful cramping and crippling darkness.

I realized that he had found it impossible to share poor Luke's maimed, broken and thwarted life; that the greatness of his devoted love for him now made it impossible for him to be under the same roof with Luke all day and every day. Of course he would have stayed if Luke had needed him, had depended on him, or could have got anything from him that he could not get from me and Giulia. That this was not the case was quite plain, for, unintentionally of course, Luke made it clear that Giulia's company pleased, diverted and soothed him more than Mark's did. (Incidentally, more than mine did either.) It would be abominable to say that Luke was in any way jealous of Mark, or grudged the fact that, here he was, master and owner of Courtesy Court, perfectly sound in wind and limb, and free to enjoy life in every way and to the full while the happiness of Luke the Brilliant was wrecked, ruined and destroyed. But at the same time, one could not help seeing what I am quite sure Mark saw, that Luke was not at all forthcoming, was not particularly responsive and grateful for all that Mark tried to do for him, and that he definitely and strongly resented Mark's attempt to put Yrotavál in his place.

And not the least amazing thing about Mark's sudden departure was the fact that he took Yrotavál with him!

As the first pain and resentment wore off, I did once or twice wonder whether Mark had taken this tremendously drastic step simply to rid me of the man. I had complained to Mark about him, told him what a curse and a pest he was, poisoning my happiness with Luke; and Mark had instantly promised to do something about it. What Mark promises he invariably performs; and I wondered whether it were possible that, failing in his attempts to make Luke see reason and either dismiss Yrotavál or completely squash him, he had actually left home, his brother and me, for the sole purpose of solving the Yrotavál problem?

I had, however, to admit that this idea was far-fetched; and when Mark wrote, I took his letters at their face value and decided that he really had left home because he couldn't stand it any longer; could not bear the sight of Luke's suffering; and, moreover, found life at Courtesy Court altogether too boring and humdrum after four years of war.

Anyway, there it was. Mark had gone; gone for at least five years; and the strong probability was that I should never see him again—the one bright spot in a blank dark and threatening sky being the fact that, to please me and to help me, he had removed the chief obstacle to domestic peace and harmony at Courtesy Court.

The more I thought about Mark, and I thought about him a very great deal, the more his conduct puzzled me.

And this in itself was curious, for he had never puzzled me before. He was so straight, so simple and honest, with nothing of the baffling complexities of mind and the enigmatical character of his brother. Why should he rush off again like this, after apparently settling down with no other object or desire than to make Luke's path easy, and devote his life to the amelioration of Luke's tragic condition? Why so suddenly, and without a word of warning? Why without any farewell, either to Luke or to me? Of course, it could not have been simply in order that he could take Yrotavál with him. Obviously not, in view of the fact that he had admitted himself to be completely baffled and thwarted by Luke's attitude, his stout defence of Yrotavál, his strong objection to any interference with the man, and his absolute refusal to consider for one moment any question of dismissing him.

Mark had admitted to me that, in view of Luke's

attitude, Yrotavál's position seemed unassailable, and that we simply could not discharge the man, since Luke professed to be so dependent upon him, as well as so grateful to him for past services.

And yet here he was, immediately after that admission, clearing the man out of the house at a moment's notice, and without a word to Luke. It was the puzzle of a lifetime—both for me and for Luke. And although my greatest puzzle, it was not my only one, for Luke himself gave me nearly as much cause for wonder and bewilderment.

In the first place, although he, of course, did not say so, he was undoubtedly glad that Yrotavál had gone. He was almost as glad as I myself was, and the man's departure was like the lifting of a weight from his shoulders and a cloud from his mind. He became more cheerful and light-hearted, and much less irritable. For the first time since he came home I actually heard him whistling and singing. He laughed and joked more, and began to play the piano again.

He also now began to wear his eye-bandage and his black glasses very much less—although, of course, I could not connect this with Yrotavál's departure. But it somehow seemed symbolic of his increased freedom and a new life of cheerfulness and well-being.

Why, I asked myself, should he have been so immovably opposed to Yrotavál's dismissal and now be obviously thankful that he had gone? As I thought of it, an idiotic suspicion which had already entered my mind—to be instantly dismissed—kept returning, the suspicion that Yrotavál had some hold over him, and that Luke, while pretending to like him, really feared him.

§3

Meanwhile, Mark wrote to me regularly and to Luke occasionally. This puzzled me at first, for inasmuch as he loved Luke far better than he loved me and, throughout their lives until Luke left the Legion they had been two minds with but a single thought, two hearts that beat as one (to wax poetic), it seemed strange that it should be me to whom Mark wrote so much, and Luke to whom he wrote so little.

I came to the conclusion, however, that this was a psychological phenomenon, very easy of explanation. Loving Luke wholly and almost solely, as he did, it would give Mark unbearable pain to write to Luke words that Luke would never read: it would be an almost complete inhibition, that and the thought that everything he wrote to his brother must be read to him by a third person.

In saying that he wrote to me very frequently—whenever he had an opportunity, in fact—I don't mean that the letters reached me regularly. It all depended on where he was stationed and what he was doing. Sometimes I got them twice a week, sometimes only one in a month, and then a whole batch delivered by one mail. At times, he would be on a long march, when it was almost impossible to write at all; sometimes he would be, for a while, in a large outpost, a big camp, or a garrison town where there were regular postal facilities; and then, later, there would be times when he was in a distant *poste,* where the tiny garrison was practically besieged, and the sending of letters extremely difficult and irregular.

Mark's letters gave me a curious mixture of delight and pain, filling me with happiness, gratitude, anxiety and a great fear.

Strangely enough, Mark made little reference to Luke's health and progress. Indeed, he scarcely alluded to him at all, until he began to show signs of anxiety as to what Yrotavál, even now, even at that distance, might be doing with regard to Luke. I gathered that Luke had written to Mark complaining of begging-letters which he had received from Yrotavál, and that Mark wanted me to reassure him.

§4

And it was soon after this fairly peaceful time that I

could not help noticing the effect that Yrotavál's letters undoubtedly were having on Luke. It was quite patent and obvious that he was worried, not to say alarmed, by them, and that their arrival quite upset him.

Sometimes I saw one of the unmistakable envelopes, and knew in advance that its contents would trouble Luke. Sometimes I found him so disturbed that, though I had not seen an Yrotavál letter, I knew perfectly well that he had had one. Their receipt caused him to have fits of extreme depression, varied by irritability and a sort of brooding, smouldering anger. This grew steadily worse and worse, and I could see that Luke was definitely being made ill by them. Had it been in my power to kill Yrotavál, I would have done so gladly.

When writing to Mark, a thing I did with the utmost regularity, spending almost the whole of every Sunday afternoon in what was my favourite task, I told him that he was right in his suspicion, fully described the situation, and spoke of my belief, nay, certainty, that Yrotavál was in some way threatening Luke. Nothing else could have had quite the same effect, for he was not only angry and worried, he was frightened.

Mark replied reassuringly, and with an anger against Yrotavál at least equal to my own. Inasmuch as Mark always said rather less than he meant, and inasmuch as he loved Luke so much more and so much better than I did, I did not doubt that his anger was as much greater than mine as was his love for his twin.

When, in one of his later letters, he assured me that all trouble from Yrotavál should cease soon and cease finally, I knew that this would be so. Nevertheless, I confess that I did succumb to a temptation which I had long resisted.

One day, going to the big table in the outer hall, on which Johnson sorted and arranged the letters, I saw, among Luke's, an envelope addressed in Yrotavál's spidery and foreign-looking handwriting.

Suddenly I rebelled. Inasmuch as these letters did Luke nothing but harm, and upset him in a way that affected the entire household, why should they be allowed to reach him? They could do no possible good, and they did very great injury. It seemed to me that I was nearly as culpable as Yrotavál himself, in not taking steps to prevent Luke's receiving them. I picked up this particular letter, hurried to my room and, with a shameful sense of doing a mean and dishonest action, opened the envelope and read its contents.

It *was* a threatening letter. It was a blackmailing letter. It demanded not only money but more money, and more frequent sending of more money. And there was a double threat. Not only was Luke to be "exposed" if Yrotavál was not satisfied, but Yrotavál would take the first opportunity of deserting, would make his way to England, would appear suddenly at Courtesy Court, and then Luke would be "for it," as the ruffian expressed it.

My blood boiled and I felt murderous. To write like this to a blind man! And not only a blind man but a benefactor.

Trembling with anger, fear and horror, I at once enclosed the letter, with a scribbled note, in an envelope and directed it to Mark. Although I was under little illusion that it might increase the speed or safety of its transit, I wrote *Urgent* on the envelope, rang for Johnson, and bade him tell Crayne to take my little car and go at once to London and there register the letter at the General Post Office.

As always, I had turned to Mark for help, and as always, I felt the better for having done so.

More quickly than I could have expected, I got his reply. In this he assured me with the utmost certainty that Luke would never again hear from Yrotavál.

How that was to be achieved I could not imagine, but I could be unutterably grateful to Mark.

Meanwhile the fact remained that Yrotavál had some hold over my husband, knew something about him which put the creature in a position to blackmail him and to fill him with apprehension, anxiety and alarm.

V

Suspicion is a beastly thing. I loathe suspicious people, and before long I began to hate myself; for not only was I unable to rid my mind of this ugly thought, but I began to entertain others.

Luke had always been wonderfully clever in his blindness. We had all agreed that he seemed to develop a sixth sense, and to make his fingers almost take the place of his eyes.

With Yrotavál's going, his cleverness had increased to the point of being almost incredible. How, without any help from a valet, did he shave himself so perfectly, knot his tie so accurately, part his hair so exactly, and completely avoid any of those slight appearances of untidiness which inevitably mark the blind? Never once did he wear a collar that did not match his shirt.

When such thoughts began to come into my mind, I simply could not help noticing that with a blue suit he wore blue socks, and with a grey suit grey ones. That, hitherto, there had never been any evidences of blindness, such as the wearing of black shoes which should have been brown ones, or having any marks or spots on his clothes, I had naturally ascribed to the fact that he had a careful and watchful valet; but the valet's departure had made not the slightest difference, and that seemed to me a strange thing. I was ashamed of myself for thinking thus, but I could not help it. One has no control over one's thoughts. One can deal with them as one thinks fit when they enter one's mind, but there is no excluding them.

And one day I got a shock, and I use the word advisedly.

Luke was sitting in a deck-chair under a big cedar in front of the house. I was crossing the lawn toward him to tell him that Giulia had rung up to say that she would not be over to lunch that day.

As I approached him, the clock over the stables struck eleven. Subconsciously, as I thought, he glanced at his wrist-watch, and for the ten-thousandth time I felt a pang as he did so. . . . They were dreadful, those little sudden reminders of his blindness. . . . He then wound the watch, and, just as I was about to call out to him, to my utter amazement he pulled the key with a click, turned the hands and set the watch right. I realized that a blind man might very well, from force of habit, subconsciously "glance" at his watch, might possibly twirl the hands idly round, knowing that the watch face meant nothing to him; but how could he possibly set them at the proper time? A blind man can use a watch by opening the glass and feeling the position of the hands, but no blind man could either tell the time or put a watch right, with the glass cover closed.

I gave him Giulia's message, then looked at the watch. He had set it exactly right.

Feeling slightly sick and faint, and inclined to tremble, I went back into the house and sat down in the hall.

I was mistaken, of course. I was a foul-minded, suspicious, beastly woman.

But it wouldn't do. At lunch the very next morning, I could not help realizing that he reached out unerringly and helped himself to butter. How could he have known exactly where the butter-dish was, have picked up the knife and taken the quantity he required? I told myself that he must have heard me use the butter-knife and put it down on the dish with a slight click.

I tried again to be angry with myself and to be properly ashamed.

Another thing that I could not help noticing was that when he was wearing nothing over his eyes he was much more accurate and untrammelled than when he was wearing the black glasses, and rather more so when he was wearing the glasses than when he was wearing the bandage. Soon I had to admit that it was patent.

One day, as we were sitting in the lounge, he tapped his pockets and said,

"Damn! Left my cigarette-case upstairs."

Without *arrière pensée,* I said,

"I've got some," and held out my long thin case which I took from the hand-bag that lay beside me on the settee.

"Turks oval; Virgins round," I said, without a thought.

And accurately, without the slightest fumbling, Luke took an oval cigarette, and my hand almost shook as I remembered what for a moment I had forgotten—that he smoked only Turkish cigarettes.

Argue with myself as I might, I could not deny the implication. How could he know exactly where the extended case was? How did he know on which of the two sides were the oval cigarettes? Had he been wearing his bandage, his hand would not have gone straight to the case. If it had, it would not have gone to the side containing the oval cigarettes. Had it done so, it could not have taken the end one without the slightest hesitation, error or fumbling.

It was simply dreadful.

I could not expel the thought from my mind. It found permanent lodgment and poisoned and darkened it with a spreading stain, as does a cigar-butt dropped into water in a glass bowl.

§2

I dallied with the idea of setting a trap which would completely decide the matter if Luke fell into it. And then I shrank from the thought with horror.

Luke was fond of chocolate-creams, rather greedy about them, as a matter of fact. Giulia Brent-Grayleigh brought me from London a box of particularly fine ones, both of us knowing that Luke would eat most of them.

I brought them out after dinner, and offered him

the box. He took one, and was disappointed to find that it was hard. Again without any ulterior motive I said,

"You'll find that those covered in gilt foil are of the kind you like; *crème de menthe.*"

Without hesitation, Luke, who was not wearing a bandage or dark glasses, took one of the chocolates wrapped in gilt foil—and continued taking them until those of that particular kind were finished. I almost taxed him with his imposture, then and there, but refrained. It was too dreadful a thing to put into words, and, whether I was right or wrong in my ghastly suspicion, the accusation alone must have caused an almost permanent breach between us, and irreparable harm would have been done.

But it was too patent, too obvious, to be ignored, and, conquering my scruples and revulsion, I determined to test him deliberately, cunningly set a trap for him, and then have a show-down.

It would be the end of our married life, but better an end of that than a continuation of this hideous suspicion and suspense.

I thought of a number of ways in which I could make him betray himself if he were deliberately shamming blindness—and found it was unthinkable. I hated myself.

And the very next day, after heavy rain, I suggested that we should go for a walk because it had turned sunny, warm, and pleasant, and he had not been out of the house for a day or two. Again, nothing at the moment was further from my thoughts than testing or trapping him; but Chance or Fate or God had decided to intervene.

We walked down the drive, well-gravelled, well-kept, and though wet, not muddy. We turned out on to a country lane to which none of these encomiums could be applied. It wasn't too bad for walking, but there were numerous shallow depressions in which water still stood. Walking beside me, Luke, who was wearing his dark glasses, avoided every one of them. Unconsciously he stepped round, or over, them.

It was absolutely clear that, looking down, he could see below his glasses. We returned from that walk with his boots no muddier or damper than mine.

That incident settled the matter once and for all, and silenced the voice of my scruples. I deliberately set myself to think of a means of trapping him and confronting him with the proof of his guilt, the exposure of his horrible swindle.

I thought at first of something dramatic, something that would provide him with a horrible dilemma. Suppose I walked into his study, a glass of water in one hand and one of iodine, carbolic, or some corrosive poison in the other, and said to him,

"Luke, I solemnly swear that I am going to drink the contents of one of these tumblers. You shall tell me which it is to be."

If he still feigned blindness and refused to tell me which to drink, I would put the iodine or carbolic or whatever it might be, to my lips and say,

"I swear I'll drink this, Luke, unless you prevent me. . . ."

And at that point I abandoned that idea. I realized with horror that I wasn't certain whether Luke would give way and confess, even to save my life. And then, more than ever, I was ashamed of myself, was filled with horror at my own baseness at thinking such evil. Nevertheless, I felt that I had better drop that scheme altogether.

But I thought of another filthy trick and I played it on him.

Now one thing that Luke had always loathed doing was confessing ignorance of any kind. He hated to admit that there was anything he did not know. In a big book-case in the lounge was a fat old dictionary. Taking it down, I searched for something concerning which it would be extremely improbable that he could answer a question. Turning the pages of the volume, I came on the word *parasceve.*

That would do. The odds were a thousand to one against his being able to tell me anything whatever about it. Taking the book to the room I called my Glory

Hole, I stuck the bottom right-hand corner of the page (on which my word occurred) to the next, so that anyone consulting the book for *parasceve* would have to tear them apart.

That evening at dinner I said casually, though feeling as treacherous as Judas,

"Luke, what does *parasceve* mean?"

Luke looked up sharply from his plate and then, with a superior smile, spoke banteringly; and I knew that he had no idea as to the meaning of the word. So far so good—or so bad.

"Come, my child, you don't mean to tell me you don't know the meaning of that, surely?"

"Well, I shouldn't be asking you, Luke, if I did, should I?"

"Presumably not; but what laziness! What neglect of ingenuity! Surely the context could have told you, couldn't it?"

"Evidently not."

"Well now, you just read it again and see if you can't find out from the context. Then dust your brains, my child, and remember your little Latin and less Greek."

"I never learnt Latin or Greek, Luke."

"No, but you know some odds and ends of French and Italian, don't you? They'll be good enough, failing Latin."

"But you tell me, Luke."

"No. No, I won't. At least, not till to-morrow. See if you can't have thought it out by dinner-time to-morrow, and I will give you a prize."

"And suppose I can't?"

"Then I'll tell you. And I'll give you a slap . . ."

And hastily I changed the subject.

Hurrying down before dinner next evening, I opened the dictionary with trembling fingers. My heart sank, and I felt both ashamed and sick when I found that the book had been consulted, the pages parted, the corner that I had gummed torn, and still adhering to the next page.

At dinner I could scarcely eat. In spite of my

certainty that I was right, and my complete conviction that this abomination must be stopped, I felt utterly disgusted with myself, and hated myself for what I was doing.

Suddenly Luke said,

"Well, thought it out?"

"Thought what out?" I pretended.

"*Parasceve.*"

"No. You'll have to tell me, Luke."

"Come, come now. What does *para* mean?"

"I don't know. What does it mean?"

"God bless my soul, what an ignorant little know-all! Case of 'She don't know nothing and she knows that wrong,' eh? Ever heard of a parasol? What do you suppose *para* means in that?"

"Well, *against,* I suppose. Against the sun."

"Clever child. But as it happens, that won't help us. What about *parallel?* What do you suppose *para* means there?"

"Oh, I don't know. *Against* again, I suppose. One line lying against another to which it is parallel."

"Wrong, my child, though ingenious. When lines are parallel they don't lie against one another, do they?"

"Well, in the sense of *over against, near,* that sort of thing."

How much longer could I keep this up? I was trembling. The dreadful hypocrisy. . . . The humbug. . . . The wicked false pretences. Getting all that he had got under false pretences. Getting *me* under false . . . No, I must not think of that.

"Ah, that's all right. *Near.* But what is one line to another to which it is parallel?"

"Beside it," I murmured.

"That's it. Now we're getting on. Parallel, lying *beside. Para*site, *beside* the person you hang on to."

God! How could he talk of parasites?

"And so to *parasceve. Para,* beside. . . . And *sceve?* You don't know?"

No, and neither did he until he consulted that dictionary and read it with those eyes that I had so pitied and wept over, mourning painfully for their cruel dreadful blindness.

"*Sceve,* my child, is the Greek for *equipment.* So we have *parasceve—beside the equipment.* And that was when the Jews sat down and ate their Passover feast. In short, parasc*eve*—no pun intended—is the eve before the Jewish Sabbath when the preparations were made for *scarabing.* Know what scarabing means? I'm sure you don't, for I've just invented the word. I must send it to the New Oxford Dictionary. *Scarab,* a beetle. *Scarabing,* beetling off."

I began to hate the sound of his voice.

"Doubtless you read the word *parasceve* used by some Bright Young Babe just down from Oxford, as an improvement on the old-fashioned term Good Friday. . . . So there we are—*parasceve,* the Eve of Good Friday. And I must give you that smacking, after dinner."

I got up and left the table, for I was trembling now with anger, and I could bear him no longer.

§3

That night I could not sleep, for I was almost beside myself; sometimes with a sick horror, sometimes with a contemptuous pity, sometimes with bitter anger.

And this last was the worst of all, for I knew that behind it were my thoughts of Mark, and a growing fear, belief, conviction, that Luke had stolen Mark from me; that, but for my marrying Luke for pity, Mark's brotherly love for me would have turned to lover's love.

I was possessed with an agony of doubt as to whether Mark had not deliberately turned his face away from me in the belief that Luke and I loved each other; and in the fear that, even if we did not, Luke might love me, and he might stand in Luke's way.

I dared not follow that train of thought. There was grief and horror and anger enough.

And then I would doubt. *Could* I be wrong? How could I ever bear myself again, if it turned out that I had misjudged him?

I would go to him, confess what I had done, and

humble myself at his feet.

But I *couldn't* be wrong, though I would have given my right hand to have known that I was. . . .

Suddenly I had an idea. He had been to see two oculists in London as well as Renier in Paris.

I would go to London; go directly after breakfast to-morrow and without telling him my purpose. When I came back I *would* tell him something—something that one of us would never forget—either that he was a swindling, despicable cur to whom I would never will-ingly speak again, or that I was a vile, suspicious-minded she-devil who would be rightly served if he refused ever to forgive her.

I hoped it would be the latter, and I promised myself a real and humble abasement. I would be honest with myself and him. I would punish myself by telling him everything, and I would beg him to punish me as he thought fit.

Breakfasting alone next morning, I told Johnson to tell Crayne, the chauffeur, that I should want the car directly after breakfast. He was a reliable man and I was quite sure he would not fail me.

"Crayne," said I, as he opened the door of the car, "you remember taking Mr. Tuyler to town, some months ago, to see an oculist in Harley Street or Wimpole Street, I expect? He went up with his valet. It was before Mr. Mark Tuyler went away."

"Yes, Madam," Crayne replied at once. "Mr. Tuyler visited two of them. One in Harley Street and the other in Wimpole Street."

"And you could find them again?"

"Oh yes, Madam. One was a corner house and the other was 57 or 59. Anyway, I should know it."

"Good. I want to go and see them both, this morning."

"Very good, Madam."

VI

"This is one of the two places to which Mr. Tuyler went that day, Madam," said Crayne, as he opened the door of the car, outside a house in Wimpole Street. I wondered if it were that in which the happy Barrett family had disported itself.

A small silver plate on the door announced in discreet black lettering that Mr. Household lived there. But here I drew a blank. Mr. Household, it appeared, had gone away for his holidays—a Mr. Haynes being his *locum tenens*—and had I made an appointment?

"Drive to the other oculist's, Crayne," said I re-entering the car.

"It is one of these two, Madam; the one on the right, I believe. Yes. That's it, Madam," said Crayne as the car stopped at a corner house in Harley Street.

A plate on the front door of this house announced that Mr. Struthers functioned here.

The door being opened by a young lady who was not a maid and was probably a secretary, I asked whether Mr. Struthers were the famous Ophthalmic Surgeon and whether he could spare me a minute, in spite of the fact that I had no appointment.

The girl, replying that this was the house of Mr. Struthers the Consulting Oculist, and that she would enquire, ushered me into a beautiful Georgian room with an Adams fireplace and ceiling. It would have been all the same to me had it been a prison-cell or a pig-sty.

Some ten minutes later the girl returned, bade me follow her, and led the way to the famous oculist's consulting-room.

From behind a big desk rose a tall, powerful-looking man, with a strong face on which the expression was neither welcoming nor particularly pleasant. Nor was what he said, for he refrained from speech altogether.

"Thank you so much for seeing me, Mr. Struthers. I am most anxious to ask you about my husband."

"Yes? Sit down. What name?"

"Tuyler," said I, spelling it for him.

For a minute or two he consulted a filing cabinet.

"No such name," he said. "Must have gone to somebody else."

Was I to be foiled and defeated again, and thrown back into my slough of doubt and suspicion?

"Is there an oculist living next door to you?" I asked.

"No."

"Then I think my husband must have come here, Mr. Struthers. A tall, fair, soldierly-looking man, rather —er—handsome. He came with his valet, a short, dark man. He's blind and . . ."

"O-h-h! That fellow. Called himself Holbeach; with a foreigner, a South American or something. Carried a white stick, yellow gloves and a bowler hat. Blue suit. Valet had a curious name—Rot . . . something or other."

"Yes. Yes," I agreed.

"Did you come in the same car?"

"Yes," said I.

He rose and went to the window.

"That's it—that's the car. I watched him get into it. Well?"

"I came to ask you whether you can tell me how bad his eyes are. Whether you think he's permanently blind."

"Yes, I can, Mrs. . . . What did you say your name was? His eyes are just as bad as he chooses to make them. As to his being permanently blind, he's not even temporarily blind. He's not blind at all. Never has been. I don't know what his game is, but he's a humbug and a fraud. I'm speaking plainly because you've asked me about him and because I don't like anyone coming here and trying to fool me. . . . You wanted the truth, didn't you?"

I again had that horrible feeling as though I were

about to faint, a physical nausea, as my heart again seemed to stop, flutter, and then threaten to choke me.

"The absolute and complete truth, please, Mr. Struthers."

"Well, there you've got it. I haven't the least idea what his graft is—unless he was lying to me in saying that he neither had a pension nor wanted one."

"No, no, nothing of the sort," I managed to say. "But I have been so anxious."

"Well, you needn't be anxious about his eyes. He can see perfectly well, and the eyes are absolutely healthy. Except for the introduction of some foreign matter they are perfectly normal, and on that I will stake my reputation."

"You couldn't possibly be mistaken, I suppose?" I begged.

"I could be. But I wasn't, in this case. I have had a good deal of experience of scrimshanking malingerers and pension-thieves during and since the War, and everybody who comes into this room goes through one or two small tests, though they don't know it. I always point to that chair that you are sitting on, placed just where I want it as regards light, and in relation to that table. No blind man could go straight to it.

"And the small table on your right is just conven-ient for hat and gloves, which are never taken from visitors. My secretary showed your husband in here herself. He went straight to that chair which I indi-cated, put his hat and gloves on that table and—he is either very stupid and inexperienced or has got care-less—he actually flicked a bit of fluff or thread or something from the sleeve of his blue coat.

"Well, as I say, I've dealt with plenty of gentlemen of that sort when I was Referee to the Ministry of Pen-sions, and while I talked to him I absent-mindedly screwed up a sheet of paper from this scribbling-pad and suddenly flicked it off my thumb—like that—straight in his face.

"He dodged it; and then must have seen that he had given himself away. However, he stuck to his point, and we went through with it. I examined his eyes most carefully, and, as I expected, found nothing wrong with them. Nothing whatsoever, except what was obviously an artificially induced irritation."

"Are your tests infallible? Can you be absolutely *certain* that a person is not blind?" I asked.

"No. No, I don't say that at all . . . In certain forms of blindness, especially those of psychological origin, there may be not the slightest sign whatsoever that there is anything wrong with the eyes."

"Then how . . . ?" I began.

"From observation of *him,* as well as his eyes. He gave himself away most obviously, and his eyes confirmed it . . . I can tell whether a man is blind or not, the moment he comes into this room. It's a look on the face, as well as the whole bearing . . . carriage . . . manner. No man can go blind and stay blind, without it showing in the expression of his face. And that alone is enough for me. Why, if a thousand men opened that door and came to this desk, and nine hundred and ninety-nine of them were blind, I'd spot the one who wasn't. Every time. I knew your husband was not blind before ever he proved it to me by what he did; and before ever I examined his eyes.

"And I'll tell you another thing, Mrs.—er—Tuyler. The valet, if that's what he is, also knows your husband isn't blind; for I watched carefully—and I suppose one developed a special faculty while working at the Ministry of Pensions. When I rang for the man, he made no attempt to give your husband his hat and gloves, which I had moved to my desk when I examined his eyes. No, your husband took them himself and marched out of the room in high dudgeon. And the attendant or valet or whatever he is, didn't open the door of the car. Your husband did that himself . . . A very clumsy impostor indeed."

"Mr. Struthers," I said, "it would be a most terrible thing if you were mistaken . . . If a blind man were called an *impostor* and . . ."

The oculist rose to his feet.

"My dear Madam," he said with an air of finality, "I am *not* mistaken. It is absolutely impossible that I should be mistaken in this particular case. If you are under any misapprehension still, why not go and test him yourself. Simplest thing in the world, for of all the impostors whom I have convicted of pretended blindness to avoid enlistment, to avoid returning to the Front, or to get a pension, your husband is the crudest and feeblest. I never saw poorer acting or greater carelessness. I might say stupidity. And if it was a joke—it was a poor one. . . ."

I thanked Mr. Struthers. For, after all, if he had not been particularly pleasant and polite, he had been honest. I also asked him if I might leave a fee.

"Well, I refused one from your husband, for I was feeling more than a little angry and contemptuous. I will accept it now. Three guineas . . . Thank you. And you can take it from me, without the slightest hesitation or shadow of a doubt, that your husband can see as well as you or I can," said the offended Mr. Struthers.

§2

My state of mind as I drove home amazed me. I had quite finally accepted the evidence of my own senses coupled with the oculist's assurance, and had ceased to resist admission of the fact that Luke was an impostor, a swindler, and a thief. Yes, a thief certainly, who had stolen much from me, if not the best and greatest thing in life.

I could not be absolutely certain that, but for his vile deceit and trickery, I should be married to Mark, but I now felt intuitively—and like most women I put intuition far before reasoning and argument—that Mark loved me, and would have asked me to marry him but for Luke's blindness and helplessness.

I ought to have been seething with indignation and fierce anger. But I was not. To my surprise, there was a glimmer of gladness in the dark turmoil of my thoughts, like a faint watery beam of sunshine breaking through massed clouds upon a black and heavy sea.

What was it? Why, now that I knew for certain, did I not feel more hurt, contemptuous, bitter, and angry?

Striving to be honest with myself, and to feel nothing merely because I *ought* to feel it, I decided that it was because I was now, in some indefinable way, nearer to Mark.

Certainly I was further from Luke. As far from Luke as I could be, for never, never again should I regard him as my husband.

It was idiotic and foolish to admit this little gleam of light and happiness, but there it was. Luke had married me under false pretences; and the fact of those same false pretences, discovered and exposed, now divorced me from him—in all but Law. It set me free. Idiotic again—to toy with that *'all but Law.'* As well say *'all but everything.'*

But would it appeal thus to Mark?

Mark was apt to be a law unto himself; and when he knew that Luke was a lying, fraudulent rogue, a contemptible impostor who had thus come between himself and me, what would Mark care about any five-cent Law? If Mark loved me, as I somehow felt that he did, and I told him that I had only married Luke out of pity, to try to compensate him, in however slight degree, for all that he had lost, what would be Mark's instant reaction when he found that I loved him?

Into what amazing by-ways one's mind can wander when the subconscious part of it is dominant. . . .

Why should I think that Mark loved me?

Why should I think that he took Yrotavál away, just to help me? Why should I think that Mark loved me in the sense of being in love with me? The wish was father to the thought, of course.

Nevertheless, if he did love me, I was free . . . free . . . When I told him that Luke . . .

And suddenly I came to life, emerged from the dull stupidity of my brown study, the conscious thinking part of my mind very much under control.

When I told Mark of Luke's horrible imposture!

How could I do such a thing? It would be absolutely devilish. It would do poor Mark irreparable harm. He would never have a grain of faith in man or woman again, as long as he lived. Not a grain of faith the size of a mustard-seed. He absolutely worshipped his twin-brother. Adored him. He had devotedly loved him from babyhood; loved him far better than ever he had loved, or would love, me.

Of course, I couldn't tell Mark. I should be ashamed of myself, and he'd be ashamed of me for doing it; more angry with me than he'd be with Luke.

Luke must recover his sight.

Of course Luke must recover his sight. Mark must be told the joyful news and he must not know that Luke had never lost it.

I would tell Luke that I had discovered his vile secret, tell him how I had first suspected him, and had then trapped him, in an honest attempt to prove or disprove the truth of my suspicion; and that I had been to see the oculist—who, incidentally, I was pretty sure had given Luke short shrift and the rough side of his tongue.

And then? Why, then—Luke and I would continue to live at Courtesy Court in peace and amity, of a sort. He could take up his permanent abode in his own room of which he was so fond, and in which, anyway, he now spent many more nights than he did in our own bedroom. And Mark, returning from the French Foreign Legion, would find that Luke had recovered his sight completely.

(When he returned! What were the chances that he would survive more years of war and such a life as that of the French Foreign Legion on active service?)

But still the little ray of hope—no, not hope—the ray of light, persisted; for I was free.

I should never be Mark's wife, but neither again would I be Luke's.

What would Mark's attitude really be, if he ever

knew?

Forgiveness, in the end, I verily believed. I did not think it was in Mark's nature to be angry with Luke for long; much less to hate him. Could I rise to Mark's heights of love and forgiveness? Perfect understanding, perfect comprehension that, understanding all, forgives all? No, I couldn't. In the first place, I was a woman, and a woman in love: in the second place, I was not Luke's twin.

What line would Luke take when I told him that I had found him out?

And should I, remembering Mark, speak to Luke gently, tell him I quite understood how War, lovely ennobling War, could have changed him so? That I completely forgave him for any wrong that he had done to me; but that he must clearly understand that, as the grounds of our marriage had been his blindness and his need, and those grounds been proved to be illusory, the marriage was as much a fraud as his blindness and, like it, must now end.

But what ever should I do if he flew into a temper; or struck an attitude of outraged innocence, and stoutly denied that he could see? I decided that I would give him the choice of dropping that line of conduct or of dropping me. I somehow felt that if it came to a choice between the truth and the retention of his creature comforts on the one hand, and clinging to this imposture and losing me and my money on the other . . .

Oh, horrible thought! Had he married me for my money?

No, no, no! What a beastly and unworthy thought. I was getting as bad as . . . Oh, God, give me a little help!

I was thankful to find that the car was turning in through the gates of Courtesy Court park.

I do not remember a single detail of that drive save my thoughts—to call that turmoil of impulses, hopes, fears and unwelcome intrusions of the subconscious mind, by the name of thoughts.

§3

I must see Luke at once, see him and get this dreadful business straightened out; and come to an understanding one way or the other. He must make confession or denial; and then I must act accordingly.

I glanced at the ancient grandfather-clock in the hall. I'd go straight and see him before I thought of food. I would not stop for so much as a cup of tea. But he'd be sleeping. The afternoon was sacred to his rest, as he slept so badly at night, since to him night and day were one. (Oh, Luke! How could you be such a lying, fraudulent faker!) When Giulia was at the house she would generally go up and read or play to him for an hour after lunch, before he went to bed.

Well, Giulia wasn't here to-day.

And Luke wasn't blind.

It would take some time to realize that and keep it permanently in mind.

I would go up to his room and, if he were asleep, I'd wake him, and with what is known as a rude awakening.

No, I must try not to get angry, bitter or contemptuous.

The last thing in the world that I wanted, or felt that I could bear, was a row, a squabble, a 'vulgar altercation.'

I must be wise and cool and careful, for Luke was so much cleverer than I, and so plausible.

Should I wait a while, until I was really calm and collected?

No. It would be dreadful. This was a thing to do at once, or never.

Telling the parlour-maid that I would have nothing until tea-time, I went straight upstairs, and along to Luke's room.

Nerving myself to say what must be said, and schooling myself to say it quietly, with dignity and without rancour, I opened the door.

Luke and Giulia! . . . Lovers! . . .

Unintentionally I had made no sound. I had stood for a few seconds preparing myself, and had opened the door swiftly and silently.

I could not believe my eyes.

Luke . . . Giulia . . . I was speechless. I doubted the evidence of my own eyes. I was incredulous and numbed.

Giulia, my friend whom I had trusted absolutely, as a nurse, as a member of the family, and of whom I had never thought the slightest evil.

Luke, to whom I had given everything, for whom I had done everything. Luke, whom I had married . . . while Mark . . .

Suddenly he looked up; his eyes met mine; and, literally and physically, he flinched; the healthy colour drained from his face as he stared.

He saw me as clearly as ever any human being saw anything at all.

"Rosanne!" he whispered, then clapped his hands to his eyes and cried something inarticulately.

Giulia raised her head in alarm, looked round, saw me, and flushed darkly.

I turned and went from the room without a word.

VII

Am I different from other women, or quite normal? I went down to the hall, seated myself in my own chair and wondered at myself.

For I was not stricken with disgust, contempt, anger, fierce resentment, or any of the feelings presumably proper to the situation. I was still numbed, of course, my feelings dulled; but, such as it was, my strongest emotion was one of amazement. Not at what I had seen; not that Giulia should be the thing she was; not that Luke should have made such return for my kindness and my sacrifice; but because the little ray of light was growing, quickly growing, to a beam, a beam of sunshine.

For surely I was now really free, free in every sense of the word; could soon be free even within the meaning of an archaic and hide-bound Law. Surely what Luke had done, first by shamefully swindling me and then by being unfaithful, was enough, even in England? Besides, if it were not, Luke would prefer divorce to exposure. If the wonderful and sensible Law decreed that he must treat me with cruelty as well as infidelity, he would undoubtedly agree to the necessary collusion, even though his halo were still further dimmed.

And then darkness gathered in again.

I could not, and I would not, let Mark know of this. Certainly not about the blindness, for he had played that trick on Mark himself, as well as on me.

Certainly not the other, with cruelty included, for that would outrage Mark's sense of decency and honour more deeply than the blindness. Oh, what could . . . ?

Suddenly Giulia appeared, and passed through the hall on her way to the front door.

I stood up and she saw me. She looked more beautiful than ever, but—she was frightened.

"Don't come again please, Giulia," I said very

quietly.

"It's *me* he loves!" she cried. "He has always loved me. He loved me before ever he set eyes on you. And I love him. I love him. I have always loved him . . ."

And then the real Giulia shone forth.

"And he married *you* for your money," she almost shouted.

"Yes, Giulia, I begin to think he did. Good-bye."

"What are you going to do about it?"

"I don't know yet, Giulia. Good-bye."

I put out my hand toward the bell, and Giulia went, with some attempt at dignity.

§2

As Giulia had asked—*What was I going to do about it?*

And as I had told Giulia, I did not know.

I must have sat in that chair for hours, staring straight before me, seeing nothing—nothing concrete, that is to say, for I saw other things all too clearly—and, in a stunned and stupid way, wondering what I was going to do.

Johnson must have brought tea, for I was aware that, with gentle reproach, he was asking me if he should make me what he called 'a fresh pot.' I remember shaking my head and being amazed that, shortly after, as it seemed, he came and announced that dinner was ready.

What was he saying? The parlour-maid could get no answer from Mr. Luke. He himself had been to Mr. Luke's room and had knocked at the door and been told to go away.

Appearances must be maintained, and it is the little familiar acts and routine habits of life that tide us over crises, and are our best helps in our times of greatest trouble.

Luke did not appear, and I went through dinner alone. As soon as I could, I went into the drawing-room and again sat and stared blankly at the future.

What was I going to do about it?

What was I going to do about Luke's living lie, imposture and deceit? What was I going to do about his shameful and shameless infidelity?

One thing, with regard to him and Giulia, I was not going to do, and that was work up the appropriate feelings if they did not come of themselves. I was not going to be the vindictive outraged wife—until I felt vindictive. I was not going to act in a wild whirl of angry determination to have my revenge and my rights —until I felt revengeful and desirous of my rights. I was not going to send instantly for my solicitor and tell him to begin divorce proceedings forthwith.

I would be absolutely honest with myself and would feel what I did feel and not what I ought to feel. . . . And I must discriminate. I must separate what I felt about Luke's deceit and cheating in the matter of his false blindness, from what I felt about his treachery and unfaithfulness to our marriage.

I think I am fairly clear-minded, logical and capable of honest thought and self-examination. Anyway, as I sat there alone in the silence, I decided that my love for Luke was completely dead, that I could never forgive him for what he had done to Mark and to me by shamming blindness.

I also came to the conclusion—which surprised me —that, with regard to him and Giulia, I was much more hurt, shocked, and amazed than I was indignant, angry and vengeful.

It was a terrible thing, of course, but the blow of this discovery was, compared with that of the blindness, but slight. I wondered whether this was because it came just after the other, at a moment when I had rather exhausted my ability to feel and to suffer. I also wondered whether it was because it was not a thing that hurt and wronged Mark as the blindness imposture had.

I decided that in simple truth it was because, horrible as it was, it set me free—from the position of being married to one man while I loved another. I realized that it set me free . . . in relation to Mark. And though I hated myself for it, I knew that, mingled with disgust, horror and sense of shocked injury and hurt, was a slight if incredible feeling of gladness. This being so, I could not and would not take a high and mighty line of outraged indignation in dealing with Luke. It was not for me to show moral superiority and pharisaical contempt of an act of which I was *almost* glad, and by which my life might perhaps be made happier.

So—what was I going to do about it?

One thing I was not going to do was ever again to live with Luke as his wife. That knowledge and certainty gave me comfort, a sense of something valuable saved from the wreck and ruin of my life.

My life! Suppose I put consideration of that aside, at any rate for the present, and thought of Mark's life.

And Luke's.

That was certainly what Mark himself would have done in the same circumstances, and I had not lived in the same house with Mark for all those years without consciously, or unconsciously, being influenced by his standards and example. Mark's rare angers and fits of indignant wrath were invariably on behalf of other people. When he was enraged against someone, it was for someone else. What would Mark do? What should I do, if I tried to be a female Mark?

First of all, forgiveness to the extent that that was possible; secondly, a general minimizing of trouble and an honest attempt to make the best of things. Luke being the culprit, Mark would forgive him altogether. In this case, he would make him recover his eyesight as gradually or as quickly as he chose; and if he believed that Luke really, truly, and finally loved Giulia, he'd do anything in his power to enable him to marry her.

Well, I'd do that. I'd tell him I knew he was not blind and that he must cease to pretend to be: and I'd ask him if he wished to marry Giulia, and I'd give him a divorce if he wanted one.

Divorce him and publicly disgrace him, against his will, I would not; but how I hoped and prayed that he would ask me to give him his freedom.

But I had better sleep on it, for I must take no

hasty step, and there was much to be considered. Finance, for one thing, if the impecunious Luke were to marry the penniless Giulia.

But on one point my mind was crystal clear, and on another, hard as adamant: clear that I must show forgiveness for what Luke had done—and understanding of his temperament and his temptations, understanding that such a man as he could have high courage and great *élan,* and yet lack the grit and backbone to hold on: understanding that such a man as he must inevitably and always be the prey of the Giulias of this world. For who shall escape his temperament?

On that I was absolutely clear.

And on the other I was hard—hard and strong on the point of an irrevocable refusal ever to return to him. There I would be firm. Surely Mark would agree to that?

As though I were Mark himself, I would go to Luke now, speak to him with real kindness and without recrimination. Just tell him simply and plainly that he must stop pretending to be blind, and that if he wanted his Giulia he should have her.

Yes, I thought bitterly, and that would be in the true tradition of the proper attitude of all his relations and friends to the great Luke.

I rose to my feet, thankful to find that I was no longer trembling. Was there in my heart any glow of self-satisfaction and self-righteousness that I had been able to attain this Mark-like attitude to the man who had wronged me so? Not the slightest, for, being honest with myself, I knew that as surely as I said,

"I forgive you and will let you have your Giulia," there followed, though unspoken by myself to me, the words,

"And I shall then be free—as Mark is free."

VIII

I stood for a moment outside the closed door of Luke's room, trying to arrange my thoughts and to decide what I should say, for I was desperately anxious to say the right thing, and in the right words. It was always very necessary to say the right thing in the right words to Luke when he was in trouble; and if ever a man were in trouble, poor Luke was now. For him, the worst conceivable trouble—being in the wrong and without excuse; desperately in the wrong and utterly without defence of any sort.

That alone would torture him, apart from any definite punishment that would follow his wrong-doing.

Now to be conciliatory, understanding and honestly friendly. Now to try to act as though I were Mark himself.

Fully dressed, he was lying on his bed, sobbing like a child.

"Luke!" I cried. *"Don't!"*

As I spoke, he turned and looked at me, scrambled from the bed, and literally threw himself at my feet.

Embracing me about the knees, he looked up into my face.

"Rosanne! Rosanne!" he cried. "I am *blind!* . . . I am *blind!* . . . Forgive me, Rosanne, for I am *blind!* . . ."

My heart seemed to sink within me, and I felt sick with disgust and misery and shame. To pretend like this, when *he knew that I knew* that he had seen me as he looked up, had flinched and turned pale—had even said my name though I had not spoken. How could he possibly sham blindness after that?

For a moment I could find no words . . . Then, as he clung to me—acting his part—babbling of his blindness —making it his excuse—using its appeal once again— my patience failed, my anger boiled over, speech

383

poured from my lips in swift and sudden spate, and I lashed him cruelly with my contempt and sudden hate.

All the bitterness and disgust I felt for his shame . . . all my sense of loss and injury . . . all my love for Mark . . . and there he grovelled at my feet weeping and crying that he was *blind.*

Lies . . . all lies, humbug, acting . . .

I tore his hands away and, thrusting him from me, I hurried from the room, bewildered, foiled and defeated by his utter—*impossibility.*

Blind! When I had proved in half a dozen ways that he could see perfectly, and when I had just had the absolute and unhesitating assurance of a distinguished oculist that he was not blind. And had I not had such assurance, had I not found him out for myself, even before I silently entered the room that afternoon and he looked up, saw me, flushed guiltily, turned pale, and then uttered my name?

How *could* I now do as Mark would have done?

But surely, even Mark would have turned against him after that exhibition of cowardly lying, swindling, avoidance of trouble and reproach.

When I reached my bedroom, I was trembling and shaking as though in the cold stage of fever. I was certainly in the cold stage of fierce anger, and I felt that I could not stay another hour beneath the same roof with this incorrigible impostor and cheat; false to his brother who worshipped him; false to me who had been willing to give up my life to looking after him. . . . Unfaithful to me—and with Giulia of all people. I wondered it was not with my own maid. Perhaps it had been.

I would order the car, go up to London and—from the hotel at which the family always stayed and where we were not numbers but honoured guests—I would write to him, tell him that when he had read this letter, as well he could, I should be glad if he'd write me an answer with his own hand and with a pen, as well he could. I would ask him what he proposed to do, for I had not the slightest intention of returning to the house while he was there. I would strongly advise him to cease his pretence of blindness, and ask him whether he wished to marry Giulia, in which case I would divorce him. I would also sting his pride—if he had any—by offering to give him and her an adequate allowance upon which to live, provided I never saw either of them again. . . .

I rose to ring the bell for Johnson, and then remembered. Appearances must be maintained. I would sleep here to-night and go to London immediately after breakfast in the morning. I would lock my door for the night, and if Luke wished to come along and whine again about his blindness, he could do it through the keyhole, the miserable, spineless rogue and liar.

IX

But the spirit of Mark, like the Hound of Heaven, followed me. During the night, and on the journey to London, I had thought of how the new state of affairs would affect me personally; of how I should tell Mark (I would not tell him of the blindness swindle, for it would break his heart, but I would tell him that Luke and I were separating, for I felt I did owe that much to myself); of how and where I should live while Luke was recovering his blindness; of whether I might not order him to recover it quite suddenly, as shell-shocked men have done; of what I should do until the decree *nisi* was made absolute; and, with longing and hope and that same gleam of joy in it all, of whether it would not be possible for me to travel to that place in Algeria which was the depôt of the French Foreign Legion. There could be no harm in that, surely; especially after Luke had married his Giulia, if that was what he intended to do.

Mark was my best and greatest and dearest friend, and surely I could travel to places where I might see him?

Day-dreams!

But when I had reached the hotel, unpacked and sat down to rest in the un-homelike, unfriendly sitting-room, I weakened. Closing my eyes, I strove to imagine that Mark was there with me, sitting in the arm-chair on the other side of the fireplace. Perhaps I was too successful, for Mark seemed rather to be pleading for Luke than to be loving and comforting me.

Against my will, I had to see Luke once more as Mark saw him. I had to understand, to make allowances, to forgive him—seventy times seven. I had to remember that Luke was not as other men; that he was an artist; that he had been spoilt from babyhood; and that Mark himself had been one of the worst offenders in this respect. Before long, I felt that, in punishing Luke, I should be punishing Mark himself, for his sin of spoiling his brother.

I was forced to remember how heroically Luke had volunteered to fight for Right against Might; to remember how he had fought with the greatest courage; to remember that he had been shell-shocked; to remember that it was quite possible that he had, for a little while, been genuinely blind after the explosion; to remember that what was hardship and suffering to a strong and stolid man like Mark, was agony unbearable to a sensitive, highly strung æsthete like Luke. All sorts of things I was forced to remember, and all sorts of sloppy sentimental tags and *clichés* would keep floating unbidden through my mind: "To err is human, to forgive divine". . . *"Tout comprendre c'est tout pardonner"* . . . "Judge not that ye be not judged". . . "If a man smite ye on the right cheek". . . though God alone knew how cruelly Luke had smitten me.

And by the time I had sat unmoving in that chair for a few dreadful hours, the worst hours of my life, I was defeated. Mark had won.

In other words, Luke had won again.

I must go back. I must forgive him. I must ask him what he wanted—and give it him with both hands. When he flung himself at my feet again, I must run my fingers through his silky curly hair and say,

"Yes, poor Lukie is blind, but we are going to make him better. And poor Lukie loves Giulia, and we are going to make everything nice and easy for him. . . ." Bah! . . .

But after a while I managed to cast that devil out too. And when I rose to my feet, with a sigh, it was only one of regret that Luke was Luke and Mark was Mark—and that I was nothing to either of them.

Well, well. . . .

§2

By the time I arrived home that evening, I was quite resigned. Not happy. Not content. But on the other hand, not angry, not bitter. Just resigned.

And honestly and truly I can say that I *had* forgiven Luke and was prepared to do whatever he wanted.

For that, I am thankful to this day.

Thank you, Mark.

For I was not called upon to act with superhuman forbearance and noble magnanimity; to forgive Luke once again; and for the thousandth time to pretend that all was as Luke could like it to be.

For Luke was dead.

I don't know—no one knows—why Luke died.

An old groom, Valentine Jermyn, who had been with the Tuylers for thirty years, last saw him alive, and gives sole testimony as to Luke's end.

As the car came up the drive, Jermyn stood in the way, shouting, with arms extended.

I could see that something was wrong. Something terrible. For Jermyn was wildly incoherent and tears were streaming down his rather rascally face. Giving credit where credit is due, Jermyn was truly and deeply moved—more so than I was—filled with horror, and broken-hearted at the death of his master, as he regarded Luke.

"What has happened? What has happened?" I cried as I jumped out of the car. . . .

"All woild and daverdy 'e looked. All moidered 'e wur. Coom rooshin' out o' the 'ouse wi' his white stick. Feelin' round wi' un and tappin', till 'e's set roight fer path to crossin'-gate. Not like usual, 'e wurn't steppin' along bold and easy, so as anyone wouldn't know un was blind. Not like that 'e wurn't s'arternoon, but all woild and daverdy, strikin' and feelin' round wi' white stick, an' bumpin' into trees an' bushes. Stumblin' over things an' blunderin' on to flower-beds. I seen un and thinkin' summat was wrong I coughs respectful an' speaks up an' said,

" *'Arternoon, Mas'r Luke,'* an' 'e says,

" *'Jermyn,'* 'e says, *'see me roight to crossin'-gate. Coom 'ere, damn ye,'* 'e says, *'so's I can get ahoold o' thy arm. . . . To crossin'-gate,'* 'e says, *'quick.'*

"An' I leads un down to crossin'-gate and he catches aholt on it.

" *'Won't ee want I fer to lead ee back to house, Mas'r Luke?'* I asks.

" *'No. Get to Hell out o' this. Go on. Go away to staables and stay there,'* 'e says. *'An' keep on gravel-path so's I hear thee agooin'.'*

"So thinkin' he was actin' funny, but not thinkin' nothing was real wrong, I goes and leaves un. . . . Sooner I'd 'ave 'acked me feet off wi' chopper ef I 'ad known what was to 'appen."

And here Jermyn pulled out a filthy red-and-white spotted handkerchief and unashamedly mopped his streaming eyes.

"Get *on,* man, get *on,*" I urged. "What happened? *Where is he?*"

"Afore I could get fifty yards away from gate, I hears little gate bump, and knawed 'e'd gone through. Then I stops and thinks 'adn't I better go back fer to see 'im safe across railway to little crossin'-gate t'other side, though I knows if 'e 'ears me 'e'll rage turr'ble fer me disobeyin' 'im.

"An' as I stands thinkin' I better go back so fur as I can see un walkin' across, but keepin' so's 'e won't know I'm follerin' un, I hears train. *By Goord!* I thinks. *'Tis train!* An' I runs . . ."

Jermyn broke down again. And I could have shaken him.

"*Yes?*" I said. "*Yes?*", trying to keep cool.

" 'Twere too late, Ma'am. Mas'r Luke 'e'd crossed in front o' train. Swung and tapped all round 'im wi' stick, 'e did, then 'e turned about to come back."

"He was run over?" I whispered, as I seized the door of the car for support.

"Not ezzactly, Ma'am. . . . Train struck 'im and knocked 'im floyin' 'ead over 'eels into ditch."

"*He's dead?*"

Jermyn nodded his head as he crammed the red handkerchief against his mouth.

"Ar!" he mumbled as I sat down on the running-board of the car. "Dead as a corp."

"Mas'r Luke!" he blubbered. "I learned un to ride. Chucked un up on his first pony . . . trained 'is first 'unter. . . . Rode be'oind 'im to 'ounds . . . An' always a foine well-plucked little b——" He broke down.

Here was another who loved Luke. This was real and honest grief.

"Where is he?"

"Up to house, Ma'am. On's bed. We took un up on 'urdle and sent for Doctor.

" '*No good,*' Doctor tells Mr. Johnson. '*Broke 'is poor bloody neck,*' 'e says. '*Aye, and every bone in his poor bloody body.*' . . . My Mas'r Luke! . . ."

And he turned and walked quickly away, sobbing.

§3

When I could think coherently, which was long after the inquest and funeral—oh, the bitter savage cruelty of that inquest, and of all such inquests—one thought perpetually persisted in my mind until it was an *idée fixe* which bade fair to drive me mad.

Had he committed suicide? Or was he play-acting— proving his false blindness before even so poor an audience as a groom and the engine-driver and fireman of a slow local train? Had he crossed in front of the train and, suddenly succumbing to temptation, turned back and flung himself in front of the engine? Or had he thought there was time to rush back, giving the engine-driver, the fireman and Jermyn something to talk about, something that everyone would talk about —and that would eventually come to my ears—of what a terribly narrow escape poor blind Mr. Luke Tuyler had had; perhaps some talk in the village of how that wife of his ought to look after him better and see that he wasn't exposed to such risks?

But if so, why had he ordered Jermyn to go to the stables, a quarter of a mile distant from where the little rural line cut off the park grounds from some pheasant preserves? Perhaps because he knew Jermyn would not obey him, after his exhibition of being 'woild and daverdy.' Perhaps because he knew that the train was due to pass within a minute, and Jermyn would see how narrow an escape his poor blind master had.

Suicide—or exhibitionism and cunning demonstration of "total blindness"?

Why should he commit suicide? In rage and fear and resentment at being found out, both in his imposture and his unfaithfulness?

No. If I knew my Luke, he would have needed better grounds than that for suicide.

Suicide—to punish me for my wickedness in catching him out as swindler and adulterer? No. Not Luke.

I came to the conclusion that in a state of hysteria, wild, as Jermyn said, he had given a silly and pointless exhibition of blindness combined with physical and mental illness, and had fallen a victim to his own folly; had misjudged the speed of the train; had tripped over a sleeper or the line itself, and so been killed.

Suicide I ruled out; and accepted the law's verdict of Death by Misadventure.

X

And now to write to Mark.

To tell Mark that Luke was dead, the hardest and most terrible thing I ever had to do.

And by the time I had finished, I found that I had not said one word to blacken Luke's memory! Not one word of his sham blindness and the wicked imposture by means of which he had come between me and Mark; not one word about his beastly infidelity, whereby he had broken the false bond wrought by his falseness.

Just that Luke was dead, killed by a train as he crossed our little private level-crossing. *And if Mark thought that I should have watched over Luke better, and seen to it that he was not left to cross the railway alone,* he would never say so, he would never reproach me for my careless care of his poor blind brother.

I knew it would be the hardest and cruellest blow that poor Mark would ever receive, hard and cruel as his life had been for years. But I felt that I must of course tell him. For me to pretend that it was an unnecessary cruelty, inasmuch as he might be killed in battle without ever knowing that he had lost Luke, was mere cowardly special-pleading on my part.

So I told him—and received no answer.

Mark's silence persisted for so long that I decided that I would go in search of him; that I would turn into fact the hitherto foolish and romantic day-dream of my seeking a Soldier of the Legion throughout Algeria and Morocco, in war-time.

§2

I could write a whole book about my adventures on that quest.

Rosanne in search of a Husband.

392

That's what it came to; but I preferred to call it Rosanne in search of Mark—just for the joy of seeing him again and talking to him.

I would have wandered all over the world throughout the rest of my life, for that alone.

I received great kindness, courtesy and consideration from the French authorities the whole way, right from Headquarters at Paris to Sidi-bel-Abbès in Algeria, and thence to the Hospital and Convalescent Camp at Arzeu.

Mark did not have to finish his time in the Legion, as the *Conseil de Réforme* invalided him out instead of sending him back to the fighting. He had been very badly wounded; and that he was in a terrible state of health, owing to fever and dysentery (and doubtless to Luke's death), was obvious to anyone, layman or doctor. Whether our story weighed at all with the gallant French officers of the *Conseil* I don't know; but after a period which seemed long to me, but was of course far shorter than it would have been had Mark had to return to Maroc, we left Sidi-bel-Abbès and, via Oran, Marseilles and Paris, returned to Courtesy Court.

§3

Mark was quite obviously in a queer state of mind.

I think he was inclined to praise God, every waking minute, that he was alive and back again at Courtesy Court, and at the same time to blame Him for the terrible accident that had robbed him of Luke, the other, and to his mind the better, half of himself.

I endeavoured to comfort him by well-meaning hypocritical talk of how it was really better so, better that poor Luke should be dead than living a life of blindness, an artist Samson, his beloved home his Gaza. But this did not appear to bring much comfort to Mark.

Well, I had got my wish, my hope, the very greatest desire of my heart—and it was dust and ashes. Mark was not happy, and, strive as I might, he grew no happier. He would fall into dark brooding moods, Mark who had never had a mood in his life. He seemed unable to read, unable to interest himself in any form of sport or game. At times, it seemed to me that the blow might prove mortal; and I knew that it was up to me to fight for him, to fight the dead Luke for the living Mark.

One evening as we sat at dinner, Mark, who was staring at the table-cloth seeing nothing and oblivious of my presence, suddenly turned to me and said,

"*Did he commit suicide?*"

"Who?" asked I, to gain time and pull myself together, to think, to walk warily, and give the right answer.

"Luke, of course," snapped Mark, scowling. Mark, who had never snapped and had never scowled at me.

"Of course not. Why should he? You know what Jermyn says. He . . ."

"Yes. I know what Jermyn says. I have made him tell me a hundred times."

It was dreadful. I knew that Mark loved me. And I knew that Luke stood, and would stand, between us unless I could prevent him, unless I could *exorcise* him, in fact. My heart ached for Mark—my whole body, mind and soul ached for him of course—but what I mean is that I suffered for him and with him. He was so miserable and broken-hearted.

"Mark," said I to him one glorious morning as we were having breakfast together, "I think I'll go back to America. But I won't go until we've found the absolutely right person for you as housekeeper. A really good housekeeper and Johnson would run the domestic part of . . ."

Mark looked up, wrenched his mind back from wherever it may have been in contemplation of Luke and his unique virtues and charm, and stared at me as though he had seen me for the first time since Sidi-bel-

Abbès, or rather the first time since ever he went away to the wars.

"*Rosanne!*" he said. "Don't be silly . . . I've been going to ask you . . ." He stopped.

"Ask me what?" I contrived to say, for I wasn't sure that my heart was not beating too loudly for him to be able to hear my voice.

He stood up and came round to where I was sitting at the head of the table.

"Rosanne!" he said in his quiet deep voice. "If you hadn't said that about America I shouldn't . . . Rosanne, you couldn't ever . . . ever . . . love me? Not after . . . Luke? . . ."

I stood up and kissed him, and he took me in his arms. I thought he would crush me to death, and half hoped he would.

"*Rosanne!*" he whispered. "Rosanne, darling. You could . . . ? You do?"

"Mark, I love you a thousand times more than ever I loved Luke."

"You'll marry me, Rosanne? . . . When?"

"Now, Mark. In the middle of breakfast, if . . ."

But I couldn't keep it up. I burst into tears, though I am not a great sniveller.

I suppose that one of the notable things about my remarkable love-affairs is that I am one of the few young persons who have received a proposal of marriage between the bacon and the marmalade.

So Mark and I were married, and settled down to live happy ever after at Courtesy Court.

EPILOGUE

But we didn't. We weren't happy at all. Not at first. Or, rather, we were not happy for long.

Luke came and stood between us as effectually as though he had been alive and living in the house. When Mark was not thinking of me, he was thinking of Luke, and I knew that more and more he thought of Luke and less and less he thought of me.

He did love me. He loved me perfectly and beautifully; and I did not, I would not and I could not, utter a word of reproach. As well blame a man for loss of manual skill after his hands have been cut off. Mark and Luke had been one, and Luke had, as it were, been torn from Mark's living side, leaving a great gaping wound. It bled, and it did not heal. Actually and truly and literally, it was a case of "In their lives they were one, and in their deaths they were not divided." Mark could no more help it than he could help the colour of his eyes.

And the utmost that I could hope was that Time would effect a change; that Time, which heals all things, would heal this wound made by the loss of Luke.

I could only hope that gradually the effect and influence of my physical presence would grow stronger and that of Luke's ghostly presence grow weaker.

Ghostly! . . . One June morning I awoke and experienced that fairly common but utterly horrible sensation of being wide awake but unable to move. It is quite useless for anyone to tell me that I fancied I was awake. I was awake. I heard the clock ticking on the table beside my bed. I heard Mark breathing in the other bed. I saw the curtains gently moving in the light summer breeze.

It was broad daylight when I awoke, and I found afterwards that it was about four o'clock. I could hear;

I could see—and I suddenly became aware, with a kind of cold horror, that I could see Luke.

He was standing at the bottom of my bed, as he had often stood in life, and was looking at me. He was staring with a look that I can only describe as one of appalling anguish and inexpressible longing. He wanted to tell me something. He yearned and strove to tell me with his eyes—and almost succeeded. But he did not speak.

It was one of the most terrifying moments of my life. By this living *rigor mortis* I was held as rigid and motionless as a corpse, utterly unable to move hand or foot.

And there Luke stood and appealed to me with a dumb yearning earnestness that was terrible to see.

I never saw anything more clearly in my life than I saw the dreadful face of poor suffering Luke.

And at last, thank God, I moved a little finger; then my hand, my arm, both arms, and broke these dreadful invisible bonds.

I sat up, found my voice and tried to speak to Luke, tried to ask him what it was that he must say.

But he was not there.

Or, rather, he was not visible.

He was there, though. Not only there, but ever present with Mark. Mark got so that he could hardly speak of anything else but Luke and the extent to which he himself had contributed to his unhappiness and death. It became an obsession with him. Luke stood between us. He spoilt our happiness and darkened our lives. And gradually I came to hate him as much as Mark loved him, for he was spoiling Mark's life. At times, I felt it would be no exaggeration to say that he was killing him—with grief, with worry, with remorse. Imagine Mark having to feel remorse about anyone or anything!

It was dreadful, the way in which he would sit and stare at a book. Read it, without turning the pages and, suddenly looking up, say something to me about Luke. It was the same with whatever he was doing.

When I persuaded him to come to the theatre, it was Luke that he saw on the stage, and when the curtain fell he would turn to me and say some such thing as,

"I don't see how it could have been an accident. But . . . It wasn't as though he . . . Yet *why* should he have committed suicide? . . . No; he'd never do that."

Then, perhaps, seeing that my face looked as tragic as his own, he'd take my hand and say,

"Not with you as his wife, darling. Who, married to you, could possibly commit suicide? But . . ."

Things were going from bad to worse, until one day I had a bright idea, an idea for which I have ever since thanked God; for it led to a solution of my awful problem. It led to salvation for Mark and happiness for both of us.

At breakfast one day, as he sat as usual, eating little, saying nothing and thinking, as I knew from the look on his face, of how terribly he was to blame for the tragedy that was Luke, there was a sudden crash as Luke's picture fell to the ground. The wire had broken—and I think that something broke in me.

"A damned good job," said I to myself, as we both sprang up. "And I'll throw him off his pedestal if it kills me. Worse, if it kills Mark's love for me."

But I had grown wary as well as watchful, and bided my time; and while I was thinking it over, I suddenly had a bright idea, a notion founded on what I had been reading about psycho-analysis. (Actually, I had examined the possibilities of trying to get poor Mark psycho-analysed!)

Since "getting it all up out of the subconscious and examining it in the light of knowledge and reason" was the central idea of that form of mental healing, I would get Mark to write a sort of brief account of his life from the time he joined the French Foreign Legion with Luke, a sort of *Memoirs of Mark Tuyler;* and in it he must write the complete but simple and unadorned truth concerning Luke and himself.

If it did nothing more, it would occupy his mind, and it might do a very great deal more. It might do what I had failed to do, prove to him that he had nothing whatever with which to reproach himself regarding Luke. Or almost nothing, inasmuch as his love, kindness and forbearance could have added but little to the harm Luke had got from the spoiling that his parents and everybody else had given him from babyhood.

Somewhat to my surprise, Mark, who had lost all interest in the care of the estate; in his work on the local Bench, Councils and Committees; in shooting, hunting and everything else, fell in with my suggestion and set to work, at first probably attracted merely by the idea of writing a eulogy of the wonderful Luke.

His mental and physical health began to improve almost from the day when, returning from his club in a rage and a serious state of mental turmoil, he began to write.

By the time he had finished, he was a different man.

And one evening, an evening which I shall remember until I die, and, I hope, thereafter, he came into the drawing-room where I was sitting, stood beside my chair for a minute, stroking my hair, and then seated himself opposite to me.

"Well, I've finished," he said. "At any rate, all I'm going to write."

He was smiling and looking almost happy.

"Poor old Luke," he said. "You know, Rosanne, he . . ."

I resolved to put everything to the touch, then and there.

"Mark," I interrupted, "Luke was false, untrustworthy, a fraud and . . ."

Mark sprang to his feet, a look of shocked consternation on his face.

"*Rosanne!*" he cried, "*did you know too—that he was never blind?*"

So he knew! I felt terrible. I felt that Mark's happiness and mine hung by a thread. I had been merely going to tell him about Luke's infidelity to me, his adultery with Giulia. What mine had I sprung beneath us? *Mark knew of Luke's imposture!*

"Did *you* know, Mark?" I gasped. "I would never, never have told you."

"Yes, I knew," he said, "and I would never have told *you*. What did you mean when you said he was a fraud . . . false . . . ?"

"He was false to me, Mark. With Giulia."

"Good God! The hound! The *cur!*"

And I could almost hear the crash with which the great Luke fell from his lofty pedestal, to lie shattered for ever on the solid earth of fact and truth.

"Rosanne, my poor darling." . . .

We are happy enough now. Almost too happy. It doesn't seem possible that such happiness can last. Mark is the Mark I knew before he went to France; and Luke has gone out of the house and out of our lives.

For a man shall leave his father and his mother—yea, and his twin brother—and cleave unto the woman whom he loves.

It is Mark and I who are one now. We never speak willingly of Luke, but I have no doubt the day will come when we shall be able to do so quite easily, I without anger and bitterness, Mark without grief or self-reproach.

For he still loves Luke.

He always will love Luke, but he is getting that love into proper proportion, and seeing Luke in proper perspective.

He will always love him—and he will always love me. I am content.

THE UNIFORM OF GLORY

being

The True Story of

A FREE FRENCHMAN'S NIGHT OUT

And over the seas we were bidden
A country to take and to keep;
And far with the brave I have ridden,
And now with the brave I shall sleep.

A. E. Housman.

TO

DR. JAMES S. AND MRS. TORFRIDA ROBINSON

AND

MRS. HEREWARD E. WAKE,

IN

TOKEN OF GRATITUDE FOR INCREDIBLE
KINDNESS

HOLNICOTE,
January 1941.

CONTENTS

CHAPTER

1   THE UNIFORM IS PUT ON
2   THE GLORY BEGINS
3   THE COLONEL'S DAUGHTER ADMIRES THE
        UNIFORM
4   THE PATH OF GLORY LEADS BUT TO . . . ?
5   STILL ON THE PATH OF GLORY
6   THE POWER AS WELL AS THE GLORY
7   REST-HOUSE ON THE PATH OF GLORY
8   GENTLE USE OF GLORIOUS POWER
9   DIVERSIONS ON THE PATH OF GLORY
10 THE WOMAN ON THE PATH
11 A STORY BY THE WAYSIDE
12 REAL POWER AND GREAT GLORY
13 BACK TO THE PATH AGAIN
14 A LITTLE MORE GLORY
15 "THE LAST ACT CROWNS THE PLAY"
16 THE UNIFORM IS TAKEN OFF

CHAPTER 1

THE UNIFORM IS PUT ON

Notoriously, it is a long worm that has no turning, and we have it on high authority that a crowded hour of glorious life is worth an age without a name.

This artless story is the veracious account of the bold turning of a down-trodden worm, and of the crowded hour of glory that he enjoyed; an hour for which he was prepared to pay in full and to grudge nothing of the payment.

Denis Ducros had seen better days, University days at the Sorbonne in Paris, and lovely long days in Provence, where, a scion of the *petite noblesse,* life had gone very well until it had gone suddenly and completely awry.

And now Denis was a servant, and a good one, who spent most of his life behind a green baize apron; much of it behind a green baize door in a little room in which he cleaned silver and his master's accoutrements; some of it behind his master's chair, where he faithfully and efficiently strove to anticipate that master's every want as he nobly enjoyed the pleasures of the table; and a little, a very little, of it in dreams.

He would have spent more time in dreaming had he not been too busy by day and too weary by night.

Nevertheless, at times, when his work was mechanical and the skilful hand polished the refulgent boot, or spur, or sword, or button, without conscious direction of the errant mind, Denis would think long thoughts that would have surprised all those who knew him, his master most of all.

For Denis, the deft valet, the accomplished houseman, the most servant-like of admirable servants, was at times strongly conscious of the fact that he had a soul above his present station, a mind above his menial tasks, and disturbing intimations of immortality.

Seated in his cubby-hole, upon an up-turned box, he would, upon occasion, see Denis not thus occupied with button-stick and brush, but mounted on a noble charger, riding at the head of victorious troops through streets lined by acclaiming crowds.

Slowly turning his cold, haughty and imperious face from side to side, he would glance up at the balconies from which bright eyes shone upon him, and white hands fluttered enchanting kisses from lovely lips.

Nice work if you can get it.

Or even in the very act of peeling potatoes, beneath the ringing scourge of the sharp tongue of the fat Natalie, the *bonne à tout faire* who loved him, he would see himself seated at a table before a tent, beneath an Army Commander's flag; and, as men galloped up, flung themselves from their panting sweating horses, and smartly saluting, gave him written messages from his Brigadiers, he would coldly, calmly and quietly issue his orders in reply. The brain at the centre of the military web, directing the battle, riding the storm. He had once seen the great Marshal Lyautey.

Very nice work if . . .

"And is it to be supposed, my little cabbage, that the potato will peel itself if you gape at it long enough?" fat Natalie would ask, and shatter the bright brief beginnings of a dream.

From time to time, though comparatively rarely, he would, when soaping a saddle, or suppling a bridle-rein, see himself arrayed in a perfectly-fitting uniform with gold five-*galoned* sleeves, such as those his master wore, entering the boudoir, a nest of silk and satin, of a lovely and most loving woman, a famous beauty, or leader of rank and fashion; and as, advancing with outstretched arms, he gracefully sank upon one knee, she would take his face between her small white hands and . . .

"*Denis!* Where's that damned scoundrel Denis?" the Colonel would roar.

And it would not be into the presence of a lovely

welcoming woman that Denis would then hasten.

For it was the Colonel's admirable way to roar loudly at Denis, it being his belief that thus, and only thus, is the best to be got from servants—menservants, that is to say—for the Colonel, albeit a brave and much decorated warrior, had never been heard to roar at fat Natalie.

What the Colonel thought of Denis, if he thought of him at all, is not known; but what Denis thought of the Colonel was that he was a super-man, a hero of romance ornamenting a prosaic world, a model and a pattern to all men.

A truly humble creature whose soul had been too long swaddled in green baize, Denis had one secret source of pride, legitimate and sustaining pride—he was undeniably very like the Colonel in appearance.

It is to be doubted that the Colonel had ever noticed this interesting fact; and indeed the resemblance was not marked when Denis in shirt-sleeves, apron and slippers was doing a job of work in which coal, potatoes, or greasy crockery played a part, and the Colonel was arrayed in the perfectly-fitting smart uniform of his famous Corps. Nor, when his hair was rough, his moustache untrimmed and his face ill-shaven, was the servant's resemblance to his master that of a twin brother.

Nevertheless, once, in the dusk—but by no means in the dark—when Denis in his walking-out uniform came suddenly upon fat Natalie by the front door of the Colonel's quarters, she had exclaimed,

"*Toi!* . . . *Mon Dieu! Salaud,* I thought it was *Monsieur le Colonel* himself."

And never, never once in the whole of his life, since the day when he had been born of a Provençal father and an Irish mother, had Denis Ducros heard sweeter words, or any sounds that had given him a tithe of the pleasure that these did.

He, Denis Ducros, *soldat première classe,* the Colonel's *ordonnance,* servant, batman, butler, horseman and valet, had been mistaken for the bravest, finest and handsomest man in the Nineteenth Army Corps of

Africa, if not in the whole French army.

He had always known it himself, and now someone else had recognised it. Fat Natalie Dupont, who greatly loved, but did not fear, him; and whom he greatly feared but did not love.

And at sunset on this Day of the Great Fête of the Republic, also the greatest day of all his life, the day on which he rose to his full stature, to the apex of his possibilities, and even to the height of his imagination, Denis stood before the mirror in the Colonel's exiguous dressing-room, and, catching sight of the reflection of his own face, was reminded of the indisputable truth. Closely his form and features resembled those of the Colonel; and, as he finished brushing the Colonel's *képi,* he did what he had never dared to do before.

He placed it on his own head.

C'est le premier pas qui coute, and this was the first step upon that path upward or downward, according to the point of view, that led to the great, the sudden, the tremendous uprising and self-assertion of the romantic soul of Denis Ducros.

The *képi* fitted beautifully; and, by stepping backward he contrived to see nothing of himself in the mirror but his *képi*-adorned head.

Most pleasing. Most satisfactory and . . . stimulating.

Why, it would only need a couple of minutes' work with the Colonel's nail-scissors to render his moustache an exact imitation of that of his handsome and debonair exemplar, a closely trimmed   lip-exposing ornament of a bronzed and martial face.

The nail-scissors were, as he knew, in the right-hand corner of the top left-hand drawer. There and nowhere else, always and inevitably, save when the Colonel was using them for the trimming of his well-kept nails.

Deftly clipping, from the corners of his mouth toward his nose, Denis quickly reproduced an admirable facsimile of the Colonel's moustache, a thorny bristling hedge that adorned, while not concealing, the firm mouth and whitely shining teeth, occasionally displayed by the Colonel's slow sardonic smile.

Denis practised one.

First slowly, and then sardonically.

Yes, that was right. That was excellent. The very smile, combining faint amusement, slight contempt, and a sense of thoughts unuttered—and just as well left unuttered perhaps.

Usually it followed upon the observation,

"*Ah! . . . Indeed?*" with which the Colonel was wont to greet some statement which, up to that moment, had seemed sane and sound and reasonable, but forthwith was seen and heard and known for the incredible puerile piffle that it surely must be.

Again stepping back to the point from where he could see nothing but his face and the *képi,* Denis regarded himself coldly, his face unwontedly austere and hard.

"*Ah! . . . Indeed?*" said he aloud, and smiled slowly and sardonically. Marvellous.

It *was* the Colonel.

There, in the mirror, Colonel Rochefort regarded Denis Ducros so coldly, so balefully, that Denis faltered, flushed with shame, and swiftly removed the *képi* from the unworthy head that presumptuously dishonoured it. And there in the mirror was Denis Ducros again, laughing at his own folly in permitting himself to frighten himself.

He replaced the *képi* and the smile—and uneasily looked away from it.

Merciful Heaven! Suppose it *had* been the Colonel there in the mirror! But he was safe in bed, poor gentleman, or Denis would not have been in the dressing-room posturing before the mirror. Safe in bed for two or three days at least, suffering, as not infrequently he did, from an attack of malaria.

As he treated these attacks according to a prescription of his own, of which the main ingredient was neat cognac, and the remainder was of an alcoholic nature, the malaria was apt to affect his liver. And this malarial affection of his liver was apt to influence his judgment.

Sometimes Denis called it his misjudgment, at others, his temper.

But as his ancient enemy had attacked him only an hour ago, and he had swiftly riposted with a tumbler full of the mixture, he was certain to be asleep and to remain in that happy state for many hours to come . . .

Denis gazed respectfully at the face in the mirror. Marvellous.

Yes, it was marvellous, but it wasn't perfect. There was something missing. Of course there was.

And Denis laughed in a manner which made his face much less like that of his master; much more happy-looking, care-free, kindly and simple.

Something missing indeed! A most important, if not essential something. And that, nothing less than the beautiful tortoise-shell-rimmed monocle which the Colonel seemed almost to throw into his eye and to hold there as firmly fixed as were the teeth in his head. As its proprietor rarely wore it in bed, it would be where it always was when not in use, in the box sacred to personal trinkets, such as links, studs, spare watch, and other jewellery, that reposed on top of the chest of drawers.

It would be rather a lark to stick it in his eye and further increase the remarkable likeness.

Most appalling impudence, but as the Colonel would never know . . .

Yes. Having gone to the trouble of trimming his moustache, he'd go the whole hog.

Well! Really! One would hardly believe it. For two pins he'd call for Natalie, bid her shut her eyes, and when he gave the word, open them and look in the mirror.

He'd wager a dozen of *pinard*[25] that she'd ejaculate with respectful amazement,

"*M'sieur le Colonel!*"

Yes; but there'd be no respect, and it would be he who would provide the amazement, when she turned from the mirror and looked at him. She'd be worse

---

[25] Cheap red wine.

than the Colonel himself, in her ferocious indignation at such outrageous rascality.

No. There could be no applauding spectators of this remarkable piece of impersonation.

A pity.

Also rather a pity that he had to screw up the left-hand side of his face just a little, for the greater security of the monocle; for its rightful owner contracted not the smallest muscle of his cheek or eye. His face gave the monocle no more encouragement, so to speak, than a wall gives a window. Yet the crystal disc sat as securely in its place as does a pane of glass in a window-frame.

However, practice makes perfect.

Unfortunately there was but little time for practice, for he had the uniform to brush, and the buttons, spurs, and riding-boots to polish, before he left the Colonel's quarters for his usual Thursday evening-out. And this was Fête Day too, and out he would go *coûte qui coûte.*

But it really was rather hard that Natalie should not see just his head—over a wall say—with *képi,* monocle and trimmed moustache.

Talk about mistaking him, in the dusk, for the Colonel!

She'd *know,* in broad daylight, that it was the Colonel, especially if she spoke and he said,

"*Ah! . . . Indeed?*" and smiled his slow sardonic smile.

Especially if he didn't drop the monocle in the effort of producing the smile. Something like the dog and the shadow, that would be. And what a waggish dog he was! He, Denis Ducros, wearing the Colonel's *képi,* monocle and moustache!

Slowly and sardonically he again smiled into the mirror.

"*Ah! . . . Indeed?*" he said, and dropped the monocle.

"*Peste!*"

That spoiled the show completely. Sad, for it was otherwise a perfect performance, and to the man with the soul of an artist, quite a little disappointment.

Of course he had the soul of an artist, or at any rate of an *artiste,* and ought really to have been an actor. He would have been another Cocquelin or another Guitry. He would have been another anything-you-like where character-parts and perfect impersonation were required.

Replacing the monocle, Denis endeavoured to screw it tightly into his eye, and to hold it there without obvious muscular effort.

No. It wasn't absolute perfection. The face was that of the Colonel all right, but it was the Colonel suffering a spasm of pain or emotion. And Colonel Rochefort did not permit his face to register the fact, when suffering spasms of pain or emotion.

"*Sacré bleu!*" An idea! The little gum-bottle on the Colonel's office-room table!

If he carefully smeared the broad tortoise-shell gallery with some of that thick gum, waited until it was nearly dry, and then carefully placed it in his eye, it would undoubtedly stick. Then he could keep his countenance as cold, austere and expressionless as the Colonel's. He could smile as slowly and sardonically as he liked, without having to spoil the effect by an anxious contraction of his facial muscles.

Yes. As a true artist for whom nothing but perfection could be satisfactory, he had to admit that the face in the mirror was not completely and truly that of the Colonel as seen in public. That look of strain and anxiety was . . .

"*Denis!* . . . DENIS! . . . *Sacré salaud!* . . ."

. . . was instantly replaced by one of infinitely greater strain and anxiety. Yea, of consternation and alarm. *Bon Dieu de Grâce!* Suppose the Old Devil jumped out of bed, strode into the dressing-room and caught him with the *képi* on his head, the monocle in his eye!

Swiftly removing *képi* and monocle, the frightened Denis flung the one on to the chest of drawers, slipped the other into his pocket, and bounded across to the door that opened into the Colonel's bedroom.

"Ah! There you are, you species of besotted imbecile," growled the Colonel as Denis entered the darkened room.

"Get me another bottle of cognac. And listen . . . Hang the DO NOT DISTURB notice on the door; and do not bring my coffee in the morning, until I call for it. Tell Madame that I shall not be present at dinner . . . that I do not wish to be awakened on *any* account."

Swiftly Denis returned with a litre bottle of the Colonel's favourite *fine*.

"Understand, you accident?" growled the Colonel as Denis deftly opened the bottle in his presence. "I am *not* to be disturbed by *anybody* for *anything.*"

"*Oui, oui, Monsieur le Colonel. Je comprends.* Not until *Monsieur le Colonel* is pleased to disturb himself and to ring."

Fading discreetly from the room, Denis softly closed the door, and, from a drawer in the Office table, took the printed card which bore the legend DO NOT DISTURB and signified to all men and one woman that, whether in office or bedroom, the Colonel wished to be alone.

That was all right. The Old Devil wouldn't budge now for the next twelve hours at least, when he would suddenly appear where least expected, neat, sleek and dapper as a young tom-cat, and ferocious as an elderly leopard.

Returning to his work, Denis took his master's handsome black-and-gold tunic from the back of the chair over which he had hung it, and began most scrupulously to brush it.

For the thousandth time he admired the beautiful *galons* of gold braid that ornamented it five-deep from cuff to elbow; the buttons and badges that seemed to be of purest gold; the lovely heart-stirring array of medals and decorations. What must it feel like to have the right to wear such a tunic as that?

What would it feel like, merely to slip it on? Just to see how it fitted. How it fitted the figure of a man who was known and admitted closely to resemble the famous Colonel Rochefort, of *La Légion Étrangère.*

What a thing to do! He was certainly going it to-night. One would think that he had opened the bottle downstairs and had been tasting its contents. Whereas he had had nothing since his tumbler of *pinard* after giving the Colonel his lunch.

What a thing to do! Nevertheless a thing to be done well if done at all.

The *képi* . . . the monocle . . . the moustache . . . the tunic . . .

And then he could behold a good half of himself. His better half, so to speak; and see how far that part of him resembled the upper half of the Colonel.

But first of all to prepare the monocle.

It was the easy and delightful work of but a couple of minutes carefully to coat with gum the flat upper rim of the gallery of the monocle, that would lie just beneath his eyebrow, and the edge of the lower one that would fit into his eye socket.

And then some smart work on his hair with the Colonel's own stiff brushes, and a beautiful polish with the help of the Colonel's own brilliantine.

It wasn't right. It went against one's conscience; but surely a man who had spent so much time and energy in polishing the Colonel's leather and bright-work, might give his own head a polish?

And then, by the Name of a Name of a Little Pink Dog, he would not only look like the Colonel, but he would smell like him.

Industriously he oiled and polished.

And now, if such an utter impossibility were in any wise possible, he looked even more like him than before—with his hair brushed straight back as the Colonel brushed his—especially when he took the *képi* off.

And now for the monocle.

Perfect. The gum neither wet nor dry, but sticky as a fly-paper. He would put it in his face and hold it pressed in tightly, until it was as firmly attached as his ear or his nose.

Seating himself in the Colonel's chair, Denis almost unconsciously assumed the exact position invariably taken by the Colonel when waiting for Denis to attach his spurs to his boots, and softly hummed a little air that was the Colonel's current favourite.

By the Father of all Good Soldiers, he was beginning not only to look and to smell, but to sound like the Colonel!

Beneath his breath he issued orders and uttered orderly-room imprecations in the Colonel's best manner.

In imagination he had Sergeant-Major Lejaune up before him, listened to that terrible man's faltering excuses, observed with cold contempt,

"Ah! . . . Indeed?"

And smiled a devastatingly slow, sardonic smile.

Anon, he rose to his feet, placed the *képi* on his anointed head, not only at the exact angle, but in the Colonel's exact manner, with the inevitable little tap on top, that crowned the work. And then, with swiftly beating heart, he slipped his right arm into the right sleeve of the tunic and, in the exact style and manner of his master, assumed the sombrely refulgent garment, hooked it beneath his chin, and fastened the big bright buttons.

A perfect fit! Comfortably tight at the waist, comfortably accommodating across the chest. No looseness anywhere. No cutting underneath the arms. Rather might he have been made for the tunic by the Divine Architect Himself, than the tunic for him by mortal military tailor.

Now for the mirror. But first to lock the door that opened on to the landing, lest fat Natalie, who had the nerve and imprudence to do anything, should open it and put her head into the Colonel's dressing-room, in search of the Colonel's batman, whom, indeed she appeared to regard as being her batman also . . .

And now . . .

"*Could* it be? Could it be that that magnificent figure was but a reflection in a mirror? And the reflection moreover of Denis Ducros? A poor servant, who was even a still poorer soldier. Could that perfect picture of a *beau sabreur,* that complete portrait of an officer and a gentleman, and an elegant but most dangerous-looking warrior, be *himself?*"

That surely was not Denis Ducros?

"*Not? Ah! . . . Indeed?*" replied the figure in the glass. And Denis all but fell away, collapsing in stricken fear before the Colonel's cold regard. Actually he shuffled back, catching sight as he did so, of his own deplorable *pantalons* and house-slippers.

Stepping forward again, he included these reassuring incongruous nether-details in the mirror portrait.

Yes, that was Denis Ducros all right, that lower half anyway, an authentic, domestic servant. He who had first been *soldat simple,* officer's *ordonnance,* then Colonel's batman, valet, butler and houseman. Madame's servant really.

What a remarkable picture!

Officer and gentleman, from the crown of his head to the middle of his body; menial domestic from his middle to his shapeless great house-shoes.

Well, he must step back once again and admire the upper part before removing the borrowed plumes that made him look so fine a bird.

Yes, it was astounding—not only the actual likeness, but the whole bearing, deportment, aura and atmosphere. Surely the personality of something fine and worthy shone through? Surely no complete clod, no mere miserable bale of cannon-fodder could have filled the Colonel's tunic and looked so really authentic a Colonel, as did the figure in the glass? Why, until one's eye reached the ill-fitting, grease-spotted overalls, and saw the hall-mark, the livery, the stigmata of domestic service and . . .

And suddenly the stifled soul of Denis Ducros cried aloud from the depths of its abasement.

Suddenly it rose upward, with a mighty surging, from those dismal deeps, threw off its swaddling clothes of cramping discipline, stood forth, and manifested itself as worthy of its great and noble ancestors, Brian Boru on the one side and d'Artagnan, if not du Guesclin, on the other.

Would the mighty warrior-king have patiently worn

the houseman's greasy trousers?

Would du Guesclin, who won the Hundred Years War—or some such prolonged argument with the English—have sat down, contented, in their ignoble baggy seat?

The blood of Brian Boru and of Bertrand du Guesclin, or of his authentically Connaught mother and Provençal father, went swiftly to Denis's head, his hands to the buttons of his trousers.

In scarcely longer than it takes to tell, the shapeless old garments had fallen—fit only to fall—and Denis, with shining eyes, compressed lips, and dilated nostrils through which he drew quick breath, seized with hands that trembled, the Colonel's beautiful red riding breeches, with their double stripe of black braid, from where they hung neatly folded over the back of a chair.

Panting with excitement, he drew them on, buttoned them about the knees, smoothed them so that they fitted there like a glove, fastened and braced them to the right height, and stood, a Colonel revealed, perfect from head to knee.

But it was not enough! His hour and his madness were upon him, and he must be fulfilled.

It was the Colonel's beautiful riding boots that were fulfilled.

As one possessed, he seized the left-hand boot, hauled out the eighteen-inch-long centre tongue of the tree, shook out the back piece, drew out the front piece and foot, hooked his fingers through the interior loops in the top of the leg, and, just in the Colonel's own manner, with identically similar grunts, and brief, pointed orisons to Higher Powers, drew the boot on, stamped his foot once, and then adjusted the knee of the black-leather-strapped breeches within the top of the boot.

As in the case of the *képi,* the tunic, the breeches, a perfect fit.

Absolutely comfortable.

Why! Had his Mama known Colonel Rochefort's Papa, he himself might have been . . .

But that was quite enough of that line of thought!

With even greater speed, Denis assumed the other boot, and having arranged boots and breeches to his fastidious liking he strapped on the silver-shining spurs that so often he had polished and fastened upon his master's feet.

Now for the mirror . . .

Now there would be something to look at. Literally *cap à pie* he would be correct.

Well! Well!

Enraptured, Denis stared.

Not at himself, Denis Ducros, so much as at Denis Ducros' reincarnation as Colonel Louis Rochefort.

Unconsciously he struck one of the Rochefort poses, left hand on hip, left foot advanced, left knee slightly bent, two middle fingers of right hand thrust between the fourth and fifth buttons of the tunic.

But there was something missing. What was it? Of course. Gloves and cane. One glove on the left hand, the cane clutched by the middle, together with the other glove.

So. That was it. Why, the greatest living portrait painter could come and paint that reflection in the glass, and not trouble Colonel Rochefort for a single sitting; and not a crapulous critic could be found to deny its perfect likeness to the man who was not its original.

Sacré Nom! If the bedroom door opened now, and the Colonel entered the room, he'd have a fit. It would be he, rather than Denis, who would collapse in fright. After one horrified glance, one agonised incredulous stare, he would cry,

"Mon Dieu! It has come! I am mad . . . God help me and forgive me."

And a man who, like Marshal Ney, had been called the bravest of the brave would flinch and quail. He'd cringe before his servant, Denis Ducros, the worthless, idle, and good-for-nothing *scélérat,* whom he was always threatening to kick back into the ranks, and whose progress he had indeed upon occasions accelerated by the not wholly playful application of one of these very boots to the baggy seat of those very fallen *pantalons.*

Almost Denis wished that the Colonel would come into the room. But not quite. No, no. He himself might be going mad, but he had not yet *quite* gone.

Nevertheless, it would be splendid fun if fat Natalie came in. He'd unlock the door. For, sooner or later, she was bound to come in search of him, if he made no reply to her agonised caterwaulings that he should come and help her with the vegetables, or something of the sort. And to come and help the good Natalie with a job, simply meant to do the job for her.

Or should he go downstairs, and, in the *rôle* of *M'sieur le Colonel,* frighten the life out of her? But there'd be no great fun in doing that, unless later he revealed himself, and that might be dangerous.

He did not think that fat Natalie would give him away, but she'd be quite capable of sticking a knife in him if he made a complete and utter fool of her, and a badly frightened one at that.

Nevertheless, Denis unlocked the door before re-turning to the most delightful spot on earth—his place before the mirror, his place from which he could see Denis Ducros as he ought to be; clad, not in shining armour as his ancestors had been, but in the shining and beautiful uniform which represented it.

Yes; there before him in the magic glass, stood the true Denis Ducros, leader of men, commander of armies, lover of beautiful ladies.

Le brave Général, Denis Ducros, who rode on white horses, into conquered cities, acclaimed by admiring multitudes, the recipient of welcoming kisses blown by small white hands from lovely coral lips . . .

His eye fell upon his green baize apron, and his discarded trousers and house slippers.

Not so good.

But away with the foolish thought.

Did not every emergent butterfly see lying beside its magnificent beautiful form, the miserable shell of the chrysalis from which it had burst forth. The life of the butterfly might be short, but it was glorious and free. The life of "Colonel" Denis Ducros might be short, but during those few minutes it should be glorious and free. For was he not glorious to behold, there in the mirror; was he not free, if only for a few fleeting moments, to imagine himself playing the part for which he was dressed; to imagine himself a distinguished and decorated soldier, whose high rank would undoubtedly be yet higher, if not indeed of the very highest in the military hierarchy?

Dreams are free, easy, cheap and fine . . .

"Pah!" he ejaculated, as he kicked the offending garments out of his sight, out of his life, his new butterfly life of a few glorious minutes, a glorious hour even.

Pacing, as the Colonel paced when thinking out some knotty problem of regimental economy, discipline or tactics, Denis strode to and fro across the little room, halting from time to time to admire himself in the mirror, to remember and practise some newly remembered attitude or gesture sacred to the Colonel. Each gave him more joyous satisfaction, more complete confidence; and each increased the *tempo* of his madness.

Then chance, or fate, intervened, using as so often she does, a woman for her instrument.

The door swiftly but softly opened, the head of Natalie appeared, even as she uttered in a venomous stage whisper,

"Denis Ducros, you lazy hound, I thought . . ." and as her bright and bold black eyes fell upon the resplendent figure before her, her tone changed as swiftly as the tenor of her words.

"Oh! M'sieur le Colonel!" she cooed. "A thousand pardons! Excuse and forgive me. I thought . . ."

"Ah! . . . Indeed?" smiled Denis sarcastically. "You thought? You must not attempt to think, my good woman. Nature has not equipped you with the apparatus for thinking."

And before Denis's cold stare, the overbearing virago who was his *bête noir,* cowered and shrank from the room.

"Ha!" ejaculated Denis in the Colonel's manner

triumphant; and, turning to the mirror, gave the right side of his moustache a brushing-upward flick with his right hand.

So the omniscient and undeceivable know-all did not know *le légionnaire* Denis Ducros from *M'sieur le Colonel* Louis Rochefort in the still-bright light of the setting sun!

Should he now go downstairs and terrify her to death; then, revealing himself for the man he was, give her a humiliation she would remember?

It was a temptation.

But away with it. How puerile. How unworthy—to use up the precious minutes of his glorious incarnation, in so base a pursuit as the discomfiture of a fat *bonne à tout faire*. What mattered it should she never know? *He* knew.

He knew that he had been mistaken for Colonel Rochefort of the Legion, and by a woman who saw him every day and all day—and hoped to see him all night.

And if a woman, why not a man? Why not all men? In that moment Denis Ducros fell from grace—and rose to the full height of his imaginative Provençal-Irish stature.

"*Ha!*" he said again, in the Colonel's own voice, excellent mimic that he was, "*Ordonnance! Denis!* Where the devil are my cane and gloves?"

"But in your hand, *M'sieur le Colonel,*" he answered himself in his own voice. "The left glove on the left hand, the right glove wrapped about the cane."

"*Ha!* Then why the devil couldn't you say so," growled Denis the Colonel to Denis the batman.

Another happy thought.

"And my silk handkerchief, species of *imbécile!*" The Colonel invariably carried a large silk handkerchief in his left cuff and frequently applied it to his nose—perhaps because he preferred the odour of its perfume to that of *les légionnaires* and other disgusting smells; or because he preferred to breathe as little dust as possible.

Taking the handkerchief from the drawer, Denis shook it out and transferred it to the left cuff of his tunic. He would know exactly how and when and where to produce that valuable piece of evidence and stage-property.

For he was going *out*.

He was going to act upon a wider stage, and before a bigger, better, worthier audience than Natalie Legros.

The well-known flourish of that familiar square of silk would carry conviction even where conviction was not needed.

H'm! An unpleasant word, conviction. But never mind. Away with it. Perish the thought, pleasant or unpleasant. He was going *out*. And *coûte qui coûte*, he was going to be a Colonel for an hour, a distinguished officer and a fine gentleman, even if he became there-after and therefore, a quite undistinguished member of a Penal Battalion.

Then, opening the outer door of the room, Denis Ducros descended the stairs from the Colonel's quarters and swaggered out into the rosy light of the beautiful spring evening.

So lovely a light, and so beautiful an evening was it, that even the hideous great yellow barracks, and the vast gravelled parade-ground, bordered by Company-offices, store-rooms, Guard-house and *cellule*-punish-ment prison, and bounded on the side opposite the barracks by lofty iron railings and great gates, looked a little less ugly and forbiddingly utilitarian than usual.

Beauty is, moreover, in the eye of the beholder; and that of Denis, viewing it from the lofty altitude of his new temporary rank, looked upon it for the first time with favour, obtaining for the first time as it were, a bird's-eye instead of a worm's-eye view.

To think that he should have lived to tread this unhallowed ground with the haughty and spurning foot of a master, a proud conqueror; and to look upon this familiar and detested scene with the gaze, as it were, of a proprietor, of one who is monarch of all he surveys.

Literally he saw the world in a new light, a roseate light indeed, as the beautiful butterfly of that humble little grub; no longer a domestic soldier-servant, but an uplifted *tête montée* Gallic-Irishman, on top of the world and on top of his form. . . .

What should he do first?

He would take a preliminary canter, or rather a dignified stroll, across the parade-ground, and match the virtue and value of his disguise against the eye-sight and observation of such of his comrades and superiors as he might encounter.

And, in that hour of his uplifting, he felt that there could arise no emergency with which he would not be most competent to cope—and in the true Rochefort vein and manner.

Confidently he strode forward on the path of glory that would lead but . . . whither?

Three *légionnaires* approached on their way from the main gates to their *chambrée.*

Now for the second test.

Drawing a deep breath, he gazed upon them haugh-tily, enquiringly, indeed suspiciously, as in the manner of Colonel Rochefort—whose attitude towards *les légionnaires,* whom greatly he loved and whom mightily he chastened—was that of one who knew their wicked hearts so well as to be only too aware that they were doing wrong, had just done something wrong, or were about to do something wrong.

The swift turn of the head, the hard penetrating glance were in the authentic vein. Would the disguise work?

It worked.

It worked most satisfactorily and completely.

Whether it would have done so as perfectly and for as long, in the broad light of high noon is unknown; but in the rosy evening light, soon to turn towards dusk, it seemed evident that whosoever beheld him, would behold Colonel Louis Rochefort. For the salutes were swift and spontaneous.

There was no doubtful look upon any of the three well-known faces. There was no hesitation, no second glance, as the respectful eyes that were turned to him resumed their stare to the front; and benignly the smartly quivering salutes were acknowledged with a finger-tip of the right hand to a gold-embroidered *képi*.

Good fellows.

Excellent fellows.

Bons camarades et bons légionnaires.

Bad men all, but bad men of the best sort. *Mauvais sujets,* but certainly not of the gaol-bird class.

Now, one of the most widely spread and completely erroneous of all misconceptions concerning the French Foreign Legion is the popular belief that, if not exactly a unique collection and assortment of crooks and criminals, it is composed very largely of this undesirable class of people. There could scarcely be a bigger mistake; and, as Denis was well aware, there are some wonderful mistakes published on this subject by those who are subsidised to slander the Legion; by journalists who have listened to the lies of the Old Soldier, more-than-willing to turn a dishonest penny and give good measure therefor; and by those equally dishonest persons who know nothing whatever about the subject.

The majority of the men of the French Foreign Legion are not criminals. But a small minority of them are, and so is a small minority of any other regiment in the world.

Anyone who thinks that this magnificent Regiment is a robbers' roost, a rogues' Alsatia, and a scoundrels' asylum, imagines a vain thing.

On the other hand, the word asylum reminds one of the indubitable fact that there is a small proportion of *légionnaires* who should be in an asylum, and these men definitely outnumber those who should be in prison.

This statement, again, must not be taken as suggesting that the French Foreign Legion consists largely of cheerful lunatics; but it is undeniably true that, while there is no greater proportion of criminals in the French Foreign Legion than there is in any other regiment, there is certainly a greater proportion of men who are what is termed "queer"; men who are slightly unbalanced, and who are, on the whole, a little more mad than the rest of us.

And of course, there are again those who, while

normally sane and sober as a judge, go completely, if temporarily, insane under the influence of *le cafard.*

And as Denis knew, the three men in the act of saluting him were representative respectively of each of these three classes.

Hans Müller, the German-Swiss, was not really a criminal, though there might be narrow-minded civilians who would regard him as one; Ivan Dobroff was not really a lunatic, though few doctors would decline to certify him as one; and Michel Aubraine was a man of well-balanced and noble mind, save when suffering from an attack of *le cafard,* the influence of which was to make him behave either as a criminal or as a lunatic, when not as both—the complete criminal-lunatic in fact.

Good fellows.

Excellent fellows.

He would have liked to greet them with a kindly, *"Bon soir, mes chers enfants! Dieu vous bénisse!"* But that would not have been in character, for assuredly it was not the habit of *le bon Colonel,* Louis Rochefort, thus to greet and bless his regimental children. Curses came much more readily to the firm lips beneath that trim little hedge of a moustache, and he appeared to regard his little ones rather as *sales cochons, scélérats,* and *salauds,* than as *ses chers enfants.*

No, Colonel Denis Ducros, must act in character, must play his part as perfectly as he looked it, and not fail to give a flawless impersonation. He must repress his benevolent and comradely instincts in the interest of his Art.

A pity though, for he highly approved these three cheerful blackguards, and would have liked to do something to add to their gaiety, to ameliorate the asperities of their path which they themselves did nothing to smooth, and to send them on their way rejoicing—to continue celebrating the Great Fête Day of *la République.*

Especially Michel Aubraine, with whom he had a tenuous tie of blood and many traits in common. He was fond of him, for they held similar views on life, and enjoyed a common sense of humour.

Michel Aubraine (whose grandfather had spelt it Michael O'Brien) had once, under the influence of *le cafard,* made Legion history by burgling the house of *Monsieur le Maire* and stealing, or, let us say, borrowing without his knowledge and consent, his complete official dress, his red, white and blue sash of office, his chain, his top-hat, his gold-mounted stick and his patent leather shoes, which were really much too small for him.

In these borrowed plumes, Michel Aubraine had called on the Commander-in-Chief in Algeria, then visiting Sidi-bel-Abbès on a tour of inspection, and had begged him, in the name of France, their common Mother, to insist that France treated her French Foreign Legion in a somewhat more motherly manner, with fewer kicks and more ha'pence.

The tale of this deed was told in *café* and canteen and *chambrée,* in *caserne* and camp, to this day, with deep chuckles, and even deeper approval.

Michel Aubraine, who, Parisian born and bred, gay insouciant *boulevardier* before his fall, was, as he said, of "Cork extraction," and probably the descendant of some Captain Michael O'Brien who had come to France to seek his fortune in the *Corps du Garde* and the French wars.

There are many people, among them canny Scots and sober Saxons, who regard the Irish as mad, and will say of the gentleman from Kilkenny or Killaloe, that he's "Irish and unaccountable."

To this type of merry madness and unaccountability, Michel Aubraine added the temperamental effervescence alleged to be particularly Gallic; and when the mood descended upon him and the fit seized him, he would do things which nobody's maiden aunt could be expected to approve.

But Denis Ducros approved; admired Michel wholly, and loved him greatly.

Nevertheless, to describe Michel as any more insane or criminal than was Denis himself, would be a complete misuse of words.

And how Denis would have loved to disclose himself to Michel!

And how Michel would have loved the disclosure! A feat after his own heart. A feat rivalling, nay excelling, his own calling on the General in the *rôle* of *Monsieur le Maire.*

A wink and a word to Michel, and he would follow Denis about, from the beginning to the end of this joyous adventure, thrilled and delighted beyond all telling.

Yes, and beyond all self-restraint too, probably. It was a temptation, but it must be resisted. Michel would know soon enough, and it would give him infinite delight to remind Michel of how, together with Hans Müller and Ivan Dobroff, he had, with most punctilious respect and impeccable smartness, saluted his old *copain,* the Colonel's batman!

Yes, he would know soon enough.

But it might be many a long day before they could laugh over it together and really enjoy the joke; for there was no denying that the butterfly's brief summer evening would almost certainly be followed by a long chill winter of discontent.

It would mean cells.

Thirty days cells, at least; and almost certainly the loss of his soft job, and the return to hoe his hard row, to live in the ranks, wherein he would be especially and extra-bitterly harried by *l'Adjudant* Buehl, Sergeant-Major Schnitzel, and by Sergeant Schumacher, all of whom he knew to hate him and to deplore his escape— from their sphere of unkind activities, to the haven of the Colonel's *ménage.*

Should he go back while there was yet time, go back before any harm was done? Go back content with having *been* the Colonel, and been so recognised by his enemy, fat Natalie, and saluted by his friends *les légionnaires* Müller, Dobroff, and, above all, by Michel Aubraine, the clever, the joyous, reckless, gay and care-free creature, the amusing rascal whom, of all men, save the grim Colonel Louis Rochefort, he most admired?

Granted that, by putting on the Colonel's uniform, swaggering across the parade-ground, and being saluted by his *copains,* he had perhaps equalled Michel's feat of calling on the General in the Mayor's clothing and insignia—should he now exceed and excel it by turning out the Guard and inspecting it?

That would be a really memorable feat.

Who was Sergeant of the Guard, to-night? What a holy joy if it were one of his especial enemies, and he could make a fool of him!

Not that it was a really healthy pastime, making fools of sergeants. No, apart from whatever official punishment he got, beginning probably with thirty days' solitary confinement in a dark cell, that sergeant would have a little of his own to add unofficially; something quite unpleasant.

And would not the worst punishment of all be the loss of his job?

For surely Denis Ducros was infinitely better off in such a position than he had been when in the ranks; a position in which he had long been exempt from gruelling marches, the wearisome and monotonous drills, guard duties and fatigues, and the boring routine of barrack life? If ever a rascally rogue of a *légionnaire* found himself in clover, or on velvet, surely it was Denis Ducros, with his light and easy duties, his considerable leisure, his opportunities of hearing so much interesting officers' gossip at table, and below-stairs gossip from Natalie; not to mention his access to an elegant sufficiency of food, wine and tobacco?

Yes, one would have thought that the most volatile of *garçons* or the maddest of "gossoons" would have been at some pains to retain so infinitely desirable a post.

But away with prudence; perish wisdom and discretion; all three but the coward's names for cowardice, and he had had enough of all three.

Was not his hour come?

Did he not know that, when the mood descended upon him and the fit seized him, as occasionally it did, he must break out, run wild, lose control, have his fling, and do the damnedest things?

For a thousand days he might be the bumble little man whose pay was a ha'penny a day, and whose right to life, liberty and the pursuit of happiness was non-existent.

But on the thousand-and-first—when the moment came—and if *le bon Dieu* alone knows what brings the moment to the real Irishman, perhaps not He Himself, knows what brings it to the hybrid Gallic Hibernian—he must arise and go to his father, the Devil; kick over the traces; cut loose; run amok; and throw his bonnet, *béret* or *képi,* over the nearest windmill.

"I must be mad," whispered Denis to himself, "even to think of such a thing . . . I *am* mad . . . Praise God from whom all blessings flow, I am as mad as a March hare. I will turn out the Guard. I will inspect it. And, Heaven and my great ancestors helping me, I will turn the Sergeant of the Guard not only out, but inside out."

Sacré véto! The Sergeant of the Guard.

Yes. He would certainly inspect the Guard and if, in doing so, he must still repress his benevolent and philanthropic instincts with regard to his comrades, the Sergeant of the Guard was another matter.

There he could do a little good of a different kind. Give himself a little real pleasure and still remain well within the scope and confines of his part.

If he could get away with it, that is.

But he could. Of course he could.

It was when an actor lived his part and actually felt himself to *be* the character he was impersonating, that he acted perfectly and carried complete conviction.

"*Ha!*" he said aloud in the very voice and manner of the Colonel, as he smartly smacked the left leg of his riding boot with his cane, and—took the second step along the path of glory that could lead but to the cells.

As he strode across the vast parade-ground, men engaged on various fatigues, or proceeding forth from barracks, in their smart array for walking-out, to enjoy the Fête Day celebrations, froze to attention if laden with bucket and broom, or, if empty-handed, saluted with the swift rigid smartness of toy automata.

As he approached the Guard-house, there was a sudden shout, swift movement; and, within one minute of the alarm, the Guard was turned out, was presenting arms with perfect precision, and standing to attention like a group of graven images.

Denis halted in his stride, meticulously returned the Guard's salute, and gravely eyed its Sergeant.

Good. His luck was in.

Of all the men he hated, and they were not very many really, he hated, yea loathed and detested, this Prussian brute, Schumacher, a bully, a brute and a ruffian if ever there were one; a base and pig-like lout whose genuine joy and pleasure it was to make trouble, bring punishment, and cause suffering.

If there were one thing he loved more than to catch the wrong-doer, and punish him as savagely as lay in his power, it was to accuse the innocent of an offence, punish him for its alleged commission, and add extra punishment for the further offence of denial and protest.

With left foot extended, left hand holding glove and cane clenched, and the fingers of the right hand stroking his moustache, Denis considered Sergeant Schumacher with disconcerting attention, or what would have been most disconcerting to anyone less sure of his unquestionable correctness than was the good Sergeant Schumacher.

"Now what would that be?" murmured Denis aloud, as he studied the motionless form of the big Prussian, and felt inwardly thankful that the latter, together with the rest of the Guard, was staring straight to his front, his mind obviously untroubled with any shadow of suspicion.

Surprised, they all possibly might be, that the Colonel, in person, should be prowling round at that time and place, but doubtful as to his genuineness they were not.

This was good.

This was great.

This was glorious.

This was worth living for; possibly even worth dying

for.

He was about to enjoy one of the most poignantly beautiful episodes of his life; enjoy it to the full; and fill each moment with enjoyment.

"What would it be?" he continued in private but most audible soliloquy. "It is not a dog. It is not a hog. It is not a frog. Yet certainly it is not a man. Or would it after all perhaps be a hog—on its hind legs?" . . .

"But no, it has hands," he observed.

"Would it be an ape of some sort then, a chimpanzee or an orang-outang?" he mused.

"Or perhaps a gorilla?" he asked of the circumambient unanswering air—or of the unanswering Guard.

The Guard stared straight to its front.

Not a muscle of the face of one of its members stirred, unless it were just a little one at the corner of the mouth of the bugler, young, foolish and comparatively undisciplined. But though no facial muscle moved, one countenance undoubtedly changed colour; for the fat and pig-eyed face of Sergeant Schumacher grew even redder than usual, achieving an almost beetroot hue.

It gave the acting Colonel infinite pleasure, to see this strong man, suppressing powerfully, bravely and silently, some emotion that bade fair to prove even stronger than he.

Surely he must explode or die?

Explode *and* die perhaps. But even on this night of nights, this was probably too much for which to hope.

"Anyway," he decided, as he prodded the Sergeant's bulging chest, "gorilla or goat, camel or crocodile, it is dressed as a man. Yes, in point of fact it is got up in a sort of parody of the uniform of the Legion—with dull straps, dingy buttons, dusty tunic and dirty boots . . .

"And, *Nom de Dieu,* the animal has actually got 'sardines on its legs,' as *mes enfants les légionnaires* would say. Stripes on its arms. . . . Upon my soul, it is actually wearing the *chevron* of a sergeant. . . . To think of such a thing happening in my Regiment!"

And words appeared to fail the Colonel for a moment.

"Well! Well! Well! But that can be remedied. If unfortunately we cannot change its face and its form, or make it keep itself clean, we can at any rate reduce it to the ranks—of those who can."

The Sergeant and the Guard stood firm, those men of magnificent discipline. They even kept their lips firm, though the eyes of some slightly goggled in their heads.

For it is not every day that it is given to simple *légionnaires* to see a well-hated superior humbled in the dust before their wondering eyes. Nor by that Being, usually as remote as *le bon Dieu,* and who was supposed by all good Sergeants—and Sergeant Schumacher was a very good sergeant indeed—to be their prop and stay, the fount and source of all their authority and power.

Removing the silk handkerchief from his left cuff, with the authentic Rochefort flick and flourish, the Colonel held it to his nose.

"The creature is a walking stink," he said. "It is a very horrible creature. A species of pollution. A mass of corruption. . . . *Pah!* But I will assuredly see—and smell—it in Orderly Room to-morrow.

"To what is the Legion coming?" the Colonel asked, as both in sorrow and in anger he regarded the swinish face of the Prussian.

"In the Legion there should be a little discipline. Definitely. And that discipline must be maintained. And primarily by Sergeants who not only know their duties, but set an example. This man evidently knows nothing and knows it all wrong. . . . And though he is, I admit, an example, it is an example of all that should be avoided by a good *légionnaire.*"

And as the Colonel was about to turn away on that sad note of disappointment and disillusion, a faint sound was heard, as of a very very minor explosion occurring at a great distance, and under what might be termed great difficulties.

The young bugler had been tried too highly. Brave he was as any man, staunch and stout and true, but not as perfectly self-controlled as later he would doubtless become. He had not yet been long enough in the Legion to become a complete automaton.

And, being a bright and merry young Dane, with a highly developed sense of humour, he was apt to laugh at the wrong thing at the wrong time, and in the wrong place. And on this memorable occasion, all three were wrong, or would have been, had "Colonel" Denis Ducros been Colonel Louis Rochefort.

What caused Stevn Knutson finally to explode was the fact that the Colonel's concluding remarks to the Sergeant, were not only couched in the Sergeant's own sort of language, but were the very identical expressions which the Sergeant had two minutes before been addressing to Stevn Knutson—and this did indeed strike this young gentleman as being not only truly remarkable, but very, very funny.

In point of fact, it was not remarkable that the Colonel should have used these particular terms and allocutions, inasmuch as they had, full many a time and oft, been used by the Sergeant to Denis himself.

But funny it was, no doubt, that so very recently the Sergeant should have said to the Bugler:

"You unspeakable species of filth! You walking stink! You pollution! You mass of corruption! I'll have you in the *boîte* to-morrow.

"This is the Legion. And I'll teach you some discipline, you little smell. I'll teach you to keep yourself clean . . ." and so forth, all because Sergeant Schumacher, who did not like the *légionnaire* Stevn Knutson, because he was quick, and clever, and humorous—had imagined that Knutson had laughed behind the Sergeant's back, a crime of which he had promptly and falsely accused him.

And now he really had laughed behind the Sergeant's broad back, for it was so exquisitely amusing to hear the bully told-off in his very own words. But the incident grew even funnier, a little humour going a long way in the Legion, for instantly the Colonel falsely accused the Sergeant of the very offence of which the Sergeant had falsely accused the Bugler!

Sharply turning back, the Colonel again transfixed the purple-faced Schumacher with his cold stare.

"*Ah! . . . Indeed?*" he said, in the authentic tones of Colonel Rochefort. "The little Shoemaker is amused? He laughs, does he? He gives a great, gross belch of drunken laughter, does he? Intoxicated as well as dirty. Possibly a connection between the two states. Dirty because he is a habitual drunkard. Perhaps he is perpetually drunk in an attempt to drown his shame at being perpetually dirty?

"At any rate, it is clear that he laughs because he is drunk; or charitably we will assume that it is so. We should not like to sentence him for gross and intentional insolence to his Commanding Officer. That would be a very serious matter, and not to be settled by a mere reduction to the ranks. No, no. That would be an affair of *le boîte;* a matter of a prison sentence perhaps; a case for a *conseil de guerre.*[26]

"It would seem hard that a man, who had by some mysterious means attained the rank of Sergeant, should be sentenced to eight years' *travaux forcées* in a Penal Battalion, for one insolent laugh. But it would not be for that, it would be for dirt, degradation and the drunkenness that led to the insolence and insubordination."

As the Colonel concluded his harsh and bitter homily, it seemed to the intelligent, if fanciful young Dane, that, for the fraction of a second, the Colonel's cold eye wavered and caught his own with a flicker of understanding.

An absurd idea of course.

With a growl in Colonel Rochefort's lowest register, the Colonel spoke his final words to the apparently stunned and stricken Sergeant.

"See that no *légionnaire* is turned back from his evening walk by reason of his being improperly dressed, dirty or slovenly," he ordered, "for the worst of them could not be as bad as the Sergeant of the Guard.

---

[26] court-martial.

"I'll deal with you in the morning," he concluded, and turned away.

It may be said that, in a way, the Guard enjoyed the remainder of their tour of duty better than did Sergeant Schumacher, though in another way they did not. For the Sergeant seemed to be angry about something, and was even less affectionate than usual. Never had the bullying ruffian who could courageously face anything except ruffianly bullying, come nearer to the suicide he sometimes contemplated, than he did that night, for his yellow streak, the hall-mark of the bully, though not wide was deep.

And as Denis Ducros turned about and ceased to face the Guard, he also found himself facing a most terrible temptation.

There before him were the great iron gates, symbol of his state of servitude, and of the iron discipline that bound him, held him, and shut him off from the world of free happy men—and women.

He had just had one of the happiest few minutes of his life. He had just done something really remarkable; something unique, and like Alexander, he sighed for fresh worlds to conquer.

Even while in the act of inspecting the Guard, he had thought of carrying on this fantastic game all over the Barracks, if he succeeded in imposing upon the Sergeant of the Guard; going into every *chambrée* of the three floors of the *caserne*; into every one of the quarters, every office, store-room, cook-house, cell, corner and cubby-hole into which he could penetrate. And finally into the canteen—until he was discovered, or completed his triumphant *tour de force,* by returning to the Colonel's quarters, restoring the Colonel's uniform and kit to their proper places, resuming his own drab livery of servitude, and hopefully awaiting the almighty rumpus, earthquake and upheaval that would follow the discovery that someone had impersonated the Colonel, and had fooled the Guard and insulted its Sergeant.

But now, an even brighter horizon dawned, and even more brilliant ideas soared up like rockets into the lurid sky of his wild imagination.

He would do all that later, but first he would leave Barracks!

He would take his evening stroll; he would promenade himself.

Was it not the great Fête Day and holiday?

Colonel Denis Ducros would take the air; Colonel Denis Ducros would walk abroad—and give the public a treat. By the souls of Brian Boru and Bertrand du Guesclin, and by the Living God of all Good Soldiers, he would indeed give the public a treat; and, incidentally, add lustre to the name and fame of the great Colonel Louis Rochefort.

And, a minute later, the strange sight might have been seen, and indeed was seen, of the Colonel commanding the Depot of the French Foreign Legion strolling out through the portal by the great gates of the Legion Barracks into the lane that runs between them and the Barracks of the Spahis.

CHAPTER 2

THE GLORY BEGINS

Along the lane strode the Colonel in the direction of the *boulevard* leading to the *Place Sadi Carnot* where the Legion band would be playing that evening.

The butterfly was in full flight.

He had emerged from his chrysalis-state in the dressing-room.

He had fluttered his beautiful wings and mentally assumed butterfly shape and colour on the barrack square.

He had sipped the sweets of the brief new existence, at the Guard-house.

And now he was up and away on the wing.

Soon he would settle and sip again of the heady honey of Power . . .

As he turned the corner, he came suddenly face to. face with *l'Adjudant* Buehl, and instinctively his hand shot up in salute.

Fool that he was! His first mistake.

First now, and probably last, for Colonels do not promptly and respectfully salute non-commissioned officers, and in the French Foreign Legion an *Adjudant* is of non-commissioned rank.

Miserable amateur actor that he was! He who had imagined himself a Cocquelin, a Guitry!

But Denis was quick; and Denis was clever. The movement of his mind was swifter than that of his hand, and just in time he turned the motion into a moustache-brushing gesture, as the *Adjudant* himself swiftly placed his cane beneath his arm, and himself saluted the Colonel with the utmost precision and correctness.

Languidly moving the raised hand, from his moustache to the peak of his *képi,* the Colonel murmured as he passed,

"Slovenly, *Adjudant.* Very sloppy and slovenly. Pull yourself together now, and try to move—and to look— like a soldier."

In justice it must be admitted that *l'Adjudant* Buehl could not possibly look more like a soldier than he already did, for the Legion contained no smarter non-commissioned officer than he. An ornament to the Regiment, a model and a pattern to all its rank and file. Scarcely could he believe his own ears. There must be some mistake; he could not have heard aright.

Never from the days when he was a smart, intelligent and ambitious *bleu*,[27] doing his recruits' course, had such words been addressed to him—and then only as a matter of mere form and routine, by a hard-driving Sergeant-Instructor, who said precisely the same thing daily, for the good of his mind, soul and body, to every recruit who passed through his hands.

He must be mistaken!

Such a shocking, unjust and cruel insult . . .

And from the Colonel too, a man who was his *beau idéal* of a fighting soldier and a *Chef de Bataillon.* And who, moreover, had hitherto been so approving and friendly.

He hadn't been at the Depôt for very long, but from the very first he had seemed to realise and to recognise that *l'Adjudant* Buehl was something a bit extra, something a little out of the ordinary, for ability, smartness and discipline, even among the non-commissioned officers of the Legion.

Why, *l'Adjudant* Buehl could have sworn that the Colonel regarded him with exactly the same feelings as those with which he regarded the Colonel.

Try to look like a soldier! What? *He,* of all men, *l'Adjudant* Buehl, with his double row of medals and decorations; his spotless record; his highest rank below that of a commissioned officer; his great reputation as a man-eating disciplinarian; hardest of the hard; smartest of the smart; his high hopes, almost amounting to certainty, of being sent to St. Maixent

---

[27] recruit.

Military College (for non-commissioned officers selected for training for promotion to commissioned rank).

Try to look like a soldier? What an incredibly cruel, unjust and wicked insult!

And *l'Adjudant* Buehl, who had spent a good deal of the best years of his life in delivering, nay hurling, cruel, unjust and wicked insults at his subordinates, did not himself suffer insult gladly.

It is far more blessed to give than to receive—as both these soldiers in that moment deeply appreciated.

Almost visibly the fine, swaggering, strutting *Adjudant* shrivelled and shrank, deflated by the piercing deadly thrust of the Colonel's sharp and bitter speech. Had the poor fellow but known it, he was for the moment looking, as well as feeling, like one of the wretched *légionnaires* whom it was his delight, if not his duty, to brow-beat, bully and be-devil.

With an almost audible gasp, he lowered his arm from the salute; and with a quite audible chuckle, Denis Ducros dropped his hand from the peak of the Colonel's *képi* as he passed on.

Almost visibly the fine swaggering, strutting Colonel swelled with pleasure, power and importance as he went on his way, pride in his port, defiance in his eye.

That would teach the over-bearing, foul-mouthed swine a little lesson. Do him all the good in the world. The only pity was there couldn't have been a score or two of his victims present to witness the bully's humiliation.

But one can't have everything, and it had been so satisfying. For it is not often, in real life, that one has the opportunity of actually saying the sort of things that, in day-dreams and phantasy, one imagines oneself saying to those whom, with good reason, one hates, despises and fears.

Still, it would have given an even sharper edge to the keen joy of the moment, had there been an audience, if of only one. Michel Aubraine, for example, or the merry and appreciative Stevn Knutson, the bugler.

In point of fact, had Denis but known it, the latter

excellent fellow, though not vouchsafed the pleasure of witnessing the discomfiture of the *Adjudant,* was about to enjoy the first fruits thereof—and behold a second scourging of the unfortunate Sergeant of the Guard. For, returning to barracks in what could only now be described as a towering rage, and passing through the portal by which the Colonel had so recently departed, *l'Adjudant* Buehl sought a victim upon whom to vent that wrath ere it blew him to pieces.

His eye fell upon the Sergeant of the Guard—also the full weight and violence of his invective—while yet that hapless man still reeled from the blow dealt by the Colonel.

Hard luck indeed . . .

"Mais que voulez-vous? C'est la Légion!" as the Legion says.

Still chuckling, the "Colonel" Denis Ducros went on his way rejoicing, glancing nevertheless with cold hauteur from left to right, and returning, in the Colonel's very own style, the salutes of the soldiers who passed him, grading the movement from the sketchiest raising of a finger, to the punctilious full salute—according to the rank of the individual, which varied from that of *soldat deuxième classe* to brother-officer of field rank.

Ah! . . . And who was this?

None other than the grey-haired, blue-nosed, *vieux moustache* known to his comrades as Père Pinard, *doyen* of his Battalion, oldest soldier, biggest liar, stoutest *légionnaire,* and champion drunk of the Army of Africa. Dear old *Pinard,*[28] who apparently had no other name than that; no other nationality, family or home than *La Légion Étrangère.* A man legendary in his own life-time, a man of tales and stories, those told about him nearly as numerous as those he himself told. A true Soldier of Fortune on whose breast glittered the medals of Tonkin, Madagascar and Dahomey, as well as those of the campaigns of Algeria—not to mention such side-line extras as the bronze cross of the *Croix de Guerre,* and the silver and gilt disc of the

---

[28] cheap wine.

Medaille Militaire, tinkling symbols of valour and war-like experience, which it was frequently his wont to pawn for wine.

He appeared to regard without pride or satisfaction his almost unique collection of war medals and decorations. It was not so much a case of the contempt that is bred by familiarity, as uninterested acceptance of their existence; things that just were—like his grey beard and blue nose. He alluded to them when pawning or redeeming them, as his *ferblanterie,* or tin-ware.

What amused and delighted those lewd fellows of the baser sort, his boon companions, was the fact that wine apparently, indeed obviously, did old Père Pinard no harm, for he could march as far and as fast as any of them; and if occasion should arise on which he had to fight all day and was permitted to drink all night, he would be as ready for the next day's doings, and as bright and early as the youngest of them.

By reason of this curious and lamentable fact he was a living refutation and a walking annoyance to *Monsieur le Médécin-Majeur,* a good *toubib*[29] with strong views on the dangers of alcohol as a cause of *cafard* and many other evils, for soldiers who work, march and fight beneath a burning sun.

It was, to his mind, a very wrong and improper thing that a man who was not only one of the most popular and most distinguished, but also one of the very best of the soldiers in his charge, should be an undeniable and incorrigible drunkard . . .

Père Pinard, magnificently sober on a few bottles of *pinard* and assorted curious spirits of undesirable origin, caught sight of the man whom he supposed to be his Colonel, and saluted with swift smartness and precision.

The heart of Denis warmed to this dear old man, this kindly simple soul, this good soldier who was *bon camarade et bon légionnaire,* to whose wonderful reminiscences drawn from his inexhaustible store of Legion lore, he had so often listened, thrilled and

---

[29] army doctor (slang).

enthralled.

The Colonel halted in his stride.

"Well, *mon cher enfant,* and how goes it?" he smiled benevolently. "Health good, slate clean, and thirst powerful?" Père Pinard, standing at the salute and looking a model of virtue and a statue of military rectitude, concealed his almost unbounded surprise and beamed his almost unbounded gratification.

Bon Dieu de Dieu de Sort! And Name of a Name of a Hairless Green Monkey! Wonders would never cease. What was happening? Could it be possible that a few bottles of red Algerian wine, a *tasse* or two of cognac, a taste or so of *tchum-tchum*,[30] a few toothfuls of *gènèvre,* and a negligible number of absinthes were making him imaginative?

Was he seeing things?

No, this was the Colonel all right.

Was he hearing things? Voices—like those heard by Jeanne d'Arc? But they had been angel voices, and whatever the *légionnaires* called Louis Rochefort, it was not "angel."

Could it be that he, Père Pinard, was losing grip, could not carry his liquor, was going ga-ga?

Away with such horrible and miserable thoughts. It was not as though he had had a skinful instead of toothfuls, mouthfuls or even bellyfuls. But it was enough to make a sober man think he might be a little drunk; for on former occasions on which the Colonel had given himself the trouble of addressing *le légionnaire* Pinard, it had not been thus that he had spoken.

On the very last occasion of all, and that only quite recently, he had called him, among other derogatory names, a Pillar of the Pot-houses of Sodom and Gomorrah; a doddering, drivelling dreg-drinker, and a tun-bellied, slop-soaking rum-sponge.

Yes, there had been a great deal more *gueule*[31] than endearment, such as this *"mon cher enfant"* stuff. In fact he had alluded to Père Pinard as one whose sole

---

[30] rice spirit.
[31] abuse.

thought and object in life was *se saouler la gueule,*[32] and *se taper la gueule.*[32]

He had roundly averred that Père Pinard was a miserable wreck, an aged ruin whose absolute chronic condition was *ayant la gueule de bois.*[32]

Yes, too much *gueule* about the Colonel's conversation altogether, at that regrettable Orderly-Room encounter.

Quite eloquent the Colonel was apt to be on the subject of poor old Père Pinard's character and habits.

And here he was, smiling at him like a father; and, like a father, was addressing him as *son cher enfant.*

There was a catch in it somewhere. And Père Pinard must either be drunk, dreaming, or both.

"*Eh, mon vieux lapin,* how's tricks?" continued the Colonel, smiling with a bright and charming kindliness, as the aged reprobate grinned and wagged his beard in lieu of tail.

Lapin!

He was the Colonel's *vieux lapin*[33] now, was he?

Only the other day, it had been rather a case of *ne pas valoir un peu de lapin* (his not being worth a tinker's damn), and of less use and value than the butt end of a dead bed-bug, as the Old Devil had clearly expressed it.

Quite good at phrases, the Colonel was; well up to his job at *fichant un poil à quelqu'un*[34] when he felt like it.

"Still no gold stripe, I see," continued the Colonel. "Not even a worsted one. How's that, now? Come, come. We can't have it. Not with that fine show of *ferblanterie.* It wants stripes to set it off.

"Only *soldat premiere classe.* No. We can't have that," he said again, smiling even more warmly. "Not with a *vieux moustache* who has served France faithfully, man and boy, for nearly half a century—Line, Marsouins, Legion and all . . .

"We must see about it, *mon ami.* We must do some-

---

[32] to be drunk.
[33] old rabbit.
[34] giving anyone a dressing down.

thing about it, *mon gars*.

"Yes. Tell Sergeant-Major Lorraine that I shall want a word with him about it to-morrow. . . .

"It is a disgrace to the non-commissioned officers of your Company that your name has not been put forward before this. Rank injustice and the old grudge-and-favouritism somewhere."

And the Colonel shook his head sadly.

"*Mon Colonel!*" murmured the abashed Père Pinard, shaken between joy at such wonderful words and fear at such apparent sarcasm.

"And I'll have a word with Captain de Grandeville about it," added the Colonel; and, with a playful tap of his cane, a kind of accolade and blessing, bade the old soldier be of good cheer, and have a night of good cheer, too, in celebration.

As he passed on, the Colonel left the good Père Pinard trembling with alcoholic emotion, and fully prepared to subscribe to the belief that the day of miracles was not passed and that the millennium must be very close at hand. In a fog of happiness and wine fumes, the elated *ancien* made his way back to barracks and to bed, resolved to lead a higher and better life. He would make a fresh start, begin again, and turn over a new leaf.

After all, he was only seventy.

And what wonderful things he could do if he were promoted Corporal, and then Sergeant. How enormously he could help all his friends, and prevent their enemies in all their unkind doings.

He would be a model Sergeant; the beloved father of his *escouade,* the admired and trusted shepherd of all black sheep . . .

Meanwhile, a few yards further on, the Colonel was aware that Mademoiselle Angélique, a Polish and polished young lady, who appeared to have no other name save Oui-Oui, was crossing the road and coming in his direction.

Little friend of all the world and of most of the half-world, she still could not claim acquaintanceship, much less friendship, with the austere and rigidly virtuous Colonel Louis Rochefort, *homme toujours très sérieux et comme il faut*. And she lowered her eyes modestly, as she stepped on to the pavement in front of him.

That Great One had nothing to say to such people as the *petites Angéliques* and *Oui-Ouis* of this world, she well knew.

Judge then of her surprise when, swift as a little bird and light as a little tickling feather, the Colonel's ungloved hand shot up from his right side and chucked her under the chin.

But what in the name of kind Saint Louis, patron Saint of all good little naughty girls, was this?

Mademoiselle Angélique Oui-Oui could scarcely believe the evidence of her own chin.

Oh, la, la! M'sieur le Colonel himself. That grim man, so cold, so severe, so disapproving. It was as though the virtuous Saint Anthony himself, promenading the Golden Street, had suddenly and playfully tickled a demure little angel passing by.

But there, they were all alike under the skin—and still more so under the rose!

And Mademoiselle Oui-Oui, smiling bewitchingly, raised her sparkling dark eyes to those of the Colonel.

"*Qu'elle est ravissante,*" he sighed aloud, as to himself.

"*Bon jour, ma chérie. Comment ça va?*" he greeted her in the tone and manner of an old friend and ardent admirer. And this latter, indeed, the humble *légionnaire* Denis Ducros had long been—from a distance.

Not for him, *soldat simple* that he was, the friendship of the fashionable Angélique Oui-Oui, who indeed only shed the light of her countenance and the charm of her conversation upon lonely soldiers of commissioned rank.

Should such an obscure person as Denis Ducros, *légionnaire* and officer's servant, ever feel that the austerities and asperities of the monastic life of the celibate warrior needed the kind amelioration of feminine society, conversation and charm, he could get him to *le village Négre* and seek it there. The romantic companionship of Arab and negro women was there available for the bold Romeo who bravely sought it. But he must not be of the fastidious, hypercritical and too discriminating type of traveller in the *pays du tendre.*

But the ha'penny-a-day *légionnaire* might just as well sigh for the moon, or a champagne-and-oyster dinner, as for the pleasure of the society of the famous Angélique Oui-Oui, *belle* of Sidi-bel-Abbès.

Yet here he was, *légionnaire* Denis Ducros, smiling upon her paternally, patronisingly indeed, and speaking to her, not as a mere suppliant, not as an equal, but positively *de haut en bas.*

"Oh, M'sieur le Colonel!" she murmured, very much as Père Pinard had done; and, although not looking in the least as Père Pinard had looked, feeling nevertheless much as he had felt on receipt of such signal honour as the kind and approving notice of stern Colonel Louis Rochefort.

"Oh, M'sieur le Colonel! Comme vous êtes gentil!"

"A happy chance! A most fortunate meeting," smiled the Colonel encouragingly, as he patted her hand. "I have for some time been meaning to call and pay my respects. I must give a party in your honour."

Mademoiselle Angélique did her utmost, by means of a private and peculiar process of her own, to blush becomingly. It was not easy, as it involved holding the breath for a rather prolonged period, and there was already a quite considerable and permanent blush established and in evidence on her rounded cheeks.

"Yes. Most certainly we must have a party," continued the Colonel. "You must bring along some nice girls, and I will bring my boys . . . All the brightest and the best of them.

"Now where shall we have it? *Chez Mademoiselle Angélique?* Or what about a moonlight picnic, a *fête champêtre?* No. I know what we'll do. We'll have a gala dinner at the Grand Hotel."

"But how delightful," murmured Mademoiselle Angélique.

The Colonel beamed in most friendly fashion.

"M'sieur le Colonel est très gentil," she faltered,

looking up a little more boldly into the kindly and affectionate eyes that gazed into hers.

"Well! Well! . . . What a world we live in," she reflected; and, again like Père Pinard, decided that wonders would never cease.

For in a life not devoid of surprises, this was a surprise indeed.

Usually of quite adequate fluency, and as ready of wit as of speech, Mademoiselle Angélique Oui-Oui was positively dumb.

Monsieur le Colonel Rochefort himself! Who next? And it was with something very nearly resembling a genuine blush that Mademoiselle smiled her joyous gratification as the Colonel patted her hand in the manner of a fond parent.

Fond certainly, if not quite parental.

"*Au 'voir donc, chère Angélique,*" concluded the Colonel. "I'll send you the invitation-cards—or, better still, I'll bring them round myself," and in his most gallant manner, or Colonel Louis Rochefort's most gallant manner, he brushed with his moustache the fingers of her right hand.

Wafting Mademoiselle Angélique an airy kiss, he then saluted and turned to resume his stroll, a warm glow around his heart, a kindly sense of something accomplished, something done to earn someone else a little pleasure, if not repose.

But scarcely had he turned to go, when a new idea illuminated his receptive mind.

Why let this charming encounter with such a nice girl be so brief? Why should it not be prolonged a while? He could hardly ask her to promenade around the town with him, for her company would rather tend to cramp his style, and his society would sooner or later be something of an embarrassment and hindrance to herself.

But he could suggest her accompanying him to the Grand Hotel for an *apéritif* and the making of all arrangements for the party.

It would give her great pleasure to walk with him, to have a drink with him, to enjoy with him the ordering of the dinner and making all arrangements for the gala, he felt sure.

It might be but a dream. It was, of course, a dream, a rosy illusion. But Angélique was unaware of that cold hard fact. She would live for a few days, or at any rate, a few hours, in a state of illusory but warm and joyful bliss.

Illusion, alas! But is not illusion finer and greater than reality?

What was it that buoyed men up, through the rough and stormy seas of life, but hopes—usually destined to remain for ever unfulfilled.

And if hope springs eternal in the human breast, let illusion also shed its soft and comforting light upon the darkness of the human path . . .

And for the space of a minute or so, such of the cosmopolitan public of Sidi-bel-Abbès as was on the spot, was treated to the stimulating and intriguing sight, as it supposed, of Colonel Louis Rochefort in hot and hasty pursuit of the well-known form of Mademoiselle Angélique Oui-Oui.

"Ah, Mademoiselle," said Denis as he overtook that young lady, "it just occurs to me . . . Shall we proceed at once and together to the Grand Hotel to order our dinner and make our little arrangements?"

"*Oh, Monsieur le Colonel!*" smiled Angélique happily. "Such an honour! But how charming! . . ."

Well! Well! Well! The good Saint Louis was going it! To think that she should live to walk down the most fashionable and popular boulevard of Sidi-bel-Abbès with the distinguished Colonel Louis Rochefort, that Monsieur so correct and impeccable, and he married too, and notoriously a model of strict domestic virtue.

Was he tired of it all?

Personally she had never tried it, but she could imagine the practice of strict virtue to be a boring pursuit and a great nuisance.

Anyway, if *Monsieur le Colonel* was contemplating a brief excursion from the strait and narrow path, she would be more than willing to accompany him into the flowery woods and dells of the realms of Romance.

And those observers who had seen the Colonel turn about and pursue Mademoiselle Angélique Oui-Oui, now, with astonishment and with breath that would not long be bated, saw him walk off beside her in pleasant fellowship, chatting and laughing with an ease that was almost abandon.

And through the portals of the best hotel of Sidi-bel-Abbès, those whose eyes followed, and they were not few, saw the adventurous couple about to disappear.

Not among these busy-bodies, but coming from the opposite direction, was Madame de Beauchamp, the wife of Major de Beauchamp of the Spahis, and an intimate friend of Madame Rochefort, the Colonel's extremely proper and serious-minded wife.

On one point, at any rate, Colonel Louis Rochefort and Acting-Colonel Denis Ducros held identical views. They both cherished a regrettable detestation of Madame de Beauchamp, that *maîtresse femme,* who considered herself the leading lady of Sidi-bel-Abbès, appointed herself its censor and the judge of its morals, was charitable to no man, still less to any woman, and was generous in nothing but rebuke.

In the opinion of Colonel Rochefort she was a most unpleasant and uncharitable person, who, in her dealings with Society, hoped for the worst rather than expected the best.

In the opinion of Denis Ducros she was just a plain *biche.* One of the plainest he had ever seen.

As the happy couple were in the act of turning to go into the hotel, they came face to face with Madame, and to both of them it was evident that, though it might be for the first time in her well-spent life, the great and good woman was wholly unequal to the occasion.

She had no words. Nothing but a gasp wherewith to reply to the Colonel's polite,

"*Ah, ma chère Madame de Beauchamp!* What good fortune! I wonder if you have met my friend, Mademoiselle Angélique Oui-Oui? . . . No? Permit me to present you to . . ."

But if Madame de Beauchamp could not utter, she could totter. Removing her horrified, indignant gaze from the Colonel's bland face, she stabbed Angélique with a viciously contemptuous stare, and made to pass on. But the deep inhalation, with which she recovered her breath after her gasp of wrath and horror, wrought evil as well as good.

Madame was large, and Madame was inclined to mitigate the appearance, if not the fact, of a slightly excessive *embonpoint,* by means of a sartorial discipline of which the key-note was tightness. Everything she wore was tight, tight almost as her compressed lips; and the deep breath which she drew through angrily inflated nostrils made everything tighter.

Too tight indeed for one terribly important button.

She felt, though none might hear, a definite and horrifying pop.

She took but a step . . . she faltered . . . halted, clutched and shuffled.

"Permit me," said the gallant Colonel, swiftly stooping, as Angélique's peal of merry laughter rang out unabashed.

Ignoring the outstretched hand and the silken pinkness which it proffered, Madame de Beauchamp recoiled, and still without a word, recovered her poise sufficiently to go on her way, without rejoicing.

"But what shall I do with them, Madame?" enquired the Colonel loudly of the broad back of the retreating Madame de Beauchamp.

"One would say the old dear is deaf," laughed Angélique, in her high and all-too-audible voice.

"Quite," replied the Colonel seriously.

"I apologise, my dear," he said. "I thought it was a lady . . . A lady of my acquaintance in fact . . . and these are undoubtedly her property."

Madame's back appeared to shudder.

"Well, if she doesn't want them . . ." smiled the practical Angélique, and swiftly performed a small miracle of folding and compression.

A moment later, laughing happily, the two passed through the swing doors into the foyer of the Grand

Hotel.

Hastily a Franco-Spanish-Arab servant fled to inform the Management that an army officer of high rank, accompanied by a lady, had entered the hotel. Swiftly the Management hurried from the little office in which it lurked, and, bowing low, smiling toothfully, and apparently cleansing its hands of all stain of sin, hurried to welcome the Colonel and to beg that he would honour it with his commands.

The Management, widely and deeply acquainted with Life, especially as it is lived in provincial towns of Northern Africa, was certainly not shocked, but was undeniably a little surprised, to discover that the lady who accompanied Monsieur le Colonel Rochefort, Commanding the Depôt of the French Foreign Legion, was none other than Mademoiselle Angélique Oui-Oui, with whom he was not unacquainted.

In fact, only the previous night, which included part of the morning of that very day, Mademoiselle Angélique had been the bright particular star of a little party at which the Management had permitted itself to relax from the anxieties and cares of Management.

But the Management's face was bland, placid and inscrutable; and the bow with which he honoured Mademoiselle—now by a strange turn of Fortune's wheel, his patron—was one of the deep respect due to a distinguished stranger.

Slightly to the Colonel's rear and right, Mademoiselle politely acknowledged the Management's deep bow with a gracious inclination of the head, and a swifter one of the right eyelid.

But neither a nod nor a wink is necessary to a clear-sighted horse, and the Management thought that Mademoiselle might, without sign or signal, have trusted him to act with the utmost discretion. However, doubtless the nod and wink were but the outward and visible sign of little Angélique's girlish levity. The wink but called upon him to regard her; to note that it really was she; to observe the social heights to which she had risen; and also to share the joke.

And the Colonel spread himself.

In a vision he also spread a table of good things, the sort of dinner of which the *légionnaire,* who has lived for years upon an unchanging diet, dreams as he sits down to his mid-day meal of *soupe* and bread, and again to his evening meal of—*soupe* and bread.

It was not that Denis Ducros, since becoming a batman, had anything of which to complain in the matter of food and drink, but he would have loved to sit down to a grand dinner more costly, more copious and more varied than those at which he served when Madame Rochefort gave a party.

Nor was it a dinner of quite that type that he wanted. He wished to provide a sort of feast that would appeal to his austerely and monotonously fed *copain,* Michel Aubraine, and his good friends Hans Müller, Ivan Dobroff, Père Pinard, MacSneeze, Ramonones and the others of his *escouade.*

That neither he and his friends, nor the lady friends of Angélique would ever sit down to any such feast at the Grand Hotel, troubled him not at all.

It was neither here nor there.

He was an artist; and, at the moment, he was giving full rein to his artistic imagination in the matter of arranging a sumptuous, beautiful and happy evening for the friends he loved and the strangers he was fully prepared to love.

He was also enjoying to the utmost the sense of power, that, in imagination, he could command.

He was enjoying too, and even more, the moment in which, and for which he lived, with its actual if brief sense of genuine reality. It was not illusion; it was not merely in his imagination that this fat *pékin*[35] was bowing before him, assenting with the utmost respect to his every suggestion, and taking his orders as does a . . . as does a . . . batman, the orders of a Colonel.

"As to the numbers, now," enquired the Management. "If *Monsieur le Colonel* would first of all kindly fix the . . ."

"Oh a score," promptly interrupted the Colonel.

---

[35] civilian.

"Ten officers and ten ladies.

"Besides ourselves, of course," he swiftly amended.

A far-away look o'erspread the ingenuous countenance of Mademoiselle Angélique Oui-Oui who was making a rapid calculation. Herself and ten more of *les girls?* Were there ten just women in all Sidi-bel-Abbès? Just the right sort, so to speak; quiet, discreet, well-behaved, and in all respects worthy? . . . There would have to be.

And if she could not raise a full team from among her personal friends and acquaintances, she could call at Madame de Beuglant's School for Young Ladies and enter into negotiations for the loan of one or two of her pupils. Nicolette, for example—and a good example.

What a lovely evening it would be. Such an event in her quiet life! Such a change!

And Mademoiselle Angélique Oui-Oui loved change. The more the better. She fully subscribed to the belief that variety is the spice of life, and she had a marked *penchant* for spice. . . .

And was there any special *plat* to which Mademoiselle gave preference? If so, she had but to mention it.

The Colonel recked not if she should mention oysters, lobsters, whitebait, and caviare. Nay ortolans, larks' tongues, Strassburg pie, and *pâté de foie gras,* things in season or out of season.

Mademoiselle had many preferences and mentioned them all.

Good! The more the merrier.

The Management scribbled hard in its little pocket-book.

And talking of merriment, what of the wines?

That was a subject quickly settled, in so far as Mademoiselle Angélique was concerned.

Sweet Champagne to begin with. Sweet Champagne to go on with. And sweet Champagne to finish with.

And after dinner some sweet Champagne.

In its little book the Management scribbled, *Asti Spumante pour Oui-Oui et les girls.*

Smiling tolerantly at so truly Angelic a preference, Denis gave joyous rein to his imagination, and once more spread himself.

His knowledge of wine was not negligible. He knew what *Messieurs les Officiers* drank at the *Cercle;* he knew what wines went with which courses; and he knew, both by hear-say and by study of prices in the Club wine-list, which were the noble wines of France.

In the light of this knowledge he now spoke of a light dry sherry *apéritif;* a rich brown sherry with the soup, a fine Chablis with the fish, a noble Burgundy with the *entrée;* a great Champagne, just twelve years old, with the joint; a generous port thereafter; and the Management must see to it that the Cognac which accompanied the coffee should be at least Napoleonic, if not real Napoleon Brandy.

And if, as he spoke of Napoleon, a shadow of his own Waterloo crossed the glowing soul of Denis Ducros, he ignored it bravely and utterly.

Was he not enjoying himself marvellously?

And was he not giving great pleasure to himself, to *cette chère petite Angélique,* and to *ce gros Monsieur,* the Management.

He was indeed.

For the joy of the Management was even greater than its amazement, which was great indeed. How he had misjudged this gallant Colonel, especially in the matter of gallantry.

What had come over him? Anyway, La Oui-Oui had over-come him, and to some purpose.

What a dinner!

The best of everything, and apparently without stint, or thought of cost. Better to be on the safe side though. And if, as apparently was the case, the sky was the limit, the fact had better be mentioned.

Did the Colonel quite realise the cost of one or two of the items so airily mentioned?

That Nuit St. Georges *par exemple?* That Mouton Rothschild? That forty-year-old Château Yquem for those who preferred it.

"Would *M'sieur le Colonel* prefer to see the wine-list?" the Management asked deferentially.

That would give him some idea of what he would be

letting himself in for.

No, the Colonel did not wish to see the wine-list. He merely wanted his orders fully and accurately carried out.

The Management bowed, while mentally rubbing its chin.

And would *M'sieur le Colonel* like an estimate? *Monsieur le Colonel* would not. As he had indicated, he required the best that the Grand Hotel could provide. The best would have to be good enough; and *Monsieur le Colonel* would look to the Management to see that it was the best.

As to the cost, *Monsieur le Colonel* expected it to bear reasonable ratio to value, and to be a fair and proper charge for wine and food of the very finest quality. It was to be a gala occasion, and its cost was not the prime consideration.

"Good enough," smiled the Management to itself, and had a bright idea.

"*Monsieur le Colonel* would of course desire that the ladies should have gifts, as is usual upon gala occasions?"

"But of course! . . . Of course! . . . I was coming to that," replied the delighted Denis, concealing his pleasure and enthusiasm at receiving this admirable suggestion.

This Management was a good fellow, unprepossessing as he looked. He might have a pendulous lip over which the tip of a red tongue continually flickered, a pasty, greasy skin, a boiled eye, and a protuberant paunch, but he had ideas.

Freely Denis admitted that but for this fat civilian he would never have thought of gala presents for the ladies.

Splendid. It gave even wider scope . . . And they should be noble gifts. Something worth having. And what was more, there should be something for *les messieurs* as well as for *les dames*. A good solid silver cigarette-case for each of the men, and for the ladies? . . .

His imagination began to run joyous riot.

What a lovely game this was.

A different kind of cigarette-case for the ladies? Smaller? Daintier?

No. Rather banal; and some of them might not smoke.

What did one give girls upon a gala occasion? Would jewellery be a little excessive? Rings . . . brace- lets . . . wrist-watches . . . That sort of thing?

He did not want to be vulgarly lavish of course, although he wanted everything to be of the best, and no reasonable expense spared.

But, of course, Angélique would know the sort of thing; and it would rest with him to decide the sort of quality and value.

"If I might be permitted to make a suggestion," continued the Management, "perhaps *Monsieur le Colo- nel* and—er—Mademoiselle would care to glance at the show-case."

"Oh, you have a stock of—ah—such things, conven- iently on the premises?"

"Yes, *Monsieur le Colonel.*"

"*Ah! . . . Indeed?*" replied Denis in a tone and manner that would have fully persuaded Colonel Louis Rochefort that he was both hearing and seeing double; and which suddenly reminded the Management that there was more than one side to the character of this distinguished and versatile officer.

If *Monsieur le Colonel* and Mademoiselle would kindly step this way, suggested the Management, wav- ing a large persuasive hand in the direction of a corri- dor.

With a brusque unkindly murmur that he had never yet learned to step in just that way, the Colonel nevertheless turned and followed the Management to where glittered a jeweller's show-case, elegant and attractive, beneath the electric light.

"*Oh-h-h,*" whispered Angélique, feasting delighted eyes upon its contents, "*Chez Tiffany, Cartier et Cie,*" for such were the names modestly adopted by the gentleman of Hispano-Israelitish extraction who kept the leading jeweller's shop in the *Plâce Sadi Carnot.*

"I will get the key if *Monsieur le Colonel* will excuse me," murmured the Management, and disappeared into his office.

"I thought of giving the gentlemen cigarette-cases, all alike," stated the Colonel decisively. "Something plain, but very good; with just the date and a little inscription. A trifling, but lasting and useful, memento of . . ."

"And the ladies?" interrupted Angélique almost impatiently.

"Ah! There you can help me, *chèrie,*" smiled the Colonel. "Suppose I leave that to you."

"*Ah-h-h,*" breathed Angélique.

This was indeed a man. A great and good man, who, praise Saint Louis, was not so good as all that.

"But with the greatest pleasure," she said. "To do *anything* for *Monsieur le Colonel* would be a pleasure."

It would indeed—to do anything of that sort especially; and Angélique made rapid mental calculations. Ten girls beside herself. A little commission from the jeweller on each, and a very distinct understanding with each of *les girls* beforehand.

And something rather extra special in the way of gala gift for Mademoiselle Angélique Oui-Oui.

"I have an idea, *Monsieur le Colonel,*" she whispered, as the Management opened its door. "Let us go to *Tiffany, Cartier et Cie.* There will be more choice at their shop. This is but a small selection."

"Excellent," replied the Colonel.

And so it was. Truly excellent. Fancy entering the finest jewellers' in the whole place with a pretty girl, and giving her *carte blanche.*

What a night he was having!

And how one thing led to another! Heaven knew what it would lead to in the end; but it is the travelling, not the arriving, that makes the joy of travel. To reach the end is but to reach an end; but to go on for a long strange journey into unknown regions, *that* was to live and to savour life.

And this was a long strange journey into unknown regions, as *le bon Dieu* could testify!

"Look," said he, as the Management made to unlock the glass door of the case, "I'll have a set of those cigarette-cases, all alike if possible. If there isn't time for that, have them all about the style and size of that one . . . I won't choose the ladies' presents here. I think I shall go along to *Tiffany, Cartier et Cie,* and have a look at what they've got there."

"I will ring them up at once and tell them to have ready the sort of article *Monsieur le Colonel* might think suitable," the Management assured him helpfully.

He would indeed ring them up, both Tiffany and Cartier, not to mention *Cie,* and point out that any sales effected in the shop would count for commission on precisely the same terms as those made from the show-case in the hotel. And there was to be no nonsense about it either . . . Indeed, in view of the grandeur of the grand total, an extra five per cent. was most obviously indicated.

More happiness.

The gentleman who was *Tiffany, Cartier et Cie* was promptly rendered as happy as was the Management itself, and Mademoiselle Angélique Oui-Oui herself, though none of them naturally was as happy as Denis Ducros, the Dispenser of Bliss.

Quickly thereafter, the business of arranging the gala dinner being now concluded, the moment for relaxation and refreshment arrived.

An *apéritif* seemed to be indicated.

What did Mademoiselle Angélique fancy, by way of a little stimulant, at this time of the day?

At this time of the day, and in point of fact, at any other time of the day or night, Mademoiselle fancied a little sweet Champagne. And her preference being made known, the Colonel bade the Management produce a bottle of its best. Or no; on second thoughts, a half-bottle of its best, of that sort, for Mademoiselle; and a bottle of the High and Dry for himself.

If the Colonel would give himself the trouble to cross the foyer to the *fumoir,* the Management would itself see to the exact fulfilment of the order, and see that the wines were of the desirable degree of coldness.

As a connoisseur, Monsieur le Colonel would realise that none of such a wine as he had mentioned was kept permanently on the ice.

With but a wave of his hand, the Colonel accepted the Management's assurance, and with a gentle pressure of the other upon the bare arm of Mademoiselle, he escorted her to the *fumoir* and a comfortable couch in a quiet and discreetly screened corner.

As he and his attractive companion crossed the broad expanse of carpet, a girl, with a sudden start, seized the arm of her companion, a smart young officer of Spahis, and at the same time lowered her head so that the shady brim of her hat concealed her face.

"*Mon Dieu! . . . Mon père! . . .*" she whispered in horrified astonishment as the Colonel and his friend, in seating themselves upon the divan in the corner, disappeared from view behind a screen.

"Well, Beloved of my Soul," drawled the young officer, "I, of course, knew you were of the most divine origin, but . . . a daughter of Heaven?" . . .

"What do you mean, stupid? Don't you see?"

"No, I only heard. You seemed to be claiming *le bon Dieu* as your parent . . . But after all, of course . . ."

"Don't be an ass, Henri. Didn't you see who that was?"

"No. The blinding dazzle from the head-lights that you have for eyes . . ."

"Oh, shut up, idiot. Didn't you see two people just come over from the foyer and go across to that corner?"

"Darling, I see nothing, absolutely nothing but you, when we are together."

This, alas, was a deviation from the truth, for glancing up, Henri had seen, smiling full upon him, the well-known face of Mademoiselle Angélique Oui-Oui, and swiftly he had glanced down again.

Angélique was a good girl, and the soul of discretion; but she was smiling like a cat that has just had a saucer of cream; and when she looked at him, grinning like that, anyone might think that she was a— er—friend of his.

So she was, as a matter of fact; but an even closer

and more intimate friend of his friend Lieutenant Pierre de Pont-Chatelrie.

And of course it would be silly and awkward to have to explain to Rochefort that the lady with whom he had exchanged smiles was but the friend of a friend, and an almost total stranger.

It would not be convincing.

And he had looked away so swiftly that he had not so much as glanced at her companion.

But *what* had Marguerite said?

Her actual words had been,

"*Mon Dieu! Mon père! . . .*" in tones of the utmost consternation and alarm.

Nonsense!

Colonel Louis Rochefort of the Legion?

With Angélique Oui-Oui?

In the Grand Hotel?

Lurking in a corner behind a screen?

Rubbish!

It is a wise child that knows its own father, no doubt; but one might assume that Marguerite knew hers when she saw him . . .

Yet old Rochefort was about the strictest and most strait-laced officer in the Nineteenth African Army Corps, or any other. From taste and conviction too. It wasn't that Madame Rochefort saw to it that he was a model of propriety and virtue, for Colonel Louis Rochefort ruled the domestic roost as he did his official one, or any other in which he might find himself.

Colonel Rochefort—*Père Fait-en-fer*—as they called him, was about as likely to be behind that screen with Angélique Oui-Oui as to be on the throne of France or the backs of two elephants.

And a good job too!

For Lieutenant Henri de Valaubon had not the faintest desire to be introduced to Colonel Louis Rochefort in the present circumstances and environment. From what he had heard of the Colonel's views and opinions, manners and customs, he did not for one moment believe that he would look with favour and admiration upon the young officer—or anybody else—

who took Mademoiselle Rochefort to the Grand Hotel and sat in a quiet corner of the *fumoir* of that place of resort, drinking cocktails with her before taking her in, or out, to dinner.

The probabilities seemed greater that he would look upon him with an ice-cold eye that would suddenly turn to one of scorching flame, ere withering the offender to dust or blasting him to ashes.

What an appallingly narrow escape!

And the young gentleman, who was by no means lacking in courage of a high order, felt the effusion of a gentle but cold perspiration upon his reasonably lofty brow.

What about a strategic movement to the rear, as a preliminary to a complete withdrawal from this overcrowded field of love—and war? Why, he had suggested the meeting with Marguerite here at the Grand Hotel as being the one place in Sidi-bel-Abbès where they would be absolutely safe; and where he would not run the slightest risk of encountering the terrible Colonel in circumstances so compromising!

When he did meet him—and that would be when he could no longer postpone the painful pleasure—he would prefer it to be in circumstances very different from these. He was madly in love with Marguerite, and it was his highest hope and ambition to marry her, but he realised that he was already sufficiently handi-capped by impecuniosity, lowly military rank, and a certain reputation for—er—wildness, recklessness, and lack of balance and discretion, without adding to that handicap by so appalling a misdemeanour as this.

Why, Colonel Rochefort probably thought that Mar-guerite had never set foot in a place like this in the whole of her young, innocent life! . . .

In point of fact, it was the *bons Papas* who were innocent nowadays—and that wouldn't help him at all if the Colonel caught them here . . .

But—wait a minute! . . . What exactly was the Colonel up to? . . . Wouldn't he be just as dumb-founded and knocked all of a heap—at being caught in here with Angélique Oui-Oui—as would be Henri de

Valaubon, at being caught in that shady (oh, entirely shady) retreat, with the Colonel's daughter?

Doubtless! And would that make him love Henri more? Henri, the brazen scoundrel who had decoyed the innocent Marguerite there, and had added to this crime the greater one of having caught Marguerite's father there too!

Definitely time to withdraw in good order, and pray that they may not be taken in flank while crossing the enemy's front.

" *'Two people,'* darling?" he murmured. "And one of them your father? . . . Who then was the other?"

"I did not notice," replied Marguerite. "I saw Father —and that was enough for me! I nearly fainted!"

"A very interesting situation," reflected the young man. "Also an interesting speculation—as to what would have happened had we all simultaneously recognised each other."

"Yes, but who could it have been?" wondered the girl. "Who *can* it be? It couldn't be Mother. I should have known her without looking at her, so to speak. Besides, she'd never come here. And if she wanted to, Father would never bring her."

"Why not?" expostulated Henri. "There's nothing very terrible in . . ."

"Oh yes, there is, *mon cher* . . . You ask them."

"Shall I go over and ask the Colonel now?" smiled Henri.

"Yes," laughed Marguerite softly. "You go over and ask him if it is not a terrible thing that he should be making assignations at a place like this."

"And if he says *'No, certainly not,'* I'll reply *'Splendid, Sir, just what I said to Mademoiselle Marguerite. And here we are.'* "

Again Marguerite laughed softly.

All very well, and all very funny no doubt, but Henri should not be so terrified of Father . . . She herself was, of course, but that was different. She was only a girl, and fathers are very terrifying animals; and, among them, *ce bon Papa* must surely hold the record.

And she had to live with him . . . For the present,

anyway.

Yes; right and reasonable enough for her to go in fear and trembling, but Henri was a man—and didn't have to live with him.

Marguerite Rochefort did herself no little injustice. For, far from being a timid and nervous person who went in terror of her redoubtable sire, she was as much his true and worthy off-spring as she was that of Madame, his wife. Rather more so, in point of fact. As Colonel Rochefort frequently and a little wistfully remarked (behind her back, *bien entendu*), she was a chip of the old block and ought to have been a boy.

Nevertheless, she had a very wholesome respect for her stern strict father, and an irrepressible urge to stand from under when trouble appeared likely to fall upon her from that direction.

So while she could, to a certain degree, sympathise with Henri's feelings with regard to the Colonel, she had no intention whatsoever of admitting the fact.

Henri loved her and she loved Henri.

Henri would give his right hand to marry her, and it was time he gave her father some slight inkling of the fact. True, he was not exactly an eligible *parti,* though by no means an obvious detrimental. Indeed, had he any money on which to marry, there was no very apparent reason why they should not do so. Still, it would be rather a strong card in her father's hand, if, on being asked for her own, the Colonel said,

"You wish to marry my daughter? *Ah! . . . Indeed?* And on what do you propose to keep her? On your pay?" and Henri had to admit that the Colonel had guessed it, the first time.

Father would scarcely trouble to answer Henri's modest request, save with one of those looks—the kind that is said to speak louder than words . . . and you could easily supply the words yourself.

Nevertheless, Henri must arise above the Colonel's horizon; become a star, however tiny, in his firmament.

Father must certainly be made aware of him, though perhaps not just yet, in the *rôle* of aspirant for the honour of membership of his family.

A tinkling of glasses and a tinkling little laugh floated across, from behind the screen.

No, definitely this was not the moment for Henri to introduce himself.

But then again, might it not be the very identical moment? Might it not be the moment auspicious and fortunate beyond belief? The moment for making an unwritten, indeed unspoken, pact with Father? . . . Something like,

"You be nice about Henri, Daddy, and I'll be nice about . . . Whatever it is that's going on."

But what could be going on? Father never went on.

"Henri," she said. "On second thoughts, don't you think it might be a good idea if we put a bold face on the matter?"

"Not if you're the matter, darling. I should hate to see a bold face on you. Besides, I loathe second thoughts. Generally worse than first. Now third thoughts . . ."

"Listen, mannikin. Don't you think it would be a good idea if we summoned up just a little courage, and frankly showed ourselves to Father, and . . ."

"But, darling, he's seen you lots of times, and I'm sure he doesn't want to see me."

"In fact you're afraid of him, and . . ."

"Of course I am, darling. Terrified to death of him."

"Then when do you propose to make his acquaintance, my dear Henri?"

"Not while he's over there," replied Henri firmly. "Let me grow a bit bigger and stronger. You know . . . finer chest . . . more presence."

"Well, do you know, it occurs to me that while he is over there is just the time, a Heaven-sent opportunity."

"Oh darling, don't bring Heaven into this. I am sure it is no place for *le bon Dieu*. Besides, my Angel, really . . . I mean to say . . . It would be so embarrassing to barge in like that. Why, it would almost have a faint suggestion of implied blackmail about it."

"Yes, just what I thought," agreed Marguerite. "Sort of '*Oo—Daddy, aren't we naughty boys and girls? Haven't we caught each other out nicely? . . . Now we'll all be so nice to each other, and live happy ever after-wards.'* "

Henri gave an exhibition of horror that was scarcely exaggerated.

"My precious child! The clean potato, I beg."

And Henri reflected that completely innocent and honourable young ladies can contemplate a line of conduct quite barred to wicked men, such as himself.

How different is the feminine mind, bless it.

Now to any decent man this was the one occasion upon which the Colonel must not be discovered. Not on any account whatever. But to Marguerite, it was the opportunity of a life-time, a glorious gift from Heaven itself, and to be exploited to the utmost.

Terrible idea! . . . What they'd better do was to go while the going was good.

There came a sound of movement from behind the screen in the opposite corner, and the Colonel and his companion reappeared, he laughing heartily and An-gélique smiling the smile of a completely successful and happy woman.

Lieutenant Henri de Valaubon bent swiftly down, drew his handkerchief from his cuff and flicked the immaculate toe of his boot.

Mademoiselle Marguerite Rochefort equally quickly bent her head slightly, so that her large tilted hat hid her face from view. But her own view from her left eye remained almost unobstructed.

"Good Heavens!" she thought. "Where did Daddy find *that?* Well, well, well! You never know. Of all people on this earth! . . . I shall be catching Mother out, next."

And without taking much risk she peeped at her erring parent.

Poor dear old Daddy! She had never in the whole of her life seen him look so happy, so care-free, young and jolly. He *was* enjoying himself!

But at that very moment, Denis Ducros, who was indeed feeling happy, care-free, young and jolly, *and* enjoying himself, laughed even longer and louder at a whispered *mot* from his dear little Angélique; and Henri thought he felt Marguerite suddenly stiffen.

He was right; and well might Marguerite do so, for she had received a further shock.

That might be her father's face and form and figure, his style, manner and bearing. It might be his uniform, but it certainly wasn't his laugh.

And indeed, so great was his happiness and joy at his marvellous success, that Denis was growing careless. Had he had the slightest idea that among his audience would be Mademoiselle Marguerite, he would have made a better job of it. He would have laughed differently, would have laughed exactly as the Colonel did, on those rare occasions when laughter overcame him; and, wonderful mimic that he was, might very well have got away with it.

But he was laughing naturally now, and the spontaneous and natural laughter of Denis Ducros was something quite different from the Colonel's laugh.

In his innocent joy at giving pleasure, he was not so much forgetting himself, as forgetting the Colonel whom he was impersonating.

Homer nodded—and Denis Ducros laughed.

He laughed as he did when sharing a joke with Michel Aubraine or fat Natalie. And that laugh did not fully consort with the dress and dignity of Colonel Louis Rochefort. It was a lovely laugh, joyous, carefree, and straight from the honest heart of a happy man. But it was not Colonel Rochefort's.

And Marguerite knew it was not.

Quickly she looked up, with a swift searching gaze, at the face of the man who was passing in front of her. Amazing!

It was her father . . .

Very nearly . . .

No, it was not quite *le bon Papa.*

Or was it?

A truly wonderful likeness, and if it were not her own respected parent, who on earth could it be?

Of course it must be Father. She must be imagining things. When the Colonel was not solidly *en famille,* and *was* feeling happy, gay and care-free, he probably did have a different laugh from the one to which she was accustomed.

What was that proverb that she had learnt at her English finishing-school in London?

"A smile abroad is oft a scowl at home," was it? Yes. Daddy certainly scowled a good deal at home. Perhaps this was how he laughed abroad.

In the act of passing Marguerite and Henri, the Colonel, his attention completely engaged by Angélique, smiled, brushed upward the right-hand side of his moustache, and drawled,

"Ah! . . . Indeed?"

Yes, that was Daddy all right; but it was a different Daddy, so different indeed that one might expect his actions and reactions also to be different.

If it were her father, something ought to be done about it—in her own interests and those of Lieutenant Henri de Valaubon: if it were not her father, still more should something be done about it.

An extremely quick-witted girl, Marguerite changed her plan of campaign on the spur of the moment.

As the Colonel and Mademoiselle Angélique Oui-Oui passed from sight in the direction of the hotel-entrance, she nudged the still bending Henri.

"All right, cowardy," she said. "Come out of hiding."

"Phew!" breathed Henri, sitting up. "My nerves are not what they were when I was young."

"Your nerve isn't," replied Marguerite, "but it'll have to serve, for you are going to meet Father. You are going to be presented to him as my Boy Friend; and you've not only got to be brave and play the part of a man, but to play the part of my Young Man."

"I am only a simple soldier," murmured Henri, "but beneath this tunic beats a . . ."

"Listen, Henri, instead of talking. Do you wish to marry me?"

"It's the only thing I do wish, darling."

"At once?"

"Sooner than that."

"And if Daddy gave us his blessing?"

"We would fly . . ."

"Where to?"

"Well, at least as far as old Père Tiffany-Cartier."

"Oh, *Henri!*"

"And we'd come out of that Robbers' Cave with the finest ring they've got in the place."

"And then, Henri?" smiled Marguerite, slipping her hand in his.

"And then we'd go and call on every friend we've got, and tell them the great news."

Marguerite rose to her feet.

"Come along, my lamb," she said.

And the lamb went meekly and bravely to the slaughter.

Colonel Louis Rochefort, *pardieu!*

"We'll follow them," she said, as she and Henri passed through the still swinging door, inside which the Colonel had paused to light the magnificent cigar respectfully offered by the Management. "He's bound to say farewell to his girl friend in a minute or two, and then we'll pounce. We'll catch him while he's still feeling all gay, and . . ."

"Guilty," murmured Henri, who privately doubted whether, if he knew his Angélique, the moment of farewell was at hand. But perhaps the Colonel had a technique of his own for these occasions. Evidently a dark horse. Well, well, well!

"Look, he's grabbed hold of her arm again," said Marguerite.

The Colonel had indeed taken Angélique delicately by the elbow.

"Here we are, my dear," he said, with a gaiety surprisingly bright and youthful for a hard-bitten veteran of so many cares and responsibilities; threw open the net-curtained door of the brilliant emporium owned by Messrs. Tiffany, Cartier *et Cie;* and entered what was to him Aladdin's Cave of Enchantment.

From behind a black velvet portière appeared, as doth the prompt attentive spider, the stout and somewhat oriental-looking gentleman who was a host in himself, being not only two men and a *Cie* in one, but a most kindly host to all who walked into his parlour.

And Denis Ducros settled down really to enjoy himself . . .

Power and Glory!

He felt as though all the Kingdoms of the Earth were at his feet.

And scarcely less happy was the excellent Angélique of whom Henri's friend, Pierre de Pont-Chatelrie, was wont to testify that her kind good heart was even better than her morals.

"Now you choose just what you like, my dear," said the Colonel. "You will know better than I what will please your little friends." And to Messieurs Tiffany, Cartier *et Cie,* he gave a stern brusque order that he should put himself entirely at the lady's disposal and endeavour to give her every satisfaction.

Messieurs Tiffany, Cartier *et Cie,* concealing with a skill that equalled that of the Management of the Grand Hotel, whatever emotions he may have felt, assured the Colonel that it was his sole remaining ambition.

And promptly the kind good heart of Angélique manifested itself, both in the loving forethought with which she selected suitable little gala-tokens for her ten girl friends, and the kindly consideration with which she spared the Colonel's pocket. So far as the ten just women were concerned, *bien entendu.*

"And now, my dear," smiled the Colonel, when ten nice little *articles de Paris* had been selected, "You have neglected yourself. We can't allow that, you know. Something rather special for my kind little hostess."

And the Colonel's unwontedly smiling face positively glowed with generous satisfaction.

So did the heart of Messieurs Tiffany, Cartier *et Cie,* though the sharp edge of his acute mind was almost dulled with wonder.

Colonel Louis Rochefort . . .

Mademoiselle Angélique Oui-Oui . . .

Something rather special for his dear little hostess! Now just how special, and how dear?

But when it came to the selection of her own trifle, the girlish face took on a look that perhaps was rather more of the ingenious rather than the ingenuous.

"Oh, just something quite small," she murmured, with a flicker of long eye-lashes in the direction of Tiffany, Cartier and every one of the *Cie*.

Again a nod was even better than a kick in the ribs to a sharp-eyed horse.

And, as though by magic, there appeared on the black velvet cushion that rested upon the glass-topped counter, something "quite small," that seemed, to the delighted eyes of the Colonel, to sparkle more brightly than the electric lights themselves.

"Ah!" said he. "A little ring, one perceives. How elegant."

Tiffany, Cartier *et Cie* agreed that it was indeed of an elegance. A diamond, in short, of the very first water.

"Water? More like Champagne," laughed the Colonel merrily, and Tiffany, Cartier *et Cie* agreed that a noble wine was indeed more worthy of mention than mere water in connection with so beautiful a stone.

"It is real?" breathed Angélique in pretty wonderment.

Tiffany, Cartier *et Cie* agreed that the jewel was indeed of a realness.

A brief silence fell on the little group.

Angélique regarded the diamond; Denis regarded Angélique; and Tiffany, Cartier *et Cie* regarded both of them, and the diamond.

Angélique forbore to ask the price of so beautiful and valuable a thing.

The Colonel forbore to ask the price of such an obvious trifle.

And Tiffany, Cartier *et Cie* forbore to mention the price, lest it prove a bomb-shell that should blow the Colonel right out of the shop.

In his previous professional encounters with the Colonel, Messrs. Tiffany, Cartier *et Cie* had found him a very exigeant and careful buyer, prone to affect contempt for the article he was examining and incredulous horror at the price asked for it.

But this was a different man from the Colonel

whom Tiffany, Cartier *et Cie* had hitherto known, admired and respected.

"*Love!* . . . *Love!* . . ." whispered the *Cie* in the dark depths of its experienced bosom. What won't Love do?

One thing it would do evidently, was to turn a middle-aged military tiger into a silly old goat.

Well, well, well!

Sad, sad, sad!

And what about another five hundred francs on to the price? To a man in the Colonel's present frame of mind such a difference between one sum of money and another would be scarcely perceptible, and if it were it would be negligible. And if it were not, he could, to show his great generosity, sympathy and commercial honesty, simply knock it off again.

Drawing toward him a little pad to which a pencil was attached, he wrote upon it the amount at which the ring had been assessed, enriched by the imperceptible or negligible sum. Discreetly he displayed the figure in such a way that the Colonel, not to mention Angélique, might have some idea of the spaciousness of the business upon which he was embarking.

With a typically Rochefort wave of his hand, the Colonel acquiesced in the financial suggestion, and dismissed it from parade.

He was not interested.

Angélique was.

And the message of her bright brown eye was to Tiffany, Cartier *et Cie* as comprehensible as it was direct.

"Yes, yes, my child," he replied, without the use of spoken words. "That's where the extra five hundred francs come in."

Angélique again fondled the jewel with her eyes and her fingers.

"And so you'd like that one, would you, my dear?" said the Colonel.

"Oh, *M'sieur le Colonel!*" breathed Angélique, words almost failing her, but not quite; for, after another brief period of wrapt contemplation, she added, almost breathless with joyful excitement,

"Might I . . . Might I . . . take it *now,* and keep it till the party?"

For an imperceptible moment, the Colonel appeared to hang in doubt, as the cold spectre of Reality tried to materialise in the rosy mists that floated about his glowing landscape of golden Illusion.

He only wished to be happy, and to make others happy; to taste the heady draught of authority, rank and power; to act the great man, greatly, if but for an hour, and to act it flawlessly, with all his little world his stage.

But he didn't want to do any harm; anything really wrong. He was an honest man, and although he and Michel Aubraine had got up to some rare tricks, and had supported each other in divers remarkable escapades, they had never done anything criminal or incurred a punishment they could not take in their stride, or received a sentence they couldn't do on their heads, as they phrased it.

No, he was no gaol-bird, and he had no desire to become one, and it rather looked as though *cette petite* Angélique Oui-Oui was leading him from the path of virtue.

That might be her business. But it was his to remain on it—within reason *c'est à dire;* and, at any rate, not suddenly to turn off at right angles.

And this would be the wrongest of right-angles— obtaining a valuable diamond ring under false pretences.

To masquerade as the Colonel for fun, for his own diversion and that of his friends, and to satisfy a tremendous urge to strut for a brief hour in the limelight, was all very well; but to rob a jeweller was quite another thing—all very ill.

Yes, the little Angélique had put him in a rather difficult position; spoilt the game a little; and . . .

But no. Not a bit of it. No positions were difficult for Colonel Louis Rochefort. Or, if they were, he would very soon turn them into easy ones.

"Oh, but *ma chère amie,*" he replied almost at once, on a note of amused expostulation. "No, no, no. That would never do. Why, it would spoil all my pleasure in giving you the little token, and most of yours in receiving it—surely . . . No, No. It's a little gala gift to grace a gala dinner, and . . ."

"But of course, *M'sieur le Colonel,*" agreed Angélique, who realised that if a bird in hand was worth two in the bush, a bird selected, tied up and paid for by Colonel Louis Rochefort, might be regarded as being in the hand. On the finger practically.

Ah! That was better, breathed Denis. That marched. Back once more into the beautiful dream—of lovely jewels, fair women, and distinguished officers whose whim, pleasure and delight it was to present the one to the other.

"Well then, that's all, I think," said the Colonel, desirous of concluding the business on this pleasant, safe and satisfactory note.

"Now will you send those things round to my house some time to-morrow?" he said to Tiffany, Cartier *et Cie* . . . "With your bill, and without fail. Colonel Louis Rochefort, Foreign Legion."

Tiffany, Cartier *et Cie,* with deferential delight assured *Monsieur le Colonel* that he would indeed send the selected ten *articles de Paris* and the diamond ring to the Colonel's house by special messenger (whose duty and pleasure it would be to await the Colonel's signature of receipt), definitely on the morrow, undoubtedly with the bill, and assuredly without fail.

And with a brusque and condescending, *"Bon,"* the Colonel turned, opened the door for Mademoiselle Angélique Oui-Oui, and—Mademoiselle Marguerite Rochefort pounced.

CHAPTER 3

THE COLONEL'S DAUGHTER ADMIRES THE UNIFORM

"Why, *Daddy!*" she said in accents of surprise which gave no hint of the fact that, for at least half an hour, she had strolled, promenaded, and shop-window gazed, in the close neighbourhood of Tiffany, Cartier *et Cie,* with one eye upon its discreet door, and one hand metaphorically upon the leash at which Henri undoubtedly strained.

For, ardent and honourable lover as he was, Henri did not wish to encounter the Colonel just now—in such circumstances (to call Mademoiselle Angélique Oui-Oui a circumstance); in the street; in Marguerite's company; nor in the *rôle* of Marguerite's would-be fiancé.

The Colonel started, a trifle guiltily—as well he might, thought Henri—and then rose to the occasion as a Rochefort should, with a fond parental smile.

Mademoiselle Angélique Oui-Oui understood perfectly, and behaved as a nice girl should in all such cases. With a charming smile, a polite bow, a soft murmur of thanks, and a discreet word of farewell to her kind patron, she effaced herself, fading away as easily as fades a dream at day-break.

"This *is* fortunate," continued Marguerite, with a kindly enigmatic smile. "I have been meaning for some time to present to you my friend Lieutenant Henri de Valaubon of the Spahis. I met him in Paris, you remember, at Madame Lecamier's, and he has just come here from a course at Saumur or Saida or somewhere . . ."

"Why, of course!" smiled the Colonel in the most urbane and friendly manner. "You told me, I remember . . . And now the Lieutenant has rejoined his regiment here . . . You must bring him to meet your Mother, at

476

the earliest opportunity."

Denis Ducros felt that this was the right line.

Must be.

What was it that fat Natalie was saying, only the other day? Something about the Colonel being an absolute ogre where young men were concerned; and that if Mademoiselle didn't soon take matters into her own hands, including a young man or two, she'd die an old maid yet, pretty as she was . . .

Yes, the right line . . . the right line . . .

Must be . . . But for how long could he hold that line? . . . Was this the end of the little escapade that had been such an unqualified success. He knew *la petite Mademoiselle* Marguerite well enough, and surely she knew him? No disguise could be good enough, no acting clever enough, to deceive a daughter; to persuade her that a man, who was not her father, was her father, surely? At a little distance, and in a poor light, perhaps . . . Say from the other side of the street, at dusk . . . But close up like this, face to face? Not a hope.

Moreover, the voice, . . . every nuance of expression. Absurd.

If one, expecting to see a member of one's family, one's daily household company, *sees* what one expects to see, instead of what is actually there, the same would scarcely apply to hearing, surely?

A clever mimic can copy another person's social mannerisms and turns of speech—but a voice, after all, is a voice; and surely a daughter knows her own father's voice, and, moreover knows when a voice that is not her father's tries to imitate it.

An order, a familiar phrase, a wonted remark, yes, perhaps—but not a conversation.

And yet, here she was, actually holding a conversation, and giving no sign that she had any suspicions whatsoever. Unless that smile really were enigmatic and ironical, and not merely made to appear so by his guilty conscience.

Henri de Valaubon made suitable sounds, a confused and murmured expression of gratitude and delight. It was not often that he was, however briefly, deprived of his nonchalance, his air of complete social equanimity, but he was on this occasion, completely taken aback, and, as later he phrased it, he was knocked clean off his perch.

Could this be the grim and unapproachable Colonel Louis Rochefort? A man with a reputation, and an unpleasant one, for being difficult whenever it was possible, and as difficult as it was possible to be.

It was also well known that anyone who approached his daughter with covetous eyes, might as well covet his wife, his house, his man-servant or his maid-servant. He had no ox or ass.

No. It was generally supposed that it would be dangerous sport to attempt to steal the Colonel's daughter.

Yet here he was, positively beaming; one might say radiating affability and geniality.

And he, too, asked himself, though merely rhetorically, could *this* be the famous Colonel Louis Rochefort?

Well, he knew it was. But what a surprise!

Marguerite on the other hand knew it was not. But what a surprise!

Who *was* the man, and what was the game?

Well, whoever it was, the game should be hers while it lasted—and it should last, at any rate, until it had served her purpose.

And what an amusing game it would be if it were properly played. She'd play her part all right—that of the innocent person completely deceived. This for Henri's benefit—and ultimately her own. It was of course, absurd to suppose that the impostor should really think he was deceiving the Colonel's own daughter, clever actor and impersonator as he might be, and undoubtedly was.

What fun to fool him that she was being fooled; to lead him on and keep him guessing—guessing at what her game might be, and yet at the same time wondering all the while whether he was actually getting away with it, and, if not, when and where she would decide to denounce him.

Who could the fellow be? And was it a daring if dubious joke for a bet, or for the sake of the tremendous *réclame* inevitably consequent upon the remarkable feat of pulling the unpullable leg of Colonel Rochefort?

Probably some wild spirit among the officers of the garrison; but it was no boyish prank, for the man was obviously every day as old as the Colonel himself.

But it *must* be Father.

Of course it wasn't.

The uniform; the face; the bearing; the manner and mannerisms, might all be those of Colonel Rochefort, but the voice wasn't—quite. Not all the time. Something in the *timbre*. And the laugh was not his. And it was more than not-quite. Daddy didn't laugh—much; and, when he did, it had little connection with amusement or any feeling of gaiety.

Daddy was not amused, nor gay.

And if it had been his voice and his laugh, it certainly wasn't his behaviour. He would not have been at that hotel. He would not have been with that woman; and most certainly he would not have been with her in Tiffany, Cartier's shop.

Those were things Daddy would not have done; and one or two that he would have done would have been to bite Henri's head off and to enquire what the devil she was doing here at this time of the evening.

He would not have been affable, genial and friendly. He would have been extremely rude, overbearing, and ferociously parental.

No, she did not know who this masquerader might be; but he certainly was not her father.

Nevertheless, he was going to play a father's part, since he'd assumed that *rôle*; and he was going to play the part of a father-in-law-elect if she had any luck at all and if she were clever enough to prompt and guide him in both these manifestations.

"And where are you off to, my dear?" enquired the Colonel, having graciously accepted Henri's respectful and grateful greetings.

"Well, to tell you the truth, Daddy, we were thinking

of having a little dinner, together, at the Grand Hotel,"
replied Marguerite brightly.

"*Ah! . . . Indeed?*" said the Colonel, brushing his
moustache, as he smiled sardonically; and so authentic were the intonation of his voice and the gesture of
his hand, that Marguerite's own faith was shaken to its
foundations, and she all but quailed.

Henri was suddenly aware of the firm pressure of
Marguerite's elbow against his own.

Henri was a soldier, one of those who seek the
bubble reputation in the cannon's mouth or even in
the Colonel's mouth, and whose trade, profession,
vocation, and calling it is to step into the imminent
breach. This looked like an imminent breach, all right,
and into it Henri stepped with both feet.

"I wonder if you would do us the great honour of
joining us, Sir," he said, wondering at his own temer-
ity. What would happen now?

"*Do,* Daddy," seconded Marguerite. "We should love
it."

Again, Denis Ducros rose to the height of the
occasion in true Rochefort style.

Fate appeared to be in most friendly mood; his luck
to be most unwontedly in; and if Fate chose to give him
the opportunity of dining in style at the Grand Hotel
with a daughter of his own, and with a Spahi Officer,
her fiance, who was he to refuse that opportunity?

Vogue la galère!

How marvellously one thing was leading to another.
And what another!

But this piquant, charming and lovely girl!

Was he, Denis Ducros, as clever an actor as all
that?

It was clearly one of two things. Either he had
deceived her, or else she was attempting to deceive
him, for some reason best known to herself.

Anyhow, she hadn't denounced him to this Spahi
Officer, and presumably did not intend to do so—for
the moment. And until she did, he would play his part
as perfectly as it lay in his power to do.

On with the game!

The Colonel glanced at his wrist-watch in the Rochefort style. A tap on the right cuff with the left hand exposing the watch, a closing of the right eye and a fixing of the watch's face with a stare through the monocle (*and,* noted Marguerite, that *is* Daddy's watch. Curiouser and curiouser).

"Well," said the Colonel, "I should love to, but . . ."

"Oh, you must, Daddy," interrupted Marguerite, and held the Colonel's eye with a cool and compelling stare.

Not menacing, threatening or blackmailing, of course; but somehow it carried a message, and Denis hastened to assure the young lady that he had merely been going to say that he wouldn't be able to give them his whole evening, much as he would like to do so.

"Never mind, darling," replied Marguerite, who was not in the habit of thus addressing her formal and austere father. "We'll just have a quick dinner if you've got other engagements. That will be long enough for Henri to tell you something."

Henri made a curious little movement; again felt the firm pressure of a determined elbow; opened and closed his mouth as doth the gold-fish, and like the gold-fish, was dumb.

"Delighted . . . Delightful . . ." responded the Colonel, equally full of wonderment, not to say consternation, despondency and alarm, as was Henri, but far too good and conscientious an actor to permit his features or manner to register these awkward feelings.

"*En avant, donc!*" he said gaily, turned with the others in the direction of the Grand Hotel, and Sidi-bel-Abbès, like Linden, saw another sight to which it was wholly unaccustomed.

It was that of the unsociable and exclusive Colonel of the French Foreign Legion, walking, in bright merry converse with his daughter and a gay young subaltern of Spahis—a less *épatant* sight than that of the Colonel strolling with Mademoiselle Angélique Oui-Oui, but every whit as remarkable and rare.

In point of fact, both sights were unique. And those

who that night beheld both, felt that here were strange portents, and that old familiar landmarks were slipping indeed.

On the way to the hotel, Marguerite took charge of the conversation, and, as Denis soon realised, did so with a kind of light and bright malice that was rather disturbing. Could she, realising that he was an impostor, be leading him to the scene of his public exposure, disgrace and humiliation? Was he to be held up to the contemptuous ridicule of the habitués of the Grand Hotel, and the angry derision of the Management and his staff?

If so, let him like a soldier fall, when they threw him out on his ear.

Let him die game.

And let him hug to himself the satisfaction and joy of having so wonderfully fooled them; and of having had his bright, brief crowded hour of glorious life.

His Hour of Glory.

But somehow he felt that this managing young woman had some other end in view. Had she been merely leading him to the scene of his downfall, she would hardly have troubled to select and follow so persistently the subject of the manifold virtues of this probably admirable, but apparently quite ordinary, Lieutenant of Spahis.

Doubtless he was the military marvel and compendium of virtues that Mademoiselle Marguerite described him to be, even if he possessed nothing in the world but the beautiful uniform in which he stood up. But he seemed, with commendable modesty, to hide his light quite successfully.

There was one thing, no-one could say that he talked foolishly, for he didn't talk at all.

And there was another thing. Whatever the young woman suspected, thought or knew, there were no doubts in the mind of her young friend. If he were sure of anything in this uncertain world, it was that his distinguished companions were not only the Colonel's daughter, but the Colonel himself. He did not give the impression of being a young man who was easily daunted or disconcerted, but definitely he gave the impression of being a daunted and disconcerted young man.

So far, so good; and if nobody penetrated the disguise of Denis Ducros this night, save the daughter of the man he was impersonating, then it would not have been a bad job of work on the part of Denis Ducros.

There might be bad results, but the work wasn't bad; in fact, it would be its very goodness which would be its chief offence.

He began to feel a little sorry for the over-awed and tongue-tied young man. He must take his part against this over-confident daughter of his, and put him at his ease.

Lieutenant Henri de Valaubon responded sensitively and gratefully to the Colonel's kindness and condescension. Gradually he grew less uncomfortably diffident; and by the time the party reached the hotel, he was chatting freely, though respectfully, with Marguerite's redoubtable and awe-inspiring father.

So, for the second time in one evening, and for the second time in his life, Denis Ducros entered the lofty halls, of faded gilt and dusty velvet, of the *Grande Hôtel d'Algérie et de Maroc,* and trod their creaking boards with the firm and confident step of one accustomed to such splendour and luxury—or of one who was an actor of real genius, thoroughly enjoying the part which he was playing. The true Rochefortian manner in which he drew off his gloves, and arrogantly thrust *képi,* cane and gloves at the hovering menial, made Marguerite marvel again, and mentally award his performance the meed of grudging yet unstinted praise.

She was in excellent form, and particularly alert in mind. She was also going to have some fun, and very profitable fun too—with a little luck and a little innocent deception of poor dear Henri.

"Will you order dinner, Daddy?" she said, when the three sat down at the table selected by the Management as the most desirable for this most distinguished but most incredible party.

(Really! The spartan and unbending Colonel Rochefort, who did not enter the place twice in a year, coming in twice in a night—and, moreover, first with the Belle of bel-Abbès, and then with his own daughter and a very junior young officer. Had it not been that the young lady indubitably was Mademoiselle Marguerite Rochefort, it would have been almost enough to make the Management doubt either the evidence of its senses or the genuineness of the Colonel Commandant!)

Promptly the Colonel excelled himself.

If he couldn't run a depôt, he could order a dinner; and it was with genuine respect for his gastronomic knowledge and understanding that the Management took his orders, and, with deep regret, had occasion to point out that delightful and desirable as certain suggested items might be, they were, alas, unprocurable. In the end it was clear that, should the dinner fall short of perfection, the failure would be in the hotel's resources rather than in the Colonel's competence and hospitable spirit. Nevertheless, it was, all things considered, an admirable dinner; and partaking of it gave Denis Ducros almost as much pleasure as he had had in ordering it.

And that had been a great moment, one of the best of that great evening. As in the case of the gala dinner, the wines were most expertly chosen. Not the wine-steward at the *Cercle Militaire* himself, could have displayed a finer knowledge of vintages than did Denis, who was interested in the subject, and who had heard so much talk of wine as he waited at Mess and private dinner party.

With the affable kindliness of the older man, sympathetic and understanding, who wishes to put his young guest at his ease, he consulted Henri, who, flattered yet diffident, gratefully admitted, what was the simple truth, that his host knew far more about wine than he did.

And as the generous ichor warmed his veins, Denis again expanded, completely throwing off the slight sensation of doubt and constraint which, beneath the cool eye of the Colonel's daughter, had threatened to cramp his style and freeze the genial current of his soul. Quickly he regained completest confidence, lost every trace of diffidence, and not only played, to the life, the part of Colonel Louis Rochefort, but *was* the Colonel.

Marguerite admitted it. The only fault she had to find with the impersonator was that he was better than the original. So infinitely kinder; so much more human; so . . . lovable; and so very, very nice to Henri.

And *how* he became the Colonel's uniform; and how the uniform became him!

This was a Dream-Daddy. The sort of father she had sometimes, in fantasy, imagined as her own. Strong and all-wise, of course, but yet gentle, courteous and encouraging. Surely the truly polite man was as polite to his wife and daughter as to anybody else. Courtesy, like charity, should begin at home. But though Daddy was fundamentally a good husband and father, no-one could say he was a kind or pleasant one.

This man might be an impostor—of course he was an impostor—but how nice if she could wake up, rub her eyes, and find that this was her real, original and genuine Father! What a Father to whom to present Henri!

What a reception for her Henri to receive!

And what a blessed vista of bliss to be opening out before her now.

Who could he be? Why was he doing it?

He didn't appear to be doing any great harm, and there seemed to be no urgent reason for her promptly to expose him, the moment he had served her purpose. So long as he wasn't doing any serious or irreparable damage, there seemed no good reason why the joke should not go as far as he chose to carry it. Not that that could be very far, of course.

He was bound to come a cropper sooner or later, and, at most, the little game could only be played for that evening.

He could hardly go on parade in the Colonel's

uniform.

Probably, had she been the ideal *jeune fille* and perfect daughter, she would have denounced the wicked man as soon as she realised that he was a fraud. But she had never professed to be that, and until she discovered real and serious harm in it, she was quite disposed to regard the joke as a joke.

And to think of a joke—on Father, of all people in the world!

But wait a moment! What about that jeweller's shop? Might he not have stung Daddy pretty badly? Of course, if it were a common swindle she'd have to do something about it. Do that Duty, with a capital D, of which Father was so fond of talking.

Yes, later on she'd have to go along to the jewellers and make a few enquiries. The joke mustn't be carried too far, and though she began to think this bogus Father was a real dear, she was, after all, her real Father's real daughter.

Meanwhile she had never enjoyed a dinner-party more, for the situation appealed tremendously to her Gallic and impish sense of humour.

The sight of Henri, respectful, humble, on his best behaviour, making the politest of deferential conversation, and behaving like a school-boy in the presence of his headmaster, was delightful.

And to see this Unknown playing Colonel Rochefort simply fascinated her.

It was such a finished performance. He was so clever—*and* so nice.

It gave her, moreover, a rather delightful sense of power, to play just a little of the cat-and-mouse game with him, and to feel that, at any moment, she could bring him up with a round turn.

The whole affair was most extraordinarily piquant and most devilishly puzzling.

And if Marguerite was puzzled, so was Henri, for a different reason.

Untroubled by the shadow of a doubt as to the *bona fides* of the Colonel, and naturally supposing him to be the person Marguerite obviously knew him to be,

Henri's puzzlement was due to the amazing discrepancy between the descriptions he had heard of Colonel Louis Rochefort and the man himself. . . .

Rude?

Surly?

Sarcastic?

Unapproachable?

Unfriendly?

Unsociable?

Inhuman?

Why the man was geniality personified.

Rude? He was most courteous.

Surly? He was urbane.

Sarcastic? He was of a delightful simplicity and transparent kindliness.

Unapproachable? He was a living invitation to easy intercourse and pleasant confidence.

Unfriendly? He, Henri de Valaubon, had never met a friendlier person; never got on more delightful terms in shorter time. He already felt that he had known him for years.

Unsociable? He was the soul of hospitality. The perfect host. Fancy anyone using the word unsociable in connection with a Colonel of that seniority who could so swiftly and completely put a young subaltern at his ease and make him feel that, for the time being, there were no barriers of rank between them.

Inhuman? He was the most warmly human person he had ever met. Look at his attitude to his daughter. Look at him now, patting Marguerite's hand. Look at Marguerite laughing up into his face.

Had she been pulling his leg with these cock-and-bull tales of a stern parent who was a cross between a hungry tiger and a sore-headed bear?

He'd have a word with the young woman about this. Why, he might have gone to this father long ago—and he'd tell her so.

On the other hand . . . Wait a minute . . . What she'd said on the subject of the Colonel was a good deal less than what everybody else said. She had loyally defended him to the best of her ability, but, at the same time, had admitted that he wasn't exactly the sunshine of the home; that she didn't positively tie him round her finger; and that Henri had better lie low, walk warily, stand from under, and generally keep out of the Colonel's way until the propitious hour struck and she gave the word to him to emerge from the depths of that profound obscurity in which junior subalterns lurk unseen, unheard.

Well, it just showed how utterly false and unreliable gossip was.

Lies. Talk about rumour being a lying jade! They were an ill-natured lot in Sidi-bel-Abbès. But there . . . no doubt all garrison-gossip was alike.

Colonel Louis Rochefort was obviously one of the very best, and, so far from being repellant and intimidating, gave one the impression that it would be quite a simple matter, if not indeed a pleasure, to present oneself to him in the *rôle* of Marguerite's suitor.

And the Colonel's thoughts at that moment were curiously and beautifully reciprocal.

Seen through the rosy haze of the fumes of excellent wine, the young man seemed in every way admirable, charming and worthy—worthy to be the fiance and, ere long, the husband of his beautiful and attractive Marguerite.

Whatever lay in his power to do, should forthwith be done to encourage their hopes and facilitate their fulfilment.

How delightful a thing, to be able in some measure to avert that malign Fate so powerful and malevolent as to make it proverbial that the course of true love never does run smooth.

He turned his benign gaze upon the fascinating girl to whom he stood *in loco parentis*.

Never until this moment had he recognised and realised her irresistible charm. But then, of course, he had never hitherto smiled at her across the rim of his eighth glass of noble wine.

But let it not be thought that though he saw her clear, and saw her whole, he saw her double.

Denis was uplifted.

Denis was beside himself.

But Denis was not drunk. Not physically drunk, that is to say, with material nectar distilled by mortals, but intoxicated with the ichor of the gods, the heady draughts of Power, that most intoxicating of all immortal drugs. Sober as a judge and a model of deportment, he yet lived and moved and had his being in a world of fantasy and unreality.

He was now no masquerading servant. He was a king, a Midas, an Alexander the truly Great, and still more an Oberon, a King of Fairyland.

No, he had never realised how wise and wonderful, witty and womanly, appealing and precious a girl was this daughter of his, long as he had known her.

She should be happy. He would make her happy, bless her lovely smiling face . . . and dear little tricks.

And the boy too. Splendid young fellow. And all his life with its joys and sorrows, victories and defeats, still before him. He would give him a victory and a joy that would o'ershadow all others, and make him, on the very threshold of his fine career, a happy and delighted man . . . fulfilled.

He, Denis Ducros, would be that fairy godfather.

What a glorious thing is Power—when rightly used.

He turned his warm and benevolent, but by no means vinous, gaze upon the object of his thoughts, and smiled kindly, understandingly; almost, it seemed to Henri, affectionately.

"Sir," he began nervously, "there is something I want most respectfully, most humbly, to say to you. It is about M . . . M . . . Marguerite and . . ."

"I know, my boy, I know!" interrupted the Colonel, with a smile of the most paternal. "I know. You love her. She loves you. You want my consent. You have it."

Henri was overcome with relief, gratitude and joy. Springing to his feet, he wrung the Colonel's hand in an access of emotion almost too powerful for expression.

"Sir!" he stammered. "I do not know how to express my feelings, my joy and gratitude. I can only . . ."

And as, most warmly, he returned the ardent grip

of the young man's hand, Denis Ducros again touched the heights and wandered singing among the shining stars that also sang.

It was a great moment.

Almost the greatest of that great evening.

Marguerite showed immense control of her emotions, whatever these may have been. Obviously they included happiness, while not appearing wholly to exclude amusement. But then she had always been an unusual girl, who took a line of her own and cared little if it were not the one she might be expected to pursue.

And, amused or not, she thanked the Colonel prettily, but refrained from kissing him, a thing which Henri himself had scarce forborne to do.

But although she was not fluent in the expression of her feelings, she quickly gave signs that she was far from being placidly unmoved.

"And you really mean that Henri and I can now consider ourselves engaged?" she said.

"Most certainly, my pet," replied the Colonel. "Why not? Why not, indeed, from this very moment? Have I not only given you my permission, but my unfeignedly heart-felt blessing? I hope and pray that, from this moment, you may both henceforth walk in a fairyland of happiness without one cloud to darken the brightness of your path. . . . Engaged? Most certainly."

And as a demure eye strayed in the direction of Henri's beaming face, Marguerite asked softly,

"And may we announce it, Daddy? At once—to all our friends? Tell them we are to be betrothed? And may Henri give me a ring? And may I wear it from now?"

"But of course, my child. Tell everyone. Let Henri take you straight to the jewellers. Come out of the shop with his ring on your finger."

And Henri, no laggard in Love, as no laggard in War, again sprang to his feet.

"We'll go to that same jewellers that you yourself visited this evening, Sir. I suppose they're the best in Sidi-bel-Abbès?"

"Yes," agreed Marguerite. "By the way, Daddy, what were you buying at the jewellers' to-night?"

And Denis Ducros was brought for a moment, back to earth, as a straight and level gaze met his.

"I, my love? Well, since you ask, I was buying a rather nice little present for your dear Mother. In fact, a *very* nice one . . ."

That was a good lie.

And he could add to it and improve upon it.

"For *Mother?*" replied Marguerite, completely taken aback; for giving valuable gifts to his wife was certainly not one of the most noticeable of Colonel Rochefort's habits.

"Yes, my child. And how amazingly *à propos* and timely it turns out to be. Do you know what I shall quite unashamedly tell her? . . . Why, that it is in com-memoration of *this* great occasion."

"What is it?" asked Marguerite bluntly.

"Curiously enough, my child, a ring. Rings are very much on the *tapis* to-night, aren't they?" he laughed easily. "Yes, it will not only celebrate your engagement, but commemorate our own. She will be quite touched when she receives it to-morrow."

"She will indeed," agreed Marguerite thoughtfully.

"You feel, Sir," asked Henri hopefully, "that Madame Rochefort will be as kindly disposed and acquiescent as yourself?"

"I am sure she will, my dear boy. I am sure she will," the Colonel assured him.

"If I say so," he added, out of his considerable knowledge, both deep and wide, of Colonel Rochefort's habit of "saying so," and his wife's custom of prompt agreement.

"Oh, yes, Mother will be glad," said Marguerite. "If only because Daddy is. She wouldn't dream of raising the slightest objection—*when she hears we've told everybody in Sidi-bel-Abbès to-night that we're engaged,* and she sees me wearing your ring.

"Come on, Henri darling," she begged, "I'm too excited to sit still another minute."

Rising to her feet, she gave the Colonel, who also

rose, a long and searching look.

"Thank you," she said. "Thank you for all your wonderful help. You have made us very happy, and have made it—er—possible for us to have a life-time of happiness together. And I *do* admire your uniform, Daddy."

Bending quickly forward, she impulsively kissed the Colonel on both cheeks; and the heart of Denis Ducros nearly burst within him.

A minute later she and Henri had departed, and the Colonel was on his way to the telephone.

"*Hullo! Hullo!* Is that Tiffany, Cartier *et Cie?*"

"*Oui, Monsieur,*" replied the suave voice of the firm.

"Colonel Rochefort is speaking."

The voice of the *Cie* became even more suave. It became warm, respectful and ingratiating.

"You know that little parcel of odds-and-ends I ordered this evening?"

The firm did indeed remember it. It would never forget it. It had given it the very greatest pleasure of a life-time to be privileged to . . .

The Colonel cut short the oily flow of compliment.

"Well, look. There was a ring, wasn't there? I've changed my mind."

Tiffany, Cartier *et Cie* groaned almost audibly.

There was indeed a ring. A *pièce de resistance.*

"Well, I want the ring directed to Madame Rochefort instead of to myself. The bric-à-brac can be sent to me under separate cover.

"My daughter is just coming along with her fiancé."

An ecstatic sound escaped from Tiffany, Cartier *et Cie,* and was quite audible at the Colonel's end of the telephone.

"Should she make enquiries about that ring, and say that she would like to see it, I have no objection. Understand? . . . The ring . . . To Madame Rochefort . . ."

Possibly for the first time in its life, Tiffany, Cartier *et Cie,* permitted a falsehood to escape its lips, and most emphatically it declared that it understood.

Fully. Perfectly.

Whereas it was extremely puzzled; and it entirely failed to understand why a valuable diamond ring, purchased with and for Mademoiselle Angélique Oui-Oui, should now be sent to Madame Louis Rochefort!

Shrugging his shoulders almost to his decorative ears, while raising eyes and palms of wonderment, Tiffany, Cartier *et Cie* permitted himself the ghost of a chuckle, and replaced the receiver as the Colonel rang off.

What a man! What a man!

To get little Angélique Oui-Oui to choose, as for herself, the ring that he intended for Madame, his wife!

Outside the telephone-box the Colonel paused a moment in thought.

Excellent. It was high time Colonel Louis Rochefort gave his wife a present. And if he didn't like the ten *articles de Paris* with which on the morrow he would be enriched, he could say so.

Doubtless he would.

Smiling to himself, Denis strode to the foyer, accepted his *képi,* stick and gloves from the obsequiously hovering attendant, and turned his haughty gaze upon the head-waiter, who with many bows, ventured to approach, bearing a discreetly folded bill upon a plate.

"Pencil," he growled, and the head-waiter having in the manner of a conjurer produced one from nowhere, he added a further ten per cent tip to the *addition,* as well as a completely undecipherable scrawl which the head-waiter was at liberty to read as L. R., since it was quite as likely to be those letters, as the more relevant D. D. of Denis Ducros.

The head-waiter, a large and greasy man whom Denis had detested at first sight, and loathed on second thoughts, bowed from the waist, bowed from the hips, almost bowed from the ankles, as mentally he allotted to his own private pocket, ten per cent of this good bill, as well as commission on the wines.

His thanks were profuse and profound.

"Give that to the Manager," ordered Denis, returning the bill, "and bring me a cigar."

In a minute the obliging man returned, not only

with a cigar but with several boxes of cigars, and from the best of these, Denis made a selection.

The head-waiter again admired a man who understood cigars as well as he did wines, and who unerringly selected the best brands.

Personally accompanying the Colonel to the entrance, the head-waiter paid honour where honour was due, by anticipating the hall-porter, and opening the door with his own hand.

Inhaling deeply, as one who appreciates fresh sweet open air after a stuffy interior, or perhaps as one who has just made successful escape from a somewhat dangerous situation, the Colonel strode on, in search of fresh adventure.

CHAPTER 4

THE PATH OF GLORY LEADS BUT TO . . . ?

What an evening he was having!

What a day to look back on, if he lived to be as old as Père Pinard!

Now what? . . .

Leave it to Fate, to Chance, to the whim of *le bon Dieu*; for to-night indeed *le bon Dieu* seemed to be feeling whimsical.

He apparently had no need to go in search of adventure, for adventure appeared to come in search of him.

The Colonel's daughter! . . .

And he had played fairy godfather to that enigmatic and forceful young woman.

And what part had she played?

Had she recognised him?

No; he thought not.

But she had used him . . . Had known him for an impostor and had used him.

Hallo! Here came the man they called Bacchus. A bad man if ever there was one. And not a bad man of the best sort, either. A bad man of the worst sort. A damned rogue in fact. And here was a chance to put a spoke in the wheel of the chariot of Bacchus. At the very least he could give the blackguard as uncomfortable a night as he had ever spent, and at the most he could put the permanent fear of Colonel Louis Rochefort into him. Especially if he were fuddled with assorted wine, absinthe, gin, and *tchum-tchum* spirit, as was more than probable.

Even if Bacchus came to learn to-morrow of the great feats of *le légionnaire* Denis Ducros, in his for ever-to-be-famous impersonation of the Colonel, he would never believe that it was not Colonel Rochefort who had stopped him in the *Rue de Daya* and given him the dressing-down of a lifetime. It would clip his wings and cramp his style for the rest of his service.

The *légionnaire,* christened Bacchus by some learned wag, suddenly catching sight of the Colonel, transformed himself from a rollicking, rolling, leering, laughing *légionnaire* into a model of military propriety and deportment, drew himself up to his full height, squared his shoulders, and achieved a salute that was positively violent in its speed and smartness.

The Colonel ignored the salute, but not the man.

"Halt! You!" he said quietly, his voice cutting in its stern coldness, his eyes like agate.

And Bacchus stood smartly to attention, a model mercenary, a perfect Soldier of Fortune, and of many campaigns . . .

Yes. That's what he's impersonating, thought Denis; he's doing the Bluff Old Soldier . . . the *Vieux Moustache* . . . the Hardy Veteran of Old Wars . . .

The damned, soaking, scrounging, swindling bully and sponge . . .

And, in a voice icy with contempt, he took this God-sent opportunity of saying what he had long thought.

"Name and number?" he demanded.

The man supplied the information promptly.

"Ah! . . . *Indeed?* And known to fools who frequent your society, as Bacchus, I understand."

"Oui, mon Commandant," smiled Bacchus, a little fatuously.

"I wonder the god doesn't strike you dead," mused the Colonel. "Such filthy blasphemy.

"As I look at you," he continued, "I see a fat-bellied, fat-faced fraud, with far too much hair on his head, and what would be far too much hair on his face, save that the beastly fungus does serve partly to conceal it.

"Yes, a horrible bush of hair, behind which is a horrible face . . . The face of the most detestable type on earth, the *faux bonhomme.*

"Do you know what you are? . . . Answer me. . . . Do you know what you are?"

"Mais, oui, mon Colonel," stammered the now alarmed Bacchus.

"So do I," continued the Colonel. "You're that God-forgotten—or God-damned—thing, a Character, who is also a humbug. . . . You pose. Yes.

"Great, fat, lousy brute that you are; gross, greedy and vile; you actually *pose*—like a pimping, posturing pansy of the lowest stews—for tourists.

"You grow that filthy mop of hair, and that filthy barrel of lard that is your stomach, and deliberately you play a part:—The Jolly, Jovial, Rollicking Bacchus . . . And you get photographed, living up to the name that some fool gave you, or that you gave yourself.

"In the canteen you roar,

" *'Behold me! I am Bacchus. Pour libations,'* and the wretched recruits, who are your victims, have to pour —or it would be the worse for them.

" *'See how popular is Bacchus,'* you bawl. And the little herd of swine that surround you, and follow you in the hope of getting the leavings that you yourself cannot quite drink, agree that you are popular, and bid the recruits, or the fool with money, to pour yet more libations, and yet more—enough for them all.

"And what do you do for the recruits in return? Eh, you foul reptile?

"You rob them. And that's only the beginning of it— and the least of it . . . You debauch, deprave and pervert the weaker ones. And what do you do to a strong one who resists and defies you?"

The Colonel lowered his voice to a very audible whisper.

"What did you do to Harald Petersen? Why did he commit suicide?" he asked; and the question was a terrible accusation and indictment, for Bacchus involuntarily stepped back a pace, his mouth opened, and the high colour of his flushed face was abated.

He gazed and gaped in horrified amazement.

"And to Grégoire Flammand?" asked the Colonel.

The *légionnaire's* eyes and mouth opened wider for a moment.

"And to Anastasiadi, the Greek? A good sturdy lad that," said the Colonel, cold hate and anger blazing from his eyes. "Shall I tell you what you did? You

followed him from the camp; and, walking silently on
sand, you came up behind him and clubbed him on
the head. . . . As he lay unconscious, you had the
courage to kill him with your bayonet. You robbed his
corpse and then buried it, an inch-or-two deep in the
sand. Next day the Battalion marched on, and poor
Anastasiadi was written off as a deserter."

Bacchus appeared to be about to faint. His lips
moved, but he was either unable or afraid to say a
word in self-defence or exculpation.

"Didn't know that I was so well-informed, did you?"
asked the Colonel, in a voice of immeasurable, inexora-
ble doom.

"No. You thought that only a few of the vile clique
that are your accomplices knew of your crimes—thefts
innumerable, persecutions, bullyings and an occasional murder. Well, you were wrong. . . . I know all about
you; and I only wish that I had known sooner.

"*However . . .*"

And to the scoundrelly Bacchus there was a world
of terrible threat in that last word. The game was up.
And the sooner he quitted the Legion the better.

Privately, Denis Ducros thought that he had not
only given a first-class exhibition of acting, but that he
had done a really useful piece of work as well.

The ruffian was evidently frightened to the very
depths of his soul.

No. Say to the depths of his being, for he had no
soul.

And Denis Ducros had enjoyed himself enormously.
Not only were there private and peculiar scores of his
own to pay off; but as he had shown the brute, he had
considerable knowledge of abominable villainies that
did not personally concern him. If he did no more than
frighten the fellow, he'd have done something; and the
probability was that he wouldn't have a comfortable
moment for many a long day to come.

Well, he'd give him a bit more of it and let him go—
with something to think about.

"Yes," he said, his gaze boring into the flinching
eyes of the amazed and terrified man, "and how did

you know that Anastasiadi had just received some extra money from his well-to-do father in Athens? . . . Eh? How did you know? . . . Answer me, you dog."

The terror-stricken Bacchus tried to moisten dry lips with a dry tongue.

"I'll tell you," continued the Colonel, "since, for once in your life, you haven't so much to say for yourself. It was that damnable rogue, the *vaguemestre*,[36] your confederate, who put you up to it. . . . Yes. I wonder how many poor devils that unspeakable swine has robbed of their wretched sous and francs—sent to them from poverty-stricken cottage homes, as often as not. When it is that sort of pickings, of which the intended recipient knows nothing, because the noble *vaguemestre* destroys the covering letter enclosed with the money, the thieving jackal can manage without your help.

"But when a man gets a letter saying that a bigger sum of money is coming under registered cover, he has to hand the draft over. . . . And that's where you come in, eh? On commission.

"And if you can't get the fellow so drunk that you can rob him, you're not above murdering him for his money."

The Colonel eyed the trembling wretch with loathing.

"Yes. I think I've got your complete *dossier,* my good Bacchus," he added. "And if there should be anything missing from it, I shall have that too, pretty soon. *And the full record of your fellow criminal's filthy breaches of trust as postmaster.*

"I'll have you both."

And as he turned to go, leaving the man apparently rooted to the *pavé,* he slowly looked him up and down from head to foot, and murmured apparently to himself,

"Eight years *travaux forcées* with the Penal Battalions? Or shot out of hand? . . . Better dead, I think, on the whole—and that *sale scélérat* of a *vaguemestre* too. I'll send them both before the Oran General Court

---

[36] postmaster sergeant-major.

Martial . . ."

And Denis Ducros went on his way rejoicing, grinning to himself while he contemplated the utter consternation and incredulous dismay of the vile Bacchus, as he attempted to realise and grasp the impossible truth that Colonel Rochefort knew all, knew everything, about him . . . that the Colonel himself, that terrible man, knew of his association with the rascally postmaster in robbing his comrades; knew of the reasons for certain curious suicides; of a few unexplained disappearances; and of three or four plain murders in barracks, camps, and side-street dives . . .

He'd pass a merry night of it!

And better still, he'd hurry straight to the *vague-mestre,* and tell him that the worst had happened, that the Colonel had, in some incredible fashion, learnt all about them—literally *all*—and that it was up to him to stand from under . . .

The Colonel almost laughed aloud as he contemplated the scene.

Bon Dieu de Grace! They'd both promptly desert that very night, if they didn't commit suicide. In either event it would be a case of excellent riddance to vile rubbish, and Denis Ducros would be as deserving of thanks and reward as would be any other public benefactor.

How many of his shots-in-the-dark had hit the target? All of them, by the look of Bacchus. Not unnaturally either, for the crimes of which he had accused him were not mere figments of barrack-room imagination, nor begotten of *caserne* gossip.

And lots of them, including himself, had every reason for feeling perfectly certain that remittances from home, financial gifts from friends, or payments due to them and sent by post, had never got past the thieving rogue who held the present office of *vague-mestre*—a post of strong temptations to a dishonest man.

So easy to swindle the poor brow-beaten *légionnaire,* to whom it would never occur to contradict, much less to accuse, a non-commissioned

500

officer. Yes, the *vaguemestre* was going to have a night of it, whatever else he had! . . .

And now what? Another little drink? Music? More of the delightful, feminine companionship? Some dancing? . . . Anything . . . Anything . . . Everything in fact . . . All in due course.

And whatever else he did, he must get the largest possible number of the boys together and give them a good time. . . . Wine unstinted. Good wine too. White and red. Colonel Rochefort didn't do nearly enough of that sort of thing—and it was high time that he improved his ways.

He should start this very night, and earn himself a much more desirable reputation for generosity to his deserving *légionnaires*.

Why, what man on earth had finer opportunities; a more accomplished collection of distinguished drinkers; an assemblage of united thirsts more worthy of the very finest efforts of a great and generous Quencher?

Well, this very night, this Night of Nights, the Colonel in the *rôle* of Quencher, should match himself against his men in their common *rôle* of Walking Thirsts; and it would be seen who won, and which outlasted the other, the Colonel's generosity or the *légionnaires'* capacity . . .

Meanwhile—to promenade himself in his Uniform of Glory and await what should befall.

And even as he made this excellent resolution, the Colonel found himself passing the hospitably open doors of the wine-shop, well, if unfavourably, known, as *The Little Dog and Lamp-post.*

Definitely there was a sound of devilry by night, a sound that plucked at the Colonel's heart-strings. For while a party of *légionnaires* was beautifully singing *Le Boudin,* a right rousing chorus, another party was equally beautifully singing an equally rousing but quite different chorus.

What a pity! What a great pity—that one's rank prevented one from entering a place where such an aura of good-fellowship mingled with such an odour of good wine.

A thousand pities that it should prevent . . .

But then . . . after all, why should it?

It was a lonely life, being a *Chef de Bataillon;* but was it quite necessarily so? Did not the loneliness arise, to some extent at any rate, from a somewhat overweening and mistaken sense of exclusiveness and dignity?

And a man who always stands upon his dignity, generally has little else upon which to stand.

To Hell with such nonsense as exclusiveness, starched superiority, and cold, stiff, unfriendliness.

The Colonel halted, hesitated, and was lost.

Or found.

Undoubtedly found entering the portals of *The Little Dog and Lamp-post*—by the eye of an earnest drinker, industriously endeavouring to empty a full wine-bottle without once removing it from his lips.

At first, as the pre-occupied and unobserving eye fell upon this astounding vision, it merely dismissed it for what it appeared to be—an astounding vision, much of the astonishment arising from the fact that so strange a manifestation should appear so early in the evening.

Why, thought the earnest and industrious soldier, this is only my—what would it be now—second, third, fourth bottle? I can't be very well . . . Seeing the Old Devil walking into the *Dog,* as large as life. Running into the *Lamp-post. Hee, Hee! . . .*

And a sudden rush of hilarity to the head caused the visionary to fail in his brave effort to empty his fourth bottle in one breathless attempt.

With the bubbling cry of some strong drinker in his agony, he banged the bottle down upon the zinc-topped table, pointed accusingly at the phantom which had arisen before his bright young eye, and began, with a hiccup, an impassioned speech.

But beyond the introductory regurgitation, it was not delivered, for suddenly he realised that the as-tounding spectre of Colonel Rochefort was no spectre at all, but the very self of that terrible man.

Yes. Advancing upon him, Miguel Gonzales, was the

Colonel himself, in gold-braided *képi,* gold-braided, five-*galon*-sleeved tunic, treble row of medal and decoration ribbons, riding-breeches and boots, and gloved left hand grasping his other glove and cane, as usual.

There could be no doubt about it, and the first instinct of *le légionnaire* Miguel Gonzales was that of any good soldier, to give prompt warning of the approach of the enemy.

Bereft of speech, and the power to rise, he kicked his *copain,* Cristobal Braganza, and pointed.

This good man was also drinking from a bottle, though not with any foolish and incontinent ambition to empty it at one fell swipe. Rather was he gently lubricating what he termed his works, while washing the day's dust from his throat with a soothing, life-giving trickle.

This silent and beneficent flow suddenly and unexpectedly changed to a shattering, breath-taking gargle.

Glancing at the Colonel, he removed the bottle from his lips and was thereupon delivered of a sound of which the amazing volume was equalled only by its incredible and gross impoliteness.

Using the bottle as a kind of wand wherewith to wave away the approaching apparition, he choked, swallowed, fought for breath, and found words.

"*L-l-look!*" he cried. "Name of the Name of the Name of a Pale Pink Hippo-pippo-pippohotamus . . . Look what's happened to us."

And blinking rapidly, the stricken warrior waved his hand to and fro across his eyes as though to dissipate the horrid and nightmarish figment of a dream, the wine-born monstrosity of delirium.

At his loud and violent cry of "*Look!*" all heads turned in the direction in which the two men stared and pointed, and a sudden and complete silence fell upon the noisy *bistro,* as the amazed revellers stared incredulous.

One after another, as the completely impossible truth dawned upon them, the *légionnaires* sprang to attention, and stood as though petrified. Petrified literally, for like rocks they stood, though one or two suggested, perhaps, those phenomena known as rocking stones, vast boulders whose unstable equilibrium can be disturbed by the touch of a child's hand.

Each grim face, whether the years of its owner were sixteen or sixty, assumed as innocent a look as was possible; and, to the Colonel's informed eye, some of the achievements went beyond the possible, for on the whole the most blackguardly villains contrived the most lamb-like and endearing expressions.

Old Stenko Schenko there, for example, looked more like a kind of missionary to the other heathen, than what Denis Ducros well knew him to be.

But the thoughts of the blank-faced *légionnaires* as they regarded their Colonel, were neither lamb-like nor loving.

Now what was this, thought they. What new sort of military heresy-hunting and sin-smelling-out was the damned old witch-doctor up to now?

Weren't there enough non-coms and pickets and military police about, that the Old Devil himself must do their dirty work?

Was there no peace on earth? Not even in one's favourite wine-shop? Where could a man take his ease? Or was there a new law in the Military Penal Code that no soldier should have any peace at all, ever? Anywhere? Anyhow?

It was a damned shame.

One fine fellow, the most rigidly upright and motionless of them all, doubtless overcome by such thoughts and emotions rather than by wine, fell back on the bench on which he had been sitting, buried his face in the greasy interior of his *képi*, burst into tears, and sobbed bitterly.

And the Colonel? The infernal back-breaking, heart-breaking, nerve-breaking old devil of a martinet, with whom Satan would almost certainly refuse to share Hell, what would he do about it? Give poor old Georges thirty days cells for a start?

What the Colonel did do, was to make his dignified

way to where Georges sat and wept.

"There, there, there, *mon pauvre* Georges!" soothed the Colonel, who greatly admired and dearly loved this old comrade of many a march and bivouac, many an escapade and fight.

"Cheer up, *mon gars,* and have another bottle of wine."

And his comrades, while still refusing to believe the evidence of their senses as to the words they had heard and the scene they were witnessing, moved only automatically and as in a dream, in obedience to the Colonel's sharp command which followed.

"Stand at ease."

"Sit down, all of you," was the next order, and obediently they resumed their seats upon chair and bench.

"A litre of white wine for each man, unless he prefers red," called the Colonel brusquely to the fat Spaniard who stood gaping goggle-eyed and open-mouthed at these most amazing proceedings, his big hands resting like a duck's feet on the wine-slopped zinc bar behind which he lurked like a gross spider.

"And send the bill in to me to-morrow," added the Colonel, as bowing frequently and rapidly, the proprietor of the *bistro,* babbling incoherently, began to snatch bottles from the shelves behind him and to plank them down upon the bar.

"There you are, *mes enfants,"* beamed the Colonel. "Drink my health, and drink heartily. And if there is any greedy and ungrateful *salaud* here, for whom a litre of wine is not sufficient, why—let him order another, the stout soldier."

And ere the stricken *légionnaires* could collect themselves sufficiently to realise what had actually happened, the Colonel, with a parting wave of the hand, a gesture that was a benediction in itself, turned upon his heel to leave them to it, free to enjoy themselves and to make merry without the embarrassment of his presence.

Automatically, and as one man, the *légionnaires* sprang to their feet. Even if the amazement caused by this incredible event had been so great as to deprive them of their reason and of all knowledge as to who and what and where they were, their sub-conscious military minds knew what soldiers should do when their Colonel turned to go. They arose as one man, and stood at attention.

"Sit down, sit down, *mes enfants,*" cried the Colonel cheerily, glancing back over his shoulder. "Sit down and drink—till you can't stand up again . . . That's the style."

Georges removed his *képi* from before his tear-stained face, and with it mopped his streaming eyes.

"Was it the Colonel or a blue elephant?" he asked.

"Both," answered his *copain;* an ungrateful remark as he was in the act of drinking the Colonel's wine. "Both, since the one is as likely as the other."

"*Was* it actually the Old Devil?" enquired another, as he removed his bottle from his lips in order to take breath.

"This is actually Old Wine, anyhow," replied a realist, returning his bottle to his lips in order to take drink as well as breath.

"The Old Devil must have gone mad. Heaven is rewarding him at last . . ." suggested another *légionnaire.*

"And us," supplemented his friend.

"Let us pray for him," suggested Miguel Gonzales.

"Let's drink up his wine, and go while we can, more likely. There's a catch in it somewhere—naturally," replied Cristobal Braganza.

"There is another *litre* in it somewhere, for each of us—if we're quick," observed Georges.

And the company settled down to what had now become the very serious business of the evening, puzzled, perturbed, yet pleased. For though dreams are dreams, and hallucinations are hallucinations, this was wine.

Eh bien! Que voulez-vous? C'est la Légion . . . and in the Legion anything, whether of earth, heaven or hell, can happen—even drinks from a crusty and crapulous Colonel.

CHAPTER 5

STILL ON THE PATH OF GLORY

Meanwhile that gentleman—or rather his admirable counterpart—strolled on, stroked his moustache from time to time, and smiled happily upon all and sundry; for he was feeling magnificent, glorious, positively on top of the world.

That little incident had done him good, and had made him really happy. It had given the boys a very great deal of real pleasure; it would cost Colonel Rochefort such a very little, with wine at three-half-pence a bottle; and look at the tremendous increase it would give his popularity!

One might in fact put it more strongly than that, and say that it would give him the first popularity he had ever had.

And how the story would spread, until there wouldn't be a *légionnaire* between Colomb Bechar and Bizerta, between Oran and Fort Zindernouf, who had not heard of how Colonel Rochefort walked into a wine-shop in Sidi, and treated all the boys to all they could hold, and any amount that they could not . . . Do his reputation a world of good. The generous fellows would be the first to admit that they had misunderstood him, and that he was as noble and as human as themselves.

They'd enjoy their wine in *The Little Dog and Lamppost,* but even more would they enjoy the thought that their Colonel was, after all, *bon camarade et bon légionnaire,* however exalted his rank.

No. Denis could not feel that there was any load upon his conscience or stain upon his character—so far—in having pledged the Colonel's credit.

Bon Dieu! What a wonderful evening it was turning out! Really worth coming to the Legion for; worth all the sweat and suffering; the gruelling work of marching and road-building; the *cafard*-inducing monotony and misery of desert out-post life.

A perfectly marvellous evening. Incredible. The night of a life-time.

And it had all grown out of his trying on the Colonel's *képi* in front of the Colonel's mirror.

An hour or two ago and he had been a servant in a green baize apron.

And now look at him. And look at what he had done. And even that should be nothing to what he would do before he had finished.

Colonel Rochefort had never had such a night. There was a man who didn't make the most of his opportunities. He ought to come out like this of a night; see a bit of life, and take a hand in it too.

Why, he wouldn't know himself if only he found himself feeling as Denis Ducros did at this moment.

He could hardly put it into words. He felt like . . . he felt like . . . Who was the fellow? Sheikh Somebody, wasn't it? *The Boulevardier of Baghdad.* Devil take it, what was his name? Well, he couldn't remember it, but he felt like him . . . Used to go about of an evening all round the town, in Baghdad, and do just what he liked . . . Have a splendid time, and give other people a splendid time too. Whoop it up for the down-and-outs, and give the pompous officials and oppressors a kick in the pants. Had power, and enjoyed it—just like Denis Ducros was doing this blessed night. Blessed night indeed! . . .

And a passing German *légionnaire,* while saluting with automatic precision and an expressionless face, was astounded to see his Colonel smiling, and to hear him humming beneath his breath,

Stille nacht; heilige nacht . . .

He, Hans Weissmann, must have been drinking, and yet he had come out from barracks without a *sou,* and he had met no comrade who could and would treat him.

Or perhaps it was the Colonel who had been drinking? And yet he knew, everyone knew, that the Colonel never drank. Not even water, it was said, for no-one had ever seen him drink on the march.

Evidently he, Hans Weissmann, had an attack of *le cafard* coming on. . . .

Yes. That had surprised the good Weissmann, smiled Denis to himself, as he passed on, still thinking of the wasted life of Colonel Rochefort.

Well, one thing was certain. To-night was doing the Colonel's reputation a world of good. He would never be the same man again—and a damned good job.

What *was* the name of that lad who used to walk the streets of his capital by night? He'd remember it by-and-bye—when he had just the right quantity of wine aboard. It ought to come easily enough to the tongue, for it was an Arab name, and he should be familiar with them by now. Yes. He'd remember him all right, for he felt just like him . . .

Ah, ha! Who came here?

Why, one of them was the man they called Bar-berouge, the man with the brightest red beard in the Foreign Legion; and the other would be that wicked *gentilhomme manqué,* known to friend and foe as the Black Snake. In point of fact he was really much more like a lithe and hungry tiger or leopard than a snake. Yes. That pair really did rather suggest a lion and a tiger taking a walk together.

Probably the two worst men in the Regiment, but nevertheless each holding the high rank and title of *bon légionnaire et bon camarade.* Bad men with whom to quarrel; but good men to do and dare, to count their lives as nothing worth, to drink, to fight, to defy authority, and to look for some rule to break.

At three paces from him, the two approaching *légionnaires* saluted smartly, one a big tall Englishman who had been an officer in a distinguished regiment, the other a black-avised Hungarian, who, not so long ago, had ridden at the head of a cavalry squadron as dashing and smart as any in Europe.

Denis Ducros admired them both, and often wished that he had their devil-may-care swagger, truculence and courage. Privately he regarded them as a pair of Lucifers, Sons of the Morning, fallen from some social paradise and high estate. Certainly they were two most interesting and intriguing men. They seemed to thrive on trouble.

Perhaps the chief of the Englishman's troubles had been whisky, and was now some unexcellent substitute; and that, for lack of whisky, he had largely to subsist on such imitations of liquor and intimations of mortality as sawdust-distilled gin; forty-metre methylated spirit (so called because of its capacity to kill an army mule at that distance); bazaar-made brandy which owed nothing to the grape; rice alcohol; and very inferior absinthe.

Failing these assorted aids to health, there was always the admirable Algerian wine, an excellent claret at a penny a pint, but not of course to be regarded by a serious drinker as a serious drink; quite good as a beverage, and for quenching thirst, but then water will do that for you if you have no liquor, and can face it.

The Black Snake, his *fidus Achates,* was in striking contrast to the Briton. Slender, sallow, black-haired, black-moustached and black-eyed, he did indeed, with his cold hard glare, his thin-lipped smile, cruel and tooth-baring, suggest an animal, fierce and treacherous and cruel, a leopard in fact. A Magyar of land-owning family, his bond with the Englishman was that of breeding, education and intelligence on the one hand, and the attraction of contrast on the other. And as Denis well knew, there was nothing and no-one feared by either, and that if the courageous reckless folly of the one, brought him into the direst danger, blackest trouble, or heaviest punishment, the other would inevitably be there to share it.

The Englishman, a very dour, surly and silent man when sober, most expansive, eloquent and violent when drunk, amused and delighted the Hungarian constantly and unfailingly; while the latter with his courtesy and excellent manners, ready wit, devilish courage and daring, well-stored mind and interesting conversation, was the only man of his *escouade* whom the Englishman could bear, and of whom he could make a *copain.*

Barberouge knew the Black Snake for a really Bad Man, who did quite a number of very decent things, while the Hungarian recognised in the Englishman a thoroughly decent man who did some very bad things indeed.

Meeting on a common ground of indomitable courage and unquenchable fighting spirit, a high standard of intelligence and a low one of morality, they just "suited each other down to the ground," as the Englishman was wont to observe when excusing himself for helping his comrade and doing something that the fierce Hungarian might have misconstrued as a friendly, gentle or kindly act. For the hard-faced Briton loathed sentiment and all such foolishness—or professed to do so.

And when he made such a remark, the Hungarian nobleman would agree that they were born to be friends, for they were both born killers, devils, rebels, raiders and rievers, their hand against every man, their arm around every woman—who was good-looking.

"What a man dares, he may do," said Count Johann Czerneski, the Black Snake.

"Aye," agreed ex-Captain Sidney Selworthy, the Barberouge . . .

The *Rue de Mascara* is shaded by fine trees, and, in the semi-darkness, the Colonel, impelled by his great and growing sense of power to mete out an uneven-handed justice, and suitably to reward the good and punish the bad—good or bad according to his own standards as a sinful private soldier—took another risk. It was one that he realised to be considerable, for these two men knew Denis Ducros only too well, and the Black Snake was a difficult man to fool. He had an eye, a perception and a brain that moved like a striking-snake.

"Ah! My fine fellows!" quoth Denis, halting in his stride, "How goes it?"

Selworthy—seeking, as the drill-book orders, a point at which to gaze, a little to the right of the Colonel's left ear, and infinitely distant beyond him—stared with glassy eye, rendered his rufous countenance expressionless, and stood with grimly tight-shut mouth, wondering what new form of *delirium tremens* was now assailing him.

The Hungarian, with the charming smile that showed his perfect teeth, replied as one gentleman to another,

"Oh, but well! But well indeed, *mon Colonel,*" successfully contriving to imply that nothing else could possibly be the case when the Colonel himself deigned to notice *un soldat simple* in the street, and actually to address him in pleasant and friendly salutation.

No on-looker could possibly have imagined that the Black Snake was fully prepared, indeed quite expecting, to hear the Colonel's quiet, gentle, and kindly voice change suddenly to a ferocious roar, his deceptively pleasant words to a stream of coldly bitter invective and vituperation.

"Good! Splendid! But when am I going to see the two best men in my Battalion getting their stripes?" asked the Colonel.

The Englishman's firm mouth fell open.

The Hungarian, smiling yet more brilliantly, answered promptly, and in a smart and soldierly manner,

"On our arms, *mon Colonel?* Or on our backsi . . . ?"

"Corporals! Corporals!" interrupted the Colonel. "There must surely be some vacancies in the *péloton* of probationary-corporals. You were both officers in your own armies before you came to this *schweinerei* of a Legion, I believe . . . In point of fact I see no earthly reason why you should not be appointed Corporals at once; both of you, without being probationary-corporals at all."

The two *légionnaires* now stared hard at the well-known if not well-loved face of their Colonel.

What was the Old Devil up to now?

One would have thought he had something better to do than stop soldiers in the street and pull their legs, bait them rather, and try to make fools of them. Not a very gentlemanly game. Nor would one have supposed it to be particularly satisfying to a person of rank and importance. Good enough for a loutish non-commissioned officer no doubt, but . . .

"And Sergeants in the shortest possible time," continued the Colonel. "And *then* you could make some of these rascally Corporals sit up, eh?"

Barberouge almost reeled, but years of drill and discipline stood him in good stead.

The Black Snake's bright smile grew faintly contemptuous.

What poor stuff from an officer who should be a gentleman! Leading them on, that he might the more suddenly trap them. One word of agreement as to Corporals being rascally, and they'd be for the Stone Jug once again.

"And after that, Sergeant-Majors, almost before you'd got accustomed to your 'sardines,' eh? And then, *mon Dieu,* you'd make some of those Sergeants jump to it, eh, what? I must speak to Captain Desboines about it to-morrow."

The *légionnaire* Selworthy silently opened dumb lips that could not pray. He had in his mis-spent life "seen things," full many a time and oft, varying from phantom rats in pink to fiery serpents in violent motion.

Was he now hearing things? Hearing his Colonel address him in kindly speech, and promising him promotion. . . . His Colonel whose voice had hitherto never been uplifted in his direction save to curse, to threaten, and to bestow harsh punishment, all in the coldest, quietest, and most deadly menacing tones that military defaulter ever heard.

And now hark at the old bastard! Cooing like a damned sucking dove. Selworthy almost broke into a favourite dirge anent a mavis singing its love-song to the morn. Instead, he laughed, checked himself, received a dig in the side from his *copain,* hiccuped, excused himself, and to his further amazement found his apology well received by his kindly-smiling superior.

"Not at all! Not at all, my dear fellow," smiled the Colonel, graciously excusing this breach of social and military good manners.

"Yes. I must speak to your Captain about it to-morrow," he continued.

The face of the Black Snake hardened. He didn't like this sort of humour at all.

"*M'sieur le Colonel* is too kind," he murmured, half way between a sneer and a jeer; for when his temper was roused, he feared neither God nor man, including that very redoubtable man, Colonel Louis Rochefort.

Yes, altogether a damn sight too kind, he decided. What was the Old Devil up to now? And thinking rapidly, the Black Snake's quick mind searched about among his more recent crimes, trying to decide which particular one, having come to the Colonel's knowledge, would more especially have enraged him.

"Not at all, *mon enfant.* Not at all," said the Colonel once again. "No kindness; merely justice . . . And where are you two fine fellows off to now?"

"Barracks, *mon Colonel.* Tattoo," replied the Black Snake. Did the old swine know that they were confined to Barracks and were at the moment wilful-missing, absent-without-leave; and that it particularly behoved them to be present and correct when the bugle for defaulters-parade went at . . .

"Nonsense! Nonsense!" ejaculated the Colonel. "Go along to *Le petit Chien et Lampadaire* and enjoy yourselves. You'll find some more of my rascals there, drinking at my expense. Tell that fat knave Ramon to give you all you want. Yes. Just as much as you can drink—and to put it down to me. Enjoy yourselves well, *mes enfants,* and when you return to Barracks tell the Sergeant of the Guard that those were my orders to you.

"Go along now," concluded the Colonel, striking the Black Snake playfully with his cane. "Make the most of your opportunity. You may not find me in this mood again," and with a short dry laugh, with which Colonel Rochefort was wont to punctuate his allegedly humorous remarks, the Colonel turned on his heel and went on his way rejoicing.

Good fellows! He hoped they'd make a merry night of it—and that their excuse to the effect that they had been misled would be accepted. Anyway, they'd have had their happy hour, their wine and song and laughter.

And as the Colonel strode off, the taciturn Selworthy found his tongue.

"Now would that anointed peacock be drunk, or am I?" he asked.

The Hungarian, licking thin dry lips with the tip of a darting tongue which did indeed remind one of that of a snake, carefully considered the point.

"*Hombre,*" he said at length. "Everyone's drunk except you and me, and we're going straight to the *Dog and Lamp-post* to remedy the defect."

"Aye," assented Selworthy sententiously. "I have never disobeyed my Colonel's orders yet, and I'm not going to start doing so to-night."

"There's a catch in it somewhere though," opined the Black Snake. "And we'll go to *The Little Dog and Lamp-post* and find out what it is."

Glancing back as he spoke, the Count saw the Colonel languidly raise a finger to the peak of his *képi,* as he received a smile and bow from a tall and angular woman, bony, grim and horse-faced, the well-known and widely detested sister and housekeeper of an officer of high rank; but the Black Snake did not hear him murmur with the utmost distinctness as he passed by,

"Now who *is* that dreadful person?"

Had he not turned his head away, the Black Snake might, however, have observed that Madame lost some of her high colour, and then more than regained it all.

"There, my sweet young thing," thought Denis Ducros to himself, as he passed the lady by, "wouldn't it interest you to know that only yesterday evening you observed that I was a clumsy creature, because you nearly knocked an entrée dish out of my hand with your bony elbow."

But the Colonel's sweet smile quickly changed to a heavy frown as his eye fell upon three elegant models of military perfection, and recognised three ambitious young Corporals, newly promoted and keen beyond measure, who, while excellent friends, vied each with the others in a smartness and sartorial perfection approaching dandyism.

To young ambition, rightly directed, Denis Ducros had no particular objection. But he had a very strong dislike for that particular form of successful climbing that uses the well-being of others as its stepping-stone.

Only too well he knew that a successful non-commissioned officer must be known as a firm disciplinarian, a man who unerringly detects military crime and unhesitatingly punishes it with all the severity in his power. And that again was all very well, but there were ambitious young corporals, who, not content with discovering crime, imagined it, manufactured it, reported it; and reported it before it was committed.

And of such were these three specimens, Prussians to a man, and determined to rise in the minimum time from Corporal to *Adjudant* on a reputation for severity, harsh discipline, and the ability to prevent wicked *légionnaires* in all their doings.

Raising his gloved hand and cane, the Colonel peremptorily signalled to the three musketeers to halt; the which, with mechanical precision, and as one man, they did in mid-stride and mid-salute.

"And pray where might you think you're going?" the Colonel enquired contemptuously, as his icy glance swept the three stolid heavy faces and met the gaze of three pairs of piggish little eyes.

"We promenade ourselves. We take the air, *mon Colonel,*" faltered the senior of the three Corporals, stammering not only in great surprise, but in some consternation and alarm, as he viewed the angry and contemptuous face before him.

"*Ah!* . . . *Indeed?*" sneered the Colonel. "You take the air, do you? Well, take eight days *de consigne* as well. All three of you. Get you back to Barracks as quickly as you can march, and I'll see you in the morning . . . Reduced to the ranks . . . *And* eight days cells . . . Do you hear me? . . . For having dirty boots, dirty belts and dirty buttons."

The faces of the three brilliant and impeccable Corporals fell, almost audibly.

"Yes. And for having dirty hands, dirty habits, dirty tongues and dirty minds," added the Colonel as he turned away and passed on, leaving behind him three of the most crestfallen men in Sidi-bel-Abbès, if not in all Algeria.

"And that'll do Michel Aubraine a bit of real good when I tell him about it," he smiled to himself. "Those swine have made a dead set at him.

"Ambitious Corporals!" he growled. "*Sales cochons* . . . Show me an ambitious Corporal, and I'll show you *un vrai bâtard d'une truie,*" and he twirled his moustache fiercely.

This action caught the roving eye of a saucy little *midinette,* who thereupon gave the Colonel *en passant* an entirely approving glance from a most obviously glad eye.

It was a challenge, and one that no true descendant of a d'Artagnan and a du Guesclin could possibly decline.

"*Mais ma chère fille!*" cried the delighted Colonel, halting, throwing a *galoned* right arm about her waist, drawing her to him and kissing her warmly upon her ripe, smiling and undeniably up-raised lips.

"*Oh! La, la! Fie l'horreur, mon Commandant! . . . Quelle méchanceté! . . . Finissez-vous donc!*" cried the laughing girl, scarcely able to believe her good fortune . . . A lovely officer of high rank in full war-paint.

And since the lips remained upturned and the smile undiminished, the Colonel finished, as requested—but in his own good time.

Yes. Undoubtedly an elevated position in the military hierarchy and the social scale has its compensations as well as its cares.

Chaque âge a ses plaisirs'—et chaque dignité aussi sans doute.

Very nice . . .

As he released the laughing *grisette,* he was aware that a group of *légionnaires* had halted, almost unconsciously it seemed, as they came upon the unusual, nay, unique sight of their grimly austere Colonel embracing and kissing a giggling young woman in the street.

"*Salutations, mes enfants!*" cried the Colonel un-abashed, as the men saluted.

"Well, how goes it?" he enquired affably . . . "Now what was your dinner like this evening?"

"Oh, but very good, *Monsieur le Colonel* . . . Our *soupe* was most excellent," stammered the *légionnaire* whom the Colonel was tapping encouragingly on the chest with his cane.

And similarly murmured in agreement all those whom incredulous surprise and amazement had not completely deprived of the power of speech.

"Oh, it was, was it? Then all I can say is that you're a set of poor fish who are damned easily satisfied," commented the Colonel brusquely. And with a snort of contempt, the great man passed on.

He did not hear, nor would I repeat, the comments of the simple soldiery . . .

And so it went, that crowded hour of glorious life. Truly and deeply satisfying, but heady.

Thirsty work though; and, as he passed an invisible house embowered in a thickly over-grown garden, whence came the appealing and disturbing strains of *Donna è Mobile,* he suddenly halted in his triumphant march.

Ah! He knew what establishment this was, and felt sorely tempted to inspect its mysteries. More so because it was sacred to officers, and strictly forbidden to *les soldats simples.* Never had its polished floors or thick-piled carpets been defiled by the hob-nailed *brodequins* of *légionnaire,* Spahi or any other lowly representative of what are known as "other ranks."

Not even a *sous-officier,* a sergeant-major or an *adjudant,* had set foot in those gilded halls.

For not only was Madame de Beuglant a rigidly scrupulous upholder of her iron rule that none but officers should pay a call upon any pupil in her School for Young Ladies, but curiously enough, the Law itself —Military Law, that is to say, was equally arrogant. It was as much a canon of Military Law that no-one below the rank of Lieutenant should ring the bell at

Madame de Beuglant's door, as that soldiers should salute their superior officers, or that they should wear a uniform prescribed for, and issued to, the Regiment which they adorned.

And, moreover, had there been no such rule made by Madame de Beuglant, and no such law promulgated by Military Authority, the officers who visited the School for Young Ladies would themselves have instituted such a regulation and have seen that it was most scrupulously observed and kept.

It was perhaps the realisation that the prohibition was of this three-fold and ineluctable order, which determined Denis Ducros to defy it.

It would be the most splendid achievement of the marvellous evening. Not only would he have been, for however brief a space, an officer, but he would have entered a forbidden place where none but officers might go.

What a tale to tell Michel Aubraine and the rest of his more especial friends! They probably wouldn't believe it, but he himself would have the satisfaction of knowing that it was true.

Perhaps he would be able to bring out with him something which would be in the nature of a piece of evidence. Something he could show them in support of his incredible story.

Perhaps a scented, lace-edged handkerchief, with initials worked on it?

Perhaps not.

He did not know whether the pupils at Madame de Beuglant's Establishment for Young Ladies used handkerchiefs like that, or gave them away as *gages d'amour*, if they did.

Anyway, go in he would; and if no-one on the morrow believed his account of what happened to him beneath Madame de Beuglant's hospitable roof, it would not alter the fact that he had actually penetrated the thrice-guarded and forbidden portals of this sacred *bouzbèr*.

CHAPTER 6

THE POWER AS WELL AS THE GLORY

Denis, with a most Colonel-like air of determination
and assurance, pushed open the gate. From it a
narrow drive led to a pillared portico over which
profusely rioted a fine bougainvillæa. Beside the front
door of the house, which probably looked more imposing and attractive by moon-lit night than by garish
day, hung an iron bell-pull supported by a chain.
Seizing this he tugged it hard, and, somewhat to his
surprise, heard one or two deep notes from a heavy bell
that evidently hung round the corner, somewhere
outside the house.

A moment later, a very big white-clad Arab materi-
alised beside him, somewhat in the manner of Aladdin's *genie* evoked by the rubbing of the Lamp.

But it was the *genie* who bore the lamp, and who
raised it, brightly burning, that he might be quite
certain as to what manner of person it was who had
summoned him from the outer darkness.

Seeing that it was no less a visitant than a gold-
braided Colonel, he salaamed deeply, his dark impassive countenance hiding any surprise he might have
felt. And as the Colonel acknowledged the obeisance by
sketchily raising one finger in the direction of the peak
of his *képi*, there followed in the semi-darkness of the
porch a piece of jugglery which he could not exactly
follow.

He was under the impression, however, that the
Arab pulled the end of a small piece of stout wire that
protruded through the door-post, thereby setting in
motion machinery both mechanical and human. For
the stout front door promptly and silently opened, apparently of its own volition, and the dark interior
behind it was instantly flooded with light, revealing a
carpeted and curtain-hung hall. To the right of this, a

door opened, and a young and beautiful girl, smiling bright welcome, emerged.

At the same moment a much less young and much less beautiful girl pushed through a bead-curtain which obscured a staircase immediately opposite the front door.

The general effect was suggestive of that consequent upon putting into the slot of a machine a penny that sets in sudden motion the apparently immobile figures which stand eternally awaiting such propulsion.

It was the less young and less beautiful figure which was set in continued motion by the pulling of the wire, and, as it advanced from the jangling and tinkling bead-curtain of which the strings were still swinging, Denis decided that, in the first place, this must be Madame herself; and, in the second, that unless appearances grievously belied her, she was a most evil and horrible hag.

Madame de Beuglant was obviously a *maîtresse femme,* a woman who would terrify and dominate anyone who was not strong enough to dominate and terrify her.

Denis however felt that the man or woman was yet to be born who could terrify and dominate Colonel Louis Rochefort; while, on the other hand, Denis well knew the Colonel's capacity for terrorising and dominating those against whom he chose to exercise his remarkable gifts in this direction.

And it was up to the Colonel's high level of arrogance and autocracy that Denis proposed to live, while within the shelter of the seminary presided over by this sinister and dangerous-looking woman.

Denis Ducros was a man of sensibility as well as sentiment, and if not remarkably sensible was unusually sensitive; and Madame affected him in much the same way as did a tarantula or a snake.

He was conscious of an emanated aura that was wholly maleficent, and he recognised in her a woman of evil power who used that power to the utmost, and to wholly evil ends.

The extremely low estimate that Denis formed of Madame was wholly intuitive, as never to his knowledge had he seen her before; while toward him her attitude and manner were more than friendly.

That Madame was surprised beyond measure, was evident.

Also that she was delighted beyond belief.

That it was a Colonel with sleeves five times *galoned* she saw at a glance, and could not doubt the evidence of her eyes; but that it should be that model of propriety and austerity, Colonel Louis Rochefort, was more than she could have thought possible, though, in her long life of the widest experience, she had learnt that all things are possible—where men are concerned.

With regard to women of course she knew that little was improbable and nothing impossible.

And yet the grim face in the shadow of the peak of the *képi* certainly appeared to be that of the famous Colonel.

The famous Colonel removed the *képi,* and with it, any doubts that may have lingered in Madame's mind. Instantly she fawned upon him with a gushing, excessive and unnatural sweetness which suggested to the simple-minded man the idea of a hard-cased hornet endeavouring to produce honey as doth the soft, velvety and industrious bee.

"My dear Colonel! What a pleasure! What an honour!" gushed Madame . . . "Charmed and delighted. Had I only known earlier . . ."

What Madame would have done had she only known earlier, was left to the imagination, but was obviously something that only a brightly vivid, not to say riotous, imagination could envisage.

"Ah! . . . *Indeed?*" murmured the Colonel non-committally; for though, on this great night when he wholly held the stage, he could have acted the part of beguiled admiring fly to Madame's enchanting and designing spider, he did not feel in the slightest degree disposed to impersonate that character. Greatly he preferred to enact the *rôle* of *blasé roué,* for whom

Madame's establishment was provincial to a degree, Madame herself something of a *type infecte,* and the *jeunes filles* whom she chaperoned, probably a dull and unattractive litter.

And so indeed they must be, he reflected. What else could be the pupils in a school of which this was the headmistress?

"*M'sieur le Colonel* wants a little cheering up," suggested Madame. "A little music, a little wine . . . a little amusing conversation with . . ."

"Yes," agreed the Colonel, still without enthusiasm. "By all means a little amusing conversation . . . with an intelligent person."

Madame's elastic smile stiffened.

What a difficult creature the man was. What did he think the place was? What did he come for? . . . Conversation? One would have thought he could get plenty of that at home. Possibly too much.

Could it be that this was a visit of inspection? Was he deeply interested in the morals as well as the manners of his officers? Sour old gooseberry . . . Well, what of it? Wasn't it Madame's admirable and beneficent aim, her delightful task in this vale of woe, to cheer the bored and down-hearted, and to brighten the days—no, the nights—of those o'er whom Life cast a shadow.

Yes; a noble duty and a rewarding, to brighten the lives of one's fellow-men.

That the lives of certain of her fellow-women might not only be dulled, but permanently blackened, in the brightening process, was not worthy of consideration. She knew how ungrateful women are. None better.

How many of the girls whom she had taken into her School for Young Ladies, and to whom she had given a thorough and comprehensive education, had ever shown the slightest gratitude, not to mention ordinary affection? One or two had indeed tried to thank her "as she deserved," to use their own ambiguous expression; but she had her own way of coping with people of that sort.

It was rather discouraging, for Madame pined to be

loved, and only asked people to be reasonable, and to act in the manner that she considered right. After all, though kindness is kindness and philanthropy is philanthropy, Madame had her living to earn; and didn't she maintain them in luxury? . . .

Now which of her young charges would be likeliest to provide this dull glum creature with what he appeared to want . . . What was it? "Polite conversation"? No. "Intelligent conversation"? . . .

There was Annette . . . But Annette was not what most people would call polite. A merry and a hearty girl. But polite? No.

Justine? A model of politeness, but definitely not intelligent. Justine thought with her stomach, and thought hard. But as Captain Montpierre was wont to remark, Justine had a complexion of soft ivory and a brain of hard ivory . . . solid right through.

No. Neither Annette nor Justine seemed indicated.

Who else was sitting around, eating her head off and wasting her time?

Odette? No. A crude and common girl. Intelligent as the devil. But common and vulgar. She could not imagine Odette sustaining a profitable conversation with Colonel Louis Rochefort. Not profitable from the Colonel's point of view, *c'est à dire*. He would quickly dismiss her as a nasty gold-digging little shark from the sewers of Paris.

With a conscious effort Madame pulled herself together. This would not do at all. This self-satisfied, self-righteous old stick was cramping her style, disturbing her calm and even mind. There are no sharks in the sewers of Paris, and sharks don't dig gold anyway.

There are rats, however, and Odette was a fair specimen. She had had a few words with her only that day—sharp words from Madame, and loud words from Odette, and Madame had been under the unpleasant necessity of showing her little Odette exactly how noisy people are rendered quiet. If there were any more trouble from that quarter she'd have to hint to Mademoiselle Odette that, though a sufficiently foolish person might try to make a habit of noisiness, a sufficiently competent one might make complete quietude both sudden and final.

No, not Annette, Justine or Odette. Bother the man. Did he think her School for the Daughters of Gentlemen was the Sorbonne, or what?

The Colonel gazed severely around the intriguing entrance-hall to this mysterious institution, which he had heard referred to both as a Young Ladies' Seminary, and as the Gilded Halls of Vice. So far he had seen only a very personable young lady, and a hag who was undoubtedly the headmistress—the Head and the Mistress—of the place; but no other signs of gilt or vice.

"Nicolette!" ejaculated Madame, as with her own white hands, soft and fat, she took the Colonel's *képi*, cane and gloves. Of course! The very girl—if she were in the right mood. Quiet as a mouse and modest as a nun. Probably very appealing to a man of the Colonel's type. Undeniably a polite girl, and reasonably intelligent . . . And as to moods, Madame herself would turn on a mood that the girl would remember—if that should be necessary. And there was one thing quite certain. The longer a girl stayed in this finishing school, the better she knew that Madame never made a promise she did not keep. And if one liked to call the promise a threat, it was all the same—to Madame at any rate.

"I beg your pardon," observed the Colonel, bringing his gaze back from dusty potted palms, brass pots, Moorish hanging lamps, fretted screens and Arab rugs, to Madame's enamelled face.

"Nicolette!" she repeated. "The very girl to interest *M'sieur le Colonel*. Oh, but of a discretion and *très serieuse, très gentil*. So truly modest and well conducted. Really *bien élévée* and *comme il faut*. But yes, *au bout des ongles*. A girl in a million."

"Must be," grunted the Colonel. "How does she come to be here?"

"But naturally—to add to her accomplishments," replied Madame promptly; and though the smile did not leave Madame's face, it seemed again to stiffen, as though her face froze suddenly. Certainly it radiated no warmth.

St. Louis smite the stiff-necked old poker-back. What the hell did he come for? This wasn't a cemetery, even if he were a walking corpse looking for somewhere to lie down.

"Perhaps *M'sieur le Colonel* might like to meet all my young ladies and select the one that most appeals to him as likely to provide him with—what was it— polite and intelligent conversation?" suggested Madame.

Doubtless *M'sieu' le Colonel* liked parades. He had but to say the word and she would order one forthwith.

On the spur of the moment, at first, she had been delighted to see him; but if he was going to be heavy in hand and difficult, he'd be far more bother than he was worth, especially as he perhaps would not wish to meet any of his young gentlemen who might happen to be calling on any of her young ladies. In fact, even now, the sooner she got him out of this hall the better.

That young Ybarronne, for example, was a very wild lad, and apt to grow wilder as the hours went by and the bottles went down.

"Come, *M'sieu' le Colonel,*" she said. "I prescribe a glass of my champagne."

That would warm the old mummy up, when Hassan had doctored it a little, in accordance with his own private and remarkable prescription.

"Thank you," replied the Colonel, still without enthusiasm. "I only drink claret."

Madame tittered.

"I thought you were going to say 'water,' " she said.

"No. Not always," replied the Colonel, following Madame toward a curtained door in the far left-hand corner of the hall.

"But doubtless *M'sieu' le Colonel* would like to offer a glass of something a little more festive than water to these young ladies, if he is feeling . . . er . . . kind," suggested Madame, as she threw open the door of a room which appeared to be a curious combination of bar and *salon.*

The drawing-room suggestion was furnished by the presence of some two or three fashionably dressed young ladies, some two or three ladies who if fashionably dressed were not young; and, strangely enough, two or three young ladies who were neither fashionably nor unfashionably dressed, as it would appear that they had abandoned the effort of dressing when they had arrived at the moment to struggle into a gown.

It was a hot night of course.

"Young ladies," called Madame, as all eyes turned to the opening door. "I have the great pleasure to present *M'sieu' le Colonel* Fait-en-fer, who has done us the immeasurable honour of visiting us this evening."

The girls rose and bowed, silently, with the utmost correctness, altogether in a manner which to the eye of this particular beholder, suggested *discipline, discipline, et toujours la discipline.* And although the Colonel's face remained austere, as politely he acknowledged their bows, his heart warmed to them.

Poor girls! Poor dears!

"Filles de joie."

At a generous estimate, and at a considerable distance, they might qualify as *'filles,'* but where was any sign of *joie?* Their faces as he first caught sight of them, far from being joyous, seemed rather the personification of sadness.

Before they had time to turn on their mechanical smiles, display their teeth, force a gleam of brightness to their eyes, the composite face of which he had caught a glimpse was expressive of hopelessness, profound unhappiness, boredom and gloom; and though, with all his soul he loathed, hated and detested Madame, he already felt that with all his heart he could love these wronged and wretched girls. Wretched, he could see they were.

Wronged, he felt sure they were.

Anyhow, they were pitiable, for they were held in as tight a grip, and as iron a system of discipline as any *légionnaire* who, did he hate his servitude, need bear it but five years. Moreover, he was a man, a soldier, a member of a noble and honourable profession, whereas these were women, camp followers, and members of a profession ignoble and dishonourable that was only the oldest in the world.

It was damnable. Infamous. Devilish . . .

It was slavery. Sheer unmitigated slavery, and more degraded and degrading than the black slavery that certain of the Great Powers were trying to stamp out. This upholstered cage was as abominable and disgraceful a place as the foul hold of a slave *dhow;* and if, as any right-minded civilised man would agree, the enslavement of black man by white man was one of the vilest criminal customs that had ever disgraced the world, what was the enslavement of white women by white men? Surely *the* most unutterably horrible of them all.

Thus, Denis Ducros, who had hitherto given the subject little or no consideration whatsoever.

But to-night he was acting a part. Nay, living a part, the part of a man of rank and power; and surely power was given to a man that he might do good with it? It was not the *rôle* of a well-intentioned Man of Power, to walk into a place like this and add the weight of his authority, the force of his influence and example, to the recognition and support of a human institution so abominable and so inhuman.

The inhumanity of man to man.

And worse, the inhumanity of man to woman.

And worst of all, as exemplified by this Madame, the inhumanity of woman to woman.

Madame . . .

The gimlet-eyed, trap-mouthed, steel-faced creature whose voice was so false, whose smile so hypocritical, who, behind a mask of hospitality, jollity and good cheer, was as coldly evil as a snake, as rapacious as a shark. If he were any judge of character, the woman was greed personified; and next to greed, her most distinguishing trait was cruelty. Or perhaps one should say—he reflected, as he glanced again at the repellently smiling face and then at the faces of the girls—that no-one, not the woman herself, knew whether she were a

living and walking Rapacious Cruelty, or an unmitigated Cruel Rapacity. Well, he'd see whether he could
give the girls an hour's pleasure.

Pleasure . . .

Joy . . .

How they must loathe the very word.

"*Filles de joie.*"

What they wanted was happiness, not joy.

What could one do for them?

Were they well-fed? Or would a good supper be
appreciated?

They didn't look starved, and doubtless Madame
was too good a business woman to let them grow
skinny, since their beauty was her stock-in-trade.

Probably their idea of a good time, or a stroke of
luck, would be peace and quiet . . . oblivion . . .

He had known what it was to ache for it himself
when, so weary at the end of a long forced march that,
had he collapsed and fallen down, he could not have
risen to his feet again.

Yes, a glass of really good wine, and a little
tranquillity. An early evening for once in a way. Late
hours, night after night, were the devil. He knew
something about that too, when Madame Rochefort
had a series of parties at the festive season, and he
had to start a day's hard work in the middle of the
night.

Well, he had been standing smiling at the girls long
enough, and that didn't help them much.

"Charmed," he said. "Delighted . . . And now what
about a glass of wine . . ."

"Champagne," specified Madame.

". . . and a little music, I was going to say,"
continued the Colonel in his coldest voice. "As to the
wine, we will have precisely what we prefer; and if
Madame will be so good as to consult the tastes of the
young ladies, and indicate her own, I personally should
like a little claret."

"But *M'sieu' le Colonel!*" expostulated Madame. "I
am indeed desolated; but I am afraid I cannot offer you
sticky Algerian claret. I fear there is nothing of that

sort in my cellar; nor should I know where to send for it."

"*Ah! . . . Indeed?*" observed the Colonel, characteristically giving his moustache an upward brush. "Remind me to tell you, before I go. Everyone who appreciates good wine should know where to send for that admirable product of our local grape. Admirable and excellent. I drink it daily."

This was a profound truth. With almost a start Denis realised it. He recognised it, smiled upon it, almost shook hands with it, so to speak. It seemed to him delightful that Truth could penetrate into this place. Delightful also, that Truth should bolster up, countenance and support his play-acting, his rendering of a leading *rôle* on the fine large stage that was Sidi-bel-Abbès.

Good, kindly truth. He patted it on the head.

"Yes. I drink it daily. Twice. Have done so for years." But he did not embellish the truth. He did not add "With morning *soupe* at ten-thirty, regulation quarter-litre, with evening *soupe* at four-thirty, regulation quarter-litre."

"But, in point of fact, I don't think I mentioned 'sticky Algerian claret,' " continued the Colonel, fixing Madame's eye with a glassy and somewhat embarrassing stare from his monocle.

"Doubtless Madame's cellars contain plenty of the best French wine; and if claret is not readily accessible, I have no objection to a vintage Burgundy. Anything . . . Anything . . . *Mouton Rothschild, Nuit St. Georges, Clos Vouguet.* Anything . . ." and the Colonel reeled off quite a little list of the best years of the best vineyards of the best districts of France.

A girl tittered.

Both Madame and the Colonel glanced at her, but there was a difference in their regard. Madame smiled bitterly.

"Odette is pleased to be amused?" she said in a voice that conveyed a message.

The girl, red-haired, with high cheek-bones, tip-tilted nose and prominent chin, faced Madame squarely.

"Very pleased. Very amused," she said. "*Ha!* . . . *Ha!* . . . and then *Ha!,* making three."

Madame eyed her for a few seconds before replying with a remarkably acid sweetness,

"It must give *anyone* pleasure to amuse you, dear child."

"Even *M'sieu' le Colonel* Louis Rochefort Fait-en-fer?" grinned the girl impudently.

Madame made a significant motion with her hand.

But the austere-seeming Colonel Fait-en-fer laughed.

"I am sure it would," he observed pleasantly. "I must remember to advise him to come and give himself that pleasure."

"Merci, *Monsieur le Colonel,*" grinned Odette. "Tell him I'll amuse him all right . . . Do him a world of good . . ."

Madame's thin lips tightened a little. These Parisian gutter-snipes took more breaking-in than some. What little Odette needed was a holiday—in Port Said.

She again made a significant and more imperious motion with her hand, a gesture which Odette again ignored. Whatever virtues Odette might lack, she possessed the greatest of all, courage; and in great measure.

Odette laughed again. Some of the other girls glanced at her in awed admiration and approval.

"And what is it that amuses Mademoiselle Odette?" smiled the Colonel.

"Oh . . . wine, *M'sieu' le Colonel.* Wine . . . and *M'sieu' le Colonel.*"

"Now I am a very inquisitive man, Mademoiselle Odette," smiled the visitor, "and should very much like to know why wine should amuse M'selle."

"It shouldn't. But it does," answered the girl. "It'll amuse *M'sieu' le Colonel* if he goes so far as to try to drink it," and Mademoiselle Odette laughed a little shrilly.

"Well," said the Colonel, "let's all be amused. Call a servant, Madame, and let us give our orders. What kind of wine do you think you will find most amusing, M'selle Odette?"

"Well, since you ask, *M'sieu' le Colonel,* it would be to find myself sharing with you a bottle of such wine as you suggested Madame should produce for you. A bottle of Madame's own private wine."

"You shall share with me a bottle of Madame's best," promised the Colonel.

"And you, my dear?" he asked a dark, stupid-looking girl of considerable beauty of a somewhat coarse and obvious kind.

"Oh, *merci beaucoup, M'sieu' le Colonel,*" replied the girl, glancing quickly from him to Madame. "*Champagne, s'il vous plaît.*"

"Don't you believe her, *M'sieu' le Général* Fait-en-fer," interrupted Odette with her *gamin* grin. "She has the distinction of resembling *M'sieu' le Général* himself in one respect. She prefers wine to champagne. Good red wine such as Madame knows so well how to select from her own corner of the 'cellar.'"

The dark girl glanced apprehensively at Madame, finding as she expected, a smile on the face of the tigress.

"*Non, non, Monsieur le Colonel,*" she said quickly, "Champagne for me, since you are so kind."

Odette's exclamation, though it delighted the Colonel, seemed to shock the delicate ears of Madame.

Perhaps to cover this distressing sound, Madame clapped her hands loudly. An Arab servant entered, and firmly she gave her order for champagne for the young ladies, and a bottle of Madame's own invalid wine for Monsieur and herself.

"A bottle, did Madame say?" enquired the Colonel, raising an eyebrow.

"Two bottles," amended Madame.

"And four more," yet further amended the Colonel, "and of the same kind."

"*Monsieur le Colonel* is too generous," observed Madame.

"One cannot be too generous," corrected the Colonel. "Very few try; and none succeed."

"We'll try to-night," he murmured pensively, as Madame and the young ladies eyed him with varying degrees of interest.

"A little music while we wait?" suggested the Colonel, looking round.

"Fifine! The gramophone," said Madame, and a somewhat negroid-looking girl, whose magnificent flashing eyes and teeth atoned for her somewhat pronounced nostrils, and slightly kinky, not to say woolly, hair, sprang up and crossed the room. She wound the handle of a gramophone, and loosed upon the heavy air, certain brassy and strident notes that soon resolved themselves into the tune of an allegedly comic song, popular at the Moulin Rouge some three years earlier.

"But I said music," expostulated the Colonel, coldly. Madame raised a hand sharply, and the girl stopped the infernal machine, and changed the record.

A minute later the well-known and, in some places, well-liked strains of *"Funiculi, Funicula,"* succeeded those of *"Monsieur, mon oncle, le bon Edouard."*

Abruptly the Colonel rose from the armchair, where at Madame's suggestion he had seated himself.

"Really!" he expostulated quietly; and again Madame raised a restraining hand, and again the music ceased. For all his air of annoyance and distaste, Denis Ducros—but for the presence of Madame and his respect for the sacredness of his Thespian art—would have loved to sing to the girls a novel (Legionised) version of the well-known words of that justly famous song. He knew they would enjoy and appreciate it.

"Monsieur le Colonel does not like the little tune?"

"No, Madame, he does not. He has listened too long and too often to the serenade of the jackals."

"Has Monsieur any special favourite?"

"None, Madame, none. I ask but that the noise be music."

Music! Madame would have liked to give him some music of her own. Give him real cause to enquire *"Qu'est-ce que c'est que vous me chantez là?"*

What the Devil did the man want? There was a pile

of good records there. No-one else had ever found any fault with them. They had been a real bargain, and Fifine had not put on any of the cracked ones; nor had the thingummy got stuck and run round and round in the same circle. That, as a just woman, she fully admitted, became boring after a time, if one noticed it. And in point of fact, it was extremely humorous when the machine, instead of singing Madame Butterfly's beautiful song in the usual way, stammered and stuttered like an aged drunk trying to tell his wife where he had spent to-morrow evening.

She wondered if one of those would amuse the Colonel. Quickly she decided that it would not.

Devil take the finnicking old dodderer. What did he think her place was? The Opera?

If he wanted music, let him go there . . . And have a bellyful.

"Perhaps some of the young ladies sing," suggested the Colonel, smiling round the circle of now definitely interested and animated faces, his eye coming to rest on one that fascinated him in its sudden, frequent, and apparently automatic, change from a mask of misery and hopeless despair, to one of politely smiling, but obviously false gaiety.

"Sing? . . ." said Madame dubiously. "Sing? . . ." What did the man think she was? A sacred canary-fancier, or what? . . . Sing? . . . Perhaps he'd like to hear that stupid lump Nicolette caterwaul to that guitar of hers. She was fond enough of doing it when she was by herself, as Madame had had cause to complain. She'd had to remind her that she wasn't on the slum music-halls of Marseilles and Barcelona now.

Yes. There she sat, mum and glum as usual, looking as though her coffin didn't fit and the vault wasn't warm enough.

"Nicolette," she said sharply. "Go and get your strum-box and give the Colonel a hot rousing chorus about *The Little Cross Where Lilies Grow* or something."

CHAPTER 7

REST-HOUSE ON THE PATH OF GLORY

The girl addressed flushed in spite of her rouge, and the Colonel noted how nervously she twisted her fingers together.

"*Segnour Diéu,*" whispered the girl to herself, as her eyes fell before Madame's stare—and the Colonel's interest was instantly awakened.

It was many a long year since he had heard that variation of "*Mon Dieu.*" Why this girl was more than a fellow country-woman.

She was a Provençal, and not very long from Provence either!

She was more than a Provençal, for Provence has many corners. She was a neighbour. Why, he might know the very village from which she came.

He must know it.

"*Segnour Diéu.*"

He savoured it to himself.

"*Segnour Diéu.*"

"Indeed, yes," he said softly. "Please sing for me, *mon enfantounet.*"

It was the girl's turn to start. And her quick glance at the Colonel disclosed what Denis Ducros considered a very lovely pair of eyes.

"*Bono Maire die Diéu,*" she whispered. "*M'sieu' le Colonel parle le Langue d'Oc!*"

"*Oui! Santouno! Mais oui,*" replied the Colonel. "*Mademoiselle est d'Arles?*" he enquired kindly.

"*Oui, M'sieu' le Colonel, je suis Arlesienne,*" replied the girl, and her smile so lit up her face, that for the moment it was bright and animated.

"Positively she looks almost happy," thought Denis Ducros.

"*Sarnipabiéune!*" he exclaimed, treating her to an exclamation she must have heard a thousand times on the lips of her father, her brother, her lover, and any of the men of her native countryside.

For though she called herself Arlesienne, he very much doubted whether she had been born and bred in that ancient Roman town, so famous for the beauty of its women.

Probably born and bred in one of the near-by hill villages. Quite probably attended Arles market with her mother, until she was old enough to go there to earn her living . . . How? . . .

In good domestic service?

Shop?

A stall of her own in the market-place?

Arles. He knew every stone of it.

La Place. He knew every inch of it. He could see it now.

The Arena. He knew every stone of it . . .

Arles, Nîmes, Avignon. *Ailas!* Would he ever see Provence again? *Malau de Diéu.* Why had he ever left the loveliest countryside in the world, for this dusty graveyard?

As he was about to repeat his request that Nicolette-from-Arles should sing, the Arab waiter, followed by a negro boy, again appeared, each burdened with a large brass tray on which stood a number of bottles of the shape dedicated to champagne, and two or three which appeared to contain claret or burgundy. The bottles looked not so much old, as weary; not as though they had lain long in dark wine-cellars, but as though they had seen considerable service in beer-gardens.

The Colonel eyed them with cold contempt.

"Just filled them?" he asked the Arab in his own tongue, and in the true Rochefort manner, with the result that the Arab was surprised, nay stampeded, into the commission of an unwonted act. He spoke the truth.

"*Ah!* . . . *Indeed?* Well, now go and empty them again."

"Where, *Sidi Général?*" asked the servant, doubtless glad to be taking his orders from a man again.

536

"Down the sink, or . . ."

Mademoiselle Odette obliged with a suggestion.

". . . over the rose-beds, I was about to say," concluded the Colonel amid the nervous tittering of the girls, among whom, encouraged or led by Odette, a mild spirit of rebellious courage seemed to be abroad.

"But before you do it," said the Colonel, eyeing the man with a steady piercing stare which seemed to fascinate and almost paralyse him, "suppose you bring half a dozen of the best champagne that Madame has, and another half-dozen of the best *vin rouge* of France —not Algeria. Madame's own, you understand."

"That is what Madame meant, is it not?" he smiled, turning to that stricken lady, who for the first time in the girls' experience of her, seemed bereft of speech.

"So much better if one can talk to these people in their own language, which Madame naturally would not understand," he added.

Yet, to those who knew Madame's history, it would not have seemed wholly unnatural that she should both understand and speak the gutter Arabic of the town-bred Arab mongrel, who had never so much as seen the black tents of the Bedouin.

Although Madame repeatedly informed the young ladies of her Seminary that she herself had gone to "school" in Paris; and had spent happy, happy years under a kind and generous Mother-Superior, who reminded her so much of herself, in a delightful School for Young Ladies, not far from the Bois de Boulogne, this was not strictly true.

In fact it was not true at all, for Madame had been born quite near the Kasbah in Algiers city; had spent her childhood in ancient and narrow alleys, speaking a language unknown in Paris; had gone to "school" at the age of fourteen, in a seminary kept by a lady who was not a Mother, and who surely was not the Superior of any woman on earth.

From this school she had gone on to a higher educational establishment, a finishing school in Pera, where she had almost learnt Greek while not forgetting the guttural accents of the old home.

In Pera, by adopting a lofty standard of conduct and pursuing most conscientiously the exact path of duty, she had risen from the humble rank of Mademoiselle to the exalted status of Madame.

So there was no *nuance* of the Colonel's Arabic that she did not understand; and for a moment she thought of spirited and piquant stories that she had heard in Pera of Constantinople, concerning gentlemen whose wine had disagreed with them—after they had disagreed with the lady who dispensed it.

"*Monsieur le Colonel* will ask for everything he wants, will he not?" suggested Madame; and the accompanying contortion of her lips could hardly be described as a smile.

"Yes," replied the Colonel simply, and again Odette laughed. The Colonel, who admired courage, smiled encouragingly at her.

Odette winked at the Colonel and hummed an air.

"That will be enough, thank you," interrupted Madame.

"But not nearly enough," contradicted the Colonel. "Let's have it all, Mademoiselle. Words and music."

"*Oh, la! la!*" commented Mademoiselle Odette; and, endeavouring to look coy, she rose to her feet and bounded into the middle of the room. There she not only sang her song, she danced it, she acted it, she embroidered and embellished it. By the time she had finished, there was but one person in the room who was not genuinely amused and laughing heartily.

Madame was not amused.

"I don't think one quite follows some of the allusions in that vulgar caterwaul, but it is not the sort of song I care to hear in my *salon*," she said.

"Mademoiselle must warn us next time, in order that Madame may depart in time," suggested the Colonel, who had appeared to thaw more rapidly with every verse, and had now shed his austerity completely.

"And now, Mademoiselle Nicolette," he said, turning to the Provençal girl, "sing for me, *enfantounet*."

"*Monsieur le Colonel*," deprecated Nicolette, "*Anas-vous-en au Tron de Diéu*," and the private smile that she flashed to him, said quite plainly, "There, *that's* a saying from home if you like; and you'll understand that it is a quotation, a message, and not a piece of impudence."

At that moment the door again opened, and the Arab with his black satellite appeared, and the Colonel used the incident, glancing from the wine to the girl, to reply with an idiomatic proverb which he knew she must have heard a thousand times.

"*Lou vin es' fa' pèr bèure,*" he said in the Langue d'Oc, and as he glanced at her, he fancied that her eyes grew brighter while he spoke. Not with tears, of course. How could the sound of her childhood's tongue cause unshed tears to rise to the eyes of a girl of this kind, in a place of this description, run by such a woman as this Madame? Surely such a girl could be but a brazen symbol of womanhood?

"And if so," cried Denis Ducros angrily to himself, "was a brazen vessel to blame that it had been fashioned in brass?"

This girl had not been brazen when she ran barefooted about some village of Provence. If she were brazen now, she had been made so by the hand of her fellow-man . . . her fellow-woman . . .

The Colonel rose to his feet.

"Now let's see," he said, picking up a bottle of champagne and studying the label and the foil that covered the wired cork.

"Ah! Not manufactured on the premises. Not a drop of Madame's own home-brew, just like Mother used to make in the stone bottles . . . Yes, this should be drinkable by those who care to drink it.

"And the red wine of France? . . . Positively imported. Actually bottled at the Château. *Premier cru* and what-not. Madame, I congratulate you . . . and ourselves," he bowed.

"It is expensive wine," observed Madame dryly, and mentally began the making out of a bill that should pay not only for the wine, but show such a dividend as would make even this awful evening worth while.

"Open them," he said to the Arab, brusquely.

"How many, Sidi?" enquired Hassan.

The Colonel's look was a sufficient rebuke, as again he growled,

"Open them."

"Madame," he said a minute later, taking up a glass of what purported to be a *Nuit St. Georges*, "I drink to the happiness of the young ladies of this seminary. Mesdemoiselles, your health, happiness and prosperity . . . May you each have the wish of your heart."

CHAPTER 8

GENTLE USE OF GLORIOUS POWER

And he looked as splendid as he felt. He was simultaneously overwhelmed and uplifted by a wave of pity, sympathy, affection and admiration.

Poor brave girls.

They were not good girls of course, but neither were the people through whose fault they were there.

No, they were not saints.

Nor were *légionnaires.* What was wrong with the holier-than-thou hypocrites and humbugs was the fact that they got hold of the wrong end of the stick. It was not because these girls were sinners that men were vicious; it was because men were vicious that these girls were sinners.

Anyway let him—or her—who was without sin, come and chuck a brick through Madame's *salon* window. Why couldn't some of the righteous ones do something *for* them for a change, instead of always trying to do something against them?

Something for them? What would most of them answer if one said to them now,

"If you could have a wish granted, what would you wish for?"

Money presumably.

Well, and if they did, so would most people if the wish were to be secret.

"Mademoiselle," he said, touching Odette's glass with his own. "Wish!"

"For what?" asked Odette, surprised by the sudden suggestion.

"For what you would like most in the world."

The girl answered almost without pause.

"I? For what I'd like better than anything else? Most of all things? . . . Why, I should like to go for a drive," she said. "A long, long drive in the beautiful, cool night

. . . The glorious fresh, sweet air. The moonlight . . . The stars . . . The cleanness . . .

"Oh these walls! These walls!" she cried.

"Odette," snarled Madame, in the voice that had the effect of the crack of a whip.

"I will arrange it," said the Colonel. "If not to-night, then another night."

And he meant it—when he spoke. He was the man of power and patronage. The girl should have her wish, and the drive should be for fifty kilometres, or a hundred.

He emptied his glass to Odette.

"And you, Mademoiselle?" he asked Fifine, having refilled it.

"I? Oh . . . It's a big question, *M'sieu' le Général* Fait-en-fer. Just one wish, and that for what one would most like in all the world? I think I should wish for . . . What? Oh, I don't know. I think I should wish for . . . For a lovely long drive by moonlight, right away from here. Far, far away to where it is . . . quiet and cool. And one could be quite alone. Where there are no . . ."

"No francs," sneered Madame. "No food, no roof, no bed. *Hein?*"

"Ah, well," sighed the girl. "Then I'd like a pile of fresh gramophone records, and none of them cracked."

"It can be arranged, Mam'selle," said the Colonel gravely. "And you, *chèrie?*" he asked, clinking glasses with Annette.

"I? *I* should like," she began with assurance and gusto, but catching Madame's basilisk eye, faltered. "I think, too, that I should love a drive . . . With someone nice . . ."

She sighed deeply.

"Someone like you," she added with an impudent grin.

"That too can be arranged," smiled the Colonel.

"And you, *ma petite?*" he asked of the beautiful but bovine-looking Justine.

"I?" yawned Justine. "Oh, I don't know . . . Don't think I want anything much. Perhaps *un amant de cœur* who adored me. Young and handsome, and very rich. And . . ."

The girl Odette gave a whoop of laughter. "Nothing much," she jeered. "Only a rich young lover who adores her."

"Yes," agreed Justine. "That's all I want . . . I think . . ."

"That arranges itself, Mademoiselle," the Colonel assured her.

"And you, Mademoiselle Nicolette? Supposing I could grant you your dearest wish, what would it be?"

The girl smiled shyly at him.

(How could a girl, a pupil of Madame's, living here in Madame's house, smile as sweetly and diffidently as that? Almost he had thought, as innocently as that, which was patently ridiculous. It was absurd. It was sentimental. That's what it was. He was a sloppily sentimental fool. 'Innocent'! . . . 'Diffident'! . . . The kitten of a cat-house! *Pfui!*)

Without hesitating, she replied,

"*M'sieu le Colonel est très gentil.* What would I like most in all the world? . . . A glimpse of my village. That is all."

And, as he met the gaze of her large eyes, still young and clear, he found himself, for some reason, unable to assure her that it should be arranged.

But he realised that if, by giving everything he possessed, and was ever likely to possess, he could truthfully have so replied, he would have assured the girl that she should see Provence again.

"And this young lady?" he asked, turning to a thin, hard-faced woman, who for some reason reminded him of a burnt-out stove.

The girl uttered a coarse and vulgar exclamation, and a sneering laugh.

"What would I like? *Zut!* I'd like some more wine."

"That is now being arranged," smiled the Colonel, as he presented her with a full bottle.

"But I expect there to be something else in life that Mademoiselle would wish for," he said kindly, as he filled her glass.

"Hell!" sneered the girl. "Yes. I'd like to go to bed."

"That also is arranged," was the reply. "Go now . . . And sleep well."

The girl angry, confused and puzzled, rose to her feet. Who was this fool that he should come here and mock her. She'd take him at his word. She'd go to bed. She'd lock her door, and he could deal with Madame. She'd take the bottle of wine he'd given her too, and he could settle with Madame for that as well.

She wasn't a slave, was she, that . . .

But she knew she was a slave.

She knew she was getting older and plainer.

She knew she was losing what looks and what attraction she had ever had.

She knew that when Madame eyed her speculatively, as with increasing frequency she did, she was considering whether the time was not approaching to start her off on the next stage of the road to Port Said.

How could she be such a fool as to dream, for one second, of defying Madame?

No-one ever defied Madame twice. She had done it once, and . . . it was hopeless. Life was hopeless . . . Hopeless . . . Suddenly she put her face in her hands and burst into tears.

The Colonel put his glass down and crossed to where the girl sat.

"Yes. Tired. I thought so. Mam'selle was quite right when she wished for sleep. Come along, my dear," and putting his hand beneath her elbow, he helped her to rise.

"Now you come along with me," he ordered, and led her from the room.

Madame said nothing, although she appeared to try to say much. Although she got up from her chair with alacrity, she sat down again with resignation.

"The sacred arranger!" she sneered, recovering speech. "Well, he has arranged for himself apparently. *Chacun à son goût!*" she shrugged; and directed Hassan to re-cork the open bottles.

"Let me see you to your room," said the Colonel politely, as he closed the door of the *salon;* and the girl mechanically led her weary way up the stairs. As she paused at a door on the landing, the Colonel opened it and said,

"Good-night, Mademoiselle. Pleasant dreams. I'll send the boy up with your wine . . . *Dormez bien.*"

Quietly he closed the door.

Well, she had her wish, anyway. Had it only been as easy to give the others what they wished for!

Within the room, the girl stood staring at the closed door.

When the Colonel opened the door of the *salon,* within a couple of minutes of leaving it, he interrupted what appeared to be an impassioned harangue addressed by Madame to her young ladies.

"Now!" he said brightly, "What about a little more music?"

At a nod from Madame, Odette rose obediently, to go to the gramophone.

"No, no," expostulated the Colonel. "No more cracked records.

"Even if cracking them does improve them," he added in the tone of a dissatisfied connoisseur.

Two more girls had come into the room in the Colonel's absence.

"Does either of these young ladies sing?" he asked, smiling upon them kindly.

"Not to friends," replied one of them perkily; while the other admitted freely that she had never sung twice to the same audience. By special request.

"But nobody's drinking. Come girls, come Madame, a glass of wine with you. Order your man to open some more bottles."

Promptly Hassan removed the corks he had inserted at Madame's behest. Being Burgundy corks that he kept for just such emergencies, this was a simple matter, but the explosions were those of damp squibs, and the Colonel was not deceived.

"Stop those damned tricks! Open fresh bottles!" he growled in Arabic—to Hassan's approval.

Though a domestic servant, and the servant of a woman, he was still sufficiently some sort of a kind of a Son of the Prophet to resent and to dislike the sight of a man, and a good man at that, being swindled by a woman, and especially such a daughter of the Devil as Madame.

Now, between men, swindling was a different matter . . . Let all men swindle, and the best man win.

"Sing again, Odette," bade Madame, the wineglasses having been replenished.

Odette sang again, and the Colonel was amused, for the song was daring, and the Colonel admired courage. To what lengths and heights—or depths—Odette's daring would carry her in this direction was a subject of interesting speculation.

But it was not the extent of Odette's repertoire which interested the Colonel at the moment.

"Very good," he nodded. "I think Odette must have her drive now," and, turning to Madame, he bade her send her servant for the best carriage he could procure.

Madame almost achieved the feat of lifting her own face, so high did she raise her eyebrows.

Was the man mad?

What on earth did he think he had come for?

To send girls off to their rooms; to send girls out for drives; to give girls real wine, and see that they drank it!

Well, if that was his idea of fun he could have it; and *pardieu,* he should pay for it.

No fool like an old fool, but this man was a fool *par excellence,* on which ever side of forty he might be, to spend his money like this . . .

To come to *her* house and start sending the girls out of it! But money's a good plaster, and a wad of hundred-franc notes can be spread over quite a big bruise. He should pay for his fun. Nevertheless, who was master here? This *blagueur* or Madame?

The point soon became quite clear.

"*Mais, Monsieur,*" said Madame, her eyebrows having slowly come again to earth, so to speak. "We don't go out for drives at this time in the evening."

"Pity!" replied the Colonel. "You should. Best time of the day."

And again turning to Hassan, he curtly ordered him to get a carriage—and no bazaar rattle-trap but one of the sort used by Officers.

Madame sprang up from her chair with an alacrity almost surprising, and with an involuntary exclamation which was quite surprising.

"But, *Monsieur le Colonel,* this is impossible!"

"Not a bit. Perfectly simple. Let Madame watch," and with a look before which Hassan quailed, he pointed that noble Arab to the door.

Hassan went. It was a pleasure to receive orders from a man like the Colonel. And a joy to see him so firmly humiliating Madame. He sped forth into the night, and quickly returned with an excellent carriage, the property of a gentleman who was not too contemptibly mean in the matter of *bakshish* to a profitable messenger.

The returning Hassan, having signified in the usual and somewhat mysterious manner that the front door should be opened, Madame arose, begged that she might be excused for deserting her honoured guest, and departed from the room. But the Colonel, quite well-endowed with his own forms of wiliness, got up and followed her, beckoning as he did so to Odette.

"Come along, Mam'selle Odette. I think I heard wheels," he said.

The Colonel was right. He had heard wheels; and he would have heard them again, departing, had he not been the quickly-acting *légionnaire* that he was. As he and Odette reached the front door, Madame was in the act of telling both Hassan and the driver of the carriage what she thought of them. Apparently she thought little, but needed many words in which to express it.

"Ah! So. Good. Not really worthy of Mademoiselle Odette, but quite passable," said the Colonel, and cast an eye over the two horses in just that all-seeing and knowledgeable manner which Denis Ducros had so often seen Colonel Louis Rochefort use when regarding his charger, before mounting it.

The driver sprang from his seat with great agility, and salaamed humbly as the rays of the lamp fell upon the Colonel's sleeve, gold-braided to the elbow.

"Look you!" grated the Colonel. "Take this Mademoi-selle for a drive. Take her in whatever direction she wishes to go, and do not turn back until she tells you to do so. One word of complaint from Mademoiselle, and you'll get no *bakshish* . . . Something else instead . . . You understand me?"

The driver assured the Colonel that he understood perfectly, and that the *Sidi's* orders would be obeyed to the letter.

The Colonel opened the carriage door and handed Mademoiselle in, with the same courtesy that he would have shown to Madame Rochefort or her daughter.

"What about a wrap, or a shawl, or something?" he said. "Madame, I wonder if you would be so good as to send for—er—something suitable. Coat . . . Rug . . . What-not."

"*Merci! Merci beaucoup, Monsieur,*" replied Odette, wondering whether this were a dream blessed by St. Louis himself. But catching Madame's eye as she spoke, she realised that this was not a dream, and that however much of a Prince Charming, *ce beau Monsieur* might be, Madame was no Fairy God-mother.

"*Mille remerciments, Monsieur,*" she continued, "*mais il fait chaud ce soir.* Pff! Much too hot. I really want nothing."

But the Colonel perhaps knew more about night temperatures than did Odette, and had too often lain down on baking hot sand to awaken later frozen stiff with the cold of a bitter wind.

"Well, we'll have a rug anyway, and then you can use it if you want it. Madame, a rug, if you please, I said."

"Perhaps the little one would like the eider-down from my own bed?" cooed Madame, and the number of the teeth that adorned her smile was, in the Colonel's estimation, thirty-two if not more.

"Perhaps so," he said, "but I think a light woollen rug would be better. Hurry up, Madame. The night is but young, but—like you and me—it's growing older."

Silently Madame entered the house, and a minute

or two later a mysterious-looking female, who incongruously enough, looked like a figure from a biblical picture, appeared, bearing in one hand a striped woven rug, while with the other she held across her entire front, with the exception of one half of one eye, the border of a comprehensive and all-concealing garment.

As he took the rug, the Colonel wondered if this excessive modesty were due to modesty, or to a regrettable ugliness of feature.

"There we are, *chèrie*," he said, putting the rug across Odette's knees. "Now go for your drive. Enjoy yourself . . . Be happy . . . And don't come back until you want to . . .

"Dawn is very lovely . . . Sometimes . . ." he added. "It is a pity you cannot get out to the real desert, and see the sun rise above the palms of an oasis . . . *Au 'voir*, Odette."

"*Mais, Monsieur le Colonel; cette Madame!* . . . She will . . ."

"Leave Madame to me. Forget Madame, and enjoy yourself," replied the Colonel.

And Odette, with feelings of deep and unadulterated gratitude such as she had almost forgotten, tried, wholly in vain, to tell this kind and courteous man what it meant to her to be treated with kindness and courtesy. Just as though she were really a woman with a woman's feelings.

"Drive on," he said sharply to the man, and turned back to enter the house.

He was feeling splendid; enjoying himself as he had never done before; savouring his power, importance and pride of place, as the sweetest draught that in a hitherto thwarted life had ever been presented to his lips.

He was like a Prince.

He was like that fellow whose name he could not remember; like one of those Kings who went about in disguise among common men, doing good secretly. Doing it for their own satisfaction, but with the gloriously satisfying knowledge that they had the power to carry out any benevolent scheme that, at the moment, should appeal to them.

Well, for the moment, he had power, the undoubtedly considerable local power of Colonel Louis Rochefort.

CHAPTER 9

DIVERSIONS ON THE PATH OF GLORY

As he turned from the front door and the salaaming Hassan to go back to the *salon,* he was aware that someone was descending the principal staircase, across the entrance to which hung the jingling bead curtain.

At any rate a pair of highly-polished and spurred black riding-boots was doing so.

And Spahi riding-breeches above them. Yes. A Spahi!

Now who would it . . . ?

Name of a name . . . It was the Spahis' Major . . . It was. Yes, it was Major de Beauchamp!

As that distinguished officer stepped through the bead curtain, he hummed a merry little tune, swung his great cloak gracefully about him—and saw within a few feet of him the grim and stern-faced figure of his enemy, the man with whom he had had bitter words, and had waged bitter official warfare. Almost he could have shot himself, with mortification, for he had frequently and publicly spoken evil of the morals of the Foreign Legion, and had condemned them as men incontinent and carnal. Men wholly unlike those mounted paladins, those centaur heroes, those models of discipline and virtue, his own Spahis.

And doubtless this wooden-headed foot-slogger was here as Senior Officer of the garrison, on some official visit.

Sort of Cantonment Magistrate, or something, wasn't he?

Peste! What a devilish piece of bad luck.

What line should he take? The gay insouciant . . . Both men of the world . . . Boys will be boys, and all that. Or pretend that he had taken it into his head to pay a visit in his official capacity and see that

Madame's little restaurant was conducted in a quiet and orderly manner, since he had reason to think his own officers looked in here occasionally—for a coffee-and-cognac and a little music . . .

Too thin . . . Rochefort wasn't a fool. He could see those hard eyes glitter and the thin lips curl with contempt, if he tried any nonsense of that sort.

Nor was Rochefort the sort of man with whom one could take the line of:

"Well, well, Colonel! Here we are again . . . What? Official? Periodical visits of inspection?" and then roar with laughter.

No . . . Rochefort was what he looked. What every-one knew him to be—a man of strictest life and most rigid principle.

But, damn it all, the fellow wasn't his Father Confessor, was he? To Hell with him.

Curse it all, he'd take no line at all, except a straight line to the front door. He'd cut him dead.

Thus thinking, and without pause, the magnificent Spahi officer, as fine a figure of a *beau sabreur* as could be found in all Africa or Europe either, strode haughtily past Denis, who, *planté là,* stood with hand on hip in the Rochefort manner and eyed him with coldest severity.

Just as Major de Beauchamp reached the front door he heard the voice of the man whom he detested and, for some reason, feared a little.

"Will not *Monsieur le Majeur* take his *képi!*" asked the cold suave voice, with more than a suspicion of mockery.

"Damn the fellow!" cursed de Beauchamp, thus halted in his stride, his gallant exit ruined.

Savagely he swung about and nearly knocked Hassan head over heels, for that ubiquitous and soft-treading minion had appeared at the right moment, bearing the Major's cap, gloves and riding-whip.

The beautiful gold-embroidered *képi* was thus knocked from Hassan's hand, and in the act of stepping forward, Major de Beauchamp trod heavily upon it.

Flustered by anger and annoyance, he did what, in his normal condition, he would never have dreamt of doing.

He actually stooped for his own *képi*.

So did Hassan, just as swiftly and suddenly.

Their heads collided with resounding impact.

Denis Ducros laughed aloud.

Major de Beauchamp sprang erect, and with a violent shove that was hardly a blow, sent Hassan reeling backward till he fell over a chair and knocked a large brass vase, containing a potted palm, from a marble-topped blackwood table that stood against the wall.

It fell upon the tiled floor of the hall with a crash that seemed to shake the house, and which shook the soul of Madame to its depths.

The *salon* door flew open and she rushed forth, a tigress in defence of her own.

Rough-housing! She knew how to cope with that if anyone did.

"*Messieurs! Messieurs!* But what is this?" she screamed, looking like an enraged macaw.

"Major de Beauchamp fighting Hassan," replied Denis. "First round is the Major's."

Hassan, thinking doubtless that discretion is the better part and that there is something in the "happy low lie down" theory of life, remained where he had fallen, his body artistically draped about the palm, which now indeed appeared to grow from him, his head reposing in reasonable comfort upon a little pile of earth.

He felt fine, and that he looked fine—lying there prostrate, wounded, bleeding he hoped, possibly dying, doing his duty. (There'd certainly be *bakshish* in this.) A simple man, humble, obscure, but faithful to the last . . . defending . . . Oh, Allah! What was this? He was going to sneeze. The earth just beneath his nose was but dust.

Violently he sneezed and abandoned the pose of the Dying Servant.

"Good! I thought *Monsieur le Majeur* had killed him

in the first round," observed Denis, regarding the body.

Madame said something that she certainly had not learned in her Passy boarding-school.

De Beauchamp said something that he certainly had learned from the rude soldiery; and marched from the house, loudly banging the heavy door behind him.

Madame and Denis eyed each other, the former with emotions which she strove to conceal, the latter with undisguised amusement.

"Evening's waking up, Madame," he smiled. "Getting quite gay, aren't we?"

"A matter of opinion and a matter of taste, *Monsieur le Colonel*," replied Madame somewhat shortly. "I do not like anything unseemly in my house. And I won't have it. We live very quietly here, and . . ."

"Quite right, Madame. I fully agree. If I were you I should remove the name of Major de Beauchamp from my visiting-list. Disgraceful . . . Coming here throwing potted palm trees at the servants . . . And then marching off without saying good-bye . . . Not *comme il faut* at all . . ."

The Colonel's reference to servants and potted palms turned Madame's attention to the still prostrate Hassan, who had decided to hope that there was still a sound chance of *bakshish* for any man who, in the proper pursuit of his lawful tasks, should be wantonly and violently assaulted and felled to the ground. A pity about the blood. A spot or two would have been worth a lot.

But there was one thing he could do, if he couldn't bleed. He could limp—and limp he would until . . .

The current of his thoughts was suddenly broken . . . An assault in the rear . . . Madame's toe.

"Are you going to sleep there all night, you lazy dog?" asked the well-known voice of the faithful servant's understanding mistress. "Get this mess cleared up, and re-pot that plant."

Turning away, she added with complete finality, and, as Hassan realised, complete truth,

"You're fined a week's pay."

Hassan watered the earth with his tears, as he re-potted the palm. . . . *Bakshish!* . . . By Allah, it was too much; and Hassan wept afresh.

On returning to the *salon,* the Colonel found it apparent that a certain unrest, not to say discontent, was manifest. The centre of the mildly cyclonic disturbance appeared to be Fifine, who seemed to feel that, though neither she nor Odette had the slightest claim or right to an evening drive, she had at least as much a right and claim as Odette.

And Odette had gone.

Then why should not Fifine go? For an hour or two Odette was as free as a bird. She had escaped from her cage. Then why not Fifine? Surely Fifine was at least as deserving as Odette.

Like Hassan, Fifine wept.

The other girls comforted her; the Colonel enquired as to the cause of her tears, and promptly bade her dry them. Of course she should have her wish, exactly as Odette had. She should go for a drive, and go at once. Turning to Madame, he begged her to be so good as to send Hassan for another carriage.

So good? Madame replied, in effect, that though undoubtedly good, she did not propose to be as good as all that.

Whereupon the Colonel, though he did not remove the velvet glove from the hand of steel, did seem to loosen it.

"*Ah!* . . . *Indeed?*" he said, a Rochefort to the life. "I can only doubt that Madame failed to hear exactly what I said."

"But not at all, *Monsieur le Colonel,*" replied Madame. "My hearing is perfect, and *Monsieur le Colonel* spoke with moderate distinctness."

"*Ah!* . . . *Indeed?*" said the Colonel once again, and yet more sarcastically. "Madame positively declines to send Hassan to get another carriage?"

Madame indicated that the Colonel had grasped the idea quite accurately.

"So Madame is thinking of retiring!" observed the Colonel conversationally, and as though changing the subject.

Madame's narrowed eyes opened a little.

"Retiring, Monsieur? Does *Monsieur le Colonel* think then that I look tired, or that my evenings end thus early?"

The Colonel yawned and poured wine.

"Retiring from business, Madame," explained the Colonel patiently. "Closing your school and sending your pupils home."

It was an absurd supposition that Madame's face seemed to him to pale a little. But its expression undoubtedly changed—for she had understood the hint.

The Colonel had given a slight nod of his handsome head, and a nod was quite as good as a wink to Madame, who was so very far from blind. This man had powers in Sidi-bel-Abbès; tremendous powers, legal powers, as well as command of the absolute and blind obedience of hundreds of men who would—remove her house, stone by stone, if he told them to do so.

And of course he had come to spy upon her.

What a fool she'd been!

Could it be that she was getting old, losing grip? Never. No.

Not if she lived to be eighty, ninety, a hundred even.

But she'd have to go carefully with this Menace.

It was a shame that women should be put upon as she was.

Always the way! The same old story. Men were the enemy, the loathsome creatures. They hated to see a woman successful.

It was a cruel shame. Just when everything was going so nicely. No trouble anywhere. Everybody happy. And such nice girls, with plenty of kind friends.

And now this . . .

What was his object? Just sheer trouble-seeking for the sake of seeking trouble? And one of the sort that makes it if he cannot find it?

Well, there it was, and no help for it. What he said, went—and anyone whom he told to go, went; "also ran," in fact.

Ah, well! she had handled men before—and got the

best of the best of them.

"Why, no, *mon cher Colonel!* Not, at least, while I have the pleasure of visits from so distinguished a gentleman as *Monsieur le Colonel* Rochefort," she said.

And let the interfering, tricky, trouble-maker take note of *that*. For, when all was said and done, he *was* visiting her house—and although undoubtedly he could ruin her, she might sing a little song about him, herself.

And was not Madame Rochefort said to be *très sérieuse*, and as genuinely strict and proper as this sacred animal pretended to be?

"Good," responded the Colonel blandly. "I somehow got the impression . . . just a foolish idea . . . that we might be losing Madame . . . But no, of course not," and with a slight change of voice and apparent inconsequence added,

"But we are forgetting about that carriage."

And steadily the Colonel looked Madame in the eye.

Madame hesitated but for the fraction of a second, and then rose to obey what was evidently a command.

As the door closed behind her, the girl Fifine rushed at the Colonel, flung her arms about his neck and kissed him rapturously, and with abandon.

Ere the Colonel had time to acknowledge and return this demonstration of affection, it appeared that the example of Fifine was inspiring and irresistibly infectious.

Justine, the beautiful, showed that, though she might think but slowly, she could act quickly—and headed the swarm. Almost simultaneously the Colonel was seized, embraced, kissed, patted, hugged, and richly endowed with every term of endearment, by the spontaneously enthusiastic group of laughing grateful girls.

Only one stood smilingly watching the scene—the Provençal girl, Nicolette.

The door opened, and Madame entered.

"*Mon Dieu!*" she whispered, at the sight. Was she wrong after all? Had she misjudged the man? . . . In every way? . . . Unless her eyes deceived her, he was now over-doing it. Kissing the whole bunch at once, and enjoying himself hugely.

Well! Well! She thought she knew something about men, but this one was a puzzler.

At the return of Madame, the bright enthusiasm of the girls waned a little, or its expression became more restrained. Nevertheless they looked happier than they had done for a long time.

The sound of approaching wheels was heard, and Madame addressed Fifine, first with a snake-like stare and then in acid mockery,

"The carriage waits, *miladi,*" she snarled.

But Fifine was not to be daunted or deterred by Madame's venomous manner and address. She sprang up, clapping her hands, and ran to enjoy her little breath of freedom.

"Ah, good!" said the Colonel, following her. "Let's see what the carriage is like."

Bowing and smiling, Hassan assured him that it was of the best; and the Colonel assured Hassan that, for his sake, he hoped it was.

All was satisfactory. Hassan had done as well for Fifine as he had for Odette; and to the driver the Colonel gave the same orders and the same cold quiet threat that carried deep conviction.

The driver was the third Arab, that night, who, while freely admitting that all things are possible to Allah, realised that he was beholding wonders.

As Fifine swept gaily away, waving her hand, kissing her finger-tips to the Colonel, and crying like an excited child, "*Merci! Merci! Merci!*" Madame's feelings completely overcame her.

She was driven to speech.

She spoke to Hassan, to his detriment and sorrow.

Once again the Colonel returned to the *salon,* lingering, ere he closed the door, to lend an appreciative ear to Madame's plaint. And this time it was quite clear that that discontent which has been termed divine, was rife and rampant. . . .

Obviously the girls had decided that Odette and Fifine had chosen the better part and they wanted a part of that part. Woman like, they wanted to do as others did. They wanted to go out and escape from this stuffy hole of a house. As Justine said, they wanted to *brrrreathe.*

The Colonel assured them promptly that, by the laws of Madame la République, which in their military manifestations it was his privilege to administer in that garrison city, they had a perfect right to breathe; and breathe they should.

Springing up, laughing, singing, and with little exclamations of happiness that did almost lend them the air of being what they were called, *filles de joie,* the girls again surrounded the Colonel and signified in what they considered the appropriate manner, their great gratitude and appreciation of his amazingly disinterested kindness.

Were there really men, pondered Nicolette, who could do something for a woman and expect nothing in return? Men who were kind for the sake of kindness, and in the true spirit of kindness; who gave pleasure for the sake of giving pleasure?

And was this one of them?

If so, he was the first she had ever met. She had known very little of men, scarcely anything of boys, indeed; until, as a gaping country fool, she had listened to the lies of the abominable half-mad poseur and liar who had made her believe she had something more than a pretty face; that he was desperately in love with her; and that she was in love with him . . .

Yes, this Colonel was *kind.*

"A drive! A drive! A drive!" chorused the girls, dancing round the Colonel.

"Well now," asked that hero, "would you like to go in pairs or all in a party, or what?"

Quickly it was decided that Marie and Greta would go together; that Tatiana, the tall, temperamental Russian girl, who was now crying for joy or for some other reason, would go alone; and that Dolores, Concepcion and Maddalena would like to share a carriage.

"What a din! What a din!" protested the laughing Colonel, as the girls made their arrangements.

So thought Madame as she entered the *salon* with her sharp and menacing cry of,

"*Girls!*" only to be swept through the doorway and back into the hall by the rush of her excited flock, now undisciplined to the point of mutiny. Indeed, to Madame, it was mutiny most complete; most appalling and villainous, that these slaves of hers should treat her with this utter disregard.

Better insolence, insult, defiance, anything rather than this complete ignoring of herself and her authority.

"*Girls!*" she screamed, again both looking and sounding like an angry parrot. "Stop! Stop! Come back at once. Come here, all of you!"

But she might as well have addressed a flight of chattering starlings, swift upon the wing, for all the response vouchsafed to her cries and orders.

Nothing remained but a vision of long silk-stockinged legs and twinkling heels vanishing up the stairs as the girls rushed to their rooms to find what they could in the way of scraps of chiffon, scarves and wraps.

Madame eyed the Colonel in doubt, fear and seething rage.

"It would appear *en effet* then, that *Monsieur le Colonel* proposes to take charge of my poor establishment."

"Just like that," smiled the Colonel.

"Please send Hassan for—let's see—three, four, oh, better say half-a-dozen more carriages; and tell him to see that each is better than the last."

"Better than the next, too," he added. "Far better. Tell him I'll have a look at them—and at him as well, if they are not to my liking."

Madame, suppressing sentiments that were better suppressed, left the *salon,* to see what could be done to induce the girls to take a more serious view of life; and the Colonel, as he poured himself a glass of wine, realised that he was not alone.

CHAPTER 10

THE WOMAN ON THE PATH

It was the girl Nicolette who had remained behind.

He poured two glasses.

"Mademoiselle is not going for a moon-light drive with the others?" he asked, as he gave her the wine.

"No, *Monsieur le Colonel,*" smiled the girl.

"But why? It would do you good, I'm sure . . . Don't you worry about anything Madame might say. *I'll* do the 'saying' to-night, for a change."

"Monsieur is too kind. But it was not that," replied the girl.

"Oh, well!" thought the Colonel, "probably expecting somebody"; and then found himself most inexplicably and unexpectedly wishing that she had not been expecting somebody, and that she had accepted his offer of a drive, and been as pleased and grateful about it as all the others had been.

"And what would Mademoiselle like to do instead?" he asked with the air of a *grand seigneur* whose protégés had but to ask and their wishes were inevitably granted—provided he felt like granting them.

"*Monsieur le Colonel* was good enough to say that he would like to hear a Provençal song," replied the girl. "If so I should like to get my guitar and sing him one or two—that he has probably heard before."

"There is nothing that would give me greater pleasure, Mademoiselle," replied the Colonel, quite truthfully—for at the moment he could think of nothing nicer than listening to a song from home, sung by a very pretty girl in the patois that had once been the real language of a great country, the patois that was his mother tongue.

And 'pretty' girl did he call her? She was more than that, and only wanted a month on a sea-beach with sunshine, pure air and plenty of sleep, to be a very beautiful girl.

She was a real type; the sort of lovely that had made Arles, Nîmes, Tarascon and Avignon famous for the beauty of their women; and it was weariness, late hours, wretchedness and general illness and misery that spoilt and obscured the loveliness of the perfect features. Thin-faced, pale, hollow-cheeked, with dull eyes set in dark rings, or rather saucers, she was but a caricature of what she would be under healthy and happy conditions, and leading the sort of life for which God had meant her.

"Do you often give them the pleasure of hearing you?" he asked.

"What, here in the *salon, Monsieur le Colonel?* Oh, no. They aren't the sort of songs that would interest the girls. Nor would Madame be entirely—er—sympathetic. But I could sing our little folk-songs to *Monsieur le Colonel* if we could be alone."

The Colonel was conscious of a slight sense of disappointment. Wanted him alone, eh? Natural enough, wasn't it? What else should he expect?

"I'll get my guitar," said Nicolette. "If it would really give Monsieur pleasure to hear some songs."

"It really would," smiled the Colonel, and opened the door.

How long was it since a man had opened a door for her; shown her a little politeness for politeness sake?

There was the sound of an avalanche descending the stairs, enriched by that of a wild tornado, the shrill high shrieks of which were provided by the voices of the girls, the ominous undertones by that of Madame, who completely failed to ride this whirlwind or to direct the storm.

Avalanche and tornado swept through and out of the house, leaving behind it a great peace. This, however, was soon broken by the never still small voice of Madame, valiant in defeat; still brave, if broken in spirit.

Catching sight of Nicolette, who was going up to her room for her guitar, Madame nodded her head in confirmation of her suspicions. So that was the idea.

But, Name of St. Louis! Did he have to empty the whole house that he might talk in private with this Nicolette creature. Would he like Madame, and Hassan and the rest of the domestics to clear out too? The whole house to himself?

What this man wanted was a town to himself. Why didn't he take a few marquees and half a dozen tents and a caravan, and have an oasis in the Sahara all to himself?

Or was she wrong, and had he bidden this one also go for a drive? Perhaps in a State Coach and four.

There were things called hearses, weren't there, in which some people took drives?

"And would one be over-inquisitive in enquiring whether *Monsieur le Colonel* intends completely to empty my poor house of all its occupants?" she asked sweetly. "Would *Monsieur le Colonel* prefer that I too went for . . . a drive?"

"Do you a lot of good, Madame," said the Colonel, showing his teeth in what may have been a smile. "But there is one girl who, I hope, is sound asleep in her bed, since she chose a little rest as what she wanted more than anything. And Nicolette is going to sing to me."

"*A-a-a-h-h-h!*" breathed Madame, on a note of deep and wide comprehension. "But that arranges itself, one sees. But *Monsieur le Colonel* could have enjoyed his music without all the unnecessary expense to which he has put himself, surely?"

"For me that is nothing . . . Nothing," replied the Colonel truthfully.

Nicolette returned with her guitar.

"Oh, you're going to strum on that thing too, are you?" said Madame, and Madame sniffed.

"One can hear them at any time," he agreed graciously. "What one cannot hear every day," he added, "are the songs of one's childhood, sung in the language in which one talked as a child."

"I am not a great player or singer," said the girl deprecatingly, as she smiled and glanced towards the Colonel.

"*Monsieur le Colonel* will excuse me," said Madame, turning to depart.

"With genuine pleasure, Madame," said the Colonel, "But if I may first so far trouble Madame, I should like her to show us to a clean and quiet room where the air is fresh, and . . ."

"All my rooms are clean and quiet—and fresh," answered Madame, as indignantly as she dared.

"Doubtless," said the Colonel. "But this one, for example, has some faint suggestion of a bar-room, hasn't it? Just a *soupçon* of a smell of tobacco, alcohol, scent, and—other odours. Ah very nice indeed, at the right time."

"What's wrong with the girl's own room?" snapped Madame, whose politeness, under the wear and tear of this trying evening, was growing thin.

"I don't know," replied the Colonel. "Nothing, I imagine. Unless it be the size and ventilation. What I want, as I just endeavoured to indicate to you, Madame, is a cool, quiet and clean sitting-room; one reasonably comfortable, in which I can hear Mademoiselle's songs without being suffocated, annoyed, or reminded of where we are."

"One quite understands, *Monsieur le Colonel.* It leaps to the eye. A setting suitable for Mam'selle and her world-famous performance. . . . One's only regret—and it will be with one while life remains—is that *Monsieur le Colonel* did not give one a little notice of his coming. . . .

"One could have had something suitable built," added Madame.

"Well, failing that," replied the Colonel, with the Rochefort rasp invading his voice, "show me another room."

"If *Monsieur le Colonel* and her Ladyship would graciously follow me," said Madame, and led the way across the hall to the room from the door of which the Colonel had seen a girl watch his first entrance into the house.

Although it probably would look different in sunlight, it had, at any rate, the appearance of being the kind of room for which the Colonel had asked; and was at any rate free from tobacco-smoke, the fumes of alcohol, or evidences of recent occupation.

"Would this be a reasonably suitable setting for the distinguished performance of . . ."

"It will do," answered the Colonel shortly. "Kindly note that we do not wish to be disturbed."

"But naturally, Monsieur. *Cela va sans dire,*" said Madame, with an edged smile. "Would not Monsieur like a little wine?" she enquired perfunctorily, as she turned to go.

"Mademoiselle?" asked the Colonel, turning to the girl, with an enquiring lift of his eyebrow.

"No, thank you, M'sieu'," smiled Nicolette, pleased at a deferential courtesy to which she had long been unaccustomed.

Madame, on the other hand, did not look pleased. Had not the fool yet learned that one of her few uses in life was to further the sale of Madame's wine?

"No wine," replied the Colonel. "But I am sure Mademoiselle would like coffee and a sandwich later. So should I. I will ring."

Madame departed.

Coffee! There were people in Constantinople and one or two other places who had found coffee an unwholesome form of refreshment! However, she promised herself a word, several words indeed, with that Nicolette. The girl had quite a lot to learn even yet.

Well, she was in a good school.

"Where would Mademoiselle like to sit?" asked the Colonel.

"This will do beautifully, thank you," and Nicolette seated herself on a *pouffe* of Moroccan leather. The Colonel settled himself comfortably on the deep wide divan, and relaxed.

Real comfort! Luxury! This play-acting, strutting and striding, was apt to grow tiring if the play went on too long. Three hours was long enough for any performance. Now he'd rest for a while. Just rest and sit back and look at himself—and at this delightful girl whom he felt he had known all his life.

What a night it had been!

And in what an amazing situation it had landed him. Lying on an infinitely comfortable divan, with a most charming and acquiescent companion anxious to entertain him and give him pleasure.

Really he was like that fellow, What's-his-name—Sheikh or King or Caliph Somebody—sitting there in lordly ease, with a *houri* in attendance to make music for his sole delight.

He was dreaming of course, probably on the plank "bed" of the guard-room.

"What shall I sing first, Monsieur?" asked Nicolette, as she strummed the air of *Sur le pont d'Avignon*.

"Why, as much of all that as you can remember. I never heard more than the one verse."

"Nor I," replied Nicolette, "though I believe some of the old people know a whole song, of which we now know only the chorus. Grandmère used to say that her grandpère knew dozens of verses."

"Quite likely," said the Colonel, "and very probably he knew a lot of old *jongleur* songs in the Langue d'Oc, and very much as the minstrels and troubadours used to sing them in the days of King René."

"I know some that are said to be quite old," said the girl. "I tried to make a collection of them when I was going on the stage."

"Oh, have you been on the stage? Actress? Professional singer?" asked the Colonel. "That accounts . . ."

" 'Going,' I said," interrupted Nicolette. "Still going for that matter."

"Didn't it come off then?" he asked.

"No," replied the girl shortly, as she struck a chord on her guitar.

"I was a complete failure," she added, as the plangent wail died away.

"Do you know the song of *The Cat who went a-fishing?*"

"*Pardieu,* yes! I haven't heard that song for a quarter of a century," laughed the Colonel. "And there was a time when I used to hear it almost every day of my life."

The girl broke into a lively air which to a stranger, or even to a Frenchman who knew neither the place where the Cat went fishing, nor the patois in which his adventures are told, would have been merely a lively air. Just a primrose by a musical river's brim.

But to Denis Ducros and Nicolette, it was something more, a whole garden of memories.

There was a little silence after she had finished.

"Do you know what I would like next?" asked Denis.

"What, Monsieur?" The girl smiled happily.

"The same song again, please," was the reply, and the delighted Nicolette sang again the song that she had first heard in her cradle.

"And now what about *In the Vineyard of Monsieur Dulac.*"

Nicolette laughed.

"Yes. He was a queer old gentleman, *ce bon papa Bompard Dulac,*" nodded Denis, in answer to the girl's laugh.

Silence again followed the singing of the *chanson* which enshrined the epic story of the notorious love affair of the respectable Monsieur Bompard Dulac, who owned the famous vineyard of Valcœur.

Song followed song, each bringing back memories, happy, painful and poignant.

A long silence fell, and Nicolette sat gazing into the past.

The Colonel stood up.

"I will not try to tell you how much I enjoyed that, Nicolette," he said. "It is a pleasure I never expected to have again. I don't profess to be a judge of music nor of singing, but I should hardly have thought you could have been a failure. For my part I found the performance . . . entrancing."

"Monsieur is too kind; and of course Monsieur is biased," replied the girl.

"In favour of Nicolette?" smiled the Colonel.

"In favour of Provence, Monsieur."

The Colonel studied the girl's face.

How in the name of God did she come to be here, a slave in the chain-gang owned by Madame. Literally a slave, bought and sold and owned for life, body and soul. And different from the other girls as though she were of some other race and breed, some other natural order of a different world.

And yet she was not. She was of the same world; the half-world.

Yet that face bore no sign of vice, depravity, nor even that feeble weakness which is so often the cause and origin of both.

It was a calm face, kind, and sweet; the mouth was generous, the eyes gentle; there was nothing hard, or predatory in its expression; nor was it a sensual face.

No, he was not idealising it. Not seeing it through a vinous haze of silly sentimentality. Nor through the golden dust-haze of a Provençal evening.

It was a good face.

And yet here she was, in Madame's house, earning her living—like this.

It must have been a long and weary road and full of strange turnings, by which she had travelled from the village near Arles, to this house in Sidi-bel-Abbès.

Poor little pilgrim!

What could her story be? Probably quite common and sordid. No. Not with that face. Not common; but no doubt the element of sordid villainy was not lacking somewhere in the tale.

The girl looked up at him and smiled.

He liked that smile.

He loved it.

Not professional. Not intentionally alluring. Not the provocative invitation.

It was just friendly, spontaneous. Kindly.

God bless his soul, he had almost called it *innocent* again.

He must be careful. He must remember that he was tough; that he was a *légionnaire;* that he neither feared, nor believed in, God nor man, much less in woman. There was a lad named Samson once, wasn't there, who had been a useful scrapper in his day. Doubtless he thought that his Delilah's smile was just friendly, spontaneous, and kindly.

Conceivably the fool had almost called it innocent; and, so far as one knew, the good soldier Samson had not met the young woman in quite such a dubious place as this.

Perhaps Samson the Soldier had . . . To Hell with Samson the Soldier and his Philistine tart.

This was a Provençal girl, with a friendly face; a good face; an *innocent* face . . .

"Come and sit by me," he said abruptly. "I want to talk to you."

And the two lost children of Provence seated themselves, side by side, on the divan.

"Tell me," said Denis Ducros, "if you care to . . . Everything . . . Or tell me nothing at all, if you'd rather."

Nicolette sat silent beside the man whose kindness was almost unbearable.

What a fool she was, to be unable to speak when she so longed to tell him of her gratitude that he should be so *gentil* to a girl like her.

It was the unexpectedness, the incredible difference. She had not known that there were men like this. Probably there were no others. And yet he was a great man; a distinguished and a powerful man. To think that such a one should have time to be courteous and kind to Nicolette, the . . . the girl in Madame's House! No doubt he was kind and courteous to everybody, but he had been, or he had seemed to be, so genuinely interested, understanding. But then he had been like that to all the girls.

It was only because she came from Provence that he had taken special notice of her.

And he had treated her as though she had been of his own world.

Suddenly she found her voice.

CHAPTER 11

A STORY BY THE WAYSIDE

"I should love to tell you . . . everything, *Monsieur le Colonel,*" she said. "If it would really interest you."

"It would really and deeply interest me," was the reply.

"I suppose Monsieur does not know Domeuil, near Arles."

The Colonel gave a short laugh.

"Know it! I know every house in it! Almost the name of every occupant of every house—and of his dog too. I can see the *brioches* and the long crusty loaves in the window of the shop of old Pierre Boulanger."

"Why, yes!" said Nicolette. "I used to go to that shop every morning, to fetch his little grand-daughter to take her to school; and he always used to give us one of those *brioches* between us, and tell us not to swallow it whole. . . . He was a dear old man."

"And got drunk every night of his life at Benoît's wine-shop, after three games of dominoes with Jean Tousseau; and was fetched home by his wife . . . *Ma foi!* But that one was something of a Sergeant-Major."

Nicolette laughed delightedly.

"I went in terror of her," she said, "though she was never unkind to me, and I had no reason to fear her. But I always imagined myself mislaying the little Hélène on the way home from school, and having to go to Madame Boulanger and confess that I had lost her. I think I should have run away from home rather than face her."

"I certainly should never have faced her," said the Colonel. "I was more afraid of her than I was of any man."

"I don't think Monsieur was ever afraid of anybody."

"I was of that one, I assure you! I used to think she was a witch and in league with the Devil. Probably was

. . ."

"And poor old crippled Gautier, the cobbler?" asked the girl. "Do you remember him?"

"Rather. Twisted and lame, and blind in one eye, and as good a workman as ever stitched leather. A humorist too, in spite of everything. Always amused, and amusing."

"And kind too," said Nicolette. "One gets the idea that deformed people are always bitter and malicious. But he wasn't."

"No," agreed the Colonel. "He had a great heart, and real courage. Do you remember how one went inside his little cave of a shop, to take him a pair of shoes to mend, and there was always a clean duster or towel on the little seat opposite to where he worked—all ready for you to sit down and have a chat? He loved to talk. The tales he used to tell of 1870. I am not sure that it wasn't he who made me a soldier."

"Yes, yes," said Nicolette eagerly. "Why, he'd even tell us girls about 1870. Not about his own doings or the fighting, but about how hard it was for the women to keep their homes going; to feed the children; and to carry on while the men were away, fighting for our France; how the women tried to do the men's work in the vineyards, in the fields; and in the forests, getting wood in the winter . . . I've sat for hours on that seat, listening to Père Gautier."

"So have I," said the Colonel. "But it must have been long before your time. I am nearly old enough to be your father."

Nicolette turned and studied his face again . . . What a nice face it was, with its steady eyes, and kindly mocking smile—the face of a *giver* among all the millions of takers.

"No, *Monsieur le Colonel,*" she said. "My father is a very much older man than you."

"Anyway, I can hardly imagine that I ever saw you when I visited Domeuil," said the Colonel. "Though it would be pleasant to think that we had actually met before—in Provence."

"That would be wonderful indeed," said Nicolette.

"But it is already wonderful that *Monsieur le Colonel* should know the place at all. And the very people among whom I grew up."

"Some wise man has already discovered that the world is a very small place, Mademoiselle."

"I suppose Monsieur must have visited Domeuil quite often," said Nicolette.

"Yes . . . Yes . . . I used to spend my holidays there. Staying near some people named—er—de Cassignac."

"*Oh!*" said the girl; and there was something in the exclamation that caught the Colonel's attention.

"Now that de Cassignac was another queer one," he said. "There was madness in that family. Been in that tiny corner of the world too long, and thought there was no one good enough to marry them, except their own cousins. A thoroughly bad man," he mused. "One of the sort they did well in clearing out, during the Revolution . . . Always a marvel to me that he kept clear of the Law . . . A wonder no one ever shot him from behind a hedge, one moonlight night. There were brothers, and husbands and fathers enough, who had reason to . . . Just as well that he was the last of his line."

He yawned and apologised.

Silence.

"Had no children at all, had he?" he asked casually.

"One," replied the girl.

"Really? . . . After I left those parts, perhaps . . . Don't say it was a son to carry on that noble line . . ."

"It was a son," said Nicolette.

"And he is following in father's footsteps no doubt," hazarded the Colonel.

"No . . . He's not," she said shortly. "I killed him."

It took a great deal to surprise Denis Ducros nowadays, but here was something quite out of the ordinary. He had heard of fiends in human form; women with lovely faces, who were devils; but he had not the faintest belief in such phenomena. In his humble opinion and wide experience, evil people had evil faces, and good people had good faces.

This girl had a good face, and on that fact he built

his faith in her.

"You did what?" he said lightly, as though she must be joking.

"I killed Raoul de Cassignac."

"Good! I am quite sure he must have deserved it." Still he asked no questions, though he drew quick and obvious conclusions.

So that was it! That was how this unusual girl was started on that dreadful road which led from Domeuil in Provence to Madame's house in Sidi-bel-Abbès.

The old, old story. The petty Seigneur's dissipated son, and the village beauty. Following in his father's footsteps.

Pity the old man's footsteps hadn't led him to an earlier grave.

Same sad old sordid story. But, for once, a damned scoundrel had got what he deserved. A marvel she had got away with it. As a rule the police haven't far to look for motives when a young blackguard of that sort gets what is coming to him. It can't be often that a village girl shoots or stabs the son of the big man of the neighbourhood, and lives to tell the tale.

"And so you killed him, eh?" mused Denis in some wonderment.

Well, this weird old World can still provide its little surprises. This dove-like girl a, well, what they call a murderess.

"Yes. Yet for some reason I don't feel like a murderess. Perhaps because it was an accident, in a way," she said, as though following his unspoken thought.

"Oh-h-h! An accident, was it?"

"Well—yes and no. It was both an accident and a murder, you see. It was an accident, because I never dreamt of causing his death in that way. It never entered my head."

"Well, if it was an accident, and you never thought of doing such a thing, why call it murder?"

"Because I had murder in my heart. Because I wanted to kill him. Because, if I had known that what I did would kill him, I would have done it intentionally."

"Well then, it looks more like the finger of

Providence, or what they call the hand of God, or something of that sort. Since, as you say, you hadn't set out to kill him."

"Set out to kill him!" said the girl. "That evening . . . I set out to meet him because I loved him. Loved him . . . there are no words . . .

"I was in love for the first time in my life, and it was the full of the moon, and the most perfect night the world has ever seen. And I thought he was the noblest, truest, kindest . . .

"Little *fool!* I thought he loved me as I did him. Truly and for ever . . . And that he . . . I thought he . . . Oh, what does it matter what I thought?

"Well, my Fairy Prince begged his village Cinderella to come up through the vineyards and meet him in the Château rose-garden by an ancient marble seat that was supposed to have come from Rome in the old days. I slipped out and went to our meeting as though I were walking straight to Heaven. He was there, sitting on the seat, waiting for me—which was something, I suppose.

"Probably he had no better sport for that evening.

"When I sat beside him he put his arms about me and kissed me. So sweetly, so kindly, and oh, had I but known it, so expertly. Such knowledge and experience of women and fools of village girls!

"I thought I should die of happiness and joy and love.

"Ah, well! I was a girl of Provence, and in love for the first time. And oh, how deep in love! And then, in his laughing whisper, he said that Roman seats were hard and uncomfortable and never made for love, and begged me to creep with him into the house, which by now was all dark and silent.

"Just up that little outside staircase and through that door we could see in the moonlight, and we should be in his room, which he'd love to show me. We should be so much more at our ease. We had to be so cautious in the garden. Servants. Watchmen. And his father often walked in the garden after dinner. He pretended to be afraid of his father, and that he had so nasty a mind that he would think ill of me if he caught us there.

"Would you believe it, Monsieur, that a girl could be such a fool? Even a village girl, ignorant and innocent as I was then; though that may seem impossible to you. Can you believe that I went into that house with him without a thought of harm or wrong or danger?"

"In point of fact, I believe anything you tell me, Nicolette, and I am perfectly certain that you were a sweet fool, innocent and ignorant," said Denis Ducros.

"What with excitement, and a little fright, and immeasurable love, I was trembling. My heart was beating so fast and so loudly that I thought people might hear it. And as he closed the door behind us, I turned and put my arms about Raoul's neck, over-come, overwhelmed with love for him . . ."

Silence.

"That was the last kiss—of love—that I ever gave a man."

Silence again.

"It was like one of those folk-tales about bewitched and transformed beasts and men. The Princess kisses the Beast and he turns into the beautiful Prince. That sort of thing. Only this was just the opposite. I kissed the Prince and he turned into—the Beast.

"It *was* a beast. A savage and horrible beast. I don't think I ever quite recovered from the shock I got that night. It seemed to me that he had gone completely mad, and that I was in most horrible danger.

"He *was* mad, and I had to fight for my life."

"He was mad, Nicolette," agreed the Colonel. "There was a *terrible* form of madness in that family. Terrible . . . vile . . . and historical. Had you heard no tales in the village?"

"No, but I knew there were tales about the old man. I never knew quite what it was, because people always stopped talking . . . And Raoul was only just back from Paris . . . And he had been gentleness and sweetness itself until he locked that door and I kissed him.

"It really was like our were-wolf stories. It really was just as if one saw a man turn into a wolf or some other dreadful beast, before one's eyes.

"And how strong he was! But so was I; and I knew I was fighting for my life. Time after time he got me down, but we struggled and fought and fell, and when he had to pause to recover breath, he still held me by the throat until I felt I should suffocate.

"After a time—how long I do not know, but it seemed a very long time indeed—I tore myself free and got away from him. I dodged behind a sofa as he rushed after me, and, as he jumped over it, he fell. As he got up, he stood for a moment between the open french windows that gave on to a little balcony. He snatched at me and with my hands against his chest, I thrust him off with all my might. To my utter surprise he fell right over backwards, crashed against the wooden railing of the balcony and went right through it and down into the garden below."

Silence again.

"I suppose he caught his heels against the ledge of the door and it tripped him."

"Broke his neck, eh?" said Denis.

"I rushed across the room, unlocked the door, ran down the stairs by which I had come up so happily, and ran all the way home. I met no one, and I got safely into my room without waking my parents.

"The next day there was a terrible to do . . . Young Monsieur Raoul de Cassignac had been found lying dead on the stones of the terrace immediately below the balcony of his room. They could see that he had fallen, or been flung against the frail wood-work of the railing, which had given way. At first they thought that he had met with an accident, but then decided that the room was in what they called a 'state of disorder'. The police were not satisfied, and were convinced that there were 'signs of a struggle'. However, they received very little help from the inmates of the Château, for these were only three in number—an ancient house-keeper, a young servant-girl, and an old man who had once been butler. These said they knew nothing at all about Monsieur Raoul's movements that evening or at any other time.

"Old Monsieur de Cassignac himself was really at Monte Carlo, and the house was practically shut up.

"Can you imagine the state of terror in which I lived? Everyone was talking about it. It was a nine days' wonder. Everyone had a theory, and hardly anyone was content with the suicide story.

"He *must* have been murdered.

"I was positively grateful to old Père Gautier who pooh-poohed the wild murder stories, and, with a shrug of his shoulders, said,

" '*Qu'est-ce que c'est que vous me chantez là?* Murder? Why? Like father, like son. He got drunk, staggered about the room catching a moth or a pink rat, staggered out on to the balcony and fell through it. *Voilà tout.*' "

"And of course nobody would have anything as simple as that," observed the Colonel. "Not while there was a chance of making a juicy murder of it."

"It was dreadful. I couldn't sleep. Every time I saw a gendarme coming towards me, I thought he was going to arrest me. I wonder I did not have a nervous breakdown. The shock I had had that night was quite enough, without the prolonged strain.

"I used to dream about the guillotine."

"Poor child!" said Denis, and put his hand protectingly over hers.

"And in the end I did the silliest thing that, in the circumstances, I could have done. Can *Monsieur le Colonel* guess what that was?"

"Yes," replied the Colonel. "I did it myself once. You ran away."

"One does not imagine *Monsieur le Colonel* running away!" smiled Nicolette.

"I had saved just about enough money to take me to Marseilles. I made my way, cleverly, as I thought, to Avignon; and there I caught the Paris-Lyons train, with a change of clothes, my guitar and barely a hundred francs."

"So that was it," thought Denis Ducros. "The simple country mouse among the rats of Marseilles. Loneliness. Poverty. Hunger. Stark starvation. And a girl, like everybody else, has the need to eat.

"And you had a very terrible time at Marseilles?"

"No," replied Nicolette unexpectedly. "Not at all a bad time, really. Of course, at first, I was very lonely and very frightened and terribly anxious about what would happen to me when my hundred francs were gone. But Providence watches over babes, and innocents and fools . . .

"For a time," she added bitterly. "In the queer cheap *pension* where I stayed, there was a girl from Nîmes who told me the best way to go about getting employment. I had idiotic ideas about 'going on the stage', as I called it. She had more sensible and experienced ones about getting a job in a cabaret-show. She thought really well of my singing and guitar playing, and offered to take me to see a man who was a kind of music-hall and theatrical agent."

Enter the villain, thought Denis Ducros. This is where the old, old story does start. Low-class scoundrelly theatrical agent and ignorant country girl at the end of her resources.

"I was so stupid that, at first, it seemed to me quite wrong that I should have to give ten per cent. of my earnings to a person who did nothing at all but tell me where there was a vacancy.

"However, Nanette laughed me out of that *sottise,* and told me the first thing was to 'find a vacancy' as I called it—before a hundred other girls had discovered it. Anyway, I went with her to see the man of whom she spoke, and found that he lived in a tiny little dirty office up the longest and steepest staircase I have ever seen. It was quite a rabbit-warren of a place, above a little café; and I didn't at all like the look of the men and women that went in and out, and up to the rooms above.

"The man turned out to be a Jew, small and fat, and very friendly. Too friendly, I thought, when he told me in the first five minutes that I was a lovely girl."

"Stock villain," thought Denis.

"He turned out to be one of the kindest men I have ever met.

"Not that I have met many kind men," she added. "But he really did have a kind heart, and proved to be a true friend. And quite disinterested beyond his ten per cent. He wasn't over-familiar, and when I went to see him, from time to time, I had no feeling that I must take someone else with me.

"He too thought well of my singing and playing; but only up to a point. He told me quite frankly that I hadn't the ghost of a chance of ever getting on to the big halls, as my voice was not powerful enough, nor my songs of the kind to appeal to the taste of the sort of people that formed the bulk of their audiences. But he said he thought he could always find me something in the *café-chantant* line, though not in the Cannabière.

"Well, believe it or not, *Monsieur le Colonel,* I actually maintained myself almost comfortably, and quite respectably, for several months, in Marseilles of all places in the world.

"Then one day I got a message from my agent, as I liked to call him, asking me to go and see him at his office the next day. I went, and found the good little man quite excited. He had got a job for me, he said, a good job. One much worthier of me than this hand-to-mouth *café-chantant* scramble.

"A real part in a real play on the real stage . . . Actually a part . . . I should be an actress.

"But I couldn't act. I knew nothing whatever about acting.

"Beyfus reassured me, however, and said that that simply did not matter.

"All I had to do was what I was now doing, only under very different conditions. What the producer wanted was a girl who could play a guitar and sing some Provençal songs. She must be pretty and have a figure for doublet and hose, as it was a period costume play.

" 'And now I ask myself,' said Beyfus, rubbing his hands together and seeming to twinkle all over, 'whether this part was especially written for you, or whether you were especially born to play this part.'

"Poor Beyfus! He was so genuinely delighted to have

got me this wonderful chance, although he knew that it would soon take me away from Marseilles, and the thought of that brought tears into his eyes.

"Poor Beyfus! He thought he was doing such a good thing for me—and he was sending me to Hell.

"I couldn't thank him enough, of course; and I was in the seventh heaven of delight, for the company had come from Paris, was opening at Marseilles, and was then going to make a complete tour of the Mediterranean.

"It seemed to me that Providence was indeed watching over me, taking me right away from France and all danger of arrest; for even here in Marseilles, I was still terrified at the approach of a gendarme, and I knew that if I were arrested and questioned, I should blurt out that I had killed Raoul de Cassignac and was glad that I had killed him.

"Do I bore *Monsieur le Colonel?*"

By way of reply, Denis Ducros put his arm about the girl.

"Well, I was a success. All I had to do was to put on the costume of one of King René's pages, sing two or three songs beneath the casement of a lady, and two or three more, in a garden-setting, to the King, as a wandering *jongleur.*

"It was all so easy. It was wonderful; and I walked on air. Almost everyone in the company was extremely nice to me, and nobody tried to be too nice.

"Then we moved on. Eventually we went across to Algiers, and life was even more interesting and exciting than in France, and I was beginning to lose my fear. I felt safe in fact; quite safe, as one of this large and happy family. Of course we didn't live in luxury or anything like it, but we did very well, and I for one had nothing whatever of which to complain.

"And what a traveller I considered myself! Nicolette from Domeuil writing letters home from Algeria. I thought I was being very artful and rather witty, when I headed a letter to my mother, '*From Africa*'. By-and-bye, I changed this to Egypt, for we went to Alexandria and Cairo—still quite successful and prosperous.

"Then our manager made the mistake of going to Constantinople where neither the Turks nor the Greeks were in the slightest degree interested in us, and the French community was either not big enough to make a theatre audience, or preferred other forms of entertainment.

"The Manager tried a Great Special Week with a change of programme every night; but, judging by the dwindling box-office returns, the public liked each play less than the last. I think the Provençal one bored them most of all. Certainly I was quite unable to feel that my Provençal songs and tunes were their idea of entertainment at all.

"In fact, we who'd had quite an appeal in French places were just dull to the Constantinople public.

"At the end of the Special Week the Manager called us all together and announced quite frankly that to-morrow the treasury would be just about empty; and that when he had paid everything, including our salaries for this and the following week, there'd be no money at all.

"This was bad, but not as bad as it would have been if he had just bolted with what money there was, and left us stranded with nothing at all. As a matter of fact, he was a completely honest man; and when he left Constantinople he owed nobody anything, and, before he went, he did his best to find jobs for us.

"It was easy enough for those of us who could dance. It seemed essential that one must dance. However well one could sing and play, one must still dance.

"My poor little stock-in-trade seemed to be of no value at all in Constantinople. And I found a different type of agent there. Not at all like my dear little Beyfus.

"I remember one fat gentleman who heard me sing and play, and almost before I'd finished, simply made a vulgar noise with his mouth and pointed with his thumb over his shoulder, at the door.

"I got a job through another girl, before my savings were quite gone, at a big café in Pera, the Greek quarter of Constantinople.

"Because I was a French girl from Provence, and

knew the old Provençal airs and folk-songs, I was dressed up as a Hungarian and had to sing the latest and silliest and vulgarest music-hall songs from Paris.

"What I hated, at first, was having to go round the tables and talk to the men, between my songs. It was my first experience of selling wine on commission; urging people who had already had quite enough wine, to drink more, for the benefit of the management; and the hours were terrible. I had to stay in that beastly place until the last patron had gone, even if that were not until day-light.

"The cabaret manager was a horrible man, just a fat beast who fawned on the patrons and treated all his employees abominably; just as though they were slaves whom he had bought.

"And besides behaving like a savage to girls who were not willing to do everything he demanded, he persecuted us with a system of fines which took nearly all our earnings, and left us with scarcely enough to starve on . . . You were either one of his 'dear little girls', or you were constantly harassed and persecuted until you felt you'd be better dead.

"But does not all this bore *Monsieur le Colonel?*"

"No," replied the Colonel. "What does bore me is the thought that this gentleman is not in Sidi-bel-Abbès.

"Yes. A pity," he mused. "We might almost do something with the good slave-owner if he were here."

Nicolette laughed.

"*Monsieur le Colonel* sounds quite dangerous!

"Slave-owner!" she said. "It describes him, for he bought us, body and soul, through our need to eat. He owned us completely, through our fear of being out of work in a foreign land; and I honestly and truly believe that he sold us like slaves.

"I'll tell you . . .

"There was a woman who used to come to the café quite frequently. Besides watching the cabaret turns, she took an interest in the girls, especially the new-comers. She was very quiet, and *très correct* and *comme il faut.*

"What my friend found curious about her was that

she always came alone. That did not seem at all strange to me, for she was not young, and it seemed to me that it was just because she was alone that she wanted to chat with us girls. I liked to talk to her because she was French, and knew Marseilles. She actually professed to know my dear little Beyfus.

"She seemed to like talking to me, and before long she would make a point of calling me over to her table. She was very friendly and interested, and asked me all about myself and what she called my career. I was just a little bit wary, and simply said I was a stage-struck Marseilles girl who had joined a touring-company and been stranded here in Constantinople.

"She was quite frank about herself too. Apparently she was a business woman who loved a little excitement and company in the evening."

"Business woman!" said the Colonel. "What kind of business?"

"She said she had a dress-making establishment. She spoke of her work-girls as though she were fond of them. I thought how nice and kind she must be as an employer. I compared the lot of anyone who worked for her with that of the employees of the *Café de Pera*. How safe her girls must feel in their jobs!

"She told me how happy they all were, singing at their work, and what gay meals they had in the big work-room when work was done. I asked her where the girls came from, and she said from one place and another, mostly brought to her by their mothers—for training.

"They all lived in the house, for she would have no one whose only thought was to get away quickly from work to outside amusements; but she provided ample leisure, and let them have friends to see them. It was just a big happy family living in a comfortable home.

"How I envied those girls!

"Then, one hot thundery night, I defied our dreadful cabaret-manager. I just could not and would not give in to him; and after an angry and ugly scene, he told me my job was finished.

"I was finished too. It was the end. I could go. I was

to go at once. That night . . . as soon as the café should close.

"Well, my new friend saw that I was in trouble, and asked me, so kindly, what was wrong. I told her."

"And what will you do now?" she asked.

"*Do?* What *can* I do? Where can I go? I have no money," I said frantically.

"She considered the situation.

" 'My child,' she said, 'are you determined to lead this café life? This uncertain, worthless way of life? . . . Why not give it up?'

" 'Give it up?' I said. 'I would do so, only too gladly. But what else can I do? Where can I go?'

"And then it seemed as if the good St. Louis himself must have led me to her, for she said,

" 'Would you care to give up all this, and join my girls in their work-room? I could not pay you much. *Au contraire,* most of them pay me to teach them their business. But you would be learning how to make a career for yourself, and you would have food, a home, and a little something to save . . . I think you would be happy with them and with me. I will see that you are well looked after.'

"I looked at her in wonder.

" 'But why? Why should you do this for me?' I asked.

" 'It so happens that I have just one vacancy,' she said. 'Our little Julie has left us to be married, and I have been looking for someone suitable to take her place. I have talked with you, and I like you . . . And you like me, *hein?* Well, come and try for a little while. You can always return to the cafés of Constantinople, if you prefer that way of life.'

"I shuddered . . . The cafés of Constantinople! . . . Each one worse than the last.

" 'Oh! Is it really true? May I really come?' I asked.

" 'We will try you,' said Madame. 'And, what is better, you shall come home with me this night. I will wait for you.'

"And so I went away with my kind friend—that night—to her establishment, where all the girls were so gay and happy in their work.

"It was quite a nice house in a turning off the hill that leads up from Galata Bridge, the *Grande Rue de Pera* I think it is; and, as we got out from the *fiacre,* my benefactress mentioned that this was her private house, not her place of business.

"I was a little puzzled, very upset by the fright I had had when I was dismissed, very relieved and grateful for this unexpected help, and so tired I could hardly keep my eyes open.

"However, she insisted on my having some little sweet cakes and thick bitter Turkish coffee, in a room she called her boudoir, before she took me up to the room in which I was to sleep that night."

A brief silence again, which Denis forbore to break. He saw it all now, and he felt savagely angry.

The poor, poor, foolish innocent little simpleton.

"I slept all night and the next day," continued Nicolette. "It was evening when I woke up. I was puzzled and a little alarmed, and yet, at the same time, stupidly content, if you know what I mean. All I wanted was to sleep and to sleep, and there seemed no reason why I should not do so."

"Drugged, in fact," growled the Colonel. "Opium, morphia, hashish, or some other filth."

"I woke again towards evening, and I suppose I had been asleep then for at least two days and nights. While I was lying awake, feeling extraordinarily stupid and drowsy, the maid, who had waited on us when we arrived the first night, came in with a tray of food. *Soupe,* a roll and some *pilaf* stuff.

"I didn't like the maid. She was a great strong horse of a woman with a cruel face and a surly manner. She dumped the tray on a chair by my bed and went out of the room without a word. I supposed she resented having to wait on me, and then I wondered if perhaps she spoke only Turkish. I was not feeling at all well, and was not hungry. I was very thirsty however, and the *soupe* was strong and good, and so was the coffee.

" 'I will get up now,' I thought to myself, and looked round for my clothes.

" *'Why, they've gone!'*, I said to myself stupidly. *'My clothes have gone!'* and almost in the act of getting up to see if they had been tidied away, I fell asleep again . . .

"Now it's a curious thing," said Nicolette. "I remember every detail of what I've told you, as though it happened yesterday, but my memory is quite blurred about what happened from that moment.

"For days and weeks, perhaps for months, I must have been about a quarter awake and three-quarters asleep, when I wasn't asleep altogether.

"Just a few memories here and there stick up, like the rocks do out of black water at twilight.

"I remember realising that my clothes really had gone, including my shoes; that my 'benefactress' came into the room, now and again, and talked quite differently from the way in which she had done at the café.

"I told her that I felt terrible, and I could only tell her that I was ill. That I felt so weak that I wondered if I might be dying . . . That I felt I must get out . . . That I must have my clothes . . . That I must go away . . .

"I was very ill of course. I was three parts poisoned, and I was frightened to death.

"The woman agreed that I was ill, and said that what I needed was a doctor. She would bring her own, for she could not have me lying ill there in her house for the rest of my life. I had come to work. Why had I not told her I was so delicate, and suffered so much from this sort of *malaise?*"

Again Nicolette fell silent.

"She brought the 'doctor'," she said at length.

"He was not a doctor," she added.

The Colonel said nothing, but the girl felt the muscles of his arm tighten across her shoulders.

"By God!" he whispered. "If I . . ."

Nicolette suddenly began to cry, and turning up her face to his, Denis Ducros kissed her on the lips.

"Don't!" he said. "Don't!"

With an effort the girl regained her self-control and dried her eyes.

"That's my little story, *Monsieur le Colonel,*" she

said. "I have no excuses to offer for myself. I was a stupid, simple, silly fool, who got what she deserved for allowing herself to be so easily caught by our dear Madame."

"*Madame!*" cried Denis. "*This* 'Madame'?"

"Yes," answered Nicolette. "This Madame. Our dear Madame who loves all her girls, and takes such care of them."

"By God!" swore Denis. "I'll break . . ."

"Too late, *Monsieur le Colonel.* You can do nothing. Nothing for any of us."

"I can do something for her, though. And I . . ."

"You have given us all a happy evening, *Monsieur le Colonel.* You have given me the happiest evening that I have had since I killed Raoul de Cassignac. Truly you can do nothing more. Be content."

"It's abominable! It's monstrous! It's almost unbelievable," he stormed. "Couldn't you have escaped from that house in Pera?"

"Not without clothes," was the brief reply.

"Couldn't you have opened the windows in your room and screamed and *screamed?*"

"It did not open."

"Could you not have broken the window?"

"I tried, with my bare hands. The little panes of glass, set in iron, must have been an inch thick."

"Couldn't you have opened the door of your room, and . . . ?"

"It was locked on the outside."

"Couldn't you have fought and fought and *fought?* . . ."

"That maid, the Turkish woman, was as strong as a strong man; and, do you know, the whole of the time I was there, I never stood on my feet without feeling so sick and giddy that I must either sit down or fall down . . .

"Please . . . Please don't think I am making excuses," she continued. "A better and a stronger character than I would have found some way out *sans doute,* or would never have got into such a position . . .

"Yes, I fully admit I was defeated. I gave in. Madame

won. She broke me, mind and body, so that I cringed when she came into the room with that dreadful Turkish woman."

"How do you come to be here, Nicolette; here in Sidi-bel-Abbès?"

"I scarcely know," replied the girl. "I lived in a kind of dream, a nightmare of horrors, until I was completely obedient and docile and had given up everything—including courage and hope—and was altogether finished as a self-respecting human being.

"Madame must have used her opium or chloral or hashish or whatever it was, quite regularly. Every day I must have had the poison in my food or coffee. Of course, if I'd been a person of any strength of character, I should have starved myself to death or deliberately died of thirst, rather than take any food or drink, knowing that some of it was drugged."

"Yes. That's what it comes to," agreed the Colonel, with a restraint that gave no indication of his fierce anger and indignation. "You were poisoned, mind and body as you say, and you were not responsible for your actions. Of course you could not commit suicide in such a horrible way as to refuse food and drink. No young girl could face such a lingering death as that. It is unthinkable."

"Well, anyhow . . . I didn't do it; and after I'd once been thoroughly drugged and stupefied, I could not think and plan and *do* anything, to help myself. I just drifted."

"Or say rather that you were drowned and your lifeless corpse drifted," said the Colonel.

"And really I remember very little after the first days in that house in Pera. As I say, it was a drugged sleep with appalling nightmares; and I had an almost unbearable headache the whole time.

"But I do remember that there was some sudden and serious trouble with the police, and Madame was in a great state of fear and anxiety. It was evidently something quite out of the ordinary, for she was then, as always, on excellent terms with the authorities.

"I never knew the facts of the matter, but a very

rich and important Turk, a *pasha* and high official of some kind, died in that quiet house in the Beyoglu quarter, and naturally there were searching enquiries.

"Apparently that always means bad trouble in Constantinople.

"The police have to make good, which means making or finding something bad; and Madame complained bitterly, for long afterwards, that the girls were not loyal, not faithful, not grateful to her, and told the police the most wicked lies. And apparently, from what I've heard her say, one trouble led to another. As if the death of a *pasha* were not bad enough, it was discovered that one of the girls was a spy—a Russian girl.

"So Madame had not only ordinary criminal-police trouble, but political-police trouble, which is far worse. However, she had friends among both, and was able to do the wisest thing—escape. She left Constantinople in a hurry and very quietly.

"I think she simply abandoned all the other girls. But she took me with her. Me and the Turkish servant woman. We went by boat to Alexandria."

"Wasn't that your chance," asked the Colonel, gently.

Nicolette shook her head.

"I was so ill that, even now, I've only the vaguest memory of being dressed, taken in a carriage down to the water-side, and on to a ship. I was Madame's sick daughter, and the Turkish woman was my nurse!

"She was so strong that when I could not put one foot before another, she carried me as though I was a child.

"It was the same when we got to Alexandria. The Mother, the nurse, and the half-sick half-idiot daughter.

"Curiously enough, one thing I can remember to this day, about that journey, with the utmost distinctness, is the terrible feeling that there was something I *must* do. I must *do* something. But I could not realise what it was. Dimly, I knew that, as you just said, this was my chance. But my chance to do what? And how was I to set about doing what I had to do? It was almost one of the worst parts of the nightmare, that indescribably awful feeling that I could save myself if only I knew what to do and how to do it.

"I know that, once or twice, I cried out, and that if anyone else was present Madame would say,

" 'Oh, the poor child! *Pauvre petite!* How she suffers! When shall we reach home, and the good doctor? . . . Give her her medicine quickly, Nurse. An injection, I think, and she will sleep.'

"But almost all the time we were in a wretched little cabin; I was never left alone; and I scarcely saw anybody when we left the ship.

"But when in the cabin I had that impulse to help myself, it was a different story. It was not 'Poor child' then. That Turkish woman was truly skilful in inflicting horrible agonising pain without causing the slightest bruise or any mark whatever . . .

"I daresay *Monsieur le Colonel* knows the pain of a twisted wrist."

"And you did not scream?" he asked.

"Only once or twice, at first. After that it was a whimper rather than a scream.

"No, believe me, Monsieur, one did not scream, or disobey those two women. Nor, for the greater part of the time, did I know where I was, where I was going, or what I was doing. The horrible little Turkish coasting-ship rolled like a tub, and I was deathly sea-sick in addition to being poisoned with the drug.

"Another thing I remember out of all the far more important things I have forgotten, was a hideous delusion that I was drowned under some terribly heavy, sticky mess that was neither liquid nor solid; and that I could only save my life by getting to my feet and raising my head above it. But the effort to stand up was terrible, as though one were lifting tons of huge chains; and when at last, with a tremendous effort, one got to one's feet, one was completely coated, a foot thick, with this awful sticky horror, and the weight of it bore one down again . . . still suffocating . . . down into it to drown and die like . . . like . . . a fly in treacle."

"That was how the opium, or hashish, or whatever

the filthy poison was, affected your brain," said the Colonel. "I wonder you did not go out of your mind, or die."

"I went out of my mind, all right," said the girl, "and I wish I had died. But I was too ill, too stupid, too drugged to put an end to it, and I shouldn't have had the courage, anyhow."

"My poor Nicolette," murmured Denis. "I should like to take our Madame and . . .

"And you came here from Alexandria?" he interrupted himself. "More trouble there for Madame?"

"I don't know. I never heard of any special catastrophe. I think it was just that Madame did not flourish. The English are a queer people. Madame does not like them."

"It is conceivable that they did not like Madame," observed the Colonel. "She may have been invited to travel further."

"Yes. She was always muttering *'Ces Anglais! Mon Dieu, ces Anglais!',* and I remember being very ill again, and being taken by train to Cairo, where Madame thought a pleasanter atmosphere might be found."

"And how long were you in Cairo?" asked the Colonel.

"There again, I really don't know. It can't have been very long; but as in the other places, I lived in a sort of dream. I was never quite awake and I slept a great deal of the time. I scarcely remember anything at all about Cairo; and I doubt if I ever once went out of the house, the whole time I was there."

"And why did Madame leave Cairo?" asked the Colonel. "I feel one cannot know too much about Madame's interesting history. Was there more trouble?"

"I am sorry to keep on saying 'I don't know'," replied Nicolette, "but I think there must have been. I think it was due to her doing something that, in Constantinople, would have been quite in order. For here again she kept on saying what imbeciles the English were, and that she'd like to see every English official pushed into the Nile, with a brick tied round his neck. Anyway, Madame began declaring that she'd go where there was less British hypocrisy and more civilisation.

"I don't think she was actually turned out of Cairo but I know we went to Algiers, for I have vague recollections of another ship's cabin, and, later, of seeing from a window a view that was familiar.

"Here again I remember something that, although it is only a memory of thoughts, is stronger and clearer than any memory of people or events. I distinctly remember coming to myself, so to speak, one day, and realising the awful difference between my life during my former visit there as an actress, with real friends, in a happy hard-working company, and my position, my life, on this second visit.

"I think it was only then that I really awoke, though only for a brief space, to the knowledge and understanding of what had happened to me. But I soon lapsed back into stupidity; a dreadful drugged drowsiness; apathy."

"And why did Madame leave the flourishing town of Algiers? I should have thought the Kasbah would have been her spiritual home," said the Colonel.

"Once again, I don't really know. But I think it was a man."

"Another dead one, or a live one this time?" enquired the Colonel.

"Very much alive. I believe he had some hold on Madame."

"Very likely, I should think."

"She talked a great deal about blackmail. . . . Oh, I remember. Yes. . . . It was the manager of the Pera café. He had come to Algiers and set himself up there in the *Café de Stamboul,* with real Turkish coffee and odalisques to serve it. Madame started going there, as she had done in Constantinople. Yes, that was it. Odette knew all about it and told me.

"Apparently, in the end, Madame simply ran away from this man. The police had nothing to do with it at all."

"I begin to think better of him," observed the Colonel. "Pity he could not have come on here."

"He was a terrible man," said Nicolette.

"And so you came here from Algiers?"

"Yes, *Monsieur le Colonel,* we came here."

The Colonel sat silent for a moment.

"It's incredible," he said. "Wouldn't one have thought it utterly impossible that a grown girl, who was neither insane nor dumb; neither blind nor bed-ridden; could be carted around the world like a piece of luggage?"

"One would, Monsieur. But, believe me, one would be wrong. Far from being impossible, such a thing is perfectly easy. . . . However unwilling or combative the victim may be . . . I would have given anything in the world, *everything in the world,* to have escaped, the moment I realised what Madame was.

"But as I have tried to show you, I had no chance. As I have said, she broke me, mind and body and soul, until I cringed at the sight of her and at the sound of her voice."

Denis Ducros rose to his feet.

"She . . . broke . . . you . . . and . . . you . . . cringed before her," he said slowly.

"Look you, Nicolette, I, Denis . . . I mean Louis Rochefort, solemnly swear that *I* will break *her,* and that *she* shall cringe before *me*—in your presence."

The girl stared at him wide-eyed.

"No! No! No!" she protested. "It is too late. We are what we are, and Madame is our . . ."

"*Stop!*" he said angrily. "You are what you are, and I am what I am. We are what Fate has made us. Tell me. Would you like to go away from here? *Would you like to go back to Provence?*"

CHAPTER 12

REAL POWER AND GREAT GLORY

"Oh!" cried Nicolette. "Oh! If only that were possible! I'd give my soul . . . anything . . . anything—if I had anything to give."

Never did Colonel Louis Rochefort speak more convincingly, with more certain assurance and more moral grandeur, than did Denis Ducros at this moment.

"My child," he said. "You shall leave here. *You shall go back to Provence.* And you shall go *to-night.*"

Nicolette leapt to her feet, and he took her in his arms.

They kissed and clung spontaneously like young lovers, and with uncontrollable emotion, devotion—and no trace of passion.

Denis Ducros felt that he loved this girl. Loved her, and would save her.

Not only would he be the great Caliph who amused himself incognito, pulling strings here and there; he would be the real Fairy Prince, of a real and living Fairy Tale which was a real tale of real life.

He would save her and set her free.

And if he never did another decent thing, he would not have lived in vain.

"Sit down," he said, "and *I* will talk."

They sat down together, his arm about her.

"Listen, my Nicolette," he began. "Is there any real reason why you should not go home? To your people, I mean."

"No," replied Nicolette, "except that I cannot leave here. How can I, without money for fares, without clothes?"

"They would be glad for you to go back to them, your parents?" he asked.

"Yes. They have always loved me very dearly, and I have always reproached myself for running away as I did . . . but I was so frightened."

"You were never suspected—in the matter of Raoul de Cassignac? That's all forgotten long ago, and . . ."

"No, I couldn't go back there," said Nicolette decisively. "Not to Domeuil. I couldn't bear it; apart from any fear. It's still my worst nightmare, even after all I've been through since. And my parents have moved to Avignon."

"Then you could go to them there?"

"Yes. If I could get away from here. But I haven't the necessary money—or anything."

"Does Madame give you no money?"

"No. *Au contraire!* We are all in Madame's debt. And the longer we are here, the bigger the debt."

"*Ah! . . . Indeed?* One begins to wonder how the poor woman lives!" said the voice of Colonel Louis Rochefort.

"However, we'll go into that with her later. Now then. There's a train leaves Sidi-bel-Abbès Station in about an hour's time, for Oran. You'll catch that train; and it'll ramble along the eighty miles to the coast in such a leisurely manner, stopping for half an hour at every station, that it won't get you to Oran much before breakfast-time.

"You will go straight to the *Hôtel de la République* for *petit déjeuner.* They'll tell you when the next boat is leaving for Marseilles, and book a berth for you. You'll get to Marseilles in about thirty-six hours; and then it won't be long before there is a train to Avignon. If you have to stay a night in Marseilles . . ."

Nicolette laughed.

What a wonderful dream!

But really rather too painful.

Of course, he meant only to be kind and agreeable, this charming and adorable Monsieur.

The station . . . The train . . . Oran . . . A ship . . . Passing the Château d'If . . . the harbour . . . Marseilles . . . France . . . Then *home!*

Monsieur le Colonel did not wish to be unkind. Furtively she wiped her eyes.

"Is that understood?" demanded Denis the Colonel.

"Oh, but yes, Monsieur. Quite understood. I go straight from this house to that of my parents—without clothes or money or Madame's permission."

The Colonel permitted himself his most superior smile.

"Not quite like that," he contradicted. "With clothes, with money, and with Madame's permission.

"And we'll arrange it now," he added, rising and opening the door.

Hassan appeared from nowhere, bowing low.

"Madame!" said the Colonel.

Hassan disappeared, and a minute later Madame sailed majestic into the hall.

"*Monsieur le Colonel* desires . . . ?"

"An outfit of clothing for Mademoiselle Nicolette, including a travelling suit, a cape, and . . . what-not.

"Also a small sum of money. Let us say ten thousand francs, in fifty- and a hundred-franc notes."

Madame stared in complete bewilderment.

"The good Nicolette would also go for a drive, and *Monsieur le Colonel* would borrow . . . ?"

"No, Madame. *Monsieur le Colonel* is not going to borrow. But Madame is going to repay. Not in full of course, for Madame could never do that in this life— though she surely will in the next.

"No. Madame is merely going to pay ten thousand francs of what she owes, to one of her girls."

"But, *Monsieur le Colonel*," protested Madame on a rising note, in which incredulity struggled with indignation and alarm.

"I? Pay Nicolette ten thousand francs? *I* pay *her*, did *Monsieur le Colonel* suggest? Why, *she* owes *me* more than that. . . . Far, far more than that."

"They all do, I expect," agreed the Colonel. "You stagger along under a crushing and increasing load of unpaid credits. That's how you live!

"Now then," he continued with an abrupt change of voice, "go and get me ten thousand francs, Madame."

"*Monsieur le Colonel* is joking! Even if I had ten thousand francs in the world, does *Monsieur le Colonel* suppose I should have it in this house?"

"Yes."

"And would it be in a little drawer in a table in the *salon*? Or on the mantelpiece, or under the front-door mat? Or perhaps in an old stocking hanging . . . ?"

"Or in an old tea-pot, perhaps. I don't know and I don't care. But I suggest a perfectly good safe in Madame's bedroom. Anyway—*get* it."

"The safe, Monsieur?"

"Look you, Madame. Wit and humour are excellent things at the right time. This is not the time. And speaking of that, my time is rather short. Mademoiselle Nicolette has a train to catch."

"Mademoiselle Nicolette has a . . . ?" gasped Madame.

"Yes. I said a train. She is leaving Sidi-bel-Abbès."

Madame's face seemed to turn into granite, her eyes into cold steel.

"And," continued the Colonel imperturbably, "so is Madame—unless she is very careful."

"I? *I* leaving Sidi-bel-Abbès, *Monsieur le Colonel?*"

"Yes."

And the Colonel's face was as hard as Madame's.

"Don't forget I can have you out of here, lock, stock and barrel, and in short order. Give me any trouble; tell me any more lies; or attempt to disobey any order I may give you—*and I'll do it.* And I'll only give you twenty-four hours' notice."

"*Monsieur le Colonel . . . I . . .*"

Was it possible that the redoubtable Madame quailed? Quailed and shrank before a man—a mere man, which is the most contemptible object in all creation.

"And I'll tell you one more thing, Madame, for your information—that unless Mademoiselle Nicolette is swiftly and suitably fitted out, and ten thousand francs paid to her, I'll send for a *péloton* of my men who'll remove the entire contents of this house—including the wall-paper and the nails, before you can scream, and they'll . . ."

Madame did cringe, as he had promised. Visibly she cringed, shrank, blenched.

The Foreign Legion!

Name of Satan! Those fearful foreign devils! Why at the order of this arch-fiend they'd do anything. Anything.

And—apart from that—at a word; at a stroke of his pen, he could ruin her. She had forgotten. She had not realised the power of this terrible man. The danger . . .

But—*ten thousand francs! Ten* thousand francs of her hard-earned money. . . . And she had been going to send it to the Bank to-morrow, as she did every month. Well, then let her imagine it had gone. He couldn't prove she had that amount of money in the house.

She plucked up spirit.

"*Monsieur le Colonel!* Once and for all, I have not . . ."

"Then, for a start, Madame, your house is out of bounds for officers of this garrison; and to-morrow you'll be out of Sidi-bel-Abbès. I will send Hassan for the picket."

Madame capitulated. Almost she collapsed. With the police she had always been able to deal satisfactorily—the police of several nations; but this was no case of a police underling anxious to improve his bank balance. This was the military; and an officer of high rank, stern, harsh, incorruptible.

And suddenly Madame had a dreadful thought, one which caused her swiftly to change her manner and her attitude. *God alone knew what the girl had told him!* And if she only told him the truth of what she knew—or half the truth, or a little part of the truth—it would be enough.

"*Monsieur le Colonel,* one can only do one's best. Doubtless I can find some odds and ends of clothes for the girl, if *Monsieur le Colonel* wishes to take her for a trip to Algiers. And I will scrape together what money I have in the house. I fear it won't be ten thousand francs, or . . ."

"It will be ten thousand francs, Madame," the Colonel reassured her, "and the clothing will be entirely adequate and suitable. I give you ten minutes," and the Colonel turned towards the room in which the girl sat nervously-biting at her handkerchief.

"If *Monsieur le Colonel* will permit Nicolette to come upstairs with me," suggested Madame, following him anxiously, "I will . . ."

"Get the clothes and the money, and bring them here," interrupted the Colonel. "You now have nine minutes."

"Hassan," he added, turning to where that acquiescent individual stood at the post of duty, "yet one more carriage. The last and the best."

"Nicolette, Madame will bring you your clothes, your money, and her permission to depart—if not her blessing on your journey."

Nicolette sprang up.

"*Monsieur le Colonel,* you do not mean . . ."

"I mean, my child, that you are going home; and you are going now," interrupted Denis grandly. "I have arranged it."

Unbelieving, half-believing, yearning to believe, the girl, in a transport of madness, put her arms about her benefactor's neck.

"*How I love you!*" she whispered.

"And I love you, my sweet, my Nicolette!" answered Denis fervently, as they clung together—a poor Daughter of Joy whom Fate had treated with the utmost brutality, and a poor Soldier of Fortune, badly wounded in the Battle of Life.

Nicolette drew back and looked into his eyes.

"You *mean* that?" she whispered. "You mean you really *do* love me a little?"

"Yes. I do mean it . . . I find I have fallen in love with you, my Nicolette. If only I had met you—there in Domeuil before you ever saw that *scélérat* of a de Cassignac."

"And, oh, if you were only an ordinary man!" sighed Nicolette. "Just a *soldat simple,* and not a Colonel."

Denis Ducros' laugh was brief and enigmatic.

"Listen, my dear," he said. "I shall retire from this high rank of Colonel that I now adorn. Retire very soon indeed, in fact. Much sooner than you would suppose. And, as soon as I can, after I have retired, I shall

return to France; and from Marseilles I shall come to—
Avignon."

"Oh!" breathed Nicolette. "*Monsieur le Colonel!* If I
could see you there, just for a minute! To try to thank
you. To tell you I was safe . . . and free . . . And to try
to express what I shall be feeling . . . I would meet
every train that came to Avignon by day or night. I
would live at the railway-station, if only in the hope of
seeing you pass by."

"Tell me where to write to," said Denis, "and I will
tell you the time of the train by which I shall come to
Avignon . . . to see you, Nicolette."

The girl's face was transfigured, and it was as
though a light shone from her eyes, a light of hope and
of love.

And the face of Denis Ducros softened, and seemed
to lose certain lines. His lips lost bitterness and his
eyes gained brightness and warmth.

Again they kissed and clung, the girl forgetting the
past, the man ignoring the future.

"You will go straight to your parents?" he said. "You
will let no other devil in human form delude you. It's a
hellish world, Nicolette, for a lovely girl alone and . . ."

"Have no fear. I shall go straight to my mother and
father, without the loss of a minute. And there I shall
wait and wait and wait—for the rest of my life, hoping
that you may come. . . .

"Am I dreaming? Do you really mean this, *Monsieur
le Colonel?*" she asked.

"I mean it, Nicolette. If I do not come, it will mean
that I am in . . . I am in . . . Well, in my grave; a grave
of some kind."

(The living death in the grave of prison. Might he
not get eight years' *travaux forcées?*)

"Please do not talk of graves . . . to-night. I think I
should die now if I ceased to believe that . . ."

"Listen, Nicolette. Would you wait eight years, if I
did not come?"

"Eighteen, *Monsieur le Colonel.* Or twenty-eight.

"And then I should not be an old woman," she
smiled.

"So you'd wait twenty-eight years, my dear?"

"I shall wait all my life. What is twenty-eight years if I am waiting for you."

Denis kissed her again.

"Well, it won't be as long as that," he said. "Nor eighteen. But possibly it might be eight. . . . On the other hand, it might be only a little more than eight months."

"Look you, *Monsieur le Colonel.* Waiting will be happiness. Thanks to you, my life is being turned from hell to heaven. From blackest misery to pure golden happiness. Waiting, waiting to see you, will be the great part of that happiness. On my knees I could ask nothing better of the Blessed Virgin than to be allowed to live, waiting—for you. Only one thing better, and that I should scarcely dare to ask—that you might really come."

"I shall come, Nicolette. I shall come."

Followed by Hassan, Madame entered, carrying a collection of clothing over one arm, and a roll of notes clutched in one hand.

The clothes she flung upon the divan, with a gesture of angry contempt. The money she offered to the Colonel.

"Before witnesses, I *lend* this money to *Monsieur le Colonel* Louis Rochefort," she said. "I do not ask for interest, but I should like prompt repayment."

"Before witnesses," smiled the Colonel. "I remark that you do nothing of the kind. You give it freely and unconditionally to Mademoiselle Nicolette, because you owe it to her. Take notice also, that you do moreover owe her about another forty thousand francs, of which we will say nothing at the moment . . .

"Unless," he added, "Madame would like to make full admission of the fact, and payment of the remainder of the sum owed? . . . Put the ten thousand francs on the table there."

One is never too old to learn, and Madame, to her profound surprise, discovered that she was learning restraint and self-control, even thus late in life. She felt she was also learning wisdom. She contrived to hold her peace, though peace was not within her.

"Dress quickly, Nicolette," he said, "and count the money. . . . Come, Madame, let us have a chat, shall we?"

"There is indeed a little I should like to say to *Monsieur le Colonel*," responded Madame grimly.

"There is a lot I should like to say to Madame," replied the Colonel, even more grimly.

And in the *salon*, to which Madame led the way, he said quite a lot; said it with point and eloquence; and said it to such purpose that Madame was almost convinced that she was not a public benefactress; was not even a real friend to unfortunate girls who had, for various reasons, left their homes and been rescued by her from the dangers notoriously resultant upon homelessness.

"Yes, my dear Madame," concluded the Colonel, just before Nicolette entered the room, "speaking judicially and impartially, without rancour, wrath or resentment, I should say that you and your kind are the most poisonous reptiles in Creation. You and your sort are the most vile, depraved and abominable bestialities that disfigure and pollute the world that God made for humanity to be happy in. You are a malignant microbe, Madame. Beside you, cancer is a mild misfortune, almost a beneficence; leprosy a trifling nuisance.

"It is not so much that you are a living Crime as that it is a terrible crime to let you live.

"We guillotine murderers for killing the body; what then should we do to you who kill souls; kill happiness; hope; self-respect; kill the life that is in the living body, leaving that body alive to suffer utter degradation?

"There is no fate bad enough for you; this world has no punishment adequate; and that, I think, is why your fate and punishment are reserved for you in the next world—a punishment quite beyond our present poor human comprehension.

"Madame, you are a foul sub-human incarnation of Evil, and a disgrace even to that section of humanity that is so much lower than the animals. When, in Hell,

you encounter Monsieur Judas Iscariot, he will doubtless feel ashamed that . . .

"Ah! Here is Mademoiselle Nicolette . . .

"Have you everything you'll want for the journey?
. . . Come along then."

Hassan entered to announce proudly that he had
produced an absolutely super carriage.

The Colonel and Nicolette left Madame standing
speechless, themselves refraining from speech as they
went from her house.

It gave the Colonel a sense of pleasure and approval
that, unlike himself, Nicolette, triumphant, uttered no
reproaches or abuse of Madame. Could there be such a
contempt as she deserved, Madame was treated with
that contempt by the girl almost young enough to be
her grand-daughter.

As the Colonel followed Nicolette into the carriage,
Madame rushed forth, having recovered her powers of
movement and of speech.

"And the bill! And the bill!" she screamed. "The
wine! The carriages! Entertainment! My time. The time
of all my girls! Is it desired that I send my little bill
direct to the house of *Monsieur le Colonel?* Or does he
prefer to settle with me now?"

"Now," replied the Colonel. "I never leave debts
unpaid. Madame may take it out of the forty thousand
francs still owing to Mademoiselle Nicolette."

"*Monsieur le Colonel!*" screamed Madame. "This is
monstrous! This is . . ."

"Devilish," supplied the Colonel.

"And one more word out of *you,* Madame, and I'll
return and have a talk with the other girls. You probably owe each of them a great deal more than fifty thousand francs. . . . Still, they'll doubtless be glad of ten
thousand francs apiece, on account."

Madame did say one more word, but the Colonel
behaved like a gentleman, and affected not to hear it.

"Drive to the station, *cocher,*" he ordered, and as
Hassan salaamed low, he delighted that admiring man
by his last words to Madame.

"Give the good Hassan ten francs *bakshish,* please,

Madame, and put it on the bill."

The delight of Hassan was unbounded. Idiot's de-light.

"There's the Law! There's the Law, *Monsieur le Colonel,*" screamed Madame, as the carriage started on its way.

"Beware of it, Madame! Beware of it!" replied the Colonel and shut the near-side door with a slam of complete finality.

As they turned into the darkness of the tree-shaded road, the Colonel took Nicolette's hand in his own, and they sat silent, the girl utterly unable to believe in this sudden amazing miracle of Love, and of release from the House of Bondage, of dreadful slavery and dark despair.

Denis, for once, was dumb; and dumb with the overwhelming need for speech.

He had fallen in love as suddenly as a man, walking in darkness, may fall in water.

Thus suddenly. Thus completely immersed in a new element . . . *Coup de foudre!*

What had he done? What had he not done, this night? This marvellous night of freedom.

In his brief and beautiful freedom he had walked into this long and beautiful bondage. Bound for ever with the golden chain of love.

He was in love. He was in love. He was in love. His heart sang.

And suddenly his soaring spirit stooped, drooped, and fell to earth.

He had plumed himself on being a mighty actor, a marvel of lost and wasted histrionic genius. He had played the Colonel!

He had also played the fool, the liar, the swindler and blackguardly cad. He had won Nicolette's love under false pretences!

Fine feathers make fine birds; and as a fine bird with golden feathers he had deluded this poor girl sitting beside him.

The Fairy Prince!

What would she say if she knew that her fairy

prince was a greasy batman, serving tables, cleaning boots, brushing clothes, doing menial jobs at the behest of fat Natalie; bowing and scraping, "No, *Monsieur le Colonel;* Yes, *Monsieur le Colonel.*"

A serving man.

Free?

A free Frenchman?

He was a slave. The slave of the Legion. The slave of Colonel Louis Rochefort.

And now the slave of a lie.

He loved Nicolette, and he could not make the foolish attempt to base their life together on a lie.

A cold sense of failure, of loss, of cruel and bitter disappointment settled upon him; and for the first time in his life he experienced that oft-imagined but sometimes very real pain, a physical aching of the heart.

He must lose Nicolette by letting her go now, out of his life, to-night. Letting her go, in the happy belief that she had been befriended by, had indeed been loved by, a distinguished man, a great man, a Colonel famous throughout a crack Army Corps.

Or, even more painfully, he must lose her by telling her the truth; by endeavouring to make her see him as he should be, a servant in a green baize apron.

He could never go to Avignon to find Nicolette in the *rôle* of Colonel Louis Rochefort, retired—whether he got heavy or light, long or short, punishment for to-night's doings.

To-night's escapade had started merely as a joke, though Colonel Rochefort might think it a joke in bad taste. To carry the joke to France would be carrying it too far.

From every point of view it was unthinkable.

What a fool he had been!

Clever Denis Ducros!

Once more he had landed himself on the horns of a dilemma; and was also firmly caught in a cleft stick of his own making.

Well, which would be the less cruel course—for her? To let her wait and wait at Avignon for the man who never came?

That would be a wicked thing to do.

To tell her suddenly, as they parted, that the man with whom she had fallen in love, the man she trusted, the first man in whom she had believed since the terrible lesson taught her by Raoul de Cassignac,—to tell her suddenly that that man was a play-acting rascal, a fraud, an impostor?

That would be a cruel thing to do—and cruelty was worse than wickedness.

Denis Ducros was not wicked, and he was not cruel.

But oh, what a fool! What a ten thousand times despicable damnable fool!

"Nicolette," he said.

"*Monsieur le Colonel . . .*"

"That's just what I was going to say, '*Don't say,*' " he smiled ruefully.

"Say '*don't say*'?" smiled the girl.

"Yes. Don't say '*Monsieur le Colonel.*' "

Nicolette pressed closer to his side.

"I feel somehow, I could never call you Louis, *Monsieur le . . .*"

"No. Don't say that either. Do you think you could call me Denis?"

"Denis? Is that Monsieur's second name?"

"No. It's his only name, Nicolette. My first name is Denis . . .

"And my second is Ducros," he added sullenly, as one who makes unwilling confession.

"*Denis Ducros?*" repeated Nicolette, in some bewilderment. "But you are *Monsieur le Colonel* Louis Rochefort."

This was difficult. This was painful. This was terrible. And beads of cold perspiration gathered on his forehead.

"Listen, Nicolette," he said heavily.

"I am *le légionnaire* Denis Ducros. I am also an impostor, a humbug, a play-acting fraud, and a fool."

"You are a private soldier?" exclaimed the girl.

"I am."

To the shocked amazement of Denis Ducros, Nicolette burst into tears.

This was what came of play-acting!

This was the real punishment for that folly. What *they* could do to him would be nothing.

"Really and truly an ordinary, common *légion-naire?*" she sobbed.

"Yes."

"Truly?"

"Yes."

Nicolette sobbed more bitterly. Her tears flowed yet more freely.

The remorseful heart of Denis sank more heavily within his gentle breast.

He must try to comfort her. Risking indignant rebuff, he put his gold-braided arm about her.

"Don't cry, Nicolette," he said. "Don't cry. At least you are *free*. There is no deception about that. And you are going home to Avignon. Don't cry."

"But I must . . . I am so happy," sobbed Nicolette. "So very . . . *very* happy."

"To be free and going home to Avignon?" he said, a little sadly.

"No. That is nothing . . . I am in a heaven of happiness—to know that *'Monsieur le Colonel'* is Denis Ducros, *le légionnaire*. . . . I thank God!" she said.

"Denis Ducros!" she whispered.

And with tears in his own eyes, and a lump in his throat, Denis kissed her.

"My Nicolette!"

This was true. This was real.

There was no play-acting about this.

He was in love with this girl, and toward her he felt as he had never felt toward any other woman. He wanted to give, and to *give*, without the slightest desire to take and to demand. And he was also aware of a feeling of pity, unfathomably deep; and Pity is the wonderful and beautiful sister of Love.

And without any amazement he found that with his new and fine love, his great and profound pity, he felt a real and true respect for her. And of that he was subconsciously but greatly glad, because he knew that without real respect, there could be no real lasting love.

Sympathy, yes; pity, yes; passion, yes—but not the love that lasts as long as life.

"My Nicolette!" he said again, and drew her yet closer to him.

"My Denis!" she whispered, returning his kiss with a warmth and strength equal to his own. "I am *too* happy. I am bewildered. I have known you for hours, and I seem to have known you for years and years. It really does seem years since you walked into Madame's *salon,* and I thought,

" 'What a handsome man! What a fine face he has! How can he bring a face like that into a place like this? He looks so restrained, so disciplined; so controlled, austere and cold.'

"I was so glad to see you, Denis; and I was so sorry.

"And then almost immediately I understood that you had merely come to see the place, to inspect it; and that while you loathed the place, and detested Madame, you were sorry for us.

"But how has it come about? How could you have done all the wonderful things you have done to-night, defeated Madame, given the girls what most they wanted, and set me free—if you are Denis Ducros, *le légionnaire?* . . . Of course they all think you are really the . . .

"You aren't making fun of me, *Monsieur le Colonel?*" she implored, gazing with love and anxiety into his eyes.

"Would you be really sorry to learn that I was?"

"That you are the Colonel Louis Rochefort after all, and not Denis Ducros? . . . It would be a dreadful disappointment. It would almost break my heart."

Again he kissed her.

"I am Denis Ducros, all right," he said. "I am no Colonel; nor anything but a private soldier."

"But, Denis . . . Denis . . . Why are you dressed like this? Why are you in the Colonel's uniform? Why did you come and make them think you were Colonel Rochefort?"

"Fate . . . Chance . . . God, Himself, I think. . . .

"Or if it is presumptuous of me to think *le bon Dieu* takes any interest in my affairs, let us say the little blind god who sees so much, the god of Love."

"I prefer to think it was the good God Himself," replied Nicolette. "Is it not true that God *is* Love? Is not *le bon Dieu* good and kind? I prefer to think it was He, and I shall thank Him all my life, every day; every morning, every night. God and the Blessed Virgin."

"We'll both thank God, then, Nicolette . . . Well . . . *le bon Dieu* saw me brushing the Colonel's uniform.

" *'Ah!'* thought *le bon Dieu, 'there's that rascal Denis Ducros; a great actor* manqué; *a wonderful impersonator; also a romantic, a dreamer, a submerged soul, drowned in the dreadful commonplace of routine and servitude . . .*

" *'Poor devil! He has made a mess of his life as so many of them do; and, being the All-Just Fountain of Justice, I'll admit he has never had much of a chance in life! I'll give him his chance now; his opportunity to do something for Me; something really worth while and useful. Also the chance to live for an hour the sort of life he would have loved and would have lived well, had it fitted in with my schemes for mice and men.*

" *'Yes, I'll give him the Stage to himself, and while he struts his little hour, he shall have a chance to realise the courage and spirit of the girl Nicolette from Domeuil. She has kept her soul alive, and in the midst of evil is untouched by evil.*

" *'That shall be his moment. If he has eyes to see, let him see. Let him act to some purpose.'*

"Thus, perhaps, *le bon Dieu* thought to Himself, and a mad idea entered my mind. Now whence do thoughts come into our minds? Obviously this one came from God, and you are right, Nicolette. What seemed a mad, wild, and idiotic notion, has resulted in—your being here beside me, our being in love.

"*Of course* it came from God—although it was no better an idea than that I should try the Colonel's *képi* on, and then his tunic . . . And the rest followed."

"But where was the real Colonel?" asked Nicolette.

"In his bed."

"And where should you suppose he is now?" Nicolette said.

"Still in his bed—I hope. He has got fever," replied Denis, "and I pray *le bon Dieu* may remember to keep him in bed until I can get back and return the clothes he doesn't know I've borrowed."

"But, Denis, won't you get into most terrible trouble?" asked the girl.

"Oh, I'm not caught yet," replied Denis evasively.

"But if they do catch you?"

"My darling little Nicolette, what can they do to me that will be more than a grain of desert sand in the scales against what *you* have done for me?"

"But, Denis, what will the punishment be, if you are caught?"

"I don't know. It depends on how the Colonel takes it," said Denis, and began to laugh.

"Do tell me what is the worst, the utmost . . ." begged Nicolette urgently.

"I should say Madame de Beauchamp," replied Denis, and laughed afresh. "That was the worst."

"No, please do be serious."

"I must. It was serious. There was a heavy fall in silk. In the street. And I shall be blamed for that."

Denis continued to laugh.

Nicolette drew away as though hurt.

"Denis," she expostulated, "please. Please answer my question. What is the worst, the utmost, that can happen to you for what you have done to-night?

"If you won't tell me, I won't go to Avignon," she added firmly.

"Well, darling, when I asked you if you'd wait eight years for me, I wasn't altogether joking," he said.

"Eight *years*! You mean eight years *in prison?* They'd do that to you, Denis?"

"I doubt it. They might, but . . . Depends on how the Colonel takes it."

"Denis!"

"You'd wait for me?" he asked.

"I shall wait for you for the rest of my life . . . But

eight years! In prison! Why, it. . ."

"Oh, nice open-air life," interrupted Denis. "Not actually in prison, you know. Out in the desert. Making roads, and forts, and other little things like that. All good exercise."

"Eight *years!*" whispered Nicolette. "Denis!"

"But it won't be eight years. The Colonel isn't a bad old sort, and I've done him no real harm. His reputation has been quite safe in my hands. Lots of people will think all the better of him," and he began to laugh. "Eight years! Good Heavens, no. More likely sixty days cells after a bit of solitary.

"Besides, I'm not caught yet," he added.

"Denis! Let's stop the carriage at once. I'll go on to the station, and you drive back to the Barracks as quickly as you can go," begged the girl.

"No. I am going to see you safely into that train, and the train safely out of the station. It would be a nice thing if the picket wouldn't let you go through!"

"Why should they interfere with me?" demurred Nicolette.

"They shouldn't. But you don't know these Legion Sergeants. They're not all Frenchmen, you know. You might very well find a bullying Prussian brute of the filthiest sort. And if it just entered his head to make you lose the train, he'd do it. Pure *schadenfreud.* Pretend your papers were out of order, or something of the sort. . . . Might say he suspected you to be the seven-foot Russian who deserted last week, trying to make his get-away after lying low in the bazaar somewhere. . . .

"No, I'm coming with you to the station," he concluded decisively.

"Oh, Denis! I shall be so anxious. So worried."

"I shall be all right. All you've got to do is to get safely home—and wait for me. I won't keep you waiting long, Nicolette."

"How I shall pray for you, Denis. Every day I shall burn candles to St. Antoine, St. Christophe, St. Michel, and to the Blessed Virgin. . . . Oh, how I shall pray for you."

"Then what harm can come to me?" smiled Denis. "Well. Here's the station. . . ."

If the Sergeant in command of the picket felt any surprise at the sight of his Colonel escorting a girl to the station with the obvious intention of seeing her off by train, he concealed it admirably, and called the Guard to order, to attention, and the presenting of arms, as though this were an unfailing nightly routine of Sidi-bel-Abbès Railway Station. . . .

As he stood by the door of the train, Denis Ducros found that, of the infinity of things he had to say, there was nothing of which he could speak coherently.

He could only beg her to take care of herself, to trust in him implicitly, and to wait for him—a reasonable time.

"I shall not expect you for eight years, Denis," said Nicolette softly, as she held his face between her hands.

"And at the end of eight years?" he asked.

"Then I shall begin to wait," she smiled.

As the train started to move and he kissed her again, *"I shall wait for ever,"* Nicolette said.

"I shall come soon," Denis answered.

CHAPTER 13

BACK TO THE PATH AGAIN

The thoughts of Sergeant Igor Schlentczic were long, long thoughts, as he witnessed the parting ceremonies between his austere strait-laced Colonel and *cette très jolie jeune fille.*

Moving only his eyes he scanned the faces of the Guard as they stood immovably to attention. Like himself, they had obviously seen nothing.

As he passed, the Colonel punctiliously, if absent-mindedly, returned their salute.

He walked on air.

Not Heaven itself could take away the solid fact, the glorious truth, that he had found Nicolette, fallen in love with Nicolette, and had actually saved Nicolette by his own wits and will-power.

There was no play-acting about that. Not but what the play-acting had been marvellous, wonderful, glorious. It would have been a hundred times worth punishment; and whatever that might be, he would not grudge or regret it. But the reality, the truth, the fact—of Nicolette—was a hundred times worth any punishment that the General Court Martial of Oran could inflict upon him—short of death.

It must not be that.

He must not die now. Now that he had found Nicolette.

But these were morbid and foolish thoughts. If the Colonel did send him to the Oran Court Martial, the utmost they would give him would be eight years with the Penal Battalions. And what was that to weigh against this new-found, wonderful happiness? Why, he'd enjoy the eight years, knowing that Nicolette would be there at the end of it.

But that again was morbid and foolish thinking. The Colonel would deal with him, himself. Probably give him all he'd got, and that was only sixty days cells.

Punishment? A mere joke.

And ever more buoyantly he trod on air.

What had he better do now? . . .

Get back to barracks as fast as he could—in the somewhat thin hope of replacing the Colonel's uniform, and satisfactorily explaining his absence if he had been missed.

No. Perish the thought! The play must go on. What sort of an actor was it who left the stage in the middle of playing his part?

He, Denis Ducros, who had waited all his life for the chance to act a big part on a great stage, to be unworthy of the opportunity when it came! To be weak, to be cowardly, to be too little for his part, to be unequal to his *rôle!*

Let the play go on—until the curtain falls.

While Denis Ducros could play the part of Colonel Louis Rochefort, he would play it for all he was worth.

As he left the station, Denis Ducros saw something that he had seen before, in different circumstances.

A pale boy in Legion uniform, obviously a wretched recruit, was standing staring with hopeless, tortured, longing eyes at the railway, symbol of escape and freedom. Obviously one of those—and there are many of them, as Denis knew—who find the beginning almost too hard for human endurance. Perhaps he was not physically equal to the strain of the day's work that begins at dawn with gymnastics, running-drill, and marching, on an empty stomach.

Perhaps he had fallen foul of some brute of a barrack-room bully, or of a corporal, or instructor.

Perhaps, and here Denis' heart was moved to acutest pity, he simply could not bear separation from the girl he had left behind him.

The boy started and stared, as though unable to believe his eyes. Was this the dread Colonel himself, bearing down upon him; the martinet of whose discipline he had heard such tales? He would know instantly that a recruit, *soldat deuxième classe,* would not have a late pass, and what was more, the Colonel would know quite well what he was doing down there.

With a brave attempt at the smart and soldierly swagger of the *vieux moustache,* the youngster saluted; and, to his dismay, the Colonel halted as he came abreast of him.

"Ah, my boy!" said he, in pleasant fatherly manner. "On late pass, I see! And taking a stroll out of town to have a look at the station . . . I know . . . I know . . . I used to do it myself when I was a young—er—ahem!—officer. But it isn't wise, *mon enfant.* It isn't wise. It only makes things harder, and God knows they're hard enough at first.

"But they get easier very quickly . . . very quickly. . . . You'll hear some of the old rascals say it's the first five years that are the worst. But don't you take any notice of them. Why in three months' time you'll be enjoying it. Absolutely enjoying it, and you wouldn't want to go back home if you could.

"Stick it out. Do your best to be a good soldier—and you'll be all right. Believe me.

"I shall keep an eye on you. Understand?"

"*Oui, mon Colonel!*" faltered the boy.

"And I expect to see you become a credit to the Regiment. You will, won't you?"

"I'll try, *Monsieur le Colonel.*"

"And you'll succeed. Take the rough with the smooth.

"If you can find any smooth," he added, with a grim smile. "But you didn't come here to look for smooth things, did you?

"Now then—back to Barracks. And remember I'm your friend."

And the boy departed, also walking on air.

A sergeant passed him, and the boy saluted smartly.

"Hey!" called the Colonel, and the astounded sergeant, scarce believing the evidence of his senses, positively galloped across the road.

"Know that *bleu*?[37]"

---

[37] recruit.

The sergeant stood statuesque and still, the back of his fingers at the peak of his *képi.*

"*Oui, mon Colonel.*"

"Then keep an eye on him. He's a good lad. Understand?"

"*Oui, mon Colonel.*"

The sergeant quite understood, or thought he did; and to himself he said, "Good Gracious!" or words to that effect.

"*Bon!* . . . *Rompez!*[38]" snapped the Colonel.

The sergeant fell away into the night, his mind interestingly occupied with thoughts of princes in disguise, missing heirs, illegitimate sons, and other colourful speculations.

"That two-*sous bleu!* The Colonel interested in him, eh? Well . . . What the Old Man said—that went. He'd have to blast the soul out of Corporal Kellermann, who, he seemed to remember, had a down on the creature."

"That would probably march, all right," reflected the Colonel. Sergeant Brausch was an ambitious climber and would put any commandment of the Colonel's before the other Ten. And it was quite probable that Sergeant Brausch, like a great many other people who had met Denis Ducros that night, would never know whether his interview had been with the genuine Colonel Louis Rochefort or not.

Anyway, he had done his best for the youngster, and at the very least he had given him a little pleasure, comfort, and brief happiness. Better still, hope. He'd feel a new man, and sleep like a child that night. Do him no harm, and perhaps do him a lot of good. And at best, it would make the wily Brausch a friend to the lad. Not a true friend of course, but a friend in need and a friend in deed.

He strode on, head in air, a giant refreshed.

Nicolette! . . . *Nicolette!* . . . *Nicolette!* . . . sang his heart.

As he approached the gate in the City rampart, he saw, passing beneath a lamp, a man of unmistakable

---

[38] Dismiss. Break off.

figure and bearing, a man whom he greatly admired and liked, Captain le Sage, whom *le légionnaire* Denis Ducros, *ordonnance* to Colonel Rochefort, knew to be a very important member of the Legion's Military Intelligence Department.

An idea entered his uplifted mind, an idea that pleased his rash and soaring spirit. He'd try himself out against the wits of the cleverest man in the Nineteenth African Army Corps. If Captain le Sage saw through him, he'd brazen it out and puzzle him. He'd have a duel of wits and wills and personalities. He'd order him back to Barracks, and tell him to consider himself under close arrest.

It would be great fun; and if he succeeded in deceiving le Sage, he'd have a pleasant chat with him, and—*bon Dieu,* what an idea—he'd make use of the brilliant officer.

He'd put him on to one or two useful things that would interest him; and on to one or two people too.

Now that would be a useful bit of sport; and, pulling himself together, summoning every ounce of his undeniably great powers as an actor, he became Colonel Rochefort more authentically than at any time that evening.

"Ah! Le Sage!" he said in the Colonel's severe and quiet voice, as Captain le Sage blew out the match with which he had lighted his cigarette.

Captain le Sage's left hand, containing the cigarette, dropped smartly to his side, while his right hand rose swiftly in salute.

"Good evening, Sir," he said. . . . What was the Old Man doing down here at this time of night?

"Going to the Station?" pursued the Colonel.

"Yes, Sir. I am rather expecting that an interesting person may arrive to-night, very incognito."

"And you're going to introduce him to himself, eh?"

"And myself to him," smiled Captain le Sage.

Now was there anything behind that poker-faced smile? wondered Denis.

No, he believed not. Even the clever le Sage saw nothing unusual. But of course it was pretty dark;

and, like mere ordinary people, le Sage saw what he expected to see. What he saw inside the Colonel's uniform must be the Colonel—naturally . . .

There was the voice, though. It must be a pretty good imitation; but if Denis Ducros, gifted impersonator, couldn't imitate a voice he heard all day long, and half the night, it would be a pity!

Le Sage must be wondering what Colonel Louis Rochefort was doing at the station at this time of night.

"I've just been seeing an interesting person off," he said. "And talking of interesting people, I want you to keep an eye on the *vaguemestre,* Stalheimer. I think you'd find a brief study of that gentleman's methods quite rewarding. And in more ways than one. I happen to know that he is robbing the men. Also that he is getting much more money than he could easily account for . . . from a foreign source."

Captain le Sage gave a quick direct look into the Colonel's eyes. This was very interesting. He didn't know the Old Man went in for that sort of thing. He had never supposed that he had an idea outside his own particular sphere of duty—wherein he was undeniably and uncommonly competent, behind that wooden facade of his.

On second thoughts, was his face and manner quite as wooden as he had always thought? He was certainly human enough to-night, and very much alive. . . . Eyes sparkling . . . Expression almost warm . . . Unusually friendly . . . Something had gingered him up . . . Well, he had just said he had been seeing somebody off. Perhaps they had opened one more bottle.

"Money comes from Berlin," continued the Colonel, "and not from kind father, loving mother, or devoted wife, for Stalheimer has no family. Not even a Rich Uncle Kurt. . . . He was a slaughter-house hand before he was a German soldier.

"Yes, he's a real *mauvais sujet,* that one; and I think that one or two of his letters, addressed to Berlin, might prove very interesting."

Certainly the Colonel was interesting to-night, thought le Sage, whatever Stalheimer was. Probably the Old Boy had been getting anonymous letters from some German *légionnaire* whose little remittances were not arriving regularly.

"German agent, do you think, Sir?" he said.

"Yes. Sure of it. And I'll tell you another thing, le Sage. He works with a damned scoundrel, as big a *salaud* as himself. That mass of corruption they call Bacchus. You know him of course? A bloated hairy fellow, a typical *faux bonhomme.*"

"I know him," le Sage answered. "A detestable brute; but I don't know anything against him."

"Well, put him under your microscope. In conjunction with the worthy *vaguemestre*. And I think you may see signs of active insect-life which will quite intrigue you."

"Well, well, well!" thought le Sage. "Out of the mouths of Colonels and Commandants they'll be convicted! Someone is certainly keeping the Old Boy posted. Mare's-nests and . . ."

"And I'll give you an address, le Sage," the Colonel's voice interrupted the current of the surprised officer's thoughts. "Make a note of it. And put a good man on to it, with instructions to contrive to be present at one or two of the little meetings that are held there.

"You might go yourself," he continued, with a dry smile, "disguised as—er—your batman, or something of the sort. I believe you'd really enjoy yourself."

Curiouser, and curiouser, thought Captain le Sage. Whoever would have thought it? One never knew; and when one did, one was generally wrong. Colonel Louis Rochefort was shedding quite a new light upon himself. Just imagine his knowing so much about his men, and particularly that sort of much!

Anonymous letters! That's what it was. And the Old Devil was coming the oracle and mystery-monger over poor stupid le Sage of the Intelligence!

"*Rue Raspail, dix bis; Rue de Daya.* Top front room. And they meet there on Sundays after evening *soupe.*"

"Thank you, Sir," said le Sage, making a note of the address in a small book which he drew from the breast pocket of his tunic.

"I expect you're wondering how I happen to have that piece of information," said the Colonel.

"I am, Sir," admitted le Sage. "I am filled with curiosity."

"*Ah! . . . Indeed?*" said the Colonel, and brushed his moustache.

"Good night," he added abruptly, and marched off, leaving an extremely clever man, extremely puzzled.

There was more in Colonel Louis Rochefort than met the eye, and a good deal more than met the ear, as a rule.

And as Denis Ducros went on his way rejoicing, he rightly surmised that he'd given his admired Captain le Sage something to think about; and there was no shadow of doubt in his mind that Captain le Sage would think about it to some purpose. He'd get that rogue the *vaguemestre* all right, and that lousy swine Bacchus, and the gang of rotten depraved parasites who did their dirty work and ran their filthy errands.

Yes. Le Sage must be wondering how Colonel Louis Rochefort knew quite as much as he seemed to know.

But in point of fact, there were precious few people in Sidi-bel-Abbès who knew as much as Denis Ducros, with a foot in either camp, and one wide-open ear in the Colonel's club, and the other in the Barrack canteen.

It was of course, speaking generally, quite against one's principles to tell tales of one's comrades to an officer, but these men of whom he had spoken were not comrades. They were despicable criminals who were a disgrace to the Regiment.

One of them was a murderer who had also been the cause of two or three suicides; and one was that lowest form of low thief who used official powers and position to rob his subordinates. And, what was perhaps worse, although Denis Ducros wasn't personally greatly concerned in such matters, they and their hireling gang were, by all accounts and many indications, traitors to the country whose pay they took and to whom they had sworn the oath of "*Honneur et Fidelité*".

No. Denis had no qualms of conscience about this

little piece of work. It was a thoroughly good job, well done.

On he strode, trailing clouds of glory.

Still the all-powerful Colonel, who interfered in the lives of men, who put down the evil-doing mighty from their seats, and raised up the humble and meek.

The potentate whom men feared and whom women were . . .

Hallo! What was this? The first of a smart procession of carriages drew up beside him, as he turned to cross the small square of the *Place Bougeaud.*

A girl sprang from it, and flung herself upon him.

"I knew it! I knew it!" she cried. "I knew it was our own dear friend, *Monsieur le Colonel.*

"Here he is, girls!" she screamed; and, as the other carriages came to a halt in the rear of the first one, the girls jumped out and came running to join Odette, and gather round the Colonel.

It could not be said that their hearts were too full for speech. Words did not fail them, nor kisses; and the heart of the Colonel was warmed within him, warmed by sympathy, affection and kindness; warmed by anger and indignation at the thought of Madame—and that such things should be.

And might not he have done more for these girls than send them for a drive?

To what was it due, but to pure selfishness on his part, that Nicolette was now speeding through the night, saved, released, set free—and these her companions, were still the slaves of the unspeakable Madame.

He felt that he had not risen to the full height of his opportunity, and that he had failed them. If he could save one, he could have saved them all.

Was it too late?

Raising his hands and waving them above his head, the Colonel, in mock despair of being heard, cried,

"*Mes enfants! Mes chères filles!* Listen! Listen! I want to make a speech."

"Speech! Speech!" cried the merry and excited girls.

"Up there, *Monsieur le Colonel!*" urged Odette, and pointed to where, behind him, stood upon a low plinth

the statue of a French general, arrayed, for some reason, in the garb of a Roman senator; about his bald
head a laurel wreath; across his stomach a close-fitting
garment of bronze; pendent from his middle a kilt of
dangling bars of metal; clasping in his hand the roll of
manuscript without which no Roman of any class was
ready to be photographed, painted, or done in enduring
stone.

"Excellent idea!" said the Colonel, and stepped on to
the plinth, sharing for the first time in his life the
pedestal of fame with a general of repute.

With laughter and cries of encouragement, the girls
gathered about him. He began to speak, and in a
moment they had fallen silent.

"*Mes enfants,*" he said, "you've had an hour or two's
freedom, and you seem to have enjoyed yourselves. Is
there any real reason why you should return to Madame's house at all?"

The girls laughed dutifully at the Colonel's idea of a
joke.

". . . Because if you don't want to go back—now is
your chance.

"Nicolette has already gone . . ."

"*What?*" breathed Odette, while the rest of the
group stood staring, speechless, stricken silent.

"I saw Nicolette off, myself, from the station, half an
hour ago. She will be out of Africa to-morrow, and in
France a day or two later."

"*Mon Dieu!*" whispered Odette. "And Madame let her
go?"

"And gave her her fare," replied the Colonel.

"At *Monsieur le Colonel's* orders, *sans doute?*" said
Odette shrewdly.

"I did suggest it . . . And what is more, I'll suggest
the same thing for all of you—or for any one of you,
who wishes to leave Madame's house," declared the
Colonel.

He stopped speaking, and glanced quickly from girl
to girl. In the brilliant moonlight he could see clearly to
read the expression upon each of the up-turned faces.

It was an expression common to them all.

Though the face were vacant, greedy, cunning, stupid, shrewd, bovine or vicious, each expressed refusal and rejection—rejection more or less contemptuous.

Before anyone spoke, he knew what the answer would be.

They would not go.

They did not want to go.

And in his heart, there mingled with regret and sorrow for them, a feeling of gladness and pride.

Nicolette was different. Nicolette was not as these.

Nicolette . . . Nicolette . . . Nicolette . . . sang his heart.

These were people quite different from Nicolette. Nevertheless he must do his best.

A girl laughed scornfully, a sound that conveyed as plainly as speech, her bitter thanks for empty nothing.

"Odette?" he asked.

The girl stared at him wide-eyed, her mouth set in hard lines.

"Wouldn't you like to go home?"

"I have no home, *Monsieur le Colonel.*"

"Oh, surely you have relations or friends, who . . ."

"My friends are in Sidi-bel-Abbès, *Monsieur le Colonel,*" said the girl shortly.

"Wouldn't you like to leave Africa?"

"In *Monsieur le Colonel's* company?" asked the girl pertly.

"I am not leaving Africa at the moment. . . . Do you really wish to remain—with Madame?"

"I wish to remain with Madame.

"And to accompany her to Hell," she added. "It will give me great satisfaction.

"*Home!*" she spat with a bitterness and venom that he found pitiful indeed.

"Fifine?" he asked. "Wouldn't you like to go home?"

"*Blague!*" laughed the girl. "*Monsieur le Colonel se moque de nous autres.*"

"No, no, Fifine. I . . ."

"And pray who will take me to my happy little home in German Poland, where we get nearly as good a time as the cattle? Not quite such nice byres, or so many mangelwurzels, you understand, but . . ."

"But one knows when one's getting white bread," grinned Annette.

"So," agreed Fifine with finality. "Believe it or not, *Monsieur le Colonel,* I prefer a fine house in Sidi-bel-Abbès to a stinking pig-sty in Solcszysch. Madame's a good many things, but she's not a German policeman.

"Home!" she added softly, and laughed, with a dreadful amusement, at the vision the word recalled to her mind.

"Justine?" asked the Colonel of a girl who stood with beautiful wide-open eyes and an also-beautiful wide-open mouth, gazing at him in placid, bovine incomprehension. "What about you? Wouldn't you like to go away from Sidi-bel-Abbès?"

"I? *Monsieur le Colonel?* Go away? Go away from Sidi-bel-Abbès? Where to?"

"Well, isn't there any place to which you'd like to go—to get away from here, to get away from Madame?"

"Mais oui, Monsieur. I should like to go to Paris," she said, and added ere he could reply,

"If Monsieur could find me a nice house like Madame's."

"A house? Like Madame's?" asked the Colonel, disappointed. "Wouldn't you like a change? A fresh start in life?"

"No, thank you, *Monsieur le Colonel,* I do very well."

"You don't want to leave Madame?"

"Madame's all right, *Monsieur le Colonel.* She's a thief, a liar, a fit wife for the Devil, and a half-caste bitch, *mais que voulez-vous?*

"What would you?" shrugged the girl, "these Madames are not angels. And should *Monsieur le Colonel* be at any time looking for an angel, it is not among them that he'll find one."

Some of the girls laughed, without great amusement.

"But if *Monsieur le Colonel* is inviting *me* to go to Paris with him, there is a train to Oran at . . ."

"I am not going to Paris at the moment, *ma belle,*" interrupted the Colonel. "But look! Wouldn't you like to go by yourself, and find a job of work which . . ."

"*Work?* What is that?" enquired Mademoiselle Justine.

Unhelpable, thought the Colonel, unemployable . . . vicious . . . born in the bone and bred in the flesh . . . from birth . . . poor doomed soul.

Complete silence held the group in the little *place.*

"Isn't there one of you who'd like to . . . escape?" he asked again. "I'll see that you get a ticket for France, Algiers, Tangier, your own country, anywhere you want to go."

No answer.

"Come on, girls," laughed Odette. "Before *Monsieur le Colonel* corrupts us. If we listen any longer, he'll make us want to cheat our dear kind Madame, who loves us so," and leaping lightly up on to the plinth, she once again flung her arms round the Colonel's neck and kissed him.

"*Dieu vous bénisse!*" she whispered in his ear, and, turning to the now laughing and applauding group, cried,

"Come on, girls. Start the procession up again. Right through Sidi and out the other side, and half-way to Saida."

Back to their respective carriages went the girls, still more like schoolboys let out of school for an unexpected holiday.

As Odette got into the last *fiacre,* she turned to the Colonel, to whose arm she still clung,

"Nicolette," she whispered. "Did you really mean that she has . . . *gone?* You've helped her to get away? Oh, I am glad . . . glad . . . glad. She was never one of us. But, oh, how I shall miss her."

"Yes," replied the Colonel. "She is in the Oran train. Going home. Safe. Now *she . . .*"

"You are a darling," she said. "You are a girl's dream of St. Louis! . . . Nicolette was different.

"You want to be, oh, so kind; but you don't understand us others. We are . . . damned . . . we are finished . . . we are doomed . . . destined . . . done for. . . . Good-bye!"

And a minute later the procession resumed its cheerful and noisy way.

"Yes," mused Denis Ducros, as he stood looking after the last retreating vehicle. "Nicolette is different."

CHAPTER 14

A LITTLE MORE GLORY

And once again, secure in this glorious certainty, he resumed his amazing journey with a light and happy heart.

A short cut through a dark, narrow and sinister alley brought him into a still-busy and crowded bazaar.

Here and there a *légionnaire,* suddenly realising that he must be drunker than he felt, thought that he came face to face with his Colonel, saluted the grim vision, and made resolutions for immediate reform.

These salutes the Colonel returned with an absent-minded raising of the fore-finger vaguely in the direction of the peak of his *képi.*

Suddenly he caught sight of a man whom he liked, admired and pitied from the depths of his vast experience. Poor Hagues! He remembered that man as a model *adjudant,* the perfect *sous-officier,* who would certainly have been sent to the St. Maixent College, to be trained for a commission, had he not suddenly taken to drink.

And, alas, he had done this as thoroughly as he did everything else; and had drunk his way down the ladder far more quickly than he had fought his way up it.

Drunk on parade—reduced to Sergeant-Major; drunk on duty—reduced to Sergeant; drunk on guard —reduced to Corporal; drunk on escort-duty and reduced to the ranks.

And now in the ranks, drinking to escape, drinking to drown the dreadful sense of failure, disgrace and ignominy. He, the smart *adjudant,* now the butt and victim of every blackguard whom he had ever punished.

"Halt there, Hagues!" said the Colonel. "I want to speak to you."

Hagues stood swaying, doing his utmost to keep stiffly at attention and at the salute.

"Stand easy. Come in here," and taking him by the arm, the Colonel actually led him into a small semi-Arab café of which the door stood invitingly open.

The fat proprietor scuttled across the cavern-like smoky room when he saw the gold braid.

Bowing low, automaton-like, he indicated the largest and cleanest divan.

"In one moment, noble Sir, the dancing girls . . ."

"Silence," growled the Colonel. "Coffee. The best. Strong. Nothing added."

That would be the best thing for Hagues in his present condition, and he personally preferred his coffee without the addition of vanilla essence, cheap cognac, Dutch oil-of-orange, a spot of hashish, or anything else.

"Six cups each, and Allah help you if . . ."

The fat hybrid galloped off, but quickly returned with a tray of his small clay cups of most excellent coffee—none better until he started improving it with assorted flavours and stimulants.

"Drink some coffee, Hagues," said the Colonel. "Pull yourself together and listen to me."

The bewildered, incredulous, and intoxicated *légionnaire* obeyed. By the time he had drunk three or four cups of the strong hot coffee, he decided that this was not a drunken dream; he realised that he was sitting in Abdullah's, face to face with Colonel Louis Rochefort—which was absurd.

No, it wasn't true. It was either absurdly impossible, or impossibly absurd. Which? He'd see the answer in a moment, through the haze of wine.

He was drunk.

He wasn't drunk.

It was the Colonel, and he was talking to him—as to a friend.

"You can do it," he was saying. "And nobody but you can do it. You've got to save yourself. I could put you straight back to *adjudant,* but what would be the good of that? You'd be in trouble again in a week. No earthly good my doing anything for you until you've done something for yourself. You stop drinking, and you'll get your Corporal's stripe back very quickly. Keep off it, and your Corporal's worsted stripe will change to your Sergeant's gold stripe, while you watch it. And soon nothing can prevent your becoming Sergeant-Major, and then *adjudant,* again, except your own weakness and folly.

"You know I'm right, don't you? You know you can climb back. And though you may not be aware of it, I shall have my eye on you. But I can't and I won't do anything for you, until you do something for yourself.

"Stop it, man, here and now—and be a man, not a hog. Damn it all, you don't want to live on the level of the animal Bacchus and his gang of sottish scum, do you?"

"*Monsieur le Colonel,*" faltered the man, "I . . . There was a letter. . . . It knocked me down into the dust."

"Get up again then," snarled the Colonel. "The dust isn't the place for a man."

"She was my . . . life. . . . She wrote that . . . And I had her put on a level with the Holy . . ."

"Don't whine," growled the Colonel. "You're not the first man who . . ."

And suppose this poor devil loved and trusted her, as he loved and trusted Nicolette?

"Look!" he said, his voice, human and sympathising, "She proved worthless, eh?"

"Worthless, *Monsieur le Colonel.*"

"Well, *mon enfant;* let's suffer and fight and die for something worthy, eh? Something worth while. Why all this misery and degradation, leading to downfall, ruin and death, for something *worthless?*

"Give everything you have—your honour, reputation, life itself if necessary, for the woman who loves you; but don't be such a fool and weakling as to throw . . ."

"*Monsieur le Colonel,* I loved her better than life itself. I loved her so that I would not marry her until I was an officer, and once again, a gentleman. And she . . ."

"And she wasn't worth it all, Hagues. But because you built up that fine pedestal so quickly—for her, why knock it down again because she is not equal to standing on it?

"Stand on it yourself, man," continued the Colonel.

"It's gone, *mon Colonel.* I am done for. Finished."

"Then I am done too—with you. Finished—with you. I am sorry, for I had had some hopes of you. I had really thought you were, in some ways, something like a man."

The Colonel leaned back, folded his arms, and stared into Hagues' miserable eyes.

"Listen, poor weakling; poor sniveller," he said. "I had actually thought it conceivably possible that, when you had been to St. Maixent Military College and got your commission, I might have seen you Captain some day; Major; and, if you were lucky, *Chef de Bataillon.* . . . But I was a fool of course. I was quite mistaken in you.

"Because one of five hundred million women is a what-shall-we-say, you at once become—what you are —a poor drunk, a disgrace, a sot and a rotten soldier. . . . *Pah!*"

The unfortunate *légionnaire* flushed, shuffled, and moved his hands and feet nervously.

"*Monsieur le Colonel,*" he began, "I am . . ."

"Yes, of course you are," interrupted the Colonel in a tone of encouragement. "You are ashamed of yourself. And you are going to start afresh. Going to turn over a new leaf. Now. Not another drop of *tchum-tchum,* or any other bazaar filth. And no more *pinard* than the regulation allowance. And—mark my words—you'll go up like a rocket, once it is realised you are back on the water-wagon, and you are on the job again.

"Don't expect anything from me—except watchfulness. I shall have my eye on you, Hagues.

"Well?" he asked sharply, and extended his hand.

Hagues hesitated to accept so great an honour, and again his face flushed.

"*Monsieur le Colonel* is too kind," he faltered, his eyes unwontedly bright. "I will do my best I promise.

"God help me," he cried and, rising, swiftly saluted, and fled, incredulous, overwhelmed, and unable either to trust his voice or control his feelings.

The Colonel!

He took an interest in the fate of such a grain of dust as Guillaume Hagues, dust blown along the road to Hell on the wind of adversity.

The Colonel himself!

What a man!

Guillaume Hagues would be deserving of his kindness. He would not fail him.

What an accursed fool he had been. As the Colonel said, he was a weakling, a coward and a cur. Imagine wrecking a successful career and ruining one's life because a woman was—a woman. As though such suicide would do him any good, or her any harm. *Assez!*

And so thought and hoped Denis Ducros as he rose to depart.

"How much?" he growled at the salaaming Abdullah.

"But nothing, nothing, nothing, *Sidi Général*," replied Abdullah, trying hard to abase himself lower and lower, while rising higher and higher in the Colonel's estimation—he hoped.

" 'How much'? I said," growled the Colonel, on his deepest note.

"Oh noble Sidi! Give your servant the honour!"

"Give your servant the bill," interrupted the noble Sidi, "and let him take it to my servant at my house," and walked out of the smoky little cavern, reflecting on the peculiarities of the ritual of credit.

He seemed to have gone a very long way, that evening, on the strength of the gold on his sleeves—though there was none in his pocket.

Poor Hagues! Would he have the guts to hold on? He might. And again, he might not, for he had undoubtedly taken a terrible knock, and he, Denis Ducros, could understand the force of it.

What sort of interest in life would he feel if, when he reached Avignon, he found no Nicolette, and learned that she had gone off with somebody else? Poor

Hagues! Poor devil! Poor, poor devil!

Well, he had done his best for him; and now he must do his best for himself. And They'd look after him all right, once They saw that he had pulled himself together, and really meant to make good. Captain le Sage had the highest opinion of him, and had told the Colonel so, at the Officers' *popotte*,[39] one evening, in camp.

The Colonel had agreed, for at that time, Hagues was not only a model *adjudant,* but the latest model.

He remembered that le Sage had advanced a theory —which was more likely a piece of private knowledge— that *Adjudant* Guillaume Hagues had been not only an officer in the Belgian Army, but a Staff Officer, and Aide-de-camp to the King.

What a downfall! And what a tragedy! Weak streak somewhere, of course. Drink probably—and that terrible form of disease which impels a normally sober and moderate man, occasionally, though perhaps very rarely, to collapse into a bout of steady and determined drinking. Just swinish.

Probably in Hagues' case it only happened under great stress and strain. Or violent emotion . . .

Hullo! What was this?

A crowd of soldiers and civilians had suddenly burst forth from a *bistro,* shouting and knocking each other down, as they struggled through the doorway.

"Run! Run!"

"Look out! He's got a knife!"

"Murder! Murder!"

"He's mad! He's mad!"

"He has killed Pedro!"

"He has cut his throat!"

"Nearly slashed his head off!"

These and other cries intrigued the Colonel, as the occupants of the place stumbled out into the alley. Positively signs of life!

And signs of death too.

It would probably be the excellent Zidenski, fighting-drunk again. He'd kill somebody one of these

---

[39] temporary Mess.

days.

"Well?" he barked, at a tall bearded *légionnaire,* who pulled himself up short in his head-long career, saluted, and blinked in amazement at this apparition.

"Zidenski! *Monsieur le Colonel,*" he gasped. "Gone mad. *Cafard.*"

"Well?" growled the Colonel.

"Got a great knife, *Monsieur le Colonel.* Murdering everybody."

"Well?"

"Mad . . . Blood . . . Murder . . . Knife . . ." gulped the *légionnaire.*

"And why have you not taken him back to Barracks?"

"Because he's mad. Because he has a knife, *Monsieur le Colonel.*"

"Any other reason?"

"No, *Monsieur le Colonel,*" faltered the big *légionnaire.*

"Yes, *Monsieur le Légionnaire,*" mocked the Colonel. "There is another reason. Because you are a coward.

"Like the rest of these scum," he added, as other soldiers either stopped, saluted and stood at attention, or, with greater presence of mind, achieved an absence of body, by promptly wheeling about and taking to their heels, on catching sight of the Colonel.

"Fall in! You, and you, and you!" he ordered, indicating some half-a-dozen *légionnaires,* "and await orders."

"You, Allones, in command," he added, addressing a grizzled *soldat première classe,* whom he knew to be the senior man present; and turning on his heel, crossed the road and entered the *bistro.*

Here was a scene of terror and confusion.

Behind the bar, across which they had vaulted, were three *légionnaires,* armed with empty bottles. Behind them again, cowered the fat little Pedro, the Spanish proprietor of the wine-shop. In corners of the room shrank soldiers and civilians, men and women, behind such fragile barricades as a couple of benches, chairs, iron-topped tables.

In the middle of the floor lay dead, dying, or sham-ming, a citizen, the peak of whose mountainous stom-ach rose far higher than any other tract of the sur-rounding area of his anatomy. Even his big, up-turned feet looked short and small.

About him, danced a little *légionnaire,* who—in spite of the facts that his eyes blazed madly brilliant in a dead white face, that foam flecked his lips, and that he brandished aloft a blood-stained knife—irresistibly re-minded the Colonel of an india-rubber ball.

He seemed to bounce as well as to bound; to re-bound as well as to leap; for his flying feet scarcely seemed to touch the floor. Undeniably, as the Colonel entered, he bounced, he rebounded, from the resilient summit of the loftily protuberant centre of the prone citizen.

On all the soldiers, with the exception of the drunken madman, discipline laid its compelling hand of steel. To a man they stood to attention, at the salute, even while death threatened them, and the homicidal maniac leapt around, about, and upon a fellow crea-ture whose fate they might at any moment share.

So sudden was the silence that fell upon the room, that even the *cafard*-stricken lunatic noticed it, and, completing the tight-rope balancing progress which he had been making along the prostrate man's body from his feet to his face, he leapt about as though to meet a new enemy, and beheld an old one—the Colonel!

The effect was instant and electrical.

He screamed, a horrible inarticulate sound, without words or meaning; raised the knife to stabbing posi-tion; and, like a panther stalking its prey and about to spring, he crept tense and crouching, towards the man he feared and hated more than any other.

Denis Ducros instinctively assumed the attitude which Colonel Louis Rochefort would have adopted in such circumstances.

With his gloved left hand in which he held his riding-switch, resting lightly on his hip, he stood at ease, the bare right hand hanging loose, but very ready. With steady level gaze he met and held the madman's glare.

Closer and closer crept Zidenski, murder in his hand and eye.

No other actor moved on that sordid stage, of which Denis Ducros saw himself the centre and the star.

One more step and the hand went back to strike.

"*Halt!*"

Crisp, clear, sudden, the familiar command fell upon the ears of the man who had obeyed it a million times.

He obeyed it.

"*About turn!*"

Prompt obedience.

"*Quick march!*"

"*Left turn!*"

"*Left turn!*"

Each order instantly and automatically carried out. The madman reached the door.

"*Halt!*"

"*Stand at ease!*"

The man obeyed.

" '*Shun!*" shouted the Colonel suddenly and loudly; and, dropping the knife, the man placed his hands, open and flat, in correct position.

"*Quick march!*"

The madman marched out through the door, into the alley.

"*Guard!*" called the Colonel, and Allones brought his squad to attention.

"You, *Légionnaire* Allones, arrest this man. Take him back to Barracks, and hand him over to the Sergeant of the Guard.

"Cells," he added grimly. "I'll deal with him to-morrow."

And, a minute later, the drink-sodden, *cafard*-stricken Bulgarian found himself in a familiar situation.

What that one wanted was another tour of active service, reflected Denis. No drink, no *cafard*. Meanwhile, no liberty, no murder. A cell was the best and safest place for him.

What a night! What a night!

Love and Death and . . . doings.

Quite a good job that he chose the Great Holiday night for his great escapade.

But he didn't really choose it.

It was chosen for him—by Fate.

No. Let him say rather by *le Bon Dieu,* who intended him to meet and to love and to save his Nicolette. . . .

Ah! Here came a nasty piece of work, and he'd give him a nasty jolt; he'd try to pay off one or two old scores. For in the days before he, Denis Ducros, became the Colonel's batman, Lieutenant Guani had, for some reason, taken a personal dislike to him, and had made a personal matter of it.

The greasy little Italian cur. All flash and bombast. Completely bogus.

For, truly or falsely, his half-company considered that he was no real fire-eater. Not of rifle-fire anyway.

Old Pinard had put the idea into appropriate words, as usual, with the casual remark that Lieutenant Guani was really more of a tactician than an ordinary fighting soldier, and had perfected the art of leading from behind, which was much superior to following in front—whatever Pinard meant by that.

However, Pinard admitted that the man was a good leader, and declared that nobody ever led a retreat better or further.

What cramped Guani's style, according to the same authority, was that the Legion never retreated, and so Guani's career had been hampered and slowed down. He had never had a chance to show what he could really do in command of a body of troops. Retreating by yourself might be spectacular, but it really led nowhere —save to the rear—and the Higher Command was not as yet sufficiently advanced in military theory to understand and appreciate the value of initiative shown in the great art of strategic retirement, without orders.

Those heavy-sterned Generals certainly mentioned an original and enterprising officer who used the tactic —but it was not in despatches.

Well, most bullies are cowards, if not all; and Guani

was a hectoring bully to subordinates and a fawning sycophant to superiors. . . .

Lieutenant Guani, a plumpish, blue-cheeked man, with protuberant eyes and over-ripe lips beneath a tiny curled moustache, gave an obvious start of surprise, and smartly saluted his Colonel, a man whom he hated as much as he dared, and admired more than he wished to do.

A sudden thought struck Denis Ducros, and made his blood boil.

He saw red.

This loathsome, swaggering, upstart brute was probably on his way to visit *chez* Madame.

Man proposes—to call Lieutenant Guani a man. For once Denis Ducros would dispose—appointing himself God's agent in the matter. And if it came to pass, obviously it was ordained that he should be just that.

He returned the Lieutenant's salute with the merest upward movement of a finger.

"Ah! *Ce bon Lieutenant Guano!*" he murmured.

"Halt you, and stand at the salute, while I tell you one or two things I have had on my mind for some time.

"You have been one of the things, Lieutenant Guano."

"Guani, *Monsieur le Colonel*" corrected the Lieutenant, and his face flushed angrily.

"I *said* Guano," agreed the Colonel.

"Guani, *Monsieur le Colonel,*" ventured the Lieutenant, who had dined well and supped better.

"My good creature, I'm not deaf. Neither am I blind, nor yet, in spite of my years and station, quite imbecile. I *heard* you say Guano. I *see* you are Guano. And I am not so ignorant as to be unaware as to what to do with Guano."

A pulse beat in the Lieutenant's cheek, but he had sufficient self-control to stand like a statue.

The Colonel appeared to be following a train of thought.

He sighed.

"Yes. Very useful . . . But not yet. Some day you'll

be buried, though. Very fertilising."

"Where are you going?" he suddenly snapped.

"Er—I was . . . I was going to a rendezvous, *Monsieur le Colonel,*" replied the junior officer, burning with resentment.

What right had the Old Devil to make puns on his name, and then to ask where he was going, when he was off duty?

"Oh! Excellent! Night march and exercises! Your men have already marched off, eh? I hope you didn't turn the poor fellows out until their holiday expired—at midnight."

The Old Man was being funny, surely. His idea of humour.

"Not a military rendezvous, to-night, *Monsieur le Colonel,*" and the Lieutenant permitted himself a little nervous giggle.

"Rather a case of Wine, Woman and Song, *Monsieur le Colonel,*" he smirked. "Holiday occasion and . . ."

"Well, I see you've had your wine," interrupted the Colonel unsympathetically. "More than enough of it. I cannot imagine that any woman could possibly desire your society. And Heaven preserve us from hearing your song.

"So there will be no more Wine, and neither Woman nor Song for you to-night, Lieutenant.

"You have my permission to go," continued the Colonel quietly.

"Back to Barracks," he added with a parade-ground rasp.

The Lieutenant's arm fell to his side. He saluted again and turned about.

"When I have told you the one or two things I have had on my mind, for some time," pursued the Colonel.

"In the first place, I wish to bring to your notice the fact that you are, in my opinion, as well as that of all your superiors, by far the most . . ."

Lieutenant Guani brightened up, stood more stiffly, and assumed the air proper to one who, with conscious modesty, receives a decoration.

The Old Man had been pulling his leg.

". . . the most inefficient, slack, lazy, incompetent and objectionable officer in the Battalion; and, almost certainly, in the whole Foreign Legion. You are a drunken, dissipated, dishonest, disreputable and detestable character, Lieutenant Guano; a bully, a braggart, and a bad officer. I don't think you'll hold your present rank much longer—certainly not long after I have sent in my next report on you.

"Those are the little matters I had on my mind concerning you.

"Now march yourself straight back to your quarters, and put yourself under close arrest. . . . You'll hear why in the morning; and you can spend the night in guessing which of the many probable reasons is the real one.

"Dismiss!"

And as the crestfallen Lieutenant, stricken, frightened and thoroughly apprehensive, turned about and took his dejected way, the Colonel smiled in the well-known Rochefort orderly-room manner.

"A taste of your own medicine, you dog," he growled, and as Colonel Rochefort was wont to do, made the motion of one who dusts his fingers.

It had been in bad taste to misuse this fellow's name like that, but one had to meet people of this sort on their own ground. He needed a touch of the whip that he was so very fond of wielding—vilely insulting remarks on subordinates' personal peculiarities, as though it were a man's own fault that he was short and thick-set, tall and lean; had a big nose, a wall eye, bat ears, or a mouth like that of a hippopotamus.

Why, the pernicious little swine used to exercise his wonderful wit on the subject of the face of a man who had been scarred and slashed when tortured by Bedouin tribesmen, had been picked up for dead, and had been decorated for the tremendous courage and resolution he had shown on that occasion!

Yes; his mutilated face had struck Guani as very funny, but it would strike the Company as something much funnier if Guani himself ever got himself a decoration for valour. . . .

Well, he'd let that animal get well ahead, and then he must really think about making his own way back to Barracks.

Positively he was beginning to feel tired.

And no wonder!

What a night!

He'd loathe to end it.

It would be with a positive pang that he would put off the uniform of glory.

Henceforth he would feel as a Colonel reduced to the ranks. But he would have had his hour, an hour which heaven itself could not take away; his crowded hour of glorious life, itself the first of many years of glorious life with Nicolette.

So no regrets . . .

It would have been a splendid and wonderful thing if he could have finished his great night on an appropriate and satisfying note, so to speak; then have just taken off his uniform, folded it up, gone to bed in peace, a Colonel fulfilled—and awakened in the morning a batman restored.

After all, uneasy walks the figure that wears the uniform of rank, and happy low lies down the humble and obscure man, be he only a batman—who has found his Nicolette.

So back along the weary road—no, no, the happy golden road—to Barracks and the green apron, *and* to Nicolette.

The golden road to Samarcand—to Avignon and to Nicolette.

Perhaps one more little drink on the way?

Thus, gaily bedight, this gallant knight in moonshine and in shadow, journeyed along singing his song —*Nicolette! . . . Nicolette! . . . Nicolette! . . .*

CHAPTER 15

"THE LAST ACT CROWNS THE PLAY"

And as he came to a large restaurant whence issued again the appealing and disturbing strains of *Donna è Mobile,* he halted in his magnificent stride.

Ah! The *Cabaret Espagnol,* a crowd of good lads still going strong; and the wine had been flowing freely.

It should again flow freely, at his command; for they must have spent their pay by now—and a bottle of it should flow down his own tightly-encircled neck.

Appropriately enough, at this moment, the music changed, and broke into the *Funeral March of a Marionette.* Appropriate, timely, and most amusing—rather sinisterly amusing. . . .

The Colonel entered in style.

Silence spread in an ever-growing circle from the door, until there was no sound in the big room, save the notes of the mocking music.

Half a hundred soldiers stood, or did their best to stand, correctly at attention.

"Stand easy! Stand easy, *mes enfants!*" he cried, "And now sit easy."

The astonished soldiers obeyed with soldierly promptitude, one or two seating themselves, somewhat heavily, upon the floor.

"A bottle for everybody," he ordered, turning to the proprietor of the restaurant.

This was the Colonel himself? The Old Devil in person?

Name of a Name of a Scalded Cat! What the Hell?

It might be the Great Fête Day of Madame la République, but it wasn't the Day of Judgment too, was it?

No. Nor did the Old Devil look as though he had come to do any judging.

"A bottle for everybody," repeated the Colonel

blithely, "of your best.

"And a still better one for me," he added with a merry laugh.

A bemedalled *légionnaire* in whom wine had weakened the bonds of discipline, habit, fear and inhibitions, called loudly for three cheers for the Colonel, and a *tohuwabohu* of joyous cries burst forth from the joyous rout. Hurrahs, mingled with *bravas, hochs, vives,* and other strange national shouts of joy and approval. Undrowned in the roaring surging sea of noise, the Colonel clearly heard a lone but dominant,

"*Rah—Rah—Rah! Attaboy!*", and glanced to where a long lean saturnine *légionnaire* stood supporting a wall with one hand, a bottle with the other, and cried aloud with open mouth and tight shut eyes.

And, hullo! Who was that sitting beside him, but the grand old rascal Michel Aubraine.

Yes, and there were Ivan Dobroff and Hans Müller with him still. They must all have got out of barracks after he left.

Now, clever Master Michel, let's see if Denis Ducros can bring off as good a one as your *Monsieur le Maire* escapade! And you yourself a witness, eh, my boy?

As the cheers died down, a lady who had seen better days stepped on to the low dais at the back of the hall.

And, as a little black-eyed Spaniard, pale and wan, struck a chord on the tinny piano, she burst into strident song.

Ere, assisted by the entire company, she had finished screeching the uncommendable ditty "*Pan, pan, le gobinois,*" the Colonel had also finished his bottle.

He ordered another.

As the lady concluded her song, the Colonel applauded loudly, beating with the empty bottle on the zinc bar by which he stood.

"*Bis!*" he cried, and the singer, proud and pleased, obliged most willingly. Even deeper and louder than before, was the chorus that the enchanted warriors supplied.

"More wine, you rascal!" ordered the Colonel. "Keep those rogues of yours busy with those bottles. Are the soldiers of France to go thirsty on the Fête Day of France?"

And, nothing loth, the proprietor drove the Arab waiters yet harder.

Having finished his second bottle, the Colonel took it by the neck, raised it on high, and bade the pianist play "*Père Dupanloup en chemin de fer.*"

There was a roar of approving laughter; the Spaniard, who evidently knew every air that the Legion knew, smiled and smote the piano with all his strength. The Colonel, stepping forward, used the upraised bottle as a baton, and personally conducted the choir and music.

The song concluded, the choir, orchestra and conductor applauded themselves loudly.

"And what shall we have next?" asked the Colonel, genially, as the applause at length died down.

"Name your favourite song, somebody."

Many were called, and all were chosen; some being led by the *cantatrice,* some being passed by her in a prudent but not prudish silence.

Breaking the peace of exhaustion which followed the singing of the last song, the doors were thrown open and there entered two senior non-commissioned officers, bearded and bemedalled men of a severity and dignity all their own, and worthy of their rank and years of service.

All eyes turned toward this apparition, the *légionnaires* torn between discipline, promptings to rise to salute, and the knowledge that the Colonel himself had given them orders to remain seated.

The *sous-officiers* stared, unwilling or unable to accept the reality of what they saw. Each knew that he was perfectly sober, but felt that nevertheless he was beholding a strange and somewhat nightmarish vision.

"*Les huiles!*" suddenly exclaimed the Colonel, turning about to see what could be the counter-attraction at which his audience was staring, "*Nom d'un pipe! Les huiles!*" to the completely incredulous amazement of the astounded *légionnaires.*

That the great and grim Colonel Louis Rochefort should come into this *casse-croûte;* that he should stand unlimited wine to the whole company assembled; that he should join in the chorus of a very low song, and then select and take an actual part in the singing of a still lower one, was enough to make the dead arise and run away.

But that he should know and use such a term as *"huiles"*—applied to non-commissioned officers—was enough to knock the fleeing dead back into their graves again.

That he, the cold hard Colonel Louis Rochefort, the aloof unapproachable aristocrat, product of St. Cyr, who had never spent a day in the ranks of the Legion, nor any other regiment—that he should know and use such a piece of barrack-room *argot* as that, was the last straw to break the back of the camel of credulity.

And indeed, as far as the two grave and reverend senior Sergeant-Majors were concerned, it was the case of the last straw which breaks the camel's heart.

But the heart of Denis Ducros was uplifted within him and he was strong, bold and outrageous with the heady fumes of good wine and brave love.

"Outside, *salauds!*" he bawled, with the well-known imperious dismissing gesture of his hand.

"Outside! Go on. Get out of here you abominable blackguards. This place is reserved for honest *légionnaires,* and for them to be able to drink and enjoy themselves in peace.

"Get out as quickly as your aged limbs can move— and a bit quicker. . . . And stay out," he shouted.

There was a roar of delighted, if slightly nervous, laughter, as, looking nearly as hurt and broken as they felt, the two *sous-officiers,* models of discipline, duty and deportment, saluted and obeyed; while the Colonel, gleefully rubbing his hands, laughed not only merrily, but most derisively.

Then, taking the hand of the fat *chanteuse,* with a cry of *"Vive la compagnie!"* he led her to a table and called for more wine—wine for the lady, wine for himself, wine for everybody.

He knew he was foundering and that the end was near; but he would go down in a blaze of glory and a sea of wine. He was bewitched, again uplifted, *tête montée,* in love.

Wine is another man and he would remain another man to the last moment.

Gone were all prudent thoughts of getting quietly into barracks, removing this enchanted uniform of glory, brushing it humbly, dutifully, and folding it away.

"Wine for *les légionnaires!"* he cried to the proprietor, who also felt he was a little bewitched, or at any rate, bemused and bewildered.

And *Messieurs les légionnaires?* They saw, they heard, and they realised—how drunk they must be. It was a Soldier's Dream of Bliss. Only a dream. But the wine was real—or seemed to be . . .

Silly . . . ! There must be a catch in it.

However, wine is wine; orders are orders; and when, once in a life-time, your Colonel sits down with you in a Bar and bids you drink, well, by all the Gods of War and the laws of the Legion—you drink.

They drank.

Those who could still drink a lot; those who felt that, as a matter of strict fact, they had drunk a lot but were still functioning; those who felt they could not drink another drop, all undeterred, drank deeply of the Colonel's wine.

The din grew louder and the fun more furious—but scarcely as furious as the two Sergeant-Majors, when, on recovering their senses, they realised that they had actually been driven away, like bazaar curs, from the wine-shop that they had considered it their duty to enter.

They, men of power and importance, ridiculed, insulted, and humiliated in front of the very men whom it was their main duty in life to discipline.

And by the Colonel himself!

Colonel Louis Rochefort, the finest stickler for discipline that ever backed-up a zealous non-commissioned officer in his arduous and difficult work of breaking and making military toughs.

"It *was* the Colonel, wasn't it?" asked Sergeant-Major Sleicher, at the end of a long and bitter silence.

"You saw him," growled Sergeant-Major Goertz.

"You heard him, too," he added.

" *'Huiles'!*" growled Sergeant-Major Sleicher beneath his breath.

"Has he gone mad, do you think?" asked Goertz.

"*Cafard,* I should say," muttered Sleicher.

"Colonels don't get *cafard,*" objected Goertz.

"Well, whether he's gone mad or not, I swear there are a few of those scum who'll think I've gone mad before I've done with them."

"Did you mark down any of the *scélérats?*"

"I did. Didn't you?"

"What do you think? There was that scoundrel Aubraine, and his two *copains,* and Zerro and his gang."

"Yes. And I saw that big baboon, Seminoff, and his jackals. I'll give Seminoff something to laugh about, as he's so fond of laughing—and plenty of time to do it in too."

"In the dark," growled the other, "with some dry bread and salt water.

"*Laugh!*" he added unpleasantly, grinding his teeth.

But if, at this stage of the affair, the rage of these noble minds burned so fiercely as to be almost uncontrollable, what was it when they met their friend the *vaguemestre* and received from him a piece of news that rendered them temporarily speechless?

Literally speechless with rage.

For when Sergeant-Major Sleicher, the more articulate of the two saw the *vaguemestre,* he beckoned him across the road, with a view to pouring out the vials of his wrath and woe.

He must tell someone or burst, and, what was more, he must tell people of the proper rank and standing—and understanding; people whose sympathy would be extremely practical. Every non-commissioned officer in the depôt was concerned in this, and must make it his business to be very actively concerned too.

Oh yes, *Messieurs les légionnaires* should have plenty to laugh at. Some of them should laugh for days —and nights.

"Hullo!" said the *vaguemestre* as he joined them. "Going back to Barracks? I've got to find Captain le Sage before I can turn in. Colonel's very ill and can't sign a . . ."

"*What?*" interrupted both *sous-officiers* simultaneously. The *vaguemestre* jumped, so fierce and menacing was the anguished cry.

"*What* did you say?" asked Sergeant-Major Sleicher.

"The Colonel's very ill, I said, and . . ."

"*Ill? . . . Where?*"

"In his sacred bed, of course!" replied the *vaguemestre* testily. "Where do you suppose? Under the kitchen sink?"

"But he isn't! He . . ."

"All right! All right! Médécin-Major Barrade is a liar then," interrupted the *vaguemestre*.

"What the *Hell* are you talking about?" burst in Sergeant-Major Goertz, a good man whose mind was not quite so strong and active as his fine body.

"I don't know. Don't ask *me*," snarled the *vaguemestre*. "Sleicher knows all about it. He knows everything. *I* was only under the impression that possibly the Colonel is ill, because Médécin-Major Barrade has given the strictest orders that he is not to be disturbed! . . . I personally don't know anything because it wasn't *I*, of course, who went to his quarters half an hour ago with an '*Urgent,*' and had my head nearly bitten off by the blasted doctor. . . . One doesn't suppose that *he* knows anything about illness, of course. Merely thinks he does. . . .

"Or about the Colonel. Merely thinks he does. . . .

"Anyway, he thinks the Colonel's so damned healthy that he has issued the strictest orders that he is not to be disturbed by anyone on any account whatsoever. Not by *anyone*. . . . Not even by me."

It will be perceived that the *vaguemestre* was, unlike Sergeant-Major Goertz, a fluent speaker; something of an orator, *en effet.*

"So the Colonel's ill? Ill in bed, is he?" said Sergeant-Major Sleicher, having patiently heard the *vaguemestre* out.

"No! No! No!" roared the latter. "He's dancing on the tiles, stark naked. He's mad. He's . . ."

"Listen!" said the Prussian, with sinister quiet. "*Monsieur le Colonel Louis Rochefort* is not ill in bed. Nor is he dancing on the tiles, stark naked."

"No! No, of course not! Never ill in his life. Never been on the tiles in his life. Never was such a person in his life," spluttered the *vaguemestre.*

"Where the Hell is he then?" he asked. "And what is he doing, since you know all about him?"

"He's in a *bistro,* the *Café d'Afrique.* Boozing with a herd of swine. When any *sous-officier* enters, he insults and abuses him, and bids the swine to laugh at him.

"The swine laugh," he added.

The *vaguemestre* stared open-mouthed at the solemn and stolid Sergeant-Major Sleicher.

"Go in and see for yourself. You'll enjoy it," advised Sergeant-Major Goertz.

"Let me see now, what have I drunk to-night?" pondered the *vaguemestre,* in the tone of one who makes careful retrospective calculation. "A little wine for the stomach's sake—with water. So it cannot be that I am so drunk that, having come straight from the Colonel's sick-bed, I am imagining that two intoxicated gorillas are telling me that my dying Colonel is drinking from a trough in a pig-sty and insulting all who pass. . . .

"No. I am as sober as Satan on a Saturday night."

The tone of his voice suddenly changed.

"Be ashamed of yourselves!" he admonished them sharply. "And get back to Barracks at once and sleep your liquor off. You'll be losing your stripes like poor Hagues, if you go on like this. . . . The Colonel boozing with the men in a low pot-house!

"You're looking for trouble, that's what. And you'll find it too. Better not tell a yarn like that to anyone else.

"He'd break you like a couple of rotten sticks," he

concluded viciously.

Sergeant-Major Sleicher dug deeply and laboriously with his huge fist in the pocket of his tunic, and, before apoplexy ensued, or his empurpled face turned black, produced a ten-franc note—big money in the Legion.

"See that?" he asked.

The *vaguemestre* replied that he did, and added that he had seen one like it before, though not waved in front of his eyes by the Sergeant-Major.

"Very well then. I'll wager *that*," and he gave the note which lay upon one large palm, a resounding smack with the other, "I'll wager *that* to a copper *sou,* that Colonel Rochefort is at this moment in the *Café d'Afrique,* boozing *and* singing with a rabble of *légionnaires*. Yes, and conducting the music—with a bottle. . . . Tight as a tick. Now then?"

"Done," responded the *vaguemestre* promptly producing a copper coin.

"Come on then," urged the two Sergeant-Majors as one man, and, a few minutes later, the door of the *Café d'Afrique* was again flung open, and through it, swelling with importance, strode the confident figure of the *vaguemestre.*

Behind him, obviously diffident and anxious, lurked, inconspicuous, two unusually unobtrusive Sergeant-Majors. They forbore to follow their rash leader into the lion-like Colonel's temporary den. Sufficient unto the moment to witness from a safe distance, and through the doorway, what might now befall.

And it was while the Colonel was himself on the dais and actually in the middle of favouring the company with a song—of which, one regrets to admit, the *chanteuse,* the pianist, and every man present knew not only the tune, but the words—that the sudden rude interruption occurred.

The Colonel indicated the fact that he noticed the man's intrusion, by an angry glare and a Rochefortian frown, but continued his song, the end of which he had almost reached.

The *vaguemestre* stared in utter bewilderment. He could see that this was the Colonel, and he knew perfectly well that it was not.

Instinct told him that this man was not Colonel Louis Rochefort.

Common sense supported instinct.

Would Médécin-Major Barrade nearly bite his head off and nearly kick him out of the place because the Colonel was far too ill to be disturbed—if the Colonel was not there at all, but was out on a bend, raising Cain in the grog-shops.

He was certain, absolutely certain, this was some new trick of these anointed devils of *légionnaires.*

But, God of Battles! *Wasn't* that Colonel Rochefort?

Colonel Rochefort, sober, he knew only too well, but Colonel Rochefort, drunk, was a sight no *vaguemestre* had seen. Was this the Colonel, drunk?

No.

And as, really rather bravely, he approached the dais, shoving his way roughly and angrily through the laughing and applauding crowd of licentious soldiery, he suddenly noticed one drunken rascal, that *mauvais sujet, légionnaire* Michel Aubraine, throw his hands up toward Heaven, then in an ecstasy of joy clasp his stomach with both arms, double up with laughter until his head almost reached his feet, and then, rising, murmur drunkenly, as he wiped his streaming eyes,

"*Magnificent! Marvellous!* I give him best! Most *perfect* piece of acting! . . . *C'est incroyable!*"

And then the *vaguemestre* knew.

He had known that he knew.

He was right. . . .

Now they should see something.

The Colonel acknowledged the applause genially, and then deigned to deal with the intruder.

"Well I'm damned!" he said, "Another *huile!*"

There was a loud laugh, and all eyes turned to the hitherto unremarked *vaguemestre.*

The angry blood of that derided man came to the boiling-point, and his rage was such that he could scarcely speak.

They'd laugh at *him,* would they?

Stepping on to the dais, he thrust the forefinger of

his outstretched hand almost in the Colonel's face.

"Y-y-y-you're a s-swindler," he stuttered.

"*Ah!* . . . *Indeed?*" drawled the Colonel, suddenly sober as a judge; and as a judge, austere, cold, hard and stern.

The *vaguemestre* recoiled.

The Colonel drew the scented handkerchief from his left cuff and held it beneath his nose.

"Get further away," he growled. "Get off this platform. Get out of this Bar. In fact, get back to Barracks, and report to Captain le Sage. He'll put you under arrest. . . . Oran Court Martial for you my man. A little matter of *stealing from the letters of les légionnaires.*"

There was a low and ominous growl from *les légionnaires.*

The *vaguemestre* quailed before the blaze of the Colonel's eye, and the import of these terrible words.

Involuntarily stepping backwards, he left the dais with unintentional suddenness, and was only saved from falling on the floor by the agile and skilful movement of a very large Turk, whose knee shot up just in time, and just in the right place.

Not only was the *vaguemestre* saved from falling backward, he was propelled upward and forward.

"Filthy *huile!*" observed the Colonel dispassionately, and that settled the matter in the *vaguemestre's* mind.

Never in this world would Colonel Rochefort have called a very senior non-commissioned officer a *huile,* much less a filthy *huile.*

No. He was being fooled. And the men were in it. What had *légionnaire* Aubraine just said?

Springing on to the dais again, he turned to the men,

"Here, you scum!" he shouted. "Frog-march this pollution of an anointed acrobat back to Barracks.

"You . . . and you . . . and you . . . and you," he pointed. "Take him. Throw him into a cell, and tear that uniform off him. Strip him naked."

" '*Huile*', eh?" he added, turning to Denis, "what

about *une bonne ration de l'huile de cotret,*[40] eh? A dose of stirrup-oil. I'll oil you, you impudent hound . . . What about a pint of *huile de ricin?*[41] . . . I'll give you oil enough to keep you greasy for the rest of your life—which may not be as long as you expect."

The *vaguemestre,* foaming at the mouth with rage, was forced to pause for breath.

"This dog's gone mad!" observed the Colonel.

"Dangerous. Throw it out."

And sweeping the wildly excited and somewhat inebriated assembly with the eye of the true commander of men, he pointed imperiously to the door.

Headed by Michel Aubraine, the *légionnaires* obeyed their Colonel. It was not every day, not even every Fête Day indeed, that they were invited, nay commanded, by superior authority to throw a *sous-officier* out on his ear.

This one fell almost at the feet of his friends who had not advanced to his support. . . .

"Well? What did I tell you?" gloated Sergeant-Major Sleicher.

"I said you'd enjoy it," said Goertz.

The *vaguemestre* picked himself up.

"Listen, you bone-headed camels. You poor, half-witted, half-blind bat-eyed beetles. You make me sick . . ." he raged.

"Go it, then," encouraged Sleicher.

The *vaguemestre* spat.

He then invoked Heaven's assistance in the retention of his sanity.

"*Bon Dieu de Dieu de Sort!*" he cried, making as though to cast his *képi* on the ground. "That's *not* the Colonel. It's a damned dog's-tail of a *légionnaire* dressed up in his uniform! *Légionnaire* Aubraine knows him too! . . . You apes . . . you asses . . . Listen! Guard that door, and when he comes out—*get him!* I'm going to run back to Barracks, and I'll send you every man I meet on the way, and the picket, *and* a party of . . ."

"*And* the real Colonel!" jeered Sleicher.

---

[40] a good thrashing.
[41] castor oil.

"Have the *Assembly* sounded, while you're about it," suggested Goertz.

The *vaguemestre* went through the motions of tearing his hair, and turned to run, at the *pas gymnastique.*

"Wait till to-morrow," he shouted. "You'll tear the chevrons off your own cuffs, you bloody fools."

Almost it seemed to the now laughing Prussians, that the poor *vaguemestre* wept.

"The good animal is imbecile," observed Goertz, in the didactic Prussian manner.

"He'll be thinking *he's* Colonel, next," sneered Sleicher.

The two men regarded each other enquiringly and somewhat doubtfully.

"Well, what do we do now?" asked Goertz. "Leave 'em to it?"

"Yes. Clear out while we can, and let the *vaguemestre* get on with it. He may have caught a cartload of Colonels by daylight.

"Not but what I am going to have another squint through the crack of that door," he added.

"They seem quiet enough now. Settled down to some serious drinking, I suppose," replied Goertz, and longingly smacked adequate lips.

Quietly approaching the door of the *Café d'Afrique,* Sergeant-Major Sleicher paused, listened, and pushed it open a couple of inches.

There was the Colonel—of course it was the Colonel —on the dais, and, in a quiet voice, earnestly addressing the now silent *légionnaires.*

For Denis Ducros had had enough.

He was tired, and he realised that, beyond telling, he wanted his Day of Days to finish quietly, decently, and in order—a weary Colonel, taking off his uniform and going to bed.

It would spoil everything—or go far toward spoiling it, for nothing could destroy the glory and the beauty of his love for Nicolette—yes, it would nearly spoil everything if, as that swine of a *vaguemestre* had said, he was seized, knocked about, frog-marched to Barracks, stripped naked and thrown into a cell.

Lucifer! Lucifer! . . .

Ichabod! . . .

As the last chorus died down, he had raised his hand for silence, and was the severe, yet still kindly Colonel once again, the man with whom no son of woman took liberties.

"Now, *mes enfants!*" he said. "That will be enough, I think. We've had a good time together this Fête Day, and now we'll call it a day—as the Day is over.

"When I give the word, you will file quietly out of the place, and march back to Barracks in a smart and soldierly manner. I wish every one of you *bonne chance.* Now then:—

"*Légionnaires! . . .*" But before he could say more, a soldier who did not appear to be drunk, but undoubtedly had drink taken, cried in a loud voice,

"Three cheers for the Colonel! By God, the very finest man that ever wore the Legion's uniform! God preserve him, and the Devil admire him!"

And the eyes of Michel Aubraine met those of Denis Ducros with the faintest flicker of an eye-lid.

"Thank you, my man," acknowledged the Colonel, and again Michel Aubraine was convulsed with ecstatic laughter as the enthusiastic cheers rang out.

Again the Colonel raised an inhibitory hand.

"*Légionnaires! . . .*" he cried. "*Garde à vous! . . . Fixe! . . .*"

And with practised skill his merry men raised their heads above the encircling rosy fumes of wine, and stood practically to attention.

"*Rompez! . . .*"

And the *légionnaires* turned about and went quietly and respectfully from the presence of their Colonel.

Sergeant-Major Sleicher hurriedly left his observation post and rejoined Sergeant-Major Goertz.

"Come on! Quick!" he said. "The Old Devil's dismissing them."

"*Of course* it's the Colonel," he added. "No doubt at all. The *vaguemestre's* been whooping it up."

"And pouring it down," agreed Goertz.

"Nice to be *vaguemestre,*" observed Sleicher, as they marched away. "No stint of the best of everything."

"But silly to flash the cash you pinch," said Goertz.

"Well, he won't flash my ten francs anyhow," decided Sleicher. "Look out, here comes the Colonel. Let's turn down here."

In the wake of the returning men whom he had been entertaining—and for whose entertainment Colonel Rochefort would very soon be invited to pay—Denis Ducros marched hopefully.

Le bon Dieu had been so truly kind and helpful this night that it was perfectly possible, almost probable, indeed, that He might grant him safe return from his wonderful escapade, his brief excursion into an upper world, clad in the Uniform of Glory, to the wearer of which all men had accorded recognition, respect and obedience.

All men . . . All women . . . And the One Woman. *Nicolette! . . . Nicolette! . . . Nicolette! . . .*

Yes, he thought, and the One Woman valued the uniform at its true worth—coloured rags—and valued *him* for what he was worth, and saw in him a fellow human-being, warm with human kindness.

Love! . . .

The men marched on. . . . He loved them too. . . . Good fellows. . . . How they responded to a little human kindness. . . . They were as quiet as lambs. . . .

Down the lane between the Spahis' Barracks and those of the Legion, through the Barrack gate, they filed at last; and there was not a man with whose deportment the Sergeant of the Guard could find cause for complaint.

And after them—the Colonel.

The Colonel flicked a perfunctory salute, and passed on in the darkness towards his house.

Behind him one came running, and his heart sank within him.

"*Pardon, M'sieu' le Colonel!*" panted a most respectful voice. "But the *vaguemestre* is most anxious to find you. Most urgent message, I believe. . . ."

"*Ah! . . . Indeed?*" said the Colonel, as he paused in

his stride. "I have already heard that he has either got *cafard,* or has had too much to drink. . . . When you see him, tell him to report to Captain le Sage, who will doubtless put him under arrest—for conduct unbecoming a *sous-officier.*

"I'll deal with him in the morning," added the Colonel grimly, and strode on.

CHAPTER 16

THE UNIFORM IS TAKEN OFF

Safe in his dressing-room, the door locked, the Colonel reluctantly removed his uniform and folded it away.

Denis Ducros, also reluctantly, resumed *his* uniform.

Before covering it with the green baize badge of servitude, he turned up the light, viewed his image in the mirror, and, in low but eloquent voice, addressed an imaginary company of—*huiles.*

"Little men!" he whispered. "Little earth-bound men, do you know what I am?"

With one accord, and one opinion, they seemed to tell him what he was.

From the heights of his wine-flown eminence, his *tête montée* glory, his vast pride of Love, he laughed his bitter contempt of those poor oppressors.

"*Imbéciles!* Goats! Asses! Mules! Camels! It is as I thought. Ignorant. Blind. *I* will tell you what I am—for I have just remembered.

"I am the great Caliph of Baghdad, and henceforth you have my permission to call me The Great Caliph, *Haroun al Raschid.*"

Yet that was not at all what they called him.

Happy as he had never been before in all his maladjusted life, Denis looked into the Colonel's room, showed himself to that convalescent, then retired, undressed, crept into bed, and composed himself to dream of Nicolette . . .

Only six more months, and his time in the Legion would be up!

Nicolette! . . . *Nicolette!* . . . *Nicolette!* . . . and Denis Ducros . . . the little Soldier of Fortune and the little Daughter of Joy, brought together, for ever, by his wearing, for an evening, the Uniform of Glory. . . .

Available P. C. Wren Titles
from
Riner Publishing Company

The Collected Short Stories

Volume One: ISBN 9780985032609
Volume Two: ISBN 9780985032616
Volume Three: ISBN 9780985032623
Volume Four: ISBN 9780985032630
Volume Five: ISBN 9780985032647

The Collected Novels

Volume One: *The Geste Novels*
 Part A: ISBN 9780985032678
 Part B: ISBN 9780985032685
Volume Two: *The Sinbad Novels*
 Part A: ISBN 9780692639382
 Part B: ISBN 9780692639429
Volume Three: *The Foreign Legion Novels*
 Part A: ISBN 9780999074909
 Part B: ISBN 9780999074916
Volume Four: *The Earlier India Novels*
 Part A: ISBN 9780999074923
 Part B: ISBN 9780999074930
Volume Five: *The Later India Novels*
 Part A: ISBN 9780999074947
 Part B: ISBN 9780999074954
Volume Six: *The English Novels*
 Part A: ISBN 9780999074961
 Part B: ISBN 9780999074978
Volume Seven: *A Mixed Bag of Novels*
 Part A: ISBN 9780999074985
 Part B: ISBN 9780999074992

Further information can be found at
rinerpublishing.wordpress.com